PENGUIN BOOKS

LOVE, HONOUR AND BETRAY

Elizabeth Kary *began her writing career at the age of fifteen and continued to write throughout high school. She graduated from the State University in New York with a degree in art education and went on to teach art to elementary schoolchildren in Rochester. In 1981 she and her husband moved to St Louis and she took a part-time job in the St Louis Art Museum that allowed her to devote more time to her writing.*

Three and a half years later she produced Love, Honour and Betray. *When it was published in the United States, this extraordinary story of love and war immediately sold over 900,000 copies.*

Elizabeth Kary has also completed a contemporary romance, Portrait of a Lady *and is now working on a second historical romance. She spends her spare time reading and is particularly interested in the American Civil War. She also enjoys travelling.*

D1321538

ELIZABETH KARY
✱✱✱

LOVE
HONOUR
AND
BETRAY

PENGUIN BOOKS

Penguin Books Ltd, Harmondsworth, Middlesex, England
Viking Penguin Inc., 40 West 23rd Street, New York, New York 10010, U.S.A.
Penguin Books Australia Ltd, Ringwood, Victoria, Australia
Penguin Books Canada Limited, 2801 John Street, Markham, Ontario, Canada L3R 1B4
Penguin Books (N.Z.) Ltd, 182–190 Wairau Road, Auckland 10, New Zealand

First published in the U.S.A. by Berkley Books, New York 1986
Published in Great Britain by Penguin Books 1986

Typeset in 9/10½pt Linotron 202 Times by
Rowland Phototypesetting Ltd, Bury St Edmunds, Suffolk
Made and printed in Great Britain by
Cox & Wyman Ltd, Reading

To
Clara V. Hill
who knew there was more to
teaching literature than
Silas Marner
and to
Dona, Regina and Carolyn
who encouraged me
first, last and always

Part One

Youngstown, New York
1812

One
✳✳✳

It was coming. The thing he dreaded most in the world was going to come to pass. Seth Porterfield's head buzzed with the certainty that the two countries to which he owed allegiance would soon be at war. He was unaware of the late spring sunshine filtering through the trees or the trillium, white and starlike, on the forest floor to either side of the trail. Instead, his thoughts were filled with the things he had seen and heard in these last days that convinced him of the inevitability of a confrontation between Britain and the United States, for the second time in thirty years. He was not sure how many other men saw the signs of danger, although relations between the two countries had been deteriorating for a long time. But in his own mind he was sure, after this last trip west, that war was not only inevitable, but imminent.

He looked up towards his Indian companion who rode slightly ahead of him on the narrow path through the forest. Even Waukee rode heavily, as if his weariness was as deep and oppressive as Seth's own. It had been a fast and trying trip along the lakes and through the woodlands to the various British and American forts and settlements along the Northwestern frontier, but it would not be long before they reached their destination. By midday Seth was to meet Henry Beckwith in a tavern in Youngstown, the small town at the mouth of the Niagara River that had sprung up in the shadow of the old French fort.

Even now Porterfield was not quite sure how he had been manipulated into the decidedly uncomfortable position of acting as the principal speaker at a political meeting to be held the next evening in Lewiston, another small town upriver from Youngstown and Fort Niagara. And though he was not certain, he thought he could discern Mitchell's fine hand in this. With the usual stir of irritation, he considered the American operative for whom he had been working, in various capacities, for the past six years. Mitchell had made a particular point of introducing him to Peter Porter, the United States Congressman and noted war hawk from Buffalo. In turn, it was Porter who had introduced him to Henry Beckwith the night he had met Mitchell at a political gathering in Black Rock. From that introduction had come the invitation to speak at Lewiston on the readiness of the frontier settlements for the advent of war with Britain. Initially he had tried to demur, but, with the Congressman smiling benignly at him, it had been impossible for Seth to refuse. It was not that Porterfield lacked information on the subject. Even if he had not travelled extensively across the length and breadth of the Northwest territory in the previous months, this last journey would have pointed up the deficiencies of the American position in that quarter. The frontier settlements were unprepared and ill equipped for any conflict. But even as he reviewed what he would say to the assembled farmers, soldiers, and tradesmen, Seth knew it would not be what they wished to hear.

He sighed heavily and removed his hat to wipe the sweat from his forehead with the back of one hand. He was acutely discomforted by the position that had been foisted upon him. In the past, his activities on behalf of American causes around the world had been conducted in a much less public manner than this one would be. Damn Mitchell, he thought irritably. The man was such a devious devil that this might all be an elaborate scheme to force him firmly and publicly into the American camp. But as a man with deeply divided loyalties, that was the one final step he was loath to take. As Seth Porterfield made his way along the trail that led towards the town of Newark, on the Canadian bank of the Niagara, and the ferry to Youngstown, he vowed that, whatever the future brought, he would not bear arms against Great Britain, the country of his birth.

But then, perhaps he had read the signs incorrectly. Who could say if the new vigilance of the British troops in the Northwest, the restlessness of their Indian allies, and the massing of militia in Ohio were irrefutable signs of impending conflict? It was possible, he tried to convince himself, that war was not as imminent as it seemed. Just as it was conceivable that the differences between Britain and the United States would be resolved by words and not weapons. At any rate, there was nothing he could do to change the course of history. He could merely decide his own role in events, should his worst fears come to pass.

Slowly he straightened in the saddle and forced the dark, confusing problems of the future from his mind. What he needed now was a hot bath, fresh clothing, a hearty meal, and a good woman to share his bed. He smiled to himself and felt his spirits rise at the prospect of a soft, willing woman held tight in his arms. A wench from the Crow's Head Tavern would do nicely, he decided. He wanted someone who would demand nothing more than a few coins and the promise of mutual pleasure, someone who would go on to another when he left on his travels again. Yes, a wench from the Crow's Head Tavern would do nicely indeed.

With renewed vigour, Porterfield urged his horse to a trot and moved swiftly along the narrow trail through the trees, towards the ferry that crossed the Niagara River from Newark to Youngstown.

✳

Henry Beckwith stood in the first-storey window of his study, watching the two freight wagons approach down the tree-lined drive. The moment they drew up in front of the house, his daughter burst from the doorway to supervise the unloading of the long-awaited shipment of furniture he had finally agreed to let her order from the cabinetmakers in Philadelphia. Smiling to himself, he observed the proceedings below as the workmen jumped to do the girl's bidding, and he marvelled at her air of command. Slowly the crates and cartons were dismantled, and one by one the handsome, shield-backed chairs and upholstered loveseats, with their gracefully tapering legs, the inlaid satinwood tables, and gilt-edged mirrors emerged from their wrappings. Charlotte had made her selections wisely, he noted with pleasure, and the final result would be a home suitable for a man who had finally achieved his station in life. He had done very well for himself, Beckwith reflected with pride, in the nearly thirty years since he'd come to this wilderness.

In 1783, just after the Peace of Paris had been signed with Britain, formally ending the War for Independence, he had left Philadelphia with what money he could scrape together and no clear idea of where he would settle. He had fought in the closing days of the war and, after the surrender at Yorktown, he had returned to the city of his birth to find that his family had scattered. Nor were there many jobs available for young men with little schooling and no trade. His ability with figures had led him to several jobs as a clerk and bookkeeper, but he found work in the dreary offices both stifling and dull. With his meagre savings tied in the toe of his extra pair of socks, he had set off to seek his fortune.

He had followed the rivers north and west, first the Hudson and then the Mohawk, moving from settlement to settlement. By the time he reached Fort Niagara on the shores of Lake Ontario, his funds were gone. Of necessity, Beckwith took a job at the trading post in the fort and soon proved adept at bartering with both white men and Indians. From that post, it was a logical move to a small store of his own in the settlement of Youngstown, just south of the fort. Over the years, the business grew, and Beckwith had done well, selling goods to the men at the fort, new settlers who followed his footsteps to the Niagara frontier, as well as those travelling further west. He had continued to expand his store and soon gained a reputation as a shrewd but fair businessman.

He had left Youngstown only once in the ensuing years, travelling to Philadelphia to visit what was left of his family and find a bride. There he met and married Philippa Drew, a demure young woman of a prominent, but impoverished Philadelphia family. The Drews were happy to settle their youngest daughter on such an ambitious and wealthy young man, regardless of where he had elected to live and make his fortune. The marriage was a happy, though brief one, for Philippa died two years later after giving birth to Henry's only child, a daughter, Charlotte Louise.

After Philippa's death Beckwith divided his time between Charlotte and his business and both prospered. He expanded the store, importing luxuries not available anywhere along the frontier, so that people often saved for months for some special item, or travelled miles out of their way to visit his establishment. Over the years Charlotte had grown from cooing baby to inquisitive child and on into an attractive and remarkable young woman, a girl with a mind of her own.

In the courtyard below, that determined young woman was giving instructions to the workmen on the correct placement of the furniture once they had carried the pieces inside, and Henry smiled as he watched her. She gestured gracefully with her long, slender hands as she spoke, and eventually resorted to moving the pieces herself in characteristic impatience. How like him she was, Henry mused, his expression soft with affection for his only daughter. Charl bore his height and his colouring, though her finely moulded features marked her as her mother's child, but on a less tangible level she resembled him, as well. She had inherited his facile mind, his ready wit and his strong will. But she was also cursed with the innate stubbornness and quick temper that had been Beckwith traits for generations. As she grew, he had hired tutors to provide her with the classical education he had missed, and he had encouraged her to master the skills of horsemanship, marksmanship and sailing. Now, as a young woman, Charlotte was a complete person in every respect: well educated, well liked in the community, and well adapted to the odd mixture of burgeoning society and harsh reality that encompassed the spectrum of life on the frontier. And during these last months, when he had finally given way to her demands and allowed her to help at the store, she had proved herself a shrewd businesswoman as well. If only she had been a son instead of a daughter, Beckwith mused, he would have welcomed her as an associate.

The expression of pleasure gave way to a fleeting frown. Charlotte was a lovely young woman, solidly and yet supplely built, with glowing alabaster skin and tumbled masses of golden hair. But, for all her beauty, she showed little interest in the usual feminine intrigues of attracting a husband. Already, she had sent several young men packing, stung by her acid tongue and devastated by a delicate disdain that instantly deflated a man's vanity. It was only the dogged Stephen Langley who persisted in courting her. And Henry did not doubt that Charl would run him off in time since she seemed unwilling to consider his suit.

Beckwith sighed and rubbed a hand across his brow. There was no question that he had raised Charlotte with too much freedom, letting her run free because he did not want to break her spirit, encouraging her accomplishments even when her behaviour and her skills were quite unseemly. Bringing up a daughter without a proper lady's influence to temper his judgement had not been an easy task, Beckwith argued in his own defence. And Harriet, the widow he had hired as a housekeeper when Charlotte was a baby, had not been up to the job of raising Charl either. In truth, she had been as beguiled by his bright, charming daughter as he, and with a child as single-minded and unbending as Charl, it had been easier to simply give the girl her head rather than discipline her. But, in spite of the few restrictions they had imposed, Charl had developed any number of positive qualities: courage, honour, intelligence, and self-reliance. They were not traits nineteenth-century society particularly prized in its women, but perhaps that was more the pity. Those things were what made Charl the uniquely admirable young woman she was. Still, Beckwith could not help wishing she had learned to play her prescribed role with a little greater conviction.

Then, just at that moment, Charl caught sight of her father at the window and waved gaily, gesturing for him to join them downstairs. Her face was flushed with the morning's exertions, and her hair had escaped its pins to tumble untidily down her back. When he saw the glow in her eyes, he was abruptly reminded of an intangible feminine warmth about her, the artless charm that instantly won over everyone she met. She possessed a genuine kindness, instinctive understanding and a deep capacity for love that tempered her fierce, independent spirit and stubborn determination.

With a smile of pride on his lips, Henry Beckwith turned from the window. He would join Charlotte downstairs and admire her purchases close to. Besides, it would soon be time to dispatch Charl to the Crow's Head Tavern to meet the man who was to be their houseguest. He well knew that propriety dictated that he meet the man himself, but there was pressing business at hand, and he was needed elsewhere. Besides, Charl would not mind stopping by the congenial country inn on the waterfront. Welcoming their guest was her job, after all, Beckwith rationalized. It was part of her role as hostess, and it would leave him free to tend to matters of his own. With the question of their houseguest's arrival resolved in his own mind, Beckwith headed downstairs.

✣

Charl Beckwith rushed into the ivory-and-blue bedroom at the front of the house with a frown between her gracefully winged brows. As anxious as she usually was to do her father's bidding, she was more than a little irritated that she had to set aside what she was doing and go up to the Crow's Head Tavern to greet their visitor. Not that Harriet, the housekeeper who had been with the Beckwiths as long as Charl could remember, was incapable of supervising the workmen who were uncrating the furniture; it was just that Charl had waited so long for the new pieces to arrive from Philadelphia that she wanted to unpack them herself. Besides, she resented this Mr Porterfield's intrusion when the house was in such an uproar in preparation for the party they would host in less than a fortnight. There was the downstairs to set to rights after the extensive painting and papering that had just been completed, the rugs to air, the menu for the party to be finalized, the wines to be chosen, and the last fittings for her gown to be scheduled, in addition to the normal duties of the household and store that would need attention. The last thing she needed right now was a houseguest underfoot. But, like it or not, Charl knew it was her responsibility to make the man feel welcome in her father's home.

As she washed her face at the basin, she speculated about the man she was preparing to meet. If he was like the rest of her father's business associates, he would be paunchy and aloof. Most likely he would treat her with galling condescension every time she opened her mouth to voice her opinion or ask a question, as their other visitors had. Nor would he willingly acknowledge that she worked at the store and had some sway over the goods her father stocked. Men were such fools, she reflected, as she stood in her chemise and stockinged feet, selecting a clean gown from the cupboard. Why was it that they were determined to treat women as if there wasn't a brain in their heads? What she did to help her father was demanding and absorbing work, and she readily enjoyed every phase of it. She only hoped that someday she would be accepted as her father's equal in the business, as she would undoubtedly have been if she had been born a son and not a daughter.

She finally selected a blue-and-white striped, muslin gown from among the others and began to struggle into it. Of course, this Mr Porterfield who was coming was not one of her father's business associates, but someone who was coming to speak at the political meeting tomorrow evening. With that realization, Charl's image changed. Porterfield would likely be pompous and stout, with a florid face that became more so as he spoke, and crisp, white hair, waving back from his brow. He had probably been an attractive man in his youth and had retained a modicum of that handsomeness into his older years. Charl already had cause to observe that men who had enjoyed carnal lust in their youth often replaced it with the lust for power as they grew older.

And why not, Charl reflected, since both fed a vain man's image of himself. As the appetite for one dwindled, the hunger for the other arose.

She doubted, however, that her father's interest in politics stemmed from that same source. It was not the desire for power that stirred Henry Beckwith, but the desire for wealth. He was a self-made man who easily recalled the poverty of his childhood, and his primary interest, after Charlotte herself, was in amassing his fortune. The store was a beginning, but he planned to speculate in huge tracts of land and make other investments along the expanding frontier. He saw the possibility of war with Britain not as a conflict to be avoided, but as an almost limitless opportunity for growth, development, and profit. Charl did not like the new preoccupation with the manoeuvrings of politics that she saw in her father, but she understood his motives. It was immaterial that she did not share his views, and he stubbornly refused to consider her opposing arguments. He had seen to it himself that Charl was well educated and well informed, but with the usual prejudices of his sex he refused to let her speak her mind. Still, she worried, both about him and about the advent of war. Should the declaration come, they would find themselves so close, both in proximity and situation, to their enemies across the river.

From her window, Charl could see that Tim, her father's groom, had brought the gig around to the front of the house, and she knew she must hurry. She flew to the mirror with brush in hand. There was no time to arrange her hair in one of the intricate hairstyles that were the fashion, so she drew a wide blue ribbon through her hair, to hold it back from her face, then wrestled the thickly waving locks into some semblance of order. Casting the brush aside, she glanced at the china clock on the dresser, then began a frantic search along the edge of the bed for her boots. Finding them, Charl hurried to the door and down the stairs to the carriage.

The drive to the Crow's Head Tavern was a short one, and Charl handled the reins with practised facility. She would have preferred to ride her horse, but undoubtedly Mr Porterfield had come to Youngstown by water and would certainly have baggage that could not be carried on horseback. She left the gig behind the store and walked swiftly in the direction of the tavern that was perched on the riverbank just above the ferry dock.

The Crow's Head was a very well kept tavern that had stood on this site for more years than even Henry Beckwith could remember. It was run by the Fisher family and offered not only clean rooms for the night, but hot, plentiful, tasty food and a hospitable atmosphere that made it a gathering place for locals and travellers alike. It was a stout, stone building with a wood shingle roof and a sign that creeked on its hinges in the lightest breeze off the river. At this time of day it was busy with merchants, farmers and travellers gathered for the noon meal. Coming into its dark, cool interior from the bright sunlight left Charl dazzled, and it was a moment before she was able to scan the tables for the man she was to meet. Conjuring up her images of Seth Porterfield, she studied the people gathered in the taproom's smoky interior. In one corner was a huge, scarred table where the locals gathered to swap stories and exchange ideas. Sometimes it was tales from the lands to the west that held the men enthralled; sometimes it was plans for planting and harvesting that were discussed. But more and more often it was the political situation between Britain and America that caused voices to rise. Even now Charl could hear the issues that had been hotly debated for months being reiterated. It was here that Henry Beckwith sat night after night, deeply embroiled in these same arguments that made tempers flare today. For Youngstown was deeply divided on the issue of a second war with Britain. And if it had been her father instead of Charl who had come to meet this Mr Porterfield, he would doubtless have joined this group, adding his views to the others being so passionately expressed.

Charl recognized Wilcox the tinker, McTavish the cooper, and Norris the gunsmith from the fort, as well as several farmers from up near Eighteen Mile Creek at that table. Once she was certain that her Mr Porterfield was not a member of that noisy group, she allowed her gaze to move over the benches and chairs that were pulled up in random pattern to the wide, planked tables. But none of the men eating and drinking there, or any of the group by the fireplace, speculating boisterously on the outcome of the game of draughts that was in progress, seemed to be the one she sought. As the proprietor, Mr Fisher, passed her with a large, circular tray of tankards balanced on one shoulder, Charlotte stopped him.

'Father sent me to meet a Mr Porterfield here,' she told him when they had exchanged pleasantries. 'Could you point him out to me?'

Fisher smiled agreeably, and his keen eyes swept across the low-ceilinged room. 'Mr Porterfield, eh Charlotte? He's a tall fellow as I recall. I don't see him just now, but he'll be along in a bit, no doubt. Why don't you find a seat if you can, and I'll send Mary over with some cider for you.'

A tall fellow, Charl mused as she made her way towards an empty table by the wall. Well, perhaps this Mr Porterfield would not run to paunch as she had expected. Instead, he would doubtless be a scarecrow of a man with stooped shoulders and a spade chin. Charl bit back a grin at the new image of their unwanted houseguest she'd conjured up. Then the smile was transformed to an impatient frown as she settled back into her chair to endure the wait forced on her by Mr Porterfield's tardiness.

✻

The ferry nudged gently against the wooden dock on the American side of the Niagara River, and the wide plank at one end of the flatboat was gradually lowered to allow passengers to disembark. Following a heavily loaded freight wagon, Porterfield and Waukee led their horses off the ferry and up the sloping riverbank. In front of the tall stone tavern, Seth paused as the Indian swung into his saddle.

'I expect to be in this area for about a fortnight,' he told his companion.

'And after that?' the redskin asked, his dark eyes intent on his friend's face.

Seth shrugged. 'That depends a great deal on what happens between now and then. I expect I'll be heading towards Quebec either to collect my belongings or –' His voice trailed off as he frowned; he was unsure of where his orders or inclinations might take him.

The Indian nodded with complete understanding of the white man's feelings. He was well aware that the question of Seth's loyalty was still unresolved and weighed heavily on his mind.

'The gathering of the bark and berries that are found only in the Onondaga's swamps will not take that long,' he said softly. 'I will be waiting on the opposite bank when you are ready, but I fear that if trouble comes, you and I will be divided by far more than a river, my brother.'

Seth looked up and saw the sadness in the brave's deep brown eyes.

'We will see what the future brings, my friend. Until then, we will ride together, as we always have.'

For an instant Seth clasped his hand on the Indian's wrist and felt Waukee's grip on his own in the age-old sign of brotherhood. Then, without a word, the redskin turned his horse up the bank and rode away. For a long moment, Seth stood watching him as he reflected on what the Indian had said. Then he turned, tied his horse to a hitching post and entered the Crow's Head Tavern.

Inside, Seth went directly to the bar and asked for a tankard of ale, downing most of it in one swallow. He looked around for Henry Beckwith and, not seeing him, ordered a second drink. Perhaps after he had slaked his thirst, he would go to Beckwith's store and find him there, Porterfield reasoned. He knew it was well past the appointed hour for their meeting, and it was possible that the man hadn't waited.

As he sipped at the second tankard, Seth's eyes came to rest on a girl sitting alone at a table by the wall. She was like a ray of sunshine in the dark room, and he straightened as he watched her. He could not remember when he had seen anyone so lovely. Her thick, golden-yellow hair curved softly against her cheeks and tumbled down across her shoulders like a gilded waterfall. Her face was creamy and pink, with the last hint of girlish roundness remaining in her features. In repose her mouth was small, but perfectly formed, with a sensuously full lower lip, and Seth found himself wondering how that soft coral mouth would taste yielding beneath his own. He was suddenly aware of how long it had been since he had made love to a woman, and he took a deep breath, letting it out slowly.

Who was this enchanting creature sitting alone in a tavern, even a tavern as respectable as this one, at midday? It was clear that she was no farmer's wife. She was too well dressed, and there was something patrician about the arch of those golden eyebrows and the line of her nose that hinted at a genteel background. Besides, no farmer would allow his wife to while away an afternoon when there was work to be done. And it was equally certain that she was not a tavern wench.

The good quality of the fabric and the fashionable cut of her gown made him think that she might be a seamstress, come to town to work for one of the local ladies. Perhaps she was a young

widow, he went on embroidering the tale as he sipped from his
tankard, forced to turn her domestic talents to making money by
the untimely death of her husband. But then, if this woman was
a travelling dressmaker, she would surely be wearing a shawl and
bonnet, and carrying a valise. Nor was it likely that a seamstress
could afford to sit idle in the afternoon either.

Seth frowned slightly and set the tankard aside. It had been a
long time since any woman had intrigued him so. Her thick, dark
lashes fluttered against her cheeks as she stared moodily into her
glass, and Seth willed her to look up so he could see the colour
of her eyes. Green, he thought, as her gaze locked with his. And,
since he had succeeded in gaining her attention, he smiled at her.

Good God! Charl thought to herself when she realized that
the man across the room had been watching her. Who does that
fellow think he is to look at me this way?

And yet, regardless of the indignation that flushed her cheeks
bright pink, she was staring back, becoming increasingly aware
of the man whose blue gaze locked with hers. He was a very tall
man and an undeniably· good looking one too, in a rough,
unkempt sort of way. Though he was broadly built, with a
wide chest and shoulders, there was not a spare ounce of flesh
anywhere on his lithe, long-boned frame. His waist was trim and
his long dark-trousered legs, above the knee-high moccasins,
looked hard and well muscled. And indeed, except for his blond
hair, waving thickly at his neck and across his forehead, he might
well have resembled an Indian in his fringed buckskin shirt. His
skin was ruddy with sun and vitality, and his features were strong.
Blond eyebrows were prominent above his thick-lashed blue
eyes, and his nose and cheekbones were finely chiseled. There
was a certain hardness to the line of his jaw, though his chin was
softened by the shadow of a deep cleft. Stubbornness showed in
the straight, narrow lips, but there were lines of good humour at
the corners that deepened when he smiled, as he was doing now.
For a moment Charl was totally aware of him, as if she could
sense him with every part of her body. The flush in her cheeks
darkened, and by an act of will she tore her eyes from his
unwavering stare.

Who was this bold stranger? she wondered in confusion. And
why did he look at her so with those brilliant, sapphire-dark
eyes? It was almost as if he wished to devour her, to memorize
every line of her face and body. Clearly he was an impudent

fellow to watch her so openly. But that did not explain her own reaction to him: the pulse that tapped erratically in her throat, or the tremor of something akin to excitement that had raced through her in those first few moments.

Slowly, anger began to replace the confusion this man inspired in her, and she took refuge in the notion that he was sadly in need of a lesson in manners.

'Has anyone told you today how lovely you are?' a deep, well-modulated voice asked quietly.

Charl looked up and was startled to find the tall, blond man standing over her, a slight half smile still on his lips.

'I'll sit down if you don't mind,' he continued smoothly as he pulled out the chair opposite her. Her eyes widened in surprise, and Porterfield could see he had misjudged the colour. They were not just green, but multicoloured, almost as if shards of glass, green, yellow, and blue, had been arranged concentrically. For a moment he felt lost in their luminous, multifaceted depths, but then her expression changed and her brows rushed together in a frown.

Up close this stranger seemed totally disreputable, his face covered with red-gold stubble and his clothes untidy.

'Yes, I do mind if you sit with me,' she began hotly. 'I'd be very glad if you would return to your station at the bar before it's necessary for me to call the proprietor. I have absolutely no desire to share my table with the likes of you.'

For an instant Seth was caught off-balance by the girl's response. Even from across the room he had sensed an intangible current of attraction flowing between them. When he had approached her, he had expected a pleasant flirtation, not an argument. Irritated by her manner, Seth felt his temper rise.

'I can see now that I sadly misjudged you, madam,' he said with a mocking nod. 'Because you have the face of an angel, I expected you to have the temperament of one. But to my disappointment, I find that though you may have the face of an angel, it is accompanied by the temperament of a shrew.' He spoke the words quietly in a deceptively soft voice, but each clipped word stung her.

'How dare you speak to me that way, you odious ruffian!' she raged, her eyes flashing. 'How dare you presume to speak to a lady at all!'

'A lady?' he drawled, as one eyebrow drifted infuriatingly

upward. 'Oh, then please pardon my confusion. It is just that I did not expect to find a lady sitting alone in a saloon like a trollop.'

Charl drew a hissing breath and stiffened at his words. It was only by the strongest dint of will that she refrained from slapping the lazy smile from his face. Who was this vulgar blackguard to speak to her this way? And why hadn't she simply ignored him and frozen him out rather than sitting here blazingly angry, casting around for the most scathing words she knew?

From the corner of her eye she could see Mr Fisher approaching. Surely she could count on him to rescue her from this despicable man's attentions.

'I see you found your Mr Porterfield, eh Charlotte?' Fisher observed as he reached their table. 'Now may I get anything else for either of you?'

Charl's flushed face went suddenly ashen.

'You? You're Seth Porterfield?' she whispered incredulously, a jolt of shock racing through her. How was this possible, she asked herself. This wasn't the kind of man her father brought into their home. This man looked like an adventurer, not a politician or a merchant. Surely there had been some mistake.

Across the table Seth Porterfield was watching the shifting emotions on her expressive face.

'Bring the lady another glass of whatever she's been drinking, and I'll have a tankard of ale,' he told the innkeeper in an even voice.

Seth Porterfield! Charl still stared at him speechlessly, unable to comprehend what business he could possibly have with her father. Had Henry Beckwith met this man? Did he know what this Mr Porterfield was like?

He had said such dreadful things to her, things no gentleman would ever say. He had called her a shrew and mistaken her for a trollop! Oh, she would make him sorry for that.

And now she was supposed to make this awful man welcome in her home, extend her courtesy to this boor! At the thought heady anger surged through her. How could her father expect her to offer this miscreant her hospitality? Yet she knew he would.

While Charl struggled with her dilemma, Seth's thoughts took their own course. It was obvious that this girl knew who he was, but how? Surely he had never met her before, and yet she knew his name and where he could be found. A natural caution took over his senses, and he watched the woman with new interest. He had long prided himself on his ability to judge people at a glance, and often enough his life had depended on that skill. But he could detect no threat in this girl who'd had the temerity to bandy words with him. Who was she, he wondered. And what business did she have with him?

Fisher's arrival with the refreshments broke into Porterfield's thoughts. After the innkeeper had been paid and moved on to other customers, Seth tipped back in his chair and regarded the blonde woman with a speculative air.

'You have me at a disadvantage, madam,' he began. 'You seem to be quite aware of who I am, but you remain a mystery to me.'

Charl felt a flush rise again beneath the candour of his penetrating gaze.

'I'm Charlotte Beckwith, Henry Beckwith's daughter. My father asked me to meet you today, since he has business elsewhere, and offer you the hospitality of our home for the duration of your stay,' she informed him crisply.

She was such a changeable woman, Seth reflected with the slightest of smiles. A few moments ago, she had been all fury and fire, but now her voice was icy cold. So this was Henry Beckwith's girl. As he recalled the man he had met only once, he could see some similarities in their colouring. Beckwith's hair was faded with grey to a sandy tan, and his complexion was more ruddy with sun. But there was something in the clear, direct eyes that was the same.

Slowly he began to relax, and the growing humour of the situation struck him. They had spoken harshly to each other, and now she would have to recant. She would be expected to act the perfect hostess and make him welcome in her home, in spite of her obvious dislike for him. No wonder she looked so cross. It would certainly prove amusing to see how she handled this situation. Nor did he plan to make it easy for her.

Impossible situation, impossible man, Charl raged inwardly as she noticed the glint of laughter in Seth Porterfield's blue eyes. It was clear that this smirking jackanapes had her at a disadvantage this time, but the next time she crossed swords with him, she would be sure to have the upper hand.

'Of course, there's plenty of room at the house, and we'd be

delighted to have you,' she went on as if there had been no
lengthy pause. 'We're right at the edge of town on the River
Road, so the house is handy to things. Father will insist you stay
with us unless you've made other plans,' she added hopefully,
increasingly aware of his growing amusement at her expense.

'My dear Miss Beckwith,' Porterfield began in a solicitous
voice that grated on her nerves. 'Your offer of hospitality is very
generous, and I'm sure you make a gracious hostess, but I would
hate to impose on you and your family. Though, in truth, I have
no other plans.' His voice trailed off, and she could see the lines
deepen at the corners of his mouth, though he had the good
grace not to grin outright. There was no doubt that he was baiting
her, and she knew it.

Oh damn him, Charl thought as she struggled to control her
anger. Now this reprehensible fellow wanted to be coaxed. Well,
he could find accommodation in hell for all she cared. She would
play this foolish game no more.

With as much dignity as she could muster, Charl rose to stand
over him and fixed him with an arctic stare.

'There are only my father and myself in the house, and I assure
you your presence will be no inconvenience. Father instructed
me to extend our welcome to you, and that is exactly what I've
done. If you have decided to avail yourself of our hospitality,
then I trust you can gather your belongings in the next few
minutes, while I complete my errands, and meet me at my father's
store. If you prefer to make your own arrangements, then I bid
you good day.'

The speech had been delivered in the frostiest tones, and when
she had finished, Charlotte Beckwith turned on her heel and
swept majestically out of the tavern.

Seth watched her go with a glow of admiration in his eyes. The
girl had handled the situation well, in spite of his taunts. But the
greater part of that feeling was inspired by a sudden physical
hunger for this lovely young woman. For as she made her sweeping exit, Porterfield had become aware of the lush body beneath
the concealing folds of the demure gown. Though Charlotte was
tall and slender, there was a sensuous fullness to her breasts and
hips, and he had caught a glimpse of trim ankles that hinted at
long shapely legs hidden under her flowing skirts and petticoats.

The tavern wenches, whose company he had contemplated
with such pleasure during the ride to Youngstown, suddenly held

no allure for him. With the hint of a smile at the corners of his mouth, he went to gather up his belongings as the lovely Charlotte had suggested. For in the next days he intended to take advantage of whatever hospitality she had to offer.

❋

Charl hoped the sounds of the meal, the tinkle of silver against china, and the men's softly murmuring voices would cover her own deliberate silence. She had planned a grand dinner for this evening, expecting that the maze of knives and forks would puzzle and embarrass their boorish guest, but Seth Porterfield seemed quite at home with the heavily laid table. Much to Charl's consternation, he seemed equally at ease in the formally cut tail coat of black broadcloth, the slate blue silk waistcoat, and the well-tailored trousers. Where they or the fine linen shirt and neckcloth had come from, she could only guess. They seemed unusual attire for a backwoodsman, and he had carried little baggage. Yet when she had announced this afternoon, as they drove back from the tavern, that they usually dressed for dinner, he had only smiled and nodded.

Charl herself had taken particular pains with her own toilette, selecting a pale, seafoam green gown with a froth of lace edging the deeply scooped neckline. Dark, forest green ribbons banded the high waist and tapering sleeves to complete the design. Harriet had toiled over her hair for nearly half an hour, finally coaxing the softly waving tresses into a shimmering cascade that tumbled provocatively down her back. With carefully curled ringlets haloing her face, and her mother's prized emeralds at her throat and ears, her intention had been to set this irritating Mr Porterfield back on his heels. And while she was aware of the flare of admiration in his eyes, his grin had been decidedly wolfish.

Now, halfway through the soup course, she allowed herself to watch him from beneath her lowered lashes. With an almost imperceptible frown she noted how well he handled the utensils as he ate. Clearly she had underestimated him this afternoon, she conceded. His attire was impeccable and his manners, when he chose to use them, were exactly correct. Somewhere he had been brought up a gentleman, and he looked, as well as acted, the part tonight. Though he was clean shaven and bathed, she would never have believed him to be the same ruffian she had found in the tavern this afternoon. And he was handsome; even she couldn't deny that. With his dark blond hair, highlighted by the mellow light of the candles, and the ruddy glow of his tanned skin in sharp contrast to his deep blue eyes, she had to admit that he was an attractive man indeed. Somehow though, the genteel dress and courtly manners seemed to point up rather than hide the rakish strength of his features and the glitter in his eyes that seemed both predatory and mischievous. There was something about the male vitality of him that nullified even her father's imposing presence and made her strangely aware of this Seth Porterfield, though she had set out to ignore him.

'Charlotte!' her father's irritated voice cut through her thoughts. 'Mr Porterfield has asked you twice about the new table in the hall. He says it's quite like the things he's seen in France.'

Colour warmed her cheekbones at her father's reproving tone as she stared mutinously at their houseguest. Somehow she found it difficult to believe that this man cared much about the latest furniture styles.

'I understand the origin of the design is French, inspired by the pieces in Napoleon's court. But then, I believe that the emperor's reign has inspired any number of new ideas,' she replied coolly. 'Have you been to France recently, Mr Porterfield?'

Something in her manner irritated Seth, but he kept his temper in check and smiled lazily at the blonde woman.

'It has been nearly two years since my last visit, Miss Beckwith. Since then things on this side of the Atlantic have kept me occupied. I do miss the gentility of Europe, however, and especially pleasant conversations with beautiful ladies.' At the comment his blue eyes met hers across the table, and he raised his wineglass in her direction, then put it to his lips.

A bright flush flamed in Charl's cheeks as she realized the biting sarcasm behind the toast, but she managed a sour smile before she looked away from Porterfield's grin. Decorum dictated her behaviour towards a guest in her home, but it was with the utmost difficulty that she kept her true feelings hidden.

Once again Seth was reminded of what an unusual woman Charlotte Beckwith was to remain cool and self-possessed in the face of his taunt. It was only the heightening of her colour that acknowledged his words, and he was puzzled by his own compulsion to goad her. This afternoon in the tavern she had shown this same mixture of spirit and self-control that intrigued him now. And he could not help but wonder what other things he would discover about the lovely Charlotte in the days to come.

He had already learned that she drove a gig with consummate skill and prided herself on her somewhat unmaidenly ability with a pistol. As they headed out of town, he had noted the primed pistol beside her on the seat and had remarked upon it.

'Father insists that I carry it when I drive alone,' she had told him. 'After all, Mr Porterfield, there are some who consider Youngstown the wild frontier.'

He had made a derisive comment about her aim, and in response she had pulled to the side of the road, indicated a dead branch some way ahead, sighted on it and fired. That her shot had been accurate from a substantial distance unsettled him. And when she told him she was even more proficient with a musket, he was wise enough not to doubt her.

Yet in spite of her avowed ability at unfeminine occupations, there was a definite woman's touch evident in the imposing house at the end of the tree-lined drive. The well-tended flowerbeds enhanced the beauty of the solidly built brick home and focused attention on the intricate details of the fanlighted entrance. Inside, everything was sparkling clean and orderly, in spite of the arrival of the new furniture. The faint scent of lemon oil polish and beeswax was discernible above the mouthwatering smell of baking bread, and Seth was immediately glad that he'd accepted the girl's reluctant invitation. He had noticed that the servants scurried to do their mistress's bidding, almost as if she was granting favours instead of assigning chores. His valise and saddlebags had been whisked from his hands the moment they entered the hall, and by the time he had washed and joined Charlotte for a light luncheon in the dining room, her eyes had been, if not friendly, at least not hostile either.

So why, he wondered, had he found it necessary to bait her this evening at dinner? What was it that was so inexplicably irritating about the toneless, impersonal voice she used to address him and the wall of reserve she set between them? Without understanding the reasons, he had been suddenly determined that if Charlotte Beckwith would not acknowledge the glow of admiration in his eyes, he would at least make it impossible for her to ignore him.

Yes, Charlotte Beckwith must be a rare woman indeed, he

reflected, to inspire this much interest on his part. It was somehow out of character for him to consider any female once he'd left the bedroom. And while he did not deny that he had thought of the lovely Charlotte in that context, it was almost unheard of for him to set aside his natural caution and allow a woman to alter his plans in any way. Yet here he was, a guest in Henry Beckwith's house, when his intention had been to stay at the Crow's Head Tavern. In truth, he had been more caught up in the humour of the embarrassing situation that Miss Beckwith had found herself in this afternoon than swayed by her frosty, reticent invitation. He was firmly settled in the handsome green-and-gold bedroom before he realized the anonymity he had unwittingly forfeited in agreeing to accept the Beckwiths' hospitality. For, in spite of the confusion of his conflicting loyalties, there were still several assignments to complete for Mitchell. But as he watched the lovely girl across the table, with her cheeks flushed and her eyes bright, Seth could not convince himself that he was sorry about any set of circumstances that brought him here.

❧

When the interminable dinner was finally finished, Charl wished for nothing more than escape to the solitude of her room, but her father insisted that she join them in the parlour, as she usually did when only her father was at home. Once there, settled in her favourite chair with her feet tucked up beneath her, Charl accepted a small glass of excellent brandy. She sipped it appreciatively, savouring the taste of it on the back of her tongue and welcoming its warmth deep inside her. Judging from the expression on Seth Porterfield's face, he was half expecting her to demand a cigar as well. And for an instant she almost did, torn between the desire to shock this unwelcome guest and the memory of how sick she'd been the first time she'd smoked one. She restrained herself and toyed absently with the ribbons on her dress.

'Charlotte, you've been very quiet this evening,' Beckwith observed as he lit his cigar with a taper, the smoke billowing up in a writhing cloud as he puffed.

'There's no reason, Father,' she said softly, her cheeks unusually pink. 'I may be a little tired, that's all.'

'I'm afraid it's my fault, Beckwith. Miss Beckwith and I got off on the wrong foot this afternoon,' Porterfield began, smiling indulgently at her as he rolled the cigar between his long, tanned

fingers. There was such a challenge in that insolent grin that
Charl found herself gritting her teeth to maintain control of her
temper. 'You see, I was so taken with her beauty, even before I
knew who she was, that I was quite forward with her. Will you
accept an apology for my deplorable behaviour, my dear Miss
Beckwith, and tell me that I am forgiven? And may I address
you simply as Charlotte, as is the delightful custom in your
frontier society?'

He was baiting her again: his blue eyes were sunny with mirth,
and the creases at the corners of his eyes and mouth crinkled as
he flashed her an appealing smile.

Her first impulse was to dash her brandy into Seth Porterfield's
smirking face, but she knew with her father here she dare not.
Nor could she tell this odious person exactly what she thought
of him, but neither was she a woman who minced words.

'What I will accept, Mr Porterfield, is the assessment of your
behaviour,' she began in a tight voice. 'Regrettably I cannot
imagine what you could say to warrant my forgiveness. As for
my name, I would rather you did not speak to me at all. But if
it is necessary to address me, Charl is what I prefer.'

'And you may call me Seth,' Porterfield told her magnani-
mously, undeterred and grinning broadly.

Henry Beckwith was appalled by his daughter's behaviour
towards his guest, though Porterfield seemed to take no offence.
What could Charlotte be thinking of to speak so to a visitor in
their home, and a friend of Congressman Porter's to boot? Good
Lord, but his daughter could be impossible at times, though he'd
tried to do his best with her. Then suddenly Henry became
uncomfortably aware of a strange current that existed between
his daughter and this man. Abruptly he broke into the lengthening
silence.

'Well then, Charlotte, if you are unwilling to enter into any
form of pleasant conversation, perhaps you will entertain us with
a little music.'

Truculently, Charl went to the pianoforte in the alcove near
the front windows and lit the candles on either side of the music
stand.

'I am sorry about Charlotte's manner, Porterfield,' Henry
apologized. 'Sometimes the girl is unbearably headstrong.'

'It's quite all right, I completely under –'

Seth's words were lost in a thunderous sweep of chords that

swelled from the deep bass to the trilling soprano, in a rhythmic roll of scales, that seemed to exorcize a bit of the girl's tension. Her first selection was a stirring piece with a distinctly martial air that effectively drowned out all attempts at conversation. Gradually the men subsided in their chairs to drink, smoke, and listen.

The girl played extremely well, Seth conceded, as he settled back and stretched his long legs before him. Mentally he tallied one more accomplishment on Charl Beckwith's side of the ledger. Slowly the tempo and tenor of the selections changed, and Seth recognized some Bach and Mozart among the pieces she played so skilfully. The candlelight, the brandy, and the music were combining to drain away the accumulated anxiety of the last weeks, leaving Seth filled with languorous calm.

Slowly he turned his head to look towards the lovely young woman at the keyboard, and, as he watched the serene expression on her pale face, he realized that she was as lost in the pleasure of her music as he was himself. The fullness of the sound surrounded him, weaving its spell until she the performer and he the listener were bound together in a communion that supplanted the conflicts of their own personalities. He could never remember being so absorbed by music, of being so aware of the melodies and harmonies blending in his head, or of being so acutely conscious of the woman who played with such power and skill. Seth felt touched by her through the ebb and flow of notes, touched, compelled and assimilated until his entire concentration was focused in the simple enjoyment of Charl's music.

Eventually the impromptu concert came to an end, as he had known it must. But before the last reverberating chord had died away, Henry Beckwith was sitting forward in his chair, demanding responses to questions he had obviously been bursting to ask all evening.

Because Seth was sitting totally relaxed and empty headed, Beckwith's inquiries caught him unprepared, and it was a long moment before he even realized what his host was saying.

'Do you think war will be declared soon, Porterfield? While our Congress dawdles with their endless debates, are those damned Britishers fortifying their possessions all along the frontier?'

'I can see you are an impatient man, Beckwith,' Porterfield began, trying to rouse himself sufficiently to make a reply. 'But those are exactly the questions I had planned to address at the meeting tomorrow night. Surely you can see that it will be better to wait until I can show you my maps and explain in detail the significance of what's been happening in the West.'

Beckwith clearly saw the other man's logic, but was irritated and disgruntled by Porterfield's rebuff, no matter the reason for it. Fixing Seth with a grim look, he went on.

'And just how is it you've come by such accurate information? Peter Porter never did explain how you came to be so well qualified to discuss both the American and the British fortifications. What makes you privy to so much confidential information?'

Porterfield knew he could hardly tell Beckwith the truth, and he lacked the energy to fabricate a plausible lie. Instead he chose a middle road. His answer was deliberately misleading, but based in fact.

'Why Beckwith,' he drawled, 'I should think that you would only have to hear me speak to understand the reason. For all intents and purposes, I'm accepted as one of them, one of your damned British. I travel where I like, and no one questions me.'

As he spoke, Seth had become aware that Charl Beckwith was watching him from where she sat at the pianoforte, an expression of frank interest on her exquisite face. And almost of their own volition his words went on, disclosing far more about himself than he'd intended.

'I was born in England the illegitimate son of a duke and a lady of the court. Of course, my birth raised a few eyebrows, and I was packed off to live with my mother's father at the family estate in Yorkshire as soon as my mother could be rid of me. They sent me to all the best schools, though. You see, even if I was a bastard, I was gentry and they felt a responsibility towards me. I never did very well though; I was in one scrape after another. Then, when I was fifteen, there was one final indiscretion my grandfather was not prepared to overlook. I was too much like my father it seemed. So they bundled me off to Quebec, to my uncle in the Army, with the hope that the military would be the makings of me.'

With the memory, Alastair Porterfield's image rose up before Seth, his grandfather's granite-hard face moulded in the familiar lines of disapproval. For a long moment he stared blankly ahead, and then continued.

'My Uncle William was something of a rake, and not all that

much older than I was. I think he came to understand me as well
as anyone ever has. I was to join his artillery unit when I turned
sixteen, but in the end I could not. Instead, William found me a
place with a party of surveyors going west to map the land north
of the Great Lakes as far as Fort Mackinac. By the time the
surveying party went back, I had made friends with the Indians
who had acted as our guides, and I decided to stay on with them.
When I returned to Quebec, William had been killed and, since
I knew the Western territories so well, I hired myself out as a
guide. In 1803, I was sent to Washington as part of a delegation
from Upper Canada to review the boundaries of the immense
tract of land Jefferson had just purchased from France. Since
then I've travelled quite a bit, both on this continent and in
Europe. I have friends on both sides of this conflict who keep
me informed. And if in my travels I watch and listen carefully,
who's to say what information I might pick up by careful observation, or glean from an unguarded tongue.'

'But, Porterfield,' Henry broke in single-mindedly. 'Do you
think there will be a war?'

Seth's eyes had been so intent on Charlotte's face as he spoke
that he had almost forgotten her father's presence in the chair
beside him. In addition to the start Beckwith's question had given
him, he was uncomfortable with the need to address a subject he
had finally succeeded in putting out of his mind. He swirled the
brandy in his glass and frowned.

'Yes, Beckwith,' he said finally, 'I'm afraid that there will be
a war between Britain and America, though I hope to God it
won't come to that. I know you, Peter Porter, and the rest of the
so-called war hawks see that eventuality as an opportunity to be
seized and welcomed: a chance for political power and financial
gain. But I warn you, Beckwith, you may well pay a very high
price for your ambition.'

Seth realized quite suddenly that he had said far more to these
two people than he had ever intended, and revealed more of
himself than was wise. What had possessed him to talk so freely?
He knew better, and with a flash of premonition he was certain
he would live to regret this indiscretion. He was a fool to be so
open with strangers. Yet even now there was something in
the emerald-dark depths of Charlotte Beckwith's eyes that was
unfathomable and compelling. The silence swelled around them,
and Seth knew he must leave the room or compound his folly.

With a quick, fluid movement he drained his glass and came to his feet.

'Now, if you will excuse me,' he began in a formal tone, 'I find I am rather tired tonight and would like to retire. Mr Beckwith, Charl, I bid you good evening.' With a slight bow he turned to go, and a moment later they could hear his bedroom door slam behind him.

Two
✻✻✻

'Gentlemen, gentlemen, may I have your attention please,' Henry Beckwith's deep voice boomed above the tumult of conversations as he called the meeting to order. Shortly the clamour of voices subsided, and the forty-odd men who had gathered in the stuffy, first-floor room of the tavern in Lewiston turned their attention to the speaker. Tacked up on the wall behind him were several large, carefully drawn maps, and slightly to Beckwith's right was a stranger who faced the assembly with a frown between his fair brows.

Even as he waited for his introduction, the tall blond man found himself wondering what light his few observations on conditions in the West could shed on a situation that had been growing steadily worse since Thomas Jefferson's presidency. This conflict had begun when both Britain and France had decided to expand the war they had been fighting to include a blockade of each other's ports. Britain's Orders of Council and France's Berlin and Milan Decrees, issued to that end, had served to impede American shipping and had caused a hue and cry from New England's shippers. Unfortunately, Jefferson's diplomatic manoeuvrings and economic sanctions had failed to change the situation. Nor was it helped by the search and seizure tactics that the British were using to recover men they claimed were deserters from their navy and who were found on American ships. Several armed encounters had ensued. As might be expected, the fledgling United States had balked at the idea that any other nation could claim the right to stop and search its ships. Inevitably, some true American citizens had been impressed with their British counterparts, and the country had clamoured for justice.

In addition to the problems of the seas, there was the question of land in Spanish Florida and British-held Canada to be addressed. Southerners and Westerners eyed these areas covetously and harboured plans for annexation, should war break out.

These things, compounded by the new nation's hurt at not being accepted as a new force in world politics, had led the United States to the point of confrontation.

The blond man's frown deepened as he turned his thoughts from broader issues to the speech he would give this evening. For what insight his observations would bring this group, he was well prepared to discuss the situation in the West. He only hoped that what he had to say would have some small bearing on the fate of the Niagara frontier in the conflict to come.

Raising his hands in a continued appeal for quiet, Henry Beckwith waited. As the last stirrings of the crowd faded into silence, he began to speak.

'Gentlemen,' he said, 'we are fortunate enough to have with us tonight Mr Seth Porterfield, who, in the past months, has travelled extensively along the length and breadth of the Western frontier. He will speak to us this evening on the preparedness of our sister settlements for the advent of war with Great Britain. I give you Mr Seth Porterfield.'

There was a murmur of voices and a flutter of applause as the tall man took his place at the makeshift podium and stared out over the crowd. The group was made up of all manner of men: farmers, tradesmen, businessmen, and even a uniform or two was visible in the mass of closely packed bodies. Seth felt uneasy in the confines of the low-ceilinged room, and already the faces in the back rows were being obscured by the film of tobacco smoke that hung over the hall. Nor, as he looked out over the group, did he find either recognition or acceptance. Somehow he had expected Mitchell to be here, if for no other reason than to gloat over Seth's discomfort at addressing such a well-attended meeting. But as for himself, Porterfield dreaded the response to his words more than the act of speaking before these men.

'For the past fifteen years,' he began, 'I have spent the majority of my time in the Northwest territory: first surveying, then living and trading with the Indians and later hiring myself out as a guide for settlers. I know that area as well as any white man, and I count among my friends people from every settlement and outpost. I returned only yesterday from a journey that included Fort Dearborn, Detroit, and Fort Malden, so I feel very qualified to speak on this subject.

'You are aware, I'm sure, that the clamour for war has come
primarily from people in the Southern states and men such as
yourselves who live along the frontier. Let me say, first of all,
that those who sought war with Britain are the ones who are
most prepared for that eventuality. You must all know that
Congress has voted to raise a standing army of thirty-five thousand men for the country's defence. To that end, General Hull
has begun to move West, stopping at Pittsburgh and Cincinnati
to requisition men for a march to reinforce the American garrison
at Fort Detroit. His arrival at Dayton was quite gratifying, due
to the fact that three regiments of militia were waiting for him.
Since then he has added substantially to his ranks. What is less
gratifying is the fact that no provision has been made either to
clothe or arm his forces. Because of that, homespun shirts have
been pressed into use as uniforms, and the arsenal at Newport,
Kentucky, has been plundered for guns. Even at that, the men
are still short of blankets, powder and shot, and many of the
muskets are in poor repair. Hull has also begun to amass supplies
for his march, but as yet there is no currency to pay for them, or
to pay the troops either. I give you these examples, not to belittle
the efforts that are being made to prepare the United States for
war, but to point up how much there is to be done.'

Seth turned to one of the maps as he continued. 'As you can
see, in any expedition to Fort Detroit, a water route would be
most expedient. But this country does not have control of the
Great Lakes or the vessels to move even the provisions, much
less the men. And in spite of Hull's recommendations that several
ships should be commissioned to patrol this vital water system,
the naval appropriations bill was recently defeated in Congress.'

Drawing a long breath before he continued, Seth faced the
crowd, but before he could move on or make his next point
someone interrupted him.

'What about the damned British?' came a voice from the back
of the hall. It was followed by a flurry of head-nodding that
confirmed the group's greater interest was in the troops they
might soon face as enemies.

For an instant Porterfield was confused. He had been asked to
speak on American preparedness, though he had planned to talk
briefly about Fort Malden. Then, all at once, Seth realized that
these men were not interested in conditions as they really were.
Nor did they care about the shortage of supplies, the lack of

qualified leadership, or the pitifully undermanned Navy. His real function at this gathering was to have been that of provocateur. These men had expected him to validate reports of British treachery along the border and to assure the group of an easy American victory in Canada. He wondered fleetingly if Mitchell had been aware of the tenor of the speech he was supposed to have given, though he was sure Peter Porter had known.

'What about the damned British?' echoed a second voice as a hostile stir went through the room.

As he faced the crowd, he knew he could continue with the report he had originally intended to give and face the group's censure, or he could tell them that they wanted to hear. He had been to enough speeches and debates in the past few months to know what they expected. It had been foolish to think that these men wanted more than that from him, and he was irritated by his own naïvety. These men were dealing in politics, after all, and not reality.

Seth straightened as he looked out over the hall. It would be wisest for him to repeat the things these men had heard over and over in the past months: that the British were responsible for Indian raids along the frontier, that their forces were weak and would be easily defeated, and that in the event of an American invasion of Canada, the people would side with the United States against the British. That would have been the expedient course, but never had Seth Porterfield been known for his prudence. Pure, mule-headed stubbornness decided him; he would say what he had come here to say. As he began to speak, though, he was acutely aware that his own accent and inflection could invalidate whatever he said.

'You demand to know about the British in the Northwest, so I shall tell you,' he said evenly. 'As ill-prepared for war as Britain's soldiers are, the Americans are more so. It is true that the number of British troops in Canada is small because the War Ministry in London is more concerned with the war with Napoleon, but the British leaders on this continent are shrewd. General Brock has seen that Fort Malden is in good repair, and there are a number of ships moored at Amherstburg, fully prepared to defend Lake Erie. General Prevost, though a less aggressive man, has made his plans as well.'

'Aye, the damned British have been preparing for some time by encouraging their heathen allies to massacre innocent women and children in settlements along the frontier,' came an angry voice from the second row.

'I don't doubt that the Indian situation would improve if the British were gone from Fort Malden,' Seth stated, 'but beyond giving them guns and liquor, the British aren't doing anything to incite the tribes. Nor are they paying a bounty for American scalps, in spite of claims to the contrary.

'In my opinion, the danger from the Indians lies with Tecumseh and his desire for an Indian nation on the Western slope of the Appalachian Mountains. He is a strong and resourceful leader who might once have been willing to negotiate the question with the United States, if she had not proved remiss in paying the annuities due the tribes from past treaties. Nor have the Indians officially taken sides.'

Seth was surprised by the growing passion of his own words as he stood glaring defiantly out over the crowded room. If he did not take care, he might well find himself being tarred and feathered by the good citizens who had attended the meeting this evening, he reminded himself. Still there was that curious rush of excitement in his blood that, for good or ill, had stirred him all his life.

'Which side are you for anyway, Porterfield?' a man shouted, and a murmur of approving voices rose around them.

'Why, on the side of peace, gentlemen,' he answered coolly. 'I'm on the side of peace, though I believe that war is inevitable. It's been stirred up by Mr Clay, Mr Calhoun, and your own Mr Porter, who have spoken so loudly and eloquently for "free trade and sailors' rights". But somehow I believe it's more than Britain's Orders of Council restricting trade, and the problems of impressment of seamen that makes them so vocal. Could it be the wish to please the expansionist desires of their land-locked constituency that inspires them to defend with such patriotic fervour both American sailors' rights and American shipping?'

Porterfield stood for a moment with his shoulders hunched, as if he expected something more than a verbal response. But the voice from the bland-faced man in the front row was conversational.

'You are a cynic, Mr Porterfield,' he observed.

Seth nodded, acknowledging his words. 'I accept your assessment, sir, and concede that at times I consider myself among those unfortunate gentlemen. Cynics are damned to see only the bare, unadorned truth in life.'

The man seemed ready to make a second comment when a voice cut him short.

'He's no cynic, Brown,' the man shouted from somewhere in the centre of the now unfriendly audience. 'My guess is he's a British agent, sent here to bluff us into thinking we're about to fight a war we cannot win, when in truth it's the other way around.'

If those words did not shock Seth, the next ones did.

'In my opinion, he's a British spy!'

The accusation came from so close beside him that Porterfield wheeled around to stare in disbelief at Henry Beckwith. Seth had nearly forgotton that his host occupied the chair near the podium, but even if he had been aware of it, he would have expected the man to remain neutral, if only in the name of hospitality. Instead Beckwith had jumped into the fray with an accusation that would clearly absolve him of any blame that might be associated with procuring such a hostile speaker.

'Can you deny,' Beckwith went on, 'that you told my daughter and me that you were born and raised in England? And didn't you also tell Charlotte that you were part of a British contingent sent to Washington to review the boundaries of the Louisiana Purchase?'

A dull red flush crept along Seth's cheekbones as he groped for a reply. But Henry Beckwith was not finished.

'Of course Charl's wise enough to ignore such bombast, but she heard you as clearly as I when you admitted that you come by your information by clandestine means: by careful observation and inadvertent disclosures. What I wonder, sir, is how much knowledge you intended to impart to us, and how much you yourself intended to learn.'

The accusation was so far off the mark that Seth's first impulse was to laugh, though Beckwith's words had stung. He had been painted both a traitor and a braggart in the same swath of accusations, and he might have reacted with anger if his situation had not been totally untenable. Instead he faced Beckwith.

'I will not even honour such claptrap with a reply, sir,' he began in a low voice, 'but it is clear that your interests lie in different channels than my own. As I see it, we have nothing left to discuss. With your permission, sir, I will take my leave. May

I also express the hope that you gentlemen will spend the rest of your evening productively. Perhaps planning for the defence of your homes should be your first priority. Because when war is declared, as it may be at any time, it will be those of you who live along the border who will pay the highest price for this opportunity to conquer Canada!'

With long, angry strides, Porterfield left the crowded, smoke-filled room and made his way down the steep stairs. Outside a storm was brewing, and the turbulence of the wind-whipped trees seemed to reflect his own emotions. Swinging into the saddle, Seth turned his horse towards the River Road. Now that he was alone, he allowed the anger he had held in check during the meeting full expression. With nothing in his mind but the need for release, he urged his mount to a gallop, and they flew recklessly through the pitch dark tunnel of trees that followed the bank of the Niagara. The exhilaration of speed cleared his head and, by the time his horse slowed to a trot, he was able to think rationally about what had transpired.

There was really no one but himself to blame for the way things had turned out. He had been a naive fool to accept this speaking invitation at face value. He might well be a creditable spy, he reflected irritably, but the intrigues of politics had proved too much for him. In the past months he had been to enough of these speeches to know what was expected. Instead, he had explained the situation in the West clearly and concisely; if only these headstrong Americans had been wise enough to listen. But instead they had wanted nothing more than empty assurance of an easy victory over the British.

Things would have been better if he had been more conciliatory once he had discovered what Beckwith and his friends really wanted. He could not say why he had felt compelled to air his own views on the subject, when he had voiced opinions contrary to his own often enough during his assignments for Mitchell. Over the years he had played so many roles, spouted so many lies, that he could not fathom why he had balked this time. But instead of retreating behind the screen of ambiguity, indifference and pretence, he had stubbornly stood his ground. He had painted a fair picture of the situation on the frontier with its dangers and drawbacks. Then Henry Beckwith had made his accusations, and everything he'd said had become suspect.

'A British spy!' Seth snorted in disgust. Christ! Beckwith's accusation couldn't be further from the truth. And the ironic thing was that the man would never know he'd been totally wrong in his assumptions. Wearily, Porterfield wondered how long it would take Beckwith's charges to be accepted as fact, and how much harder it would make the job he had come here to do.

Well, he had no one to blame but himself for giving Beckwith the information to make his speculations seem plausible. If only he had kept his peace instead of pouring out his life story to Charlotte Beckwith last night, he wouldn't be in this difficulty.

Damn Henry Beckwith, and damn the girl, too! Somehow this was all her fault. She had discovered and exploited some unsuspected weakness in him. With her half-enticing, half-disinterested ways, she had somehow compelled him to cast aside his natural caution and open himself to her. The plentiful food and drink, her extraordinary beauty, and her sweet music in his ears had dazzled his senses and made him feel relaxed, secure, and anonymous. And he had revealed too much. He had been a fool, Seth was forced to admit; but it was her, Charl, with her sea-green eyes and her thick, yellow hair, that had made him one. And in time he would see that she paid the full price for the treachery she had worked on him.

The wind was stronger now, scudding clouds across the moon, and flaring Seth's cape out behind him as he and his horse thundered down the road between the trees and the river.

※

Charlotte had heard the wind rise and could feel the heaviness in the air that heralded the approach of a storm. Somehow the wind sounds were more pervasive in the empty house, and she was aware of the ceaseless rustle of the leaves outside her window. Both her father and Mr Porterfield had ridden to Lewiston for the meeting Mr Porterfield had come to address, and in spite of herself she was curious about what he might have to say. She had been surprised to hear his frank admission that he opposed a second war between Britain and America, and she wondered if he would be so forthright at tonight's meeting. At any rate, Seth Porterfield seemed like a man who would be sure of his facts and would present them clearly and concisely. It was odd, she reflected as she brushed out her hair, that the only thing she and their houseguest could agree on was an issue that was causing dissent everywhere else.

With a sigh Charl put down the hairbrush and took a turn

around the bedroom, pausing at the window. Outside she could see the leaves and branches of the maples churning in the wind. It was going to storm, and she could not help but wish that she was somewhere where she could feel the fresh wind on her face and see the jagged shards of lightning splinter the night sky. She had always loved storms, and if she was not already dressed for bed, she would have gone outdoors to more fully appreciate this most violent and awesome of nature's spectacles. Even in her cosy room, she could sense the storm coiling back, preparing to unleash the fury of its pent-up energy. In a way her mood was apace with the weather, for she herself felt anticipatory and restless.

Perhaps she would read, she decided, and remembered that she had left her book on the piano in the parlour. Slipping into a silky wrapper, she left her room and went down the dark staircase to retrieve it. The oil lamp in the entry hall cast enough light into the sitting room so that she found the slim volume of poetry easily. She was just recrossing the hallway to the stairs when the front door burst open, banging back on its hinges.

Seth Porterfield loomed in the doorway, massive and forbidding. His hair was wildly wind blown, his face was set in a grim mask, and his eyes were blazing blue fire in the semi-darkness. Charl was instantly aware of the tension in the man and of the intensity of his hostile glare upon her. Whatever was the matter with him, she wondered, as she stood frozen, half in curiosity and half in fear.

'I – I came to get my book from the –' she began to stammer in explanation, but before she could finish the sentence, Seth pushed her back against the open door and kissed her savagely.

For an instant Charl was too stunned by the force of his movement and the unexpectedness of his attack to react to the brutal, angry pressure of his mouth against hers. Finally, she began to struggle, pushing ineffectively against his broad chest, her book lost somewhere on the floor. When she tried to evade him by turning her head away, he mercilessly bent her back, fitting the whole of her body against his. As he did, his fingers tangled in her free-flowing hair, forcing her face towards his so that her lips were even more accessible to him. His tongue plundered the sweetness of her mouth as he leaned closer, trapping her between his rigid body and the open door, putting her totally at his command.

Why is he doing this? Charl wondered dizzily, as she tried
unsuccessfully to twist away. What had she done that he should
treat her so? He seemed so angry, so savage. His kisses seemed
meant to punish and chastise, though Charl did not know how
she had earned his wrath. In the spinning recesses of her mind
she fully recognized her danger and the need to break away, but
this man was so strong, so determined. As he held her hard
against him, the kisses became deeper, bruising her tender
mouth, ever more hurtful and more demanding.

Charl felt herself grow weak as her breath came in short,
shaky gasps, and her knees went liquid beneath her. Her heart
thundered in her throat and at her temples as she struggled
uselessly in his crushing embrace. Then her resolution crumbled
and she could fight no more. He was too strong, too strong.

Half-fainting, Charl swayed against him as her resistance ebbed
away. In the trembling, dissolving weakness she clung to him,
and her lips opened willingly beneath his unrelenting mouth.
And in the depths of that despairing surrender, she began to
respond to him. A pleasurable flush rose to envelop her, and the
weakness became a growing languor in her limbs. There was a
fragile, unfurling expectancy in her now, as she became aware
of the man who held her with suddenly tender ferocity. She felt
her womanly softness mould along the hardness of his chest and
thighs, felt the effortless strength of his arms around her. Charl
found the silkiness of his hair beneath her questing hands, and
his scent, of tobacco and shaving soap, rose up around her. There
was a slight, faint aftertaste of brandy on his mouth, and she
seemed more intoxicated by it than she would have been by the
liquor itself. Her head was swimming, and the distant warnings
of impending disaster were swept away by the waves of sensation
that buffeted her. She was totally caught in the wordless spell of
desire that Seth Porterfield had cast so relentlessly over her.

In the darkness of the deserted hallway, Seth was as intensely
aware of the girl in his arms as she was of him. He had known
the exact moment of her surrender and had felt the lips she'd
held tight with resistance go soft and yielding beneath his own.
In that moment, he had been drowning in the same rush of liquid
fire that swept through Charl's veins, and he had revelled in the
perfect flow of her long-limbed body against his. Abruptly he
had realized the state of her undress: of her full, firm breasts, so
tempting to caress beneath the flimsy layers of fabric that were

all she wore. And the stab of physical longing that he felt for this sweet, infuriating vixen was unlike anything he had ever known.

As he'd ridden towards the house in a fury of frustration, he'd stoked a raging anger at Charlotte Beckwith and her father that would likely have died to embers of hatred or disillusionment by morning. But through the parlour windows he had seen Charl's pale, ghostly figure and had burst in on her with mayhem in his mind. It had somehow been Charlotte Beckwith's fault that all his plans had gone awry. When he burst in on her, he had meant to make her pay for the divulgences she'd forced from him, and the weakness he perceived them to evidence. He had wanted to hurt and humble her with the tyranny of his kisses. And in the beginning, it had been as he'd intended. Charl had suffered the degradation of his carnal use of her. But then everything had changed, and he had lost his detachment.

Somehow, they were suddenly clinging together, equal in desire, straining ever closer, bound in a strange alchemy that subtly altered them both. For a time they were lost in a maelstrom of searching kisses and searing caresses, where nothing mattered to either of them but the other.

Afterwards, Porterfield wondered what would have happened if they had not stopped, drawing back trembling and very aware of what had ignited between them. What would have happened if he'd taken Charl to his bed? Seth asked himself. Would he have made love to her? Could she have prevented it? What had happened between them was frightening in its intensity and unlike anything he had experienced with any other woman. He did not understand what had happened or why they stood a little way apart now, silently watching each other. It was almost as if their bodies had bridged a gap between them that could not be spanned in any other way.

Then suddenly he was angry again: angry because he did not understand his own emotions, or hers. He was angry because he had not taken advantage of her when he had the chance and because he did not know what to say to her now. Why did she continue to watch him with a half-frightened, half-hopeful expression in her sea-green eyes, that made him feel oddly guilty for what he had done? Somehow it was as if she had bested him again, and he scowled at her, his own eyes hard, cold chips of ice.

Turning abruptly he climbed the stairs, taking them two at a time. At the top he paused to look back. She stood just as he had left her, with her back to the open door. In the semi-darkness he could see the pale oval of her face and the uncertainty in her luminous eyes. There was a quick impulsive moment when he nearly returned to her side. But by then the sobering power of reality was in control once more, and he vowed he would not be manipulated by her again. There was no way to explain the strange effect Charlotte Beckwith had on him. But it was clear that she was a person to be avoided in the future, if not because of his responsibilities, for his own peace of mind. With resolution he turned from the beguiling woman at the foot of the stairs and entered his room.

※

Once the door to Porterfield's room banged shut, Charl became aware of her wrapper flapping against her ankles as she stood in the doorway; of the lightning that flashed, momentarily flooding the garden with an eerie violet glow; of the rain that came spattering through the trees. Only now the growing fury of that early summer storm seemed as nothing when compared to the tempest of her own thoughts. Moving automatically, she closed and secured the door and retrieved her book from the floor. With deliberate calm she went to the back of the house and dispatched a groom to care for Mr Porterfield's forgotten horse. She took refuge in these simple tasks to keep the memory of her encounter with Seth Porterfield at bay. But once she had returned to the solitude of her room, she had no defence against the riot of emotions that engulfed her.

Unbidden, she recalled the feel of Porterfield's lips on hers and the strength of his embrace with a clarity that made her blush. Never before in her limited experience with stolen kisses had she felt anything akin to the melting weakness and surging exhilaration that this man aroused in her. When they had drawn apart, Charl sensed that what had passed between them was somehow incomplete: part of a greater whole that would have heightened, then resolved, the compelling sensations that enveloped her.

Tutored at home, and raised by a father alone, Charl had little knowledge of what went on between men and women. She knew the technicalities of the act, as all country children did, and she had read the poets' vague waxings on the glories of love, but she had no idea about the shared intimacies and the pleasures they could provide. Now that Seth Porterfield's kisses had awakened desires she had never known, she was both avidly curious and strangely compelled to seek the answers to a myriad of questions in the circle of his arms.

Charl slipped off her wrapper and climbed into bed, although she suspected that sleep would be a long time coming. Frowning, she tucked her hands beneath her head and stared up at the crocheted canopy above her.

Why, she wanted to know, had she responded so strongly to this particular man? Seth Porterfield was someone she hardly knew; nor was he a person she particularly liked. Yet her reaction to him had been intense and all consuming. Was it only him, Seth alone, who could affect her so? Or in time would she find that other men could stir these same passions in her? Were Seth's responses to her as unique and compelling, or was this usual and to him totally unremarkable?

And why had he stormed into the house and kissed her as he had in the first place?

Charl knew she had done nothing to encourage the man; for the most part, she had barely been civil to him. Of course, she had been dressed in nothing more than her night dress and wrapper, but neither garment was revealing enough to provoke him. And why had he seemed so angry with her? He had not offered one word of explanation for his actions; nor had she wits enough to demand one. She should probably tell her father and let the two men settle the question of her honour between them. Yet she knew she would not say a word. There was no real harm in what had passed between them, and she was plainly unwilling to forfeit the opportunity to seek answers to her questions.

It was clear that Seth Porterfield had not begun to kiss her out of desire. But for what other reasons did a man kiss a woman?

She was certain that Seth had not kissed her with desire at the start. In the beginning it had been almost as if he meant to insult or shame her by his actions, but then everything had changed between them. Had it been her own wanton response to him that had altered the situation? she wondered. Her face flamed with embarrassment at the obvious answer, as shame swept through her. Did he think her wayward because of the reaction she had been unable to control? He had been neither gentle nor loverlike, but she had accepted his kisses with obvious relish. If he had mistaken her for a trollop because he had found her sitting alone in a tavern, what must he think of her now?

Rolling onto one side, Charl buried her burning face in the pillow, seized by a paroxysm of embarrassment. Dear God! After the way she had acted, how could she ever face the man again?

Yet she knew she would find the courage to do so because she needed to see him. She needed to talk to him, maybe even kiss him, in order to understand the chaos he had so readily aroused in her. There were so many questions in her mind that she knew she must do more than face him; she had to ask him her questions as well. The question that nagged at her most persistently was whether the same feelings would return if he took her in his arms again. Strangely, she both feared and hoped they would.

Charl had never shrunk from a challenge, and even as the doubts plagued her, she decided on her course. In the morning she would conspire to get Seth Porterfield alone and simply ask him to explain himself. In doing so, she hoped that he would address her own confused emotions as well. And if he did not answer her questions then, she would have to find the courage to ask them herself. With her decision made, she snuggled deeper beneath the coverlet, determined to sleep. But as it was, she lay awake for a very long time.

※

Seth rose early, determined to have more success with the remainder of his mission to Youngstown than he'd had during the first phase. Clearly, he had been out of his depth in the capacity of a political speaker, but his own stubbornness and Beckwith's accusations had turned his initial blunders into an unmitigated disaster. At least the rest of his assignment would rely on his strengths, he reflected thankfully. From now on he would be seeking information, first from Fort Niagara, and later from the British encampment across the river at Fort George. For years these two military installations had stood on opposite sides of the border, always manned and at the ready, but at peace. If war was declared, they would face each other as enemies, both attempting to control the mouth of the Niagara River and the strategic land and water routes between Lake Erie and Lake Ontario.

Absently, Seth soaped his face and opened the bone-handled razor in preparation for shaving, as he reviewed his situation.

He would have little difficulty penetrating the American fortifications because Mitchell would have sent word ahead. The necessary reports on the manpower and weaponry available to the fort would already have been prepared for him. It would be the complex discussions of tactics and strategy that would remain: the parts that for Seth were the most challenging and compelling. Defences needed to be evaluated with an unbiased eye, and offensives needed to be planned for review, first by Mitchell and later by the War Department. In this assignment, it was Seth's role to act as go-between.

Obtaining this same kind of information about the British stronghold at Fort George would undoubtedly prove more difficult. He would need to gain the confidence of the ranking English officer and get him talking freely about his command. It was in this capacity that Seth, with his English background and manner, had proven most effective in the past. It was also the role that pained his conscience most acutely. In spite of his American citizenship and loyalty to her causes around the world, he did not want to undermine the interests of the country of his birth. Why he felt such loyalty to a nation and a society that had spurned him, he could not say. He only knew he could not reconcile himself to supporting one side against the other if war was declared.

With difficulty he forced the question of his splintered allegiance to the back of his mind. There it would continue to nag him until the circumstances forced a decision upon him. But until that time, he had a mission to complete for Mitchell and the United States that he could not ignore.

Frowning, he turned his thoughts to the situation at hand. His foremost problem was finding an entrée into the confidence of Fort George's commander. Then suddenly his mouth quirked upward in a wry smile. Perhaps Henry Beckwith had unwittingly provided him with the perfect solution to this particular dilemma. He would have to see what came of last night's accusations, if they were bandied about or ignored. But if they became common knowledge, as he expected they would, he might use them to his advantage in convincing the British officer of his loyalty. To win the man's trust he might be forced to assume the guise of an British spy.

With care he drew the straight razor along the line of his throat, tested the smoothness with his fingertips and went on to the next lathered section below his jaw.

Of course, if he decided to assume the role of a British agent, it would probably jeopardize the last phase of his assignment. But then, perhaps his chance to gauge the public's response to the possibility of war had already been compromised. He was no longer a nameless, faceless vagrant who could mingle in the taverns and at the markets, saying little and hearing much. Henry Beckwith had robbed him of his anonymity, and Seth could only guess the consequences. Besides, Mitchell had other men who could report on these things and the newly formed militia units along this frontier. But he had few men who could infiltrate Fort George and learn its secrets. Irritably, Seth realized the choice had been taken out of his hands.

As he wiped the last of the shaving soap from his chin, he met his own red-rimmed eyes in the mirror. He had not slept well. The events of the previous evening had disturbed his rest, and he felt vaguely aggravated and out of sorts.

He had lost control, both of the meeting and of himself last night, and frankly that irked him. Porterfield was a man used to manipulating situations and people to his advantage, but this time things had gone dangerously awry. Admittedly, he had not clearly understood his function at the meeting and that had put him at a disadvantage. But in spite of that, he should have been able to make his point dispassionately: the United States was not prepared for war. Instead he had badgered his listeners, sacrificing his considerable persuasive powers in the name of the unadorned truth. What had possessed him to be so outspoken?

Leaning his palms against the shaving stand, he closed his eyes.

And in addition to the disaster at the meeting, there was his treatment of the girl to be considered. His behaviour towards Charl Beckwith had been totally reprehensible and he would not be surprised if her father met him at breakfast with a challenge for his daughter's honour. Though he could not convince himself that Charl was completely blameless in encouraging his disclosures the other night, he was forced to admit that he had chastised her for his own shortcomings. Nor was he any closer to understanding his own uncharacteristic reaction to her than he had been when he left her in the hall. It was clear that there was only one way to deal with her unsettling presence in the days to come. He would have to do his best to avoid her.

He had made two inexcusable blunders in quick succession that might well jeopardize his real reasons for being in Youngstown. Both had been based in his own arrogance and lack of self-control: a potentially deadly combination that could not only doom his mission, but cost him his life as well.

Seth took a long breath and exhaled slowly.

He had made two mistakes, and there was nothing he could do to rectify either one of them. He had no choice but to go ahead with his plans now. The rest of this assignment must proceed without incident, and Porterfield intended to make very sure that it did.

Three
✣✣✣

Charl sat at the breakfast table with her father, nervously waiting
for their houseguest to appear. Henry was preoccupied with a
pile of papers that were propped up before him, and in the silence
memories of the previous night's encounter filled Charl's mind.
How would Seth Porterfield respond to her in the cold light of
day? she wondered. Would she see pleasure and warmth in his
eyes when he looked at her, or would there still be the odd
mixture of confusion and anger in their sapphire-blue depths that
she had seen last night? And in addition to those two questions,
there were the myriad of others to be answered when she finally
managed to get him alone.

She had dressed with particular care this morning, selecting a
rosy-pink gown that she knew was becoming and that showed off
her creamy skin to advantage. Charl shifted in her chair and
glanced out of the window. Would Seth still find her desirable
this morning, or had the deep flush of passion that had risen
between them paled and faded with the night? It seemed strange
that this morning she was waiting so eagerly for Seth Porterfield
to appear, when only yesterday she had done everything she
could to ignore him. She crumbled a roll and pushed the eggs
around on her plate in a pretence of appetite she did not feel.

Charl drank from her cup, straining to hear Seth's step on the
stairs. 'I can't imagine what's keeping Mr Porterfield,' she said
sharply.

Henry Beckwith glanced up in surprise at his daughter's tone,
his bushy eyebrows rising to form half-moons above his eyes.
'And just what do you want with Mr Porterfield?' he demanded.

'It only seems good manners for a guest to be on time for
meals,' she answered quickly. 'I don't want any more of him than
that.'

'He left very early this morning, didn't have a bite to eat, not even coffee', Harriet put in as she brought fresh muffins up from the kitchen.

'Doesn't it seem that Mr Porterfield should have let someone know that he would not be here for breakfast? Father, that man is no gentleman!' Charl railed, more upset than she cared to admit at missing their houseguest. 'Why ever did you invite such a man into our home?'

'I'm not sure myself,' Henry admitted. 'At least it sets my mind at rest to know you find Porterfield so distasteful.'

Her green eyes widened.

'Why?'

Henry ruffled the napkin in his lap.

'Because he's an English spy!' he replied.

'What?' Charl gasped incredulously and then began to laugh. 'Whatever gave you such an idea?'

Henry did not appreciate her levity.

'He as much as told us so himself the other night,' he put in defensively. 'He was born in England, grew to manhood in Canada. And he told us outright that he had been part of at least one British delegation. What else could he be? It's as clear as day.'

'Father, that's ludicrous!' she exclaimed. 'Whatever else Mr Porterfield may be, I'd wager he's no spy. Didn't he say that all he wanted was peace between Britain and the United States? If that makes him a British agent, then there are a vast number of us living along the length and breadth of this country. Do you consider me a traitor as well, Father, because my most fervent wish is that this thing can be settled by peaceable means?'

'Then if Seth Porterfield is a loyal American, why did he persist in telling us how ill prepared we are to fight a war with the British?' Henry challenged. 'Not one other speaker I've heard in these last months has been so pessimistic.'

'Perhaps what he told you at the meeting is the truth as he sees it,' Charl countered. 'Besides, as I understand it, you wanted to hear about fortifications and preparedness in the West. Loyal American, loyal Canadian or loyal Englishman, what do Mr Porterfield's politics matter if his reports on those conditions are accurate?'

'How did Seth Porterfield come to speak at your meeting anyway? And what happened last night?'

'For some time we have wanted someone to tell us honestly about the situation in the west. Consequently when Peter Porter introduced me to Porterfield at a political gathering in Black Rock and mentioned that he was well acquainted with the situation in the West, I asked him to speak to us.'

'But what happened last night at the meeting?' she persisted.

'And why are you so curious, missy?' her father asked, eyeing her.

'Mr Porterfield came home early and seemed quite – um – agitated,' Charl replied truthfully.

Henry chuckled. 'As well he might be. His views on the situation in the West were not well received, and before he had finished his speech, he was shouted down. Several men accused him of sympathy with the British, and I could not help but add my insight to theirs.'

'Oh, Father!' Charl exclaimed with exasperation. 'Who accused Mr Porterfield of being a British agent?'

Henry's ruddy face seemed more florid than usual.

'John Taylor,' he replied, 'but I suggested he was more a spy. Hush now, girl,' he went on when Charl would have spoken. 'You heard the man admit that he gained his information by clandestine means, and who but a spy –'

'That's ridiculous!' Charl interrupted hotly. 'If Mr Porterfield is a spy, why would he tip his hand so carelessly by telling us his business?'

'Well, I believe he's taken a bit of a fancy to you, Charlotte,' Henry replied, and Charl's cheeks flamed guiltily at the observation. 'At any rate, it puts my mind to rest to know you've taken no fancy to him in return. If only I could ask him to leave this house –'

'And why can't you?' Charl asked, anxious for any subject that would turn the conversation from her reaction to Seth Porterfield, though Seth's expulsion was the last thing she wanted at that moment.

'Since it was Congressman Porter who introduced us, it might not be seemly to evict even so tedious a guest. Perhaps the blackguard will realize he's not welcome, either with us or in Youngstown, and will have the good grace to leave of his own accord.'

'Well, Father, as much as I find Mr Porterfield a trial, I think you've done the man an injustice in accusing him of being a British spy.'

'You women!' her father broke in condescendingly, anxious to forestall the continuation of an argument he was clearly not going to win. 'You never think the worst of anyone; your mother was exactly the same. It's as well we men look out for your best interests, or you'd all be sorely misused by the scoundrels of this world.'

Charl opened her mouth to protest, but her father hurried on.

'You are planning to come to the store later to write those letters for me and see to next month's orders, aren't you?' he asked, setting aside his napkin and rising to leave. 'I'm going to be away most of the day as well, and it might be wise for you to be there in case Freddy needs help.'

Without waiting for her reply, Henry bustled out, closing the door behind him. The sound of the latch seemed to galvanize Charl, and she hurled her fragile teacup at the stout panel in frustration.

For the moment Seth Porterfield, accused British spy and unwelcome houseguest, was forgotten as the old frustration at being born female surged through her.

How could her father insinuate that she was some empty-headed chit who needed protection, turn aside the validity of her arguments against the war that threatened to engulf them, and then blithely turn his responsibilities over to her? It was not fair, she raged. She was as capable as any man. She could read, write, reason, and figure, nor was she lacking in business acumen, as she'd proved over and over in these past months. Allowing her to work at the store had been an indulgence at first, but her father had come to depend on her help. And yet, in spite of her considerable ability, he expected her to marry some fool man, have a baby every year, and be content with her lot.

Still, Charl meant to have her way in this. She was her father's only child, and in time the business would come to her. If only she could continue to work by her father's side and elude the attentions of grasping, single-minded men like Stephen Langley, she might well gain what she wanted most out of life: complete independence.

With a sense of mission Charl rose from the table and moved towards the door, anxious to be on about her duties. For a moment she looked down at the delicate teacup lying broken on the carpet. With a defiant toss of her head she stepped over it, as her father would have done.

❆

The first buildings at Fort Niagara were built by French fur traders in the early part of the eighteenth century, and, as Seth Porterfield passed over the drawbridge, with its windlass and counterweights, and through the Gate of Five Nations, he was very aware of the fort's history. The gate and gatehouse, named for the five nations of the Iroquois confederacy, were constructed of heavy grey-brown stone, as was the rest of the fort. Passing the formidable south redoubt, Seth saw the broad, grassy parade ground spread out before him. It was filled, even at this early hour, with smartly drilling troops arrayed in their deep blue uniforms. Lining the southern, eastern and western walls were series of batteries, armed with all manner of guns that gleamed dully in the sunlight. To Seth's left were barracks and the soldiers' mess as well as the bakehouse and various shops.

At the far end, with its rear wall at the slope of the riverbank, sat the first building on the site, the impressive three-storey 'Castle'. The fur traders had petitioned the fierce Iroquois for permission to build 'a stone house for trading'. Instead they had constructed a small, but very effective fortress, complete with barred windows and gun emplacements in the dormered roof. Though the Indians suspected that the French had built more of a defensive stronghold than the chiefs had intended, they never knew for sure. Redskins were not allowed beyond the ground floor trading post, and all other windows on that level were shuttered on the inside, both for defence and to hide the 'Castle's' secrets from prying eyes. Today, the Frenchmen's castle was a fortress within a fortress.

Moving with quick resolute steps, Seth skirted the grassy parade ground. His narrowed eyes missed nothing as he walked in the direction of the main building. He noted everything, from a group of chattering laundresses hanging their clothes on lines strung between two barracks buildings to a detachment of artillerymen, wrestling an obviously new carronade gun into an advantageous position on one of the ramparts. With an emotion that vacillated between satisfaction and dread, Seth realized that these Americans were preparing for war, just as their British counterparts were.

Seth entered the Castle through the main door, gave his name to the sentry, and expressed his wish to see the commander. The soldier immediately disappeared, and while he waited, Seth noted the feeling of invulnerability that the building seemed to transmit.

The entire place was built of that same grey stone, with thick walls and vaulted ceilings. There were only two entrances, the main one behind him and the door that led to the trading post on his right, so that this building could be used as a last line of defence in case of attack. There was even a well in the centre of this hallway, which had been dug in case of siege, and a chapel on the floor above.

Instead of taking a seat on one of the benches that lined the hall, he moved absently to stare down into the brackish, black water at the bottom of the now-abandoned well. The Castle had indeed been a stronghold for the French in the New World, though the British had captured it shortly before Quebec fell in 1759. Fort Niagara had come into American hands at last by the treaty that ended the Revolutionary War. Who could say what changes the fortunes of war might bring to this old, strategically located fortress? In truth, who could guess what changes the advent of war might bring to any man alive today, or any woman? Again, the terrible inevitability of conflict weighed him down, and Seth was filled with dark pessimism. Somehow he must find a way to resolve the question of his divided loyalties and allegiances before his world was splintered by a conflict he could neither face nor avoid. In this case Seth knew he could not apply the cool logic that had always been his touchstone, because these feelings were far from rational. Nor did he know what other criterion he could use to decide his course. He was so caught up in his musings and his own dark emotions that it was a moment before he realized that the sentry had returned and was waiting to show him to the commander's office.

The room where he was taken was small and stone walled, just as the hallway had been, with a heavily studded door that closed securely behind him. In spite of the pleasant June morning, there was a small fire in the grate to dispel the chill. As he waited, Seth wandered to the high window in the north wall. Outside there was a sheer drop to the lake far below, where the water boiled up in an angry froth around jagged, grey boulders. From this vantage point, Seth could see the swirling blue-green tide that marked the place where the lake and river merged. The French had indeed selected an ideal site for their Castle: on a point of land that not only guarded the channel, but that was also impregnable from the rear.

Turning from the window, Porterfield studied the contents of the room, hoping to discover something about the man who commanded the fort. There had been a recent change of personnel, and he did not know who had been assigned to the post. He could only hope that the man would be cooperative and receptive to some of the suggestions he intended to make. The desk and furniture were of standard issue, and the officer had not added much to his austere surroundings. He enjoyed his tobacco, Seth concluded from the humidor and pipe perched on the edge of the desk, and judging from the placement of the ink pot and pen, the man was right handed. Seth frowned, realizing the reason there was so little of the man's personality evident was that the office was inspection perfect. And that in itself was a telling trait, Seth reflected. Porterfield's speculation was cut short when a familiar voice spoke his name.

'Seth Porterfield! When I heard you were in town, I wondered if you'd turn up here.'

With surprise, the blond man turned to stare at the officer who had just entered from the adjoining room. He was easily as tall as Seth, but of slighter build, and his uniform fitted his slim body snugly. His long angular face was split in a broad grin that showed whitely from beneath a bushy, brown moustache.

'Will Hubbard,' Seth greeted the officer, clapping him on the back. 'Colonel Hubbard, that is. By God! When did you become a real soldier?'

'Sit down, Seth,' he said, indicating a chair near the desk. 'It's a long story. By thunder, it's good to see you.'

Seth grinned back at the man who had taken his place behind the desk. It had been almost two years since he had worked with Hubbard in France. They had been unofficially attached to a delegation negotiating with Napoleon's government for the release of American ships captured under the Berlin and Milan Decrees.

'It seems as though these past few years have been good to you, Will,' Porterfield observed, accepting a cigar from the humidor and a light from the twig that Hubbard extended towards him.

'They have,' the other man admitted as he lit his pipe. 'Leaving Mitchell's service is the wisest thing I've ever done. I quit right after that French affair. There are too many risks in that kind of work for a married man.'

Seth was thunderstruck. Hubbard had always seemed so

detached and so aloof that he seemed an unlikely candidate for matrimony. 'Married man?' he echoed.

Will grinned again. 'You must remember Janette, the innkeeper's daughter at that last pension where we stayed outside Paris.'

Seth nodded, conjuring up an image of the slender, curly-haired mademoiselle with eyes like pools of midnight.

'Janette's my wife now and is due to make me a father in August,' Hubbard told him proudly.

'That's wonderful,' Porterfield interjected, 'but how did you get her out of France?'

'I took her with me when I left.'

'On that repossessed brigantine?' Seth was incredulous, and Will's grin broadened in reply.

'It was commandeered, and you know it,' he laughed, and then sobered. 'I was glad to get her out of there any way I could. France is at the brink of disaster. Napoleon has drained the country dry, and if the British persist, I believe it's only a matter of time before Bonaparte is defeated.'

'And if that happens, will Janette be any safer here?'

'Here I can see to Janette's welfare. There?' Hubbard's silence spoke volumes.

Seth nodded. 'Would you mind if I called at the officers' quarters to see Janette when I leave? It would be pleasant to renew our acquaintance.'

Hubbard frowned. 'I don't think you should. The less Janette knows about you being here the better. Besides it might be unseemly for the commander's wife to be the acquaintance of a British spy.'

Seth coloured. 'Rumours certainly travel swiftly,' he observed.

'How the devil did that one begin?'

'I was a fool!' Seth said simply, his lips compressed into an angry line.

'That's not like you,' Hubbard replied, puffing on his pipe.

'I met Henry Beckwith's daughter –' Seth began.

'And a beauty she is, too, though a bit headstrong I've heard,' Will put in, smiling wryly.

'Yes, that's a fair appraisal,' Seth agreed, a vision of Charl flashing into his mind. 'She asked me to stay with them and made it impossible for me to refuse.' Porterfield's voice trailed off, and Will watched his old friend speculatively. 'Accepting the invitation was my first mistake. Unfortunately I compounded the error by talking too freely to Beckwith and the girl. Somehow I managed to reveal that I was born in England and raised in Canada. The next thing I knew Beckwith was accusing me of being an English spy.'

Hubbard accepted the oversimplification at face value. 'Well, a beautiful woman can do a great deal to wear down a man's reserve,' he offered.

'More likely it was the liquor,' Seth put in glumly, unwilling to admit that the Beckwith girl stirred him. 'Regardless of the reason, I was a fool to talk so freely.'

'Yes, I suppose that's so,' Will agreed. 'If I know Mitchell, he has other things for you to do while you're here besides address that meeting and pick up my report. Will these rumours make the rest of your assignment more difficult?'

Seth shrugged. 'You're right, there are several more things I must do while I'm in Youngstown. Mitchell hasn't changed a bit.'

Will chuckled. 'No, I bet he hasn't. Still, I don't envy him his job: trying to keep an eye on this entire border, waiting for it to explode when war's declared.'

'Then you think war's inevitable?' Seth asked, and Will's nod confirmed his worst fears.

'God knows we're not prepared for it. Our generals are all old men, veterans of the revolution most of them. West Point has turned out so few officers in the past decade it's pitiful. Why don't you give up what you are doing, Seth, and take your commission? There's no question that you've earned it, and we're going to need you.'

'I'll consider it when the time comes,' Seth replied evasively. 'Right now I want to go over this report with you. I'm to see Mitchell in a few days, and I've much to do between now and then.'

'Well, give him my regards,' Hubbard laughed, as he produced several closely written pages from a strong box, and they began their discussions in earnest.

Their meeting went on all morning and well into the afternoon. Hubbard sent out for coffee and a meal from the officers' mess, but the two men stayed closeted in the office, bent over the desk, thick with charts and maps. They speculated on the deployment of new troops that would likely be sent to Fort George in the event that war was declared. They argued at length about the best use for the men and guns at Fort Niagara and fought mock battles to discover the weaknesses in the plans they laid. Seth questioned Hubbard closely about the effectiveness and strength of militia units along the frontier.

By two o'clock Seth felt he knew every significant fact about the fort and the surrounding area. He was confident, too, that most of the plans and alternatives that they had discussed were valid. Finally, Porterfield eased himself back into one of the armchairs before the desk and read over Hubbard's report. He read with great concentration, his narrowed eyes moving slowly over the carefully penned lines. When he was finished, he handed the pages back to Hubbard.

'You'd better burn that now, Will. We don't want a document like that one lying around.'

Hubbard's angular features registered surprise and then recognition. 'I had forgotten that you can do that trick with your memory,' he said.

Seth shrugged. 'There's no trick to it. It's just the way my memory works; it always has. If I need to recall that report, it will come back to me word for word, as if I were reading it off a page. I don't understand why or how it works; it's a gift, I suppose.'

Will Hubbard shook his dark head in wonder and then turned away to feed the pages of the report to the smouldering fire. Seth watched thoughtfully as the pages were consumed, though it was evident there was something else on his mind.

'I want one more thing from you, old friend,' Seth said after a moment.

'You need only ask,' Will assured him as he watched the last of the pages wither and turn to ashes.

'You were right when you guessed that Mitchell has much more than this for me to do while I'm in Youngstown. He wants the same kind of information you have given me from Fort George, across the river.'

'And just how do you propose to get it?' Will asked, settling in his chair on the far side of the cluttered desk, certain that Porterfield had a plan.

'I think Henry Beckwith may have offered me a perfect opportunity to infiltrate their defences. His accusations may prove an unexpected boon if I encourage the misconception that I'm a British spy. Who would have more reason to make contact with the fort's commander than an agent on an assignment from Quebec?'

'You realize, don't you, that though this may offer you access to the fort, and maybe even the information you want, your role could become a very dangerous one if war is declared?'

Seth nodded. 'It could, but this is not a part I intend to play for very long. I expect to be far from Fort George and Youngstown when war is declared.'

Will shook his head, his face sombre. 'Don't count on that, Seth. This thing is coming faster than any of us suspect.'

'You always did worry too much, Will,' Seth observed with a grin.

'It's always wise to consider the ramifications of anything you do,' Will began prudently, but Seth's laugh cut him short.

'I've lived my life doing what I had to do, and damn the consequences. I doubt I'll change much at this stage.'

Will was aware that he could not alter Seth's plans, but he had voiced his warning anyway. He knew Seth enjoyed the exhilaration of the game, the chances and the bluffs, far more than the victory itself. And he both admired and feared for his friend's recklessness. It was pointless to argue once Porterfield's mind was made up, and Will acquiesced gracefully.

'What can I do to help you?' he finally asked.

Minutes later Hubbard went to his office door. 'Guards!' he bellowed down the corridor.

Two armed men forced their way through the milling crowd of soldiers and civilians who had appointments with the post's commander.

Angrily, Will pushed Seth into the passageway and addressed his men. 'Escort this man directly to the front gate and see that he has no more chance to pry into our affairs. If he comes to the fort again, I want him brought to my office immediately.

'And as for you, Porterfield,' he said, eyeing the tall blond man with open hostility, 'I find some of your answers suspect, but I have no proof that you're working for the British. Be aware that I will be watching your movements, and if my suspicions are confirmed, we'll have a cell prepared and waiting for you.'

'You undoubtedly realize that no declaration of hostility exists between your country and Great Britain, don't you, Colonel?' Seth asked silkily.

'But by God, if war is declared, you watch your step,

Porterfield. You remember that we hang spies!' Will stormed. 'Now get him out of here.'

The two guards hurried to obey and prodded Seth in the direction of the main door, past the startled crowd. When Colonel Hubbard's door banged shut and Porterfield and his escort were gone, the people began to mutter and speculate about the little drama they had witnessed. So the fort's commander had been questioning a man he believed to be a British agent. What was the world coming to? And wasn't this Porterfield the same man that Henry Beckwith had accused of being a British spy, only last night? It was rumoured that the man was staying at the Beckwith house, so surely Beckwith would know. But if he suspected that the man was a spy, why had he offered the hospitality of his home? Had this Porterfield been discovered trying to infiltrate the fort's defences? Someone thought so. They buzzed among themselves, speculating, and then accepted those speculations as fact, just as Porterfield and Hubbard had intended they would.

In his office, Will was very pleased by their little performance and had enjoyed the opportunity to test his dramatic skills once more. He had not lost his touch, he reflected, and for a moment he was overtaken by a rush of nostalgia for the days when he and Seth had worked together for Mitchell. They had lived recklessly and boldly, intoxicated by an awareness that any day could be their last. It had been a fast and exciting life, but Will had given it up forever the day he married Janette. Nor was he sorry: not now, not ever.

As the conversation buzzed in the corridor outside his office, Hubbard made some speculations of his own. There had been a good audience in the hall, and he'd wager that by bedtime half of Youngstown would have heard about the scene he and Seth had staged. By noon tomorrow his friend would be a marked man all along the Niagara frontier. He only hoped that Seth would not get caught up in a situation that was beyond his control.

Will rubbed the back of his neck wearily. The hours of poring over the maps had taken their toll, and he was tired. But before he could begin to attend to his appointments, he needed to find the guard who had admitted Seth to his office this morning and swear him to silence. The fewer people who knew how Porterfield had entered the fort and came to be in the commander's office, the safer Seth would be.

Four

✳✳✳

Charl sat on a tall stool at a desk near the back of Henry Beckwith's shop. It faced the street, and from her perch she could watch the people in the store and those who passed by outside. It was at this desk that Charl wrote the orders and letters, in her firm, legible hand, that kept the shelves stocked and the business prospering. When Henry was too busy with his other investments, she kept the ledger as well.

She enjoyed working here where she could see and hear what was going on and greet the customers personally. It also kept her nearby in case the store became crowded and Freddy Latham, their clerk, needed extra help. Currently, he was carefully measuring out delicate, blue lace trim under the watchful eye of the Widow Farley.

'Is Amanda to have a new gown, Mrs Farley?' Charlotte asked across the store.

Turning, the dour-looking woman met Charl's smile with a frown. The Widow Farley was one of those who heartily disapproved of Charl's involvement with her father's business. She had protested long and loudly that her Amanda would never engage in such an unmaidenly practice.

'Just a little something special for the party next week,' the woman answered shortly.

'I'm sure she'll look lovely.' Charl smiled again, thinking of poor Amanda festooned by her mother so that she more closely resembled a wedding cake than a girl. Charl suspected that the widow wanted her daughter to be the belle that she had never been, and she forced Amanda into that role with no thought about whether the girl enjoyed it or not.

Charl looked down at the partially finished letter on the desk, picked up the pen and sat poised over the paper. 'As noted in your letter of the tenth,' she read aloud to herself.

But somehow her mind slipped away from the letter, and instead of the black, businesslike words, Seth's face floated before her. She imagined him with that bright, hot glow of desire in his eyes and a lazy half smile curving his lips. An odd melting sensation curled in her middle as she recalled the fierce, yet tender, way his mouth had moved on hers. A warm flush mounted to her cheeks at the memory and she blinked the vision away.

'Your letter of the tenth . . . ,' she read aloud.

The door to the store opened, and her eyes flew from the page to see who had come in. It was not Seth, as it had not been Seth all morning. She exhaled sharply, reminded once more that she had been waiting almost breathlessly for the moment when she could confront him.

If only she could see and talk to him, maybe he could answer the myriad of questions that plagued her, and she would feel calm again. Where had he been this morning? Where was he now? She stared intently out of the window, willing him to appear. Maybe if she went over to the Crow's Head Tavern, she would find him there.

No, no, she argued with herself. She would not give him the satisfaction of seeking him out, nor would she make herself so obvious before the whole town. He was a scandal already, and she would not risk her good name for the sake of a few questions.

Sighing, she looked down at the letter. In one margin she had doodled his initials. Carefully drawn and beautifully embellished, they looked up at her, clear evidence of where her mind had been. She was behaving like a schoolgirl, Charl chided herself. You would think by the way she was acting that she had never been kissed before. Yet she had to admit that the few stolen kisses that Stephen Langley had managed had not prepared her for the response Seth Porterfield elicited from her.

'Oh, damn him!' she muttered to herself, but with sufficient venom to make both Freddy Latham and the Widow Farley look up askance. She caught her breath in exasperation and tore the paper before her to bits, fluttering it into the waste-basket when she was done.

'Freddy, I can't keep my mind on these letters right now. I'm going to have my lunch and some tea. Can I make some for you?' she asked, sliding off the stool and going towards the storeroom in the back where the Franklin stove stood.

'That would be nice, Miss Charlotte. It's well after twelve.'

'Oh, is it? Time seems to have just flown by this morning,' she lied.

The afternoon was somewhat better. Although she jumped every time the door opened, she was better able to collect her thoughts, and finished several of the letters.

As time wore on, Freddy's mother came in. Mrs Latham and her son were as alike as parent and child could possibly be. They were both tall and spare with the same straggly, ginger-coloured hair drawn severely back from their narrow faces. Because the store was not busy, they stood talking quietly for some minutes. Then the old woman's face became animated and she began to gesture.

Across the room, Charl caught Seth's name in the conversation. Slipping from the stool, Charl went towards them.

'Excuse me, Mrs Latham. I thought I heard you mention Mr Porterfield's name just now. He is staying at our house and I –'

'Well, I for one cannot imagine your father giving shelter to such a man!' the dour woman exclaimed. 'The very thought that he would invite a British spy into his home and jeopardize our community by extending his hospitality to a scoundrel and a traitor is an outrage!'

'But Mr Porterfield is not a British spy,' Charl put in. 'It was wrong of Father to accuse him.'

For a moment Mrs Latham seemed confused. 'As far as I know, it was not your father that accused him; it was Colonel Hubbard at the fort.'

'What?' Charl gasped. 'Colonel Hubbard! How do you know that?'

'I was there myself,' the spare woman began, 'sitting in the hallway waiting for a chance to speak to Colonel Hubbard about poor Sergeant Latham's pension, God rest his soul. All at once the colonel shouts for guards, and they came at a run.' She paused for breath, aware of the intent look on her listeners' faces. 'Then the Colonel turns to the guards and says, "Escort this man to the gate and see that he has no more chance for snooping around." Then he turns to your Mr Porterfield and says, "I have no proof you're working for the British, but you watch your step. We hang spies."

'They led him out right past where I was sitting. Grinning he was, and as handsome as the devil himself. He sent shivers up and down my spine, he did,' the woman finished with a delicate shudder.

Charl smothered a smile and reflected wryly that shivers of fear were not the usual kind Seth Porterfield inspired in women.

'There must be some mistake,' Charl replied. 'I've spoken to Mr Porterfield at length, and while he opposes a war between Britain and the United States, I can't believe there's any truth –'

'Oh there's truth in the accusations,' Mrs Latham broke in, 'it's just that you refuse to see it. You girls are all alike. None of you can see past a man's handsome face or hear the lies in his words. With age a woman may well lose her beauty, but she gains wisdom that far outweighs the value of a fair face.

'That one is no good, and will only cause trouble here. So mark me well, Miss Charlotte, or you'll come to grief.' Finishing her ominous prophecy with a nod of her head, the old woman turned her back on Charl and calmly resumed the conversation with her son.

Spluttering, and clearly dismissed, Charl stormed back to her desk muttering furiously. She was not sure if she was more angry about the unjust accusations against their houseguest or that Mrs Latham had somehow sensed her unwilling attraction to him.

'Old witch!' she mumbled under her breath as she glared at the woman's back.

After this conversation it became even more impossible to concentrate on the columns of numbers to be added or the letters to be written. In addition to the questions about their encounter in the hall, there was now the more pressing need to know where Seth Porterfield's allegiance lay. Carefully, she reviewed her reasons for believing in him and found them sound. But beyond the dictates of logic, she had heard an inflection of mingled concern and dread in his voice when he spoke of war between these two countries that convinced her beyond any doubt of his sincerity. If he felt such conviction about the advent of war between Great Britain and the United States, he could not be a British spy, she reasoned.

Still Mrs Latham's words plagued her. Was it possible that the old woman was right? Did her feelings for Seth, whatever they were, blind her to the truth of the accusations?

Where was he? Charl needed to see him now more than ever. She still wanted to ask him about what had happened the night before, but now she also desperately needed reassurance that she had judged him correctly. Knowing it was unlikely that Seth would seek her out here, Charl set her pen aside and tucked the paper inside the desk.

'I'm going to post the letters I've finished, Freddy. I'll do the rest tomorrow. If anyone comes looking for me,' she added almost hopefully, 'please send them to the house.'

✳

After being deposited somewhat roughly outside the Gate of Five Nations, Seth made his way into town. He stopped at the Crow's Head Tavern for a tankard of ale, using the time to decide on his next move. The taproom was fairly empty, and he drank thoughtfully. The barmaid, who said her name was Mary, flirted with him outrageously and told him that most of the gentlemen were at the parade ground at this time of day, drilling with their militia units. It seemed a good idea to see these volunteers for himself, so he paid the girl, leaving a heavy tip which she tucked provocatively into her bodice.

He followed the girl's directions to the field at the edge of town that was used for marching and target practice. Seth found a seat on a tree stump along the western perimeter and watched the unskilled units drill.

The troops were ill equipped, carrying every variety of weapon from long squirrel guns to ancient muzzleloaders. They lacked any unifying insignia, and most of the clothing identified the men more closely with their occupations than with their fighting unit. They marched badly, straggling out into an unruly line and colliding comically when right face was confused by some with left face. But what was worse was the way each man wanted a say in decisions made about the troop. These men had elected their officers and clearly expected them to function as elected, and not as military, officials.

This lack of discipline was what worried Seth most. It was probably partially due to the weak officers, selected more for their popularity than for their ability, but the major flaw lay with the men themselves and their complete ignorance of proper military behaviour.

Although he had never been a soldier himself, Seth knew and understood the importance of discipline. It was the flawless discipline that made the British army the most powerful fighting force in the world.

If the order was given to take a particular hill, the British soldier obeyed, regardless of the danger, until either the hill was taken or everyone was dead. With this motley group of militiamen, it was more likely that a discussion would ensue about the merits of taking that particular hill as opposed to another hill over there. These men, or perhaps their fathers, had fought for the right to free speech, but in the case of the military there was no room for democracy.

It was not long before Seth's presence at the edge of the parade ground was noted and remarked upon. By the hostile way the men eyed him, it was evident that they had heard and believed Henry Beckwith's accusations. To avoid trouble, Seth sauntered out of sight, marvelling at how quickly gossip spread. In the trees to the north of the field he found a more secluded place for his observations.

As badly as the militia marched, and as reluctantly as they obeyed orders, Seth was surprised to find that they were exceptional marksmen. Almost every man hit the target consistently and with what might one ·day prove to be deadly accuracy. If anyone had sufficient patience, time and motivation to turn these marching civilians into real soldiers, they might well become a force to be reckoned with.

❊

Seth took his supper at the Crow's Head Tavern and spent the evening drinking ale and listening to the buzz of conversation in the taproom. He had always prided himself on his skill as an eavesdropper, and before the tavern began to empty, he had learned who sold goods to the British at Fort George, who intended to seek refuge across the river if war was declared, who favoured annexation of Canada, and whose bastard the local trollop was carrying. In this one evening, he had learned as much about this little town as some of its inhabitants knew.

Clearly he was anathema, and no one approached him except Mary, who kept his tankard filled. Obviously, everyone had heard of either Henry Beckwith or Will Hubbard's accusations, and if that was so, soon the people of Newark and Fort George would hear of them, too. And when the time came, he intended to use those rumours to his advantage.

Some time after the crowd in the taproom had thinned, Mary came to where he sat and wordlessly took his hand. She led him up the stairs to her small room on the second floor under the slope of the roof. The chamber was scantily furnished, but the bed was wide enough for two, and when she closed the door behind them, Seth was well aware of what was about to happen. Smiling shyly, Mary slowly unfastened and stripped away her clothes. When she was naked, with her thick brown hair tumbling down her back and her full breasts, pale and creamy in the moonlight, she was quite pretty.

This was what he needed, Seth decided as he undressed and joined her between the rough sheets. It had been far too long since he had spent the night with a woman. It had been this need that had driven him to such despicable actions with the Beckwith girl. And surely it was his unsatisfied hunger that had made him respond so ardently to her.

He began to kiss and caress Mary gently, smiling to himself as he felt the fire flame in him and in her. She was open and willing, and soon they were clinging together.

But when it was over and he lay with Mary's head resting lightly on his shoulder, it was Charl who filled his thoughts. He remembered the feel of her silky gold hair between his fingers and the shine of her eyes, like emeralds in the dark. In his mind he could almost feel the length of her body against his and the roundness of her breasts crushed close against him.

Mary exclaimed that he was stirring again, and he turned to her, glad that their movements blotted out the unwelcome vision of Charlotte Beckwith that was inexplicably in his mind.

❧

To Charl the evening was endless. Seth Porterfield did not return for dinner, and she was torn between irritation at his unexplained absence and an eagerness for his company that she could not seem to quell. Her father retired to his study immediately after the meal, leaving Charl to find her own diversions. Normally she had no difficulty in amusing herself, but tonight she was tense and expectant. For a long time she paced around the parlour, unable to muster sufficient powers of concentration to either read or sew. Nor could she seem to stay away from the windows, where she stood waiting for Seth to return.

She devised absurd games for herself, making up the rules as she went along. If she could count all the way to one thousand very slowly, Seth would be standing in the doorway to the parlour when she was done. If she could name all the countries in Europe and their capitals, he would say he had been thinking about her all day long. Whether it was due to her lack of resolution or his contrary nature Charl did not know, but Seth Porterfield refused to appear. Charl chided herself for her preoccupation with his comings and goings when it was clear that he had easily put her out of his mind, but it did not help. She still found herself waiting impatiently for him to arrive.

For a while she played the pianoforte, but her fingers stumbled so badly that she finally decided to go to bed. Though she lay for a long time with her eyes resolutely closed, she heard the clock on the landing strike three before she drifted into a fitful sleep.

The misty, grey light of dawn had begun to filter between her curtains when Charl came suddenly awake. As she lay motionless, with her heart thudding against her ribs, she was not sure what had roused her. Then, from somewhere came a softly whistled tune. She slipped from her bed and went to the front window, resting her palms on the casement as she looked out. Below, Seth was coming up the drive, looking dishevelled but remarkably well rested. Judging from the gay tune and the way he sauntered along, he was well pleased with himself. She was about to call out to him, when she realized, with a certainty that made her stomach sink, just where he must have been.

Trembling, Charl turned from the window to seek her bed and pulled the covers high to block out the sound of Seth's jauntily whistled song. As she huddled there, shivering uncontrollably in the damp morning air, she could not imagine what she'd wanted to say to the noisome man who was their houseguest.

※

On her way to the store the next morning, Charl planned a stop at the Crow's Head Tavern. Their party was only days away, and she needed to revise the list of beer, rum and whisky that Mr Fisher would furnish them from the inn's stock. She had tried to discuss these matters with her father this morning at breakfast, but beyond the maintenance of his own wine cellar his interest in such things was limited. Besides, Charl had served as his hostess so long and so competently that he merely blustered good-naturedly and left all the decisions in her hands.

Seth Porterfield never did put in an appearance at breakfast, and because Charl knew the reason for his absence, she burned with fresh anger. She was not sure whether she was more upset because he had treated her like a wanton or because he had turned from her to one of them. But in either case she was furious, and the revisions offered her a welcome diversion from her own thoughts.

She found solace in the leisurely walk along the riverbank into town, and she enjoyed the play of sunlight on the gently rippling water. Above her birds wheeled in ever-widening patterns against the turquoise sky, and the light breeze carried the faint scent of honeysuckle to her. It was a fine day, warm and pleasant with the promise of summer, and when she reached the Crow's Head, she was reluctant to go indoors.

Once inside the tavern's dim interior, Charl greeted Mary, the Fisher's serving girl, and asked to see the proprietor. For a moment Mary disappeared into a back room, then returned to the task of wiping tables.

'Mr Fisher will be along in a bit, Miss Charlotte,' Mary told her.

Charl wandered aimlessly through the maze of furniture as she waited, aware of the silence in the usually crowded taproom and the scent of stale beer that hung in the air.

'That Mr Porterfield,' Mary began as she came closer to where Charl was standing, 'he's staying with you, isn't he?'

Charl looked up sharply feeling inexplicably wary at the other girl's question. 'Why, yes, he is,' she replied.

'He's quite a handsome man, don't you think?' Mary continued. 'And he's undoubtedly a gentleman.'

'At least on the surface,' Charl conceded. 'Has Mr Porterfield been spending much time here?'

Mary's head came up sharply, and her smile was hard and feral. 'Oh, he surely has,' she purred, 'afternoons, evenings, most of the night.'

A crimson flush rose in Charl's cheeks at the blatant admission. She had guessed how Porterfield had spent the previous evening, but she was not prepared to learn with whom he had passed the hours between midnight and dawn.

'Do you envy me, Charlotte?' Mary continued. 'Aren't you at least a little jealous that I can attract a man like Seth Porterfield when it's obvious you cannot? He's a fine strong man, too, and he knows how to bring a woman pleasure in the dark. But then what would you know of that? And what could you offer a virile man like that, with your modest blushes and pretty ways?'

'Stop it!' Charl hissed at last. 'I have no desire to hear about your dalliances, or Mr Porterfield's either!' But Mary's words had aroused strange emotions in Charl, emotions that were part unsatisfied curiosity and part inexplicable anger.

She was casting about frantically for something more to say when the door to the tavern opened, and the subject of their disagreement stood silhouetted in the glare. Each girl took a step backwards as Seth moved between them, taking Mary's arm and steering her towards the far side of the room.

For a few seconds Charl stood stunned by Porterfield's unexpected intervention, and then her anger drained away to leave her feeling shaken and vaguely sick. But then Mr Fisher was greeting her, and Charl was forced to pull herself together as best she could. What she said to Fisher, she hardly knew, since most of her attention was focused on the pair across the room. Just as Charl was turning to go, she saw Seth gently run a finger along Mary's cheek in a gesture that sent pain twisting through her. He had never treated her with the tenderness he showed this other girl, she realized bitterly.

Once outside, Charl clung convulsively to the hitching post, taking in great gasps of air. It had been a thoroughly unpleasant scene inside the tavern, and her two sleepless nights abruptly caught up with her, making her feel achy and old beyond her years.

She had started up the hill towards the main street and her father's store, when a familiar voice reached her.

'Wait, Charl,' Seth called out.

Wearily, she turned to watch him approach. She did not want to talk to Seth now, but he was giving her no choice in the matter.

'Are you all right?' he asked as he came up beside her.

'I'm just fine,' she replied coolly. 'Thank you for your concern.'

'Mary told me what she said to you,' he began.

'All of it?' Charl asked icily, though her cheeks were hot. Resolutely she turned towards the main street.

'Enough to understand what took place,' he told her, easily matching her pace. 'I would like to explain.'

'I'm really not interested in your licentious escapades, Mr Porterfield,' Charl said, walking even faster.

Seth grabbed one arm and roughly pulled her to a stop.

'Damn you, woman. I'm trying to say I'm sorry that you became involved in something that was really none of your affair.'

'You're quite right, Mr Porterfield; where you spend your nights is none of my concern. But as long as you're a guest in my house, I'll thank you not to come strolling up the drive at daybreak, whistling like a jaybird for all the world to see.'

Charl caught her breath in horror at her unintentional disclosure, and Seth gave a whoop of delighted laughter.

'Charl, my love,' he said with a wicked grin, 'I'd have come home sooner if I'd known you were staying up for me.'

Mortified, Charl flushed to the hairline.

'You woke me with your whistling, you fool!' she began furiously, reaching out to slap his smirking face.

He caught her hand easily and held it tight between both of his as he smiled at her, his eyes filled with barely suppressed glee.

'At least you could deny where you'd been,' she blazed at him.

'And why should I deny it when Mary seemed determined to kiss and tell? I'm glad to learn that you have better manners, though. At least, I assume you've held your tongue since your father's not called me out.'

'I never – He doesn't –' she sputtered.

'Charl, listen,' he broke in. 'I didn't catch you to start another row. I wished to apologize for what happened with Mary and to make sure you were all right. I suppose that while I'm about it, I should apologize for what happened the other night in the hall. But I'm not a bit sorry.' His voice had suddenly gone soft and silky, and for a moment Charl was sure he was going to kiss her right there in the street. Involuntarily she swayed towards him, lost in the azure depths of his eyes. Then his hand was under her elbow steadying her, and he was solicitously asking if she was feeling faint.

'I'm fine,' she assured him as she pulled her arm away.

'Let me walk you wherever you're going anyway,' he insisted.

'I'm going to my father's store. I work there,' she proclaimed defiantly, watching for some reaction from him.

'That's quite unusual for a woman,' he observed noncommittally.

'I suppose it is,' she agreed, 'but Father has always encouraged me to learn new things, and in some ways he treats me more like a son than a daughter. My interest in the business pleases him, and I enjoy being able to use my talents.'

'I've often thought that women should be allowed to use their talents more freely,' he grinned.

'That seems an unusual point of view for you to take,' Charl commented. Then, glancing up at him, she realized the double meaning in his words and blushed again.

She turned to him, her eyes blazing. 'You are a despicable man!'

'I know,' he agreed with a teasing smile. Somehow his night with Mary had done nothing to dim his desire for Charl. She was absolutely enchanting this morning with her cheeks flushed pink and her hair curling enticingly from beneath the brim of her yellow straw bonnet. For the second time in as many minutes, he felt the urge to bend and kiss her frowning mouth until it lost those hard contours. Instead, he took her hand.

'I'm sorry for making fun, and I do agree with you. Women are far more capable than most men are willing to admit. I've often wondered how they put up with their lot. It's rather refreshing to meet someone who is trying to change things. Are there many difficulties?'

Charl looked at him sharply, trying to discern whether he was being patronizing or if she could accept his statement at face value. She wished he would let go of her hand because the faint, warm feeling it gave her to find her hand in his was quite distracting.

'Yes, there are some problems,' she replied. 'Father's associates are reluctant to deal with a woman, and the ladies in town are askance. But I enjoy the things I do at the store, and I intend to keep on working.'

He watched her intently for a moment and then smiled.

'You are an unusual woman, Charl. I'm struck by that more every day. I admire what you're doing, and I hope you won't let anyone deter you.'

She was flustered by his unexpected praise, and her voice was soft and breathy when she replied. 'Why thank you, Mr Porterfield. Here we are at the store. It was nice of you to escort me.'

'It was my pleasure,' he assured her. The time had come for them to part, but neither one of them wanted that.

'Will you be home this evening?' she asked, wanting to detain him.

He hesitated and shook his head.

'No, I think not. I have a great deal of business to take care of in the next day or so.'

Reluctantly, Charl withdrew her hand from his warm one.
'Then I wish you well with it. Good day.'

'Good day to you, Charlotte,' he said, and waited until the
door closed behind her before he turned away. What he'd told
Charl was true; he did have a great deal to do before he met
Mitchell at Black Rock in two days' time. But even as he made
his way back towards the ferry to Fort George, Mitchell's assignments were far from his mind.

*

Seth spent the day in Newark, the Canadian town near Fort
George, attempting to mingle inconspicuously with the people
to learn what he could from the local talk. But as the day wore
on, it became evident that his fame or infamy, had preceded him.
Although nothing was said, he could sense a certain deference
in their behaviour towards him, and he was sure that the people
of Newark believed him to be a British spy. Now if only the
soldiers at the fort could be duped as easily, Seth thought, as he
dined at the village inn, his plan might work.

It was a simple plan, but bold and audacious as his plans usually
were, that depended on nothing more than his own ability to
play his role convincingly. It would be easier if Colonel John
Milton, the commander at Fort George, had heard and believed
the stories that Porterfield was a British spy. But even if he had
not, Seth was prepared to prove his identity.

Seth carried stolen papers, signed by Major Felix St James,
military envoy to Canada, that could be altered to suit his
purposes. He would present the papers, hope that they would be
accepted, and proceed from there. Of course, there were myriads
of things that could go wrong, but in the past Seth had been very
lucky with this kind of ruse.

Besides, it would be amusing to use St James' own signature
against him. Seth thought momentarily of the man who had long
been his enemy and of the embarrassment this could conceivably
cause him. But the embarrassment was nothing compared to the
price Seth would one day extract from St James for William
Porterfield's murder.

Felix St James had been the commanding officer of William's
artillery unit when he had first been posted to Canada. From the
very beginning, there had been an inexplicable animosity between
the two men. St James was a hard officer, strict, demanding, and
cruel in the punishments he handed down. He and William, as

second in command, had argued bitterly and often about strategy and the treatment of the troops. But their frequent disagreements were somehow not the basis for St James' hatred.

When Seth had arrived from England to join the artillery troop, St James had conspired to refuse him admittance. In retrospect it seemed almost as if Felix had transferred his hatred of William to anyone who bore the Porterfield name. St James had tried unsuccessfully to deny Seth his position with the surveyors, too, but with his acceptance by the group going West, Seth had slipped beyond Felix's sphere of influence. Unfortunately, William did not.

Months turned to years while Seth remained in the West, living and trading with the Indians. When he finally returned to Quebec with his boat piled high with pelts, he found that William, and all but two of his artillery crew, had been killed when a defective cannon had exploded. Seth had gone to the military headquarters in the Château St Louis to demand information on the accident. After reading the reports and talking briefly to Captain St James, he had left, grieving but satisfied. It was several days later, when Seth encountered his uncle's former sergeant in a tavern, that Seth heard quite a different story.

The sergeant had been with the artillery crew the day William died, and he had lost his left arm in the accident. Now the man found work where he could, though untrained and disabled as he was, he made a meagre living. That evening, with an interested listener who willingly kept his glass refilled, the grizzled sergeant reminisced about happier days when he'd served under William. Eventually, he came to speak about the tragedy that had taken place.

'They was new guns, fresh from the foundry in Scotland. Captain St James ordered your Uncle William to inspect them and fire them a few times before they was set in place. Knowing the danger of firing new guns, the lieutenant looked them over careful like, and the first three fired off neat as you please.' The sergeant took a long pull on his rum, and Seth motioned for a refill. 'But when we set off the charge on the fourth one, the barrel exploded, sending hot powder and fragments everywhere. The lieutenant didn't suffer none, boy. It was him that set fire to the touchhole. A fragment took him just above the eye; he was dead before he hit the ground. Some of the others weren't so lucky, and that ain't a pretty way to die.

'The corporal and I was farthest from the blast, and both of us survived, though I was hardly left a whole man and he lost his foot. The army don't have any use for either of us now, and life ain't been easy,' he finished, drowning his self-pity in another glass of rum.

'I was sorry about your uncle. Lieutenant Porterfield was a fine officer, though a little wild in his ways. And I wanted you to know the truth about what happened so that you can see to Captain St James yourself.'

'Captain St James?' Seth had asked in confusion. 'What do you mean?'

'It was after my arm was mostly healed,' the sergeant continued, 'that the captain's aide showed me the papers.'

'What papers?' Seth demanded. 'What papers are you talking about?'

'They were the papers that came from Scotland on the ship.'

'Invoices?' Seth suggested.

'Yes, the invoices,' he nodded. 'The ship's captain wrote on them. It seems one of the guns broke loose on the voyage and was damaged. It was on those papers, clear as day; that gun was not to be used.'

'Are you saying that Captain St James knew one of the guns was defective when he assigned William to inspect and test them?' Seth breathed.

'Yes,' the sergeant replied.

'But why?'

'There weren't no love lost between Captain St James and your uncle,' the one-armed man speculated as he finished his rum.

Seth ordered him another.

'Dear God, sergeant, you're accusing Felix St James of murder.' When the other man did not reply, Seth went on, thinking aloud. 'I've got to get hold of those papers if I'm to prove that St James deliberately endangered William and those men and ultimately caused their deaths. How can I talk to St James's aide?'

The sergeant lowered his glass.

'I reckon you can't. He met with an accident shortly after he showed those papers to me. Stepped in front of a team of horses, he did.'

'And what about the invoices?'

The sergeant laughed. 'I'd bet a year's wages that they'll never be seen again.'

Undeterred, Seth had made inquiries both at Château St Louis and along the waterfront. Though he never succeeded in locating the invoices, he found the captain who had transported the guns. What the sergeant had told him proved correct. The cannon that exploded, killing William and the other men, had been damaged en route to Quebec. The captain had indeed notified the military of that fact, too. With a signed statement from the captain in hand, Seth had searched for the one-armed sergeant, whose testimony would link Felix St James to the crime. But the sergeant had been found, the day after their conversation, floating face down in the St Lawrence River.

Reconciled to the fact that he could never prove that Felix St James had killed his uncle, Seth left Quebec. For a time he worked as a guide for settlers moving west, and later was asked to join a delegation bound for Washington. But Seth never forgot St James' treachery. He made discreet inquiries and learned all he could about his adversary. For he knew the time would come when he would face his uncle's killer. And when he did, Seth intended to see that William Porterfield's murder would be avenged.

Seth sat back in his chair in the inn's common room and sipped his drink thoughtfully. Perhaps he would not need the paper with St James' signature to gain admittance to the fort, but if he could use it for his own purposes, so much the better. Seth finished his wine and left some coins on the table as he rose to go. His plans were made; he would visit Fort George in the morning.

Five
***

The next morning, when Seth joined the Beckwiths for breakfast in the large, sunny dining room, it was obvious that he had interrupted an argument. Charl's face was flushed with anger, and the expression her father wore was one of consternation. They paused in their battle only long enough to greet their houseguest and for Charl to pour his tea before hostilities resumed.

'I tell you, Charlotte, you will attend Mrs Langley's party,' Henry proclaimed loudly, as if sheer volume could change the girl's mind in the matter.

'No, Father, I will not! I do not intend to travel all the way to Manchester for what will undoubtedly be a dull affair.'

'I promised Gloria Langley that you would play at her musical, and you will not disappoint her. God knows, the programme probably won't be much without you. Besides it wouldn't do you any harm to curry Mrs Langley's favour this once.'

'Nor would it do you any harm if John Langley thought well of you,' she countered.

Henry did not acknowledge her words, but went on persistently.

'I intend to see that you go, Charl, even if I have to change my plans and take you myself.'

'You only want me to attend so that you can throw me together with that nephew of hers,' Charl accused.

'And what's wrong with Stephen Langley?' Henry demanded, her accusation obviously hitting home.

'Do you mean in addition to the fact that I loathe him?' she inquired, and Seth was forced to stifle a chuckle at her scathing disdain.

'You could do much worse, my girl. Stephen's a fine young man: wealthy, educated, well thought of –'

'But I loathe him, Father!' she exclaimed in exasperation.

'See here, Charlotte, you're twenty-one years old, and it's high time you thought about marriage. Mr Langley is quite taken with you. If you showed any interest in him at all, he'd be happy to have you for his wife.'

'I don't care about getting married, Father,' Charl replied passionately, 'and especially not to Mr Langley. Can't you see that we'd never get along? Stephen is stubborn and single minded, and so am I. Besides he eyes the store far more covetously than he eyes me.'

In the pause before Henry could reply, Seth spoke up.

'If that's so, Beckwith, then it's clear the man's priorities are confused.' His bland observation brought hot blood to Charlotte's cheeks, and Henry frowned at him before he went on, abandoning the subject of Stephen Langley for the moment.

'I still expect you to attend that musical tomorrow night, Charlotte.'

'Oh, Father,' the girl broke in, changing her tactics, 'there's really too much for me to do here to get ready for our own party on Saturday. If I go, it will take all day tomorrow to reach Mrs Langley's house and all day the next to make the return trip. It's too far to travel.'

Beckwith regarded his daughter sternly. 'You will go, Charl, or I swear I will cancel the party here,' he said quietly.

Charl's face fell. She had been looking forward to giving this party for months and had worked hard on the preparations. She enjoyed her role as hostess and would be embarrassed if the gathering was cancelled on such short notice. But she did not doubt her father's threat. They were too much alike, and she knew how far he would go to get his way.

Beckwith sensed his victory but knew better than to rush her decision. As she considered her options, Charl picked up her teacup, postponing the inevitable moment of capitulation.

'All right, I'll go,' she finally agreed, when she could stall no longer.

'Ah, that's better. I'll try to rearrange my schedule so I'll be free to take you as I promised I would. I hate to miss my meeting with Mr Grant, but I guess that can't be helped.'

'Forgive me,' Seth broke in, 'perhaps I can be of some assistance. I must meet a friend in Black Rock tomorrow night. If you will entrust Charlotte's welfare to me, I can accompany her to

Manchester tomorrow and stop by to retrieve her on my way back the next day.'

Charl shot him a murderous look, and Seth smiled pleasantly in reply as he waited for Henry's decision. He could not say why it gave him such pleasure to see the girl's plans thwarted, but he enjoyed having the upper hand this once.

In silence, Henry considered Porterfield's offer. He neither liked nor trusted the man, and since the night of the meeting he had resented his continued presence in his home. But now at least he was to be of some use in offering him a solution to one of his problems. He had not been looking forward to the trip to Manchester or his daughter's sulky moods en route. And he had never much enjoyed Gloria Langley's stilted parties either. Besides, his meeting with Mr Grant might well prove both important and profitable. He was sure that Charl would be safe enough with Porterfield. He was a gentleman for the most part, even if he was English, and Charl could take care of herself.

'It's very kind of you to offer to take Charl to Mrs Langley's. I know you'll take good care –'

The rest of the sentence was lost in the thunderous slam of the dining room door, as Charl stormed out of the room.

Seth chuckled softly in the silence that followed the girl's furious exit.

'She likes to get her own way in things I see,' Porterfield observed dryly.

'You don't know the half of it, sir, not the half,' Henry replied, shaking his head slowly from side to side.

※

The ancient, silver-brown boards of the ferry deck rose and fell slightly under Seth's booted feet as it rocked its way across the Niagara. The tattered old man pulling the huge oar at the stern hardly seemed strong enough to drive the flat-boat, but it moved swiftly to midriver. Looking towards the lake, Seth could see the sun's reflections on the rippling green water. Small boats huddled along both banks, and a large, double-masted lake schooner was visible just beyond the mouth of the river, headed to the Lewiston tramway for unloading. The Niagara was a busy river, at least as far as it was navigable, and of great importance to the Western frontier. For the hundredth time Seth thought about the proximity of the two forts, separated only by the width of the river, and the two towns that would undoubtedly suffer great damage if war was declared. When war was declared, he corrected himself, scowling into the water.

From the river the two forts were a study in contrasts. To the right the square, grey-brown blockhouses of Fort Niagara rose above the trees, strong and sturdy, seeming warlike and invincible. To the left Fort George sat low behind the undulations of the hillside. The spiked log walls, barely visible at the crest of the slope, gave the only evidence of any fortification.

Seth well knew the strength of the American fort. The day spent with Will Hubbard had been very enlightening on that score. Now he needed that same information about the strengths and weaknesses of Fort George.

As he waited for the ferry to nudge the Canadian bank, Seth felt the familiar hard kernel of excitement forming inside him. Somehow it radiated strength along his nerves and muscles and made him seem more aware and alive. Danger had always galvanized him, giving the world a superior reality he relished that made him both more cool-headed and more reckless. The sheer audacity of his plan to infiltrate the fort made him smile to himself. It was totally without subterfuge and relied only on his own ability to play a role. As he moved up the hill towards the front gate of Fort George, he noted the shape and contours of the land, the height and protection given by the trees and the curve of the river, storing them in his perfect memory to be examined and assessed later.

A V-shaped log ravelin protected the main gate from frontal attack, and as Seth passed between the spiked log walls, he realized how well the earthenworks were placed to provide maximum protection for the troops within. Facing the parade ground, filled now with artisans and soldiers, he made quick calculations on the size of the fort. At first it seemed more like a large, log-fenced field than a military installation. There was an open, busy feel to the place that would have reminded him of a country fair if it had not been for the guns along the walls. The fenced area was roughly rectangular with six bastions, one at each corner and two more about midway up each side. Each bastion deployed five guns of varying sizes. To his left were three large log blockhouses, the first floors of which were obviously being used as barracks for the troops. Across from them was a small clapboard building, where a red uniformed sentry stood on guard. Seth moved slowly in this direction, observing a number of men practising artillery firing drills on the grass.

At the guardhouse Seth presented himself to the lieutenant in charge and expressed his desire to see Colonel Milton.

'May I ask the nature of your business with Colonel Milton, Mr Porterfield?' the young officer asked in a thickly accented voice that reminded Seth quite suddenly of his childhood in Yorkshire.

For a long moment he took in the crisp, crimson uniform with its spotless white breeches and bright buttons and found himself wondering why he wasn't wearing one like it instead of coming here to spy on these brave, well-disciplined men.

'It's a private matter,' he said, unaware of how long he had paused. Drawing the folder paper with Felix St James' signature from inside his coat, he continued. 'You might give this to Colonel Milton as a means of explanation.'

'Please wait here,' the officer said, indicating a bench near the door of the small room. When Seth was seated, the man took his black shako from the table and went out.

Another guard sat at the table loading cartridges. It was a familiar enough procedure. Seth had often watched William do it, and had done it himself many times, but now it seemed to fascinate him. The private's stubby fingers moved with practised ease to settle a lead ball at the concave end of the short dowel. Then, taking a carefully cut wedge-shaped wrapping paper, he rolled them inside. A string was tied at one end of the paper to hold the ball in place at the bottom while the dowel was removed, leaving a neat paper cylinder. A measure of powder was added to the tube on top of the ball, and the paper was twisted to a point at the top. It took the man only seconds to complete the cartridge, and it joined many others in a box on the floor beside him.

More proof that the enemy was preparing for war, Seth thought, his eyes fastened on the box of ready cartridges. The enemy in this case was England, his home. The spirit of excitement that had buoyed him up earlier evaporated, leaving in its place aching confusion. Perhaps Hubbard had been right the other day. With war so certain, maybe it was time to stop dealing in intrigue and settle his loyalties once and for all. What would happen if tomorrow night he told Mitchell he was finished spying for the Americans? Could he find a place to sit out the war or at least take some time to sort out his allegiances?

The young lieutenant returned, smiling broadly, breaking into Seth's thoughts and bringing back the problems and dangers of the moment.

'Please come this way, Mr Porterfield. The colonel will see you immediately,' he said, obviously impressed by the order to bring the visitor at once.

Seth followed the man, noting the U-shaped building that served as officers' barracks. It was built of rough-hewn logs on the outside, but inside the walls were furnished richly with oak panels or plaster. They passed through what was apparently the officers' mess and then a small, cluttered office before entering Milton's quarters.

The room was well furnished with pieces obviously shipped from England: heavy, well-made, expensive pieces. Along one wall was a wide four-poster bed with a quilted coverlet and at the foot of it an officer's trunk. Under one white-curtained window stood a slant-top desk, and near a second window a paint box and easel with a half-finished painting clamped in place.

Milton sat at a table near the fireplace with one foot propped up on a rush-seated chair. He was a small man, whose grey-flecked hair belied a youthful face and body. Even when he was seated, his military bearing was evident in the square line of his shoulders, and when he spoke, his voice was resonant and clear. He was not a man to be easily duped, Seth decided, and steeled himself for the conflict to come.

'You'll excuse me if I don't rise. I was wounded in the knee at Castalla in Spain, and every now and then it plagues me,' John Milton apologized as he extended his hand across the table to Seth. His handshake was firm and brief.

Seth assessed the man carefully. It was a certainty that he had been in Upper Canada long enough to have met Felix St James, if not when St James had commanded the artillery unit, then later when receptions had been given to celebrate his appointment as envoy from the Crown. Seth chose to gamble.

'Major St James sends his best wishes, Colonel Milton,' Seth said keeping his face blank.

'I doubt he remembers me,' Milton frowned. 'We met only briefly at one of his receptions.'

'I'm sure he remembers you, sir. He mentioned your painting,' Seth went on gambling again, knowing that St James was an avid patron of the arts with several pieces in his collection done by fellow officers. Art was not an unusual pastime for British officers, in that military information was often communicated by detailed maps and drawings. For many, the skills developed at the Royal Military Academy at Woolwich and in the field carried over into their personal lives.

Milton smiled a bit self-consciously, flattered that he had made an impression. 'We did discuss art, as I remember.'

For a moment Seth felt almost light-headed with relief. He had played for high stakes and won, initially offsetting the other man's suspicion. The warm, strong sense of excitement was back, and he looked forward to the rest of the interview.

'Mr Porterfield, is it? It seems I've heard that name recently,' Milton went on, seeming genuinely unsure.

For a moment Seth hesitated, wondering if he could bluff Milton into thinking he was mistaken, but he decided that sticking closer to the truth was the safer course. He'd taken too many chances already. 'There have been some rumours, sir,' Seth answered honestly, waiting for a reaction.

'Ah, yes, from the other side of the river. So they think you're a British spy?' Milton's eyes were cold and thoughtful.

'Yes, sir.'

'Well, are you, Mr Porterfield?' One eyebrow quirked as he spoke, but otherwise the colonel's expression remained neutral.

Seth was startled by the directness of the question. Milton was a very clever man, he realized. To deny the rumours would put his relationship with St James in a questionable light, but he sensed that an affirmative answer would be just as damning.

'I am not at liberty to discuss the matter, sir,' Seth said, weighing his words. 'I am here on a mission for Major St James. That is all I can say.

'The rumours were an unfortunate outgrowth of a conversation I had with a young lady. Her father overheard and drew some conclusions of his own, which he refused to keep to himself. Colonel Hubbard questioned me also but could not prove any of Mr Beckwith's accusations.'

'Am I to assume that Major St James will not be pleased by the rumours?' Milton asked, his eyes hooded.

'No, sir,' Seth admitted, easily imagining St James' wrath in a like situation. 'I don't relish the idea of explaining this to him. Major St James is a strict officer, and I would be grateful if he didn't find out about the rumours, sir,' Seth finished with just the right tone of appeal in his voice.

'Very well,' Milton agreed. 'I have heard he is a most severe officer. If the rumours impede your mission, he will know soon enough.'

'Thank you, sir,' Seth said, looking down for a moment in what seemed to be gratitude.

'Now what is all this about?' Milton asked.

'Am I to assume you do not have the report ready?' Seth countered, putting the other man on the defensive now.

'Report? All this says is that I am to cooperate with the bearer of this paper!' Milton boomed, clearly not liking the defensive position.

'I was under the impression that a messenger would be sent ahead, informing you about what I would need to know.' Seth paused and Colonel Milton shook his head slowly, looking confused. 'No one arrived with a request for a concise count of troops, supplies, munitions?' Milton continued to shake his head, and Seth frowned deeply.

'Damnation!' Milton grimaced, his eyebrows drawn together. 'It seems as if I send out reports on those things every other day. What do they do with them up there in Quebec?'

Seth shrugged and muttered something about military inefficiency. 'Very well,' he went on, 'a tour and some facts will do. Are you able to conduct me around, sir, or would you prefer one of your senior officers to –'

'Damnation!' Milton snapped again. 'I'm not an invalid. Just hand me my walking stick, and I'll take you around myself,' he said, indicating a brass-tipped ebony cane standing against the wall. He came painfully to his feet and hobbled towards the door, his carriage straight and military in spite of the limp.

'We have five hundred and forty-four men, thirty-six artillery pieces and eight hundred pounds of powder here at the fort,' he began, obvious pride evident in his deep voice. 'Aren't you going to make notes?' he asked, pausing.

'I have a very good memory, sir,' Seth said as he followed Milton outside.

Six

✻✻✻

Seth met Charl in the stable very early the next morning. She was dressed in a carefully tailored riding habit of the darkest green, with a small brimmed hat to match. Her hair was coiled back under the hat with tendrils escaping at her cheeks. A lacy ruffle rose at her throat.

'You are a vision this morning,' Seth commented. 'But I expected that we would be taking the carriage to Manchester rather than riding.'

'As long as I must make this dreadful trip, I thought I might at least enjoy the ride,' she told him. 'I've packed a valise with the things I'll need for tonight's party. I hope you don't mind, but I've taken the liberty of having your horse saddled.'

He nodded his approval and noted the small leather bag tied to the back of Charlotte's saddle next to a hamper.

'I've packed us a picnic too,' she added as one of the stable boys helped her to mount her horse.

'That is very thoughtful,' Seth said, swinging into his own saddle.

They travelled quickly, cantering along the bank of the river. Charlotte seemed to be in a better mood than Seth had expected her to be. Watching the sunlight on the river, he caught snatches of a song she was humming and wondered idly if it was something she would play at the party.

By midmorning they had reached Lewiston. As they passed along the short, deserted main street, Seth noticed the tavern where the disastrous meeting had been held. Watching Charl from the corner of his eye, he wondered how much she knew about the meeting and its aftermath. He had little doubt that she had heard the rumours about him and was curious to know if she had believed them.

They guided their horses along the edge of the town where it nestled against the base of the escarpment, which rose a steep, grey rock ridge, several hundred feet high, that was bisected by the course of the river. For miles it ran across the lake plain on both sides of the border, forming a treacherous crease in the landscape.

They toiled up the rocky road cut from the hillside that was screened from below by the growth of trees. It had been an Indian portage only years before and was too steep for riding, so they dismounted and walked, leading their horses. They reached the top breathless after the climb, and when she had caught her breath, Charl suggested that they stop to eat. 'I know it's not noon yet, but I am getting hungry and I am very thirsty.'

Seth agreed and she led him off the road and through the bushes that grew along the top of the cliff until they came to a clear space. Below them spread the Niagara River, shining green in the sunlight between its steep, red, sandstone banks. The tree tops flowed lush and verdant to the edges of the river, like a gently shifting carpet on the plain below. The spire of a church and several slate roofs broke through the leafy cover, evidence of the town at the base of the escarpment. The deep brown of the freshly ploughed fields marked its perimeters. Scattered over the landscape were more ploughed fields, some yellow with hay or pale green with new corn. They made a random pattern, laced with trees and hemmed by roads and fences that led the eye north towards the lake, its expanse of steely blue stretching on to the pale horizon.

'It's beautiful!' Seth said softly after a minute.

'I love it here,' she smiled, delighted with his appreciation of something she considered special.

'We had better tie the horses,' she suggested, taking down the hamper and blanket. 'We are on a point of land, and it falls off dangerously on three sides.'

Seth took the reins to her horse and tied them while she spread the blanket and began taking out food. There was cold chicken, boiled eggs and some cheese, thick slices of buttered bread and fresh strawberry tarts. She uncorked a bottle of cider and poured it, offering Seth a glass as he sat down beside her, stretching his long legs in front of him on the grass.

'This looks good,' he commented. 'I didn't expect such a feast, but I am hungry.'

They chatted companionably through the meal, laughing

together as if they were old friends. As the sun rose higher and it got warmer, Charl took off her jacket and hat and settled back on her elbows, watching the plain below stretching off towards the vista of lake and sky. The wind was cool and brought the smells of earth and growing things, and the sky was like a soft blue mist hanging high above them. The contentment of that moment was like something tangible between them, and it seemed very natural when Seth leaned close and kissed her gently. Just as naturally Charl responded, softly opening her lips under his. For a shivering moment, they sat motionless, their mouths barely touching. Then Seth pulled her carefully into his arms, stretching the length of his body against hers in the grass.

Smiling, he looked down at her. She was intensely aware of his closeness, the warm, male scent of him, the hardness of his body and the incredible, unfathomable blueness of his eyes. Breathlessly she waited. Without moving, she felt drawn towards him, her muscles growing taut. Then his mouth came down to hers, and he was kissing her: first her lips, then her cheeks and eyes, and down her neck. She moved a little under his lips, her pulse beating dizzily against her temples. When his lips covered hers again, she met his tongue with hers, shyly, and moaned deep in her throat as he pressed her down against the soft earth.

It was the same as before. The responses to Seth's warm exploring mouth were the same ones that Charl had experienced that night in the hall. Only now she abandoned herself to them, feeling her heart pound and relishing the sweeping weakness that made her tremble. It was as if he had the power to make her feel things she had never felt, as if her nerve endings were newly aware of sensations. His hand gently stroking her arm through her silk sleeve sent ripples of sensation through her, tightening her nipples. The warmth of his breath against her ear seemed to travel down her neck and spine, leaving a glowing trail to her loins.

It was the same. Even while he kissed her, filling her senses and compelling her body, a corner of her mind grasped and revelled in that thought. And she wondered why it was so. Dreamily, the idea circled through her brain, and even while she responded to him, some small part of her mind demanded voice for her questions.

Unaware of her thoughts, Seth worked on the ruffle tied at her neck, loosening it to expose her white skin. He moved his lips lower to kiss the expanse of throat, breathing the sweet, citrus fragrance of her. Why, he wondered, did this woman stir him so? What was it that made each of his reactions to her so sharp and delicious? He caught her carefully coiled hair, loosening it over her shoulders, and buried his face in the golden softness. His mind was so full of desire that he barely heard her speak his name and was only marginally aware when she began to push against him.

'Seth, wait,' her voice came again, slowly penetrating his thoughts. She was struggling gently in his iron grip.

'What the deuce?' he muttered, and was suddenly furious. The bitch had been teasing him! That thought tore across his consciousness and drove like needles in his blood. Angrily he flung her away, breathing hard, unaware of the confusion in her eyes.

'I suppose you're saving yourself for your marriage bed!' he accused sarcastically, his eyes narrowing.

'No, I –' she paused, blushing. She did not want to ask her questions now. The tender moment was past and instead of the gentle, passionate man whom she wanted to answer her questions, there was a cold, angry stranger, ready to mock her naïvety.

'I had some questions,' she began, raising her chin and plunging in characteristically.

'Virgin's questions, I'm sure,' he mocked her. 'Perhaps you had better save them for your wedding night,' he advised, his voice like ice. He stared intently towards the lake, his anger turned inward now. When would he learn to leave her alone? he wondered. There had been something about this girl from the moment he set eyes on her that disturbed him and diverted his attention from more important matters. Intentionally or unintentionally, Charl always managed to set his plans awry, and he was at a loss to explain his own reactions to her. A moment ago she had seemed a willing partner, carrying them both to the heights of passion, and now she wanted only answers to her maidenly questions.

'I don't intend to have a wedding night,' she said, her mouth growing tight. 'I'll never marry. There is too much to lose.'

'Too much to lose? Do tell.' He raised one eyebrow as he questioned her and observed that her mouth grew tighter still.

She had not intended to discuss her plans for the future with anyone, least of all Seth Porterfield, and certainly not now when he was angry and in a caustic mood.

'I'm waiting,' he prompted her. 'It seems as if you owe me some explanation.'

Fury broke through her common sense. 'All right!' she shouted at him. Then, controlling her voice, she continued. 'You know I am interested in my father's business. I've always spent time at the store, ever since I was a little girl. I love the work: the planning, the figuring, every part of it. It excites me and it makes me feel worthwhile. Father allows me to work there only because I am his daughter, but what he really wants is a son-in-law to bring into the business. If I should marry, my father and my husband will take over the holdings and I will retire, like a good wife, to raise a family and tend a home.' She paused but could read nothing in Seth's expression. 'If I never marry, I can continue with a life I enjoy and, because I am an only child, eventually Father's business will come to me. I do not intend to lose either the promise of my inheritance or my independence by marrying someone like the self-serving Mr Langley. I will remain my own woman, Mr Porterfield, and I will do what I must to achieve that end,' she declared, her face set.

Seth watched her for a long moment, struck once more by the intelligence and determination of this unique female.

'You never cease to amaze me, Charlotte,' he admitted, looking at her in frank admiration. She was so different from what she seemed, or perhaps she was just different from what he expected her to be. She was thoughtful in a frivolous age, strong when most women affected a helpless demeanour, honest and truthful when he himself practised deceit. As he watched her, his eyes softened, and he began to smile.

'You had some questions, I believe,' he said quietly, his gaze intent on her face.

Somehow the things that she had wanted to know were far from her mind now.

'After the other night I was curious –' she began in confusion, very aware of his eyes on her.

'So this was along the lines of an investigation?' His teasing voice led her on.

'No, no, not exactly. When you kiss me I feel –' she broke off, her face flushing. 'There is something special that happens between us, and I need to know –' she began again, stopping short. 'I have so many questions!' she exclaimed in exasperation.

Seth laughed softly, and she felt her face grow hot again. 'You're curious about what goes on between men and women, and you wonder about how my kisses make you feel, is that right?' he asked, sounding strangely instructive and patient.

'Yes,' she admitted, her lashes hiding her eyes.

'There is not much I can tell you, Charl. What happens between any man and woman is unique and special, but if you want to understand the whole of it, you must let me make love to you. I want you, Charl; you must know that. But I won't force you to do anything you don't want to do. The decision is yours to make,' he told her, his voice very even.

'I don't know what I want,' she said quietly, her deep green eyes coming up to his face.

'I know you don't,' he answered, a wave of desire rising in him so strongly that it was impossible for him to move away from her. Blindly he reached out, and when she did not resist, he kissed her again and again.

As they lay together in the grass, he took them both to the depths of passion until their world spun around them, a blur of gold and green and blue. He kissed her deeply, while she clung to him. Her silk shirt opened under his eager hands, and he lowered his head to her creamy round breasts and tight rosy nipples. She pressed her soft body up against him, feeling his hardness and his strength, and whispered his name against his ear. He knew very well what he was doing to both of them, and her response was even stronger than he had expected it to be. Slowly and gently he drew away and looked down at her, lying still and limp in the grass. Her eyes were closed, and her lips looked smudged with kisses. He stroked her hair.

'Charlotte?' he said softly. Her eyes fluttered open as if the lids were too heavy for her, and she smiled. 'Charlotte, we must go now.' She nodded and her eyelids shut again.

He laughed and got to his feet. The horses were munching grass contentedly on the far side of the clearing, and he went to untie them. By the time he returned, Charl was dressed, and the hamper was repacked. Only the cascade of thick, glowing hair that tumbled down her back gave evidence of what had happened between them.

Seth helped her into her saddle and swung into his own.

'You must decide about this soon,' he said, catching her bridle.

'I know,' she replied, as she met his eyes. For an instant their gazes held, and then she turned away. Carefully they followed the path back along the edge of the cliff to the road that led towards Manchester.

❊

It was midafternoon when they pulled their horses to a halt outside Gloria Langley's stately Georgian home. The white picket fence made a frame for the symmetry of the two-storey house with its circular drive and gave the impression of wealth and importance to the structure. It was an impressive building. The rich, tan stuccoed walls glowed gold in the sun and contrasted with the white pilasters and cornices that framed the façade. They had ridden only partway up the drive when the fanlighted door burst open and a tiny, raven-haired woman came out.

'Oh, Charlotte!' Mrs Langley cried as they stopped at the foot of the steps. 'I'm so delighted you could come. You will be the best musician to play tonight. I am sure you will make the party a success all by yourself.' Then her eyes lighted on Seth, and a dimple crept into her cheek.

'And who is this, Charlotte, dear? Your father never mentioned another guest to John, although he's welcome, I'm sure.'

'I'm Seth Porterfield, ma'am,' he said, smiling as he slid from the saddle. 'I regret I cannot stay. Mr Beckwith asked me to escort Miss Beckwith on my way to Black Rock.'

Flirtatiously Gloria Langley raised her amber eyes to Seth's face and smiled provocatively. 'Well, it's a shame you can't stay. I'm sure we would love to have you.'

Watching them from her perch on the sidesaddle, Charl felt angry and ignored. In spite of the fact that Gloria Langley was well past her prime, she was still a beautiful woman. Her blue-black hair was fashionably disarrayed and seemed lustrous against her ivory skin. And, in spite of her tiny stature, her body was lush, with full breasts and hips. Seth's towering form made her look even more petite and fragile and, as Charl watched them, openly flirting with each other, she felt irritation stir within her.

Unhooking her knee from the saddle, Charl slid to the ground, landing awkwardly in a flurry of dust. Seth and Mrs Langley looked up from their conversation as if they were not sure where she had come from.

'You should have let me help you down,' Seth admonished her.

'I thought you had quite forgotten about me!' she snapped, shooting him a murderous look.

She saw the sunny gleam of mirth in his eyes, and his mouth fought a smile. 'Never, Charlotte, my love,' he said softly, as he turned away from Mrs Langley. 'Let me help you with your bags,' he offered in a louder voice. 'I must be on my way if I'm to be in Black Rock by nightfall. I will be by for you tomorrow afternoon, Miss Beckwith, and I would be pleased if you were ready,' he finished brusquely.

'Oh, I'll be ready, don't worry,' she answered sharply.

'Perhaps you could stay to tea tomorrow,' Mrs Langley suggested.

'We shall see,' Seth replied. 'I can't think of anything more delightful than tea with two lovely ladies. But it is a long way back to Youngstown, and I don't know if we'll be able to spare the time.'

He turned to the small woman and took her tiny hand in his large brown one. 'I can't think when I've met a more charming lady,' he said, smiling at her in an intimate way that left Charl fuming. 'Until tomorrow then, Mrs Langley. And good-bye, Miss Beckwith,' Seth called out as he climbed into the saddle again, but Charl was already storming into the house.

The room that the maid indicated for Charl's use was exquisitely furnished in pale lavender. Like the rest of the house, it was tasteful and expensive, speaking well of John Langley's success on the frontier. He had come to the area long before Henry Beckwith had left Philadelphia and, with a large land grant to bolster his own wealth, had done very well. He was highly respected by all who knew him, but his marriage to the beautiful Miss Gloria Winton of Baltimore, a woman half his age, had caused tongues to wag. Charl did not remember Mrs Langley's arrival on the frontier more than ten years before, but Gloria had caused a sensation. She had arrived in a sleek new carriage at the splendid house John Langley had built for her. In a way, it was her coming that had marked the beginning of any real social life in this wilderness, and she gave and attended parties with the zeal of a crusader. For the most part she had been a good wife to John Langley, but now, as he approached sixty, there were whispers that Gloria enjoyed other relationships.

Charl had just sent the maid off to press her gauzy, green party dress when Gloria Langley fluttered into the room.

'Oh, Charlotte, darling, I'm so glad to have you here. Are you quite comfortable, my dear?' she asked, perching like a small blue bird on the edge of a violet velvet chair.

'This is fine, Mrs Langley. Thank you. The bedroom is beautiful,' Charl said without enthusiasm.

'Oh, you must call me Gloria since we're more or less of an age,' she said, flattering herself. 'And when you marry Stephen, we'll be in the same family,' she went on in a high musical voice that reminded Charl of a melody struck randomly up and down the scale.

'I never said I'd marry your nephew,' Charl replied evenly.

'Oh, you'll lead him a merry chase, but in the end it will be a good alliance, and you'll have him,' Gloria prophesied.

'But I don't love Stephen,' Charl insisted.

'You'll find love doesn't necessarily make a good marriage, my dear. A husband provides security and position. I had learned that lesson before I was your age, but you'll learn it in time. And Stephen will be patient. He's quite enamoured with you."

'Every woman needs love,' Charl argued.

'Oh yes, every woman does, but after a woman is married, there are other ways to find satisfaction: society, a home, children –' Her voice trailed off.

Lovers, Charl finished the sentence mentally, and was shocked at how well that thought fitted with what Mrs Langley said next.

'Enough of this serious discussion,' she began. 'I came up to find out who that divine Mr Porterfield is. He's quite the most dashing man I've met in years!'

Seth – dashing? That wasn't quite the adjective she would have chosen, Charl thought. Infuriating, arrogant, confusing, perhaps even compelling were all words that would have described their houseguest. But dashing; Charl was not at all sure that she would call Seth dashing.

'Actually I don't know too much about him. He's been staying with us for about a week. He and father have business. He spoke at a meeting in Lewiston,' Charl told Gloria, being purposefully vague.

'He's not the British agent, is he?' Gloria asked and clapped her hands together in delight. 'Oh, how marvellously romantic! I don't think I've ever met a more deliciously handsome man, so

tall and strong and blond, and now to find he's wrapped up in
some kind of intrigue! Charlotte, what's wrong with you? Don't
you find him exciting?'

'You're acting like a schoolgirl!' Charl told the older woman
severely, angry at hearing someone else extolling Seth's virtues.

'Oh, perhaps,' Gloria smiled prettily, 'but I'll wager he'd make
a superb lover. Are you shocked?' she asked, watching Charl's
face. 'I suppose you are, but a woman needs a physical side to
her life, too. Once she is made aware of them, there are desires
that every woman has. And a man like Mr Porterfield is just what
she needs to satisfy them. Oh, he'd make a poor husband. There's
a quicksilver quality about him that will never be pinned down,
but I wager that a single night in his bed would keep a woman
warm all winter,' she finished.

'Please, Mrs Langley! What you've said is most unseemly!'
Charl gasped, flushing brightly.

'Charlotte, you needn't be embarrassed. You'll marry Stephen
soon and then you'll understand what I'm talking about,' she
said, patting Charl's hand as she rose.

'Is there anything else you need before I go?' Gloria asked
solicitously.

'I'd like a hot bath and a chance to practise my selections for
tonight,' Charl answered automatically, her mind on their earlier
conversation.

'Of course. I'll send Susan up with some hot water, and the
pianoforte is in the parlour when you're ready. You might rest
a while, too, dear. You seem tired.'

'Thank you, Mrs Langley,' Charl said, glad to see the other
woman go.

Moving to the window, Charl stared out across the carefully
trimmed lawn, hardly seeing it. In her mind the events of the day
swirled together, like colours in a kaleidoscope, Gloria Langley's
words superimposed against her memories of Seth's kisses.

'I'll wager he'd make a superb lover . . .' the high voice chimed
in her thoughts. 'There are desires that every woman has . . .'

How could the older woman possibly have known what she
was thinking, Charl wondered. Seth wanted to make love to her,
and in one brief conversation Gloria had assured her that it would
be all right, had in effect sanctioned the act. It was normal for
her to feel and respond to Seth as she did. It was not wrong to
want him to kiss her and touch her. A sense of relief washed

over her. The instinctive reactions Seth had aroused were not the responses of a wanton, but those of a woman.

She rested her forehead against the cool windowpane, thinking how grateful she was to Gloria for calming her uncertainties. It was so strange that the older woman had known how she felt about Seth. It was almost as if she shared Charl's feelings.

Thunderstruck, Charl turned away from the window, her fingers pressed to her open mouth. Gloria did share Charl's feelings for Seth. It was suddenly so clear. Gloria Langley wanted Seth, her Seth, as a lover! Coming to Charl's room to welcome her had been Gloria's ploy to learn more about him. But in the end she had tipped her hand, and now Charl knew what the older woman really wanted.

With that realization, confusing and conflicting emotions flooded Charl. For the first time in her life a tide of pure aching jealousy swelled in her. Possessiveness and doubt linked to form a tight band around her ribs, restricting her breathing. It was suddenly very important to her that Seth still wanted her after he had met the elegant, sophisticated, and obviously available Mrs Langley. Would he still want her? she wondered.

Charl had never thought of herself as the object of a man's desire, but Seth had unleashed not only an array of puzzling sensations, but a jumble of unfamiliar emotions as well.

She moved across the room to the long gilt-framed mirror and peered into the glass, wondering what Seth saw when he looked at her. What was there in her that inspired his desire? And did he feel the same thing when he flirted with Gloria Langley? Charl was coming to accept her own responses to Seth Porterfield, but, instead of that acceptance resolving her questions, it only deepened her confusion. And she could not help but wonder if it would be necessary to make love with this compelling stranger before she could understand her own feelings and satisfy her curiosity.

Charl had been so deep in thought that she had been unaware of the maid's presence in the room, but when she turned from the mirror, she found her bath awaiting her. She undressed quickly and stepped into the tub. The warm scented water offered solace to her tired body, but as she slid deeper into the copper tub, her mind began the round of questions once again.

Seven

When Seth rode into Black Rock, only pale purple smudges of clouds were left along the Western horizon to mark the last of the sunset. Overhead the sky was turning a deep marine blue, and stars were becoming visible. He was late, and Mitchell would not be pleased.

'The devil take Mitchell!' he muttered. Mitchell's wishes had played too important a role in his life for the past few years. He had gone where Mitchell told him to go, done what Mitchell told him to do, but now that was ending. It had been a period of his life full of adventure and intrigue, a time of travel and exploration. It had paid well too, not that he had much put aside, but tonight it was over. He was no longer able to tolerate the feeling that in order to serve one of the countries he loved, he must betray his loyalty to the other. He would give Mitchell the information he carried in his head and then tell him that he was through.

On the tedious ride from Manchester, where he had left Charl, he had turned the idea of quitting over and over in his mind. He had weighed the advantages and disadvantages with cool logic, but in the end it had been his emotions that had forced the decision upon him. He could not continue with this job while his loyalties were fragmented.

Seth had not always felt this conflict. There had been no question of allegiance on the assignments to France and Spain or into the Spanish territories to the South and West. He had gone willingly, enjoying the new lands he explored and the dangers that he faced. There had been complete loyalty to the fledgling United States during these missions against the larger European powers. In his dealings with them he had been reckless, daring, and clever and had been commended once by President Jefferson himself. But in these last months, when he had been spying on British settlements in Canada and on the Indians with whom he had lived, he had felt a deep conflict. Now with the war a virtual certainty, he had made his decision.

What he would do after tonight was unclear. He would be eligible for a captain's commission in the Army if he wanted it, but to fight against Great Britain in uniform would be no better than what he was doing now. He needed to find somewhere to sit out the war, some place where his loyalties were not constantly being tested. There was beautiful land in the mountains beyond the boundaries of the Louisiana Purchase, or to the southwest where the Spanish held lush grasslands and arid deserts. Perhaps he would go even further West to the Pacific coast, where the icy green water turned to shimmering foam against the rocks.

He would find his haven, far away from the war, but first he would return to Youngstown for a few more days with Charl. As he considered his future, he almost wished he could discuss all this with her, share his hopes with her as she had with him. But most of all he wanted to make love to her. That desire had haunted him ever since the day he watched her across the room at the Crow's Head Tavern, each encounter with her strengthening his need. He wanted to see her naked before him, her hair tumbling over her shoulders and across her breasts. He needed to feel her writhing under him, calling out his name in a voice thick with passion, while he took them both to climax. He could not leave Youngstown before that happened.

As he eased himself down from his horse in front of the shabby, white frame tavern where Mitchell kept a room, he was well aware of the many hours he had spent in the saddle. His muscles ached, and his vertebrae felt fused together from the constant motion. He was tired and needed a hot meal and a drink. Leaving his horse with the stableboy, he entered the tavern's taproom. The beamed ceiling was low, and he had to duck his head to get in the door. Inside, a wave of smoke and heat enveloped him, and the din of many voices seemed loud after the solitary ride. Even before he had a chance to orient himself, Mitchell appeared before him.

'Where the hell have you been?' he demanded. 'I expected you this afternoon.'

'It's a long ride from Youngstown,' Seth shrugged.

At first glance Mitchell hardly seemed a man who could organize and oversee the complex intelligence network that honeycombed the entire frontier, from Quebec west to Fort Mackinac.

He was a small man, whose round face and heavy shoulders gave him a stocky, solid air. His age could have been forty or sixty, and his thinning, grey hair seemed a direct contrast to the smooth, ruddy face. On the surface he looked like a farmer or a tradesman, placid and innocuous. But the black eyes behind their round spectacles gave evidence of a canny intelligence and ruthless ambition. Seth had worked for Mitchell at intervals for six years, and even now he was not sure if Mitchell was the man's first or last name. He was an enigma, seeming to exist in only one context.

'I've very little time to spare on your excuses, Porterfield,' he said tersely, and led Seth to the back of the room where open stairs went up to the second floor.

'Can't I have a drink or a quick meal?' Seth asked as he moved to follow the smaller man.

'I don't want your report muddled with liquor,' Mitchell retorted as he opened the door to a small room near the end of the corridor. 'There are paper and ink on the table. Write out a full report on all your activities, if you please. When you are done, I'll see about a bit of dinner for you,' Mitchell promised.

'Why don't I simply tell you what I know, and you can write the report,' Seth proposed, not looking forward to the next few hours.

Mitchell laughed shortly and without humour. 'I don't have your memory for details,' he said, lighting the lamp on the table. 'Get busy.'

Before sitting down Seth stretched, his fingers easily brushing the ceiling of the sparsely furnished room. 'You don't really live here, do you?' he asked, but Mitchell only frowned in reply.

With a sigh Seth sat down at the table and picked up the pen. Dipping it into the inkwell, he paused and closed his eyes. After a few moments of concentration the first page of Hubbard's report came into focus behind his closed lids. Slowly he opened his eyes and began to copy what he saw so clearly in his mind, oblivious to the room around him. Mitchell watched, mildly amazed as he always was by what the other man was able to do. It was a valuable gift, he thought. Some time later Mitchell left, but Seth was too engrossed in the work to notice.

It was well after two o'clock when Mitchell returned to find Seth asleep at the table, his head pillowed on his crossed arms. Beside him were three lengthy reports, written in his bold, distinctive hand. Two were on the fortifications at the Niagara River installations. A third dealt with his assessments of community sentiment, militia readiness, leadership potentials, and other pertinent topics. Mitchell read them through, nodding to himself, before he woke Porterfield.

Groaning, Seth shook his head to clear the sleep from his brain. 'What time is it?' he asked, squinting at the light. 'It seems as if I just finished those.'

'You probably did. It's only three.'

'A man is never well rested in your employ,' Seth complained.

'If you are not well rested, Porterfield, I sense it is for other reasons,' Mitchell responded. 'I have ordered a meal for you so at least you cannot accuse me of starvation.'

'Thank you,' Seth replied dryly, and at that moment there was a knock at the door. A serving girl entered with a tray of food and set it down in front of Seth.

'You may go now,' Mitchell told her. As Seth began to devour the greasy stew, Mitchell questioned him in detail about the information in the reports.

Finally satisfied, Mitchell sat back and lit his pipe, drawing raspily on it until the bowl glowed orange. 'You've done an especially good job on these, Porterfield,' he said quietly, and Seth looked up from his meal to see if he had heard correctly. It was unusual for Mitchell to compliment his men, and it aroused a ripple of suspicion in Seth.

'Thank you,' he replied guardedly.

'The ploy of passing yourself off as a British spy was a stroke of genius,' Mitchell went on with a look of what seemed to be genuine amusement on his broad face. It did little good to wonder where Mitchell got his information; he seemed to know everything that went on along the frontier. 'I understand Will Hubbard helped you carry it off.'

'Yes, he did. Will asked me to give you his best when I saw you,' Seth went on, an inexplicable feeling of apprehension beginning to creep up his neck.

'Good man, Hubbard. It was a shame to lose him.'

Mitchell shifted in his chair, leaning forward to rest his elbows on the arms. In silence he clasped his hands across his middle and studied Seth over the top of his spectacles. His black eyes were intense, and it was difficult to sit motionless under his scrutiny. Seth's feeling of uneasiness grew.

'You want to bolt, don't you, to quit the service?' Mitchell finally asked in a low voice.

At first Seth was surprised at the question; then there was a flash of anger and finally a feeling of resignation settled over him. Mitchell knew everything. He nodded.

'You haven't liked what you've been doing for some time; I've been aware of that. But damn it, man, you're so good at this!' Mitchell said intently.

'I can't go on spying against Great Britain,' Seth began, knowing it would be impossible to explain his feelings to Mitchell.

'I know England is your home. You forget I met you a long time ago,' Mitchell went on.

'I don't plan to take my commission either. I just need to be away from this conflict. I feel a loyalty to each country, and I can't reconcile what I'm doing with what I feel.' There was strain in Seth's voice as he spoke.

'I understand,' Mitchell said, 'but I'll need you for a while longer.'

Seth looked up sharply, unable to believe what he was hearing. He had never expected Mitchell to refuse his resignation.

'Now just let me finish, Seth,' Mitchell went on, when the other man would have spoken. 'As you know, the declaration of war is imminent. God knows, Congress may have declared war already, and we just don't know it. When that happens, all hell will break loose. Hull is out there in the west marching around, damn, old, inefficient war horse. No matter what they think in Washington, that campaign to Fort Detroit is doomed to disaster. For a while after that the worst fighting will be here, along the lakes, where enemy territory will be so close.' His eyes fixed on the younger man and he spoke softly. 'Seth, I need a man I can trust, someone who knows the land along the border as well as you do to carry messages between here and Quebec. Masquerading as a British spy has established the perfect identity for you. Along the frontier you can move with impunity, and your memory is an added advantage. Carrying any kind of incriminating papers across the border will be dangerous. With your strange talent, there would be no need for those risks. Surely you can see why I can't let you quit the service just yet.'

For a moment Seth held tight to the edge of the table in front of him until the red haze of anger faded a bit and the urge to tighten his hands around Mitchell's throat began to lessen. Who

the deuce was Mitchell to tell him he couldn't quit? His life was
his own. He was free, had always been free, to do what he chose
to do. He would leave, get up and walk away from all this, and
Mitchell could not stop him. In a single fluid motion, he came to
his feet, towering above the seated man, and strode towards the
door. Behind him he heard the unmistakable sound of a pistol
being cocked, and he froze with one hand on the latch.

'I'm sorry, Porterfield, I can't let you leave just yet. If you
make any move to open that door, I'll kill you.' Mitchell's voice
was cold now, and there was no doubt that he meant every word.
'Please come back and sit down. Our discussion has not been
concluded.'

Moving slowly under Mitchell's deadly, black eyes, Seth returned to his chair and Mitchell uncocked the pistol, putting it
in his lap.

'You can't make me work for you!' Seth blazed at him.

'I promise you that in six months you will be free to do as you
please, and you will have accumulated a substantial sum for your
trouble. But for the moment I am afraid I must compel you to
do as I ask, regardless of your feelings,' the smaller man said
calmly, one finger tracing a design on the stock of the pistol.

'I will need you to go to Quebec as soon as war is declared.
Take the Indian if you wish, but move quickly before the border
closes. It might be very unhealthy for a suspected British spy to
meet a mob caught up in a patriotic frenzy. A man could get
hanged in those circumstances.' He met Seth's eyes levelly, the
implied threat clear.

'In Quebec stay with Madame La Soeur, as you usually do.
There will be someone in the Place d'Armes at nine o'clock every
morning, waiting for you to make contact.'

'And what will be the nature of my treacheries?' Seth inquired
hotly.

'Collecting information, acting as courier, nothing more.
Knowing your sensibilities, I will leave overt acts to others,'
Mitchell added generously.

'I won't do it! If you let me leave this room alive, I swear I
will get on my horse and you will never see me again!' Seth
vowed, his voice low and dangerous.

'I doubt that,' Mitchell smiled blandly. 'If you leave, I will
have a bounty put on your head, of ten thousand dollars let's
say. With that much money at stake, interest will surely continue

for some time. The circulars are certain to be sent outside the country too, perhaps to the Spanish territories and California.'

'And what will the charge be?' Seth asked icily.

'Murder,' Mitchell smiled.

'Murder,' Seth repeated, pale with rage.

'A senator's son, as I remember,' Mitchell prodded.

'It was self-defence; you know that. And you sanctioned it! He was selling information to –'

'All that is immaterial. There are still those who wish to see the crime solved, the boy's father for one.' Mitchell's voice was quiet and conversational.

'You Judas!' Seth hissed, as he felt Mitchell's trap closing around him.

'Of course, I hate to use this method to insure your co-operation, Porterfield. By the time we get word of the declaration of war, I think you will go to Quebec quite willingly. Just remember, it's only for six months; I give you my word on that,' Mitchell finished.

'As if your word was worth anything at all,' Seth snapped.

'Actually it is worth quite a bit,' Mitchell assured him, unoffended.

Seth rose stiffly, and Mitchell watched him, one hand resting on the handle of the pistol in his lap.

'I will be with the Beckwiths for a few more days,' Seth said, controlling himself with difficulty. The desire to crush out Mitchell's life was still strong in him.

'Then you will be on to Quebec,' Mitchell prodded.

'Perhaps,' Porterfield replied.

Mitchell rose too. 'You will go,' he said confidently, opening the door for his visitor to leave.

Seth wanted to defy this smug, manipulative man. He wanted to walk away, travelling so far and so fast that he would never be found. But even as he contemplated it, Porterfield knew there was no escape. Mitchell knew him too well and had constructed this trap flawlessly. To Seth, escape would never be the same as freedom because he would refuse to live his life on the run. Mitchell was right. He would go to Quebec; he had no choice.

Outside, the sky to the east was glowing pink with dawn. Seth stood on the porch of the tavern and took several shaky breaths. Things had not gone at all as he had planned. He was trapped into doing what Mitchell dictated, and in six months, six hellish months, he might be free.

Wearily he started towards the stable. It had been a long night.

*

Seth was not sure how long he had been riding when he began to notice the strong shafts of light filtering through the trees. As he moved into a clearing, he squinted up at the sun to determine the time. It must be midmorning, he estimated, and he had left Black Rock at dawn. It bothered him that he had not been aware of the passage of time, but he had been too preoccupied trying to find a way out of Mitchell's trap. There was none, he had decided. It was hopeless.

If he left the service, as his conscience dictated he must, Mitchell would see that he was hunted down. Even if he did manage to escape, he knew that he would always be looking over his shoulder, always running. And as difficult as the next six months would be, it seemed better to work for Mitchell than to spend the rest of his life wondering when he would be caught. In retrospect, Seth knew Mitchell's word was good; this would be only a six-month assignment. Just as Mitchell's threats were to be believed, so were his promises.

It was frustrating to know that instead of leaving his life of intrigue behind he would have to become further embroiled in the conflict he hated. Once war was declared, the dangers he had faced before would be multiplied. He had always considered himself a courier or an investigator, not a spy, but even those activities would be labelled treason when war was declared. And if he was discovered, he would hang.

Even in his own bleak mood, he did not fear the gallows. He was very good at what he did, and it seemed unlikely that he would be caught. When he considered the situation, he realized that the trap would lie more in his disguise than in his discovery. As soon as he began his masquerade as a British spy, he would be a man without a country. He would be despised by the Americans, even while he worked for their cause, and if he was accepted by the English, it would be only until his duplicity was discovered. He frowned. In a way, that had been his lot from the beginning, always to be caught between two worlds.

His frown deepened as his mind slipped backwards in time and images of things past flashed across his consciousness. He had never truly belonged anywhere. His parents both denied their bastard son, hiding him away in the countryside, remembering the boy only as an irrevocable mistake. As Seth grew older, Felix St James had barred him from joining William's artillery troop. He had belonged neither with the surveyors headed West nor with the Indians whose lifestyle he had tried to embrace.

Seth had been happiest during the three years he had spent exploring the western territories with Meriweather Lewis and William Clark. He had been just twenty when he met Lewis. In spite of his youth he knew the western lakes region better than most men, and he had been sent to Washington with a delegation from Upper Canada to review the boundaries of the Louisiana Purchase prior to its approval by the United States Congress. Lewis had been an American who worked with the delegation, and Seth had liked the quiet, precise man immediately. Apparently, Lewis had been impressed by the young man's knowledge and ability, because one night he had invited Seth to join him at a tavern. There they met Captain William Clark. After several tankards of ale and much talk, Lewis proposed that Seth join the expedition that was being formed, by order of President Jefferson, to explore the lands west of the Mississippi River, all the way to the Pacific Ocean.

The prospect of such an adventure excited Seth, and, although it meant becoming an American citizen, at the time that seemed like a small price to pay for such an opportunity.

In the spring of 1804, the twenty-seven men set out up the Missouri River on a keelboat. In the next two years the party travelled across the Rocky Mountains, rising huge and rugged into the clouds, and descended the western face to follow the Columbia River to its mouth, where it entered the Pacific. Seth had loved the icy green of the ocean and the taste of the thin, clear air on the mountaintops. He had been fascinated by the steaming, bubbling sulphur springs and by the new varieties of animals and plants they encountered. He had been part of a great adventure, and the memories of the beautiful country he had seen would be with him always.

He had met Mitchell through Meri Lewis sometime after their return. Seth was at a loose end once the expedition was over, and Mitchell had offered him a job. He was vaguely aware that the papers he would be paid so handsomely to carry must be something special, but he did not dwell on the contents. He welcomed the chance that Mitchell offered to visit Spain, and if he must carry these documents to do so, so be it. There had been no trouble that first time, nor the second, and soon he was travelling almost constantly with Mitchell's packages and papers. It was not until he had taken a letter to a particularly unsavoury section of Paris, and had nearly been stabbed for his efforts, that he asked Mitchell exactly what it was that he had been delivering.

'You are carrying some confidential reports,' Mitchell admitted reluctantly when questioned.

'Matters of security?' Seth wanted to know.

'Yes,' Mitchell spoke slowly, as if weighing the word.

'You are aware that I am only recently a citizen of the United States?' Seth inquired.

'I know a great deal about you, Porterfield. You were thoroughly investigated even though your friend Lewis recommended you for this assignment,' Mitchell finally told him. 'Your English background and manner make it seem unlikely that you could be an American agent.'

'Am I an American agent?' Seth asked, eyeing the other man.

'A courier,' Mitchell corrected.

'Well, it is kind of you to inform me of my true role, at last.' Seth observed dryly. 'Am I to expect more assassins in the future?'

'Probably not, if you continue to act only as a courier. The only reason you were bothered this time was because the house where you delivered those documents was being watched,' Mitchell finally explained.

'And what if I chose to act as more than a courier?' Seth asked, wondering how wise the question was as soon as it left his lips.

'Each assignment would have its own risks,' Mitchell answered, meeting Seth's eyes. He had been impressed by the young man's daring and had suddenly decided to offer him a real challenge.

'We could use some observers in France just now,' he finally said.

'And what am I to observe?' Seth asked, intrigued.

'Many things,' Mitchell had answered. And so it had begun, a series of assignments that had taken him to Egypt, Rome, France, and Spain, to Mexico and to the Spanish territories. There had been times of danger: once he had been captured breaking into an ambassador's house, and had been attacked on several occasions by those who opposed the United States, but he grew to welcome the danger. He became almost intoxicated by the strong sense of excitement that came with living by his wits.

His reverie was broken as Tonawanda Creek appeared suddenly before him, and his thoughts snapped back to the business at hand. Gently, he urged his horse down the slight slope. The stones in the creek bed were slippery and covered with moss, and he guided the animal carefully through the chest-high stream. It was not far to Manchester from here, and he was pleased with his progress. As his mount climbed the opposite bank and moved on to the trail, Seth's thoughts returned to the past.

It had been almost two years earlier that he had met Senator Jim Clayborn's son Billy. Mitchell had arranged that, just as he arranged everything. Seth had been admitted to an exclusive gambling house in Virginia. Once inside, it was easy to spot Billy Clayborn. He was bending over a gaming table, the centre of a crowd who had gathered to watch the young man who lost so graciously. At first Seth was struck by the physical beauty of the young man. His firm, patrician features were perfect in every way, and his body was slender and graceful as he reached forward to settle a tottering tower of chips on the green baize cloth. But when he looked up, his eyes were hard and bitter beyond his years. As Seth watched the boy from across the room, he realized that Billy was drunk, almost to the point of incoherence. Moving towards the table, Seth weighed his pile of chips in the palm of his hand, then placed them on the table next to Billy's.

'Pardon me, sir,' Billy began in a thick, liquid voice, 'This is my game. Perhaps you could select another table,' he suggested.

'I find blondes lucky,' Seth smiled, indicating the girl who dealt the cards.

For a moment the boy eyed him. 'Well, perhaps playing with you can change my luck. It's been abominable all evening. If I win this hand, I will buy you a drink, my friend,' he told Seth.

'Deal on, my lovely,' he said with a slight mocking bow.

For that one hand the cards fell Billy's way, and when the blonde raked up Seth's pile of chips, Billy turned to him and smiled.

'A drink?' he asked.

'If you don't mind. That was my entire fortune,' Seth answered, indicating the mass of chips in front of the dealer.

Billy laughed and went to the long marble bar. 'Your name, my friend?' Billy asked, raising his glass shakily.

'Seth Porterfield,' came the answer.

'To Seth Porterfield, a man capable of changing my luck,' he toasted, downing the glass in one swallow.

'To your luck,' Seth said, sipping his own whisky and watching Clayborn over the rim of his glass. All at once, Billy seemed to grow very pale, and sweat formed on his forehead and above his lip. The boy's eyes rolled up in his head, and he pitched backwards, sprawling on the floor.

When no one moved to help him, Seth pulled the limp youth across his shoulders and carried him outside. Just as he was wondering what to do with Billy, an old black man stepped out of the shadows, shook his head, then wordlessly led Seth towards an expensive new carriage.

'I'd like to see the young man safely home,' Seth told him. 'Just let me get my horse.'

'No need, sir. I put him to bed by myself before,' the man answered.

'I'll come anyway, if you don't mind,' Seth said quietly.

Billy's rooms were luxurious and in one of the best sections of the new capital. He had not regained consciousness on the long ride back to the city, but he had begun to snore loudly. When they arrived, Seth shouldered Billy's slack body and followed the black man up the plush staircase, depositing the boy unceremoniously in the ornate bed.

While the Negro tended the horses, Seth poured himself a drink and made a cursory search of the rooms. Mitchell was sure that Billy was stealing secret papers and selling them to the highest bidder, but Seth found no evidence of such intrigue. The rooms were what they appeared to be, Billy Clayborn's bachelor digs, provided by thoughtful parents for the private entertainment of young women.

In the weeks that followed, Seth brought Billy home many times and he began to feel, if not a friendship, at least a responsibility for the wayward boy. He continued to search the rooms on these occasions, but he began to think that for once Mitchell was wrong. He said as much to Mitchell one afternoon when they met on the lawn of the Capitol.

'If you believe Billy Clayborn innocent, you are a fool,' Mitchell had said disgustedly, 'and you will see how big a fool you are tonight. I have information that the French undersecretary will be at Clayborn's at ten o'clock to exchange fifteen thousand dollars for some papers dealing with our proposed

trade agreement with Britain. You will take the papers instead,'
Mitchell told him.

'How is Clayborn getting these documents?' Seth wondered,
unable to imagine the inept boy involved in such an activity.

'Senator Clayborn is the chairman of several powerful commit-
tees, and as such he has access to many secret papers, some of
which he uses at home. Billy simply takes what he needs.'

'Doesn't the Senator realize what is happening?' Seth asked
incredulously.

'Would he admit it if he did?' Mitchell asked in return. 'If he
or any member of his family was embroiled in a scandal, he
would have difficulty getting reelected. It is as simple as that. So
he overlooks the boy's activities.'

Seth paused to digest what Mitchell had said. It made sense
and fitted in with the impression he had of the spoiled, unhappy
young man.

'Is there liable to be trouble?' he asked.

Mitchell shrugged. 'That depends on how you handle it. Try
to get to Clayborn's before the Frenchman,' he suggested. 'If the
boy becomes a problem, you can eliminate him.'

Seth's eyebrows arched up in surprise. 'You don't mean kill
him?' he asked. He had been in difficult situations before and
had done what he'd had to do, but Mitchell's words took him off
guard. Seth had no desire to hurt Billy.

'Taking the papers from him will only stop him temporarily –'
Mitchell's voice trailed off.

'I can't understand how the boy got involved with this in the
beginning,' Seth went on, anxious to change the subject. 'All he
seems to care about is drinking and gambling and an occasional
night with a woman.'

'And he needs money to enjoy all of those things,' Mitchell
observed.

'Strangely enough, Billy Clayborn doesn't seem to enjoy them.
He seems driven to do them, as if he couldn't help himself. And
he'll keep on doing them until they destroy him.'

Mitchell stared at the other man for a long moment. 'Perhaps
that's what he's seeking, self-destruction,' Mitchell speculated.

Seth had thought of those words many times since then. They
had echoed in his mind as he watched Billy Clayborn draw his
pistol that night two years ago. He had seen the boy's shaking
hands and had felt the ball slam into his own arm before he had

fired the lethal shot that had left Billy sprawling on the thick, blue carpet. As he stood staring down at the dead boy, feeling sick and disgusted with himself, he remembered Mitchell's words. And as he rode along the trail between Black Rock and Manchester, they came to him once more.

Unlike Billy, Seth had no wish for self-destruction, and he knew that he would do what he must in order to survive. Mitchell might trap him for the moment with the events of that night long ago, but in the end he would escape.

Unexpectedly, Gloria Langley's house loomed up before him at the end of the drive. With an effort he began to pull his thoughts from the entangling past to the present. Already the petite, dark woman was in the doorway to greet him, and automatically his lips curved into a smile to answer hers.

❅

Charlotte stood impatiently by the bedroom window, dressed once again in her riding habit. Her valise was neatly packed and sat on the floor by the bedroom door beside the wicker hamper. She was anxious to leave Gloria Langley's sumptuous house and waited impatiently for Seth to come. Last night's party had been a dazzling affair with a buffet and wine after the musical, but she had not enjoyed herself. She had played very well, but her conversation with Gloria, coupled with her own confused thoughts, made her tense and edgy. By the end of the evening the older woman's effusive manner had become almost unbearable, and Charl longed to go upstairs to bed hours before the last guest went home.

Gloria had also contrived to make Stephen Langley Charl's escort, and he had been constantly at her elbow, hanging on every word. His efforts to manoeuvre her into corners where they could be alone were sometimes both comic and infuriating. And by the end of the evening she was tired of the constant battle to keep him at bay.

It was not that there was anything really wrong with Stephen Langley. He was quite handsome in a bullish way, with thick dark hair growing low over his forehead and a heavy, solid body. But Charl did not like the single-minded way he went after what he wanted, in this case her. There was no subtlety in his pursuit. Indeed, she suspected that subtlety was quite beyond his powers of understanding. He did not realize that women liked to be charmed and flattered, and he dogged her every move, demanding that she accept him and acquiesce to his wishes. It was rumoured that in business this tenacity manifested itself in a frightening ruthlessness in dealing with all who opposed him. Charl realized that to some women this drive and determination would prove exciting, but to her it represented Langley's need to always have his own way. She well knew her own stubbornness and was wise enough to realize that such a union would be disastrous. Even more basic to her repeated refusals of his suit were the plans that she had made for her own future. Marriage to Langley would crush those hopes. He would never allow her to continue working at the store, and she knew that she would never love him enough to give up her dreams of freedom and independence.

At any rate she was glad the evening was behind her. She knew her duties as hostess at the party on Saturday night would exempt her from more of Stephen's unwelcome company. As she was reminded of all the things that remained to be done at home, she became even more anxious to begin the journey to Youngstown.

She continued to stare out of the window, to the road where Seth eventually came into sight. Watching him ride up the drive gave her a warm, contented feeling, and she smiled softly as he came closer. He had been on her mind almost constantly since they'd parted, and she was overwhelmingly glad to see him. In the sunlight he looked as if he could have been cast from some precious metal. His skin on his face and arms was warm gold, and his hair seemed only slightly darker. At that moment he was very handsome and desirable to her.

Gloria had already greeted Seth by the time Charl came into the hall, and she was delighted to hear him say that they could not possibly take the time to stay for tea. His voice was cool and distant as he spoke to the other woman, and Charl was relieved that his flirtatious manner was gone. Quietly she waited at the foot of the stairs for him to notice her, anticipating the warmth of his smile. But even when she spoke his name, he did not acknowledge her. Instead he stood staring with opaque eyes, as if he was trying to remember who she was. Charl felt strangely off-balance at his lack of response, and her uncertainty grew when he spoke to her.

'I'm glad to see you're ready,' he said in the same vacant voice he had used with Gloria. 'Is your horse being brought around?'

Stunned by his indifference, Charl could only nod, trying

desperately to contemplate the change in Seth. What had happened in the scant twenty-four hours since he had left her? Why did he look at her like a stranger when only yesterday he had wanted to make love to her? Had he meant the things he'd said on the escarpment, or had he merely been caught up in the passion that had existed between them?

Charl began to watch Seth's face as Gloria chattered on about the party: discussing the guests, what they wore, the food and the music. Although he nodded and smiled at Gloria's words, the actions were mechanical. From the glazed expression in his eyes, Charl guessed he understood little of what the animated Mrs Langley was saying.

As soon as the groom brought Charl's horse from the stable, they said their brief good-byes and set off for Youngstown. Seth immediately lapsed into a brooding silence, and Charl was not even sure that he realized she was following obediently behind him.

Studying him carefully, she realized that there had indeed been a startling change in him overnight. It was more than the weariness caused by a long ride, although that was evident, too. She could see pale violet shadows under his eyes, and there were lines of fatigue around his mouth. Something about the way his broad shoulders hunched as he rode spoke clearly of how tired he was, and she wondered if he had slept at all. But she sensed that it was more than physical exhaustion that made the deep vertical line form between his eyebrows or the skin stretch taut across his cheekbones.

He was clearly a man with something on his mind, something serious and upsetting. Nor could she help but wonder where he'd been. Bit by bit she came to suspect that he was oblivious to his surroundings and found his way totally by instinct, his mind occupied by his own dark thoughts.

As she watched him, a protectiveness grew inside her, and in an instant their roles changed. There was a sudden vulnerability to Seth Porterfield that had not been there before, and though she did not understand the reason for the change in him, she knew she would watch over him until he was himself once more. Moving surely, she took the lead, but if Seth was aware of the change in their positions or in their roles, he gave no sign. And his air of introspection was as deep as before.

Eight
✤✤✤

Although everything was ready, Charl fussed nervously over the centrepiece on the dining room table. People would be arriving for the party soon, and she wanted to make sure of each detail. As she rearranged the flowers on the sideboard, she caught a glimpse of herself in the mirror that hung above it and was pleased to realize that her new gown was very becoming. It was fashioned from filmy, turquoise muslin, draped over an embroidered underskirt of white voile. The scooped neckline plunged so low that it nearly reached the high empire waist and exposed a creamy expanse of her breasts and shoulders. The gown's sheer turquoise sleeves were drawn tight with wide white cuffs that buttoned to the elbow. She liked the colour of the dress, and she paused to wonder if Seth would notice.

He had been polite and distant since the day he had escorted her home from Manchester, and it was only the conviction that he had things on his mind that kept her from wondering what she had done to offend him. His eyes were always opaque now, and there was an inattentiveness that puzzled her. She only wished she understood what had happened to cause this change in him.

She sighed softly and began to realign the rows of silverware Harriet had laid out for the buffet that would be served later in the evening. As she worked, her long, slender, white hands fluttered over the table in a flurry of nervous activity. Charl was unaware that anyone had entered the room until Seth caught her hands in his, stilling their movement. As she looked up at him, standing so tall and straight beside her, she felt strangely fragile. She was a tall woman, used to meeting men eye to eye, but his height overwhelmed her somehow.

Standing close enough so that he could smell that faint lemon scent she wore, he wondered how he could have been so wrapped up in himself these past few days that he had ceased to be aware of her. Her beauty was warm and vital, melting his indifference, and he felt in touch with his surroundings for the first time since his meeting with Mitchell. Never a man given to long periods of introspection, Seth felt as if he was emerging from a cocoon of self-absorption. He was suddenly very glad to be alive and in the company of such a lovely young woman, regardless of what the future held for him.

He looked at her hungrily and with new awareness. Her gown was exquisite, the turquoise shade bringing out the blue flecks in her eyes and matching the delicate, aquamarine pendant that hung at the curve of her breasts. Her heavy golden hair was curled enticingly around her face and then drawn back with braided ribbons to cascade provocatively down her back. Her lips smiled, and her eyes smiled, and for a moment Seth wanted nothing more than to crush her against him and claim that smile with his lips.

'You look lovely tonight,' he said, his voice vibrant and warm.

Feeling shy, all at once, Charl lowered her eyes, a blush of pleasure creeping onto her cheeks. 'Thank you,' she answered.

Just being close to her made his spirits soar dizzily. 'You make me feel so happy,' he said suddenly and then caught himself. What was it about this particular woman that made him say such revealing things about himself? He had talked too freely that first night, and he was ready to open himself to her again. The next thing he knew he would be telling her about Mitchell and his assignment to Quebec. He drew back, troubled and confused by his own actions, but Charl flashed him a smile of such warmth and understanding that his momentary discomfort passed.

She peeked up at him from beneath her thicket of lashes, a dimple creeping into one cheek.

'You will dance with me tonight, won't you, Mr Porterfield?' she asked in a voice that was softly teasing.

'Miss Beckwith, I will be happy to dance with you any time, anywhere,' he answered sliding one hand around her waist to assume the correct dancing posture and lead her through a graceful turn. She smiled into his eyes and tossed her hair, flirting with him openly and welcoming his response. They moved gracefully through the complex figures of a contredanse, the lack of music not lessening their enjoyment at all.

'Charlotte! What are you doing here when your guests are arriving?' an angry voice asked from across the room.

Seth turned to face the dark, heavily muscled man at the door who stood glaring at them, and he felt Charl's back stiffen under his hand just before she stepped away. There was cold fury in the man's face, and Seth felt his own hackles rise in response. Even before Charl's introduction confirmed it, he had guessed that this was the persistent Stephen Langley, and he instantly understood her dislike for the man.

As Charl completed the introductions, each of the men watched the other, sensing that here was a rival for the attentions of this woman. Seth did not like the cruel curve of Langley's mouth, and he took exception to the proprietary air he tried to exercise over Charl. As he took the measure of the other man, Seth realized that even if he was not attracted to her himself, Langley was not someone he would want Charlotte to marry.

Breaking the stare he had fixed malevolently on Seth, Langley turned to Charlotte. 'Your father wants you to come to the door. I was one of the first guests to arrive, but my aunt and uncle and several others were just behind me. You should be in the hall to greet them.'

'Stephen, I don't need anyone to remind me of my duties as hostess,' she began frigidly, but he cut her short.

'I am sure you are the soul of propriety, Charlotte,' he soothed. 'Let me escort you to the hall now, and I will help you welcome your guests.'

Charl's chin came up sharply at his words, and her lips were drawn into a tight line. Stephen was trying to manoeuvre around her again, and it was clear to her what he wanted to do this time. If he greeted guests in her home and acted as host, it would amount to a declaration of her intention to marry him. And that was one bargain she would not seal, by inference or in fact. She would not be manipulated by Stephen Langley tonight, and she would never marry him! Charl fought to control her temper, and then an inspiration came to her. Over Langley's shoulder, she met Seth's eyes.

'Stephen,' she said sweetly, 'I really think it would be more appropriate if I greeted my guests with Mr Porterfield. After all, he is a visitor in my home, and I am sure he will not know many of the people who are coming tonight.'

Langley bristled, and there was a moment when Charl tensed, too, waiting for his reaction, but he controlled himself. He knew she was getting the better of him and thwarting his plan to make it seem as if they would marry soon. What was worse, she had chosen to greet her guests with Porterfield instead. Of course, it was quite proper for Porterfield to be with her at the door, but that did not assuage Langley's anger. His dark eyes glowed ominously, but before he could make a reply, she offered her hand to Seth.

'You will let me make a few introductions, won't you, Mr Porterfield?' she asked coyly.

'I'll be glad to meet your friends, Miss Beckwith. I trust they are not all like Mr Langley,' he said, taking her hand in his and stepping around Langley's menacing form. 'And perhaps later you will allow me the pleasure of another dance,' he went on as they left the room.

Langley glared after them, seething. He was furious with the stubborn chit for disrupting his plans for the evening. He had made up his mind to monopolize Charlotte from the beginning of the evening to the end, not letting anyone else near her. If he could do this often enough, people would begin to consider her his property even though she continued to refuse his offers of marriage, and in time he would win her for himself.

Stephen could not remember a time when he had not sought her favour. Even in childhood Charl had always been the most desirable of companions, accomplished in the things that mattered – swimming, running, and sailing – she had been fearless, climbing the tallest trees, walking through the graveyard after dark. He had always thought she was extremely pretty, too, with her fat yellow pigtails and sunburned cheeks. But even then she would not have him as her best and only friend. So he had been forced to bully her, paying her in pain and cruelty for her rejection.

He had gone away to school and had returned much altered, yet very much the same. Now he understood the importance of Henry Beckwith's position and property, and he realized the advantage of allying himself with Beckwith's only daughter. But the beautiful woman Charl had become drew him as well. He set out to win her and pursued her ruthlessly, driven by a morass of emotions. But until tonight he had never had a rival for Charlotte's attentions.

Fury blazed in him again when he thought of how he had found her when he arrived. She had been in the arms of Seth Porterfield. Didn't she know what kind of a man Porterfield was? Surely she realized he was a British spy. Langley balled his fists. He was not about to let such a man spoil his chances with Charlotte Beckwith! Stephen would admit that he had lost the first skirmish in the battle for her attentions, but he would resort to any means necessary to win this war. His shaggy brows drew together over the bridge of his nose as he considered how he would rid himself of Seth Porterfield's unwelcome presence. There were a number of possibilities. Still deep in thought, he moved towards the clamour of voices in the front hall.

❋

Charl minced painfully around the makeshift dance floor in the parlour, trying with only moderate success to keep her toes from beneath her partner's feet. Still she supposed she should be grateful to John Buchanan, a colleague of her father's, for asking her to dance. It was the first time she had been away from Stephen all evening. He had claimed her in the hallway as soon as the flow of guests had become a trickle and her initial duty as hostess had been discharged, and he had relinquished her hand to the old man now only because there had been no way to refuse him. As they moved through the figures and turns of the quadrille, Buchanan wheezed reminiscences of the women he had danced and partied with in his youth. Only half listening, Charl was thankful that the conversation required little effort on her part, and her mind wandered freely.

Stephen had been impossible all evening. Although she supposed she had asked for this treatment by refusing to greet her guests with him, it infuriated her. He had literally held on to her all evening, scowling away any man who came to ask her to dance and acting in a most possessive way. He had also seemed preoccupied and sullen, and even if she had wanted to be with him, his mood would have put a damper on the evening. She sighed. She supposed she should be grateful to this portly perspiring man for rescuing her, at least for a few minutes.

She was aware of Seth across the room, but even he had not dared Stephen's wrath to dance with her. Well, he had helped her once tonight, and she appreciated him standing beside her to welcome the guests. It had been quite amusing to see the shock on people's faces when she introduced him, and from their open-mouthed curiosity, it was obvious that everyone had heard the rumours about the 'British spy'. As she thought back, there was something that had bothered her, though. Colonel Will

Hubbard and his French wife had arrived towards the end of the crush. They hadn't been stationed at the fort very long and had not socialized much because of Mrs Hubbard's condition, so Charl did not know them well. As she greeted them, she saw the woman's eyes dart to Seth's face with a look of happy recognition, and Charl had sensed a change in his demeanour as well. She had been aware of a spark in the air, and then Colonel Hubbard had asked her a question, and her attention had been drawn elsewhere. That vague impression nagged at her. It was almost as if Mrs Hubbard knew Seth, but that was impossible, wasn't it?

'May I have the rest of this dance with our hostess, Mr Buchanan?' a familiar voice asked. For a moment Charl was newly aware of the British tint to Seth's speech and the way he clipped his words. But then, half the people she knew spoke accented English, thick with a Scottish burr or with the catch of German, giving evidence of their origins. At that moment it did not matter what his politics or loyalties were. What mattered was that she and Seth would finish the dance they had begun earlier and he would hold her in his arms.

The music eddied around them, gently turning them this way and that. Seth danced lightly and well, and his firm hand on her back carried her with him as they moved across the floor. They did not speak but danced smoothly, caught up in the flow of notes, until the tune ended.

'Let's escape before your Mr Langley catches up with us,' Seth whispered conspiratorially, grinning down at her. Catching sight of Stephen's flushed, angry face through the crowd, Charl nodded, and Porterfield pulled her towards the front door.

Once they stepped outside into the warm June night, the voices and music seemed muffled and far away. Even the vision of Stephen's angry face receded when Seth put his arm around her and led her down the drive. It was lined with all manner of vehicles, pulled up under the trees, their diversity revealing much about the make-up of frontier society.

Walking slowly, enjoying the soft breeze and the scent of honeysuckle in the air, they crossed the main road and stood together watching the river move past. It was dark and quiet except for a shimmering path left by the moon on the water and the lapping of the waves at the bank below them.

Seth turned to watch the woman at his shoulder. The moonlight had frosted her yellow hair with silver and shadowed her face to highlight the fine, strong bones beneath her ivory skin. Gently, he brushed his lips against her mouth and heard her indrawn breath. Stretching up, she lengthened the kiss as her arms crept around his neck and he pulled her tight against him. There on the riverbank they clung together, the kisses deepening as their tongues played gently, their bodies pressing closer in a perfect unity with each other, and with the soft, sweet-scented darkness of the night.

'Oh, woman,' Seth whispered as he trailed burning kisses along her throat, 'how you stir me. I'm sorry there's been no time for pretty speeches and chaste kisses, and I know I've hardly courted your favour. But, Charl, I want to make love to you, and I believe that's what you want, too.

'Tonight, after everyone's asleep, I'm going to come to your room. And unless you bar the door against me, Charl, I'm going to answer all the questions you've asked me and teach you all I know about passion.'

His husky words left her breathless and giddy so that she had no strength to resist him when he drew her close and kissed her lingeringly.

'I'm coming to your room tonight, Charlotte,' he repeated. 'Do you understand?'

She paused and nodded. 'Yes, Seth, I understand.'

It was impossible to read her expression in the moonlight, and he was suddenly uncertain of her. For one last time he bent his head to claim her lips. And it was only when he felt desire flame between them that he was satisfied.

As always, the power of his kisses had robbed Charl of her will, and she felt bereft and incomplete when he raised his mouth from hers. They stood without moving for one long moment and then finally stepped apart.

'We must go back to the house now, Charl,' Porterfield reminded her. 'They're probably all wondering where we are.'

Reluctantly Charl agreed.

They walked up the drive hand in hand, and as they approached the house, the sounds of voices and laughter swept out to greet them. It was almost time to set out the buffet, Charl was thinking, when a movement to her right drew her attention. Suddenly, Stephen Langley sprang from the shadows brandishing a knife. Instinctively, she stepped between him and Seth.

'Get out of my way, Charlotte,' Langley hissed. 'I'm going to kill that bastard.' Stephen's eyes were slitted, his bulky shoulders hunched forward in the age-old posture of attack.

'You'll do no such thing!' she told him fiercely. 'Put that knife away.'

'Let him come, Charl,' she heard Porterfield say. 'I'm not a man who dies easily.'

She watched Stephen's eyes track Seth and felt the blond man tensed and manoeuvring behind her.

'You dog,' Langley shouted as he lunged. 'I'll see you in hell for this.'

Charlotte stepped between them once more, sure that Langley would not harm her. 'Stop it, Stephen!' she begged, but Seth's cold voice cut in.

'You needn't protect me from him, Charl,' he said, but she stood her ground, terrifyingly aware that Seth was unarmed.

'And you,' Langley went on, 'why were you taken in by him? Everyone knows he is an English spy.'

Charl felt as if she had been waiting all evening for those words to be spoken. It was as if they were all playing roles, reciting predetermined lines, waiting for their audience to arrive. Behind Stephen Charl could see people spilling out the door of the house, drawn by the loud voices. Their faces were curious and excited as they came down the driveway towards them, an audience to make the drama complete. The feeling of unreality was strong in her, as if she were caught in a living nightmare.

'I saw what you let him do to you,' Stephen continued, jealousy fanning his anger. 'You enjoyed it, too.'

'Stephen, please!' Charl implored, aware that the guests were almost within earshot of his harshly whispered words.

'You allowed me a few chaste kisses, but with him you played the whore!'

'Shut up, Langley,' Seth muttered hotly. 'Leave Charlotte out of this. If you have an argument with me, then let's meet and settle it, but leave the girl alone.'

'Are you challenging me to a duel, Porterfield?' Stephen asked, straightening a bit and letting the knife slip off his fingers and into the shadows. It was plain that this was what he had wanted.

'Yes,' Seth answered evenly. His face was cold and unreadable when Charl turned to try to dissuade him. 'An affair of honour is not what you deserve, Langley, but I'll be glad to meet you, at whatever time and place you choose.'

'What's going on here?' Henry Beckwith demanded when he reached the three people who were silhouetted so revealingly in the moonlight.

'Your houseguest has challenged me to a duel, Henry,' Langley answered. At his words a rustle of excitement passed through the crowd that was assembling beneath the trees.

'Oh, Father! You must stop them. This is all a terrible misunderstanding!' Charl cried, her voice taut with anxiety.

One look at his daughter made the words he was about to say catch in Henry's throat. Her eyes were wide and shiny with fear, and she was curiously dishevelled. What had been going on out here? What had Porterfield done to her? Had Langley been forced to defend her honour? Her concern was evident. Was Charlotte afraid Langley would be hurt in a duel? Was it possible she cared more for Stephen than she would admit? All these thoughts flashed through Henry's mind before he answered her. 'Charlotte, there's nothing I can do. If they have agreed to meet, it is settled.'

'Is it settled, Langley?' Seth's cold voice inquired.

'Yes,' Stephen answered.

With an incoherent cry Charl ran towards the house, one hand clapped tightly against her mouth to stop the sounds of horror that rose in her throat.

The men glared at each other, barely noticing her departure. 'Pistols at dawn?' Langley suggested.

'Fine,' came the answer.

'My second will call on yours later tonight,' Langley said.

For a moment Seth was struck by his isolation here. His eyes sought Will Hubbard at the edge of the crowd. Will shot him a long look and then turned away. No, Seth thought bitterly, Will could not acknowledge their friendship.

'Beckwith,' he began, 'I know how you feel about me, but will you stand by me tomorrow?'

There was a long pause before the answer came. 'Very well.'

※

Charl stopped pacing the length of her bedroom to look out of the window towards the river. Could it have been only hours before that she had stood on the bank with Seth, watching the moonlight on the water? Was it less than a lifetime ago that he had told her he would come to her? Even now she was not sure what she really wanted. Somehow her affairs of the heart paled in comparison to her turmoil over the duel Stephen and Seth would fight at dawn.

She shivered and hugged the satin wrapper more tightly around her body, but it was not the cold that made her tremble. In a few hours two men would face each other under the willows at Five Mile Meadows with pistols in hand because of her, because of her! And one of them would likely die. She turned away from the window to resume her pacing. There should have been something she could do to stop the duel, but suddenly the situation had been past fixing. It had become a matter of honour.

She did not understand men and their honour. As a woman she knew the most basic truth: that only life mattered. Maybe it was because a woman laboured to bring new life from her body that she instinctively understood how precious a man's brief span of years could be. Life was not a gift to be squandered on the field of honour. And with all her heart Charl believed it was more important to survive than to die for some vague principle. No one, not Seth, not Stephen or her father, had understood that, and her pleas to stop the duel had been ignored.

She did not dare to examine her feelings beyond the intense desire to see the duel stopped. She only feared. She feared for Stephen, although she knew she did not care for him, and she feared for Seth. Beyond that her emotions were undefinable. She knew she could not stand to have either man die.

She had been too deep in thought to hear the door open and close softly, and it startled her to see Seth standing near it, watching her. She ran to him, and his arms closed around her.

As he held her, he realized that she had come to him more for comfort than from desire, and he pulled her close, resting her head against his broad chest. She was trembling, and he willed the heat of his body to warm and soothe her, and they stood quietly embracing for a long time.

Slowly, he felt her muscles relax, and the trembling stopped. How like a child she was at that moment, trusting and defenceless, and he wondered if he would be taking advantage of her need for comfort if he made love to her. But he wanted her, and although he was not afraid to face Langley, it was possible that this might be his last chance to make her his.

Gently he drew her head up, away from where it rested against his chest, so he could kiss her. His mouth came down on hers softly, savouring her sweetness. He felt her melt against him as he lingered over her lips, and he seemed to be drowning in sensations himself. She was so soft to his touch and so accessible, dressed only in her flimsy night clothes. His hands moved to her waist, where the sash to her wrapper slid through his fingers to the floor and the wrapper followed it. Trying to calm his ragged breathing, he began to undo the long line of pearl buttons that fastened the front of the lawn nightdress.

His face was grave in concentration as he worked on the tiny buttons, and Charl smiled to herself. She had left the door unlocked because she needed to see him before tomorrow at dawn, and in doing so the decisions about so many things were made for her.

His warm fingers brushed against her breast as he worked on the buttons, and she shivered with anticipation. She knew she was being swept along by the sensations that enveloped her, but she did not care. Although the delicious sensations Seth evoked were new and unique to her, she knew that in their way they were as old as time. And for a moment she was caught up in the image of women through the ages baring themselves to their men, turning their faces up to be kissed just as she had offered hers to Seth tonight. At that moment Charl felt a need to abandon herself to Seth, to risk the things that women have always risked: their bodies, their respectability, and their hearts, to learn the secrets of life from men. She suddenly wanted to become a part of the unending chain of girls made women by their men, moving towards life and away from their own mortality.

When Seth finally slipped the nightdress from her shoulders, Charl's doubts and fears were gone. Nothing mattered, as she stood shyly before him, but this moment between them. Murmuring a jumble of endearments, he swept her up in his arms and carried her to the bed. Then he lay down beside her, covering and shielding her body with his own. For a very long time he kissed her, demanding nothing but her acquiescence. His mouth was tender against hers, nibbling gently at her parted lips, letting his tongue tease hers until he felt her willing response. Only then did his lips move on to her cheeks and temples, her throat and ears. She shivered beneath him, but not with cold.

Guiding her hands, he made her unbutton his fine linen shirt and slide it down his arms. Shyly but curiously, she began to run her palms over the warm skin of his chest, feeling the soft, prickly, gold hairs brush against her fingers.

'Your hands are cold!' he complained softly, but held them in place when she tried to pull away.

She explored him slowly, the hollows above his collarbones, his strong, sinewy arms, the rock-hard muscles of his chest and back that flexed and slid when he moved. She memorized the texture of his skin, the breadth of his shoulders, and as she touched his body, he touched hers, too. He stroked the satiny skin along her back and thighs and cupped one perfect breast in his palm as he brought the nipple erect. When he heard Charl's indrawn breath, he lowered his head and circled the hardening nipple with his tongue. His mouth moved over her: warm, nibbling, burning, tickling all at once, and Charl went limp and liquid with sensation.

She found his nipples, hidden in the mat of fair hair on his chest, and touched them experimentally.

'My God, woman,' he whispered hoarsely and forced her hands lower until his trousers had joined the shirt on the floor at the side of the bed.

She had never seen a naked man before and averted her eyes, but he made her look at him. There was a rugged beauty and a leashed power to the flat planes of his body, and a menacing promise in his erect manhood that both terrified and intrigued her. She looked down at her own softly rounded body lying along the length of his.

'There's a big difference, isn't there?' he teased her. 'The biggest difference is here,' he said and touched the joining of her legs. She gasped, but his insistent hand moved gently against the triangle of pale hair.

'You mustn't!' she whispered, her eyes wide.

'Oh yes, oh yes, I must,' he insisted, and as if by his will, her legs opened under his hand. His fingers slid deeper, touching, probing, stroking, making waves of warmth rush through her body. Seth seemed to know the things she craved even before she knew them herself. His fiery touch awakened desires within her that she had never dreamed were there. She was nearly mindless with the exquisite need his caresses aroused.

'What are you doing to me?' she whispered against his ear.

'I'm making love to you, woman, as I've wanted to since the

moment I set eyes on you.' His voice was rough with passion and deep with a sincerity he could not hide.

'Oh, Seth,' she breathed, kissing him deeply as she clung to him, anxious to share the wonder he had helped her discover.

'Touch me,' he demanded. And though she shook her head in silent negation, she was powerless to deny him. Her fingers skimmed across his ribs and belly until she held his manhood in one trembling hand. With firm, sure strokes he taught her how to please him, rewarding her efforts with a shuddering sigh of pleasure. As she did as she was taught, he began to kiss her breasts as his fingers touched deep inside her, making her ache. He was not so gentle now, but it did not matter as she moved instinctively against him, seeking something she did not understand.

'Oh please, please!' she moaned, confused by her own need.

'Yes, Charlotte. Oh God, yes,' Seth mumbled brokenly, turning her on her back and kneeling between her legs. She felt his manhood probe the joining of her thighs, gently at first as Seth fought to hold his own passion in check, and then harder, pressing deep into her soft body. He muffled her moan of pain against his lips and held her still with his weight until her struggles ceased. When she was quiet, he began to move slowly, rocking against her until the memory of that first swift pain began to recede. In its place came a need to arch against him, to take up the rhythm of his movements. She was swept along, twisting, taking him deeper into herself, until a flare of heat moved through her, searing her skin and scalding her veins. It carried her up in a flare of sensation that enveloped her. But even as the fire raged through her, Charl knew that she was not alone in her passion for Seth was clinging fiercely as he throbbed deep within her. The blaze of satisfaction became a gradually diminishing glow that died to embers, leaving them both spent and consumed. But even as she lay lost in wonder, a new understanding rose from the ashes of their passion that promised a new beginning.

Seth lay heavily, yet comfortably over her, and as she stirred, Charl kissed the shoulder that was pressed conveniently against her chin. He stretched, smiled, and lay beside her, watching the golden-haired woman contentedly.

Her eyes were dreamy and soft in the glow from the candle, and he could not keep himself from touching her. She is so beautiful, he thought. Her body was long and strong, but deliciously rounded, with full, perfect breasts and a slender waist. Her skin was pale ivory and the texture of rose petals.

'Do you have any questions now?' he asked, his voice softly teasing as he remembered the day on the escarpment. She paused, drew a long breath, and her chin came up.

'Why did you hurt me?' she asked earnestly, a flush beginning to spread along her cheekbones.

'I didn't mean to hurt you,' he replied, 'but it always hurts the first time a woman makes love. There was a virgin's membrane inside you that I broke when I entered you. That was where the pain came from. It felt better afterwards, though, didn't it?'

The flush was spreading now and she would not look at him, so he pulled her against him, cuddling her until the embarrassment passed.

'Is it always like that at the end?' she asked in a small voice, and he smothered a grin as he answered.

'For men it usually is,' he said in his most instructive voice. 'Sometimes it is like that for a woman and sometimes it is not. What you experienced is called an orgasm.'

'Oh,' she said and retreated into silence, pondering this new knowledge. But before long his hands were moving over her again, tracing designs on her naked flesh, stroking, caressing until the new, familiar feeling began to build in her and she turned to touch him, too. He was both gentle with her and more daring, making her writhe under his hands. She was still shy, but her hands and mouth seemed to instinctively know the places that pleased him. When he entered her, she clung to him until they reached the shattering heights together.

The candle had long since gutted out when she felt him leave the bed.

'Seth!' she called out in the dark, and his hand gently silenced her. 'It's not dawn yet,' she whispered, suddenly terrified.

'I have things to prepare,' he told her.

'Please don't go! Please don't meet Stephen,' she pleaded, her voice shaking.

'Charlotte, you know I must meet him. It's a matter of honour.' Gentleness and exasperation were mingled in his reply.

'Stephen has no honour. He showed that last night when he came after you with the knife. Stephen sees only what he wants, and it doesn't matter what he must do to achieve it.'

'Our seconds will see that everything is fair,' he brushed away her concern.

'And who of those men is your friend? They don't care if you die!' she argued.

'Will you accuse your father of dishonour?' His voice was cold, and she sat silently as he finished dressing. Her father was an honourable man, yes, but she knew him to be ruthless, too.

The dim figure came to sit on the edge of the bed and pulled her close.

'How do you feel?' she asked.

'Fine,' he answered, his voice puzzled.

'I mean about the duel,' she asked again. She felt him shrug.

'I don't know: frightened, excited, confident, perhaps a little angry,' he told her, his lips in her hair. 'Don't worry.'

She hugged him. 'Be careful,' she whispered as his mouth closed over hers.

'I will,' he said. There was a smile in his voice as he moved towards the door. 'I have to go. If your father catches me coming out of here at this hour, he'll be the next to call me out.'

As soon as Seth was gone, Charl jumped out of bed. She knew what she must do. Quickly she pulled on her riding clothes and tiptoed out into the hall. Lights showed under her father's door and under Seth's, telling her that they were doing whatever men did to prepare to meet on the field of honour. Without a sound she made her way down the stairs and out to the stable.

Nine
✳✳✳

Charl rode directly to Five Mile Meadows in the filmy pre-dawn light. Although duelling was against the law, if men still chose to meet to settle their differences in the traditional place at the willows by the stream, the law seldom interfered. The actual settlement at Five Mile Meadows was further up the road, a scattering of houses that had no importance of its own except that men killed each other nearby. There was fog creeping along the stream bed, and the duelling willows were woven with feathery patches of mist. The air was cold and damp, and Charl could feel it in her lungs when she breathed.

She did not want to be here on this chilly June morning, before dawn. She had come only because she could not stay away. Soon two men would meet here to kill or maim each other because of her, and for jealousy and misplaced honour. And she knew she must see it. It would have been impossible for her to stay at home waiting to hear the outcome of this duel. Yet she wished she was anywhere but here.

It was getting brighter, and the colours in the landscape were becoming noticeable in the grey light. She knew she must hide quickly before anyone arrived, for if her presence was discovered, she would be sent home and the duel would go on anyway.

Half a mile farther downstream was a small, semicircular grove of apple trees, thickly hung with wild grape vines and brambles. In the midst of the thicket she tied her horse and walked back towards the willows. There was an overgrown gully that ran roughly parallel to the stream where she could hide. Looking through a curtain of grasses and wild flowers, she could see the willow grove perfectly. The men would be like actors on a stage to her, their concealed audience. She would even be able to hear their voices.

The early morning dew had quickly penetrated her clothes,

and she shivered as she waited. It was not long before the first carriage drew up under the trees. Stephen Langley and his second, a young man Charl knew slightly, Roger Hamlin, alighted, followed by a third man she recognized as a doctor from Fort Schlosser. Her stomach clenched at the implication. It was traditional to have a doctor present, as it was traditional for men to meet under these willows. As her father's carriage drew up, she realized that even the use of that vehicle was dictated by custom. A man brought a carriage to a duel in case his body had to be taken home afterwards. The images that flew at her made her bite down on her lips in horror, but with the arrival of the duellists she could not leave her hiding place undetected, even if she wanted to.

Charl felt a warm stab of pain under her ribs as she watched Seth step down from the carriage. She had shared his body and his kisses such a short time ago. His face was grave in the dawn, and a vertical line was etched deeply between his brows as he spoke quietly to her father.

She could see the glow of gold stretching along the horizon to the east, and the shiny black carriages began to reflect the pinkish cast of the sky. Both Seth and Stephen were silently removing the long cloaks and handing them to their seconds. Their coats, waistcoats, and cravats followed, until both men stood identically attired in white shirts and dark breeches. Hamlin walked towards Seth carrying the carved mahogany box that Charl knew held Stephen's father's matched set of duelling pistols. Breathlessly, she watched Seth select one and check it thoroughly. As he did so, another man rode up quietly behind her father's carriage. At first Charl was too engrossed in watching both men prepare their pistols to notice who he was. Then with a start of recognition, she realized it was Constable Greene.

For a long moment she wondered why he was here, then it suddenly became frighteningly clear. He had come to arrest Seth Porterfield for murder! Constable Greene's presence made Seth's position untenable; either Stephen would shoot him, or he would hang for killing Langley. There was no way out. It was a brilliant, simple plan to benefit those who wanted to be rid of a man they suspected of being a British spy, and she wondered who had devised it. Had it been Stephen or perhaps her own father? She did not want to believe that her father would condone this treachery, but he obviously did. And she knew there was no way to warn Seth of those plotting against him. Even if she showed herself now, they would not let her talk to him.

Terrified, she watched the two men move towards the centre of the grove where the doctor would start the count. Seth's profile was outlined clearly against the rising sun as he stood with his back to the bulkier man. The doctor spoke to the duellists quietly, and then the count began as the two men strode away from each other.

'One . . . Two . . . Three . . . Four . . . Five . . . Six . . . Seven,' the voice cut loudly through the golden dawn.

'Eight.' And as Charl watched, she saw Stephen begin to turn, his body growing into a wider silhouette against the bright sky. With deadly precision his arm came down to aim.

She leaped to her feet.

'Nine.'

'Stephen! No!' she screamed as he fired.

Simultaneously there was a blast of flame and the sound of explosion. A cloud of dust rose at Seth's feet where the ball had hit.

Instantly Seth realized what Langley had done, and he turned completely to face the man, his eyes wild with fury. Slowly he lowered the pistol to sight on Langley. Stephen stood his ground, but his face was deathly pale. Now Porterfield would kill him. The moment hung suspended endlessly in the silent dawn. Then Seth turned the pistol towards the rising sun and fired.

With a cry Charl crumpled to her knees, both hands pressed against her mouth.

'You don't deserve to live, Langley, but I won't have your blood on my hands,' Seth shouted in a voice as cold as the death that Langley had feared. 'You leave Charlotte Beckwith alone. I don't want her name on your lips ever again, or I will come back and finish this with you.' He turned, throwing the pistol into the brush and moving quickly towards the place where Charlotte had been hidden. But she had already staggered off towards her horse, sobbing inconsolably.

❊

Charl arrived home cold and shaking, far ahead of the men. She had galloped all the way from Five Mile Meadows, blindly jumping fences and streams, trying to escape the thing she had witnessed. Harriet met her at the kitchen door and ushered the trembling girl upstairs, clucking disapprovingly. It was evident

that the grey-haired woman knew where Charl had been, but she
kept her questions and comments to herself. Once in the bedroom
Harriet rang for a bath and began to strip off her mistress's wet
clothes and brush out her tangled hair.

Charl was immersed in the hot, soothing water when her father
knocked at the door to inquire if she would accompany him to
church. Fury and disillusionment flared in her at the thought of
the travesty of honour he had been party to this morning at dawn,
and she knew she could face neither his hypocritical denials nor
his admission of compliance. She realized she must confront him
eventually, but she hoped she could wait until she'd gained
control of her frayed emotions. Still she could not understand
how he could condone such an illicit act and then go off to piously
worship God.

Thankfully, Harriet had gone to the door and muttered something to Henry about not 'giving people another chance to gawk
at the girl'. He left, alone.

Charl sipped at the mug of a strong, steamy concoction that
Harriet had given her. For the first time in her life her father had
done something she could not accept. He had shown injustice
and malice in his dealings with others, and it troubled her deeply,
adding to the turmoil within her.

As Harriet brushed the heavy wet hair, she insisted Charl drink
another mugful of the toddy – this one laced even more liberally
with whisky than the first had been. The last thing Charl remembered was sinking down on to the big bed as the room spun
dizzily around her.

She slept all afternoon under the effects of Harriet's toddies.
Towards evening she opened her eyes to find Seth sitting on the
side of the bed, smiling at her. She smiled drowsily in return.

'Are you awake?' he asked, grinning at her struggles to keep
her eyes from closing.

'I think so. What time is it?' She squinted up at him. Why did
he seem so fuzzy and out of focus?

'About six,' he answered.

'Six?' she puzzled. 'You're too early –'

He laughed. 'Quiet, woman. I had the devil's own time getting
in here to see you. If that harpie had any idea I was in here last
night –' his voice trailed off.

Last night, she remembered and smiled contentedly. He remembered too and felt a tightening in his loins.

'I came to thank you,' he continued gravely. 'You probably saved my life this morning. If you had not called out when you did, Langley would have had me.'

'And if you had shot him, you would have been dead in time anyway,' she said sleepily.

'Charlotte, what are you talking about?' He frowned, wondering if she knew what she was saying.

Why couldn't she keep her thoughts straight? Charl closed her eyes to improve her concentration and felt herself drifting away instead. She opened her eyes.

'The constable, Constable Greene, was there. A death by duelling is considered murder under the law. If you had killed Stephen, he would have taken you in,' she told him bluntly. He caught his breath.

'Charl, are you sure?' He gently grasped her arms and bent closer.

'M – m – hum,' she answered and began to drift away again. 'Why am I so sleepy?'

'The toddies Harriet gave you.'

'Am I drunk?' she wanted to know.

He chuckled. 'Sleeping it off, I'd say.'

She blinked. 'You're all dressed up,' she observed. 'Where are you going?'

'Colonel Hubbard is having some men to dinner at the fort to discuss what will happen if war is declared,' Seth told her.

'I remember now,' she nodded. The war, in the turmoil of the last twenty-four hours, she had almost forgotten.

'Thank you,' Seth whispered again, his face just inches from hers. 'Go back to sleep now.'

'Will you come tonight?' she whispered back, and then was shocked by her own forwardness. Whatever was the matter with her?

His smile was like sunshine. 'If you're good,' he answered. 'Now close your eyes.' She obeyed him and he gently brushed her lids with his lips. She felt as if her eyes were sealed shut with his kisses, and almost immediately her breathing deepened. She was asleep again before he was out of the door.

❉

Cigar smoke filled the long, stone wardroom in the main building at Fort Niagara. Men had gathered there from all along the Niagara frontier to hear plans for defence of the region, if war was declared. Seth Porterfield sat towards the rear of the room, thoughtfully swirling his brandy and listening abstractedly to the plan Colonel Will Hubbard was explaining to the group. He knew this plan front to back, as he did various alternate and contingency plans. How stunned these men would be to know he had helped Will Hubbard devise most of them.

He smiled bitterly to himself. He had been very successful in convincing everyone he was a British spy; Mitchell would be pleased. There had been surprise and consternation in the air when he entered the wardroom, but no one had tried to bar his way. Still, the hot hatred in the men's eyes told him how well he had played the role. He had played it so well that it had already almost cost him his life, or at least his freedom. If it had not been for Charl, he would either be dead or in jail now. And it was through her that he had learned how dangerous his position here really was. He would have to leave soon, he realized, but he wanted just a few more days with her.

He smiled down into the amber liquid, remembering the passion they had shared. He had never known a woman to give so freely, touching and caressing, returning pleasure for pleasure. There was a natural sensuality about Charlotte that made him wish the meeting was over so he could go to her again. Silently he toasted her: to her beauty, her passion, her bravery, and her intelligence. At the same time he knew, as much as he liked and desired her, it would end here. Mitchell had seen to that. In a day or two he would be gone, and she couldn't even know where or why.

Grimly he turned his attention back to what Colonel Hubbard was saying, and he tried to focus on the map he and Will had marked to show areas to be developed as batteries when the war came.

Suddenly a young sentry burst into the room. For a minute he looked startled by the size of the group, but he recovered himself and went directly to the colonel. The soldier whispered something to Hubbard, and he nodded, looking grave.

Will turned to the group of men. 'If you gentlemen will excuse me for a few minutes, I have a messenger in my office I must see at once. I will return as soon as possible, and we can resume our discussion,' Hubbard said formally, and he followed the private out of the door.

Instantly the wardroom was alive with noisy speculation. The

men's faces were flushed with excitement. Even those who
opposed the war seemed animated and caught up in the anticipation. Seth sat tensed and silent, smoking his cigar, all too sure
about the news the messenger had brought.

Will was back quickly and held up his hands for quiet. 'I've
had some news that will affect us all,' he began. Across the room
his eyes met Seth's, and he nodded imperceptibly. This was it.
'On June 18, the Congress of the United States declared war on
Great Britain.'

A clamour of voices rose in the room. 'This is the twenty-
seventh. Why didn't we get word before now?' someone shouted.

'I am not sure about the delay. Even now the information is
unofficial. The messenger was from Black Rock. It seems that
today some men from Fort Erie captured a small vessel on the
lake, and that is how the American forces found out about the
declaration,' Will told them, frowning deeply.

There was a swell of angry voices that filled the room, and
several men were on their feet asking questions. Seth took
advantage of the confusion to slip outside. He must get across
the border, now, tonight. With that one thought in his head he
raced towards his horse.

The Beckwith house was quiet, and he reached his room
undetected. He would have time to throw a few things into his
saddlebags, but that was all. He was convinced that if he was
caught, it would be his life, and neither Will Hubbard nor Mitchell
would be able to intervene.

As he crossed the hall, he noticed Charl's closed door. For a
moment he hesitated. He wanted time to say good-bye to her,
time to hold her in his arms once more, but he knew it was time
he dared not take. He would have to wake her, tell her about
the declaration of war. She would have questions. Then she
would want to know why he was leaving. And what could he say
to her? No, it would be better just to go and let her draw her
own conclusions. He turned away from the door. He knew he
was right to leave without seeing her, but it was with great
reluctance that he went down the stairs.

※

Charl woke with a start, clear headed and totally aware of her
surroundings. The room was completely dark, but she could see
the sky to the north glowing red and orange, and she knew
immediately that something was wrong.

She sprang from the bed, looking frantically for her clothes. It must be someone's barn burning, she thought as she dressed, but she could not recall hearing the fire bell ring.

She flew down the stairs two at a time and ran towards the stable.

'Miss Charlotte, where are you going, dear?' Harriet called after her as she sped through the kitchen.

'There's a fire! The sky towards town is all lit up. You can see it from upstairs,' she answered as she went out of the door.

'There's no fire, Miss Charlotte!' the woman shouted after her. 'It's the war.'

Charl skidded to a stop halfway across the yard. 'What did you say?' she demanded, thunderstruck.

'It's the war. They've built up a big bonfire on Main Street to celebrate,' Harriet told her.

Charl came closer and gripped the woman's shoulders. 'You're sure? They declared war on Britain? How do you know?'

'Tim came and told us. He came to get Mr Beckwith's horse. He's out in the barn; you ask him.'

Flying across the yard Charl intercepted her father's driver at the stable door, catching the reins of her father's roan in her hand. 'Tim, is this true? Has war been declared?'

'Yes, miss, they got word tonight at their meeting at the fort. The messenger came riding in while they were there. They're meeting in Lewiston tonight, your father, Mr Barton, and the other men. Your daddy sent me back to exchange the carriage for his horse,' Tim told her as she stared at him in disbelief.

'Miss, Mr Beckwith needs his horse right away,' he prompted her.

'Of course, Tim. Thank you for the news,' she said, dropping the reins and stepping back to let him pass.

So it had come. Henry Clay and his war hawks had finally forced the country into war. From where she stood she could see what was now enemy territory across the river. Would there be fighting along the Niagara? Could the cannons from Fort George reach her home? Would people she knew die in battle?

She moved dazedly towards her horse's stall with the idea of saddling him to go into town. A sound from the doorway made her look up. It was Seth, still dressed in the black tailcoat and fawn breeches he had worn to dinner at the fort. Perhaps he could tell her more about what had happened. She was about to step out of the stall to question him when she saw him take a pistol out of his saddlebags and tuck it into the waistband of his trousers, closing his coat over it.

The implications of what he was doing hit her like a blow. He was leaving. War had been declared on Britain, and he was sneaking away into the night. There could only be one reason for his actions, but her mind rejected it.

Breathlessly, she watched him move across the stable to where his horse stood saddled and ready for his escape. His face was in shadows, but there was an air of tension to his movements.

Charl stepped out of the stall, towards him. 'Where are you going, Seth?' she asked, fearing the answer.

He spun towards her in an explosion of movement, pulling and levelling the pistol at her as he did. For a moment he stood hunched and tense, eyes alive and searching her face and the darkness behind her. Warily, he tucked the pistol back into his waistband and relaxed.

'Charlotte,' he said solemnly, 'you could have been the first casualty of the war.'

'I'm sorry,' she mumbled, but her mind grasped only that he was leaving. As she stood there, she knew that regardless of what his answer was, she had to ask him one question. Her chin came up sharply, and she caught his arm. 'Seth,' she whispered, looking up into his face, 'are you going away because my country has declared war on yours?'

He looked down at her. There was confusion and hope and despair on her face and in the blue-green depths of her eyes. For a heartbeat he stood trying to memorize her sweet face: the softness of her mouth, the roundness of her cheeks, and the clear sea green eyes that held hope and promises of a future he had only to stay with her to claim. He realized suddenly that she was the sort of woman a man could build a life with, and he ached to take her in his arms. He wanted to tell her the truth about himself, explain where he was going and why. But he could not. He had to forget what had happened between them and leave her thinking he was a traitor.

Without a flicker of emotion he said the words that would make her his enemy. 'I must get across the border before it closes. If I'm found here, they'll have every right to hang me.'

She flinched away from him. The terrible suspicions and accusations were now indisputable fact. 'You are a spy!' she breathed, backing away from him. 'A traitor! They all said so and I didn't believe them, Stephen and my father.' She laughed bitterly. 'I told them they were wrong; I defended you. Oh, I was such a fool!'

She turned from him with tears in her eyes that she would not let him see and rested her forehead against the rough wooden door at the end of one of the stalls. Suddenly, in front of her eyes a pitchfork came into focus, standing against the bars. Instinctively one hand snaked out to grasp it, and she turned back to face him with her weapon held high.

'I'm afraid, Mr Porterfield, that instead of leaving, you are going to be unavoidably detained,' Charl told him, her voice and eyes gone cold. 'Throw down the gun!' she ordered, and he moved slowly to withdraw it from his waistband and drop it to the floor.

He had betrayed her country and her, she thought. It was clear that the night they had spent together meant nothing to him. Everything he'd said had been lies, right from the beginning. He had deceived them, made them think he was something he was not. And she had been the biggest fool of all. He had found her weaknesses so easily, and he had exploited them ruthlessly to get what he wanted. Anger and hurt were so mixed up inside her that she understood only that she must hold him here until someone came, until she could turn him over to the authorities.

Seth watched her, knowing full well how dangerous Charl was at this minute. He did not underestimate either her determination or her anger. She was beyond reason, and he doubted that he could appeal to her emotions. Still it seemed incredible that a woman who had given herself to him freely less than twenty-four hours ago, and then saved his life, might be in a position to kill him now.

She held the pitchfork tightly in both hands, pointed directly at his chest. The tines shone dully in the dim light, like deadly fingers reaching out to tear at him. He eyed it warily.

He was intensely aware of the minutes slipping by, and he knew he had to get away. If they found him here, he would have no chance. And with what he had just told Charl, they would have the evidence to prove their suspicions. He did not want to hang.

Moving swiftly, Seth reached out to grab the pitchfork from her, hoping to surprise and overpower her. But Charl had sensed what he would do and moved too quickly for him. Stepping back, she raised the fork, catching the fleshy part of his forearm with one of the sharp prongs, tearing his flesh through the protection of his shirt and coat. They both stepped back startled: Charl at the unsuspected violence in her own nature and Seth at the searing pain that raced up in his arm.

Her eyes were defiant, and their message was plain; she would hold her ground. As Seth manoeuvred around her, he found himself studying her with new respect. She was a worthy adversary, he found himself thinking, as he noted her height and the breadth of her shoulders. He remembered the strong, sinuous body moving against his own, and he knew she would not be easily overpowered. She left him no choice.

Smoothly, he feinted to the left, and as she turned to counter his move, his right fist came up to hit her. She went down heavily, the pitchfork clattering between them. He kicked it away and bent to examine her. Her eyelids were closed, and he touched them and then the edge of her jaw where the blow had landed. Convinced that she would be all right, he became aware of the blood dripping off his hand and onto the floor. Tearing back the coat and shirtsleeve, he exposed a jagged cut, running nearly the length of his forearm. Using his neckcloth he bandaged it, swearing under his breath. The wound burned like fire, but he knew it was not serious. What he needed now was to get away.

He began to search the stable floor for the saddlebags and the gun he had tossed aside and was startled when Charl began to moan. She was regaining consciousness and could surely set up enough of a din to make his escape difficult, if not impossible. Pulling a knife from his boot, he cut a length of leather from some tack and knelt beside Charl to bind her hands.

Her eyelids were fluttering as if she were trying to make some sense out of what was happening. As he crossed her line of vision, Seth noted her sharp intake of breath, and she began to struggle against him.

'Damn it, Charl, hold still!' he ordered angrily, but the girl continued to pull her hands away from him. His mouth drew into a thin, furious line as he roughly caught her wrists and pulled the leather tight around them. Even semiconscious she struggled against him. What was he going to do with her, he wondered.

Before he had time to decide, Charl began to scream, a long, high-pitched sound, more than slightly tinged with panic.

Clamping his hand over her mouth, he pulled her violently to her feet, holding her tightly against him.

'Be silent!' he threatened in her ear but she continued to struggle, biting his hand and making small noises in her throat. He was cursing steadily now, clamping his hand more tightly over her nose and mouth to cut off her air. She began to arch and twist against him, fighting to breathe. His arm closed around her ribs, and soon the struggles stopped and she went limp in his arms.

I can't leave her here, Seth thought wildly. I'll have to take her with me.

Dragging Charl, he crossed the stable, finding the pistol and stumbling over the saddlebags as he went. With one hand he slung the bags over the horse's rump, and with the other he supported the unconscious girl until he mounted. Then he dragged her unceremoniously up in front of him in the saddle.

❧

When Charl came to her senses again, they were beginning the descent from the high bank at the edge of town, down the wagon road towards the ferry. With mixed anger and terror she realized what Seth intended to do. Using her as a hostage, he was going to board the ferry and slip across the border to Canada and safety. Frantically she tried to think of something she could do to prevent his escape, but with her hands tied and with his arm clamped tightly around her ribs to hold her on the horse, she was helpless.

From the town there came the sound of shouts and gunshots. To their right, she could see the hot orange glow of the bonfire reflected on the sides of buildings that faced Main Street. She turned her head to look at the back of her father's store as they made their silent way towards the ferry. If only there were someone she could signal for help, she thought. It seemed that everyone was at the bonfire celebrating the start of the war. The start of the war! Her mind reeled; she couldn't believe that war had actually been declared. The noise from the town grew louder, and some cheering could be heard. With difficulty, she forced her mind back to the situation at hand. She had to find a way to get away from Seth, or at least attract attention to his escape. But there was no one nearby, and her scream would surely go unnoticed in the din of the celebration.

'Feeling better, my dear?' Seth inquired in her ear. There was a note in his voice that she had not heard before. It seemed more resonant, more alive, and she wished she could see his expression. 'I hope you have no intention of screaming for help, not that anyone would hear you above that racket. You see, I have a very sharp knife here that could silence you quite effectively.' She felt a sudden sharp pressure between two of her ribs and she gasped involuntarily.

His voice went on softly, caressingly, filled with that same vital quality. 'I can see you've decided not to expose me, Charlotte, after all we've meant to each other.' She stiffened at the laughter in his words and drew breath to reply angrily, but the knife bit deeper, breaking the skin along her ribs.

'Not a word, Charl. I do not want to hurt you, but I will if you don't do as you're told,' he threatened.

'Monster!' she hissed between her teeth, and he tightened his arm around her ribs. For a moment lights danced before her eyes as her breath was cut off; then abruptly he let her go.

Seth swore softly under his breath, and as she looked more closely, she could see the reason. Mr Taggart, the ferryman, had not gone to town with the others but had stayed at the ferry dock. Seth had meant to steal the flatboat and cross the river undetected, but now that would be impossible. Hope flared inside her for a minute. Perhaps between them they could overpower Seth and prevent his escape.

His voice was soft and reasonable as he spoke. 'I suppose you know the ferryman, just as you know everyone else here.' He paused and she nodded. 'Then tell him to do as I say, or it will go badly for both of you. I only want to cross the river, and it would be foolish and dangerous for either of you to try to stop me.'

Desperately, she looked back towards town. There would be no help from that sector, and Mr Taggart was an old man. In reality, what could an old man and a girl do to prevent this armed, dangerous man from using the ferry to escape? It was useless, Charl decided. Let him cross the river and end this nightmare.

'All right,' she finally agreed, noting how deserted the landing was as they rode up. The pressure of the knife against her ribs was suddenly gone, but before she had a chance to move, she felt the cold, round muzzle of a pistol at her temple. She gasped involuntarily.

'Two passengers to cross the river,' Seth called out.

The old man looked up, squinting into the shadows. 'No more river crossings, not tonight, not for a long time to come,' Taggart answered, coming forward.

'I'm afraid there must be one more,' Seth said, as the horse pranced from the shadows into the moonlight. Recognition and comprehension were clear on Taggart's craggy face as Seth continued. 'Miss Beckwith is my prisoner. If you do not wish to see her harmed, you must do as I say.'

Taggart's eyes met Seth's icy blue ones across the length of dock, then travelled to Charlotte's white face. There was a purple bruise on her jaw and across one cheek. Her hands were tied, too, and there were bloodstains on her blouse. The damned Englishman had hurt her, Taggart thought angrily.

Charl was surprised by the calm tone of her own voice. 'Please do as he says, Mr Taggart. This scoundrel would think nothing of killing us both.'

Seth tensed at her words, and the barrel of the pistol went tight against her temple. Closing her eyes, Charl wondered if she would hear or feel the blast when he pulled the trigger. For eternal seconds they stood motionless, frozen like a tableau in the bright moonlight, until the old man snorted his assent and defeat. What could be done? The spy clearly had the upper hand.

The horse's hooves sounded hollowly on the wooden gangway and on the deck of the ferry as Seth rode aboard. In a way it was over now, Charl thought. Nothing stood in the way of Seth's escape, and once he reached Canada, he would set her free. Now that he was getting what he wanted, he would not harm her unless she provoked him. When they reached the other bank, they would both be safe.

The flatboat moved swiftly out into the river, catching the current and sweeping them towards enemy territory. For a second there was a flash of reflection near the tiller, and Seth was off the horse immediately, pushing aside some boxes to reveal an ancient muzzleloader leaning against the rail. He tensed for a moment, and Charl held her breath, wondering what he would do. Then with a quick, economical motion he threw the gun, arching it out across the water, to splash down into the deepest part of the river.

'I'll not have you shooting me in the back once I'm safe in Canada,' he told Taggart as he moved to mount behind Charl again.

She watched the Canadian bank approaching, and she could begin to make out some shadowed shapes that lay hulking and dark in the moonlight. It was almost over. In a few minutes Seth would make good his escape, and she could return home to safety. But for how long would Youngstown be safe? How long would it be before there would be fighting in her own town? How long before the artillery would begin to bombard her home?

The ferry nudged gently against the Canadian dock, and under Seth's hard eyes Taggart lowered the gangway.

'Thank you very much for your trouble,' Seth said sarcastically, raining coins down on the deck. 'I hope we haven't inconvenienced you too much.'

He tightened his arm around Charl. 'One more thing. Tell Henry Beckwith I'm taking his daughter with me as a hostage.'

'No! Seth!' Charl gasped, before he silenced her painfully with his grip.

'Assure him I'll take good care of her as long as no attempt is made to follow me,' he went on. 'I'll send her back when I have no more use for her.'

'Seth, no, please! Let me go!' Charl begged, but he was already guiding the horse down the gangway. She tried to turn to kick and claw at him, but he held her fast, controlling her struggles as he turned the horse up the road towards York.

Taggart stood helplessly and heard Charlotte's long, anguished scream echoing back to him as the spy and his hostage vanished into the darkness.

❊

They rode all night, moving north, following the lakeshore on a rough road that was little more than a wagon track. Once they were safely into the forest, Seth put away the knife he had pressed tight against Charl's ribs to keep her silent. She began to struggle at once, but his iron-hard arm held her effortlessly in place, and her anger and frustration grew. She swore at him and called him all the names that she could think of, but he seemed totally unaffected by her rancour. She soon found it was useless to scream questions at him, and pleading with him did not help either. Seth just held her while she raged, moving farther and farther down the trail.

Finally, panting and exhausted, Charl slumped against him, her head nodding heavily at his shoulder. For the first time in her life she felt totally defeated, and tears began to sting her eyes.

'Why won't you let me go?' she asked brokenly. 'Where are you taking me?'

He was unduly pleased by the subdued tone of her voice; perhaps now the struggles would stop. 'I will send you back to your father when I am through with you. That is all you need to know for now. Do as I tell you, Charl, and it will go much easier on you.' There was a threatening note in his granite voice, and she did not doubt the sincerity of his words.

'I hate you, Seth!' she whispered, as her defiance ebbed away and she closed her eyes against the tears she was determined not to shed.

They kept moving until the sky began to grey with dawn, picking their way along the same overgrown trail. Finally, Seth turned the horse into the woods and stopped beside a small stream.

'We'll rest here,' he told her as he pulled her roughly to the ground. Charl was numb with exhaustion, and when he set her on her feet, she stared at him vacantly. Realizing that she was almost beyond coherent thought, he swept her up in his arms and carried her to a flat grassy place that was to be her bed. A moment later he was back to drape a blanket over her; then he set about unsaddling and hobbling the horse before he joined her on the grass.

'I'm sorry. This is the only blanket I have,' he told her as he pulled it up over them.

Charl hardly heard his explanation and was only marginally aware of his arm around her, pulling her into the curve of his body, before she fell into a deep, dreamless sleep.

Ten
❈❈❈

She awoke slowly, aware first of the sunlight in her eyes, then of the smell of earth beneath her, and finally of the crackle of a fire. Without moving, she opened her eyes. Seth was bending over the small fire, turning some animal on a spit made from branches. He was bare chested, dressed only in buckskins and moccasins, a blood-soaked cloth wrapped tightly around his right forearm.

She stirred and sat up, suddenly aware that her hands were still tied in front of her.

'So you are finally awake,' he observed conversationally, coming towards her. Anger filled her as she realized where she was and why.

'Let me untie you,' he offered, but she glared at him, frowning. Without comment he quickly unfastened the leather strap and began to chafe her hands between his own to increase the circulation. Charl bit her lip to keep back the gasp of pain as the blood came stinging back into her fingers. She pulled her hands away and began to shake and flex them while Seth went back to the fire.

Charl got unsteadily to her feet, feeling bruised and sore. After disappearing into the bushes for a few moments, she returned to the stream to splash her face with icy water and wash her hands. She could smell their food, which on closer inspection she recognized as a rabbit cooking over the fire, and decided that her escape could wait until after they had eaten.

Wordlessly, Seth offered her half the fare when it was ready, and she ate ravenously. The crisp, sweet meat seemed incredibly delicious, and she was unable to think when she had eaten last. Too much had happened too quickly, and she couldn't seem to get her jumbled thoughts and emotions straight in her mind. The only thing clear to her was the need to escape from Seth. She could not comprehend why he had abducted her in the first place, but she knew she must slip away before they travelled too much farther from Youngstown. She had no idea where they were now or how far they had come the night before. She was sure that the lake was nearby, and she knew that by following the shoreline she could get home. The question was: Could she get away from Seth? She well knew his determination, and she wondered if she could somehow outwit him.

His voice cut into her thoughts, and Charl looked up sharply. 'If you're quite finished, I'd like you to bandage my arm before we move on,' he said. It was neither a request nor a demand, and after a pause she began to unwrap the bloody, stiffened neckcloth from around the arm he extended towards her.

The fabric was stuck in places, and she could see his jaw tighten against the pain as she dissolved the blood with water. Looking down at the jagged gouge that ran the length of his forearm, from wrist to elbow, she momentarily forgot her anger. She had done that to him! It appalled her to think that there was enough violence in her to do such a thing to another human being; she had never suspected that facet of her personality. Then the anger came back, smothering her momentary remorse. Why should she be sorry she had hurt him after all he had done to her? Still, his uncivilized behaviour was no excuse for her actions.

Carefully and thoroughly, she washed away the dried blood and examined the wound. It would benefit from stitching, but there was no way to do that here. Still, there were no signs of infection, and that was good.

'You are lucky it bled as much as it did,' she told him, intent on what she was doing. 'Wounds that happen in stables often cause serious illness, but this one bled itself clean, and it should heal quickly.'

He watched what she was doing dispassionately, as if the arm belonged to someone else. Her eyes were cast down as she worked, and she bit her lip as she applied the bandage torn from one of his shirts. As he watched her, he read contrition in every line of her face, and he felt himself relax. He had been afraid she would fight him as she had last night, but today her resistance seemed to be gone. She was pale, except where a bruise purpled along her cheek and jaw, and subdued, ready to do as she was told.

She helped him to shrug into the buckskin shirt he had been wearing the day she met him at the Crow's Head. Somehow he looked more natural here, dressed like this, than he had ever looked in his carefully tailored tailcoats in her parlour. And for good reason, she reminded herself. He was a savage, capable of any act; he had proved that last night.

Standing, Seth moved towards the horse, lightly, noiselessly, seeming perfectly at home in the forest. She gathered the strips of shirting together, while he saddled the horse and smothered the small fire in preparation for leaving. He took the neatly folded bandages from her and tucked them into the saddlebags. Then he threw them over the horse's rump.

Charl was sure that he would bind her hands, but when he ordered her to mount and then swung up behind her, she realized her hands would be left free. Hope rose in her, and she smiled to herself. He must think he has tamed me, she thought. And if that was the case, he would soon grow careless. She smiled to herself. She would wait for an opportunity and then she would escape.

※

It was sunset when they broke from the forest onto the wagon track. They had slept all day, and Seth apparently planned to travel all night. For a moment Charl wondered why he was being so cautious, now that he had reached the safety of Canada. Then her thoughts turned away as she glimpsed the lake reflected grey and yellow and gold through the trees. It was clear now, as it had not been last night, that the road followed along the lakeshore. Again she smiled to herself. It would be easy to find her way home once she had escaped from Seth. She would slip away from him and hide in the forest until he tired of looking for her; then she would simply follow the shoreline back to Youngstown. It would be easy, but she must act quickly before they left this trail.

The horse pranced along as if he had been refreshed by the rest, and Seth seemed relaxed and in a good mood. He held her loosely against him and spoke softly, pointing out various kinds of trees and plants that grew along the edges of the trail. It was evident that he felt very much in control of the situation. And it was only by a supreme effort of will that Charl kept her body from going rigid with anger and anticipation. The light was dimming, and she waited until the vegetation thickened at the edges of the trail before she made her move.

Suddenly and savagely, Charl pushed against Seth's right arm to free herself, feeling him flinch away as she did. Nimbly, she slid from the horse, landing on the balls of her feet, and was running through the underbrush almost before Seth realized what she was doing.

'Charlotte!' she heard him bellow behind her. A moment later he was off the horse and running after her. She fled headlong, too frightened to plan any kind of evasion. Bushes clutched at her clothes, and roots reached out to trip her, but she was sure footed and fast, spurred on by the sound of Seth crashing through the brush behind her. After a few minutes the sound of his movements receded, and she felt the distance between them grow.

Finally at the end of her endurance, she stopped to crouch behind the trunk of a fallen tree, her muscles trembling. Silently she gasped for breath as she listened for the sound of pursuit. When her breathing slowed and her heart stopped hammering in her ears, she became aware of the profound silence of the forest at dusk. Breathlessly she listened, but everything was still. Her spirits soared. Was it possible Seth had given up? Joy swept through her. She was free! She was free!

Slowly, she rose, still listening, but filled with relief. The thick silence swelled around her. Seth had given up! She could hardly believe it. Quietly, she skirted a clump of bushes. She would move south parallel to the shoreline until she judged it was safe to return to the wagon road. She doubted that Seth would waste time retracing their route from Youngstown if he had given her up so easily. Perhaps he was as glad to be rid of her as she was to be free.

Her mind had already turned to the problem of crossing the river when some small sound to her right made her turn. Through the deepening grey twilight she saw Seth, standing silently, watching her. He was a terrible apparition, and she froze like a frightened doe, her eyes widening to take in his expression. His face was hard with fury, his eyes narrowed, and his mouth formed into a grim line.

Her heart seemed to stop beating in her chest as she stared at him. For the first time since she had met him, she was terrified by what he might do. She knew now what he was capable of, and she realized that she was defenceless against his superior strength. The rage in his blue eyes reached towards her with a force of its own. In blind panic she bolted away, but she had run no more than a dozen steps when Seth caught her from behind, dragging her heavily to the ground.

'Bitch,' he growled as he rose above her. 'You bitch! Just what the deuce do you think you're doing?' He was shaking her, leaving bruises on her soft skin and making her teeth rattle. Under the violence of his grip her silk shirt came open, baring her breasts as the buttons were wrenched from the fabric. His eyes widened as he stared down at her in searing fury and flaring desire. Sensing the danger, Charl began to struggle.

'Seth!' she cried out, that single word conveying her shock, her horror and her hate. His mouth roughly silenced her as he straddled her hips so she would not escape him again.

In a frenzy of emotions that bore no single name, his hands moved over her, across her lush breasts and beneath her riding skirt to the warm, moist recess between her thighs.

He's going to rape me, Charlotte's mind screamed, even while his lips muffled hers. The inevitability of the act only made her fight him harder, using her teeth to bite and her nails to rake his face. She felt him gasp in surprise and pain as he caught both her wrists in one hand, shifting his weight to pin her down. She could feel his desire grow hard and full against her hip as he pressed closer. Then his lips left her bruised mouth to trail across her throat and breasts with ravishing intensity. As he moved, she glimpsed his face, rigid with uncontrolled rage and flushed with all-encompassing passion until the two goads that drove him were one.

'Oh, Seth! No! No, please!' she begged, the full scope of her helplessness and fear expressed in her desperate, husky words. The tone of voice more than her meaning penetrated the madness that engulfed him, and Seth went suddenly still, hovering above her on trembling arms. Charl lay beneath him without even breathing, terrified by the bared teeth and slitted eyes that gave evidence of his savage emotions. He was like one demented, driven by anger to drop any guise of civility he'd ever possessed. As if frozen, she stared up at him, seeing the pulse tapping wildly in his throat, the veins that stood out in his temples and the sweat that slicked his brow as he fought his way back from the brink of the abyss. The return to sanity was hard won, but some semblance of rationality finally dawned in his face and she drew a breath at last. Then with a shuddering moan deep in his throat he collapsed against her and lay still.

✻

When Seth's brain began to function again, it was full dark, and it took him several moments to remember where he was. Charlotte was beginning to stir under him, and he came to his feet in one smooth movement, pulling himself together as he stood over her.

'Get dressed,' he ordered, furious with her for the time she had made him waste and with himself for his loss of control.

'If you've left me anything to put on,' Charl answered, trying to summon anger to make her weakened limbs respond. Her blouse was beyond repair and could be held together only by tying the two tails in front under her breasts.

'Hurry!' he growled. Reacting on pure instinct, she spun angrily to strike at him. Roughly he caught her wrist and twisted it against her body, making her cry out.

'I'll not have any more of this, Charlotte!' he told her, his face so close to hers that she could feel his warm breath across her cheeks. 'I mean it. You will do as I tell you and forget these mad ideas of escape, or I will make you very sorry. You do believe that, don't you, Charlotte?'

'Yes, I believe it! You've gone out of your way to show me what a brute you are,' she answered, too angry now to care what he did to her. 'You can abuse me however you want, but I will never do what you tell me. And you had better keep a hold on me every minute because I intend to get away from you at the first opportunity. I hate you, Seth Porterfield! You are scum, dirty, traitorous –'

Involuntarily, his hand snaked out to strike her, but he caught himself in time. Instead he tightened his grip on her wrist and dragged her off through the dark. How he knew where he was going Charl had no idea. But he moved steadily, heedless of the roots that tripped her or the branches that scratched her skin.

Breaking through the underbrush on to the trail, Seth let out a low whistle, and there was a distinct whinny in response. Still pulling Charl along, he strode off in that direction until he found the horse grazing contentedly at the side of the path. His steely fingers still held Charlotte's wrist as he rummaged in the saddlebags. Finding the rawhide he had removed hardly more than an hour ago, he bound her wrists. In the pale moonlight that filtered through the trees his face was rigid, with hard lines around his thin mouth. He looked sinister and forbidding now that Charl's bravado had faded. She felt fear and hatred knot her stomach, and she began to wonder if she had the strength to continue to defy him.

Without a word he swung her into the saddle. Then he gathered the dangling reins and climbed up after her. She tensed to avoid contact with his body, but his arm came around to pull her closer. As he held her, Charl felt a warm stickiness against her skin and realized that his wound was bleeding again. This time, the sense of remorse she had felt before was gone; she was no longer sorry she had hurt him. He was a vile man and deserved whatever happened to him. It seemed impossible that she had ever seen him in any different light. She had not believed his wickedness, once, but now she knew him as the traitorous liar he was.

He had seduced her, hurt her, and lied to her for his own ends; now he was continuing to exploit her. For the moment there was little she could do to prevent him from using her, but as they cantered down the trail towards York, she vowed never to surrender to him. In the end she would see him beaten at his own game, and she would have her revenge.

✳

Charl stood where Seth had told her to stand, her hands tied, waiting for him to finish breaking camp. Her face was set in bitter, angry lines, and her eyes were stormy as she watched him, but she did as she was told.

In the two days since he had abducted her from Youngstown, she had learned that she must do as he said or face the consequences. And he could make the consequences very unpleasant indeed. A rush of hatred went through her. Since the first day, when she had tried to escape and failed, he had been harsh with her. He had forced her to bend to his will in every situation, until now she reluctantly obeyed him. Simmering with anger she recalled his rough hands pushing and forcing her to do what he wanted. He had even tied her up when he went hunting or fishing for their nightly meal so that she could not run away.

Oh, how she hated him. Now that he made no effort to disguise his personality, she realized what a beast he really was, and she cursed herself for not seeing his true nature before this. She had been a fool to believe anything he said.

He had as much as admitted to her that he was a British spy, sent to Youngstown to gather information. Again she was furious with herself for ever believing in him. Everyone had been right about Seth, her father, Stephen, even old Mrs Latham, but she had stubbornly refused to see it. She had been infatuated with Seth, and that had blurred her judgement, but now she clearly saw what a despicable man he really was.

Only a villain would kidnap a girl from a home where she was loved and protected and drag her out into the wilderness, to use her for his own ends. She had been a hostage to facilitate his escape, and she had expected to be free when he reached safety. But now it was clear that he was not going to let her go. She was his prisoner, and as such he exercised complete control over her.

It was this control over every aspect of her life that made her fight him most bitterly. He decided where and when she would eat and sleep. He took her far away from her home when he knew her only desire was to return there. He made her do what he wanted by the sheer physical power he had over her. She hated him most for that power he exercised so freely and for the appalling intimacy in his lightest touch.

Since the night she had tried to escape and Seth had almost raped her, there was an implied threat whenever he came near. His physical presence was encroaching and overwhelming, and she could not bear to think what might have happened if he had not regained control of himself. Nor did she doubt that he was still capable of doing the deed. His hands unerringly found her whenever she was within his reach, and he seemed to be constantly testing them both by pressing the limits of their endurance. He would pull her close, caressing her breasts or thighs until his face was flushed and his breathing ragged or until she fought her way free in righteous indignation. Yet there were times when his touch still made her go weak and melt inside. But she hid them well, for to acknowledge his control over her body and her senses would be the final degradation.

Seth came towards her, the saddlebags in one hand. As he tossed them up on the horse, he turned to her.

'Are you ready to leave, Charlotte?' he asked conversationally.

'Only if we are going back to Youngstown,' she snapped.

'I hate to disappoint you, my dear, but we are headed in quite a different direction,' he said calmly.

'Seth, please let me go. Untie me and I will go back to Youngstown by myself. It's not that far, and I can find the way,' she pleaded. 'You don't need me with you now; you are safe. I must be a terrible burden to you. Let me go,' she went on, hating the desperate note in her voice but unable to control it.

He looked at her for a long moment. His pale, opaque eyes seemed to bore into her, as if he were considering what she said. Her chin came up as she glared at him defiantly. Then his hand reached out to touch her face, slid down her neck under the tangle of hair, and finally stopped to cup her breast.

'I'm not ready to let you go yet,' he told her, his eyes darkening with desire. His reasons for keeping her with him were very clear. Then he seemed to master himself, and he went on. 'Besides it is a long way back to Youngstown, and I could hardly let you go alone, on foot and without food or a weapon. You would not be safe.'

'As if I am safe with you, you scoundrel!' she hissed, and pulled away.

'You needn't call me names, Charl. You are safer with me than without me. Just as I was safer with you the other night. Eventually I will send you back, but for now you are my prisoner and you will do as I say.'

'I will never do as you say! I hate you!' she spat at him.

'Be that as it may, I think it's time we were away. The sun is already rising.' Effortlessly, he swung her up into the saddle and mounted behind her.

They had begun to travel in the daylight now, moving along the shore of Lake Ontario eastwards towards York, the capital of Upper Canada. They rode in stony silence, and Charl kept her back straight, trying to avoid touching him. But he seemed to enjoy the contact with her, and he pulled her back to rest against his chest. As the horse plodded on, his hands began to wander over her, almost absentmindedly, caressing, stroking, until she bit her lips in frustration and anger. How dared he? How dared he? She trembled with fury, but by now she knew she was helpless against him.

As the sun rose higher, the day grew hotter. The air turned thick with humidity until the muggy heat seemed to press all around them. There was no breeze, and the lake lay still and silvery in the sun. Even the trees that laced together overhead offered no comfort but seemed to hold the thick air down upon them like a weight.

By early evening when they made camp, Charl's hair hung damply against her neck, and her clothes stuck to her body. The campsite was on a low bluff overlooking the lake, and once their meagre possessions were unloaded, Charl turned to Seth.

'Untie me!' she demanded. 'I want to bathe.'

He felt his temper flare up at her manner, but he shrugged it away as he cut the leather from her wrists. A swim would feel good after the heat of the day, and he knew he could hardly deny her one and then go himself.

'I'll join you as soon as I get a fire started,' he told her.

In the past days of enforced intimacy Charl had overcome her usual modesty; still she turned her back to undress, leaving the ragged remains of her blouse and skirt on a log. Seth watched her with glowing eyes. Her body had such clean lines, long and sleek, yet enticingly rounded. Why was it, he wondered, that everything she did made him want her?

'If you stand there naked, I'll have to assume you're looking for more than a swim,' he teased her.

'You seem to think that me, standing anywhere, dressed or undressed, gives you the right to force your attentions on me,' she flashed angrily.

'I don't suppose you have any soap.' She turned to face him with her hands on her hips, and he drew a shaky breath. There was a pink glow, reflected from the sunset, on the tops of her breasts and along the curve of her belly. She was so beautiful that he could hardly take his eyes off her. She was like some wild creature, all pink and gold with sun, her hair tumbling down her back.

He would like to make love to her when they were both cool and clean from their swim, he decided through the haze of lust that fogged his thinking. Then, in irritation, he bent to rummage in one of the saddlebags. He found the cake of soap, tossed it to her across the clearing, and watched Charl move gracefully down the path towards the lake.

Her hair was soapy and piled on top of her head when he joined her in the water. It was cold at first, startling and fresh against his hot skin, and he dived and swam around lazily before he paddled over to get the soap from her. She rinsed quickly and tossed her hair back out of her eyes. As he lathered himself, he watched her swim, her long, smooth strokes taking her from one grey-blue patch of shadow into water orange with the reflected sun. She swam well, strongly, like a man. And she dived cleanly, knifing her body down without hesitation.

He frowned as he watched her. These had been unpleasant days, and he had asked himself more than once why he hadn't left her at the ferry as he'd intended. He had no idea why he had brought Charl with him. She seemed to have some strange power that made him do things he did not want to do and take chances it was not wise to take. It had been like that since the first day at the Crow's Head. He had agreed to stay in Beckwith's home, and nothing had gone right since then. Disaster followed each of his faulty decisions; he knew that by now. But here he was, halfway to York with Charl his unwilling captive, defying him at every turn. Nothing was simple with her along, and he wondered what kind of trouble she would bring him in the future.

Irritation ripped through him, partly at himself, but mostly with her. Charlotte Beckwith had to be the most infuriating woman he had ever met. She could fire his temper with only a look or word, and he was constantly fighting himself for control. Since the night she had tried to escape and he had nearly raped her, he had kept his temper by an act of will. He remembered the furious red haze that enveloped him, the brutal way he had treated her. How close he had come to violating the soft, tempting body Charl had once offered him with innocent eagerness and complete trust. Even now he did not understand his own emotions. He only knew he hated himself for what had almost happened and for the terror he had seen in Charl's eyes.

Seth was well aware that he could not change the past, but he was determined to maintain his self-control. Yet Charl never gave him a moment's peace, and he was constantly at war either with himself or with her.

Sighing, he left the precious soap on a rock at the water's edge and swam to where she floated motionlessly on her back. Her hair fanned out around her like the petals of a flower moving slightly with the current of the water.

Silently he dived beneath her, snaking one arm up around her waist to pull her under. She fought and kicked at him until he let her go, but bobbed to the surface laughing. For a moment their animosity dropped away, and she swam after him as he dodged and dived to get away. She caught him with a burst of speed and sank him with her hands on his shoulders, screaming as he pulled her down, too. They broke the surface together, and she slid away, splashing at him. He pretended to ignore her, settling down on his back, knowing that she was just out of his range of vision, ready to attack. But no attack came. After a few moments of lying, tense but vulnerable, he raised his head to look around. She was nowhere in sight. He waited for her, but as he did, he felt his stomach begin to tighten. He scanned the surface of the water again, carefully watching the lengthening shadows. There was no sign of her.

Where was she? He dived quickly, scanning around under the surface. He was beginning to feel apprehensive now. If this was some kind of trick . . .

He dived again, deeper this time, carefully watching the shifting patches of light and dark. At the edge of his vision he saw her, like a struggling shadow, being pulled inexorably down by what must be a strong undertow.

Surfacing, he began to swim towards her, and almost immediately he began to feel the current pull at him, too. He swam with it, letting it draw him towards its centre and Charlotte. He dived again and felt the flow suck him down. He could see Charl below him now, her arms no longer struggling but swaying bonelessly, like seaweed. Seth swam faster, reaching out towards her, but she seemed constantly just out of his grasp. It was as if the lake was toying with him, drawing him deeper, until it claimed both their lives. He made a sudden desperate grab for her and found her limp wrist under his fingers. Kicking furiously, he struggled towards the surface, but the current that had helped him reach her held him down. Using his free arm and his legs, he worked against the force of the water, towing the girl behind him, fighting for the smooth, light surface above him. His chest hurt and the blood was pounding in his ears when he felt the air on his face and he pulled Charl up beside him. Gasping in the sweet, fresh air, he trod water, carefully holding Charl's face so she could breathe. The undertow had pulled them out in the lake until the shore and safety seemed impossibly far away.

For what seemed like hours Seth struggled towards the distant land, alternately swimming and floating, not daring to wonder if the girl he towed with him was alive or dead. Finally at the end of his endurance, he felt the gravelly bottom under his feet, and he half dragged, half carried Charl to the shore. The world spun dizzily around him, and for a while he was aware of nothing more than his own raspy breathing and the pounding of his heart. Then the sound of Charl's coughing and her sobbing breaths began to invade his consciousness, and he moved towards her. Her body seemed to be convulsed by the deep gasps for air, and he moved to comfort her. She turned to him, her breathing easing, and clung to him, trembling. She did not know or care who he was just then as long as he was warm and alive. And if he was alive, then she must be alive, too.

He cradled her against him for a long time, sitting on the sand, holding her like a child. His lips were in her hair, and he crooned to her, soft soothing sounds that gradually brought her back to reality. Slowly, the unconscious fear receded, and she became aware of who and where she was.

Charl finally raised her head and looked deep into his eyes. He seemed so kind, so comforting, and she felt the tears gathering in her throat. More than anything she wanted to stay in his arms and sob out the terror she had felt trapped underwater. She wanted to tell him about it, to talk it out until the fear had gone. She needed his comfort and his strength. But from somewhere in the stirrings of her conscious mind came the conviction that she must not show him even this moment of weakness or she would be lost.

She knew now who he was and what he had done to her. She remembered why she was here and that she hated him. She pulled away from him and straightened, trying to summon anger to overcome her weariness and fear.

'I suppose I should thank you for saving my life,' she began in a voice that sounded pale in her own ears, 'but I won't. This was probably my only chance to escape from you.'

She was surprised at her own bitterness. His eyes flashed dangerously at her, and then his face turned hard and expressionless.

'You needn't thank me, Charl. I don't owe you anything anymore, nor do you owe me,' he told her harshly.

'Good! I'm glad because I'd hate to be in your debt.'

'Damn you, Charlotte!' Seth exploded. She flinched away from him automatically, not knowing what to expect. He rose and snatched her up in his arms, carrying her roughly up the slope to where the campfire glowed invitingly in the semi-darkness. She cried out, afraid of what he might do, but instead of hurting her, he wrapped her in the blanket and put her down near the fire. Swiftly he dressed and began to throw together a rough meal, moving compulsively, as if he dared not stop. When the food was ready, they ate silently, tension thick in the air.

'Charlotte,' Seth finally said in a voice that sounded weary, 'Let's call a truce.'

She eyed him suspiciously, surprised by his words. What was he up to? She watched his face, but it was unreadable in the flickering firelight.

He went on. 'We are headed for York; you must realize that. I'm going on to Quebec from there. If you behave yourself until we get to the city, I promise I will see what I can do about sending you back to Youngstown.'

Doubt swirled around her. What trick was he playing on her now? What did he have planned? Did he think he could fool her into letting down her guard?

'Why are you doing this?' she finally demanded.

He shrugged. 'I'm tired of struggling with you, I suppose. You've proved your point. You won't voluntarily submit even though I can control you. It's a stalemate, and I'm weary of the game. I'd planned to let you go when we got to York in any case, so I suppose I'm willing to trade that knowledge for a few days' peace.' He paused. 'And I do find it a little disconcerting to realize that you'd rather drown than travel with me.' There was mockery in his tone, and if she had been able to listen more carefully, she would have realized that the words she had spoken in desperation had wounded him.

Instead, she frowned in response, wondering what he hoped to gain by this tactic. Could it be that he meant what he said?

'Come, Charlotte. I'm giving you what you want,' he prompted her irritably.

'How do I know that you will do as you say when we get to York?' she asked, her face intent.

'You'll have my word,' he told her.

'Your word? Your word, Mr Spy!' She laughed mirthlessly. 'I was fool enough to believe what you said once before.'

A cloud seemed to pass over his face, and his expression tightened. 'Spy or not, you will have to trust me, Charl.'

She looked deep into his eyes, remembering that she had trusted him once and she still ached with that betrayal. For a moment the problem at hand dimmed in her mind, and she voiced the question that had hung between them for days. 'How is it you can be a spy?'

Emotions she could not fathom flickered across his face, and when he finally answered her, bitterness echoed in his voice. 'I

cannot explain it all to you, Charlotte. There comes a time when
no matter what you want personally you have no choice about
what you do. A situation becomes inevitable, and you simply
choose your side and do what you must.'

'I don't understand,' she whispered, unable to break away
from the intensity of his eyes. She felt suspended, mesmerized,
drowning in their blueness. She wanted to trust him, to believe
in him and in the agreement he offered, but she was afraid.

'Well then, Charl? Will we have a truce or not?' he asked
gruffly, looking away.

'All right,' she agreed, feeling betrayed the moment she spoke
the words. She sighed. What did she have to lose after all? If she
did not fight him, he would not hurt her. She knew a truce would
not change the hate she harboured for him. In the end he would
decide whether to let her go or keep her prisoner, regardless of
what she promised.

Suddenly an aching weariness came over her, and her energy
ebbed away. Too many things had happened too quickly. If Seth
meant what he said, this should have been her victory; instead,
everything seemed bleak and hopeless.

'I am very tired,' she said thinly, thinking that she had never
felt such a deep and debilitating exhaustion. 'I'd like to go to
sleep if you don't mind.'

'Of course,' Seth answered solicitously. 'It has been a difficult
day for you.'

Annoyance at his words rippled through her, but she had no
strength to respond. In some ways his kindness was as difficult
to bear as his anger.

Sighing deeply, she lay down near the fire and pulled the
blanket tighter. She pillowed her head on her arm and closed her
eyes. 'Good night,' she said quietly.

'Good night,' came Seth's voice from behind her. For a long
time she lay very still letting the hot, silent tears course down
her cheeks until she finally fell asleep.

Seth sat staring into the flames while the fire burned to embers,
purposely keeping his eyes off the sleeping girl. They had made
a truce of sorts, and in two days, or three at the most, he would
be rid of her. It was just as well. He would find someone in York
who was sailing to Youngstown, and he would send her home.

Wearily rubbing one hand across his eyes, he sighed. It was
better this way. He was not even sure what he had intended to

do with her. Charl was difficult to control, and he could not trust her alone in Quebec. He must have been mad to even consider taking her there with him. What would he have done with her while he was on assignments for Mitchell? He groaned inwardly. He dreaded to think what Mitchell would have to say about this.

Scowling, he looked off into the darkness. He had not thought this out but had gone ahead recklessly, as Charl was prone to make him do. What was it about her that confused his judgement so? If he kept her with him, she would probably end up getting him killed. It was best that they part company at York. He was sure of it.

Seth stretched and moved to lie down next to Charl, drawing her gently into the curve of his body. She was sleeping soundly and seemed well in spite of her brush with death. He put one arm around her possessively. He had saved her life. In some primitive way that made her belong to him, and he felt responsible for her well-being. He sighed again. He would discharge that responsibility, he vowed. He would see her safely on her way back to Youngstown. It was what she wanted, and it was what was best for both of them.

Wearily he pressed his cheek against her cool hair and let the waves of sleep sweep in to claim him.

Part Two

✳✳✳

Quebec City

Eleven
✳✳✳

It was the sound of birds singing in the trees overhead that woke Charl the next morning. She lay quietly listening, feeling newly aware of their sweet sound. Seth's warm body was no longer snug against her back, and she could hear his muffled footsteps as he moved around the clearing. She was not ready to face him after all that had happened the night before, and she continued to lie with her eyes closed, feigning sleep.

Her thoughts were a jumble and she wanted to sort out her feelings before she had to deal with his unsettling presence. The memory of the clutching undertow still hung like a cloud over her mind. She knew she would never forget the sensation of being pulled deeper and deeper into the water or the terror of watching the clear surface, and her life, slip further and further away. There had been the feeling of helplessness, of struggling against a force too great for her. And then in those moments before everything became dark and indistinct, there had been the certainty that she was going to die. Involuntarily, she shuddered.

She had Seth to thank for being alive today; she knew that. For a moment, Charl luxuriated in the warmth of the sun on her skin and the sharp, tangy smell of her green grass bed. It was only because Seth had risked his life to save her that she was not dead. This morning she might be nothing more than some bit of flotsam tossed up somewhere along the shore of the lake if it had not been for him. She might never have been able to see her father or her home again, might never have had the opportunity to fulfill the promises she had made to the future. Tears rose under her eyelids, and her heart began to beat wildly. She had come so close to death. With an effort she willed herself to calm.

Seth had been so kind to her last night, she remembered through a haze of terror, so kind and so gentle. He had held her and comforted her, and she had nearly weakened and clung to

him. Now he wanted a truce between them. What possessed him
to propose such a thing after these past days of conflict, she
wondered. Had he come to accept that she would not let him
control her? Or did he see the quivering vulnerability just below
her shell of defiance?

She did not understand what drove him, what made him kind
one minute and brutal the next. She had seen so many faces of
Seth Porterfield she could not be sure what parts of him were
real and which were not. And, most important, she didn't know
if she could trust him to send her home as he had promised he
would. Was it possible that he had been humouring her last
night? Had he told her what she wanted to hear to make her
calm? Could it be that he had tired of her resistance and would
lie to gain her cooperation? Perhaps this morning his motives
would be clear and she would be able to tell if he was sincere in
his desire for peace between them.

At any rate she needed to be up. In a way she was surprised
that Seth had let her sleep so long. He had driven them mercilessly
for three days, and she could not help but wonder how much
farther it was to York.

Languorously, Charl stretched and opened her eyes, then went
icy cold with shock. A tall Indian was squatting by the fire
searching through Seth's saddlebags. Without thinking she sat
bolt upright, clutching the blanket around her, filled with anger.

'What are you doing?' she demanded, surprised by her own
audacity.

The Indian looked up, unperturbed. Then, leaving the saddlebags on the ground, he came towards her, moving with an
unconscious grace that was both predatory and beautiful. He
came easily to his knees in front of her, looking into her widening
eyes. Silence stretched between them as each watched the other
intently.

'You have lovely hair,' he finally said, reaching out one bronzed
hand to touch a tangled curl that fell across her breast. His
English was perfect, and in some strange way his accent and
inflection reminded her of Seth.

She continued to stare at him, too stunned to move even when
he had reached towards her. It was strange but she felt no fear,
as if she sensed he would not harm her. His face was kind and
hard, all planes and angles: high cheekboned, heavy-browed,
and hawk-nosed. His mouth was wide with straight, chiselled

lips, and his eyes were the colour of bittersweet chocolate.

'You're not going to hurt me, are you?' she finally asked.

A flicker of warmth came into his eyes, and he shook his head.

'I am Waukee,' he said in the same soft, cultured voice. 'Seth Porterfield and I have ridden together for a long time. I will accompany you to Quebec.'

Charl felt irritation stir inside her. It was just like Seth not to mention Waukee to her. What did he care if she woke up terrified to find an Indian in camp? She frowned irritably and instantly dismissed all the grateful thoughts she'd been thinking on Seth's behalf.

'I am Charlotte Beckwith, as Seth may or may not have told you. Fortunately I will not be going to Quebec. Seth is leaving me in York,' she told him flatly.

He nodded once, a short, sharp, definite motion that seemed to conclude the matter.

'I was told who you were,' Waukee said, raising one eyebrow. In spite of herself, Charlotte could not help but wonder exactly what it was that Seth had said to the Indian about her.

'You are to dress and prepare for our journey to York,' Waukee went on. 'Seth is anxious to arrive, and we will not stop again until we get to the city.'

Seth was obviously in a hurry to be rid of her, Charl thought, with an odd feeling of pique. But then, the sooner they arrived in the capital, the sooner she would be out of his clutches and on her way home.

'Where is he?' she demanded.

'He went to catch some fish for our meal. It is best we eat before we leave,' Waukee explained evenly.

'Very well,' she agreed, struggling to rise. The folds of the blanket were tangled around her feet, and he offered her his hand.

'Thank you,' she said gratefully, accepting it. Gathering her clothes from the log where she had left them, she slipped into the bushes to dress. She must be a sorry sight, Charl reflected, as she pulled on her tattered things. Her blouse and underclothes were little more than rags, thanks to the impatient Mr Porterfield, and her skirt was only a little better. What would people think if she arrived home in this state? They would think she had been seduced and abducted by a British spy, she answered herself bitterly. Her reputation would be ruined, of course, and she would be the source of gossip for months to come. It had not occurred to her until that minute that her ordeal would not be over when Seth set her free. She would have to face the good people of Youngstown. Grimly she pushed the thought away. She would deal with that in time, for now only her freedom mattered.

Returning to the clearing, she tried to comb her tangled hair with her fingers, but found it impossible. Giving up in exasperation she tramped off towards the lake to wash her face and hands.

Seth was coming up the beach as she reached the water's edge. Apparently his fishing had been successful, because several pike dangled from the line he held in his hand. She studiously ignored him until he came up to where she was wading.

'Good morning,' he said pleasantly. 'I trust you slept well.'

Angrily she turned to him, her eyes flashing. 'Why didn't you tell me about Waukee?' she demanded.

His first impulse was to snap back at her, but he controlled himself and shrugged. 'I'm sorry. I had other things on my mind last night. Besides, I didn't expect him to catch up to us for a day or so. I hope he didn't frighten you too much.'

Charl calmed down a little. 'He did give me a bit of a shock,' she admitted. 'Is that breakfast?'

He nodded. 'It might be lunch, at the rate things are going. Put on your boots and I'll teach you how to clean fish,' he offered.

'I already know how to clean fish,' she told him archly as she waded towards him.

'Ah, Miss Beckwith, you're a woman of so many accomplishments,' he grinned. 'You never cease to amaze me.'

'But, Mr Porterfield, it has always been my intention to confound you,' she said prettily, her eyes twinkling.

He roared with laughter. 'You do, Charlotte. You do,' he told her. He waited while she tugged on her boots, then led her back to the campsite.

Together Charl and Seth fixed the meal while Waukee whittled intently on something. He had brought some potatoes, and Charl baked them in the coals while Seth cooked the fish on sticks over the fire.

It seemed good to be able to put aside the animosity between them, and Charl could begin to feel the tight knot of tension inside her ease. Seth's manner was easily bantering, and she knew she was responding to his unaffected charm and lazy smile. The suspension of hostilities did not change the way she felt about him, she told herself, but neither could she bear to live in a constant state of war. It would not hurt to be civil to him for the next few days until he sent her home.

It appeared that he had been honest about that, at least. From the comments he made to Waukee it was evident that he really meant to arrange for her passage to Youngstown. Seth and the Indian talked about their plans for their trip to Quebec while they ate, and the plans clearly did not include her.

It was odd to watch the two men together. They were like opposite sides of the same coin: one dark as a shadow with raven black hair and dusky skin, while the other was as fair as the summer sun. In their lean, strong faces Charl could see the subtle differences in their character. There was the rakish glint of adventure in Seth's expression, while Waukee's eyes were dark and steady. They were both tall and strongly built, but with a certain lean grace that marked them as men of action. As Charl watched them across the smouldering fire, she could sense the strong bond of friendship that existed between them, and she found herself wondering how it had been forged. She knew some of Seth's background from the things he had told them that night in the parlour, and as she watched the two men together, she tried to recall everything he'd said then. Had Seth lived with Waukee's people when he went West with the surveyors? If that was the case, why was Waukee here now? Was it possible that the Indian was affiliated with the British, too?

She was suddenly aware that Waukee was moving towards her, his hands behind his back and his eyes shining. She stared up at him inquisitively.

'I hope you will accept this small gift I've made for you,' he said, smiling as he extended a roughly carved wooden comb towards her. 'I am sorry I had no time to refine it.'

Charl's face flushed with delight as she reached for the comb. 'Oh, thank you!' she smiled, and immediately began to tug the snarls from her hair. 'It seems good to be able to see to my appearance again. I've felt so dishevelled these past few days. Thank you so much!'

Across the clearing Seth watched her as she smoothed her tangled locks, frowning to himself. There had been a hairbrush in his bags all this time, but it had never occurred to him to offer it to Charl. These past few days he had been oblivious to her comfort and her needs. He had been aware only of her defiance and his lust for her. As he watched her curl one silken strand of hair around her hand, he realized how ragged her clothes had become. For the first time he noticed the bruise along her jaw and the purpling marks he had left on her wrists. In the days since they had left Youngstown, he had looked at her often but never quite seen her. He had been aware of the woman who fought him so stubbornly, and the spirit he needed to subdue, but he had ceased to be aware of her as Charlotte. She had been an adversary, and he had treated her as one. Now there was no hint of that enemy left in her. She seemed so vulnerable to him to be delighted by the simple gift of a comb.

His expression tightened. There was no excuse for the way he had treated Charlotte, he told himself. As uncooperative and infuriating as she had been, he had no reason to brutalize her. He had acted like a savage, not a rational man. Irritation stirred inside him as he watched her pat her hair into place, then turn to smile gratefully at Waukee.

He would buy her some new clothes once they had reached York, Seth decided. He could hardly send her home looking like this anyway. Besides, Charl was too beautiful a woman to be dressed in rags.

Seth threw a stick into the fire and stood up; they needed to be on their way. Charl immediately sensed his impatience and moved to gather their meagre belongings in preparation for breaking camp.

Minutes later they were ready to leave. The fire had been smothered, the saddlebags packed, and the horses watered. As Seth helped her into the saddle, Charl realized that in a few days' time she would bid him good-bye forever. He and Waukee would travel on across the lake and down the St Lawrence to Quebec while she returned to her life in Youngstown. Although she could never forgive Seth for many of the things he'd done, or for the duplicity he'd practised on her, she owed him a deep debt of gratitude for saving her life. Slowly she turned to him and laid one hand on his arm, smiling warmly into his eyes.

'Thank you,' she said softly, the simple words conveying a multitude of meanings.

Seth found he was suddenly rather short of breath as he looked up into her face. Quickly he swung up into the saddle behind her and tightened one arm possessively around her waist, realizing with a jolt that it was going to be very difficult to let her go once they reached York.

*

To Charl's surprise they rode north from the campsite, picking their way through the forest until they came upon another, more travelled road to York. It seemed as though Seth had been avoiding settlements, and Charl could hardly help but wonder why. Perhaps he had wanted to give Waukee a chance to catch up with them, she reasoned. Or maybe he had been afraid that her father would come after them in spite of what he had told Mr Taggart, the ferryman.

Once on the main road to York, they travelled faster, not stopping at nightfall but moving on until the stars shone brightly against the blue velvet sky. Trees and fences moved past them, lurking silhouettes of their daytime reality, and the waning moon gave a half-light to the ribbon of road ahead of them. It grew cooler with the darkness, and the clear sky seemed to allow the day's heat to float away into space. Charl was thankful for Seth's warm body against her back, protecting her from the chill as they rode swiftly towards their destination. Near dawn weariness overtook her and she went limp, leaning heavily against his chest, deeply asleep and oblivious to the miles they travelled.

By midmorning they had reached the town. It was a bustling settlement and the seat of government for Upper Canada. York, a jumble of brick, frame, and log homes and businesses, was clustered between the busy harbour and the stone fort, owing its prosperity to one and its protection to the other.

They went quickly to a boardinghouse that Seth knew, and he made arrangements for a room for Charl. She still slept deeply, cradled in Seth's arms, and he carried her carefully up to the room the landlady had rented them. She stirred as he gently undressed her and tucked her between the clean sheets, but fell back to sleep almost immediately. Determinedly, he fought the weariness that made him want to crawl in beside her.

'You sleep like the dead, my dear,' he told her, as he propped a hastily scribbled note on the crude dresser. Impulsively, he bent and brushed his lips across her forehead before he left.

It was late afternoon when Charl awoke, confused and alone in a strange room. She flew to the window and peered out into the golden light. Her view included a stable and another house partly hidden by a tall hedgerow. They must be in York, she reasoned. But where had Seth and Waukee gone? Panic raced through her. Had they abandoned her? As she turned away from the windows, her eyes fell on Seth's saddlebags, slung over the back of the chair, and the panic receded a bit. They would be back, she realized, chiding herself for being so foolish. Then a new thought struck her, and the panic rose again. She rushed to the door and tugged at it frantically; they had locked her in. She was still Seth's prisoner. Charl leaned her forehead against the stout wood with tears welling in her eyes.

'Damn him! Damn him!' she muttered furiously. How could Seth continue to treat her this way? Then through the wavering mist of tears, she noticed the key. It had not occurred to her that the room might be locked for her protection. Gingerly she turned the key, heard a satisfying click, and opened the door a crack to peer out. There was a long narrow hallway lined with identical doors, lit by a single window at one end. This must be some kind of inn or boardinghouse, she decided. Satisfied, she closed and locked the door again, leaning back against it to survey the room. It was small and somewhat shabby, but spotlessly clean. The large, low-backed featherbed dominated the space, but there was also a small, rush-seated side chair and a dark, rough-hewn dresser with a spotted mirror in a thick frame. For the first time she noticed the piece of paper leaning against the glass, and she snatched it up.

Dear Charlotte,
    There are many arrangements to make. You are safe here. We will be back as soon as we can.
                                    Seth

She stared at the message written in the strong, legible hand and felt her tension ease. There was something reassuring about the writing. It looked solid and dependable on the foolscap page, and she smiled to herself. Probably Seth was out now seeing about her passage home as he had promised. She would be dressed and ready when he returned, she decided. After washing her face and hands with water from the ewer, she began to look for her clothes. Inexplicably, they seemed to have disappeared, and she wondered angrily if Seth had taken them to ensure that she would not try to escape. Dumping the saddlebags on the bed, she procured Seth's last clean shirt to cover her nakedness. It was too big, of course, hanging down to midthigh, but at least it offered her some clothing. There was a knock on the door, and Charl sprang to her feet in confusion.

'Who is it?' she called out.

'The maid, Miz Porterfield, with your bath,' came a voice from outside.

Mrs Porterfield indeed, Charl fumed. Naturally the landlady and her staff would assume she was Seth's wife. She went to the door and unlocked it to admit a drab, grey-haired women dragging a copper tub.

'Billy will be up with your bathwater,' the maid informed Charl, eyeing her unlikely costume. 'Perhaps you'd best hop in bed and cover up until he's done,' she suggested, rather pointedly. Charl obliged while a strapping lad entered and poured two bucketfuls of steaming water into the tub.

When he was gone, Charl began to sort the rumpled clothes that she had tumbled on the coverlet. 'I'd like Mr Porterfield's things laundered, please,' she told the woman. 'And I'll need a needle and thread, for I've some mending to do. I also want my own clothes as soon as possible, and then a hot meal.'

The maid looked quite disconcerted by Charl's air of command and answered reluctantly. 'Mr Porterfield said to throw away your clothes, mum. He said he'd be buying you some new things.' Then she added in a sympathetic tone, 'And it's a shame about the Indians.'

Charl fought down a giggle. Whatever had Seth told these people about her?

'Thank you,' Charl said, controlling her face. 'Just take care of these things, will you?'

'Certainly, mum,' the maid nodded and gathered up the laundry.

When the woman was gone, Charl locked the door with an air of satisfaction; it seemed good to be able to lock the world out. She slipped the shirt down her arms and hung it around the side chair before she lowered herself into the steamy water. The lemon verbena soap made her think of home, and she luxuriated in the smooth lather and the sweet, tangy smell. Lazily she drifted in the warmth of the tub, her mind turned dreamily to thoughts of home. Some time later, she dried herself with the soft towels and slipped on the shirt again to wait impatiently for her meal.

It arrived on a tray, a generous plate of chicken and dumplings with creamy gravy and peas. For dessert there was an apple tart still warm from the oven. She ate ravenously, pleased by the hearty fare.

Feeling content and magnanimous after the meal, Charl picked up Seth's tailcoat. Sitting by the window in the fading daylight, she studied the jagged tear in the sleeve. A shudder ran through her when she remembered how it had happened. It did not seem possible that she could have hurt Seth as she had. Even in her worst moments of temper she had never thought herself capable of violence, but here was the undeniable proof. His arm was healing well, but he would always bear the scar of what she had done.

She looked down at the coat in despair, her feelings of well-being suddenly evaporated. What was becoming of her? What terrible future was Seth leading her to? Under his influence she had forfeited her virtue and committed this violent act. God only knew the depths of depravity to which she might sink if she continued her association with him. Tears rose in her eyes but she brushed them away and took up her needle and thread. With skilful, deliberate stitches she straightened the sleeve working until the frayed edges were carefully hidden and the outside lay smooth and even. Determinedly she worked, repairing the fabric of the jacket as she desperately hoped to reconstruct the ravelled fabric of her own life.

❊

When he came down from Charl's room, Seth found Waukee in the stable at the rear of the house, feeding the horses. He began to fork hay into the stalls while the Indian went for water from the trough in the yard.

'Is she settled?' Waukee asked when he returned with the bucket full.

'She's comfortable and still asleep,' Seth answered, pausing to lean on the handle of the pitchfork.

'The first thing we need to do is find a boat we can buy. A mackinaw would be best, but it must be small enough so that we can handle it alone.'

'If you would like, I will go down to the harbour and see what I can find,' Waukee offered.

'Good! I should take care of Charl's passage to Youngstown first. I'll feel better when that's done. Perhaps someone at Fort

York can tell me if there have been any arrangements made for Americans who are stranded here.'

Waukee looked quizzically at his old friend. 'You have made no plans for returning the girl to Youngstown?'

'No.' Seth's voice sounded irritable. 'I wasn't planning to bring Charl with me, and I didn't decide what I was going to do with her until the other night.'

Waukee raised one dark eyebrow but said nothing more until the horses were bedded down. 'Shall we plan to meet later?' he inquired.

Seth squinted out at the sun. 'That's a good idea,' he agreed. 'I will meet you in front of the harbourmaster's office at two o'clock. Do you know where that is?'

The Indian nodded as they left the barn. The two men moved briskly towards the centre of town and the harbour. It felt good to walk after the hours in the saddle, Seth found himself thinking. As always, the streets of York were busy with all manner of vehicles and all manner of men, from buckskinned Indians to prosperous merchants. The town would probably grow as a result of the war, he reasoned, just as it had prospered when it became the capital of Upper Canada sixteen years before.

On the main street, Seth left Waukee and turned west towards the fort. Surely the military had been keeping watch on any Americans who remained in town and would be aware of their plans for returning to the United States.

As Seth approached the earthworks that surrounded the palisaded walls of Fort York, he could see what an industrious effort was being made to reinforce the defences that had been built some twenty years before by John Graves Simcoe, the first governor of Upper Canada. Seth had heard rumours that renovation had been started the previous year when Major General Sir Isaac Brock had taken command, and now that work was nearly complete. Unconsciously, Seth frowned. If reports could be believed, this Brock was an excellent officer with both tactical and administrative skills. His very presence on the frontier between the United States and Canada would bode ill for the American cause.

Seth was stopped by a sentry at the gate to the fort for a cursory questioning and then sent on his way. As he moved in the direction of the administrative offices and officers' mess, he passed several buildings that were obviously soldiers' barracks.

From their size and number, he made a quick mental tally of the approximate strength of the garrison, filing it away for future reference.

He waited impatiently in the whitewashed anteroom outside Brock's office, while a pompous young lieutenant concluded his business with another man. Then, stepping up to the aide's desk, Seth gave his name and made his request to see General Brock.

'And what, may I ask, is the nature of your business with the general?' the boyish lieutenant asked blandly.

'I want to inquire about passage to the United States,' Seth replied.

The lieutenant gave a derisive snort.

'Surely you realize, Mr Porterfield, that such passage is impossible between countries at war. Besides, why should you trouble General Brock with such a question when any ship's captain would tell you the same thing?'

Seth's annoyance stirred at the man's manner, but he held it in check and answered politely. 'I thought that there might have been some Americans stranded here when war was declared, and I wondered if provisions had been made for a safe return to their country.'

'My good man, it has been more than a fortnight since we received word of the declaration. The last of our Americans left several days ago. Tell me, is the passage for you?' the lieutenant asked, regarding Porterfield with suspicion.

'No, it is not for myself but for a young American lady of my acquaintance.'

The young lieutenant's eyes narrowed as he studied Seth as if he was trying to discern the truth in his words. 'If the passage were for you, sir, I would suggest some gentlemen of ill repute who are undoubtedly continuing to make the journey to the States with contraband. They are an unsavoury lot, however, and I doubt if a young lady would be safe with them. Are you able to accompany her?'

'Unfortunately not. I have pressing business in Quebec.'

The lieutenant shrugged. 'If you like, I will give you several names anyway so that you may judge the calibre of these men yourself.' Seth watched as the young officer scratched several names on a paper and handed it to him. 'These men frequent a waterfront establishment aptly known as the Serpent's Cave. Don't go there alone after dark.'

Nodding, Seth accepted the list and pocketed it. 'Thank you for your trouble, lieutenant,' he said.

'I do hope that your young lady finds her way home safely,' he replied.

'So do I,' Seth muttered grimly as he turned to go.

Seth had not anticipated any problems finding safe passage for Charl, and as he strode in the direction of the harbourmaster's office, his mind worked furiously for other possibilities. Undoubtedly coaches ran to Newark, but a coach would not solve the problem of getting Charl across the Niagara River; nor did Seth want to send her on that journey alone. He had no doubt that she could take care of herself, but he felt a keen sense of responsibility for her well-being that would not be discharged until he was sure she would reach her own doorstep. He would try to contact the smugglers, he decided, and perhaps he would find one man he could trust to deliver Charl safely. For the hundredth time he cursed himself for being fool enough to bring her with him. If he could not send her home, the only alternative would be to take her to Quebec with them. He knew, without thinking about it, that Charl would never approve of such a plan, and he dreaded the prospect of proposing it to her.

Waukee was waiting for Seth in the appointed place. His wide mouth was curved slightly into a satisfied smile.

'It appears you met with some success,' Seth observed.

'I have located a small mackinaw boat, yes. It could use some sealing, and several of the ribs need to be reinforced, but otherwise it is just what we want. The repairs could be completed in time to leave tomorrow if your affairs here are concluded.'

Seth frowned deeply and said nothing as Waukee led him down the dock to where the mackinaw was moored. His spirits rose as he saw the boat bobbing jauntily beside the pier, and he turned to smile his approval at the Indian. They looked it over carefully, checking the sails and the lines. As Waukee said, it needed some minor repairs, but otherwise it was seaworthy and exactly the right size for two men to handle on the trek along the lakeshore and down the St Lawrence River. Seth negotiated the price with the owner, and a bargain was struck. In the meantime Waukee compiled a list of things they would need to complete the repairs and provision the boat. They bought the naval stores, and Waukee set to work strengthening the cracked ribbing while Seth went to order the rest of the supplies for delivery in the morning. The two men worked together all afternoon, reinforcing the stays and sealing the hull with tar. It was after dark when they stopped to eat.

They bought meat pies from a vendor at the end of the dock and sat watching the mackinaw move gently with the waves as they ate.

'How much more do you think there is to do?' Seth asked between bites.

'Well,' Waukee paused to consider, 'the inside is secure, but we need to haul it out and seal the hull as well.'

Seth nodded. 'How long will that take?'

'We should be done by morning,' he answered.

'Let's haul it out and then go to the place the lieutenant told me about. Maybe there I can finish making arrangements for Charlotte's passage to Youngstown. That will give the hull time to dry before we tar it,' Seth suggested, coming to his feet. Waukee rose too and climbed into the boat, manoeuvering it towards the skidway beside the pier. When the boat had been hauled in place, the two men walked the distance to the tavern. It was a squat frame structure, leaning so far to one side that it seemed on the verge of collapse. The paint had long ago weathered away, leaving the siding a dingy grey. It seemed that the place was every bit as unsavoury as the young officer had said it would be.

Seth entered the dim, crowded taproom and made his way towards the grille at the rear where the proprietor was dispensing liquor. He ordered a tot of whisky and inquired about the men on his list. One of them was not in the tavern, but two others were sitting at a table across the room playing cards. He ordered a bottle of liquor and went towards where they were seated. As he crossed the distance, he noticed Waukee had followed him in and was leaning unobtrusively against the wall near the door. Many waterfront taverns would not serve liquor to Indians, but apparently this one was not so selective.

'I would like to talk to Jeb McGee or Lou Miller,' he said as he reached the table.

One man looked up, his rheumy eyes studying the tall stranger. 'What you want them for?' he wheezed.

'Are you McGee or Miller?' Seth asked in reply.

'McGee. Who're you?' he went on suspiciously.

'Porterfield. I'd like to buy you a friendly whisky,' he said, nodding towards an adjacent table.

McGee nudged another man who was slumped halfway across the table, obviously far gone in drink. 'Miller,' McGee said quietly, 'fellow here wants to talk to us private like.'

Miller stirred, thrust himself to his feet and lurched towards the next table. Seth signalled for glasses and sat down.

Once the drinks were poured, Seth turned towards McGee, who seemed the more coherent of the two. 'You still making trips across the lake?'

'Cross the lake where?' McGee said vaguely. 'There are lots of places across the lake.'

'To Sackett's Harbor, Youngstown?'

'Hell, no! There's a war on 'tween us and them. Ain't you heard?'

'I understand you make the trip anyway,' Seth insisted softly.

'Can't imagine who told you that,' McGee eyed him. 'Why you asking?'

'I have something that needs transporting,' Seth said, already sure that he could not entrust Charl's safety to men like these. It had been a mistake to come here.

'What kind of merchandise?'

'A woman,' Seth answered, then went on. 'That doesn't matter, though, if you're not making the trip.' He gathered himself to rise as Miller's head came up.

'Woman, hey?' he spoke for the first time, his yellowed teeth showing in a leering grin. 'Wouldn't mind taking a woman wherever she wants to go. If it's a young filly, we'll make it half the price.' He laughed, his eyes bright with interest.

Seth regarded the smuggler with disgust, noticing the black, stubbly beard, the large, dirty hands. It made his skin crawl to think what might happen if Charl took passage with these two. He would have to find another way to get her back to Youngstown. 'I really don't think we can strike a bargain after all,' he said as he rose.

'Your lady too good to travel with us?' Miller snarled. Seth drew breath to reply, but before he could voice the word, Miller's pistol was in his hand, the barrel amazingly steady. Seth had not expected such an encounter, nor had he judged Miller to be a belligerent drunk.

'We don't take kindly to insults here,' he went on. 'Ain't no woman too good for us.' He leered again. 'Most of them thank us when we're done, don't they, McGee? No matter how unwilling they were to start.'

White hot anger rushed up Seth's spine and exploded somewhere between his temples. Without thinking, he launched himself across the table at the armed man. There was a blast as the gun went off, but the bullet lodged harmlessly in one of the overhead beams as Miller went over backwards in his chair under Seth's attack. McGee lurched to his feet, his pistol drawn to help his friend, but an arm came around from behind him to balance a knife at his throat.

'Drop the gun,' the Indian whispered menacingly. McGee's hand went limp, and the gun thudded to the floor.

Miller lay a sprawling mass at Seth's feet, his drunken bravado gone. Waukee let McGee go.

'What'd you do to Miller?' McGee growled.

'Nothing,' Seth answered, the unreasonable anger fading. 'He's just drunk. I didn't even hit him.' Seth picked up the empty gun and handed it to McGee. 'See that he doesn't threaten anyone else with this.'

Steadily, the two tall men moved towards the door of the tavern, the crowd parting to let them pass. Wordlessly, they made their way back to the mackinaw, each man busy with his own thoughts.

When they reached the boat, Seth stripped off his buckskin shirt as he prepared to resume work on the mackinaw. One by one he lit the torches that were stuck in the sand at the sides of the skidway. Waukee watched this thoughtfully, then moved to where the other man was bent over inspecting the hull.

'You took a very foolish chance back there at the tavern,' he said.

Seth looked up, his mouth set. 'The man drew a gun on me. What else should I have done?'

'You acted in anger, not in self-defence,' Waukee observed coolly. 'And the man was drunk.'

'It was something he said.' He shrugged. 'Are you questioning my actions?'

'I think it's the girl that's bothering you,' Waukee went on. 'You say you don't want to keep her with you, but you can't bring yourself to send her away.'

'The girl means nothing to me!' Seth flared. 'I can't wait to be rid of her! But I certainly can't turn her over to men like those, can I?' His face was stormy.

'No. She can't go with them,' Waukee agreed.

'Then what the hell can I do with her? If you have any ideas about how to get her back to Youngstown, I'd welcome them.'

'You could take her back. Or I could,' the Indian suggested.

Seth's eyes narrowed as he glanced up at the Indian; then he looked away. 'I must leave for Quebec tomorrow, and you know it will take both of us to man this boat.'

There was a long pause, filled with the sound of waves lapping against the shore, while Waukee studied his friend.

'Then there is no choice but to take her with us,' Waukee said at last.

'Now all I have to do is explain that to Charl,' Seth replied grimly.

Twelve
❀❀❀

Charlotte felt the bed sag, and then a pair of warm lips closed over hers. In the moments before she came fully awake, she responded instinctively, her arms going tight around the neck of the man beside her and her mouth opening willingly under his.

'Seth,' she breathed as her eyes fluttered open, and she was pleased to find the man she had expected smiling into her face. 'How did you get in here?' she mumbled, and then, coming more fully awake, struggled to sit up.

'I have the other key,' he informed her, holding it up for her to see. Then he bent to kiss her again, but she fended him off with her hands. He sighed and broke off his attack for the moment. 'I suppose you haven't been out of that bed since I tucked you in yesterday morning.'

Charl realized suddenly that the sun was streaming in the window and it was fully daylight. 'Yes, I have, but I couldn't go too far without my clothes, could I? What time is it? Where have you been all night? Have you arranged for me to go home?'

Seth's eyes went suddenly opaque at the last question, and Charl felt her stomach knot with apprehension. Had Seth lied to her? Was it possible that even after all he had promised that night on the shore, he would refuse to send her home now? And if he had lied to her, what could she do? Was she to remain his prisoner indefinitely?

She sat up straight, meeting his gaze. 'You might as well tell me,' she said evenly.

Seth sighed again and looked away. 'There isn't any way I can send you back to Youngstown from here, Charl. Regular shipping has stopped because of the war, and the men running goods across the lake are an unsavoury lot. You would not be safe with them. If I had more time, perhaps arrangements could be made, but it is imperative that I leave for Quebec today.'

'Then I'll stay and make my own arrangements,' she told him firmly. 'Just give me enough money to pay my passage and go on to Quebec. I'll be fine.'

He took her hands in his and looked at her for a long moment as if considering what she had said. Mingled hope and dread flared within her as he regarded her in silence. 'Charlotte, I know you will find it hard to believe,' he said quietly, 'but there are men even more evil than I am. These are the men that you would have to deal with in order to find passage home, and I simply cannot allow that. It would be too dangerous for you.'

She tore her hands out of his grip. 'And what would they do to me? Threaten me? Beat me? What could they possibly do to me that you have not already done?' she flung at him.

He went white with anger, recognizing that there was truth in her accusation. When he finally spoke, his voice was calm. 'I'll not debate this with you, Charl. You are going to Quebec with Waukee and me. That way I can be sure you are safe. I promise you, I'll send you home from there as soon as I can.'

'You promised! You promised that I would be on my way home now. Admit you lied to me to gain my cooperation just as you have lied about everything else that has passed between us. I hate you, Seth Porterfield, for your dishonour and your duplicity. I will not go to Quebec with you!' she shouted at him, trying to wriggle free of the entangling blankets.

Swiftly he pinned her to the bed, catching her clawing hands and twisting them to her sides. He held her effortlessly immobile, crushing her into the feather bed with his weight. 'Damn it, Charl! We have fought this battle before, and you know you will not win. Do as I tell you and you will not be hurt, but I intend to have my way in this, for your own good. Either you will go with us peacefully or I swear I will knock you senseless and take you anyway.'

'You rogue!' she spat at him, the rage and frustration like leaping fire in her eyes. She was beaten, as she well knew. Why couldn't he just admit that he had lied to her? Why did he persist in this story that there was no safe passage available?

Seth felt her muscles relax, and he released his hold on her. Angrily, she turned from him, trying to master her tumultuous emotions. While she struggled for control, he moved around the room gathering his belongings.

She hated him. Dear God, how she hated him! For a few hours

she had actually believed he would do what he promised. That seemed to be her weakness, trusting and believing Seth Porterfield. (More the fool she!) Charl felt the tears well up, but she fought them back. If this was to be her fate, to be dragged all over the countryside by this vile man, she might as well accept it stoically. She had tried once to openly oppose him, but she had failed. Perhaps now it was best to accept the situation even though her acceptance would never override her abiding hatred for him. Nor would she ever stop looking for a way to escape.

Seth's voice interrupted her thoughts. 'Charlotte, where are my clothes?' he asked as if he expected to hear she had burned them.

'I sent them with the maid to be laundered; I hope to have them back this morning. And I mended your black coat,' she told him, turning back in time to see his expression soften. 'There are still some bloodstains on the cuff, but perhaps they can be sponged out.'

Surprise flickered over his features, and he seemed about to say something when there was a knock on the door and the maid entered with the breakfast tray.

'Morning, mum,' she muttered, as she set the tray on the foot of the bed.

'We will need Mr Porterfield's clothing if it is ready,' Charl said. 'And another cup for his coffee,' she added.

The clothes and cup were delivered shortly, and they shared the breakfast in silence. The coffee in its pewter pot was strong, hot, and good. Charl ate the fresh raspberries and cream while Seth devoured the corn muffins and jam.

'Did you buy me some new clothes then?' Charlotte inquired as they finished eating.

There was a flash of surprise on Seth's face at her friendly tone of voice, and then his expression clouded as he replied. 'I did, but I doubt if they're what you expected.' From a package on the chair he took a lacy white camisole and some delicate underdrawers and held them towards her.

Charl felt her face flame, but she proceeded calmly. 'Those are very nice. What else did you buy me?'

'I didn't know if those were the correct undergarments for a lady to wear with buckskins or not,' he said, extending the fawn-coloured breeches towards her.

'You can't expect me to wear those!' she exclaimed, her eyes wide with shock.

'Well, we're in for a week or more of sailing to Quebec in an open boat, and somehow a silk dress didn't seem very practical,' he explained, looking somewhat chagrined.

Suddenly Charl laughed. It all seemed so ridiculous. What did it matter how she felt or what she wore? Seth could make her do what he wanted anyway; it did no good to oppose him.

Slowly the peals of laughter died away, and she began to wipe her eyes on the back of her hand. Somehow Seth looked so nonplussed by her outburst that she began to giggle again.

'I trust you bought me a shirt, too,' she said, biting her lip to keep back the grin she could not control. Watching her as if she were not quite sane, Seth put the package on the edge of the bed. He seemed so startled by her behaviour that she burst out laughing again. There was a clear edge of hysteria in the sound, but at the same time the laughter seemed to exorcize the tension that had been building between them.

Bit by bit Charl regained control of herself. A stitch in her side caught her breathing short, and she panted for air as she wiped her streaming eyes.

'I'm sorry,' she gasped and giggled again. 'I can't imagine what got into me.'

'Just get dressed!' Seth told her gruffly. Pointedly, he turned his back on her and began to pack up the clean clothes.

She clambered out of bed and began to dress, first slipping on the flimsy underthings. They were very sheer, whisper soft against her skin. She felt her cheeks grow hot as she realized Seth was watching her in the mirror. Quickly she pulled on the buckskin trousers, seeking to shield herself from his regard, but they fitted almost too well, and her flush darkened as she realized how clearly they outlined her hips and the shape of her legs. The shirt was fine white linen, embroidered with a red and blue design on the collar and down the front. Tugging on her boots, she studied herself in the foggy mirror.

'This isn't what the well-bred young lady is wearing this season,' she informed Seth wryly.

'It does look uncommonly good on you, though,' he replied. Something in his voice made her turn to look at him, and her face grew hotter still at the glow in his eyes.

He smiled lazily at her, thinking how much he would like to

crawl into the big bed with her. It would be wonderful to make love to her and then sleep endlessly, snuggled against her.

Wearily he picked up the saddlebags.

'There are a jacket and hat in the package for you, too. Did you find them?' he asked.

She nodded, peering into the mirror to fix her hair. He lounged in the doorway somewhat impatiently. 'Waukee is loading supplies into the boat, and our bill here is paid,' he prompted.

Charl preened for another moment until she saw the frown begin to form at the corners of his mouth. Then she tucked the comb into a pocket, picked up the rest of her new belongings, and brushed past him into the hallway, her chin held high.

*

York was the biggest place Charl had ever been. She had spent her entire twenty-one years in or around Youngstown, with occasional trips to Lewiston or Fort Schlosser. Once Henry Beckwith had even taken his daughter as far as Black Rock, but none of these places had prepared her for the bustle of a town the size of York. From the moment they left the boarding house, Charl entered an exciting new world. The street was narrower than those in Youngstown, and the houses crowded close to the road and each other. The homes, whether built from brick or stone or wood, were taller, too, and each was framed by a small garden that gave it a quaint foreign air.

At the end of the street they turned on to a busier one that seemed to run steadily downhill towards the waterfront. In the distance Lake Ontario lay glistening in the sun under a cloudless sky. As they walked on, Charl noticed that many other streets ran down the hill towards the harbour. It seemed almost as if the entire town leaned a little in that direction as if in attendance to the hub of activity that the docks had become.

The farther they went, the busier and more crowded the streets became. Aware of Charl's wide-eyed interest, Seth slowed his pace so she could take in everything York had to offer. The thoroughfares were jammed with carts and wagons of every description, from polished carriages to heavy delivery drays pulled by huge, shaggy horses. Boxes and barrels were piled high on the planked sidewalks, and they were often forced to step into the dusty street as they made their way towards the centre of town.

Shops lined the streets, and Charl stopped to look in every

window, exclaiming over the beauty and variety of the merchandise offered for sale. She seemed as delighted by the windows displaying navigational equipment as she was by the ones showing stylishly feathered bonnets. She drooled childishly over the pastries in a bakery window until Seth took her in and bought her one, tangy with apples and cinnamon. She munched contentedly as they walked, stopping to admire a pale blue dress with a high, lacy collar and puffed sleeves. It was the most glamorous dress Charl had ever seen, and she stood for a long moment imagining how she would look and feel in such a gown. She glanced down at her own rough attire with disgust and sighed. There was too much in York to see and enjoy for her to worry about things she could not change, Charl decided, brushing away the irritation.

At one shop further down the street they paused to discuss a mahogany settee, upholstered in pale jade silk, that Charl liked. She pointed out the gracefully scrolled lines of the caned back and the slender, tapered legs, but Seth thought the piece too delicate for prolonged use. He vastly preferred a sturdy straight-legged affair with humped back and rolled arms. They argued good-naturedly until the proprietor came to assist them in their selection. Their last stop was in a dry goods store where Seth bought Charl some ribbons for her hair.

'Ribbons aren't worn with buckskins,' she told him coldly. He bought several colours anyway, unperturbed by her sarcasm, including blue-green ones to match her eyes.

The streets were clogged with people under the noonday sun, and Charl was more interested in them than she had been in the shop windows. Businessmen brushed past them in their conservatively cut tailcoats and top hats, projecting an air of efficiency and prosperity. Tradesmen in their rough work clothes and aprons mingled in the crowd, and delicate ladies, with their servants in tow, swept down from their open carriages to run errands to the cobbler or dressmaker. Charl had never seen such stylishly dressed women with their small, curly heads rising above their shawl-draped shoulders. Their pale pastel gowns looked good enough to eat, and Charl devoured every detail, each tuck and every ruffle. Seth could easily see the longing in her eyes, and he wished for a moment that he had bought her something else, to please her vanity, instead of the more practical buckskins.

Closer to the waterfront they wandered through a farmer's

market where the sweet-tart fragrance of strawberries was like perfume in the air. It was here that the women of the town came to buy their fruits and vegetables, or bargain with rosy-cheeked farmers' wives for fresh eggs or live chickens still squawking in their cages. Charl was so amazed and excited by everything she saw that she had quite forgotten how she had come to be in York.

Towards the piers the fishmongers took over the marketplace, each vendor extolling his wares and adding to the general clamour and confusion. The smell of fish was everywhere, and Seth hurried Charl along, impatient now to get to the boat. Still she would not be rushed, stopping to examine the tables piled high with clams and lake fish and to watch the fishermen and sailors unloading their cargoes. Reluctantly, she let Seth lead her down the dock to where the mackinaw boat was moored.

Having grown up on the lake, Charl was familiar with this type of boat, and she had learned to sail on one only slightly smaller than this mackinaw was. These boats combined some features of a sailboat and a canoe. Made from layers of birch bark over a cedar frame, they were light, shallow-drafted vessels. The mast and sails could be used only in light wind, and paddles or oars were used at other times. Narrowed at both ends, they were stubby, awkward-looking craft but ideally suited to lake and river travel.

Waukee greeted them with a smile and offered his hand to Charl to help her board the boat. She could see that it had been provisioned, and an improvised bed had been made from blankets and animal skins in the bow. This was not to be a luxurious trip, she thought wryly, then put the thought out of her mind.

Already Seth was casting off the lines, and Waukee was pushing away from the dock with one of the paddles. Charl's heart sank as they got under way. Somehow she had hoped that at the last minute something might change and she would be able to go home.

Seth made the step from the dock at the last possible second, perching precariously on the gunwale for a long moment before he stepped into the boat and took up a paddle.

They moved swiftly into the channel, passing the islands that protected the mouth of the harbour and gliding out into the open water. Dismally, Charl watched York fall away behind them, knowing that her last chance at going home was fading as fast as the town on the horizon.

There was a light breeze, and as soon as they had cleared the islands, Seth ran up the sail while Waukee set a course east towards the St Lawrence River and Quebec. Once they were under way, Waukee went to the makeshift bed and lay down wearily. Watching him, Charl wondered if either man had slept the night before. She eyed Seth. He looked tired, she decided. As she thought about it, she realized that it had probably been close to forty-eight hours since either Seth or Waukee had slept, having ridden all the previous night.

As they sailed, the wind caught at Charl's hair, sweeping it across her face and into her eyes. To tame it she began to braid it, binding both fat, yellow plaits with blue ribbons. Silently she watched the shoreline slip by, an undulating green and brown stripe in the distance.

'Will you let me sail?' she asked suddenly.

Seth eyed her dubiously. 'Do you know how?'

'Of course,' she informed him. 'I grew up on this lake, and I got to be quite a good sailor before Father began some nonsense about it not being a very ladylike activity.'

'One more accomplishment to add to the list, Miss Beckwith?' he teased her.

'One more, Mr Porterfield. Will you yield the tiller?'

He nodded and they exchanged places. He seated himself comfortably, stretching his long legs and resting his head against the gunwale. 'Just run parallel to the shore,' he told her.

She handled the tiller well, and with a gentle adjustment on the main sheet the boat picked up speed. Seth raised one eyebrow. It was obvious that she knew what she was doing, and he could feel himself relax as he watched her. Somehow she looked very natural at the helm, her thick golden plaits hanging carelessly across her breasts and her face coloured by the sun. An image nagged at the edge of his memory, and then he began to smile as he made the connection in his mind.

'Sitting there like that, Charlotte, you remind me of some ancient Viking maiden,' he said, his smile deepening, 'sailing us safely to uncharted lands.'

Her eyes widened and then she began to laugh merrily, the sound like crystal in the clear air.

'It was the hand on the tiller that convinced me,' he informed her, straight faced.

'I may be a throwback, I suppose,' she smiled. 'My father's

people were from an English village on the North Sea, so perhaps there is a Viking in our background.'

'The Porterfields are from Yorkshire, so perhaps we both have Norse blood in our veins. Maybe that is why our landlady back in York believed that you were my sister.'

'Your sister!' she exclaimed and laughed again. 'So that's what you told her. I wondered.' She adjusted the tiller and looked back at his long-boned body slumped across the deck.

'Somehow I can well imagine a Viking raider in your ancestry. The urge to rape and pillage comes so naturally to you,' she told him pointedly.

He smiled slowly at her and stretched, refusing to rise to the bait. 'I haven't felt a need to rape and pillage in days,' he said and then fell silent, watching the horizon.

The sun felt warm and good on his face, and the wind ruffled his hair. He could hear the hiss of the water rushing under the keel, and after a while Charl began to sing to herself. He listened contentedly. The tune was familiar, and her voice sounded clear and sweet in his ears. The sun was bright, reflecting on the water, and he closed his eyes against the glare, lulled into a sense of well-being by the gentle, steady movement of the boat under him.

Soon Charl was aware that Seth's breathing had begun to deepen, and his thin, determined mouth softened as he fell more deeply asleep. His hard body seemed to mould bonelessly against the shape of the hull, and his thick amber lashes cast shadows on his cheeks in the bright sun. But even in sleep his features never quite relaxed as if he were always internally alert. Charl watched him for a long time, still singing softly, praying that the deep, heavy cadence of his breathing meant that he would not awaken easily. Then, moving slowly, she began to come about, pulling in the sails and changing their heading until they sailed south across the lake towards her home.

The sun was in his eyes, like a glowing orange ball against his closed lids. He stirred and moved his head trying to escape the brightness, but his body seemed to have been turned to stone. Forcing his eyes open, Seth sat up, thick-headed and confused. He had been asleep and dreaming. Dreaming of what, he wondered. The image eluded him behind the veil of sleep, and he fought his way back to coherence.

How long had he slept? Two hours? Maybe three? He had not

meant to give in to the weariness, but with Charl at the tiller there had been nothing to keep him alert. He glanced in her direction. There seemed to be little she could not do, he conceded.

Where were they? He looked over his shoulder towards where the shoreline should have been and felt his stomach sink. It was not there. He looked again, turning his head slowly, searching the horizon in every direction for even a narrow strip of green. There was no land anywhere in sight. How could Charl have strayed so far off course, he wondered dazedly, bringing one hand up to shade his eyes.

How long had he slept? he asked himself again. It must have been longer than he had thought at first. It was sunset. He'd slept four hours, maybe five. It had been the sunset in his eyes that had awakened him.

He stared stupidly at the crimson disk sliding slowly into the water to the west. To the west, he was facing west. The realization came to him with the force of a blow. If he was facing west, they were sailing south across the lake, not eastward towards Quebec. He looked questioningly at Charl, and she raised her chin, the fires of defiance blazing brightly in her eyes. She had changed their course on purpose!

'Damn it, woman! What have you done?' he thundered at her.

Charl glared at him, tight-lipped and smiling. For a moment a kind of incandescent fury surged through him.

'You've sailed us out into the middle of the lake, haven't you?' he shouted at her as he pushed her away from the tiller. 'Don't you realize this is not a proper boat for lake sailing! We could be killed in your damn escape attempt.'

'I don't care!' she shouted back.

Waukee was stirring in the bow, sitting up as confused as Seth had been minutes before.

Angrily, Seth was hauling on the main sheet in an attempt to change course quickly. The boom snapped across the boat, and they heeled dangerously to port as they came about.

'You're the one who'll drown us!' she accused, but the boat righted itself quickly.

'Quiet, woman! Give me the slightest provocation, and I'll be only too happy to throw you overboard and let you swim home,' he threatened furiously as he tied off the lines. 'How far have we come? Damn it, Charlotte! Answer me!'

'I don't know. You slept for a long time.'

Waukee came from the bow towards them. 'What has happened? Where are we?' he asked.

Seth explained tersely, his voice low and dangerous. Waukee listened carefully and nodded, glancing up at the sky. 'We are headed in roughly the right direction. Once it's dark we will be able to steer by the position of the stars. The lake is calm and the wind is brisk. If that continues, we should make up the distance before morning.' He gave Charl a long, measuring look and continued. 'I will sleep until it is full dark and then take the helm for the night.'

Porterfield agreed and Waukee returned to the bed in the bow and lay down to sleep for another hour or so.

They sailed quietly into the gathering dusk: the Indian sleeping on his bed of furs, the woman staring fixedly to the south as if she could visualize her home just beyond the horizon, and the spy cursing himself for his own carelessness. It had been a serious mistake to have fallen asleep, but it had been a bigger one to have underestimated the girl. By now he should know that he could not trust Charlotte. He had been a fool to let himself be lulled into a false sense of security by her moments of acquiescence. He could not trust her; that was the simple fact, no matter how outwardly compliant she seemed. He must not forget it again.

In a way, he felt a grudging respect for her stubbornness. She could not have expected to succeed in her escape; the lake must be thirty miles wide at this point. But Charl had tried anyway. She had waited cunningly for an opportunity to get away. And when one presented itself, she'd had courage enough to attempt it.

He glanced at her in the semi-darkness. She was still staring intently to the south, but not with the longing he might have expected in another woman. There was a proud thrust to her chin that said more clearly than words that she was not defeated.

A smile touched the corners of his mouth as he watched her. He understood that kind of pride. It had ruled him all his life, making him strong and self-reliant but acting as a trap as well. He had never learned to bend to another's will, nor had Charlotte. She was as determined and single minded as he was, and that led inevitably to conflict and confrontation between them. The insight hardened his resolve. Charl might very well be one of the most beautiful and charming women he had ever encountered, but it was plain he could never trust her.

※

Beneath the waning moon, the mackinaw moved swiftly eastward, making up the distance they had lost in Charl's wild flight across the lake. The Indian was a skilful sailor and navigator and, while Seth slept on the bed of skins, Charlotte sat near the man at the tiller, watching and occasionally asking questions. Waukee talked freely, once he had begun, and explained the rudiments of plotting a course by the stars. He also pointed out various constellations, vividly visible in the clear night sky, and told her legends about them that left her enthralled and amused.

It was very late when she finally went to stretch out on the fur pallet. She lay down gingerly, but even in his sleep Seth seemed to sense her presence. His arm came around her waist possessively, and he pulled her close to him. Charl sighed in exasperation, but his warmth next to her was welcome. And as she drifted between sleep and wakefulness, she marvelled at how well her body fitted into the curve of his.

Cloudless blue sky domed high overhead, and the sun was at its zenith when she awoke. For a moment she was not sure where she was. She had expected to see the crocheted canopy of her tester bed above her, but the gentle movement of the boat and the softness of the furs brought back her memory. Languorously she stretched and sat up, blinking at the brightness. The thickly treed shoreline passed low to the north and gave evidence that they were back on course for Quebec.

Wordlessly, Seth handed her a piece of dried beef and a chunk of bread for her breakfast, and she dipped herself a drink from the lake, pausing to wash her hands and face. She ate hungrily, realizing that she had eaten nothing since the pastry Seth had bought her in York.

Charl looked towards the land, wondering how far they had come and how long it would be before they reached their destination. She knew that the city of Quebec had been founded by the French in the seventeenth century at the westernmost navigable point on the St Lawrence River. It had begun as a fur trading post and had eventually grown to be a stronghold for the French in the New World. In many ways its role had remained the same after its capture by the English, and it now served the British as a gateway to the Great Lakes and the West. Beyond those few facts she knew little or nothing about their destination, and she was avidly curious.

She eyed Seth sitting towards the stern. He had been totally uncommunicative since she had awakened, and she felt her irritation stir. She was not going to let him ignore her, she decided. He had dragged her along on this escapade, and she had a right to know what was to become of her.

'Seth!' she began a trifle more forcefully than she had intended. He looked up sharply, meeting those clear, direct eyes and noting the stubborn set of her chin. He scowled at her tone, but she was undeterred by his expression and went on briskly. 'I demand to know where we are.'

'You demand, miss?' He paused to let one eyebrow drift infuriatingly upward. 'I'm not sure that you're in a position to demand anything. Let's just say we are as far towards Quebec as I might have hoped we would be by noon today.' His face went closed and blank as he spoke, and unreasonably she grew furious.

'Damn it, you despicable, arrogant bastard. I have a right to know where we are, at least!' she fumed.

'Charlotte, watch your language in front of Waukee. What will he think of such an outburst?' Seth admonished her, putting up one hand as if to ward off her words.

The girl glanced at the Indian holding the tiller, and although his face was solemn, there were dancing lights of humour in his eyes. Somehow the thought that either one of them might consider her behaviour amusing made her angrier still.

With iron determination she fought down her temper. 'I – I don't think it's unreasonable for me to ask where we are.'

Seth watched her, noting the lowered eyes and the soft voice. She played this game very well indeed, he thought. How easy it would be to let himself be taken in by her again. He regarded her cautiously and speculatively for a long moment. There was really no harm in telling her what she wanted to know.

'We are about thirty miles east of York, no thanks to your efforts,' he said suddenly.

Her eyes came up to his face. 'And how far is it to Quebec, please?'

She had only wanted to know where they were going, he realized. Nor was that an unreasonable request for her to make.

He frowned deeply. What was it about Charl that raised his ire and made the simplest question a confrontation?

'It will be four or five days to Kingston at the head of the lake. There's not much of a settlement there, but we'll stop for provisions. Then there will be four more days down the river to Montreal and another day or two to Quebec. That is assuming that the weather holds and the wind is from the right quarter.'

Charl nodded thoughtfully, then glanced back at him. 'Is there any danger?' she asked.

'Storms, capsizing,' he answered irritably. Trust her to ask some damn stupid woman's question.

'From the war, I mean,' she put in.

He stared at her for a long moment. Perhaps it was not such a stupid question after all; he had pondered that himself. 'I doubt it,' he said finally. 'Neither side has had time to react to the declaration of war. Oh, there may have been some isolated incidents of fighting or a skirmish or two, but it's too early for there to be trouble on the lake. It takes time for a fleet to be mobilized; we should reach Quebec without incident.' He smiled reassuringly.

'But there will be fighting on the lake eventually and on the Niagara?' Charl's brow puckered with the question.

'Yes, of course. It's inevitable.'

'Then why are we headed to Quebec?'

The question was an earnest one, obviously filled with the need to understand the world that was crumbling under her feet. Nor could he find an easy answer to it. To tell her simply that Mitchell had ordered him there was clearly impossible. He drew a long breath.

'Are you sure you want me to explain all this? It gets rather complicated,' he asked, buying time to frame a reply.

'I am neither a child nor a dullard, unable to comprehend the things around me,' she informed him, raising her chin. 'Proceed.'

'Very well,' he began. 'There are two opposing forces that will affect the lakes region now that war has been declared. The Americans will be trying to invade and annex upper Canada, and the British will attempt to capture and control the Mississippi Valley. Either way, the St Lawrence and Great Lakes water system is of strategic importance to these goals. Any troops that are landed to further British aims will come into Quebec and will need to follow the waterways west.

'General Prevost in Quebec fears that in order to prevent the transport of these troops an attack will be launched to capture Montreal and Quebec,' he explained.

'But you don't believe that's what will happen,' she observed.

'No, but Prevost does have history on his side. During the revolution the Continental Army under General Montgomery did advance and capture Montreal.'

'And Quebec?'

'Quebec is impregnable. No one has captured Quebec since General Wolfe scaled the cliffs in 1759 to rout the French.'

'What do you think will happen?' she asked curiously, caught up in the discussion.

'I think the United States has made a very grave mistake by declaring war on Great Britain. And I think she'll be lucky to get out of it with her sovereignty and her territory intact,' Seth stated flatly.

'Even though Britain is carrying on a war with Napoleon in Europe?'

'And what will happen if Napoleon is defeated and all of King George's troops are brought to bear on this fledgling nation? How long will she stand when redcoats come up the Chesapeake to meet those sweeping down across New York? Or perhaps troops will land at the mouth of the Mississippi and march north to rendezvous with others sent south from the Great Lakes. If that happens, your nation will be neatly cut in two and defeated.'

'Have you laid out your battle plans for the British yet?' she flared at him, her voice thick with bitterness.

'They haven't asked me.' Seth laughed shortly, flashing a warning look at the Indian. 'At any rate, no matter what happens, the important decisions will be made in Quebec and that's where I must be,' he finished. There was an echoing silence, filled only with the sound of the waves and the wind.

'What will happen to Youngstown?' she asked in a small voice, her eyes dark with worry.

'It will be in the direct path of the fighting. There is no way it can escape unscathed.' He looked into her stricken face and wished that there was some way he could change the inevitable. His words had been more brutal than he had meant them to be, but Charl would need to face the truth sometime.

With a small cry, she turned away from him, gripping the

gunwale until her knuckles went white. For a very long time she stared dry-eyed towards her home as if she could already see the dark smoke of devastation curling upward on the horizon.

Thirteen
✻✻✻

It was nearly sunset when they lowered the sail on the mackinaw and paddled into a protected cove for the night. After securing the boat, they waded to shore carrying the blankets and food they would need to make camp. Seth had caught several trout during the afternoon and soon had them cooking on spits over the fire while Charl prepared vegetables and boiled water for tea.

The day had been hot and clear, and in the fading light Charl's face and arms began to grow scarlet with sunburn. She brushed away Seth's questions of concern, unwilling to admit her discomfort, as if it represented some kind of weakness in her. Instead she went ahead with preparations for the meal, ignoring the additional pain that being near the fire caused.

When they had eaten, Seth came towards where she sat combing out her plaits. She frowned at him as he squatted down in front of her. 'Waukee made this for you,' he told her, extending a tin cup filled with a gooey concoction. 'It doesn't smell very good, but it will take some of the sting out of that sunburn.'

Gratefully, she glanced across the clearing at Waukee, and he gave her an encouraging smile. For a moment she was torn between the need to ease her pain and the desire to maintain her independence from the two men. In the end, her pride was stronger.

'No. I'm fine, really,' she began, shaking her head.

'Damn it, Charl! Don't be so stubborn. You're not fine and we both know it. Now unbutton your shirt. I've no time to argue with you,' Seth muttered gruffly. Resigned, she did as she was told. The gentleness of Seth's hands on her skin belied the bluster in his voice as he smoothed the balm into the angry red V above her camisole where her shirt had been open at the throat. Then he applied it down her arms and across her forehead and cheeks in impersonal, economical strokes.

'You'll wear your hat tomorrow,' he told her, 'and I'll rig some kind of shelter for you to use at midday.'

'You needn't fuss over me.'

'I know,' he smiled, 'but I won't have you accusing me of any more abuse. Is this helping?'

She nodded as a cooling tingle began to replace the scorching heat of her skin.

'What is this?' she asked, wrinkling her nose at the odour.

Seth shrugged. 'Bear grease, mint, some other herbs. It's an old Indian remedy for burns of any kind.'

'You didn't sunburn,' she observed accusingly.

He laughed at her tone. 'I'm used to the sun; I've used a great deal of this in my day, though,' he consoled her and came easily to his feet.

'Thank you,' she said, rising to stand beside him.

'For what? Tending your wounds? You've tended mine.'

'Only the wounds I've inflicted myself,' she whispered softly, not able to meet his eyes.

His voice was suddenly very gentle. 'Of all the ways I've injured you, this is the only hurt I've been able to heal. No matter what you think, Charlotte, I have no desire to cause you pain.'

For a heartbeat, the clearing was very still as he stood looking into her face. Then he turned abruptly and strode towards the shore where Waukee had gone to check the boat.

✻

It was very late when Seth awoke, and he was on his feet before he realized that the dark shape huddled by the fading embers of the fire was Charl.

'Charl?' he called out softly. 'Charlotte, what's the matter?'

'Nothing,' came the muffled reply. As he moved towards her, he could see that she was shivering. 'It's just that I'm so cold.'

He sank to his knees beside her, feeling her face and neck with the back of one hand. Her skin was like fire.

'It's the sunburn,' he diagnosed. 'Come with me.'

He drew her slowly towards his pile of blankets, picking up the tin cup where he had left it by the fire. He wrapped another blanket around her shoulders, then opened the buttons on her blouse with practised hands.

'Hush!' he whispered, anticipating her protest. He began to

smooth the unguent across her chest, up her neck, and into the curves and angles of her face. He did her arms next, and she found that in spite of the cooling properties of the balm, she was warmer and no longer had to clench her teeth to keep them from chattering.

'You'll sleep next to me tonight. I'll keep you warm,' he offered.

'No, I . . .'

'We'll only sleep,' he promised, guiding her down next to him on the bed of pine boughs. His arms came around her shoulders, and she felt warmer almost immediately.

'I wouldn't want to do more than sleep with someone who smells like a grizzly bear,' he teased in her ear. He felt her elbow nudge his ribs as she stretched out beside him. He chuckled softly. 'We'll only sleep, my girl. Dawn will come too soon for both of us.'

He felt her gradually go limp against him, and he lay listening to her deep, even breathing for a long time. Strangely, he was no longer sleepy, but held Charl as she slept, wondering what the future held for both of them. He could not anticipate what kinds of assignments Mitchell might have him undertake once they reached Quebec. As much as he had opposed continuing in the role of spy, he had to admit to himself that the prospect of the intrigue excited him. He was curious to know if Hull had reached Detroit and if a battle had been joined with the British from Fort Malden. He contemplated his feelings about being in battle himself and then brushed the thought away. He doubted that Mitchell would expose any of his agents to that particular kind of danger. Like Charl, like everyone, he couldn't help wondering about the ways this war would change his life. Looking down, he could see the pale curve of Charl's cheek in the darkness, and he pulled her closer. This damn war was changing her world, too. If he sent her to Youngstown, she would surely be caught in the middle of one campaign or another. And how, he asked himself, could he send her back, knowing that by doing so he would put her in constant danger? Finally he slept, content, for this night, at least, to have Charlotte Beckwith safe in the circle of his arms.

✧

The house where Seth took her was not far from the harbour, in the section of Quebec he had described as Lowertown. It was on a narrow, cobbled street that ran uphill to end at the base of the cliff. Somehow, the building's three storeys seemed dwarfed by the heavy rock face that loomed above it. There was a certain similarity between this house and other ones they had passed on their way from the boat, but Seth had hurried her along and Charl had no chance to observe them. Now, as they stood waiting for the door to be opened, she took the opportunity to study the sturdy, grey stone structure. It was a tall, narrow building, standing close to the street and its neighbours on either side. The small-paned windows on the ground floor were heavily shuttered in bright red to match the paint on the wide planked door. On the first floor the windows were larger and more numerous, but the shutters were still evident, looking like sentries in bright scarlet coats. The top floor windows were dormered and set into the steeply peaked roof. There was a narrow passageway between this house and the one on the right that led to a yard and a stable behind.

They heard the rasp of a bolt being slipped back, and the heavy door opened to reveal a tiny, black-haired woman. Her face lit in surprise and delight when she recognized Seth, and she flung herself into his arms, chattering gaily in French. He replied in the same language. It was only when Seth set her back on her feet in the doorway that she noticed Charl standing several paces behind. Her dark eyes registered amazement at the girl's presence and then sincere welcome.

'Gabrielle, permettez-moi de vous présenter Mademoiselle Charlotte Beckwith,' Seth said with a comic bow. 'Charlotte, this is Madame La Soeur.'

'Enchantée de faire votre connaissance, Mademoiselle Beckwith,' the woman said graciously, her message evident in spite of the fact that Charl did not understand a word of what had been said, except her own name. Even that had sounded strange and exotic in the woman's low, throaty voice.

Charl turned wide-eyed to Seth for translation, unable to sustain her charade any longer.

'Charl, no French?' he asked incredulously, shaking his head at her. 'Either thank you or hello would be an appropriate response.' She said thank you, smiling uncertainly at Madame La Soeur.

The mistress of the house opened the door wider to allow them to enter a long, narrow, stone hallway. She called a series of

names and some instructions over her shoulder, then began a
series of rapid questions that at least partially concerned Charl's
presence with Seth. He laughed and began to answer, but a
joyous shriek from the head of the stairs cut him short and a
fiery-haired girl of about sixteen flew into his arms. He spun her
around happily. By this time a short, heavy, white-haired woman
and a sturdy boy had joined the group crowded around Seth.
They all were laughing and asking questions at once, and Charl
stood back feeling like an intruder. Seth answered them one by
one, making them chuckle at the responses Charl could not
understand. Finally he turned to her, and his smile told her she
had not been forgotten. Taking her hand, he pulled her into
the circle of strangers. Their eyes were alive, curious, but not
unfriendly.

'Charlotte, this is the La Soeur family, Madame Gabrielle La
Soeur, Anne, and Jean-Louis.' He paused and turned to face the
older woman. 'And may I also present Marie Droilette, a family
friend.' Charl smiled uncertainly, wishing that she were bathed
and properly dressed to meet these new people.

But Seth draped an arm casually across her shoulders in mute
approval and went on in French to the others. With his arm
reassuringly around her, Charl felt less like an outsider, and she
listened quietly to the words she could not comprehend. As the
conversation became more lively, she began to watch the people
carefully, hoping to satisfy her own curiosity.

They were clearly glad to see Seth and welcomed him back as
one of their own; yet she could see he was no kin to them. There
was genuine affection in their faces and voices when they spoke
to him, and the boy and girl addressed him with an almost
brotherly familiarity. It also seemed as if he had been missed in
his absence. Who were these people to Seth? she wondered.

The woman, Madame La Soeur, was older than Seth, by
perhaps a half dozen years, but her small stature and graceful
carriage made her look hardly older than her children. Her hair
was sooty black and was drawn severely back into a chignon that
emphasized the heart shape of her pale face. The girl, Anne, was
the image of her mother except that her hair was a warm, deep
red rather than black. The boy was more sturdily built and
already towering over his mother and sister, but his long jawed
face confirmed his membership in the family, as did his dark hair
and brown eyes. Charl peered curiously at the white-haired

woman. Her kind, rosy face was seamed with good humour, and
the lines that webbed from the corners of her eyes and mouth
deepened as she smiled at Seth. She said little, allowing the
others to ask the questions while she regarded the tall man with
affection.

Seth pressed Charl's shoulder reassuringly as if to tell her he
was still aware of her beside him. She smiled gratefully in return.
Anne had launched into some complicated story, gesturing
broadly to the amusement of the others. For a minute Charl
listened carefully and tried to comprehend a bit of what was
being said, but the rapid foreign words and phrases skitted past
her like leaves blown by the wind, defying understanding.

Instead, she turned her attention to her surroundings. This
was an old house, she decided. The dark floors had the patina of
wood worn smooth by years of traffic, and she had noticed when
they entered that the stone walls were very thick. From where
she stood she could see the plastered interior of the parlour to
her right. It was a dimly lit room because of the heavily shuttered
windows, but with a fire roaring in the huge stone fireplace it
would be warm and hospitable, suffused with an air of quiet
gentility. The pieces of furniture she could see through the
doorway were of good quality but were worn and out of date,
and the carpet was threadbare in places. Still everything was
glowing with care. She could see another doorway down the
hallway and guessed that there was a dining room behind the
parlour. At the end of the passage, added to the rear of the
house, was a kitchen of the same grey stone.

Charl was suddenly aware that the conversation was ebbing
around her, and she looked up at Seth questioningly. He smiled,
then asked Madame La Soeur a question. She nodded in reply
and turned to issue orders that sent the others scurrying in all
directions. Firmly, he took Charlotte's hand.

From the noisy confusion of the hallway Seth led her up the
well-worn pine stairs with the air of a man who was very much
at home. They passed the first floor hallway with its once bright
carpet and trudged on to the second floor. There was no carpet
in the hall here, and Charl realized that in better days these
rooms had been the servants' quarters. Three heavy wooden
doors led off the landing. Seth opened the one to the right and
motioned her inside. It was a small cosy room, tucked up under
the slant of the roof. The grey stone of the west wall met the

roof beams at waist height, and a tall, narrow window was set into the pitch of the roof to form one of the dormers on the façade of the house. There was a small, open fireplace, which was made of the same grey stone on the facing wall. A narrow pine mantel above it held two pewter candlesticks and a crested silver tankard The other two walls were freshly whitewashed, and the waxed pine floor shone in the sun. Everything was scrupulously clean, from the yellow and blue calico quilt on the wide double bed to the rag rug on the floor. There were few furnishings: only the heavy walnut bed, a small, round table with its two slat-backed chairs, and a campaign chest. A bowl and pitcher sat on the floor by the hearth. Still, it was a welcoming room with the sun streaming in through the dimity curtains. As they stood together just inside the doorway, Charl could see an expression of well-being come into Seth's face.

Charl realized with a jolt that in some strange way this tiny room came as close as any place in the world to being his home. Her expression softened. How little she actually knew or understood about him. Seth had been her constant companion for more than a fortnight. She had eaten with him, slept with him, laughed with him, and fought with him. He had taught her things she wanted to know and explained the forces that would change her life. On one hand he had been protective and gentle, and on the other cruel and uncaring. In their travels he had shown her wonders she might never otherwise have seen, but she had seen them as his prisoner. She knew all his faces, all his disguises, and had experienced his chameleonlike changes of role and mood, but she did not understand the kind of man he was. Nor did she understand why he had brought her with him.

He turned to her as if to speak, but a knock at the door interrupted him.

Madame La Soeur entered and immediately began a rapid discourse in French while Jean-Louis carried in a copper tub. It seemed that either she or Seth or both of them were to have a bath. It was difficult to tell since Charl could not understand a word of the conversation. She glared at Seth and Madame La Soeur as their speech became more animated, and they began to laugh together over something the woman had said. Seth commented to the boy who was filling the tub with hot water, and they laughed again. Charl stared morosely at the floor. She had been anxious to get to Quebec. The discomforts of the mackinaw, sleeping on the ground, cooking over an open fire and the complete lack of privacy had become increasingly trying for her. She had also hoped that once in Quebec she could find some way back to Youngstown. As she sat listening to a conversation she could neither understand nor join, she missed the brief camaraderie that had existed among Waukee, Seth, and herself. Suddenly, a feeling of isolation swept over her, and she wondered if she would ever be able to find solutions to her problems in so foreign a place.

The tone of Madame La Soeur's voice changed, and Charl looked up as the older woman handed a pale pink wrapper to Seth. She moved towards the door, calling a final rejoinder over her shoulder as she left, and he chuckled, turning back to where Charl was sitting on the bed.

'Don't you realize how impolite it is to speak a language not everyone understands?' she fired at him.

'It is not my fault your education was lacking.' He shrugged indifferently. 'I find it incomprehensible that for all your tutors you never learned to speak French.'

'I read and write both Latin and Greek,' she told him defensively, her chin high.

'Latin and Greek,' he echoed, smiling that slow smile that infuriated her. 'I was never very good at Latin. The masters used to cane me for not having my declensions done properly. But in the end, it has been more practical to know French.'

He had come to stand in front of her, looking down into her frowning face. 'Would you like me to teach you French?' he asked, his voice gone soft and silky. When she did not answer, he went on, 'Voudriez-vous vous baigner, mademoiselle?'

'Stop it!' she flared. 'Leave me alone.'

He knelt down next to the bed in front of her so his face was level with hers. 'I only asked you if you wanted a bath,' he told her in that same soft voice as he reached out to undo the buttons on her shirt. His fingers brushed her breasts through the thin camisole as the blouse fell open. Charl began to tremble.

'Please!' she whispered imploringly, her eyes fixed on her clasped hands in her lap. He had not touched her in this way since the day Waukee had ridden into camp. Surely he did not intend to begin abusing her again.

He sighed and stood up. 'Madame La Soeur left a wrapper for

you. That bath is yours, too. I will take mine when you have finished,' he informed her, the softness in his voice gone.

'Will you leave while I bathe?' Charl asked as she rose, clutching the soft, pink velvet robe against her chest.

Seth laughed briefly. 'No, but I won't bother you. I have some papers to look over that accumulated while I was away.' He swung into one of the chairs by the table and began opening envelopes and studying the contents.

Convinced that he was really busy, Charl turned her back and began to undress. The tub was large and the water hot and scented. In seconds she forgot Seth's presence as she luxuriated in the soapy warmth. She washed her hair, working up a foamy lather, then scrubbed the rest of her until the gritty, sandy feeling had left her skin. It was wonderful to be really clean again and to bathe in warm water rather than the chilly lake. She sighed with satisfaction.

'Seth,' she said, peering over her shoulder at him, 'could you get me a pitcher of clear water to rinse my hair, please?'

He looked startled by her request but got up without comment and went obediently, leaving his papers spread out on the table. Charl stared after him in surprise. She was not sure what response she had expected, but his compliance startled her. Before she could ponder it, he was back to help her rinse away the soap and solicitously hand her towels. Then he began to empty and refill the tub, obviously anxious for his own bath.

Charl slipped into the worn, pink velvet wrapper, tying it as best she could. Madame La Soeur was a much smaller woman, and the robe was too short and fell open, revealing more breast and thigh than Charl would have wished. Still it had been generous to offer what had once been a very expensive garment for Charl's use.

She took the hairbrush from the jumble of Seth's belongings that had been dumped from the saddlebags on to the top of the chest. It was strange to realize that in the past days his things had become hers as well. Settling herself on the bed, she began to brush her hair dry with long strokes that began at the nape of the neck and moved towards the already curling ends an arm's length away.

Seth stripped unself-consciously, leaving his clothes slung over a chair, and slid into the tub with a satisfied sigh. He sat motionless for a few minutes as if deep in thought, then began to wash industriously, whistling under his breath. Through the curtain of hair she watched his movements. His back was to her, and she enjoyed the flex and slide of his muscles under the sun-bronzed skin as he scrubbed. She could see the heavy cording across his wide shoulders, the angle of his shoulder blades, and the valley of his spine. She watched the broad slope of his back, the way it narrowed as it went downwards across his ribs and disappeared below the level of the water. She liked the way the thick, blond hair curled shaggily down his strong, brown neck. When he turned, she could see a bit of his profile, too, and the lines of his jaw covered with the newly grown mat of red-gold beard. Watching him, she felt curiously warm, and she found she wanted to reach out and touch him. Her hair brushing had slowed as she studied him, and she started when he spoke her name.

'Charlotte,' he said, without glancing at her, 'will you wash my back?'

Colour crept up in her cheeks as if she had been caught doing something wrong, and she stammered, 'Oh Seth! I'd really rather not.'

He turned to glare at her, his mouth tight. She came to her feet. It was really not worth arguing about, she chided herself.

She reached over his shoulder for the soap, brushing against him accidentally, and a tingle raced through her. She was suddenly very aware of him sitting naked before her, and she flushed in confusion. With as much composure as she could muster, she began to soap his back. It was impossible not to notice the texture of his skin under her hands and his clean, male scent that rose up to meet her. Dizzily, she wondered what would happen if she leaned against him and slipped her hands down to caress the planes of his chest. Her fingers ached to slide down his rock-hard arms and to feel his muscles tighten under her palms. And with a clarity that startled her, she remembered the feel of his lips burning on hers.

Good heavens, she thought. What was the matter with her? This was Seth Porterfield, the man she hated. How could she possibly contemplate the touching and stroking that would inevitably end in his possession of her? It was shameful to think such things. But below her outrage, the deep core of honesty within her could not deny the wild, uncontrolled attraction she felt for this particular man, and she had to admit to herself that he stirred her in a way she could not fully comprehend, that even while she hated him, she wanted him in a primitive, wanton way that she could not control. That knowledge shook her to the very base of her beliefs. She had never meant to want any man, least of all one who took from her things she was not willing to give. Still she could not deny that she felt drawn to Seth. On the heels of that realization came the conviction that he must never suspect how she felt. She could never show him this weakness because he would surely use it against her, just as he had used all her weaknesses in the past.

'That feels good,' Seth said in a voice that was heavy and relaxed. His words abruptly brought Charl back to what she was doing, and she nearly dropped the flannel. He must not guess what she was thinking, caution whispered. She began to wash away the soap briskly.

'You were more gentle a minute ago,' he complained. She answered noncommittally and dropped the cloth into the tub with a splash when she was done. He scowled at her for splashing him, and she giggled as she returned to the bed.

He emerged from the tub and padded to the window, leaving puddling footprints on the polished floor and drying himself languorously. He was like a graceful, tawny cat, she thought, stretching and basking in the late afternoon sun. Somehow she could not help watching him. He turned unexpectedly to meet her eyes, and a flush crept into her cheeks. Smiling, he came towards her, a large towel knotted around his hips. The bed gave under his weight as he sat down beside her. Charl felt her heart begin to race, but she sat perfectly still, keeping her face slightly averted.

His hand cupped her chin, and he turned her face to his. 'You are so beautiful, Charlotte!' he said softly, warmly, meltingly. 'God knows I will probably be sorry that I brought you here with me, but right now I'm not.'

'Seth, please!' she breathed, a strange fluttering beginning in her.

'Please what, Charlotte?'

'Oh, please don't. Please don't do that.'

His thumb slid gently up and down the side of her neck, and she felt the heat rise in her. It should not be so easy for him to do this to her, she told herself. Still she sat motionless while his fingers traced feather-light patterns on her face and throat. One index finger brushed her partly open mouth, and she closed her eyes, waiting for his lips. They came down on hers a moment later, not roughly as she had come to expect his kisses to be, but gently and with a strange tenderness to their touch. His kisses were not a demand now, but a question asked over and over until her blood boiled with the response. Surrender came with a sweet, searing pain that rose from her loins, up through her body and down her arms, leaving her weak in his embrace.

It doesn't matter, her whirling mind whispered, and the hatred that had been written on her soul was erased by her need. Leisurely, he opened her robe to explore her body, as if he was seeing it for the first time, lingering over her breasts and between her thighs. Charl was swept along, touching him, stroking him, moving in concert with him as if part of some passionate ballet. She gave herself to him completely only because she could hold nothing back. They came together with exquisite slowness, and he entered her gently in a way that was both fulfilment and promise.

She looked up at him with wide green eyes, misty with tenderness and passion, and softly caressed his bearded cheek. Her fingers trailed down his neck and across his chest, and she felt him tremble. The trembling came in Charlotte, too, and they began to move together. From that moment there were no thoughts, only sensations raging through them. Then there was a warmth glowing inside her, burning along her limbs, that ignited violently, carrying her up in an incandescent blaze of passion that seemed to fuse them together. Seth took her higher still, until she felt she would be torn apart by the sweet chaos inside her own body. Wildly, she called out his name, clinging to him, her fingers biting into the muscles of his shoulders as they began the dizzying spiral downwards together.

They lay for a long time in the growing darkness, unable or unwilling to say anything that would break the drowsy bond that held them together. Seth refused to let the realities of his life intrude upon these few minutes with Charlotte, and he was content to simply stroke her hair. She was the most sweetly passionate woman he had ever known. She instinctively understood that giving and receiving pleasure were inextricably mixed, and when she abandoned herself to him, as she had this afternoon, she truly sought to please him. For that brief time they were simply Charlotte and Seth with no doubts or loyalties or suspicions to spoil what passed between them. He pressed his cheek against her hair, breathing her sweet, lemon fragrance, and wished that they would never return to their former roles. But too much had passed between them. He sighed. They had these few minutes, at least.

'Seth?' came the soft voice at his shoulder.

'Don't speak,' he whispered, rolling towards her and sliding his forearm under her head. His mouth found hers in the dark, and he kissed her slowly, savouring her honeyed lips. They could not return to their former roles just yet, he decided. His free hand came to the crest of one full breast, and he began to stroke it gently as his tongue sought hers. He felt the excitement grow in her, and his desire rose to match it. For a few more minutes this physical bond between them could keep reality at bay, he thought. Then her hands came to caress him, and for a long time he was lost in unthinking passion.

✻

The hazy grey light filtering into the bedroom woke Seth, and he lay drowsily enjoying the comfort of the feather bed after so many nights of sleeping on the ground. He was hopelessly tangled with the fair-haired girl who shared his bed, and he smiled contentedly as he watched her. Even after the night they had shared, he found her desirable, with her peachy-gold skin and the tangle of pale hair pooled on the pillow. Still, he knew there were matters to be settled, and he must get up. Gently, he tried to extricate himself, moving one slender arm from across his chest and sliding his leg from under her thigh. Her head was on his shoulder, and his wrist was shackled by one curling, golden lock. When he drew away, she opened her eyes questioningly.

'Sleep,' he whispered, brushing her lips softly, but her arms came up to hold him, and he was drawn back down beside her. His pulse quickened, and it was with great reluctance that he pulled away.

'I must go, Charl. I have things to attend to that cannot wait. Sleep a while longer; I'll send someone up with breakfast.'

'When will you be back?' she asked, unwilling to be left alone in this strange house.

'I'm not sure. Be patient, and I'll bring you a present,' he promised, smiling into her heavy-lidded eyes.

'Where?' she began, but he cut her short with a kiss.

'I have no more time for questions,' he told her lightly. 'Back to sleep with you.'

'Yes, Seth,' she answered, sounding strangely obedient as she nestled back into the pillows.

Quietly, he washed and dressed, tucking the papers from the table inside the campaign chest and locking it. It would not do for Charl to see them. Although their contents were not incriminating, she was quick-witted enough to see discrepancies between what he had told her and what they said. He felt restless this morning, tensed and jumpy with anticipation. He would be meeting Mitchell's man at the Place d'Armes at nine o'clock right under the noses of the British. Perhaps after he knew what would be expected of him in the coming weeks, he could relax; but now he was plagued with uncertainty. With a last look at the sleeping girl, he left.

Seth clattered down the stairs, aware that the other members of the household were already up and about their duties. Gabrielle La Soeur was alone in the kitchen at the rear of the house when Seth entered. He slid onto the bench across the table from her and greeted her cheerily.

She looked up from her coffee as he sat down and arched one black eyebrow at him.

'You certainly seem well rested,' she observed dryly. 'It is a shame you slept through supper last night, though. Marie made her special veal stew, and it was delicious.'

Unaccountably, Seth felt himself flush and was puzzled that her teasing bothered him. 'May I have a cup of coffee?' he requested gruffly to cover his discomfort.

The woman rose to pour him a steaming cupful and set a plate of croissants in front of him on the wide trestle table, eyeing him silently. He took one, broke it in two, and buttered both halves with deliberate motions. He paused to sip the strong, dark coffee, then ate one of the halves.

'You would like to know what the girl is doing here, wouldn't you, Gabby?' he said finally.

'I will gladly extend my hospitality to any of your friends, Seth, with no questions asked. You know that,' she answered noncommittally.

He studied her across the table. She had changed little in the past fifteen years since he had first come to live in this house as a boy, and he could see why William Porterfield had come to love her. She carried her small frame gracefully and seemed to possess a tranquillity of spirit that made her pale face seem always serene. Her inky dark hair was carefully knotted at the back of her head, with never a strand out of place, and her eyes were flat and candid. Nothing ever seemed to ruffle Gabrielle, and she had been good for William all those years ago. She had tamed his volatile nature as nothing or no one had ever been able to do. If he had lived, things would have been very different for her. She would have been the wife of a ranking British officer, treasured and cared for, not a widow alone, subsisting on the money from the sale of her husband's blacksmith's shop and the stipend William left in her name. Seth paid for the room and his meals, but he was well aware of how difficult it was for her to make ends meet. But somehow she managed to feed and clothe them all, though the house was badly in need of repairs.

Gabrielle La Soeur was a rare woman, strong, resourceful, intelligent. And trustworthy, he added to the list that until then had also described the girl who slept upstairs. His thoughts came abruptly back to the problem at hand. He must talk to Gabby about Charl.

He sipped his coffee absently and took another croissant, unaware of the half left in front of him. He wondered how much he should tell her. He frowned. Regardless of what he said, she would surmise the rest.

He had not been able to keep his work for Mitchell a secret from her for long, and he had come to trust her implicitly. Occasionally she had even carried messages to other agents for him. Gabby felt no loyalty to the British rule in Lower Canada, as was the case with many of the old Quebecois families, and he knew he was safe in this house. His greatest fear was that she and her family might somehow come under suspicion because of their association with him, so they maintained the fiction that he was no more than a boarder of long standing. On the surface it was a convincing ploy, but any kind of a deep investigation would easily reveal the truth. He had made plans twice to leave, but Gabrielle would not let him go. He understood her reasons. In Seth she held the last tangible association with William Porterfield, the man she still loved, and she could not bring herself to break that bond.

He looked up from his musing to find Gabby still quietly sipping her coffee. He motioned for another cupful, and when she had poured it, he began.

'The girl is an American. I abducted her when she tried to

prevent my escape from Youngstown the night we heard about the war.'

'Pardon me, but why were you forced to escape from your own country?' she queried, her eyebrows drawn together.

'I posed as a British spy to obtain information. Mitchell thought the ploy worked so well that I should continue it. Charl was certainly convinced,' he explained wryly.

'Oh,' she said, resting her small pointed chin in one hand, waiting for him to go on.

'I planned to send her home from York, but by the time we arrived, there was no way I could do that.' He paused, frowning abstractedly. 'So I had no choice but to bring her here with me. Perhaps I will be able to arrange passage for her from Quebec, or I could take her back to Youngstown myself if the opportunity arises.

'The journey here was difficult for Charl, but she adapted well to the way we were forced to travel. The passage down the river is not easy at the best of times –' His voice trailed off as he remembered her lovely face highlighted by the flames as she cooked over the campfire and her slim back straining with effort as they paddled through the rain. The hint of a smile curved his hard mouth.

'Do you love her?' Gabrielle asked quietly, observing the change in his expression.

The question knifed through his thoughts, and Seth was both startled by the idea and shocked by the implications. His eyebrows rose as he stared at Gabrielle, and at first he could not think of a thing to say.

'I thought that because she shares your bed –' she went on calmly, but Seth suddenly found his voice.

'Good God! No! I don't love Charlotte! She's the most difficult woman I've ever met.' He laughed. 'Nor does she love me. As a matter of fact she tells me with some regularity that she hates me. In a way I can't blame her. I've hardly played the gallant where she's concerned.'

'But you keep her with you –'

'Only to be sure she's safe. Charl has a penchant for trouble,' he explained.

'I see.' Gabrielle said slowly. 'Then it's very noble of you indeed to keep her by your side all night just to keep her from some scandalous misadventure.'

Seth felt the colour rise in his face. This conversation was clearly not headed in the direction he had intended it to go. He changed his approach.

'Gabby, Charl knows nothing about what I am doing in Quebec, and I must ask you to help me keep her from discovering the truth.'

'I will not tell her anything,' the woman stated flatly.

'I don't mean to suggest that you would.' He paused. 'Charl is not a stupid girl. Any misplaced word, any inflection could give me away. Even the children could say something that might make her suspicious. If it were not so important, I would not ask this.'

'What is it?'

'Gabby, I want you, Marie, and the children to speak only French when Charl is within earshot.'

'Only French? That is not difficult; we speak French most of the time as it is. But your Charlotte will not be able to understand a single word!'

'Exactly,' he nodded.

'Surely you realize how isolated that will make her feel.'

'I know.' Seth sighed, sounding genuinely sorry. 'But this is the only way I can be sure that she won't discover too much about me. My life could very well depend on this, Gabby,' he prompted her.

'But why can't you tell her the truth? It is her country you fight for, isn't it? Surely she would not betray you,' the woman reasoned.

Seth's brows rushed together. 'Will you do as I ask, or won't you?' he demanded as he came to his feet. His face was stormy and his jaw was set. For a moment Gabrielle La Soeur was stunned by his resemblance to William Porterfield. How often she had seen that same expression on William's face, she thought, and how often she had watched it soften with tenderness.

She sighed. 'I will do as you ask.'

'Good,' Seth replied. 'I must leave now. I would be grateful if you took Charl some breakfast in a little while.' He turned to go.

'I'm sorry, Gabby. I wish it was not necessary to treat Charl this way, but it is. Believe me.'

Gabrielle watched his broad back disappear down the corridor and heard the front door close behind him. She was amazed by Seth's uncanny resemblance to William. Sitting across the table from him just now, she could almost imagine that William had returned to her. Dear God! How long had it been since William was killed? Could it possibly be twelve years, twelve years of loneliness and longing? And how long would it be until the memories faded? It seemed like only yesterday that the tall British officer had brought his nephew to board with them. Seth had been fifteen then, tall, all arms and legs, with a closed, wary look around the eyes. And there had been William, dashing and splendid in his scarlet tunic and black shako. She remembered how immense he'd seemed when she opened the door for him. He'd carried Seth's heavy trunk on one shoulder, as if it weighed nothing at all. William had heard that René La Soeur, the blacksmith at the fort, had rooms to rent, and he had taken one for his nephew who was soon to be arriving from England.

Gabrielle had loved William from that first meeting. Her noble, but impoverished Quebecois family had been pleased with the match they had arranged for her with the enterprising blacksmith, and René had been a good husband. She had been happy with him, and she loved Monique and Anne. But then the handsome British officer had intruded on her life, and everything had changed.

For the first few months he came often to spend time with his nephew, and she watched him win over the aloof, defensive young man. A warm, friendly bond grew slowly between Seth and his young uncle, and it pleased her to see how patient William was with him. She had heard stories from René about the notorious Lieutenant Porterfield, about his gambling and his excesses with liquor and women. But she was sure that any man who made the effort to gain the trust of such a difficult boy was a good man at heart. Bit by bit she began to join William and Seth as they talked quietly in the garden. Occasionally, when the girls were napping and Seth was busy studying, she was able to talk to William alone. These were the moments she treasured.

Then suddenly René was dead, his skull crushed by a horse he was shoeing, and in her confusion Gabrielle turned to William. She was a woman alone, barely twenty-two, with two small children and a baby on the way, and she needed a man's help. Under William's guidance, she sold the blacksmith shop and invested the money so she would have a small steady income. William and Seth worked together to make repairs on the house and stable, and soon William was spending all his off-duty hours at the little house on ruelle du Porche.

She could see the change William's presence effected on Seth. The young man was learning to handle weapons and tools and studying military history in preparation for his induction into William's troop on his sixteenth birthday. Under William's encouragement and praise, Seth seemed to develop a pleasant, easygoing manner that was a vast improvement over his moodiness. Monique and Anne thrived, too, and William seemed unaccountably at home in the role of surrogate father. When Seth went west with the surveyors after being denied admission to William's unit by Felix St James, Gabby feared she would no longer see William. But he continued to arrive as often as his duties would permit, and after the birth of Jean-Louis they became lovers.

Gabby had never known more happiness than she knew during those two years. She and William had planned to be married when he received his next promotion, but he had died before their dreams could be realized. He had left her with memories and a trust fund in the amount of his small inheritance. For, although he was from a wealthy family, as second son he had no claim on the vast Porterfield fortune.

Gabrielle wiped the tears from her eyes and blew her nose. It had been a long time since she had cried for William. It was just that Seth had reminded her so much of him, sitting across the table from her as William used to do. Seth had that same look about him. The Porterfield look, William had called it: the strong, long-boned build, the brilliant blue eyes, the sharply defined features, and the cleft chin. There was a startling similarity between the two men that reminded her, more clearly than she wished, of the happiness that had almost been hers.

With a final, determined sniff she put away her handkerchief. It did no good at all to cry, she chided herself. She squared her small shoulders and took down a tray, turning away from the memories by activity. Seth Porterfield had brought a strange woman into her home, and Gabrielle was avidly curious about her. She had promised Seth that she would speak only French to the girl, and she would keep her word. But sometimes the difference in language was not the barrier one would expect. Quickly Gabrielle put together a breakfast tray with fresh blueberries and cream, several golden brown croissants, and fresh churned butter.

To this she added a large pot of tea, sugar, and two of her best china cups. She picked up the tray and moved steadily upstairs. There was much to be learned about Charlotte Beckwith, and it was obvious she would not learn it from Seth.

Fourteen

✳✳✳

Even the brilliant sunlight already probing into the narrow streets of Lowertown could not relieve Seth's restive mood. He would be glad when he made contact with Mitchell's man and knew exactly what was in store for him in the next months. Only then could he begin to resolve the rest of his situation. As he climbed the Champlain stairs towards Uppertown, he thought ruefully of the girl he had left sleeping in the house on ruelle du Porche. Much of her future, as well as his, depended on the outcome of this meeting.

He was not totally satisfied with the promise of silence he had forced from Gabrielle, and he knew he was being unfair to Charl. But, in light of the girl's unpredictable nature, he could not let her guess his reasons for being in Quebec. Perhaps Gabby was right; it might soon be necessary to tell Charl the truth about his mission. After all, he was here on behalf of her country, and she should be willing to keep his secret for that reason if not because of any loyalty she felt towards him. Still, he could not dismiss the strong feeling that telling Charl the truth would be a grave mistake. He scowled absently at his own thoughts, unaware of the cheerful greeting from a shopkeeper who was sweeping the steps outside his store.

Damn! Whatever had possessed him to bring the girl with him, he wondered for what must have been at least the hundredth time. He would not be in such a quandary if he had only himself to consider. Why was it that she alone had the power to thwart him and divert him from his purpose? What was it about her that sent all his carefully laid plans awry? Her presence in Quebec could easily turn this mission into a disaster; he would have to be wary of everything he said or did.

Even while he cursed her, a vision of her softly contoured face rose up before him, and a smile tugged at the corners of his mouth as he remembered the pleasures of the night. Damn her, he found himself thinking, damn me. Perhaps the dangers and inconveniences she represented were worth the risks after all.

He was a bit early for the rendezvous and circled around to enter the Place d'Armes from the eastern end. At this hour it was full of people, and it was not difficult for Seth to lose himself in the crowd. Moving easily between groups of farmers, businessmen, and soldiers, he surveyed the two imposing structures that fronted on the square. Before him, clinging to the edge of the cliff, was the fortresslike Château St Louis, standing grey and austere just as it had since the first half of the seventeenth century. In earlier days it had served as the residence of the governors of Lower Canada, but now it was used primarily for civil and military offices. Beside it rose the governor's current home, a stately mansion built some forty years earlier to meet the growing social demands of the office. It was here that Sir George Prevost lived and ran the affairs of the province. Behind the mansion was a carefully tended formal garden that was opened on Sundays for the enjoyment of the citizenry.

Seth lounged against the wall of one of the lesser buildings that edged the square and intently watched the milling people, seeking a face he might recognize in the crowd. There were all manner of people here this morning, moving to and fro, greeting their friends and pausing in the sunshine to talk before disappearing down side streets to go on about their business. From across the square came an English officer, resplendent in his scarlet coat and grey trousers, his cocked hat tilted rakishly over one eye. He was striding purposefully through the square, oblivious to the groups that drifted across his path. Something about the man's lean, sinewy body and stiff-shoulder carriage drew Seth's attention and kindled painful memories. From the distance he could clearly see the deep auburn hair of the man's sideburns and the distinctive aquiline profile. Seth stiffened. This was the man he hated most in the world, Felix St James.

Natural caution, more than common sense, kept him from approaching the other man, but his eyes never left that hard, gaunt face.

Some day, he vowed, some day, St James, you will pay for William's murder. As he watched the officer's progress, hatred seeped like miasmic vapours into his brain, obscuring everything but the searing desire for revenge. Hardly breathing, Seth saw

the sentry snap to attention as St James approached and disappeared into the Château St Louis. After the British major was
gone, Porterfield became slowly aware that he had gone rigid,
clenching his fists at his sides and trembling with suppressed fury;
with an effort he forced himself to relax.

So St James was still in Quebec. It was not really surprising.
His appointment as royal envoy to the military staff of Quebec
was a recent one, but it had startled Seth to see him nonetheless.
As his head cleared, Seth realized how important it was to avoid
any future contact between them. In the past St James had gone
out of his way to make trouble for Seth, and he had been
responsible for William's death. Why the man harboured such
hatred for the two Porterfields Seth did not know, but he could
not afford to draw the attentions of such a man to his current
activities. And then, too, there was the stolen paper with St
James' signature that he had used to gain admittance to Fort
George. If he found out about that, he could raise some very
dangerous questions. At the time its use had seemed like a
harmless ploy, but then he had not expected to be sent back to
Quebec.

Determinedly he turned his thoughts to the business at hand,
putting Felix St James out of his mind for the moment. With great
care he scanned the square and almost immediately recognized a
burly, roughly dressed tradesman as someone who had contacted
him before. Gradually, he fell into step about ten yards behind
the man and then followed at a safe distance as they turned right
out of the square and proceeded downhill past the Quebec
Seminary with its high, iron gates. Ducking into a shadowed
alley, the tradesman waited for Seth.

'Third door on the right,' he instructed, then turned on his
heel and was swiftly out of sight.

Seth entered the narrow, dark building without knocking and
moved cautiously to a set of double doors on his left. He tensed,
thrust one open, and stepped inside the darkened room.

Sitting on a chair by the far wall he could see a man silhouetted
in the dimness. His heart lurched as he realized that man was
slowly levelling a pistol at him. Instinctively, Seth reached for
the knife tucked into his boot, freezing in mid-motion as the
sound of the pistol being cocked echoed in the empty room.

'What is your code name?' came the voice from the darkened
corner.

Seth straightened. 'Coeur de Lion,' he answered.

The man gave a short laugh. 'Another of Mitchell's noble allusions, I see. You may light the candle, Porterfield.' The lone candle sitting on an upturned box came to life, and Seth had the impression that the man whose face was hidden in the shadow of a wide-brimmed hat was studying him in its pale yellow glow.

'I think I would have known you from Mitchell's description,' he said finally.

'Who are you?' Seth asked.

'Joubert,' came the reply. Seth coolly raised one eyebrow. Mitchell's second in command, he thought. This mission must be something important.

'We had begun to despair that you might not arrive in time. I understand that you were reluctant to return to Quebec with a war on.' There was a hint of scorn in the soft voice, but Seth chose to ignore it.

'That is true,' Seth conceded, wondering how that particular bit of information had reached Quebec so quickly, 'but Mitchell can be very persuasive. I left Youngstown the night we heard about the declaration of war.'

'And when was that?' came the faceless voice.

'June 27.'

Joubert whistled softly under his breath, shaking his head from side to side in disbelief.

'Well, you are here in time at least.'

'In time for what?' Seth questioned, his eyes probing the darkness under the hatbrim.

'The last of the Americans who have been living in Quebec sail at dawn tomorrow for New York. They were to leave July 1, but fortunately Prevost extended the deadline by fourteen days.' Joubert paused to lean forward in his chair, and for an instant the candle flame reflected in his eyes. They glowed like embers in the shadowed face, and then the reflection died. 'We have reserved a space for a Mr Seth Porterfield, a lumber merchant.'

A baiting smile curved Seth's mouth. 'Then it is fortunate I arrived.'

Joubert ignored the insolent comment.

'I understand you received a packet from a man upstream. Is that correct?'

'Yes.'

'We also have a good deal of information for you to carry to Mitchell in New York. Is it also correct that you remember everything you are asked to carry?'

'That is correct.'

'I have never heard of such an ability, but Mitchell seems to have great faith in it,' Joubert said, taking a sheaf of papers from a large leather envelope on the floor and handing them to Seth. 'What must you do?'

'Read them over,' Seth told him simply, moving closer to the light. Silence fell in the tiny room as Seth's eyes moved slowly over the pages, memorizing their contents. Finally he handed them back to Joubert.

'Are you finished?' he asked.

'Do what you will with those,' Seth said, smiling slightly. 'The facts are safe.'

Joubert went on dubiously. 'The most important things to tell Mitchell are –'

'That two thousand troops are arriving in Quebec the first week in August and that twelve thousand militiamen can be mustered in the event of an attack up the Hudson. You needn't worry, Joubert,' Seth assured him.

He could sense a frown on the other man's face. 'You were selected for this assignment, Porterfield, because of this strange ability of yours and because you were granted United States citizenship and have the papers to prove it.' Joubert paused, then took several more papers from the leather folder and extended them to Seth. 'These will augment your proof of citizenship. They state your reasons for being in Quebec and include your permit to buy and transport lumber products.'

Seth bent his head and seemed to be going over the documents carefully. Ever since Joubert had told him where he was being sent, his mind had been working feverishly on a plan to take Charl with him. This seemed like the perfect opportunity to return her to the States. If he could take her as far as New York, Mitchell would see that she reached Youngstown safely.

'I will also need travelling passes for a young American lady who will be accompanying me,' he mentioned casually, not glancing up from the permits.

Joubert's voice deepened angrily. 'Surely you are mad, Porterfield!' he exclaimed. Seth stared at him blankly, as if he didn't know how difficult it would be to prepare the necessary papers on such short notice.

'I will not take the risks to get forged papers so your whore can travel with you,' Joubert snapped.

Seth subdued the quick stirring of anger. 'The young lady is not my whore,' he stated crisply, 'but the daughter of an influential American. Unfortunately she was visiting in Canada when the border closed and has not been able to return to her home. I am sure that Mitchell would want you to help her.'

'Is it true?' Joubert asked speculatively.

'Yes,' he answered levelly. The circumstances of Charl's 'visit' were none of Joubert's business.

There was a long silence between the two men as Joubert watched Seth, waiting for any small betrayal in expression or demeanour. There was none.

'Perhaps the papers could be taken care of in time,' Joubert said. With difficulty Seth hid the gleam of triumph that flashed in his eyes. This was working out perfectly, and it would be better than anything he could arrange on his own. With any luck at all he would be able to turn Charl over to Mitchell in two weeks' time, and he would be free of her disturbing presence.

'Of course, her papers would have to be in order, too,' Joubert went on.

Seth looked up sharply. 'She was visiting Canada. She has no papers of her own; there was no reason for her to have any proof of citizenship with her.'

The other man's voice was cold and conclusive. 'Then there is nothing to be done,' he stated with finality.

Seth's eyebrows rushed together, and his scowling look was full of anger.

'I intend to take the girl with me, Joubert. If you will not help me, I'll find some other way to do it!' Seth threatened.

'No! I forbid it!' Joubert answered sharply, coming to his feet. His flushed face was visible for an instant in the candlelight.

'This mission is too important for you to jeopardize on behalf of some woman. This information must reach New York as soon as possible, and you represent our best chance of getting it there. Think of how many lives depend on this.'

Joubert paused in his pacing and turned to face Seth. His eyes burned out of the shadows. 'I don't care whose daughter she is! You will not take her on-board that ship! We know papers will be checked and rechecked before the voyage begins. For God's sake, man, listen to reason! Should they find any irregularities in your papers, you will both end up in the dungeon at Château St Louis if they don't hang you first.' Joubert paused. 'If the risk does not matter to you, think of the girl. How do you think the British will treat her if they suspect she is an American spy?'

The men glared at each other across the tension-charged room. Rationally, Seth knew Joubert spoke the truth, but it was difficult to put aside what had seemed like a perfect opportunity to return Charl to her father. His desire to be free of her had coloured his judgement, and he had not considered the dangers he would expose her to if he took her with him. The image Joubert conjured up of Charl at the hands of an officer like Felix St James was a sobering one and made him realize his folly. He could take chances with his own life, but it was wrong to endanger Charl or this vital mission to further his own interests. Why hadn't he been able to see that from the first? Once again, he had proved that Charl could destroy his objectivity and drive him to make foolish mistakes.

'Perhaps when you return to Quebec, we will be able to help the girl,' Joubert offered, sensing the struggle going on behind the other man's eyes.

'You're right, of course,' Seth admitted evenly, his expression carefully masked. 'She will be quite safe here until we arc able to make other arrangements.'

They concluded their business quickly with the transfer of passage tickets and a large sum of money.

'Mitchell will contact you at the City Hotel in New York,' Joubert told him finally and extended his right hand to Seth.

'I wish you luck, Coeur de Lion. Perhaps some of Mitchell's allusions are correct after all. It is quite gallant of you to offer your protection to a young lady in such dire straits and to fight so valiantly for her passage home. We will see to her needs in the future, I promise you. In the meantime, she must consider herself fortunate that you are seeing to her safety.'

Seth stared speechlessly at the other man as he slipped quietly out the door, closing it silently behind him. Suddenly Seth laughed aloud at Joubert's words. Gallant indeed! Charlotte certainly would not agree with Joubert's assessment of their situation. He laughed again, somewhat bitterly, as he realized that he would somehow have to explain his forthcoming absence to Charl. She would never accept it without question, and he would need to steel himself for the argument that was sure to come. He shrugged. He had tried to secure her passage to the States, and he had failed. He could do no more than that. Quietly, he left the room, turning his thoughts to the myriad other matters to be settled by dawn tomorrow.

❧

When the knock came on the door to Seth's room, Charl was sitting in the centre of the wide bed, clutching the covers around her. She had been vainly trying to reconcile the events of the night with the feelings of anger and abandonment that morning had brought. It seemed impossible that Seth could have treated her so tenderly and then simply left her to shift for herself in a strange, unfriendly place. By now she should be used to such treatment, she reminded herself, but somehow she had expected more consideration from him in this case.

The knock came again.

'Just a minute!' she called out as she searched through the tangle of bedcovers for the pink wrapper. Silently, she prayed that whoever was outside would understand her tone of voice, if not her words, and wait until she answered the door. Belting the robe around her, she crossed the room.

'Bonjour,' Madame La Soeur greeted her as she entered the room carrying a tray of food.

'Good morning,' Charl responded with the logical reply.

'Désirez-vous le petit déjeuner?' the dark-haired woman asked, motioning towards the tray.

Charl nodded. Gabby moved smoothly to the table and set the tray down in front of one of the chairs, then seated herself in the other.

Charl flushed in confusion. Was she to eat her breakfast with this strange woman watching her? Gabrielle took one fragile china teacup and saucer from the tray, placed it in front of herself, and lifted the pewter teapot.

'Du thé?' she asked.

Charl sank into the other chair in amazement. Madame La Soeur was going to join her for breakfast, and she was treating the occasion as formally as any tea party Charl had ever attended. Mutely she nodded.

'Oui, s'il vous plaît.'

'Oui, s'il vous plaît,' Charl repeated, her eyes wide.

Gabby smiled warmly at the girl. 'Du sucre?' she asked, offering the sugar bowl.

'No,' Charl said.

'Non, merci,' Gabrielle nodded encouragingly.

'Non, merci,' came Charl's echo.

Gabby set the sugar next to the teapot on the table and pushed the tray an inch or two closer to Charl.

'Mangez!' she ordered.

The meaning of the simple command was obvious to Charl. She quickly smoothed the napkin onto her lap and picked up her spoon, realizing that she was famished. She had eaten nothing since breakfast yesterday, and the flaky crescent-shaped rolls and purple berries floating in cream looked delicious. Only good manners kept her from wolfing them down.

Sipping her tea Gabrielle watched Charl eat. Trust Seth Porterfield to abduct a beautiful woman, she observed with a small smile. Yesterday it had been difficult to tell about the girl's looks. Her hair had been tucked up under a shapeless felt hat; she had been dirty and had worn men's clothes. But now, clean and dressed in the pink wrapper, she was exquisite. Her hair was like sunset and moonbeams, red and pale gold in the light, and her complexion had that same healthy golden pink glow. Her features were strong, even, lovely, and her eyes were large and expressive behind the sweep of dark lashes. This Charlotte was a large woman, tall and solidly built. A perfect match for Seth's towering form, Gabrielle found herself thinking. The wrapper did little to conceal the girl's high, full breasts. Still her figure was slim, with a small waist and shapely legs. She was obviously every inch a lady, and a spirited one, too, if Gabby had correctly guessed at the things Seth omitted from his story. She smiled again, wondering if in this handsome woman the formidable Mr Porterfield had met his match. Unaware of the thoughts behind Gabrielle's smile, Charl smiled back.

'Thé, s'il vous plaît,' Charl said slowly, using almost her entire French vocabulary.

Gabby laughed with delight. 'Bien, Charlotte!'

'Charl,' she corrected.

'Gabrielle.'

The women smiled warmly at each other for a minute, then Charl's eyes clouded. This woman's kindness only reminded her of how isolated she was here in Quebec. She realized once again how far she was from her home and loved ones and how dependent she was on Seth's vacillating moods. A stifling wave of homesickness rose in her chest, but she valiantly fought it down. When she looked back at Gabrielle, she could see compassion and concern in her dark eyes, as if the woman had been able to read Charl's thoughts. Charl wished she could express how much this visit meant to her.

Gabrielle easily saw the confusion and loneliness in Charl's face, and she inwardly cursed Seth for the promise he had extracted from her. The girl clearly deserved better treatment than she was receiving from Seth, and Gabby could not understand his need to deny Charl communication. Gabrielle had an unfailing sense about people, and in the few minutes she had spent with Charl, she had come to like her. The American was bright, well mannered, and spirited. But she was also caught in a situation she could not hope to control. First of all, Charl needed a friend to trust and talk to, Gabby decided. And if they could not talk in English, then they would have to speak in French.

'Attendez!' she said. Charl looked up intently.

'La chambre,' Gabby pronounced clearly, throwing her hands wide to indicate the room.

'La chambre,' Charl repeated, realizing immediately what Gabrielle was doing.

'Bien,' Gabrielle nodded her dark head. 'La chaise,' she said, standing up to point to the chair.

'La chaise.'

'La fenêtre.'

'La fenêtre. The window,' Charl went on.

They continued the lesson for more than an hour. By the time the teapot was empty and Gabrielle rose to go, Charl knew the French words for everything in the room, and a few simple sentences besides.

'Merci, Gabrielle,' Charl said, laying one hand on the older woman's arm.

'Ah, vous êtes mon amie maintenant, Charl,' Gabrielle said smiling.

Charl was unsure of the words, but the meaning was clear. They were friends now.

'Au revoir,' Gabby said, moving to the door, the tray balanced on one hip.

'Au revoir, Gabrielle,' Charl replied.

At the threshold Gabrielle stopped. 'Charl?'

'Seth, sh-sh!' she warned, one finger over her lips.

Charl laughed. 'Oui! Seth sh-sh!' The lessons would be a secret.

Alone in the room once more, Charl spun around happily, hugging herself, her doubts gone for the moment at least. She had found a friend in Gabrielle La Soeur. Granted, they could not talk and share secrets in the usual sense, but that was not to say that they couldn't communicate. And Gabrielle was teaching her French. Charl had always been good at languages, and she prayed that her facility had not deserted her in the years since she had left the schoolroom. Slowly she moved around the bedroom, touching each object and naming it with its new French word. Le mur, the wall. La porte, the door. Le lit, the bed. With each object she was able to name her confidence grew. In learning to say even these first few words in French she was regaining control over her life. Somehow she would manage to live and perhaps even find some happiness in Quebec. Then, in time, she would arrange her passage home. She was sure of it. Humming softly to herself, she began to tidy up the room.

Fifteen
✳✳✳

As Seth made his way along the ramparts towards Lowertown, he paused to look down across the mouth of the Charles River, where it entered the St Lawrence, and watch the busy Quebec harbour. Canoes and rowboats were drawn up along the shore, mackinaws and sloops were tied at the several narrow piers that jutted into the harbour, and the large double and triple-masted ships were anchored in deeper water near the mouth of the channel. Absently, he watched the midmorning activity along the docks as all kinds of merchandise were unloaded for use in the city or transport west. Tomorrow, with luck, he would sail out of this harbour bound for New York, carrying information vital to the United States' war effort. The tension he felt earlier had vanished and in its place was the familiar simmer of excitement in his blood. He welcomed the danger this assignment promised and felt it course like some intoxicant through his body. His facile mind moved over the problems at hand, and he quickly decided on the things that must be done to prepare for the voyage.

His papers and passage had been taken care of for him. That left only his personal needs to meet and Charl to attend to. Frowning, he put thoughts of her aside for the moment. He would need to purchase clothes suitable for a merchant. They should be of good quality, but a man who had undoubtedly risen from a job as either clerk or a lumberjack would lack the polish of a gentleman, and his clothes would reflect that. He should be shaved and barbered, he thought, rubbing one lean knuckle along his bearded jaw. And he would need a trunk of some kind. Even a refugee would be able to bring a few possessions with him. Clothes, books, a few tools, and a ledger or two would make a convincing collection. He knew a forger who could have the ledgers ready by tonight if the price was right. Seth just hoped that no one questioned him too closely about lumbering. He had only a vague idea of how the industry was carried on in the Quebec backwoods and barely knew the difference between a board foot and a footboard.

The larger task would be to provide for Charl in his absence. She would stay in his room at the La Soeur house, of course. He was sure he could depend on Gabby to provide food and lodging for her, but he could not expect Gabrielle to be responsible for Charl's actions. He had not been looking forward to that task himself. Charl was a headstrong woman at the best of times, and the idea of leaving her unattended for what would probably be well over a month made him uneasy. Perhaps he should turn her over to Joubert and let him deal with her fits of temper, Seth thought wryly. After all, it was Joubert's fault that Charl was being left alone in Quebec.

As he stared out across the harbour, his eyes unconsciously sought and found one particular mackinaw tied up along the wharf. He contemplated it thoughtfully. Perhaps Waukee would keep an eye on Charl for him. The two had become friends on the trip downriver, and the Indian seemed to understand the girl in a way Seth never had. The longer he considered this solution, the more sensible it seemed. All he had to do was get Waukee to agree. Determinedly, he walked towards Hope Gate, anxious to see Waukee at the boat and settle the matter of Charlotte Beckwith between them.

As Seth made his way down the narrow, wooden pier, he could see his friend sitting in the boat mending the sail. He was bent over the canvas working with a long curving needle to sew up a two-cornered tear in the flowing cloth. When Seth called a greeting, the Indian looked up in surprise.

'I had not expected to see you for some days,' he said honestly as Seth stepped on to the gunwale and into the mackinaw.

Seth was aware of the wall of reserve that had sprung up between them during the last leg of their journey, and he was suddenly reluctant to ask Waukee for help. Still, he could think of no better alternative. Speculatively, he watched the other man, knowing full well that Charl had caused the breach between them, and for a moment he was at a loss as to how he would bridge the gap. Again Seth frowned. Perhaps Waukee would agree to his request more for Charl's sake than because of their relationship.

His mouth thinned and he drew a long breath. There was nothing to do but explain.

'I have received an assignment that will take me away from Quebec for some weeks,' he began. Briefly, he outlined what he wanted Waukee to do in his absence. The Indian listened without comment until Seth finished, then nodded.

'And is there no way for Charlotte to accompany you?' he inquired. 'It seems an ideal way to return her to Youngstown.'

'None,' Seth stated with finality. 'I wish I could be rid of her so easily, but I cannot take her with me.

'It will be much better for her if you visit her and escort her if she needs to go out. She likes you, and she needs to see at least one friendly face in this city of strangers.'

Waukee stared past Seth to where the sunlight sparkled on the rippling water.

'Yes, she likes me,' he agreed. His eyes came to rest solemnly on Seth's face, and he studied the fair-haired man with great care. What were Seth's real feelings for the girl, Waukee wondered, noting the pucker of discontent on Seth's brow.

Reluctantly he agreed. 'All right, I will do as you ask, Seth. I will see to Charl while you are away.'

'Thank you. I am not pleased with the role I must play, but I have no choice in this matter,' Seth told him sincerely. 'And now I know she will be in good hands.'

The Indian nodded briefly again. 'Tell Charl I will visit her tomorrow.'

'I will.' After a pause Seth turned to go, not knowing what more there was to say.

'Have a safe journey.' Waukee's words came so quietly that Porterfield was not sure he had heard correctly.

Slowly Seth turned back towards the other man, his face softening as he smiled into the Indian's black eyes. He extended his hand, and Waukee gripped it warmly in return. Regardless of what had changed the relationship between the two men, at that moment their friendship was as strong as it had ever been.

From the harbour Seth made his way across Lowertown to rue St Pierre, in whose shops, it was said, a man could find anything he could ever want provided that he had the price to pay for it. Seth needed some new clothes for his role as lumber merchant, and he should buy a few things for Charlotte. She could hardly spend the next weeks in Gabrielle's borrowed wrapper. He wished he had time to take her shopping with him. Her delight over the shops in York had been immense, and Quebec's stores had so much more to offer. It would have pleased him to watch her eyes light at the fashionable gowns and bonnets for sale and the bolts of rich materials available. And he found he was almost sorry that he would not be able to introduce her to the city of Quebec. It would have been a pleasure to share in her explorations of a place that would seem so foreign and exotic to her.

For the first time he realized that he really did not want to leave her. It seemed paradoxical that he had spent the morning trying to rid himself of her, and now he discovered that he did not want to go himself. He frowned, finding that thought vaguely disturbing. But then, he had just grown accustomed to her. What man would not want a woman like her nearby? Charl was a beautiful and spirited creature who intrigued and excited him even while she opposed and infuriated him. And when the time came, he would send her home gladly. Once she was no concern of his, he would forget her.

In the meantime, forgetting her was a luxury he could ill afford. He was not looking forward to telling Charl about the journey, and he certainly could not explain where he was going. Perhaps it would be better to return to the house with a few parcels to divert her, he reasoned. If she was preoccupied with some new clothes, she might be less likely to object to his leaving her alone in Quebec. And, for once, he had the means to be generous. He'd buy her a new dress, or maybe two, he thought with a grin. Whistling to himself he entered a dressmaker's shop.

❧

The tiny second floor room at the La Soeur house grew warm as the late afternoon sun poured through the open window, and the curtains cast undulating shadows on the pine floor. Charl looked up from the book she was reading to watch them curl and flap in the breeze and to wonder, for what must easily be the twentieth time, when Seth would return. There had been only so much to fold and pick up in the tiny room once Jean-Louis had come to take away the tub, and it was by sheer luck that she had stumbled across the cache of books tucked between the handsome burl campaign chest and the wall. Finding them in Seth's room surprised her. He had not struck her as a man who read books, but there was a fine assortment including politics, philosophy, poetry, religion, and literature. They were obviously well read, and there were notations written along the margins of many pages in Seth's hand.

The novel she had selected from the pile helped her pass the time, but as the afternoon came to a close, she grew more and more impatient. It seemed that she had spent too much time lately shut up in strange rooms, waiting for Seth Porterfield to return. Charl rose, leaving the book open on the quilt, and paced restlessly to the window. Where was he, she wondered, her irritation growing.

At that moment there was a noise on the stairs, and Seth nudged the door open with one broad shoulder and entered, his arms filled with parcels. He grinned a greeting at her and dropped the packages on the bed, but Charl could do no more than stare wide-eyed at him.

This did not look like the man who had left this morning. Some strange kind of transformation had occurred while he was gone, and a ripple of uneasiness passed over Charl. The soft mat of beard she had grown to like was gone, and his shaggy, sun-streaked blond hair had been cut short. It made him look faintly boyish, as men with fresh haircuts always did, but there was a severity to the style that seemed somehow staid and stodgy. His suit of clothes heightened the illusion. Both coat and trousers were cut from a sombre grey broadcloth in a style that was slightly outmoded. Nor did they fit well, the coat drawing taut across his wide shoulders and hanging loosely at the waist. The waistcoat and cravat were conservatively black, and there was the air about him of someone who had money but no idea of how to dress.

'What new mischief are you planning?' Charl asked bluntly as she faced him, her hands on her hips.

He smiled down into her suspicious face. 'I would have thought that any woman would want to see her new clothes, before she went on to other matters,' he teased, hoping to buy time.

'Seth Porterfield! I know you, and I know when you're scheming,' she accused hotly.

His smile flashed again, and he spread his hands wide, as if he had nothing to hide. 'I'm only scheming to making you the most beautiful woman in Quebec, and I've bought a few gewgaws to that end. Though, God knows, you don't need them.' His voice had begun to soften, and Charl was tantalizingly aware of the warm current that flowed between them. With an effort she ignored it.

There was something afoot. She was sure of it, and she would not let herself be diverted.

'Seth, why don't you just tell me what this is all about?' she prodded pointedly, raking him from head to toe with cold eyes.

As usual, her stubbornness was making him angry, and he threw away all the soothing words he had planned to say. 'I'm going away tomorrow, and you're staying here,' he announced harshly.

There was a flash of mingled panic and disbelief on her face; then outrage swept away everything.

'Where are you going?' she demanded furiously. 'How dare you drag me hundreds of miles from home and then abandon me?'

'Charl, you might as well stop shrieking like a fishwife and calm down,' he said reasonably, although his eyes were flinty. 'If I had my way, I wouldn't go, but I have no choice in the matter.'

'Calm down! I don't ever intend to calm down. Not while you hold me against my will,' she shouted, trembling in anger. 'You're a cad, Seth! A lying, treacherous, spying . . .'

Her expression showed sudden comprehension, and her eyes narrowed. 'That's it, isn't it? You're going on some vile spying mission and all this,' she swept her hand up and down in a gesture of utter disdain, 'is in the way of some disguise.'

'Where I'm going is no concern of yours.'

'Well, I'll not stay here, waiting for your return like some faithful puppy,' she vowed, the cold weight of panic heavy in her chest. There was a ragged note of hysteria in her voice as she went on. 'I'll run away! I swear I will. I'll find my way back to Youngstown, too. I won't stay alone where I can't even make myself understood, where no one knows me. I mean it, Seth! I won't stay here!'

He reached across the distance that separated them and caught her roughly against his chest, not sure if he meant to subdue or comfort her.

'You have no choice in this either, Charl,' he said fiercely. 'You'll stay here even if I have to leave you locked up in this room!' At his words she began to struggle against his hold, straining to break his grip on her, but he held her fast.

'Do as I say, Charl, and things will go easier for you.'

'You've told me that before,' she whispered, going suddenly still beneath his hands.

'And if you had been wise enough to heed my words, you would have saved yourself a good deal of grief,' he finished quietly.

With grim tenderness he smoothed a stray tendril of hair away from her cheek. Her unexpected vulnerability left a strange, breathless warmth in his middle and made him speak gently to her.

'I've asked Waukee to visit you every day or so, and Gabrielle will see to your needs.' He paused, watching her, but she would not look at him.

'I didn't plan to leave you like this when I brought you to Quebec, but I have no choice. I wish to heaven you could come with me now, but you can't.'

If Charl had been less caught up in her own turmoil, she might have realized the truth in his words and seen the almost bleak expression in his eyes. But only one thought went around and around in her head: Seth was leaving her alone in Quebec. In the face of that realization, all the burgeoning confidence in the future fled, and a suffocating dread rose in her throat. How could he do this to her, she asked herself, fighting back the tears that burned behind her downcast lids. Some day she would repay him tenfold for the things he had done to her.

The silence stretched on and on between them as Seth waited for some reply. The flapping of the curtains seemed as loud as gunshot in the quiet room, and he realized, all at once, that he was holding his breath. He exhaled sharply and frowned down at the woman in his arms.

'Charl,' he began, 'I want your word that you'll be here when I return.'

'No!' she said softly but with a kind of cold finality that raised his ire again.

'You will remain here,' he assured her harshly. 'Since I was fool enough to make myself responsible for you, I intend to see you're safe. As long as you stay in this house, I know I need not worry. And perhaps when I return, I will be able to take you home. Now, I need your word.'

Charl mutely shook her head from side to side, her expression truculent.

Seth's mouth narrowed with exasperation. Damn stubborn vixen, he fumed. How could she seem so vulnerable one minute and be so hard and implacable the next? Well, he would not be taken in by what must be a pretence of weakness or diverted by her soft, melting ways. He'd have her word before he left, or, by God, he would lock her in.

'All right,' he growled, 'have it your way for the moment. I am going downstairs to talk to Gabby. While I am gone, I want you to dress for dinner. I hope the things I bought will fit; I had to guess about sizes.'

'I don't want anything you selected for me!' Charl spat at him as she pulled away, her anger returned.

Seth grinned at her. It was almost good to face her temper after her moments of vulnerability and the rush of confusion they had caused in him. At least he knew how to handle her outbursts.

'Don't you think you'd better see what you're refusing?' he asked as he moved towards the door, his eyes sparkling with mischief.

Charl snatched up a package from the bed and hurled it at him. 'You can't buy my cooperation!' she shouted.

He laughed, noting the attractive flush anger had brought to her cheeks. Slowly he raised one eyebrow and let his gaze move insolently over her. He grinned again, his white teeth flashing in his tanned face, as if he was pleased with what he saw.

'I have no plans to buy any part of you,' he told her, pausing to let his eyes linger on the deep V where the dressing gown strained across her breasts. His smile deepened and he met her angry stare. 'I was thinking of these as more of a rental fee,' he said, as he shut the door.

Charl's face went crimson with the implications of that remark, and she threw several packages at the heavy oak door in frustration. How could Seth be so flippant about their situation? How could he tease her about being his mistress? Didn't he know how she felt about the role he had forced on her? It was obvious she meant nothing to him, or he would be more sensitive to her feelings. At any rate, he needn't be so outspoken about the temporary nature of their relationship. Oh, Seth was odious, she fumed. And now he expected to placate her with a few clothes as if she was a common trollop! As she sat at the edge of the bed, hot, angry tears flooded her eyes, and she clenched her fists in her lap, fighting for control of her emotions.

'Some day, Seth!' she threatened through stiff lips. 'Some day you will pay for my humiliation!'

As her anger cooled, the tears dried, and she found her eyes drawn unwillingly across the floor to where one of the packages had fallen open. Spilling out from between the layers of brown paper were ruffles of pale aqua muslin. Charl poked at them with her toe. Frowning to herself, she bent to pull the dress free of its wrapper, too curious to resist one look. Involuntarily, she sighed as she held the garment up in front of her. It was a lovely gown, pale and fresh and styled in a most becoming fashion. The neckline was low, squared off and edged with the same frothy white lace that trimmed the small puffed sleeves. The skirt fell softly from the high waistline and ended in three tiers of narrow ruffles that were also trimmed with lace.

Unable to stop herself, Charl unbelted the wrapper and dropped it to the floor, then lowered the dress over her head. The fine lawn lining slid softly over her naked body, and she was aware of the sensuous feel of the fabric against her bare skin. The fit was nearly perfect, and she pirouetted in the centre of the room, feeling the gentle sway of the gown on her breasts and thighs. There was no mirror in the tiny, masculine room, but Charl needed no mirrored confirmation. The gown made her feel beautiful, and that was enough.

Without volition, she opened the other packages, exclaiming over the light, cream-coloured cashmere shawl and the petit point reticule. She quickly located a package of underclothes. After removing the aqua gown and laying it gently on the bed, she put on one of the light, lacy batiste chemises and a soft embroidered petticoat. There were sheer lisle stockings in the package, too, and she stroked them up her slim legs and fastened them with ribbon garters.

There were two more dresses in the tumble of packages on the bed, and she tried those on, too. The first was a plain apricot cotton with a black velvet tie at the neck and a drawstring under the breasts. The other was a yellow mull, flowered in blue and green, with a bibbed yoke and long buttoned sleeves. Trailing blue and green ribbons tied at the high waistline, and there were matching ribbons for her hair. All the clothes fitted remarkably well, including the soft black kid slippers that laced across her instep.

Seth had thought of everything (except a nightgown, she realized with a rueful smile). His purchases had included hairpins, rice powder papers, and even scented soap and cologne. There was a tortoise shell comb and brush for her use, too. If she accepted his gifts, there would be little more that she could want, and Charlotte was amazed by his generosity.

She knew that she should not accept the clothes, of course. No lady accepted gifts of clothing from a gentleman. But then, perhaps she could no longer be considered a lady. And she was sure that Seth had never been a gentleman.

She smiled to herself. What a sly devil he was! He knew very well that she could not refuse clothes as lovely as these. And he did have good taste. She would grant him that. But if he thought he could still her protests with these few gowns, he was sadly mistaken. She would keep the new clothes, she decided, but she would accept them as her due, not as a bribe for future favours or as a payment for past mistakes.

※

By the light of the single candle Seth finished shaving and slipped into a clean shirt, neatly tying his cravat. It was several hours before dawn, and he would easily be aboard the American refugee ship by time to sail.

He closed the bone-handled razor, put it and several other personal items into the saddlebags, and buckled them closed. The small trunk he had purchased was packed and waiting for him down by the front door. One quick glance around the room confirmed that he was nearly ready.

He lifted the lid of the campaign chest to return his shaving mirror to its proper place and took out the papers he had tucked inside yesterday. Quickly he skimmed over them and burned all but two of the pages, leaving their smouldering ashes in the empty fireplace. With silent steps he crossed to the dormered window and ran the fingers of his left hand along the edge of the stone sill until he felt a slight, round depression. He pressed gingerly and pulled. Noiselessly, the sill slid forward to reveal a cavity the width of the window and about three inches deep. He had discovered this secret compartment when he was a boy, never imagining then that he would make such good use of it as an adult. From inside he took his citizenship papers and placed them in the pocket with Joubert's passes. Then he tucked the two remaining papers from the trunk inside the opening with a dozen or so others and pushed the sill back into place.

Finally, Seth turned towards the bed where Charl lay deeply asleep. His gaze lingered reluctantly on her face, subtly shadowed in the candlelight: the arched golden eyebrows, the rosy curve of her cheek, the pale coral mouth turned in the slightest of smiles. She would be safe here while he was gone. Mentally, he reviewed the provisions he had made for her in his absence. Gabby would see to Charl's immediate needs. The girl would be sheltered and cared for, and Waukee would come by to offer companionship. The situation was not ideal, but it was the best he could do on such short notice.

In the end, Seth had forced Charl to promise to remain at Gabrielle's until he returned to the city. Looking back, he realized that it had been more through the strength of his will than his powers of persuasion that he had convinced her. And even as he assured her that his demands were being made in the interests of her own safety, he had to admit to himself that his motives were not completely altruistic. Last night, when she had entered the dining room wearing the new aqua gown, he had been dazzled by her beauty, and he had realized, with a shock, just how much he wanted her. The hours they had spent together and the times they had made love were simply too few to satisfy him, and he was not ready to let her go yet.

Later, they had lain in the deep quiet that followed their passionate coupling: curved together like complementing parts of a whole, caught in a contentment that suspended their differences. In those tranquil moments, Seth had gently turned her face to his.

'Charlotte, promise me you'll be here when I return,' he had whispered.

'Oh Seth!' came her voice, thick with confusion and resistance.

'You'll be safe here,' he coaxed softly. 'And when I return, I'll do my best to find you passage to Youngstown.'

Charl had shaken her head, as if trying to resist the intensity of his demand, but Seth would brook no refusal.

'Promise me!' he had whispered, moving to claim her lips, branding her with his searing fire. 'Promise me!'

He could not let her go just yet, he unwillingly acknowledged. Then, driven by forces he stubbornly refused to name, he had fitted his body to hers and ruthlessly forced his passion upon her. His determination to have his way was meant to quell any resistance Charl could muster, and as his caresses grew more intimate, her will to oppose him seemed to drain away. That she had been overwhelmed by his nearness, robbed of coherent thought by devastating physical sensation, overcome by the force of his personality, was evident. But even as he bullied her with his sensual skill, defeated her with the dizzying power of his touch, his arguments had been based in irrefutable logic.

'You will be safe in Quebec; I promise you,' Seth had murmured against her throat. 'And there is no way to return to Youngstown without me. Give me your word, Charlotte. Say you'll stay in Quebec while I'm gone.'

Pressed intimately beside her, he had sensed her capitulation long before she agreed. 'Yes, yes, I promise! I'll be here when you return!' she had finally gasped, the words coming because he had willed them, not she. And even as she whispered the promise he was seeking, Seth's mouth had sought hers in a kiss that was both a reward and a bond.

Now, as he stood watching Charl's lovely, tranquil face by the light of the flickering flame, he wished he understood why she had finally agreed. It seemed so unlike Charl to submit. As unsure as he was about his own motives in demanding the promise, he was even less sure of her motives in giving it. Had she seen the logic behind his insistence that she stay in Quebec, or had she given her word without any intention of keeping it? He eyed her as she slept. She had made the promise, but could he trust her to keep it? He scowled blackly, then shrugged. It would do little good to worry about that now. He had given his word, as well. If she was not here when he returned, he would follow her. And God help her when he found her.

Shaking off the pensive mood, he tugged on the grey jacket and picked up the saddlebags. He patted his pocket to be certain that his papers were safe and then started towards the door. Lingering in the doorway, he looked back to where Charl slept and then extinguished the candle. There was nothing more he could do to ensure her safety while he was gone. The arrangements were made, and for the next weeks he relinquished all responsibility for her. Charlotte Beckwith was no longer his concern, and he intended to put her out of his mind.

Sixteen

✻✻✻

Once Seth left on his mysterious journey, Charl's days took on a pleasant, leisurely pattern that seemed apace with the glorious July days. Her time was divided between helping Marie and Gabrielle with the household chores and discovering the wonders of Quebec with Waukee. She was delighted by the vital, bustling city he showed her, and together they explored its narrow, cobbled streets and alleys. At first they toured Lowertown, visiting the market at La Place Royale where the midsummer produce was brought for sale. There were sweet, crimson cherries, deep purple blueberries, and raspberries piled high in their baskets. Mossy pea pods, fuzzy green and yellow beans, and emerald cucumbers spilled from the backs of farm carts, and colourful sprays of wild flowers bloomed in bouquets beside them. There were fresh-baked breads and pastries for sale, crisp and golden brown in the sun. One man sold fat, yellow cheeses, as large as melons, and smoked sausages that hung like linked festoons from the sides of his stall. Another farmer specialized in maple syrup, tapped from his own trees and boiled to its heavy brown sweetness by him and his family during sugaring off in April.

Craftsmen came to the market, too; wood carvers and potters, weavers and cobblers all came to offer their unique wares. There were always people in the square near the old church, but on Wednesdays there was hardly room to move in the crush that came to sample Quebec's bounty.

Charl soon discovered the shops on rue St Pierre and was amazed by the variety of goods for sale inside. They easily surpassed anything she had seen during her brief stay in York. Living in Youngstown, essentially a frontier community, she had never dreamed of the richness and luxury available to those who lived in more cosmopolitan areas. She found sheer silks and gauzes from the East, woven with shimmering gold and silver threads; light, warm woollens from England and delicate lace from Belgium and Spain crowded together on narrow shelves in one store. In another shop were fragile, subtly shaded blown glass pitchers and goblets from Portugal and cut crystal decanters, whose prismed surfaces reflected rainbows in the sunlight. Charl was delighted by the intricately patterned ginger jars and beautifully carved teak tea chests that could be found in Quebec's more exclusive shops. She liked the tiny spice store with its rich, tangy smell and the dressmaker's where Seth had bought her gowns. It seemed that she would never cease to find new things to excite, fascinate, and amuse her only a few paces from her own doorstep.

Then Waukee took her up the Champlain stairs to Uppertown and opened the world inside the city wall to her. Public buildings and churches, more ancient and impressive than any buildings she had ever seen, dominated this part of town. The Château St Louis and the Governor's Mansion seemed the epitome of the grey stone architecture that was so much a part of Quebec. The church spires probed upward into the turquoise summer sky, rising bravely from the world of men into the realm of nature.

When caught up in the vitality of Quebec, it was difficult to believe that the settlement was more than two hundred years old. Still there was a fortresslike permanence to the city that gave clear evidence of its history. Together, Charl and Waukee wandered the streets that twisted and turned, confined by the high grey stone walls that ringed the city. They explored the city above the cliff as thoroughly as they had the one below. Going on errands for Gabrielle, to the blacksmith or cooper, they passed the Ursuline Convent, where Montcalm was buried, and strolled through the Governor's formal gardens, ablaze with the blooms of summer.

Wherever they went in Quebec, Charl was aware of the all-pervasive British military presence. Quebec itself was a walled city in the medieval fashion, and batteries lined the cliff to the north and east. To the southwest was the rocky crest of Cape Diamond rising steeply above the settlement, its guns defending the river and the fields outside the city wall. Seth's observation that Quebec was impregnable came to mind often as Charl watched the British reinforce existing fortifications and construct new ones. And it seemed to her that his assessment had been correct.

The British troops drilled daily in the Place d'Armes or on the Plains of Abraham just outside the city wall. As she watched the precise, well-disciplined moves of the crack British troops, she remembered with despair the ragtag unit of farmers and tradesmen who had drilled so diligently on the grassy field outside Youngstown. How could those pitiful militia men, with their odd assortment of weapons and uniforms, expect to stand against these efficient, well-equipped men? Had Seth's dire prophecies about the outcome of the war been correct? she wondered.

Except for the renewed military activity, Quebec seemed untouched by the war. There were guns fired at noon and sunset from Battery Royale in Lowertown, but the sound soon became familiar and, ironically, quite soothing. If it had not been for the continuous concern for her father's safety, Charl could have put the war out of her mind. No word had come from the west, and Charl existed in an agony of uncertainty, caught between the desire to hear something of Youngstown and the realization that if word of her home reached Quebec, the news would not be good.

Still, time passed pleasantly with trips in the mackinaw downstream to the Ile d'Orleans or Montmorency Falls for leisurely, daylong picnics. Waukee continued with the knife lessons he had begun on their way to Quebec. In the afternoons they practised in the small garden behind the La Soeur house until Charl's skill with the weapon amazed even the Indian.

The friendship that had begun on the boat flourished in the long summer days they spent together. There was an easy companionship between them that made even their silences comfortable and relaxed. Charl's basic honesty was compatible with Waukee's forthright nature, and they could discuss anything, anything except Seth. Since the night that Waukee had questioned her about her relationship with Seth, he had hardly mentioned the other man's name. Charl sensed that the Indian did not approve of the way she had been treated, but she did not realize that an estrangement had grown between the two men because of her. She knew only that Waukee seemed to understand and accept her in a way that Seth never had. Charl was secure in Waukee's friendship while her reaction to Seth was constantly in transition. It was only now and then, when Charl looked up unexpectedly to find Waukee eyeing her intently, that she questioned his feelings for her. But his expression changed so quickly, growing solemn or mischievous, that she had no time to analyse what she had seen.

Charl was beginning to feel very much at home in Gabrielle's house. The French lessons continued daily as she helped Gabrielle cook or clean, and an understanding grew between the two women that transcended language. Charl was soon able to grasp snatches of most conversations and form simple sentences on her own. Marie and Anne helped her, too, by practising grammar with her as they sat by the fire in the evenings.

When Charl had time to think about it, she was amazed by how quickly she had adapted to her new life, and she realized that she was happy. She was exploring, and learning, and experiencing new things daily, things she would never have encountered if she had stayed in Youngstown. There was an irrepressible excitement about getting out of bed every morning that she had never known before.

Charl had not counted on missing Seth. The day she awoke to find him gone she felt only anger: anger at his mistreatment and anger at her own weakness for agreeing to remain in Quebec. But, as the days progressed and the anger faded, she missed his diverting presence. It was difficult to lie alone in the wide bed these warm summer nights without thinking of Seth. She hated her body's betrayal, but when the strange, wild longing rose in her, she ached for the familiar press of his hard form against hers.

Even more, she missed being able to share her daily discoveries with him. Charl knew he loved Quebec, and it would have pleased her to explore the place with him. There would have been stories and odd bits of history woven into her explorations if he had been her guide. She was anxious to show off her growing mastery of French, too. She wanted to watch the surprise dawn on his face as she formed her first halting sentences and to hear his rich, warm laughter rise with pleasure at her accomplishments. Charl needed Seth's reassurance, too. Fear for her home dogged her night and day, but she sensed that if news of an attack came from the west, Seth would have the information to end her uncertainties.

She missed him, Charl admitted reluctantly to herself. Even in his absence he had proved his power over her. Ironically, he'd had to force her to promise to stay in Quebec until his return, and now she anxiously awaited the day.

One afternoon, when Waukee was unable to come, Charl

began to put her things away in the burl campaign chest as Seth
had said she could. The persistent whisper of the summer rain
that washed the sandy streets and left the air heavy with the smell
of earth made her feel efficient and industrious. Already she had
removed Seth's clothes and separated them into two neat piles,
one to be returned to the chest and the second to be mended.

At the bottom of the chest lay a richly inlaid walnut box. For
several minutes she held it in her lap, examining the complex
marquetry designs, unsure if she should open it. Gingerly, she
tried the catch, and when it slid easily, she lifted the lid. Inside
was an odd collection of military items: a half dozen or more
gold buttons, a brass gorget, a pair of dress spurs with their tiny
silver rowels, all resting on a pair of white gauntlets, still creased
with the shape of the owner's hand. Charl examined the things
carefully, then set them on the floor beside her. Carefully folded
under them was a crimson officer's sash. Her fingers caressed the
heavy, expensive silk as she lifted it gently from the box. In the
bottom was a pile of letters bound together and addressed to
William Porterfield. These things had belonged to Seth's uncle,
Charl realized. Slowly she riffled through the letters, noting that
some bore Seth's bold script while the rest were written in a hand
somehow similar to his but more scrawled and spidery. With a
small frown she set the letters aside as well, and reached into the
box for the last item, a gilt-framed miniature. She turned it slowly
towards the grey light that filtered in the window and caught her
breath with surprise. The man in the frame could easily have
been Seth! Except for the British uniform and the sandy brown
hair that curled across his brow, the resemblance was uncanny.
This man had the same strong features, the same cleft chin, the
same startlingly blue eyes that Seth had. Even the expression
was the same, filled with reckless vitality. Charl studied the
miniature in her hand, wondering what kind of man William
Porterfield had been. Was he like Seth, arrogant, cold, and
unbending?

She had seen a picture of this man somewhere before, and her
brow puckered as she tried to isolate the memory that nagged
her. She rose, taking the miniature with her as she picked her
way between the piles of clothing. Perhaps Gabrielle would be
able to tell her where she might have seen William Porterfield
before.

It was Gabrielle's habit to spend several afternoons each week in her room, working on accounts or writing letters to her parents in Château Richer or to her married daughter in Trois-Rivières. She was working on just such a letter to Monique at her graceful rosewood desk when Charl entered.

'Bonjour, Charl. Pleut-il maintenant?' she began, glancing up from her letter.

Charl was about to answer that it was still raining when her eyes fell on the miniature sitting on top of Gabrielle's desk. She moved closer to get a better look, then turned to face her friend, her expression one of puzzlement.

'Gabrielle, est-ce William Porterfield?' Charl asked, extending the miniature in her hand that was identical to the one on Gabrielle's desk.

Without warning, Gabrielle's eyes filled with tears that spilled over their edges, leaving shining silver paths down her pale cheeks. Charl came to her knees beside Gabrielle's chair and took the older woman's hands in her own, upset by her friend's distress.

'Oui. Cet homme est William Porterfield, l'oncle de Seth,' she explained painfully. Her words were barely audible as she went on, as if compelled to account for her possession of the miniature. 'William était mon amant. Il est mort.'

'I know he's dead,' Charl whispered, horrified by the hurt she had inadvertently caused.

'Il y a douze ans,' Gabrielle told her brokenly.

Twelve years! Dear God! Gabrielle still mourned a man who had been dead twelve years. Their love must have been something rare and fine, Charl found herself thinking with mingled envy and pity. Surely William Porterfield had been an exceptional man to win the love of a woman like Gabrielle. He would have to have been strong and honourable, good and kind. In the tiny portrait he seemed so like Seth, yet in fact they must have been so different.

Slowly, Gabrielle drew her hands away from Charl's comforting grip and searched her pockets for her lace-trimmed handkerchief.

'Assez,' Gabrielle said, as much to herself as to Charl. 'Je ne pleure plus jamais William.' She met Charl's eyes, easily reading the sympathy and regret in their green depths.

'Je regrette . . .' Charl began, but Gabby cut her short with a shake of her head.

'Non. Je vais bien maintenant. Quittez moi, s'il vous plait. Je désire être seule.'

Charl turned towards the door, the miniature clutched tightly in her hand. Small wonder that Gabrielle wanted to be alone after the blunder she had made by asking about William Porterfield. If only she had known, Charl thought. If only Seth had told her about William and Gabrielle, but there had been so little time before he left.

She closed the door to the second floor room and went back to work on rearranging the campaign chest, but her mind was busy with other matters. This explained Seth's close relationship with the La Soeur family, but it raised a dozen other questions that only Seth could answer. Irritably, she refolded one of his shirts before she packed it away. Damn him for leaving her in the middle of all this without any explanations. Seth was infuriating, unreliable, and she wished that he would hurry back.

*

In New York, Seth trudged unsteadily up the two flights of stairs to his room at the City Hotel. It was very late, and he was aware that he had drunk too much whisky as he gambled away the evening in the backroom of one of the saloons further up Broadway. He had won, though, he rationalized, weighing the gold pieces in his pocket. Now what he wanted was sleep. Already, a headache had begun to throb above his eyes, and he would be glad to reach the solace of his room. He fumbled with the key in the lock and closed the door behind him. Without lighting a lamp he made his way to the bed, loosening his neckcloth and dropping his jacket over a chair. He had nearly reached the large mahogany poster bed when the unmistakable press of a pistol came hard against his spine.

'Good Christ!' he muttered, more irritated by the inconvenience of an armed guest than alarmed by the danger.

'About time you returned, Porterfield,' came a familiar voice as the pressure of the pistol left his back.

'Damn you, Mitchell,' Seth began hotly, turning towards where a spark flared to light the lamp. The brightness from the flame sent searing pains into his head, and he squinted at the other man.

'Been out on the town, Porterfield?' the grey-haired man asked blandly.

'I needed some diversion,' Seth sneered, dropping heavily into the chair. 'You've let me sit here nearly a week, cooling my heels, while I waited for you.'

'You've hardly cooled your heels,' Mitchell observed, offering Seth a cup of coffee poured from a silver coffee service on the table. He took it gratefully, hoping it would ease the pain in his head. 'I hear you've visited half the whorehouses in New York and almost as many taverns.'

Seth felt his colour rise. Mitchell knew entirely too much about what went on.

'This coffee's cold,' he complained, pushing the cup aside.

'I'm not surprised; I've been waiting a long time.' Mitchell frowned at the tall man slumped in the wing-backed chair. 'It seems I should get some more. Doubtless you'll need a bit before you can give me any kind of coherent report.'

Seth's mouth tightened as he cast about for a suitably sarcastic response, but Mitchell had left to order more coffee before one came to him.

Dismally, he pressed the heels of his hands against his eyes, willing the throbbing in his head to stop. It didn't.

Dear God! He did not want to deal with Mitchell tonight. His aching head and his alcohol-dulled brain were no match for Mitchell's rapierlike tongue and facile mind. He groaned and let his head rest against the high-backed chair, staring blankly ahead.

What was the matter with him? He never drank more than a glass or two. But the waiting had been so dull, the deceptions had seemed so senseless, and the cards had fallen so easily in his favour. He had simply accepted the drinks that were offered as a release and an escape. He passed a hand across his eyes. Had the women he had sought out these past nights been a release and an escape, too? he wondered. And why was it that suddenly a fifty-dollar-a-night harlot no longer seemed . . .

Seth pulled himself out of the chair and went to the washstand. He needed a clear head for what was ahead of him tonight. Water from the ewer splashed into the deep blue delft bowl. He held his breath for a moment before he plunged his head into it. The cold water felt shocking and good on his flushed face. He breathed deeply and shook the water out of his eyes before submerging himself again. Groping for a towel, he took several more deep breaths and then tucked it around his neck as he made his way back to the chair. With a sigh he leaned back, stretching his long legs and letting the rivulets of water from his hair soak his shirt.

The water had cleared the fog in his brain, and his headache had receded slightly. Now, if only he wasn't so tired.

Mitchell reappeared at the door. 'The coffee will be up in a few minutes,' he reported, taking the chair across the hearth from Seth's.

The blond man nodded wearily. Mitchell studied him with care, noting the shadowed eyes and the deepening crease between his brows. He had never known Porterfield to drink before, not that the man was reeling drunk, by any means, but a man who lived by his wits needed to be alert at all times if he was to survive. An agent as effective as Seth was would never forget such a basic truth. There must be something bothering Porterfield, Mitchell reasoned, stirring uncomfortably in his chair. Perhaps it had been a mistake to force the Quebec assignment on him if his loyalties were truly divided. But then, who would have been better qualified? Mitchell frowned. He would make the same choice again. There was no one who could be as effective in Quebec as this man was. And when Porterfield's six months were up, it would be impossible to replace him. Still Porterfield was getting reckless; take the matter of the girl, for example.

There was a discreet knock at the door, and Mitchell answered it. A small, grey-haired maid stood in the hallway with the coffee. Mitchell gave her a few coins and took the service to the table.

'Come, my good man. Have some coffee to clear your head and tell me of Quebec,' he invited.

Seth took the cupful of the steaming liquid and sat down at the table in the yellow glow of the hanging lamp.

'I wasn't in Quebec long enough to form much of an impression. We had only just arrived when Joubert insisted I go off again.'

'Tell me about your passsage down the river then,' Mitchell suggested, his eyes bright behind the thick lenses of his spectacles.

Seth nodded in agreement and began to talk. After the best part of an hour had passed, Mitchell sat forward.

'And you saw new fortifications at Fort York and at Coteau-du-Lac?' Mitchell questioned.

'Yes. There seems to be a full garrison at Montreal, and the fort at Trois-Rivières was well manned. I noticed some regimental insignia that I had not seen before in Quebec, but I didn't have a chance to identify it.' Seth shrugged and paused, waiting for more questions. Mitchell only frowned intently, seeming far away. The room grew very quiet.

'Has anything happened in the west?' Seth finally asked.

'With Hull, you mean? Damn it, no!' Mitchell shook his head with exasperation. 'At least there's no word yet. Someday they'll find a better way to dispatch information. Fool couriers take weeks,' he mumbled. 'We have reports that General Brock has left York for Fort Malden, and that bodes ill for our cause. He's a brave man and a superb officer.'

'You mean that you believe Brock could defeat Hull?' Seth asked.

'With regulars, militia, and the Indians behind him, yes, I think it's possible. And if Detroit falls, so will Michilimackinac and Fort Dearborn,' Mitchell prophesied darkly.

'But there's been no other fighting?'

'Isolated incidents,' Mitchell answered, rising to pace around the room. He had never been a man to remain still for long, Seth observed.

'I heard that General Dearborn and Prevost have been negotiating a truce,' Seth commented noncommittally.

Mitchell snorted. 'It will last until autumn. By then the war-hawks in Congress and along the frontier will be screaming for an invasion of Canada. Dearborn will be forced to make some move before the snow flies.'

Seth had been careful to keep his face blank throughout the discussion, but Mitchell must have sensed his concern for he turned almost accusingly to the younger man.

'But then, you have a special interest in the Niagara region, haven't you, Porterfield? In Youngstown, perhaps?'

There was a flush that spread along his cheekbones, and Seth knew it was useless to make any denials. He had not wanted to discuss Charl with Mitchell, but now he had no choice. With an effort he made his features impassive and waited for Mitchell's questions. He'd be damned if he would volunteer any information.

Mitchell stood motionless for some minutes, just outside the circle of lamplight that so revealingly illuminated Seth's face. He could hear voices from the street below and vaguely smell the coffee cooling in the cups. He hoped the silence would unnerve the younger man, but Porterfield seemed coolly unaffected.

'Why did you abduct Henry Beckwith's daughter?' he finally asked.

'Charlotte surprised me in the stable as I was trying to make my escape from Youngstown. I seemed to have no choice in the matter. I either took her with me or remained there to wait for the hangman.' Seth shrugged. 'If I could have told her the truth about my identity, it might have been different.'

'Then she still thinks you're a British spy?' Mitchell asked.

'It seemed safer to let her continue with her illusion although she berates me regularly for my vile pursuits,' Seth admitted, smiling in spite of himself at the thought of Charl's vilifications.

'Damnation, man! This is no laughing matter!' Mitchell boomed.

'You don't know the girl, then?' Seth asked, the smile becoming a grin.

'I only know her father's wild to get her back. He's written to every Congressman in Washington and made my life a living hell!'

'Well, she's a spirited chit. Had it been any other woman who surprised me in the stable that night, she'd have quietly fainted. But not Charl. She planned to hold me captive with her pitchfork until they came to hang me as a spy.'

A smile played briefly at the corners of Mitchell's mouth. The girl must be a real spitfire to take on a man like Porterfield.

'If she's so much trouble, why didn't you send her back on the ferry once you reached Canada?'

This was the question that Seth had been dreading. His smile faded. 'I don't know,' he said simply.

'What do you mean, you don't know?' came Mitchell's quick response.

'I don't know. I took her with me; at the time it seemed the only thing to do. I know now that it was a mistake. But then?' He shrugged his broad shoulders wearily. Even Mitchell would never realize how much Seth wished he understood his own motivations.

'Have you made any attempt to return her to Youngstown?'

The blond man nodded. 'I tried to find passage for her from York, but I wouldn't let her go anywhere with those lake scum. I wanted her to arrive home safely. Then I intended to bring her to New York with me, but Joubert forbade it.'

'Did you have any trouble on the voyage?'

'None,' came Seth's curt reply. 'I doubt that there was any real danger.'

'Oh, the danger was real. But Joubert employs a master forger,

and your citizenship papers are genuine. No, Joubert was probably right about leaving the girl in Quebec. She had no papers
of her own, I presume.' Seth shook his head. 'I thought not. Well,
send her back to her father as soon as you get an opportunity. For
now she's safe in Quebec,' Mitchell instructed as he went to get
his leather folder from a small table near the door.

Inwardly, Seth breathed a sigh of relief. The interview had not
been as bad as he expected it would be. Now all Mitchell would
want him to do was write out the reports.

'What I can't understand, Porterfield, is why you would fight
a duel for Charlotte Beckwith's honour at dawn and then, later
that same day, do something to sully her virtue for ever,' Mitchell
observed, coming back towards the table where Seth sat waiting.

'I'll not discuss the girl anymore!' Seth warned murderously.
His face was so full of fury that Mitchell stared in amazement.
Porterfield's reaction was completely out of proportion to the
casual comment he had made, and Mitchell was instantly suspicious. What was going on between Porterfield and the Beckwith
girl? This might well warrant further investigation.

'You can't deny that the girl is ruined,' Mitchell prodded.

'I'll deny anything I please where she's concerned.'

Mitchell's eyebrows rose slowly, arching high above the rim
of his spectacles. 'Even the paternity of her child?' he asked
speculatively, waiting for some reaction from the other man.

Seth paled visibly at the words. 'Charlotte Beckwith will bear
no child of mine,' he said unsteadily, giving Mitchell the lie.

'Then send her home soon, Porterfield,' he advised, stepping
closer, 'for even I can see that you care more for the girl than is
wise.'

When Seth opened his mouth to protest, Mitchell slapped a
foolscap tablet on the table in front of him.

'Write your reports!' he ordered. 'But mark me well, you send
the girl home. You're preoccupied, and you've taken too many
chances lately. I wasn't sure what was wrong with you, but now
I'd wager it's the girl that has caused the change. You get rid of
her, Porterfield, or she'll be the death of you,' Mitchell finished,
then sauntered across the room to a chair by the hearth and lit
his pipe.

Seth's jaw hardened and he clenched his fists at his sides, too
angry to even answer Mitchell's charges. It was his fault that
Charl was in Quebec. If Mitchell had not forced him into this

mission, he would be on his way to California or Mexico by now, and Charl would be with her father in Youngstown. Now Mitchell calmly ordered that Charl be sent home with no thought for the difficulties in getting her there. To hell with what Mitchell said. He'd handle Charl as he saw fit. This was none of Mitchell's concern, in any case.

It was a long time before Seth was calm enough to concentrate on the reports, and it was fully daylight before they were finished. He glanced over at Mitchell, who snored gently in his chair, his hands crossed on his slight paunch and his face strangely cherubic. Watching him so, it was hard to believe that this unremarkable man wielded such awesome power. As if sensing Seth's thoughts upon him, Mitchell opened his eyes.

'Finished with those?' he asked pleasantly as he stretched. Slowly he rose and came to collect the pile of papers from the table. Leaning his elbows on the back of one of the chairs, he scanned over the reports with a discerning eye and slid them into the battered leather writing case.

In another man the expression on Mitchell's face as he prepared to go might well have been read as concern. Slowly he turned to Seth. 'Return to Quebec, observe, report to Joubert, and wait,' he instructed. 'Send the girl home, Porterfield. There are bad times coming for all of us, and she can only do you harm.'

Seth nodded, too tired to argue, and locked the door when Mitchell was gone. Without hesitation he headed towards the wide four-poster, shedding his clothes as he went. Wearily he fell across the coverlet that had been turned back by the maid the night before and pulled up the sheet.

Tomorrow he would leave for Quebec. It would take him several weeks to make the journey, and by the time he arrived, he would have to have decided what he was going to do with Charlotte Beckwith. Damn! That girl was the blight of his life. Sleepily, he turned his face into the pillow. Mitchell had raised some damn unsettling questions. Charl couldn't possibly be carrying his child, could she? He groaned at the thought and pulled the extra pillow over his head. Before he made any decision about sending her home, perhaps he'd better ask Charl if she was with child.

※

Overhead the branches of the elms intertwined to form a long cool tunnel above the narrow lane. Through the leaves the sunlight dappled the earth in slowly wavering patches of brightness, and at the edges of the trace, the buttercups, bachelor buttons, and Queen Anne's lace swayed in the breeze. With one hand Charlotte Beckwith brushed a strand of wheaten hair away from her flushed face as she followed the tall Indian along the well-worn path. There was a tight knot of sadness in her throat, as they made their way towards the main road to Quebec, that could not be banished by the beauty of the countryside and the brilliant sunshine. In truth, the pleasant day spent picking peaches in an orchard at the edge of the river was the cause of the girl's unhappiness. Being in the country again and watching the sunlight glistening on the blue-grey expanse of river had reminded her painfully of Youngstown and had renewed the homesickness she had experienced when she first came to Quebec. Wisely, the Indian had sensed her mood and had left her alone with her feelings. Now she lengthened her stride to catch up to him and match his loping gait.

Reaching his side, she adjusted the heavy market basket filled with peaches on her arm and smiled up into his swarthy face.

'Waukee, do you think Seth will really take me back to Youngstown when he returns?' she asked earnestly.

The Indian slowed his pace and regarded the woman beside him. She seemed so young and vulnerable with her thick, yellow plaits hanging down her back and her serious sea green eyes intent on him.

'I don't know, Charl,' he answered honestly. 'If he promised he would take you back, then eventually he will. Although you doubt my words, I know Seth Porterfield to be an honest man.'

She exhaled sharply in disbelief. 'How is it he can be so honest with you when everything he tells me is suspect?' she wanted to know.

Waukee was silent, unwilling to say more but irritatingly aware that there was much more to be said. Stubbornly, he compressed his lips, deciding that if Seth Porterfield would not tell this girl the truth, it was not his place to do so. For some minutes they walked in silence.

'How long have you known Seth?' Charl asked abruptly.

'Known him?' There was a long pause as the man considered what he would say. Characteristically, he chose the truth or at least as much of the truth as he could safely tell. 'Fourteen or fifteen years,' he answered. 'My father was guide for the surveying party that went west in 1798.'

'And Seth was with that party. Is that how you met him?'

Waukee nodded. He spoke reluctantly, unwilling to expose the secrets of the man who had been his friend for so long. Slowly, the story began, and his voice naturally took on a depth and cadence that added richness to his words and cast a spell of silence over his fascinated listener.

'I was fourteen then,' he remembered, his eyes clouded with memories, 'and for the first time I was allowed to accompany my father. He was a well-known Shawnee guide and told stories of exploring the lands to the West, where the mountains rose so high as to be crowned by snow all year long. He spoke of rivers swift and wide and of animals that grazed in fields of grass so tall and vast that they looked like the sea rolling in the wind. I was to become a guide also, and, while he led the surveyors and mapmakers, I was to begin to learn the lakes and rivers that belonged to our people.

'Seth was with the surveyors, and because he was only a year or two older than I was, we became friends. He had just come from England and knew nothing of living in the wild. It fell to me to teach him.' An amused smile curved his wide mouth at some memory he chose not to share. 'Not that Seth was always a willing student, but he learned his lessons well, as you know. There are few white men who match his ability to live in the wilderness. In return, he taught me to read and write English.'

'But why are you travelling with him now?' Charl asked, sensing that there was more to the story.

In Waukee's mind the images were as clear as they had been that day fourteen years ago. He remembered the stream foaming over the rocks, the whisper-soft sound of his moccasins on the grass, and the stirring of the wind in the trees. The bear he had come on accidentally was equally clear in his mind. He could still see her hovering protectively beside her cubs at the water's edge. her coat like a heavy brown mat hanging on her body, and her eyes red with rage. Even the heart-stopping panic came flooding back. Her challenging howl had echoed in the narrow canyon of trees as she charged. He remembered the slippery rocks beneath his feet as he pounded along the creek bed and the rasp of his own breathing in his ears. Then came the terrible, endless moment when he fell, and the bear was on him. Her face loomed above him, and he could see her mouth flecked with foam, open in a snarl, and her sharp fangs ready to rend his flesh. In that last moment he read black death in her eyes. A claw caught his shoulder, and the world exploded in a haze of pain. From somewhere he heard a voice cry his name, and then the crushing weight of the bear was gone from above him. The memories were distorted and jumbled with pain after that, but he could clearly remember Seth standing over him, covered with blood, his knife still drawn and concern etched on his face. Then the Indian had lost consciousness.

Somehow, Waukee found the words to tell Charl of that day half his lifetime ago, and the girl listened without interruption until they stopped.

'And Seth saved your life?' Charl asked softly.

'Yes,' he answered. 'From that day he has been my brother. I have shared my home, my food, and my horses with him. When I can, I travel with him as well.'

'And do you share Seth's views on the war?' she asked, her voice gone cold.

'My people fight for the English under Tecumseh,' came the noncommittal answer.

Silence fell between them as they turned from the shady lane onto the wide, dusty road that led back to Quebec.

'Why didn't Seth stay with your tribe instead of returning to Quebec?' Charl asked after some minutes, determined to satisfy her curiosity about him while she had the chance.

'Seth is seeking something,' Waukee said softly. 'At times I doubt if he even understands what it is he wants, but until he finds it, he will never know true peace.'

The Indian's dark eyes searched her face carefully, as if his strange words carried some special meaning for her, but she could not fathom what it might be. Unaccountably, she felt uncomfortable under his scrutiny. To hide her confusion, she reached into her basket and offered him one of the golden peaches they had picked earlier in the day. Then she selected one for herself and bit into the fuzzy fruit. Juice trickled down her chin, and she wiped it away with the back of her hand.

'These will make marvellous peach cobbler,' she chattered nervously, anxious to break the tension that existed suddenly and inexplicably between them. 'And I can hardly wait to taste them in one of Marie's pies.'

Waukee laughed. 'You seem to have found some measure of contentment here in Quebec, haven't you, Charl?' he asked as they walked.

The girl nodded. 'As much as I want to go home, I am not unhappy here,' she reluctantly admitted. In silence they completed the walk back to Quebec.

As they crossed Place d'Armes, they passed an old man selling newspapers in the square. In Quebec the newspapers were printed in French, but this man sold the *Gazette de Montréal*, which was published in English.

'Waukee, could I have a newspaper, please?' Charlotte asked. Seth had left specific instructions that Charl was to have no money of her own although he had left a substantial sum with both Waukee and Gabrielle for her use.

'The Montreal paper is at least a week out of date by the time it reaches here, Charl. Look, this one was published on July 20. Its news is probably more than two weeks old,' he pointed out.

'I don't care,' she insisted stubbornly. 'I would welcome even old news if I could read it in my own language.'

Frowning, he agreed, and he reached for the leather pouch at his belt. With a brilliant smile, Charl took the paper and tucked it into the basket with the peaches.

*

It was late in the evening, after she had bathed and prepared for bed, when Charl remembered the newspaper and slipped downstairs to retrieve it from the kitchen. Returning to the room, she moved a pair of candlesticks to the top of the campaign chest and drew the Windsor chair they had brought up from the parlour closer to the light. With a satisfied sigh she tucked her feet up under the hem of the ruffled nightdress Gabrielle had bought her and began to read.

Carefully, she scanned the front page. Although war had been declared, no battles had been joined, and the several articles on it dealt mostly with local reactions to the declaration and the construction of new fortifications. The *Gazette* had printed a rumour that Lt General Prevost was negotiating an armistice with the American commander, and Charl cheered to that news. There were other stories dealing with the preparations being made in the west, but they gave her no more information than what she had been able to get from Seth. And she was amazed by the accuracy of his observations.

On the second page a headline caught her eye: 'Last American Citizens Sail from Quebec.' With a strange tension creeping up her neck, she began to read:

On July 14, the last American citizens from Montreal, Quebec City, and the surrounding countryside sailed on the ship *Nightwind*, bound for the port of New York. The evacuation was ordered by Lt General Prevost to take place by the first of July, but the deadline was extended by a fortnight to provide the refugees time to prepare themselves for the trip.

One hand came slowly to Charl's mouth, and her throat constricted with disappointment. They had arrived in Quebec before July 14. If only they had known about the refugee ship, she might well be on her way home by now. Tears rose in her eyes, blurring the words before her.

Dear God! She wanted to go home. Her father must be frantic by now, and she wanted to run to him for protection from the harsh realities of life, just as she had run to him as a child. She needed the security of the solid brick house she had lived in all her life to shelter her from danger. Somehow she felt she could find a haven from a world gone mad in the familiar surroundings of childhood. She sought the balm of familiarity when everything around her was caught up in the turmoil of the coming war. Rationally, she knew that even those places familiar and dear to her were not safe, but as the waves of homesickness washed over her, she knew she would take any risk to ease her father's worry and go home again. Sighing, she brushed away the tears and read on.

The article ended with a list of refugees. Idly, she scanned over the names, not expecting to recognize any of them. A third of the way down the second column one name leaped out at her from between Samuel Haslett, wheelwright, and Andrew Engle, cobbler.

The name was Seth Porterfield, and his occupation was fraudulently given as lumber merchant.

Charl stared at the words until everything else on the page blurred and receded, leaving one phrase to penetrate her consciousness. She fought the dawning comprehension, and her eyes moved desperately between the headline above and the name below as she sought some less damning conclusion than the one that was immediately obvious to her. Frantically, she searched for some other reason for Seth to be on this ship because her heart rejected what her mind had already accepted as fact. Unwillingly, she recalled the night in the stable when Seth had told her he was a British spy and the afternoon he had returned to this room looking as if he had dressed in someone else's clothes. With an echoing sob she crumpled the paper between her fists.

Of course, Seth had boarded the ship as an American refugee, probably with forged or stolen papers, on his way to spy on her country. It was likely he had reached New York by now, she raged, where he would carry out his mission, whatever it was. When he left, he knew he was headed towards her home, towards Youngstown, the one place in the world where she wanted to be. And knowing that, he had left her in Quebec as his prisoner.

Anger, sorrow, and betrayal twisted in her chest as the strangling, shuddering sobs shook her. Drawing her knees up to her chest, she gave herself to her despair, mourning her captivity and the death of her trust in Seth Porterfield. For she had begun to trust him again, to forget his lies and believe the things he said. And what was worse, she realized through the pain, was that she had come to care for him. Her sobs grew louder, and she no longer tried to choke them back, knowing that the thick stone walls and the sturdy door would keep the secret of her grief.

The sky was growing light when she stirred from her chair and made her way to the bed. The storm of emotions had left her spent and broken, unable to think of anything but the soothing balm of sleep. As Charl stretched across the bed, she felt empty and too tired for either the pain or anger she had experienced before. Her swollen eyelids sagged with weariness, and she welcomed the oblivion of sleep. Sighing deeply, she let her troubles drift away, aware that they would return with the morning.

※

Consciousness came back to Charl slowly with the sound of vendors crying their wares from the street below. The heat of the day had already begun, making the filmy nightdress cling to her, and she was surprised that she had slept so late. Sleep still clogged her brain and beckoned her back to forgetfulness, as if she could close her eyes and deny the problems of the day. Determinedly, Charl sat up, knowing full well that something was wrong but unable to name her dread. Beside her on the bed her fingers found the crumpled newspaper. With a pain that threatened to sear her in two, her memory came flooding back. Sighing, she closed her eyes as if to reject what she had found on its smudged pages.

Wearily she rose and poured water from the pitcher into the bowl and began to wash, her mind clouded with confusion. There was no doubt about what the discoveries the night before meant. Seth had deceived her again, more cruelly this time than ever before. Beyond the anger and the hurt was the question she had not even dared ask: What would she do now? Surely this discovery negated any promises she had made to Seth, but she had no idea of how she could escape from Quebec. She realized it was useless to ask Waukee to help her; his loyalty to Seth was stronger than his friendship for her. Charl thought next of Gabrielle. Could she convince the Frenchwoman to defy Seth and aid her in her escape? And if she did, was it possible for an American to slip away from this British stronghold in the middle of a war? She could not even consider how she would reach Youngstown once she had left Quebec. She forced her doubts into the recesses of her mind, and her chin rose stubbornly. She would return to Youngstown somehow, she vowed. What other course of action was open to her now?

As she descended the stairs, the sound of the heavy iron knocker on the stout wooden door echoed through the house. Because it was late and Charl was not sure where the other members of the household might be, she quickened her pace. Rushing down the final flight, she saw Gabrielle come from the kitchen, wiping her hands on her apron.

The words spoken by the person on the other side of the door were lost in a mumble, but Gabrielle's words floated up to Charl, crisp and clear.

'I am very sorry, but you must have the wrong address. There is no one here by that name.'

Charl crept down several more steps as the visitor spoke again.

'I tell you that I know no one by that name,' Gabrielle said indignantly in English that was accented but amazingly precise. 'I assure you that I am well acquainted with everyone in my household, and there is no one here by that name. Now good day!'

With a slam Gabrielle closed and bolted the heavy door.

Turning, she noticed Charl on the stairs for the first time and stopped, frozen by the accusation in the girl's green eyes. Gabrielle knew she could no longer pretend she spoke only French because the American had obviously heard the entire conversation.

'Charl, I can explain . . .' the older woman began, but Charl bolted up the stairs, unwilling to listen. As she raced up the stairs behind Charl, Gabrielle cursed Seth for the deception he had forced on her. She had known it was wrong to try to isolate the girl, and she had done her best to make her feel at home. Now Charl had discovered the truth, and the friendship that had grown up between them was in jeopardy. Reaching the head of the stairs, Gabrielle forced her way into the room before Charl could snap the bolt or turn the key in the lock.

With tears of anger in her eyes, Charl turned to the older woman. 'How could you lie to me?' she hissed. 'I thought you were my friend.'

Gabrielle realized suddenly that the girl's eyes were red from weeping, and she wondered what other secrets she had unwittingly discovered.

'Charl, listen to me –'

'No! Seth lied to me, but I thought I could trust you!' Her voice caught in her throat.

'Seth?' Gabrielle asked, comprehension coming as her dark eyes rested on the newspaper spread open on the tumbled sheets. Even before she located the headline and the damning list below, she knew what Charl had found.

So the girl thought that they had all turned against her. And with good reason, mused Gabrielle.

Charl had thrown open the lid of the campaign chest and was rummaging inside, tossing aside shirts and chemises in her single-minded search.

'What are you doing?' Gabrielle demanded.

'I'm taking what's mine and I'm leaving!' she panted. 'I'm going home to Youngstown. You may tell Seth Porterfield, that blackguard, that I hate him and I'll see him dead for what he's done to me.'

Charl straightened suddenly and pressed her hands to her eyes, her shoulders shaking in silent sobs. Gabrielle rushed to her, and Charl allowed herself to be led to the bed, clinging to the woman who, in spite of her deception, was still a friend. For a long time they sat together, the fair-haired woman weeping beyond control, and the dark-haired one offering what comfort she could.

'You must not leave, Charl,' Gabrielle said determinedly when Charl's tears had ebbed.

'And what am I to do? Shall I wait here for Seth to return so he can tell me more lies? Do you know where he is?' Charl demanded.

'He's in New York,' Gabby answered.

'In New York! Why didn't he take me with him if he truly intends to take me home?'

'He wanted to, but he could not,' came the brief answer.

'Because he goes as a spy, and he's afraid I might spoil his game. He swore you to speak only French for the same reason, because he was afraid I might learn his secrets. Isn't that right?'

'Yes,' Gabrielle answered and gritted her teeth in irritation. Why couldn't Seth have told this girl the truth?

'I am leaving!' Charl said as she began to snatch up some of her belongings. 'I was on my way downstairs to ask you to help me. I can see now that you won't.'

'No, I won't, but not for the reason you think. What you propose is impossible. How can you expect to travel more than five hundred miles alone through the wilderness in the middle of a war? You would not survive, and I will not let you risk your life on such a scheme.'

The girl stopped in the centre of the room, caught in a flurry of indecision, the enormity of such an undertaking overwhelming her.

'And if I stay here, I only lengthen my captivity,' she said bitterly.

'Charl,' Gabby pleaded, 'stay. I will talk to Seth. If he refuses to take you home, I swear I will help you get back to Youngstown safely if you still want to go.'

'There is nowhere else in the world I will ever want to be!'

'Then let me help you.'

Charl answered slowly, shaking her head in confusion. 'Oh, very well,' she said softly.

Seventeen

�֍֍֍

Jean-Louis La Soeur was gathering eggs in the tiny stable behind the house on ruelle du Porche when Seth Porterfield led the sturdy roan he had bought in Montreal between the houses and into the barn.

'Seth!' the boy greeted him jubilantly, setting the egg basket aside. 'Mother did not expect you back for another week.'

'A man learns to step lively with a war on,' he said noncommittally.

'Curry my horse, will you? And see that he gets an extra ration of oats. You may find a few pence beside your plate at dinner if you do it well. There's someone I'm anxious to see.'

Nodding, the boy took the reins from him and led the horse towards one of the two box stalls at the rear of the stable. Seth gave the roan a final pat and walked briskly towards the house.

In the kitchen Gabrielle looked up in surprise from the bread dough she was kneading as he greeted her.

'You're back sooner than I expected,' she observed, wiping her hands on her apron. 'Did you have a good journey?'

He did not even pause to answer. 'Is Charlotte upstairs?' he asked, and Gabrielle was amazed by the eagerness in his face.

'Yes, but . . .' Before she could finish the sentence, he had headed down the hall towards the front of the house. Gabrielle exchanged a worried look with Marie, who sat on a stool by the door churning butter, and hurried after him.

'Seth, wait!' she called out, but he chose to ignore her as he started up the steps. She sighed and turned back to the kitchen. Gabrielle had thought to warn him of the fury that awaited him in his room. Perhaps if he had been prepared to face Charlotte, he could have found some way to mollify her and avoid the confrontation that was now inevitable. For in the days that had passed since Charl discovered Seth's deceptions, her disillusionment had turned to bitterness and her hurt to hatred. She had steeled herself to confront Seth, fanning the flame of anger until it raged through her, consuming any feelings of tenderness she had ever known for the man who had seduced and betrayed her.

Seth sprinted up the stairs, taking them two at a time, stopping on the landing outside his room only long enough to smooth his ruffled hair. The door was slightly ajar, and he pushed it wider, smiling in anticipation.

Charl was seated in a Windsor chair in front of the fireplace, her hands busy with some bit of sewing. She was wearing the apricot gown he'd bought her, and he was pleased with how well it complemented her rosy gold colouring. Her hair was drawn back from her face to highlight the symmetry of her features and hung in soft, shimmering waves down her back. He spoke her name softly, enjoying the sound of it on his tongue, carefully shaping the vowels and consonants that were the essence of her.

Slowly her head came up. He read surprise in the arched brows and slightly parted lips. But when he met her eyes, there was a look of such deadly, cold hatred in their depths that it froze him where he stood. Confusion and disappointment welled up inside him.

He stared back at her across the space of the room, but the expression in the green eyes did not soften. Slowly he came towards her with his lithe, tigerish walk, until he stood above her. Watching her expression, he bent to rest one hand on each arm of the chair.

'I trust you've been well in my absence, Miss Beckwith,' he drawled, his face only inches from hers.

Charl had feared she would weaken when she confronted him, falling victim to his sweet words and charming smile once again, but she did not.

He saw her mouth go tight, and she slapped him with all the force of her arm. The blow was hard and had come so unexpectedly that he staggered back a step and stood looking down at her. One hand went up to the swiftly reddening palm-print on his lean cheek, but, surprisingly, he was not angry.

'This is not exactly the kind of homecoming I had expected,' he said dryly.

'But all you're liable to get from this quarter,' she hissed back at him.

'What, may I ask, have I done to incur your wrath?' he asked, resting one hip on the lid of the campaign chest and crossing his long legs at the ankle.

It infuriated her that he could be so unaffected by her rancour. She had expected to face his flaring temper, at least, but he seemed utterly calm.

'I know where you've been!' she stated bluntly.

'Where I've been? Where do you think I've been, Charlotte?' He crossed his arms on his chest and regarded her with interest, his eyebrows raised in mock innocence.

'You've been in New York,' she accused.

'New York? What an extraordinary idea.' His voice was smooth and calm, but he was making no denials. 'Where did you come by that bit of information?'

Rising and pushing him aside, she flung open the top of the campaign chest and withdrew the crumpled newspaper. Wordlessly, she handed it to him and was pleased to see his face harden as he read the article she had marked.

Damn! he cursed silently. Who could have forseen that she would come across something like this?

'Yes, I was in New York,' he stated, outwardly unruffled but realizing for the first time how deeply angry she must be. 'Why does that anger you?'

'You liar!' she whispered, her eyes flashing emerald lightning. 'You left me here!'

Charl was not going to give him a chance to explain, he realized, even if he could. Her conclusions had all been drawn, and unfortunately most of them had been correct. By his own hand he had made himself a villain, at least in her eyes, and in order to explain himself he would need to tell her things she could not know. He watched her stormy face, caught in the irony of the situation. The more he tried to protect her from what he was, the more cause he gave her to hate him. He smiled grimly and mentally prepared himself to bear her accusations. But Charl was not done with her revelations yet.

'I also discovered something else,' she told him.

'Oh? It seems you've been quite busy while I was gone,' he observed, his calm beginning to desert him. Warily he glanced towards the window sill. If she had discovered his cache of papers, he could be in grave trouble.

'Gabrielle and her family speak English as well as French,' she stated flatly. 'But then, you knew that. It was only to be kept a secret from me.' Her brows rushed together.

'Tell me, Seth, why was it so necessary for you to keep me isolated and dependent on you? What were you afraid I would discover?'

Charl was too quick, too aware, too determined, Seth found himself thinking. It was only by the grace of God that he'd kept the secrets he had. One day she would learn too much, and then her knowledge would imperil them both.

Mitchell had been right. Charlotte Beckwith was a danger to him, but not because he cared for her. Someday she might well have the power to expose him and, feeling as she did about him, she would do it without a qualm. He read the next words in her eyes even before she spoke them.

'I hate you, Seth!' Her voice came out low and full of enmity. 'You've played your cruel games with me for the last time. I swear, if it's the last thing I ever do, I'll see you hang for your treacheries.'

He almost laughed at her words, even while his mind reeled with the depth of her loathing. How well her threats mirrored his own fears, yet he could understand her feelings. He had been intentionally unfair with her, had deceived her, telling himself it was for her own good. Now she hated him and with good cause.

Suddenly, he wanted nothing more than to escape from that room. He had returned to Quebec seeking a haven where he could retreat and prepare himself before the war demanded his energies. He had wanted this woman to soothe him and fulfill his needs before he sent her home, but somehow things had gone awry. He moved towards the door.

'Are you going so soon?' Charl asked, her words dripping sarcasm. 'There is one more thing I would like to tell you before you go.'

Seth faced her, his eyes wary.

Slowly, she came towards him and poked one finger into his chest. She looked up at him almost seductively, but her eyes were like smouldering ice.

'You can have no more secrets, Seth,' she said softly, 'parce que je comprends chaque mot que vous dites en français.'

It was not true. Charl did not understand every word he said in French, but it would be many days before he would discover that. He reacted with shock to her words, his mouth dropping open and his eyes going wide and incredulous. Involuntarily, he took a step backwards, and Charl began to laugh although her expression was hard and bitter.

Damn unpredictable wench, he thought. Why was it that he always underestimated her? With a muttered curse he whirled and fled from the room, escaping from the girl's taunting laughter.

Seth thundered down the stairs only slightly faster than he had ascended them minutes before and stormed into the kitchen where Marie and Gabrielle were shaping the bread dough into loaves to be baked in the vaulted brick oven.

'What happened here while I was gone?' he demanded.

'Nothing that you did not prepare us for before you left,' Gabrielle answered sweetly as she continued shaping the loaf with her hands. She had once lived with the legendary Porterfield temper and could not be bowed by it now.

'Damn it, Gabby! I want to know how Charl came by that newspaper.'

She paused to open the oven door with a wad of towelling and placed a newly risen loaf inside.

'Waukee bought it for her,' she said, brushing the perspiration from her brow.

'Waukee!' Seth echoed, growing more furious by the minute. 'I thought I could trust him to keep Charl out of trouble.'

Gabrielle turned to face him, her own temper straining a little. 'You don't seriously think he would have bought the paper for her if he'd realized what was in it?'

Seth calmed slightly. He knew that Waukee would not deliberately expose him, regardless of past differences. Another thought struck him, and his anger flared again.

'How did Charl learn that you spoke English?' he wanted to know.

'I did not realize that Charl was behind me when I answered the door, and she overheard a conversation in English. I could hardly deny that I spoke her language after that,' she answered.

'And I suppose you taught her French, too.'

'Yes, I did! You went away and left that girl without friends and with no way to communicate her needs. You forbade me to speak English to her, so I had no choice but to teach her the bit of French she needed to manage. And a good student she's been, too,' Gabrielle said, stretching up to her full height, which was easily a foot less than his. Her dark eyes were steady as she faced him.

'You've treated that girl abominably, Seth, and there's no excuse for it. She's a fine woman and certainly deserves better. If you'd told her the truth from the beginning, none of this would have –'

'Oh, stop!' he interrupted. 'I should have known you women would stick together.' Disgustedly, he turned towards the door, nearly knocking Jean-Louis down in his haste to escape Gabrielle's recriminations.

On the street he turned right with no clear idea of where he was going. He needed to find somewhere quiet where he could gain control of his temper and collect his thoughts. Near the waterfront, he found a tavern frequented by dockworkers and rivermen that was deserted at this hour in the afternoon. He ducked inside, paused to let his eyes grow accustomed to the dimness, bought a tankard of rum, and found a table near the wall.

He took a long swallow of the liquor and closed his eyes, willing his calm to return so he could think logically. He had never expected to walk in on such havoc when he left New York. He'd even been anxious to return to Quebec and had travelled all night more than once to hasten his arrival. Now he found that everything had changed in his absence. He snorted in disgust and drank down another inch of liquor, staring distractedly across the empty room, a scowl twisting his face.

As much as he wished to deny it, he'd been impatient to return to Quebec because of Charlotte. He had been sure that once she was no longer his responsibility, he could put her out of his mind, but her memory had accompanied him everywhere. On the ship to New York the blue-green water had reminded him of her eyes. As he gambled in the backrooms of the saloons on Broadway, he had wished for the touch of her soft, cool hand on the back of his neck to bring him luck. Even the peace of his campsites had seemed strangely empty without her. Never had a woman so entangled his mind until his thoughts could hardly be called his own. It had been that lovely, wildly responsive woman he had left in Quebec who had haunted his memory and brought him rushing back. But now, in her place, he found a screaming shrew.

Did she hate him for the pain he had caused her? Would she

always despise him for the bruises that had been so slow to heal on her body or the scars that he had left on her pride?

Would she list among her reasons to hate him her kidnapping, seduction, or the mutual passion that had made her his mistress? And did she realize that he was as entrapped by that passion as she?

Seth drank deeply from the tankard before him, his thoughts focused on the truth within himself. He had never known a woman he desired more than Charl Beckwith. When they came together in passion, it was as if something unique was forged between them, something he could not explain. He had sought the whores in New York, trying to deny the attraction he felt for Charl, but he had failed. Never in his life had a woman stirred, tormented, and satisfied him as Charlotte did. It was as if she had been created just for him, to fit his body and fulfill his needs.

And now she had turned against him because he had lied to her.

He drained his tankard and clapped it loudly on the table, realizing that the tavern was becoming crowded. How long had he been sitting here while he drank his rum? And how much longer would he sit here still, waiting for the courage to face the woman in his room?

'Barmaid!' he shouted above the din, waving his empty tankard.

Would it really have been any different if he had told Charl the truth? he asked himself. And when should he have told her, that night in the stable, in York when he was not able to find her passage home, or before he left Quebec? Could the truth have saved them from the confrontation this afternoon?

He ran a hand through his hair as he watched the barmaid make her way towards his table.

Why was everything so difficult with Charlotte? Other women had easily succumbed to his good looks and his lazy charm. Why was it that Charl was always so ready to oppose him? He stared down into his empty tankard, wanting more rum to dull his brain and silence his questions.

She had raged at him before, but somehow this time was different. This time the bond between them had been irreparably broken by his actions and the tenderness irretrievably lost. Charl Beckwith had just cause to hate him, and nothing he could do would change that.

The barmaid broke into his black thoughts as she set a fresh rum in front of him, and he regarded her groggily as he rummaged for the money to pay her. She was vaguely pretty, with lank blonde hair and eyes that seemed almost green in the half-light. In the depths of his pocket his fingers closed around a small velvet box, and he withdrew it along with the coins. For a few seconds he stared at the black box as if he could not remember what it was; then he gave it to the barmaid along with the price of the rum.

'For you,' he said thickly, meeting her questioning eyes.

The girl pocketed the coins and slowly opened the lid of the box. He watched the change in her face when she saw the contents.

'Oh, sir,' she said reluctantly, 'you don't want me to have this.'

'Yes, take it!' he replied shortly.

'Oh, it's too lovely for the likes of me. Something like this is meant for a real lady.' She closed the lid and extended the box towards him, her eyes sad, but he would not take it back.

'Please,' he insisted, 'I want you to have it.'

The man must be far gone in drink to give away something of such obvious value, the girl thought.

'If you're sure,' she wavered, her basic honesty warring with her desire for the lovely piece.

He nodded and watched the barmaid carefully reopen the box. With a smile that was hard and full of irony he expressed his approval as the girl fastened the delicate gold chain around her neck and adjusted the perfect ivory cameo to lie in the hollow of her throat. Seth had bought it from a jeweller the morning he had left New York with the hope that it might please another lady as much as it did its eventual recipient.

'Thank you, sir,' the girl said.

His smile was bitter. 'It looks beautiful on you, my dear. Now, if you'll bring me a bottle of your best rum, I'll not disturb you for the rest of the evening.' As he watched her scurry off to do his bidding, he drained his tankard again.

❧

Seth had been in Quebec hardly more than twenty-four hours when word of fighting began to trickle in from the west. At first General William Hull seemed on the verge of capturing Fort Malden on the Detroit River, but as days passed and no news of Hull's victory arrived, the British were buoyed up by new hope.

Then a report of the surrender of the Americans at Michilimackinac to Captain Charles Roberts arrived, and the British were able
to claim control of Lake Huron and the lands to the west. On the
heels of that news came word of General Brock's victory over
Hull at Detroit and of the Indian massacre of Americans at Fort
Dearborn.

As the days passed, Charl came to dread the arrival of any
news from the west, almost wishing for the torturous days of
uncertainty. Her fear of battle along the Niagara was now eclipsed
by the blind panic she felt as word of the massacre at Fort
Dearborn spread. Although six hundred miles farther east,
Youngstown had known the horror of Indian hostilities in the
past, and the thought of that kind of warfare frightened her more
than the idea of an invasion by the civilized British. She knew that
somehow Seth had additional information about these events, but
she was loath to inquire. She had set her mind to avoid him at
all costs and could not bring herself to ask him for additional
news. Nor did she care to hear any more of his dire prophecies
about the outcome of the war now that his initial theories had
proved correct.

Quebec itself accepted the news with mixed reactions. Needless
to say, the military faction rejoiced in each new victory, and the
lights at the Château St Louis and in the Governor's Mansion
burned late in celebration. The troops took on a new jauntiness
as they realized that the endless drilling would serve a purpose,
and they prepared with newfound enthusiasm for the coming
war.

The citizenry was less pleased. By many of the Quebecois,
who felt no loyalty to the British, the victories were marked with
dread. They represented the beginnings of an unpopular war in
which they could see little gain. Wars inevitably led to ruined
land, squandered money, and senseless loss of life. There would
be no glory in winning for these simple farmers and tradesmen.
So as the British officers toasted their victories at the Château St
Louis, the men of town gathered in their taverns and speculated
on how the war would alter their lives.

In the midst of all this came word of an armistice, signed
August 9 by Lt General George Prevost and General Henry
Dearborn. Charl greeted this bit of news as the only ray of
sunshine in a dark world, taking comfort in the fact that for a
month's time Youngstown would be safe. She would not let

herself consider what might happen when the armistice was over, but was content to put aside her worry for thirty days.

There was no cessation of hostilities in the war that raged in the tiny room on ruelle du Porche. The combatants faced each other daily in loud verbal barrages or with stunning silences. There was little hope of victory in the conflict; nor would either party surrender.

Seth had returned to the La Soeur house that first night, much the worse for drink. His stumblings and muttered curses as he attempted to undress quickly awakened Charl, and she lay still in the darkness trying to form a plan of action. In the end she decided to present her back to him and hope for the best. After what seemed like a very long time, Seth came to bed. The weight of his large body on the feather mattress rolled her against him, and she scrambled away quickly.

'So you are awake,' he mumbled thickly. She was suddenly aware that he was naked beside her, and in spite of her aversion to him, a shiver of excitement went through her. It was quickly followed by a second as his hand swept up under her arm to cup her breast. Obligingly her nipple hardened against his palm, and she silently cursed her own weakness.

'Charl, my love, where did you get this wretched nightshirt?' The intensity of the disgust in his voice was almost comic. 'I'm sure it wasn't with the things I bought for you.'

She sat up suddenly, anxious to break the physical contact he had initiated, and turned to face him. He grinned back lopsidedly.

'My God, you're lovely in the moonlight!' he said softly and reached for her again.

'Keep your hands off me, you drunken sot!' she told him coldly. 'If you touch me again, I'll scream the house down; I swear I will. Why don't you leave me alone and find somewhere else to sober up? This is my bed.'

His eyes were hooded as he watched her, and his smile was drunkenly serene.

'This was my bed first,' he reminded her, 'and at least I was generous enough to share it. Besides, madam, I am far too muddled tonight to find somewhere else to lay my head. Now, if you have no desire for my affections, you must excuse me as I plan to go to sleep.' With those polite, distant if slightly slurred words, he turned his back to her.

She stared after him furiously, wishing she could think of a suitably scathing comeback. It irked her that, as intoxicated as he was, he had somehow bested her. With a toss of her hair she turned her back and lay down. It was not long before she slept again.

Sleep did not come so quickly to Seth. At first he lay awake because he dared not close his eyes and let the room spin nauseatingly around him, but he was also painfully aware of Charl beside him. Staring into the dark, he wished he knew the words that could destroy the wall of hate she had erected between them. He hungered for the feel of her, soft and yielding against him. But even more than her body, he wanted her good will. It was so easy to fence with words, he decided sleepily, but so difficult to find the ones that would make things right between them. As he drifted between sleep and wakefulness, he tried many phrases in his spinning brain, and, oddly, most of them sounded like apologies.

The next day passed in stony silence, with Charl busy in the kitchen helping Marie and Gabrielle put up grape preserves. Seth was plainly unwilling to broach any subject with his throbbing head and uncertain stomach to hamper him, but by bedtime both parties were ready to join battle again.

When Seth entered the bedroom, Charl was already wearing the long nightdress and had brushed out her hair. Although the gown was of modest cut, he could see the sway of her breasts through the light fabric, and a stab of desire went through him. His eyes followed her hungrily until she climbed into bed and snuffed the candle. In the darkness Seth began to undress.

'Mr Porterfield,' came Charl's cold voice from the bed, 'I do not intend to share my bed with you another night. Find somewhere else to sleep!'

'It is my intention to sleep here,' he told her, his tone firm, 'so if you've no desire to share this bed, I suggest it is you who should be seeking other accommodations. However, I am perfectly willing to be generous, and you may stay if you like.' He hung his shirt on the back of the chair and sat down to remove his boots.

She glared at the dim figure silhouetted in the moonlight.

'If you were a gentleman, you would not put a lady out of her bed,' she said.

He chuckled softly, and she could see his grin as he came towards the bed, having divested himself of the rest of his clothes.

'I think we established long ago, Charlotte, that I am no gentleman.' The bed gave under his weight, and Charl stiffened to avoid being rolled towards him.

'Then give me your word that you will not touch me,' Charl negotiated.

'No,' came the soft reply.

Charl spluttered angrily beside him, but his voice went on smooth and sure.

'I intend to touch you everywhere until you burn with desire for me, as I do for you. I plan to melt your resistance with my kisses until you have no more strength to oppose me.'

'Oh!' Charl said, unsettled by the memories his words brought to mind. His manner was lightly teasing, but she had no doubt that his threats were real. A warm shiver of excitement raced down her spine, for as much cause as she had to hate him, she was still strangely attracted to him.

In self-defence she skittered out of his reach by climbing over the footboard to the floor, dragging her pillow and the patchwork quilt with her.

'Arrogant ass!' she muttered furiously from the foot of the bed. 'I've no desire to stay here and be manhandled, so I guess I will find somewhere else to sleep.'

'Very well,' he said in a voice that sounded angry. 'I hope you enjoy your rest.' She heard the bed creak as he rolled over, and there was the rustle of covers as he settled in.

Determinedly, she left and closed the door, pausing on the landing to decide where she might sleep. It was too late to disturb Gabrielle, Marie, or Anne, so she padded down to the parlour and tried to make herself comfortable on the sofa. It was narrow and at least a foot too short for her, but she lay down, pulling her knees up to her chest and shivering under the thin quilt. Who would have thought it could be so cold in August? she wondered as she drifted off to sleep.

It was some time later when she awoke to find a tall, black shape towering above her. With difficulty she muffled a scream as she was snatched off the sofa, quilt and all, and held in arms that were rigid with anger.

'Damn you, woman!' Seth muttered furiously in her ear. 'If you must have my word, then I give it. But come back to bed!'

He was carrying her steadily upward, giving her no choice in the matter, and she began to struggle against his chest.

'And how can I be sure I can trust your word this time when it's been no good in the past?' she asked, driven by an unreasonable anger of her own. He stopped dead, and she felt the arms beneath her shoulders and her knees turn to iron. For an awful moment she thought he was going to drop her, but he resumed his climb.

'In this I can keep my word You're not all that desirable.'

She was strangely piqued by his words and whispered back the first thing that came into her head. 'It's a shame you didn't discover that sooner, or I wouldn't be in this mess.'

Again he went totally still, and Charl could almost hear his heart beating. 'What do you mean by that?' he demanded.

She stared up at him, confused by his reaction. 'What do you think I mean?'

'You're not going to have my child?'

Her mouth dropped open with shock. Although she was not naive, it had never occurred to her that pregnancy might be the outcome of their activities in bed.

'Good Lord! No!' she gasped.

'Are you sure?'

'Yes!' Her nod was one of conviction.

'That's good,' he commented dryly. 'I'm not ready for fatherhood.'

In the room at the top of the stairs he settled her on the far side of the bed and lay down beside her.

'I have given my word not to touch you, but it would not be wise to tempt me unduly,' he warned her.

'You need not fear,' she replied sharply. 'I can't think of anyone whose advances would be less welcome than yours.' With that she turned her back and pulled up the sheet.

The first skirmishes in the war on ruelle du Porche were indecisive, and occasionally there was a lull in the fighting when Seth would disappear overnight and occasionally for days at a time.

Charl was busy now, helping with the preparation of food for the winter. It seemed ironic to her that the hottest days of the summer should be spent preparing for winter. Still she did not mind the time spent in the kitchen with the other women, and they chattered endlessly in a mixture of French and English, sharing an easy camaraderie. They worked for hours tending kettles of preserves. Charl's hands became raw from the brine they used to make pickles in the heavy earthenware crocks. They dried fruit, pears and apricots, and left grapes in the sun to turn to raisins. They made several batches of a spicy brown relish called ketchup that required dozens of thinly sliced green tomatoes to be boiled with onions, vinegar, and maple sugar. After enough had been stored in the root cellar for the family's use, Gabrielle sold the rest to a Mr Emile Savard who kept a stall in the market in the Place Royale. He came often to inspect the production of the ketchup, but it soon became evident that his interest was less in ketchup and more in Gabrielle.

Although Charl did not mind sharing in the housework or helping with the bottling and preserving, she was anxious to leave Quebec. When Seth failed to make any mention of a journey to Youngstown, she called in the promise that Gabrielle had made to talk to him.

It was with this purpose in mind that Gabrielle approached Seth in the stable one day in early September. She stood for some minutes watching him curry the big roan, noting that he seemed tense and tired. The battle of wits that raged between him and Charl was taking its toll on both of them, and she wished that she could effect a truce. Gabby knew that Seth vacillated between a desire to placate Charl with gifts and kindnesses and anger that she should remain so steadfast in her hatred of him. Two new dresses had appeared in Charlotte's wardrobe, and there were often trinkets or flowers beside her plate at dinner. The pianoforte in the parlour was suddenly and mysteriously in tune, after years of disuse, and new musical selections were found on the music stand. Seth had even borrowed a horse one day and offered to take Charl riding. Her refusal had been curt, and when he left with Anne in tow, his mood had been understandably stormy. At times he seemed almost to be courting the girl, but nothing he did won her favour or breached the barrier she had erected against him.

Gabrielle wondered, as she stood in the stable watching him, if he wouldn't be almost relieved to be rid of Charl.

'Seth,' she began gently but pointedly. 'Things have changed so since you brought Charl to Quebec. Don't you think it's time to take her home?'

He paused in his brushing of the shiny brown coat and looked down at her, reading understanding in her face.

'God knows I'd like to, Gabby. I'm tired of fighting her night and day, but there's trouble brewing along the Niagara, and I'll be damned if I'll take her back there to be in the middle of it.'

Gabrielle chilled to his words. She had no desire to see Charl in danger either. 'Are you sure? The armistice –'

'The armistice will be over in a matter of days.' He shook his head. 'It was never meant to be an overture to peace, as Prevost claimed, but a prelude to war. Brock has been recalled to Fort George, and General Van Rensselaer has been put in command of the New York state militia. The battle lines are already being drawn on both sides of the Niagara River and I don't have any intention of putting Charl into that situation.'

'Seth, you do care about her,' Gabrielle observed softly.

He laughed and set aside the curry comb. 'I simply have no desire to see her hurt.' He came slowly towards the French woman.

'Gabby, can't you make her see that here in Quebec she's safe? In Youngstown she'd be in constant danger.'

'You know it won't change a thing,' Gabrielle said regretfully. 'She has her mind made up. She would rather cast her lot with her family and friends than stay here alone, out of harm's way. And I can understand how she feels.'

Seth's voice was weary. 'I know. I know. But talk to her please, will you? She won't listen to me now, even when I do tell her the truth.'

Gabrielle had been right about Charl's reaction to the explanations she tried to give.

'And when does he plan to take me home?' Charl demanded before she stalked out of the kitchen. 'Does he expect to keep me here until the war is over?'

Gabby watched helplessly, wondering if there was any solution to the problem that kept these two people at odds. Charl had every right to want to go home to Youngstown. But could Seth be faulted for wanting to protect the girl? She shook her head with worry, sipping a cup of tea absently. If only she could think of some way to ease the tension between Charl and Seth, they might be able to recognize the deeper emotions that stirred them both.

Upstairs, Charl almost welcomed the chance to rail against Seth Porterfield and his treatment of her. In the days and nights since his return, Charl found it increasingly difficult to sustain her hatred for him. His gifts had been generous, and his kindnesses many, each one eroding her antagonism a little. Still she was determined that she would not be bought off or won over by his insidious charm, as she had been in the past. She had good reason to hate him, she told herself as she recited the litany of his sins. But gradually the breaches in her armour began to appear, made by his wit or his kindness or perhaps her own susceptibility. It was only her stubbornness and her determination to avoid him that kept her staunchly opposed to him. And at times the angry words she flung at him were devoid of that emotion.

The month of September began to slip past with its warm, golden days and chilly nights that hinted at the approach of winter. Crisp mornings left the garden beaded with crystal droplets of dew that sparkled with the first rays of the sun, and the cerulean sky was swept with the wispy clouds of autumn.

Charl and Gabrielle made daily trips to the market, carrying baskets of squash, potatoes, or apples to be stored in the root cellar below the kitchen. Since the children had returned to school, Seth often accompanied them to help with the heavier loads and cumbersome bushels of vegetables, but he would then leave the house, reappearing only in the evening. Charl sometimes wondered where he spent his days, but she was too busy helping Gabrielle and Marie with the last preparations for cold weather to waste much time on such thoughts. Sweetcorn and apples were dried by hanging them near the fire, strung or woven together in order to make them easier to store on nails in the rafters, much as the apricots and pears had been. And for days the air was redolent with the sweet-tart tang of apples, either bubbling to sauce in the black iron kettle over the fire or being turned into pies or pastries that were a tribute to Marie's artistry with sugar and flour.

As busy and as full as her days were, her nights were long and restless. From dark until dawn she could not avoid Seth, and she was intensely aware of him beside her in the double bed, although they rarely spoke. Any words that had passed between them of late had been biting and cruel, and Charl found that as her feelings of hatred began to dissolve, her comments became more cutting and venomous.

Seth was not sleeping well either, she knew with the certainty of someone who shared his bed. And as she lay awake, she was not sure if it was her own frustration and confusion or his tossing and turning that robbed her of her rest. Many nights, as she lay watching the shadows on the ceiling, she was aware that Seth was awake beside her, and it took all her strength of will not to turn to him for comfort and companionship in the darkness.

Charl recognized that she was living in a world of pretence, where her anger had become no more than a ruse to protect her from herself. And she knew that her actions no longer reflected her true emotions, but she did not know how to let down her guard. She had fought Seth so hard and so bitterly that there seemed to be no way to offer peace without leaving herself totally unprotected. And she could not do that. So she avoided him in the daylight, ignored him in the dark, and watched the chasm between them widen day by day.

It was the nights when Seth slept deeply, exhausted by one of his mysterious journeys, that were the worst for Charlotte. Then she could watch him freely, his features softened and vulnerable with weariness. With her finger she could gently trace the mocking curve of his brow, the straight nose and the firm, narrow lips and let the tenderness well up inside her. Nothing had been resolved between them in the weeks since his return, and nothing had changed except her feelings for Seth. She wanted desperately to hate him, knowing that hate was a far less dangerous emotion than the others that threatened to overwhelm her, but she could not. On these nights when he would curve unconsciously against her, pressing close to her body, she would lie with tears in her eyes, wishing that she could deny that she loved him. But she could not.

Eighteen
✳✳✳

The Bach concerto filled the cosy parlour with strong, stirring phrases of music that seemed a counterpoint to the tranquillity of the domestic scene. The firelight reflected on the pale plastered walls, turning them saffron and apricot and deepening the shadows on the heavy beams in the ceiling. Somehow the mellow glow from the flames revived the colours in the worn carpet, bringing the rich jewel tones to life once again and highlighting the intricate carving on the arms and legs of the chairs and tables.

On the floor in front of the fire the boy and girl played a game; their laughter and exclamations at the turn of a card were the only sounds that intruded on the music. The old woman dozed peacefully in her chair, her lined face collapsed in sleep. At the far end of the room sat the mistress of the house and Monsieur Emile Savard, the merchant from the market at Place Royale. He had been a guest for dinner and now sat contentedly smoking his pipe as he watched Gabrielle work on a piece of embroidery. Monsieur Savard was a shy man who, in his own quiet way, was seeking someone to replace the wife who had died some months before. It was evident by the way his eyes followed Madame La Soeur that he felt he had found that woman, and he was completely captivated by her. Only the blond man seemed unaffected by the peace in the room as he stared fixedly ahead, oblivious to the book in his lap and the thin, dark cigar that burned to ashes between his fingers. There was a tension to the set of his broad shoulders and an intensity in his blue eyes that would have alerted the woman at the pianoforte had she not been so lost in the pleasure of her music. Her eyes were closed as her slender fingers skimmed the keys, loosing a melody she had learned long ago. In the light of the candles that stood on either side of the music stand, her ivory skin glowed flawlessly and complemented the amber shade of her hair.

The concerto ended with a powerful sweep of chords, and almost immediately the girl began to play a light, rollicking tune. The melody roused the blond man from his thoughts, and he smiled as he recognized one of the bawdy ballads he had taught the girl himself. Seth tossed the stub of the cigarillo into the fire and directed his gaze to the woman at the pianoforte. The music brought back warm memories of their trip to Quebec, and, coincidentally, he had been thinking of the Indian who had accompanied them. Waukee had disappeared only a few days after Seth had returned to Quebec. At first, his absence had not seemed unusual, since he had intended to travel north to gather herbs but, as the days turned to weeks, Seth became concerned. In one of the few civil conversations he had had with Charl since his return she asked about Waukee. And he hadn't been able to tell her anything. He only hoped that the Indian had not gone west to rejoin his people. Reports of raids along the American frontier by the Shawnee and several other tribes under Tecumseh filtered into Quebec with some regularity, and the descriptions of the brutality and damage done by the Indians made Seth's blood run cold. He could not imagine that the strong, gentle man he called his friend could be a party to such devastation, but as the length of Waukee's absence grew, Seth began to worry. Never would he want to face Waukee as an enemy.

As the tall grandfather clock in the hallway began to chime nine o'clock, Emile Savard gathered his short legs under him and rose to go. Gabrielle shooed Anne and Jean-Louis up to bed and gently awakened Marie, who followed them upstairs. A few minutes later Gabrielle closed and bolted the front door behind Emile and then retired herself.

Seth came to stand beside Charl at the pianoforte, turning the pages of the music as she directed.

'You play very well,' he complimented her as she finished the new piece and began to stack the music on the top of the pianoforte.

'Thank you,' she replied with a slight smile. For once there was no hostility in her eyes, and Seth was reluctant to initiate a conversation that would undoubtedly put it there. He watched her, warmed by her nearness and her beauty, but when she turned to go to bed, he caught her arm. She looked up questioningly.

He knew there was no way to put off what had to be said.

'Charl, I'm going away tomorrow.' He saw her expression

change. 'It's possible that I'll be in a position to get a letter to your father if you care to write one.'

'Are you going to Youngstown?' she asked eagerly.

'You know very well I can't set foot in Youngstown,' he frowned.

'Nearby, then?' Her eyes were bright. 'Oh, Seth, please take me with you. I won't be any trouble. I swear it. I'll help you sail. I'll cook for you and make camp.' Her cheeks were flushed, and there was an animation to her face that had been missing for weeks.

'I know I've been impossible since you came back, but I promise I'll do whatever you say if only you'll take me home.'

His face was hard and unreadable, hiding the effect her words had on him. For a moment he was tempted to take her with him, despite the dangers she would face in Youngstown, simply so he would not have to watch the warmth in her eyes turn to cold hatred. But his mind was made up. In spite of what she might want, he was responsible for her, and he would do what he must to keep her safe.

'No,' he said quietly.

'But why?' With a single word he had dashed all her hopes. Her expression turned from one of hope to entreaty and then to anger as she realized that he meant what he said.

Taking her rigid arm he led her to the sofa and made her sit down beside him.

'I want you to listen carefully because I am only going to explain this once,' he said with exaggerated patience, as if he were talking to a child.

'There is going to be a major battle along the Niagara soon.' Charl's face paled, and he tried to ignore the stricken look that came into her eyes. 'We know that Dearborn has received orders to invade Canada, and that could touch off fighting all along the border. I understand why you want to go home, but I won't take you there now to be caught in the middle of this campaign.'

'Your concern does you credit, of course,' she said icily, 'but when do you plan to take me home?'

He regarded her beside him. The angle of her head and the set of her jaw were haughty, regal, angry.

'I don't know,' he answered honestly. 'When it's safe. Not now.' His tone turned mocking. 'My motives are really very gallant, Charlotte. I don't want you hurt. If your father were privy to my thoughts, even he could not fault me.'

'If my father were privy to your thoughts, he would have called you out long ago. And I know there's not a gallant bone in your body.'

She changed her tactics suddenly, and her wide eyes came up to his face, soft, promising, with golden lights dancing in their blue-green depths. She leaned closer.

'Take me home, Seth. There's nothing to gain by keeping me here, and you know that I can take care of myself.'

He laughed softly, strangely aware of her seductive powers and angry that she was using them like an accomplished coquette. What had happened to the sweet, naive girl he'd met in Youngstown? His anger grew as he acknowledged the only possible cause for the change in her; her loss of innocence was his fault. But even while he castigated himself, he was curious to see how far she was willing to carry the flirtation. He said nothing but watched her closely, his sapphire eyes smouldering with mixed anger and desire.

Charl lowered her lids in confusion, and a look of uncertainty crossed her lovely face. For a moment he thought she would give up the game, but then a deceptively sweet smile came to her lips and she laid a palm on his sleeve.

'Seth, please, it would mean so much to me to go home,' she whispered. Her eyes were round and entreating behind the thicket of dark lashes. She bit her lower lip, her even white teeth tugging at the pale, coral mouth in an invitation that any man could read. 'I've been homesick . . .'

Anger pounded in his temples, and desire turned his blood to flame.

Damn her for resorting to this kind of trickery, he thought. And damn me for being susceptible to it.

'I would be so grateful . . .' she was saying.

'How grateful would you be, Charlotte?' he asked, the timbre of his voice low and rich with anger.

'What?' she faltered.

'I said, how grateful would you be if I took you home?' His hand had come up to cup the back of her head, gently but firmly holding her in place as his other arm circled her waist.

Panic flickered across her features. Charl had not been sure what she hoped to accomplish with her actions, but she realized suddenly that things were swiftly moving beyond her control.

'Why I . . .' she stammered, breathlessly.

'Would it be worth a kiss?' he taunted. In the depths of his blue eyes emotions raged that she could not comprehend. 'Or maybe two?'

He drew her inexorably closer until his lips brushed hers. A tremor passed through her body as he deepened the kiss, and then, as if suddenly aware of what was happening, she pushed him away.

His voice was filled with bitter mockery as he looked into her flushed face.

'If you plan to make this kind of a bargain with a man, my dear Charlotte, you must learn to give freely of your body.'

She drew breath for a scathing reply, but he pulled her down on the sofa beside him, covering her mouth with his own. Stubbornly she resisted him, but his lips were like velvet, soft, tantalizing, and her will to oppose him was slowly trickling away. His tongue probed her mouth, caressing hers, and she felt as if she were melting under his assault like ice in the hot sun.

He chuckled softly with satisfaction, pressing kisses down her neck while his fingers sought the buttons on her bodice. The gown opened under his hands, and with careless haste he pushed aside the chemise, freeing her breasts. She arched against him as he kissed her nipples, tangling her fingers in his thick hair and urging him on. Dimly she realized that in the past weeks, when she had denied him this wild, sensual pleasure, she had denied herself as well. With a trembling sigh, Charl gave up any thought of stopping this passion before it reached its culmination.

Reading her total surrender, Seth came abruptly to his feet, ignoring his body's demands that he make love to this girl who stirred him so. Below him, she lay half naked on the settee, entrapped by the sensual web he had woven so skilfully around her. He watched as she opened her eyes, dazed and confused by his withdrawal. Dizzily she sat up, her gaze moving to the sardonic expression that twisted his face and masked his anger.

'You're a novice at this, Charl, and I've just taught you a valuable lesson.' His voice was purposely cruel. 'Whores seduce their clients, not the other way around.'

Her brain was still clouded with passion, and she frowned, trying to make some sense of his words.

'What do you mean, Seth?' she asked. 'How can you say such a thing to me?'

'Offering enticements for favours? That certainly makes you a whore, my darling Charl.' He moved to the fireplace, took a thin cigar from a humidor on the mantel, and lit it with a taper before he continued. 'Would you have let me make love to you if I had agreed to take you to Youngstown?'

'No, I . . .' Outrage and confusion struggled in her breast.

'Well, it really doesn't matter,' his voice was deceptively cold, 'because I'm not taking you anywhere with me. And if you still want me to deliver a letter to your father, I warn you, it had best be written soon.' Without giving her a chance to reply he strode out of the room, and a moment later she heard the back door slam behind him.

A groan of anger and humiliation rose in her throat, and suddenly she was crying, noisily, without any attempt to restrain her sobs. There had been a grain of truth in Seth's accusations, she realized, but her actions had been closer to the instinctive cajoling of a child than the ruthless manipulations of a designing woman. Trust Seth to think the worst of her and then to point out her inadequacies as well. Why was it that he took such joy in humiliating her? she wondered. He never let an opportunity pass to demonstrate how he could control her, and he ruthlessly exploited her obvious weakness for him. She took a shaky breath and brushed the tears from her cheeks.

For a moment her thoughts tumbled senselessly. Then as she calmed herself, she began to think what she must do. First, she would write a letter to her father. Word of her safety must reach him as soon as possible to ease his worry. And then? Well, she would find a way to make sure Seth took her to Youngstown. He had unwittingly dictated the terms of his bargain on this matter, and Charl had already paid the full price. She had given herself to him freely; now he had only to comply. Willing or unwilling, he would take her home, but it would take cunning to make him fulfill his part of the bargain. Charl knit her brows in thought. If she could follow him undetected as far as Trois-Rivières or Montreal, he would have to take her the rest of the way to Youngstown, she reasoned recklessly. She was well aware of the dangers she would face on such an expedition, and she knew she was gambling everything on Seth's reluctance to take time to return her to Quebec, but she had no choice. In a matter of weeks the rivers would be covered with ice, and the trails would be made impassible by snow. If she did not leave now, she would have to stay in Quebec until spring. Resolutely, she climbed the stairs. She knew what she must do.

In the stable behind the house Seth shared no like sense of purpose. He leaned against the door to the roan's stall, feeding him a handful of oats and stroking his velvety muzzle absently. His anger had cooled, leaving him tired and vaguely disillusioned.

He was plainly stunned by the change he had seen in Charl tonight. Where was that guileless girl he had met at the Crow's Head Tavern? he wondered moodily. What had happened to that curious child-woman with her innocent questions about passion? The Charlotte who had faced him tonight seemed hardly related to the girl she had been only a few short months ago. Then she had been ingenuous, startled by the stirrings of her own desire. Tonight she had played the tart, promising everything with her eyes, bargaining shamelessly for the thing she wanted most.

He shook his head in wonder. As much as he might regret his part in this transformation, he was excited and beguiled by the woman she had become. Charl's desire for independence had intrigued him, and he had been captivated by her beauty, but her motives had been as transparent as glass. Now she had become a many-faceted woman, glowing with life, reflecting the subtleties of her world with diamondlike clarity. As sudden and as disconcerting as the change had been, he was not sorry it had occurred. She had grown up, and as the days passed, she would continue to grow, becoming more complex, more brilliant, and more compelling.

In the darkness he puffed on the slender cigar until the tip glowed bright orange, then exhaled, watching the feathery stream of smoke rise towards the roof. He would give her some time to compose a letter to her father, he decided, settling himself on a barrel by the door. There was probably much she needed to say. Later, he would go up and prepare for his journey.

More than an hour had passed when he went inside and climbed the stairs to his room. The door was shut tight, and it took him only one try to realize that Charl had slipped the bolt on the inside. As futile as he knew it was, he set aside the candle he'd carried up from the kitchen and assaulted the sturdy panel with his shoulder. It did not budge.

'Charlotte!' he whispered furiously, leaning against the solid wood. 'Damn it, Charl. Open this door!'

He waited, but there was no sound of movement from within the room.

'You're going to be very sorry if you don't open this door immediately, Charl!' he threatened ominously. Another minute passed, but the bolt was not slipped back.

In blind frustration he shouldered the door a second time, but with no better results than he'd had the first. Gritting his teeth, he pressed his ear to the smooth wood. There were slight whispers of movement on the other side.

'What are you doing in there?' he asked sharply. There was no reply. 'Charl, I have to be ready to leave at dawn tomorrow,' he said reasonably, keeping his voice calm with an effort. 'Now let me in!'

Seth could hear soft footsteps approaching the wooden barrier. In a minute he'd have his hands on her, and he'd find out what all this foolishness was about.

'I've packed your things for you,' came Charl's cool voice from the other side of the door. 'Your saddlebags are hanging over the railing. Have a pleasant journey.'

Muttering an oath Seth swung around and noticed the saddlebags hanging neatly over the railing at the far end of the landing beside his heavy buckskin jacket and his blanket roll. Moving the candle to the top step, he sat down and riffled through the bags. At first glance it seemed that Charl had been quite thorough. Then he noticed the neatly folded piece of parchment tucked into one of the pouches. Quickly, he withdrew it and skimmed the carefully penned lines, a frown blunting his brows.

He moved to the door again, the paper in his hand. 'If you don't let me in, I'll destroy this letter to your father,' he warned.

There was a pause. 'I don't care!' Charl answered defiantly. 'Whether you take that letter or not, my situation will be the same. Go away!'

Seth had the impression that she did care very much what happened to the letter, but he knew he would not call her bluff.

In the hallway he leaned closer to the door and imagined her doing the same on the opposite side. Suddenly the whole situation seemed ridiculous, and he grinned to himself in amusement and exasperation.

'Very well, my lovely Charl, then this is good-bye.' His grin deepened and his voice was coaxing. 'I had hoped to say good-bye with a kiss, but something seems to have come between us.' He heard her giggle. 'So I bid you a fond farewell.'

'Farewell,' she said softly. There wás a long silence. 'Seth?'

'What?'

'I hope it's not too long before I see you again.'

He stared at the blank door in amazement. There was a sincerity in her voice as she said the words that made several unaccustomed emotions collide in the middle of his chest, and he wished he could see her face. He almost asked her what she meant, but he realized that this was neither the time nor the place to discuss it. Nor could he picture himself whispering endearments into a keyhole. Resolutely, he gathered his belongings and picked up the candle. There would be time enough to find out what she meant when he returned.

With her ear pressed to the wood she could clearly hear him leaving, and she smiled mischievously to herself. What devilry had brought the last words to her lips she could not say, but they filled her with reckless abandon. With any luck she would see him in about three days' time at Trois-Rivières. Already she had donned the shirt and buckskins she had worn on the trip to Quebec and tied her necessities into the cashmere shawl. The neat bundle of possessions and her jacket and hat waited on the table so that she could snatch them up when she heard Seth leave. She would need to stop only long enough to add some food to her bundle before she followed him. Smiling smugly, she curled up on the coverlet and opened a novel. Without Waukee to help with the mackinaw, Seth would have to travel by land, and she doubted that she would lose him between Quebec and Trois-Rivières.

Charl was not quite sure what it was that jerked her awake, but as she sat up in the middle of the bed, a wave of panic washed over her. She had not meant to fall asleep, and now perhaps she had missed Seth's departure. There was a misty greyness to the sky that heralded the approach of dawn, and Charl rushed to the window, peering down into the street. Nothing stirred.

Pacing silently she considered her options. She could creep downstairs now and chance meeting Seth, or wait here and hope that he had not left. From somewhere in the bowels of the house she heard a door slam, and she was spared the decision. Breathlessly, she crept to the window and watched the empty street. It was some time before Seth emerged from the narrow passageway between the buildings, leading his horse. He paused in front of the house to adjust the cinch. He was wearing the heavy buckskin jacket against the early morning chill and looked tall and strong and handsome. A jumble of emotions seemed ready to overwhelm her as she watched him, but then Seth turned to look up at the dormer. With a small gasp she pressed back against the wall even though she doubted that he could see her from below.

Her heart thudded in her chest, and everything else was forgotten in the excitement of outwitting him. A look of triumph glowed in her eyes as she snatched up her belongings from the table and went to the door. With extreme care she slipped the heavy iron bolt that had kept Seth out the night before. She would have to hurry if she was to keep up with him. The doorknob spun beneath her eager fingers, but the door would not open. Frantically, she set her heels and pulled, but the heavy panel would not move. With a lurch of certainty she stared at the empty keyhole, and she suddenly knew what it was that had awakened her. It had been the sound of the key turning in the lock on the other side of the door.

With a curse she flew to the window. On the street below Seth looked up, his hands on his hips and a grin spreading across his face. When he saw her, he removed his hat and swept it downward, making a deep bow to acknowledge that he had seen through her schemes again. Muttering, she worked at the fasteners on the casement window, but by the time she flung it open, Seth had disappeared up the street.

❊

By noon Charl had been pacing the tiny second floor room for hours, caught up in her impotent rage, alternately storming and weeping with vexation. Again Seth had outwitted her by thwarting her plans to escape, and she was furious. Once, just once, she would like to outmanoeuvre him and catch him off his guard. Then, when she had him at her mercy, she would make him pay for all the times he had humiliated her. For a second, there was a malicious gleam in her eyes, but it quickly faded. As badly as he treated her, and as angry as he made her, Charl knew she would never do anything to hurt Seth. And it was because of this sudden softening of her feelings for him that she needed desperately to get away.

There was the grate of the key in the lock from behind her, and Charl turned from the window to confront her liberator.

Cautiously, Gabrielle pushed open the heavy wooden panel to face Charl.

'It's about time you set me free, jailer!' she spat, her green eyes sparking.

'In the note Seth left with the key, he said not to let you out before noon,' the Frenchwoman said evenly.

'So that's too late to follow him west!' Charl accused.

'Yes, so it's too late to follow him if that's what you had in mind,' Gabrielle agreed, shaking her head. 'Try to understand that Seth only wants to protect you.'

'Protect me?' Charl laughed bitterly. 'Gabrielle, can't you see past his lies? He wants me in Quebec to serve his own purposes.'

The two women faced each other in the tiny room, each certain that the other was wrong about the blond man's motives.

'What I see, Charl, is that he cares enough about you not to want to see you hurt,' Gabby said in a low voice.

At her words, Charl's heart began to drum in her chest, and she turned away from the dark-haired woman, wringing her hands. If only she could believe that Seth cared for her, she would stay with him gladly. But he did not care. Only last night he had insulted and humiliated her by exploiting the inexplicable confusion his kisses had the power to cause in her. In the end it was she who had weakened. It was she who had surrendered and had begun to care. And if she did not escape from Quebec soon, she would be at the mercy of a man who would use her love against her.

Pain was in her eyes as she turned back to the Frenchwoman who regarded her with concern.

'Gabrielle, you must help me leave Quebec!' she said beseechingly. 'You told me once that if Seth would not take me home, you would help me. Please, Gabrielle, I need that help now.'

Gabrielle heard the desperation in Charl's voice and frowned. If only these two had more time together, perhaps they would be able to resolve their differences and discover their real feelings for each other. It seemed so obvious to her that they were both bound by the same frustrated emotions. Or perhaps it was their fate to be separated for ever by their own wilful natures. For a moment she could not look at Charl as she tried to think of some way to evade the promise she had given. She had made it to comfort the girl when Charl discovered that Seth had gone to New York. But now that hastily given promise had become something more.

Gabrielle moved to stand beside the bed where Charl sat staring hopelessly at her hands.

'I don't know what I can do to help you,' she said truthfully. 'I have no money for passage or bribes. I know no men of importance to advise you or woodsmen to guide you. It was a promise I did not expect to have to keep.' Gabby's expression was sombre. 'But I will try to think of some way to help you even though I don't think you should go.'

Charl smiled sadly.

Gently, Gabrielle brushed back a stray lock of golden hair from Charl's cheek, sympathy stirring inside her. The girl was clearly torn between feelings of love and hate for Seth, and it was clear that a resolution to the conflict would not come easily.

'I must take some old clothing for the poor up to the Ursuline Convent,' she said gently, hoping to change the subject and divert the girl. 'Why don't you come and walk with me? It will do you good to be out.'

Charl nodded, anxious to retreat from her gloomy thoughts. 'I need to wash my face and comb my hair; then I'll be downstairs,' she promised.

The day was as warm as summer in spite of the morning's chill, and Charl's spirits rose with each step they took up the hill to Uppertown. From below the hulking rockface, the trees appeared appliquéd on to the azure sky. The elms and maples shone russet and gold, the chestnuts bright orange, and the oaks nearly crimson, in sharp contrast to the pines that always eluded the frost's seduction. The women scuffled through the leaves that had gathered in drifts at the street corners like a harlequin snowfall, past the ornate iron gate of the Quebec Seminary and the grey-stoned splendour of the Basilica de Notre Dame. It had been several weeks since either Charl or Gabrielle had been farther than the market at Place Royale, and they dawdled in the sunshine, revelling in their freedom. At the convent, where Anne attended school, Gabrielle gave the bundle of clothing to one of the sisters, and they made their way home across the Place d'Armes.

The square was busy, as it was at most hours of the day, but this afternoon there seemed to be a large number of British officers enjoying the glorious Indian summer day. Charl could not help but be impressed by their splendid appearance, even if they were the enemy. Their scarlet coats were brilliant in the sun, with their white crossed belts and the regimental colours on their collars and cuffs in sharp contrast to the cardinal red. Their boots shone black as night, and the cocked hats with their proud plumes gave a dashing martial air to the men, making them seem more dauntless and romantic.

'William must have been such a fine man,' Charl said impulsively, a tinge of wistfulness in her voice.

Gabrielle nodded, following Charl's gaze with a wistfulness of her own. 'Yes, he was a fine man,' she said slowly, 'strong and kind, but only a man.'

There was a long pause before she continued, and she regarded the girl at her side from under lowered lids. Perhaps it was not her place to speak to Charl of such things, but it was evident the girl was tortured by emotions she would not acknowledge. And she seemed to have unintentionally offered an opportunity to speak up. Choosing her words with care, Gabby went on.

'There were times, though, when William was stubborn and wilful and arrogant. He made me angry, but I loved him anyway.' Her voice was rich with emotion. 'William was a man, no more, no less, just as Seth is.' She turned to face Charl, her dark eyes intent on the girl's face.

'It is not how great a man is or how patient or how kind that makes him worthy of your love. It is how great his love is in return.'

Charl shook her head from side to side, ready to protest, but Gabrielle went on.

'You doubt that Seth loves you, but he does. It is in his eyes when he looks at you so strong and clear it cannot be mistaken. Perhaps he does not even realize it yet, but he loves you.'

'I do not want his love!' Charl said. 'I do not love him!'

Gabrielle laughed softly. 'Oh, chérie, that is why you so dread his return. You can no longer hide what you feel, and you must tell him that you care.'

Charl's eyes welled with tears. 'He does not deserve my love!' she insisted stubbornly.

'But you will give it anyway because you cannot hold it back. Remember that Seth is only a man with his own doubts and fears. Expect no more of him than that.'

With an exasperated cry Charl fled across the square, leaving several of the British officers watching her retreating figure with interest. Gabrielle followed after Charl, smiling to herself. She had done the right thing. What Charl needed now was time alone to come to terms with her emotions. She had reluctantly admitted to loving Seth; that would be a good start. And perhaps, by the time he returned, Seth would have realized his love for Charlotte, too. Gabrielle gave a slight Gallic shrug. One could hope for the best anyway.

In the weeks that followed they spoke no more of Seth, but as Charlotte tossed and turned in the wide, lonely bed, she could not forget Gabrielle's words. How could Gabby be so sure that Seth loved her? she asked herself a hundred times. Even in his most tender moments Seth had never done anything to indicate that it was more than desire that stirred him. Nor was Seth a man given to display his feelings. If he did care for her, it would not be an easy thing for him to admit. Daily Charl went through the motions of her life, and nightly she lay awake tortured by the same question: Did Seth Porterfield love her? Never could she settle on an answer. And she, who had always been a gambler, suddenly found the stakes too high. She had no choice if she was to remain her own woman; she had to find a way out of Quebec.

Waukee returned, as suddenly and as inexplicably as he had disappeared, to brighten Charl's days. The warm comfortable bond was renewed between them, and things went on as if he had never been gone. There were sails on the river and rides into the country now brilliant with autumn.

It was on one of these outings that Charl, driven by the desperation of another sleepless night, began to talk of Youngstown. Sitting companionably on a stone wall near where the horses grazed, Charl thoughtfully twirled a stem of Michaelmas daisies, watching the tiny purple flowers spin between her fingers.

'You seem preoccupied today,' Waukee observed, noting that there were pale violet smudges beneath her eyes and that her skin had lost much of its peachy glow.

'I want to go home,' she said simply, without looking up.

He watched her closely, tenderness growing in his dark eyes. It hurt him to see her so unhappy. Charl was the reason for his continued presence in Quebec. He had only intended to gather the medicinal herbs that grew north of the city and return to his

people, but somehow she held him here, caught up in the belief
that somehow, some day she would have need of him.

'What does Seth say about taking you home? I half expected
that I would return to Quebec and find you gone.'

Her expression was bitter. 'He says there is danger in Youngstown from the war.'

'There is,' he confirmed.

She shook her head. 'That may be so, but it is not for my safety
that Seth keeps me in Quebec. He only wants me here to be his
mistress!'

Charl spat the last word, and the Indian was surprised by her
venom. In spite of the things she had told him that night on the
bank of the St Lawrence, he had sensed that there was something
special between Seth and this woman. As he watched her bleak
expression, he conceded that he must have been wrong.

'Waukee.' The eyes that came up to his face were the dark
green of a pine forest. 'Would you take me home?'

He should have been expecting the request, but it caught him
off guard, and he floundered in confusion. For whatever reasons,
his friend wanted this woman in Quebec. That should have been
the end of it, but her unhappiness haunted him.

'Charl, I can't. You must understand –'

She silenced him with her fingers on his lips, her touch as light
as a butterfly's wing.

'Please, just think about it. I know I have no right to ask you –'
She stopped abruptly, recognizing emotions in his face that she
had not expected to see there. Almost instantly they were gone,
but she was shaken by what she read in his eyes.

'Perhaps we should go,' he said gently. 'There's a storm coming
in from the west.'

She followed the direction of his gesture and noticed the lumpy
grey mass of clouds quickly crowding out the blue sky.

'Yes, the wind's rising, too,' she agreed. 'Let's go.'

They returned to the house on ruelle du Porche late in the
afternoon, laughing, flushed and breathless from their race with
the rain.

'You'll think about what I asked you, won't you?' Charl said
as she bid him good-bye at the kitchen door.

'Charl, I . . .'

'Just think,' she prompted.

'All right. I'll think about it,' he agreed reluctantly.

Her smile was sunny, and his mouth curved upwards in response.

'And I'll see you tomorrow for a sail.'

'Yes,' he smiled again. 'Good-bye, Charl.'

Slowly she closed the door behind him, preoccupied with the prospect that she might convince Waukee to take her home. Then she turned to find Gabrielle glaring at her. Charl had never seen anger on the woman's usually serene countenance and stopped in surprise.

'I'll not have you coming between those two,' Gabby warned. 'Seth and Waukee were friends before you arrived, and they will still be friends when you are gone.'

Charl stared wide-eyed at the Frenchwoman, knowing that she could make no denials.

'If you're still determined to leave Quebec, there's a man you might go to see. I did not realize that he was still in Quebec until the other day when I saw him at the Place d'Armes. He has always had a reputation for getting whatever he wants, and maybe he'd be willing to do the same for you.' There was disapproval in Gabrielle's voice, but Charl ignored it.

'What is his name?' she asked.

'His name is Felix St James, and you should be able to find him at the Château St Louis.'

❧

The British officer looked up from the neat stack of papers in the centre of the large leather-topped desk. His aide stood uncertainly in the doorway, a look of reticence on his boyish face. The officer frowned, knowing that the young lieutenant's presence meant that there was someone else who wished to see him.

It had been a particularly busy afternoon, spent settling commissary accounts and listening to complaints from the populace about the troops billeted in town. He knew that there were more pressing duties for him to attend to than the ones of bookkeeper and mediator that had been foisted upon him when Major McKenzie was ordered west, but at the moment those took priority. He glanced briefly at the reports on his desk dealing with the efforts to combat an incredibly effective American spy network that was operating within the walls of the city and perhaps within the Château St Louis itself. He knew he must finish reading them before he would be able to join his fellow officers at the Barron's

Club on the far side of the Place d'Armes for dinner and an evening of cards.

'Yes, Jenkins. What is it now?' he growled, glancing up from the papers.

The young lieutenant came in and closed the door, his ingratiating manner irritating the officer all the more.

'There is only one more person to see you, sir,' Jenkins reported reluctantly.

The officer slapped one palm down on the desk in aggravation. 'And who, pray tell, is it now?' he snapped. 'I thought I'd already heard the wails of every scandalized French mama and tavern keeper in Quebec.'

'Oh no, sir. I doubt if it's anything like that. It's a young lady, sir, and a pretty one at that.'

'So you saved her for last?' the man inquired, straightening in his chair.

'To finish your day off pleasantly sir. At least I think she will. She wouldn't tell me the nature of her business.'

The officer allowed the slightest twist of a smile. 'Then perhaps you had better show her in, Lieutenant Jenkins, so that I may discover what it is.'

Jenkins turned and left, only to return a moment later escorting a young woman.

'Major Felix St James, ma'am,' he said stiffly, and left, closing the door behind him.

The girl paused in the centre of the room, and St James took the opportunity to study her. She could not be much more than twenty although she carried herself with an easy grace unusual in one so young. For once Jenkins had been right, he observed. The girl was lovely with her silky blonde hair and lush body.

From behind the desk he moved to indicate a chair.

'Won't you have a seat, Miss . . .'

'Beckwith, Charlotte Beckwith.'

'Ah, Miss Beckwith.' He paused as if fitting the name to its owner, watching her from beneath his slashing dark brows.

Charl stared back with equal intensity trying to assess this Major St James. He was the one person in Quebec who could help her get home safely if only she could convince him of her plight. So much depended on the next minutes. In spite of her resolutions, her stomach clenched with apprehension, and she wondered if she was doing the right thing in trying to leave the city. Firmly, she brushed the thought away and turned her attention to the man across the desk, sensing that he was not a man to be dealt with lightly.

He was in his early forties and bore the features and carriage of the English aristocracy. He was rapier-thin but with wide shoulders and a sinewy strength that seemed evident in even his most casual movements. In the last rays of sunlight that filtered through the tall windows overlooking the Place d'Armes, he seemed like a line drawing rendered in sharp strokes of sepia. His deep auburn hair curved like a corona around his high, regal brow and hawklike features. His cheekbones were sharp and prominent and the shadowed cheeks were like crevices in his lean countenance. Her eyes moved to his mouth, and Charl hoped to read his character in the curve of his lips. Seth's mouth, thin, firm, determined, with a hint of humour and softness at the corners reflected his nature exactly. St James' lips were full, proud, sensual, but there was a disturbing flicker of cruelty in the slight smile. Slowly, she met his gaze. Behind the hooded lids his eyes were deep red-brown, and they glowed almost as if a small flame shone out of their depths. The hairs on the back of Charl's neck rose in some primitive response to him, but she forced a smile on to her face and waited for his next words.

Felix St James had been regarding his visitor as closely as she had him, trying to decide what had brought such a beauteous creature to his office on this chilly October afternoon. Her classic features spoke of good breeding, though there was nothing frail or delicate in her, and she moved with the grace of a young Diana. The dark blue gown, trimmed with bands of lace, was becomingly simple and contrasted well with the long, gently curving curls of golden hair. As he watched this young woman, with her hands folded demurely in her lap, he was aware of desire stirring within him. He felt a need to possess her, just as he needed to possess anything beautiful and of obvious value. Allowing his eyes to rove over her freely, he knew that sooner or later he must take her to his bed.

Putting the thought aside, he smiled at Charl over the steeple of his fingers.

'Well, Miss Beckwith, what is it that you require of me?' St James asked.

Nervously Charl moistened her lips. She had prepared herself to explain the situation, but she had not expected to face such an imposing man. It was as if his mahogany eyes could see right through her and all the half-truths she had planned to tell. Still, she could not falter; there was too much at stake.

She moved slightly forward in her chair and met his gaze squarely.

'You see, Major St James, I find myself in a difficult predicament, and I had hoped that you could offer me a solution.'

'Indeed?' St James inquired, one eyebrow slanting sharply upward.

'I am an American citizen, sir,' she went on. 'When war was declared between our two countries, it was my misfortune to be visiting in Canada. I have made several attempts to return home, but thus far I have met with little success.'

'And where precisely is your home?'

'In Youngstown, New York, sir.' Charl was breathing easier now that she had begun and Major St James seemed friendly and concerned. 'Near Fort Niagara. My father is a merchant there.'

He nodded thoughtfully.

'We sent a ship of refugees to New York in August, I think it was. It is a shame that you did not come to me sooner.'

There was a flash of anger in her green eyes before she looked away.

'I arrived in Quebec too late to gain passage,' she told him.

He watched her closely. She was not telling the truth, he was sure of it, but her face did not betray her. There was more to her story than she was willing to admit, and she had begun to intrigue him. It would be amusing to draw her out.

'Is some other member of your family with you, Miss Beckwith? Someone else who will also need passage to the United States?' His face was bland, but she was sure he had begun to bait her.

Perhaps it would be better to get her shame out in the open immediately, Charl reasoned, rather than wait for it to be exposed by slow degrees.

'No sir. I am in Canada alone, under the protection of a British gentleman,' she said briefly and willed herself not to blush.

His eyebrows inched upward again, but she held her chin high.

'Pardon my inquisitiveness, Miss Beckwith,' he drawled, 'but just how did you come to be in Canada and under the protection of this gentleman?'

Now the heat rose in her cheeks, and she burned under the insinuation of his question. Did he think she was a common trollop coming to seek his favour? Her mouth drew taut as she struggled to control her temper. It would do her little good to storm out of his office as she longed to do. Involuntarily, she thought of Seth and wished fervently that she had never laid eyes on him. It was his fault that she had to sit here and be humiliated.

Her chin rose a bit higher.

'I assure you, sir, it was through circumstances beyond my control!' she snapped.

His full lips curved upward, and his eyes sparkled with satisfaction. The girl was proud and had spirit, in spite of her obviously degrading situation. She might not be as pure and virginal as she seemed, but she was no soiled dove either. There was a depth and power to her that had begun to fascinate him, and he was anxious to question her further, secure in the knowledge that she must answer him if she was to achieve her ends.

'And may I ask why you wish to leave Quebec if you have a gentleman willing to offer you his protection?'

Charl was as aware as he was that she would have to endure his questions if she hoped to enlist his aid. But it did not stop her from levelling a glance of pure loathing in his direction. She took a moment longer to compose herself, then faced him without flinching.

'I have never been in Quebec by my own choice, but of late life has become intolerable. I miss my father and my home. With the war on, I want to be in my own country, not sheltered by my enemies.' Her voice rose imperceptibly, and St James felt the deep emotions behind her words.

For a moment he was almost moved by her declaration, but he would not be diverted from his probe.

'Will your protector allow you to leave Quebec?'

'He is away now. I had hoped to be gone by the time he returns,' she said truthfully, lowering her lashes to hide the confusion that swept through her unexpectedly. What would Seth do if he returned to find her gone? Would it matter to him? Would he miss her?

'And when will he be back?' St James wanted to know, breaking in on her thoughts.

'I'm not sure. Please, Major St James, is there safe passage available to the United States?' she asked finally.

'And if I cannot help you obtain passage, what will you do?'

Charl was tired of his questions, and she knew that this arrogant man was toying with her. For a moment she was torn between anger and the need for his cooperation; but she had come too far to give up now.

'I shall start out on my own,' she answered levelly.

St James gave a gust of laughter. 'Don't be absurd, my dear. Such a journey would be impossible for a woman.'

Her eyes were as cold and hard as polished agate as she answered him. 'I assure you, sir,' she began, 'I can live in the woods, shoot a gun, and sail a boat if necessary. If I follow the river and then the lakeshore, there is no doubt that in time I will reach my home.'

He was regarding her speculatively, but she could read nothing in the shadowed face. 'If you are indeed capable of that why come to me?'

'Because I realize the way is long and difficult and the land is hostile to a woman alone.

'I came to see you, major, with the hope that you would help me. I can see now that I was mistaken.' She rose to go in a swirl of skirts, her beautiful face truculent, stormy.

She was magnificent, St James found himself thinking as he watched her sweep towards the door, passionate, wilful, beautiful, and worth possessing, at least for a time.

'Miss Beckwith, wait, please.' His voice stopped her at the door. 'I did not mean to indicate that I would not help you. I only wished to fully understand your plight.'

She turned to face him, regarding him coldly, and he found himself admiring her self-control. He was offering her exactly what she sought, but with her haughty expression she made it seem hardly acceptable. Slowly, she returned to her seat before the desk. Somehow her features seemed sharper and her emotions were carefully masked.

'Then there is something you can do for me?' she asked.

St James paused to light a lamp against the deepening dusk.

'You must realize, Miss Beckwith, that since war has been declared, there are no direct relations between your country and mine. There are, however, certain neutral ports to which you might sail and then book passage on an American ship.'

Charl carefully lowered her lashes as if considering the feasibility of such a plan, hiding the jubilation and relief that surged through her.

'That seems like a sensible suggestion,' she said and then paused.

'I will be frank with you, Major St James. I have no money at present, but I will gladly pay my passage once I reach my destination. Do you suppose such an arrangement could be made?'

'Oh, Miss Beckwith, I would gladly lend you the money myself,' St James offered, waving one hand as if brushing away the magnanimous gesture.

Charl studied him, weighing the ramifications of such a loan. 'That is certainly a generous offer,' she replied noncommittally.

'Well then,' he smiled slowly, 'shall I look into the possibility of your speedy departure, Miss Beckwith?'

Charl rose to leave, arranging the creamy shawl around her shoulders. 'I can think of nothing that would please me more, Major St James.'

Coming around the desk in two long strides, he escorted her to the door. 'Why don't you come by on Friday, and I will let you know what arrangements can be made,' he suggested.

'That would be fine. Thank you,' she said softly. Now that the bargain was made, she felt a surge of regret that brought a tightness in her throat.

The twin embers of his dark eyes bore into her as he brought her hand to his lips. At his touch that same primitive shiver of fear raced through her, as if he represented some terrible threat to her well-being. Mustering her courage, she met his eyes and smiled. After a moment he reached past her and opened the door.

'Jenkins!' he ordered.

'Yes, sir!'

Charl had the impression that the young lieutenant had been hovering just outside, waiting to be summoned.

'Jenkins, see Miss Beckwith out and then come to me. I have one or two more things for you to do before you return to the barracks.'

'Yes, sir!'

St James turned back to Charl.

'And I shall look forward to seeing you on Friday, my dear.'

'Until Friday then.'

Once alone in the Place d'Armes the enormity of what she had done struck Charl. Everything she had wanted since she had been abducted was now within her grasp. She could leave Quebec, escape Seth, and return to Youngstown at last. She had accomplished everything she had set out to do. There was every reason for her to be jubilant. Why was it then that her victory left her nothing but emptiness?

Felix St James stared intently over his steepled fingers in a characteristic pose of deep concentration, oblivious to the reports that awaited his attention or to his aide's return to the office. Though his eyebrows were drawn over the bridge of his nose, there was a sliver of a smile on his lips as he thought of the young woman who had just made her exit. It had been a long time since a woman had piqued his interest as Charlotte Beckwith did. There could be no doubt that she was lovely, but it was the fiery nature beneath that haughty exterior that intrigued him and made him want to possess her at any cost.

As a man grew older, he began to realize that there was more to a woman than a perfect face and body. To hold a man for more than a night or two a woman must possess intelligence, wit, and a rare combination of strength and spirit. Although she was young, St James sensed these things in the beautiful American and he meant to make her his, for a time at least.

The corners of his mouth rose, and his eyes glowed almost red in their sockets as he anticipated the pleasures he would discover when he took Miss Beckwith to his bed. She was not the kind of woman who would submit easily, and yet there would be passion in any response she gave.

Slowly, the smile withered and a deep frown came in its place. Someone had already made the lovely Charlotte his mistress, St James realized. A tide of unreasonable jealousy rose in him. Suddenly he was curious to know the identity of this other man.

'Jenkins!' he snapped loudly, startling the young officer. 'I will need a roster of ships leaving Quebec in the next weeks: their homeports and their destinations.' He paused.

'And Jenkins.'

'Yes, sir.'

'Miss Beckwith has a protector here in Quebec. I want you to have one of our men find out who he is.'

Nineteen

✻✻✻

Seth Porterfield pulled his horse to a stop on the jutting ridge of land that overlooked the St Lawrence just upstream from Quebec and sat watching the activity on the river. Slinging one long leg across the saddle and leaning on his knee, he stared pensively at the boats and barges that moved below him. The trees on the opposite bank were nearly bare, and in the late afternoon sun the birches' white trunks and branches were like chalk lines sketched against the pines. It would not be long before winter arrived to smother the land with snow and choke the river with ice floes, effectively forestalling the war that had changed his life. Perhaps in the winter's lull he would be able to come to terms with his actions in the battle at Queenston Heights.

Bleakly, Seth wondered if he could ever reconcile the betrayal of his English heritage or if he would regret the decisions he made so impulsively at Queenston to the end of his days. He still loved the country of his boyhood, with its rolling green countryside and its genteel ways. He felt a sweeping nostalgia for the old and familiar things it represented. But he also knew that from the moment he stepped into the transport at Lewiston to cross the Niagara with the Americans, he had made his choice. With the first shot he fired at the redcoats, he had lost the right to call himself an Englishman. That realization left an aching hollowness within him. He had never intended to give up his birthright. Bitterly, he cursed the imprudent judgement that had involved him in the battle and the blackmail that had forced him to return to Quebec at the outbreak of the war. If he'd had a choice, he might well be in California or Mexico by now, safe and untouched by this conflict.

Despite his reluctance, he was committed to the American cause in a way that he had never been before. He had risked his life, spilled English blood, and he could never claim neutrality again. When his six months in Quebec were over and his job for Mitchell was done, Seth would continue to fight for his new country.

The sun was sinking lower, and the shadows in the river gorge were deepening, claiming more and more of the grey walls in their dusky veil. The wind blew along the crest of the bank, driving the gold and brown leaves before it, and Seth shivered in spite of the heavy buckskin jacket. Still he could not bring himself to move on into the city.

How complicated his life had suddenly become, he reflected darkly. And how little control he seemed to have over his fate. It had never been like this before. He had always been in command, coolly calculating, if somewhat reckless. But now he was no longer ruled by logic. Some strange impulse he did not understand seemed to govern his actions, and even his most carefully laid plans went awry. Charl had come into his life that way, half by accident and half by design. And he had even less idea of how to deal with her than he did his new allegiance to her country.

Seth had not been able to forget the words Charl had written in the letter to her father. Although they were no different from the things she shouted at him daily, seeing them in black and white gave them new meaning. One passage had haunted him from the first time he read it.

I have been treated as you might expect, but Mr Porterfield has seen to it that I am sheltered, clothed and fed. I can tell you in truth that I am well, if not happy.

Staring down into the blue-grey water, Seth had to admit that he had done little to make Charl happy. He had deceived her, denied her, and used her for his own ends. But then, he rationalized, he had not set out to make her happy. The leather saddle creaked in complaint as he shifted his weight. Why had it become important that he find a way to make Charl happy? he asked himself. And how was it that his own contentment had come to be so closely linked with hers?

The answer to that question was suddenly very clear to him. Without realizing it, he had come to care for Charl. The thought startled him with its simplicity and its truth. He had only cared deeply for two people in his life. One had been William, with whom he shared a bond of blood; the other was Waukee, with whom he shared a bond of friendship. Now, without warning, this woman had intruded on his life, and he found that he cared for her, as well. What she thought and felt and said mattered to him. He recognized that this was something more than the physical desire he had felt for other women, and it went beyond his need to possess her and make her his.

Perhaps I love Charl, Seth found himself thinking abstractedly. With a scowl he forced the thought away. He had never loved anyone, he reflected bitterly, nor had he ever known love. Not even his mother, the beautiful Elaine, had cared for him.

'I never wanted him!' he could remember his mother shouting at his grandfather on the steps of the manor house at Seahaven as she prepared to leave him there. Her blue eyes had been stormy, and her silverfloss hair had glinted in the light as she faced her father.

'He was a mistake, a dreadful mistake! But I have my life ahead of me, and I'll not be saddled with a brat to raise!'

His grandfather had said something low and angry, and his mother had fairly leaped into the waiting coach and driven away. After that he had lived with his stern, forbidding grandfather, under the care of a succession of nurserymaids, housekeepers and tutors. From that time on his mother had drifted in and out of his life like a cloud across the sun until he was sent to Quebec in disgrace.

Seth closed his eyes tightly for a moment, amazed at how those memories still had the power to wound him.

No, he did not love Charl; nor did he believe that there was a capacity for love within him. What he had done, for the first time since childhood, was to make himself vulnerable. He had allowed someone to get close to him, to matter to him. And that someone was Charlotte Beckwith.

He scowled again in disgust. Of all the women in the world he could have chosen, why was it this one who had captured his mind and heart? He was well aware that Charl hated him, and yet he had come to care for her. Seth shook his head slowly at the irony of the situation, realizing there was nothing he could do to change his feelings. They had crept up on him, insidiously penetrating his defences, until they were too strong to alter or deny. All his life he had known the dangers of making himself vulnerable, and still he was lowering his guard to the one person who would have reason to want to hurt him. Without intending to, Charl had made a fool of him again.

He could not let Charl know how he felt about her, he decided defensively. There was only one thing she wanted from him anyway, and that was passage to Youngstown. Before he went away, it had been difficult to face her hatred day after day. But now, caring for her as he did, it would be impossible. For once he would give in to her demands. Because she mattered to him, he would take her home.

Seth straightened in the saddle and guided his horse back onto the trail to Quebec, his decision made. For the first time he could freely admit that he did not want to let Charl go, and yet he would, knowing it was best for both of them.

The dusk was deepening, and the sky was streaked with the blue and mauve of approaching night. The wind had risen as well, and there was the bite of winter in its gusts. Anxiously he anticipated the glowing warmth of the La Soeur kitchen and the happiness in Charl's eyes when he told her she was going home.

It was sometime later, as he was crossing Place d'Armes, that he caught sight of a tall woman descending the steps of Château St Louis. Even in the twilight the golden colour of the girl's hair and her proud carriage left little doubt in his mind about her identity. He was also curious and slightly uneasy about any business she might have at British Military Headquarters. He prodded the big roan to a trot and overtook Charl on the cobbled hill that connected Uppertown and Lowertown. Coming up alongside her, he caught her around the waist with an easy motion and pulled her up in front of him on the saddle.

In self-defence Charl brought her elbow back to catch him squarely in the stomach, robbing him of his breath and prematurely ending his admonitions on the dangers of walking alone. Except for his great strength and his determined hold on her, Charl might have slipped away. Instead, she turned, ready to claw her attacker, until she recognized who it was.

'Seth!' she exclaimed, her eyes widening with surprise and pleasure. Then, recovering herself, she suppressed a giggle at his obvious discomfort.

'Did I hurt you?' she asked solicitously.

Seth caught his breath with difficulty.

'What are you doing wandering the streets at this hour, madam?' he demanded at last.

Charl knew that tone of voice well, and her pleasure at seeing him quickly evaporated. In its place was a kind of bleak resignation. Things between them would never change.

'I had some errands to do,' she said evasively.

His arm tightened at her waist, but his voice was calm and conversational as he guided the big roan down the hill and through the streets to the La Soeur house.

'Oh? What kind of errands?' he inquired. 'I was not aware that the shops were open so late.'

Charl's mouth was suddenly dry with fear, and she sensed the suspicion beneath his quiet questions. She had forgotten that he could be like this, so threatening and so terrifying. Her pulses leaped, and she was sure that he could feel her heart pounding against her ribs. She knew that guilt was written plainly on her face as she cast about frantically for some excuse to give him.

Why had he chosen this particular time to return? she wondered in dismay. If he had been delayed for a few more days, she would have been gone.

'Gabrielle asked me to take some clothing up to the Ursuline Convent,' she babbled, seizing on the first thing that came into her head. 'The sisters do so much for the poor. And then I stopped to – to . . .'

'To visit with someone at Château St Louis?' he finished helpfully.

The colour drained from Charl's face, and she was curiously light-headed for a moment. Dear God! Was it possible that Seth had seen her coming from her meeting with Felix St James? And if he had, how could she prevent him from finding out about her plans to escape?

'I – I . . .' she stammered, although she knew it was useless to make any denials. If Seth had seen her leaving Château St Louis, he would not be satisfied by anything less than the whole truth.

The grim expression on his face and the set of his jaw confirmed Charl's worst fears. As Seth guided the horse down ruelle du Porche and between the houses, she tried to prepare herself for his questions. In the stable he dismounted and helped Charl down, retaining the grip on her wrist even after she was on her feet.

'Now,' he said quietly as he faced her, 'why don't you tell me the truth about where you've been?'

She knew him too well to be fooled by the calm tone of voice, and in mounting panic she tried to pull away from him. Although his hold on her wrist did not hurt, she was helpless against his superior strength. In frustration she kicked at him, her toe meeting his shin with surprising force. Grunting in pain Seth released her to rub his leg. In that split second Charl made a mad dash for the back door of the house, knowing that Seth was not far behind her.

'How was your meeting with Major St James?' Gabrielle asked as Charl burst into the kitchen.

'Oh, Gabby!' Charl groaned at the ill-timed question the Frenchwoman had unwittingly asked.

'Why were you with Felix St James?' Seth demanded from the doorway.

Gabrielle's eyes went round with shock at the sound of his voice, and Charl froze where she stood, knowing that there was no chance to keep her secrets now.

'Seth, you mustn't be angry with Charl,' Gabrielle began. 'I sent her to him.'

'Don't interfere, Gabby,' he told her as he crossed the room to where Charl stood frozen in place.

Seth towered over her: so huge and menacing, an angry scowl twisting his face. As Charl glared defiantly up at him, she wondered how she could both love and hate this man. He was the antithesis of everything she had hoped for in a lover, and yet she was irresistibly drawn to him.

'Tell me, damn you!' he growled, his eyes moving over her like hot blue flames as his hands tightened on her arms.

She pulled away from him, her own eyes blazing. Charl knew she might well jeopardize everything she had gained this afternoon if she told him the truth, but she could not stop herself. She wanted to hurt him: to let him know how much she loathed and despised him, as at that moment she truly did. He needed to know how desperately she wanted to escape him.

'I went to see him about leaving Quebcc,' she panted in anger, 'about escaping you! I had hoped to be gone by the time you returned so I would never have to see you again!'

Charl stood for a moment after her outburst, trembling with rage. Then she bolted for the stairs.

Seth followed her, reaching the door to his room before she had time to slide the bolt in place, and he forced his way in. Charl tried to elude him, but he caught her arms, becoming suddenly aware that her face was wet with tears. With that realization his anger drained away like water out of a sieve, and he stood staring down at her in astonishment.

He had never seen Charl cry before: not from frustration or hurt or fear, and he was unprepared for the emotions it stirred in him. It was as if he were melting inside, going soft and breathless with tenderness, feeling guilty and ashamed that he had hurt her.

Charl's eyes came up to his face. They were swimming with tears, like silver-green pools reflecting the last light of day. In the dimness her features were softened and indistinct, and the sound of her ragged breathing was loud in the quiet room. His hands moved tentatively and ineffectively on her arms in some vague attempt to comfort her, but the tears continued to fall, making shimmering pathways down her cheeks and dripping off her chin. Never in his life had Seth felt so helpless. He cared about this woman, and yet everything he did caused her pain.

Wrapping his arms around her he pulled her close, gently stroking her face, her back, her hair. There was concern on his face, evident in the unaccustomed softening at the corners of his mouth and the tension on his brow. And then, because he did not know what else to do, he bent his head and kissed her.

It was a soft, gentle kiss, but at the touch of his lips a current seemed to pass through Charl, forcing her to acknowledge her need for this man. Gabrielle was right, she realized. In spite of the anger he aroused in her, she could not deny that she loved Seth.

There was the taste of tears on her mouth and wetness against his face as he held her. And then, quite suddenly, her arms slipped around his neck and she was melting against him: the length and softness of her moulding to his lean, hard body. The speed and intensity of her response startled and confused Seth. Minutes ago Charl had been loudly proclaiming her hatred for him, then weeping because he had hurt her! Now she was turning to him with rising passion.

There was an inconsistency in her behaviour that made him wary, and he knew he should heed the voice of caution that whispered warnings in his ears. But then her hands were tracing his cheekbones and tangling in his hair to draw his head down for her deepening kiss. And all at once the warnings seemed indistinct and far away.

Seth knew he was losing himself in her: in her sweet taste and lemon fragrance, in the depth of her desire and the passion of her response. With the last shred of reason he wished he understood what had caused this change in her. He should be suspicious of what she was offering him, but he could not believe that there was pretence in the heat of this passion.

It was as if she came to him in a dream, all wild and willing, when before she had been combative and reluctant. Charl was filling his senses and bending to his will as if she simply sought to please him. Desperately, he wanted to be sure of what this meant. Was it possible that, in spite of her harsh words, Charl felt something for him?

'Charl, wait,' he whispered huskily.

She gave a soft laugh, pressing closer and pulling his head down for her kiss. Then her tongue was gently probing his mouth, circling his, and her hands were tracing delicate designs on his bare skin under his shirt, sending shivers of delight radiating through him. In his head the questions seemed to fade and dissolve in the flood of sensations that raged through him.

Later, later, he thought. For now he was burning with his need for Charl, aching with his desire to be one with her. And Charl seemed to know it, seemed to share his need.

Her nimble fingers were opening the buttons on his shirt and sliding it down his arms to lie in a crumpled pile on the floor. His own fingers were clumsy and he swore in exasperation as he worked the tiny fasteners at the back of her gown.

'Damn it, woman! You wear too many clothes,' he mumbled against her ear.

Grinning mischievously, Charl pushed him back on the bed to remove his boots and trousers. Then, stepping out of his reach, she began to divest herself of her gown, her stockings and her shift, letting them float downward until they lay like discarded petals at her feet. Slowly, she came towards him, her breasts swaying slightly with her movements and the thick sheaf of golden hair tumbling nearly to her waist.

Eagerly Seth drew her down beside him on the bed, nuzzling against her neck as his hand moved over her silky skin. His eyes were cloudy and heavy-lidded with passion as his lips followed the path his hands had taken. He felt her nipples harden and bud against his tongue, and his fingers probed the moistness between her legs. Charl gave a little breathless moan deep in her throat, and he knew that she was as eager for this joining as he. Slowly Seth moved to cover her body with his, opening her thighs and sheathing himself in her until they knew perfect unity.

Charl was intensely aware of him filling her, answering her body's craving and making her feel complete in every way. What was passing between them was an act of love more tender and intimate than either of them could ever hope to express in words. And as she accepted him inside her, she knew she could never hope to leave him. Nor would she want to, for in the depths of his eyes she saw for herself the love that Gabrielle had said was there. Gently, she urged him deeper, and they began to move together.

A slow, exquisite pleasure came to trap them both and carry them beyond any restraint. For, as they moved to heighten sensations, the more compelling the sensations became, until the wild, spinning pleasure crashed in on them. They were caught in a white-hot spiral of passion that arched them up and swept them down until all but the last shred of consciousness was torn away. Slowly, the tide of sensations ebbed, leaving them spent and trembling in each other's arms.

It was infinitely pleasant to remain tangled together as their passion had left them, drifting between sleep and wakefulness. The languorous heaviness in their limbs precluded any kind of movement, and it was a very long time before either of them spoke.

'Seth?' Charl finally whispered in the dark.

There was a long hesitation before he answered, as if he was reluctant to move beyond the communication of their bodies.

'M – m – m, what?'

She smiled, sensing the contentment he felt curved beside her. They had just shared something rare and special, but Charl wanted more than passion from this man. She wanted his love, his understanding and his trust. As she framed the question in her mind, she knew that his reply could easily destroy the fragile bond that united them now.

'Seth, please, will you tell me where you've been?'

Almost imperceptibly Seth drew away, and Charl felt his reluctance to answer her question. And, at the same time, she knew that she must wait in silence for his reply.

Inside his head Seth was fighting a brief, difficult battle with his own nature. He had learned early never to trust, never to share, never to make himself vulnerable to anyone; and he could not help feeling wary of her question now. Nor could he be completely honest with her, for her own sake. Still, he realized that there had been a drastic change in their relationship during this last hour, and he knew he could not do anything that would cause a resumption of the hostilities between them. Charl had given herself to him with great tenderness and had afforded him more pleasure than he had dreamed possible. She had risked everything to bridge the gap between them. Surely he could tell her the truth about this.

'I've been in Queenston,' he said finally.

Charl tipped her head to look up at him in surprise.

'Were you there for the battle?'

Silently he nodded.

Charl bit her lip, keeping back the score of questions that clamoured in her head, demanding answers. Seth had taken the first step towards establishing an understanding between them; he had not lied to her about where he had been. She must move slowly now, not pushing him, not demanding that he tell her too much.

And she must keep her own conflicting emotions in check. Charl could not let herself think about what his role at the battle might have been. He was an Englishman, and his sympathies lay with her enemies. Somehow, she could not let that destroy this new beginning.

'Tell me about it,' she urged him.

Reflexively, his arms tightened around her, and Charl was aware of a strange tension coiling within him although she was at a loss to understand it.

It was difficult to be objective, but Seth knew he could not let Charl guess his part in the battle. Nor would he be able to tell her of his encounter with Stephen Langley and its fatal outcome. Perhaps no one would ever know exactly how Langley had died. They might think it was cowardice that had driven him over the edge of the cliff or that he had lost his way in the smoke and confusion of the battle. Seth closed his eyes and drew Charl closer, newly aware of the sweetness of life.

'The battle at Queenston Heights should never have taken place,' he began in a voice that was flat but faintly tinged with bitterness. 'There was no military advantage to be gained by the invasion of Canada and yet the American general, Van Rensselaer, insisted on the attack.'

Charl listened silently, clearly picturing the events of that day in her mind's eye. She imagined the adventure and daring of the night attack as the boats slipped noiselessly across the black water, the cannonades echoing along the river gorge and the flashes of gunfire that pierced the dark. She listened to Seth's account of the intensity of the fighting on the ridge as British reinforcements arrived from Chippewa and Fort George, and the bitterness of the American surrender.

Seth's voice trailed off in the darkness, and the room became very still. As the silence grew, Charl could sense him retreating from her, bit by bit, but she was helpless to prevent it. A few minutes ago she had been so sure of him, but now her doubts returned.

Seth felt uncertain, too. Only this afternoon he had been ready to let her go, to guide her back to Youngstown himself; but after this unexpected welcome, the thought of losing her was almost unthinkable. Still, if he really cared for Charl, he should take her home, he reasoned. There was no future for her in Quebec, and perhaps little safety once he began meeting with the notorious Frenchwoman who had offered to sell British secrets to the Americans. But if he was to let Charl go, he could not continue to lie with her like this, with her softness pressed along the length of his body. Already, he could feel desire stirring in him again. Abruptly, he rolled away from her and stood up, tugging on his trousers. Padding across the cold floor to the mantle, he lit the candles and tossed another log on the fire, buying time to sort out his feelings.

After stirring the fire to flames he turned to face Charl, trying not to notice her tousled hair and her opulent curves only partially concealed by the covers.

'I've decided to take you back to Youngstown,' he announced without preamble.

Her eyes widened in surprise at his words, and she stared at him speechlessly.

Why was he letting her go now? Charl wondered, her thoughts in turmoil. Didn't Seth want her anymore? Or was he making this offer only because she had gone to Felix St James?

'You've decided!' she exclaimed angrily, without stopping to think about what her words would reveal. 'Damn it, Seth! Are you always going to make decisions without consulting me?'

Now it was Seth's turn to stare in total confusion. How could Charlotte be angry when he had given in to her demands?

'You mean you don't want to go?' he spluttered.

Charl spoke without meeting his eyes. 'No, it's too late.'

'Too late? Didn't you go to see St James just this afternoon to find a way to leave Quebec?'

'Yes.'

'And now you want to stay?'

'If you want me to stay.'

He frowned as he watched her. 'Pray tell, madam, what caused this sudden change of heart? You've hardly given me a moment's peace since we left Youngstown with your demands to be taken back. In one day you have two offers of passage, and then you decide to stay. Why?'

The colour rose in Charl's cheeks, but she could not find the right words.

'Charlotte! Answer me!' he blustered, his voice a trifle unsteady.

Her sea-green eyes came up to his face.

'Isn't it enough that I want to stay?'

He shook his head, his face intent. 'I want your reasons,' he persisted.

Confound his stubbornness, Charl thought furiously. Why couldn't Seth just accept this change without questioning her motives? She had wanted to say the words for the first time in tenderness, not in anger. The flush in her cheeks darkened, and her flashing eyes met his.

'Damn it, Seth!' she began hotly. 'Even after all that's happened, I care for you. That's why I want to stay. I know it's madness but . . .' Her voice faltered and she stared at him, awaiting some response.

There was none.

Panic churned through her. She had opened her heart to him, and now he was silent. Had she misread the look in his eyes as they made love? Didn't he feel some tenderness for her?

Her mouth was dry as dust as she went on defensively.

'And why did you suddenly decide to take me home? Was it because Felix St James offered first? Or is it because you just don't want me anymore?'

Seth continued to watch her in silence, the expression on his face never changing, his eyes never leaving hers.

'I care for you, too, Charl,' he finally admitted, his voice little more than a whisper.

For an interminable moment they were frozen in place by his words. Then they were moving closer, coming together half on, half off the bed in an embrace full of wild discovery. There was a new sweetness to the kisses and embraces given and returned with love and trust, and they clung together for a long time.

'Then you want me to stay?' Charl asked breathlessly, smiling up into his eyes.

'God, yes!' Seth laughed. 'If you'll be happy here with me. Forgive me if I didn't make that clear.'

He pulled her down beside him on the bed and held her close.

'Seth?'

'Now what, woman?' he asked in mock exasperation.

'You didn't offer to take me home just because I went to see Felix St James?' she asked.

'No,' he answered hesitantly. 'Of course, I didn't want that devil to get his hands on you, but I had decided to take you back to Youngstown before I heard about the plans you made with him.'

'Why?'

For a moment Seth nuzzled against her hair, soft, fragrant, and cool against his cheek.

'Because I couldn't bear to see you unhappy any more,' he said simply.

They lay curved together on the bed, warm and drowsy, secure in the cocoon of their own contentment. Outside, the wind rattled the window, and a light rain had begun to fall. From the bed Charl watched the fire gnawing at the logs and listened to the pop and sizzle as they were consumed. It was too soon to think about the ramifications of this afternoon's revelations. Charl knew only that she was happy for the first time in months. Still her questions persisted.

'Seth?'

He rolled over to face her, easily recognizing her inquisitive tone.

'What questions do you want answers to now, woman?' Although his voice was gruff, he was smiling and his gaze lingered on her lips, as if he would rather give her kisses than answers.

'Why do you hate Felix St James?'

To evade the question he bent his head and kissed her slowly, letting his hand roam freely over her body. He wanted to make love to her again, not discuss Felix St James.

'About Major St James?' she reminded him breathlessly when the kiss was done.

Seth sighed and made a face.

'You're the most nosy, stubborn, persistent wench,' he complained.

'Felix St James is a very old and very dangerous enemy,' he began, choosing his words with care. 'He is cunning and treacherous, and he also has a remarkable ability to manipulate people.

'From the beginning he hated my uncle William, making his life miserable as only a superior officer can. When I came to Quebec, he transferred some of that hatred to me. He saw to it that I was barred from William's artillery unit and tried to prevent me from going west with the surveyors. I don't understand his enmity for the Porterfields, but I have learned that he is a man who will stop at nothing to avenge a hatred.' Seth's voice came to an abrupt halt as if he was afraid he would say too much. His face was stony and closed in the candlelight.

Charl silently digested what Seth had told her, and an involuntary shiver went down her spine.

'That's not all, is it?' she asked.

He paused. 'No,' came the answer, 'but if you're going to stay with me, you must learn to accept some things without question. Do you understand that?'

He was asking her to trust him, she realized. Slowly, she nodded.

'And you can accept it?' he persisted.

'I'll try, Seth. Honestly, I'll try.'

'Good,' he whispered, his eyes glowing bright with desire as his hands began to wander over her. 'Are there any more questions?'

Charl shook her head, unable to think of anything but what his touch was doing to her.

'Good,' he whispered again as his mouth closed over hers.

❊

The morning after Seth's homecoming Charl awoke slowly: aware first of the daylight filtering between the dimity curtains, then of the enveloping warmth from the man beside her, and finally of the contentment she felt deep inside. For the first time in months the snarl of emotions that had held her rigid was gone, resolved by the events of the night before. In the growing brightness she let her eyes rove over the cosy little room under the eaves, with its sturdy stone walls and simple furnishings. Surely no place on earth, no matter how grand, would ever be as dear to her as this tiny chamber she had shared with Seth. Finally, her gaze came to rest on the big man who slept deeply and peacefully beside her. Tenderness rose like a soft, warm wave to curl around her heart as she studied those strong, familiar features.

'I love you, Seth!' she whispered experimentally, trying the words for the first time. She liked the shape of them in her mouth, and a bubble of happiness seemed to swell inside her at being able to acknowledge her feelings at last.

Smiling, she nestled back into the pillows. Who would have thought that one night could change everything between them? The galvanic rage that arced between them, and the stunning passion that took its place, had cleared the air like a summer storm, allowing the tender admissions that might never have been made otherwise. How close she had come to leaving Quebec and Seth behind her. Surely it had been nothing short of a miracle that had led to this resolution of their relationship.

Languorously she stretched, letting her mind wander as she drifted between sleep and wakefulness, revelling in her sense of well-being. It was some time later that Seth stirred and peered sleepily over the crest of his pillow at her.

'Good morning,' she whispered, her face glowing with happiness.

'I thought you were a dream,' he whispered back, his eyes clouded with drowsy confusion.

'No dream, my love,' she said, dropping a light kiss on his lips. But before she could move back to her pillow, his hands had tightened on her arms, holding her in place beside him.

'And last night was no dream either?' he demanded, his voice deep and serious. 'Is it true you came to me willingly and promised to stay in Quebec?' His face was hard and he spoke in deadly earnest as if reaffirming some cold-blooded bargain that had been negotiated between them.

A crimson flush stained Charlotte's cheekbones. For an instant she was uncertain of what to answer, and terribly afraid. Had she somehow misjudged what had passed between them? Should she deny the truth in the things she had said, blaming them on their moments of passion? Her mouth was dry, as she pondered what her reply should be. Pride demanded that she negate her promises. If Seth did not care for her, did not want her, perhaps it would be better to ignore what had happened and leave Quebec.

Angrily she clenched her teeth. No! She would not lie about what had transpired or what she felt. She loved this man, and regardless of what he wanted she would not disavow that love. If he had second thoughts about the events of the night before, let him be the one to make the denials.

'Yes,' she admitted, 'I came to you willingly last night, and I will stay with you in Quebec if you wish.'

Charl's heartbeats seemed to thunder in the silence that stretched between them. Then Seth snatched her against him in a hug that might easily have crushed a more fragile woman.

'Thank God!' he muttered against her hair.

'Does that mean you want me to stay?' Charl demanded when she had regained her breath.

He seemed a little breathless too.

'After last night if I had awakened to find that you wanted to go back to Youngstown, I don't know what I would have done. Shackled you to the bed perhaps.' He shook his head.

'I will take you back to Youngstown, Charl. I promise you that. Please, just trust me for a little while longer. Someday you'll understand everything, but for now please trust me.'

His sapphire-blue eyes were solemn as they caught and held hers. At that moment she would have been lost to his will even if it had not been what she wanted, too.

'I believe you, Seth,' she whispered.

'You won't be sorry,' he vowed, in the seconds before his lips closed over hers.

In the days that followed, Charl came to realize that she had been wrong in thinking that she and Seth had finally reached a point of resolution in their feelings for each other. The breathless passion and the tender admissions on the night of his homecoming had served to span the yawning chasm that separated them; but instead of being an end to the journey they had begun so long ago at the Crow's Head Tavern, it had only set them on another road to be travelled. This was a smoother road, to be sure, for they had discovered they could look to each other for help. But there were still discoveries to be made and understandings to be reached between them.

November brought heavy, grey skies with intermittent sun and bone-chilling cold. But without the threat of the snows that would soon force the populace of Quebec to huddle indoors, Seth worked on repairs to Gabrielle's house. Climbing on to the roof, he patched the leaks and replaced the wooden shingles, heedless of Charl's admonitions from the street below. The repairs to the stable roof were less harrowing, and Charl came to accept the lithe, catlike grace that allowed him to cling effortlessly to the steep pitch of the roof as he worked. He fixed one of the stalls and reinforced several rafters in the loft. At times both Emile Savard and Waukee came to help, but for the most part Seth worked alone, enjoying the satisfaction of an honest job well done.

Savard's relationship with Gabrielle had begun to blossom into love, and he spent much of his time in her company. Charl began to suspect that spring would bring a wedding for the older couple, and she was delighted for them. But she wondered if Gabrielle could ever forget her love for William Porterfield. His picture remained in the same place it had always occupied on Gabrielle's desk, and there were times when she eyed Savard with a clearly speculative air.

Charl was always busy these days, assuming Marie's tasks in addition to her own as the cold weather set the old woman's joints to aching and made her less and less able to get about. When Charl worked in the kitchen with Gabrielle, they would chatter like schoolgirls in the odd mixture of French and English they had come to adopt for their conversations, but when Charl worked alone, she had time to reflect on the things she was discovering about Seth day by day.

In the past Charl had always seen the hard inflexible part of his nature, but finally she was beginning to learn about the man within. At first there had been only the outward displays of desire to hint at emotions that had been hidden for so long. But slowly she was discovering the wellspring of warmth and affection that he had been forced to conceal because of the life he'd led.

They talked for hours. Sitting by the fire in the evenings, as Charl busied herself with mending and Seth worked to reclaim the tools and harnesses that had lain too long in disrepair, they discussed the events of the day. They took time together at noon for a cup of tea and a brief conversation before they went on about their business. And as they lay together, cuddling close in the dark after making love, they spoke quietly and at length on more personal topics. It took time, but slowly the obstacles between them were overcome and Seth began to talk of his family and his life in England.

Sheltered in a loving home, Charl was appalled by the tales he told of the childhood that made him the man he was, and she gradually began to realize how difficult it had been for him to reach out to her. Even all these years later, Charl felt searing anger for the heartless coquette who had borne and then deserted Seth and for the peer who had fathered and then denied him. How these two callous people could spurn the affections of a child, with no thought of what scars their rejection might leave on him, Charl could not understand. She would somehow make it up to Seth, she decided with stubborn determination. She would show him the affection he had never known and prove to him that she could be trusted.

Seth spoke with mixed bitterness and affection of Alastair Porterfield, the grandfather who had ostensibly raised him. From what Charl could gather, they had seen each other seldom in the years when Seth was growing up. On those occasions the older Porterfield was unduly stern with his young charge, and it was evident Seth had lacked any security or acceptance in his early life. Still, his memories of Seahaven, the Porterfield manor in Yorkshire, were happy ones.

'If you come around the bend in the drive just at sunset, the stone house on the ridge seems to have been cast from bronze,' he recalled one day as he sat at the trestle table sipping tea, while Charl rolled out the pastry for the sausage and vegetable pie that would be their evening meal. Rubbing a smudge of flour from her nose, she watched his glowing eyes as he went on. 'The smell of the sea is always in the air, and from the windows in the great hall you can watch the breakers foam up on the beach and hear the waves.'

In her mind Charl could see the kind of place he described: graceful stone architecture with arched windows reflecting the light like a thousand diamonds, perfect, rolling lawns, a formal boxwood garden, all silhouetted against an endless stretch of sky and sea.

'The coast is gentle in Yorkshire, sprinkled with inlets and rocky beaches where I swam as a boy. I used to ride for miles along the shore on my horse, forgetting my supper, my studies, everything but the incredible sense of freedom.'

He was lost in his musings now, and Charl listened with tenderness in her eyes.

'The hills are so green, and the grass is like a velvet mantle covering the earth. The soil is too stony for farming but sheep and cattle do well.'

He paused for a moment, his lips curved gently with thoughts of a home he could never claim.

'My family have never farmed, though,' he continued. 'Back as far as anyone can remember, the Porterfields have gone to sea. Grandfather sailed around the world with Captain James Cook, and when they returned, he used the routes they had discovered to make his fortune. By the time my mother was born, he had tripled the size of the Porterfield fleet. With that fortune and faithful service to the Crown came more lands, a title and access to the highest circles of English society.' Unexpectedly, a flash of bitterness crossed his handsome features. 'Of course, that led to my mother's downfall and my subsequent birth.'

He rose suddenly, thumping the mug down on the table. It was evident he felt he had said too much.

'I have wood to cut,' he announced gruffly, tugging on his jacket.

Charl followed him to the door and watched as he viciously attacked the wood pile, chopping as if he could find a release for all his bitterness in activity.

Seth was not an introspective man, she readily discovered. He had never had to explain himself to anyone and spent most of his life unconsciously hiding from his own emotions. Because of this, it fell to Charl to draw understanding from the stories he told.

'I was a rascal at school,' he laughed one night after Jean-Louis had been reprimanded for his behaviour in class. 'I played outrageous pranks, stayed out late, smuggled in cigars and rum that made half the house sick from overindulgence.'

Charl could easily imagine the kind of schoolboy he'd been. He would have faced his masters with his blue eyes conveying total defiance and with the same stubborn set to his jaw that she'd seen so often. Perhaps rebellion had been the only way for him to gain recognition from the society that would not accept him otherwise, but it had also tempered his outlook with cynicism.

As she came to know more about him, Charl began to realize that Seth was an extremely complex man, and she wondered if she would ever completely understand him.

During those icy winter days before the snows came, Charl was happy in a way she had only guessed existed: content and serene and secure in Seth's unspoken love. And because she felt as she did, she gave freely of her own love, filling her man with a contentment he had never known.

Every day was a balm to Seth's spirit that gradually eased the bitterness inside him. And, without consciously making the decision, he lowered the barriers he had created to protect himself. With Charl there was no need for subterfuge, and he began to relax and enjoy life without being constantly on his guard. If Seth had never known love, he had only to look into Charl's eyes to see it in its fullest measure. She always made time for him regardless of how busy she was with her chores: time for a cup of tea to warm him and a few soft words to bring a smile to his face, time for a gentle touch that promised the passions of the night, time for the mending that kept his buttons magically in place and his socks free of holes. They were little things, inconsequential things, but things that gave him a security he had never known in his life. And he was no longer alone.

He had never recognized his own loneliness until now, never realized the singular nature of his existence until Charl had unwittingly changed everything. Looking back, he did not understand how he had survived all those years without her. There had been William and Gabrielle and Waukee, but none of them could offer the completeness he found in Charl's love, and he could not imagine life without her.

How a man could be both strong and weak, both independent and bound, both determined and yet yielding Seth was just beginning to understand. He only knew that in discovering the depth of Charl's love he was discovering himself.

A day or so after Seth's return, Charl sat down to write a brief, polite note to Felix St James thanking him for his trouble on her behalf. She knew Seth would not approve of such a message, but after much thought she decided it was necessary:

Unexpectedly I have had a change in plans and no longer require your assistance in booking passage from Quebec.

Briefly, she wondered what Major St James would think when he received such a missive, but just then Seth had come into the kitchen to tell her that the delicate, chestnut filly he had bought for her to use was saddled and ready for their ride downriver. With one swift motion she had tucked the note into the pocket of her skirt so that she could give it to Jean-Louis for delivery to the Château St Louis the next morning on his way to school.

The snows began in mid-November. There were a few tentative flakes earlier that disappeared as they touched the ground, but one grey day the first smoky waves of white rolled in to outline the roofs and streets with a delicate, pale filigree. By slow degrees the persistent flakes began to fade the colours of the earth until trees, rocks and buildings alike were cloaked in a gauzy veil of white.

It was the snow that finally drove Waukee from his home in the mackinaw to the relative warmth of the La Soeur stable. He had been offered the comforts of the house but had refused them with a noncommittal shrug, thus retaining his independence from the housefolk.

In the cold, early winter days the two men took to the forests seeking the game that was plentiful in the woods around Quebec. Soon their hunting began to provide delicious extras for the La Soeur table: rabbit or squirrel stew, duck in maple syrup sauce, venison roasts, and wild turkey. During those long days together the friendship between the two men returned to its former status, and a strong camaraderie was again evident between them. Waukee was pleased that Seth and Charl had resolved their differences and seemed content in their company. It was only occasionally, when Charl glanced up at the Indian unexpectedly, that she was aware of a look in his eyes that she easily recognized but did not want to understand.

Seth still disappeared from time to time. When this occurred, Charl tried not to wonder where he was or what he was doing. He had asked her to trust him, and she made the effort to do so, refusing to consider that when he was absent without explanation, he was probably spying against the United States. Guiltily, Charl realized that if a choice had to be made between loyalty to Seth and loyalty to her country, she would certainly choose the man she loved.

Charl missed Seth when he was gone and worried about his safety. He had never confided in her about his activities, but undoubtedly there was some danger involved. If something happened to Seth while he was away, how would she ever know it, she wondered as she tossed and turned in the wide, lonely bed. And how could she ever live without him now that he had become so essential to her?

It was strange the way things had turned out. She had prized her independence beyond all else, and Seth had made her his captive. She had disliked him heartily from the first moment she noticed him at the Crow's Head Tavern, taking exception to the insolent perusal of an arrogant stranger, and yet he had come to be the man she loved. In the scant six months since she had met him she had twined her body and her life with his. Like a tuberose climbing a stout trellis she had changed her direction, her outlook, growing more and more bound to him until she could no longer hope to continue alone. And yet in the act of climbing, changing and bending, she had reached new heights of contentment and happiness.

Even when the absence had been a short one, Seth's homecomings were cause for celebration. Seth might bring home a bottle of wine that they would share, curled in bed together. And after they had drunk it, Charl would abandon herself to him, hiding her relief at his safe return in the depths of their passion.

After one such protracted absence, Charl met Seth in the stable, having heard him come into the yard. She rushed at him from the doorway, flinging herself into his arms, heedless of the snow that clung to his heavy fur coat. The hug became a kiss that melted and sizzled with a heat of its own and left them both slightly giddy and breathless.

'You shouldn't be out here with just a shawl to keep you warm,' he scolded her.

'I'm so glad to have you back!' she exclaimed. 'I couldn't wait until you came inside.'

Opening his fuzzy coat he pulled her against him to share the warmth of his body.

'So you missed me, did you?' he asked, his gaze intently searching her face.

In her eyes he found the reassurance he sought.

'A little,' she teased him, nestling closer to his broad chest and sliding her hands around him to lock behind his waist. 'I wish you didn't have to go away.'

'I think this will be the last time.'

'It will? But why? Has something happened?' The questions tumbled out in spite of her determination to hold them back. She wanted to trust him. She did trust him, but there was so much he would not explain.

'We've been invited to a ball,' he announced, abruptly changing the subject to divert her from things he could not answer. 'It will be a Christmas cotillion at the end of December in the Governor's Mansion,' he went on, watching her excitement grow.

'Oh Seth!' she breathed.

'May I presume that you would like to attend?'

'Oh yes! But how did we get invited?' In dismay she bit the question short, not sure that she would like the answer. Instead her eyes went round and innocent, although mischief glittered in their sea-green depths.

'But Seth,' she said in a guileless voice. 'I haven't a thing to wear.'

'M-m-m, I think I can afford one new gown,' he told her, a smile tugging at one corner of his mouth.

'And a pelisse?' she wheedled.

He laughed.

'What a beggar you are, Charlotte. Yes, you may have a pelisse. I've been meaning to buy you something warm to wear. And perhaps we can find a pair of satin slippers, but nothing more!'

His gruff tone did not fool her. She laughed too and hugged him tightly, turning her face up for his kiss. His lips were cold against her mouth, but the kiss was sweet and warm. Without warning, the wild, dizzying tide of desire claimed them. Under the cover of the heavy coat his hands moved with gentle persistence across her shoulders and down her back until he cupped her buttocks, pressing her against him. She could feel his desire growing hard and full between their bodies, and she felt herself respond to him.

Breathing heavily Seth set her away from him. 'Damn it, woman!' he muttered. 'Get back to that kitchen, or I swear I'll make love to you right here in the straw.'

She laughed and nestled against him provocatively. 'I think making love in the straw might be quite romantic,' she grinned invitingly, the teasing twinkle bright in her eyes.

His mouth thinned in exasperation.

'Wanton!' he accused as he bent to kiss her again. 'I think the

weather today might cool your ardour a bit. Besides I want my
food first and you later. What are you going to feed me?'

'Well, I've got cinnamon buns baking,' she suggested, 'and
there's some ham and fresh eggs . . .'

'Then get to work, woman!' he said, propelling her in the
direction of the house. 'I'm starving. I'll be in as soon as I've
seen to the roan.'

'Yes, sir!' she answered and skipped across the drifted yard.

In the light of the lantern he had lit against the encroaching
dusk she could see Seth unsaddling the horse. From the kitchen
door she watched him, and a feeling of contentment seemed to
settle over her at the sight. He was home. He was safe. And he
was not going away again.

Twenty

The snowflakes that drifted past the lead-paned windows in the fading twilight were as large as goose down and seemed to muffle the sounds from the street below. Tonight she and Seth were to attend the ball at the Governor's Mansion, and in these few moments alone Charl tried to suppress her inexplicable anxiety. She had attended grand occasions before without being assailed by the fluttering stomach or the icy hands that troubled her now. It irritated her to be so edgy when all she wanted was to enjoy the evening with Seth. It had been so long since they had even danced together. Dreamily she remembered the party in her own home just before war had been declared. She had danced with him for the first time then, walked with him by the river, and spent the night in his arms. Only that evening had set into motion a series of events that had taken her from Youngstown and had nearly destroyed any feelings they had for one another.

Quickly, she dismissed the thought. Tonight would be wonderful, she insisted silently. She would be beautiful in the exquisite gown Seth had bought for her. They would dance and drink champagne, and when they returned home . . .

Gabrielle was suddenly in the room breaking into Charl's thoughts with her infectious gaiety. Listening to her throaty laughter, Charl realized that Gabrielle was far more excited by the ball than she was herself.

'Chérie, you haven't even begun to dry your hair yet!' Gabby admonished as she spread the freshly pressed gown on the bed. 'What have you been doing?'

'Daydreaming, I guess,' Charl answered guiltily as she sank to a low-backed chair by the fire and began to draw the brush through the thick strands of damp hair.

'Here, let me do that,' Gabrielle offered as she took the brush from Charl's hand.

'Now you must promise me that you will tell me all about the Governor's Mansion when you return home,' Gabrielle bubbled as she worked. 'And you must take notice of the gowns worn by all the ladies, especially the Governor's wife, and that wicked Madame Verreault.'

'Madame Verreault?'

Gabrielle nodded. 'They say she has been mistress to half the English officers in Quebec. She's sure to be there tonight because she is the current favourite of General Prevost himself.'

Charl laughed. 'I thought you never listened to gossip, Gabby.'

She gave a brief shrug.

'There is not a woman alive who doesn't enjoy a bit of a scandal.'

'And how will I know this notorious Madame Verreault when I see her?' Charl asked, caught up in Gabby's gossip too, her apprehension about the evening fading.

'Ah! She will be the most beautiful woman there,' Gabrielle replied with assurance. 'She is very petite, and her hair is so pale it is nearly silver. I saw her at the dressmaker's on rue St Pierre once. She is like a doll, like a porcelain doll, fragile and incredibly beautiful. And her jewels!' Gabby rolled her eyes expressively, 'bought for her by lovers all over the world!'

'Then what is she doing in Quebec? This is the last place on earth I would come if I was kept by rich lovers,' Charl observed.

Unperturbed by Charl's comment, Gabby went on.

'She arrived here about a year ago. Some say she was exiled from France by Napoleon himself for threatening to come between his sister and Joachim Murat, the King of Naples. Others say she fled from Europe with her aristocratic father in the face of the French invasions.' Gabrielle shrugged again as if to indicate that it did not matter which story was true.

'Well, I certainly will look for her,' Charl assured the other woman with a wry smile.

'Are you ready for your dress yet, chérie?' Gabrielle asked as Charl went to stand before the tall mirror near the foot of the four-poster bed. It had been decided that Charl would dress for the ball in Gabrielle's room so that Seth could complete his toilet in the privacy of the little room upstairs.

'Yes, please,' she answered, staring unseeing at the tall, flaxen-haired woman in the glass.

The dress that Seth had bought her for the ball was easily the most elegant she had ever owned. It was fashioned from sheer alabaster silk, the high-waisted skirt cut slim across the front with gathered fullness in the train at the back. The neckline was scooped low and wide to highlight the slope of her ivory breasts and shoulders, clearly visible above the décolletage.

Slowly, Gabrielle lowered the dress over Charl's head and began to do up the fasteners in the back while Charl adjusted the small puffed sleeves. The dress was perfectly plain except for the wide row of lace that edged the hem and the sides of the train. It was a dress designed more to highlight a woman's beauty than display the dressmaker's art, and Charl's gold and pink colouring was a perfect foil for the pale simplicity of the gown. Gingerly, she smoothed the delicate material over her curving hips and then, more slowly, over the flat plain of her stomach.

Gabrielle had been watching Charl's expression with knowing eyes.

'Charlotte, when are you going to tell Seth about the child?' she asked softly.

Her eyes wide with amazement, Charl met the other woman's gaze in the mirror. It had only become evident a few days ago that she must be carrying Seth's child, and there had been no time for her to accept that knowledge herself.

'How did you know?' she breathed, incredulously.

The Frenchwoman led her to the dressing table and pulled out the bench so that Charl could sit down, then began to brush the thick mane of golden hair into some semblance of order.

'I have three children of my own,' she laughed. 'I know the signs. You've stopped eating breakfast, but you're ravenous all the rest of the day. You've begun to need a nap in the afternoon. Ah! Don't deny it! I've caught you twice this week curled up on the bed before dinner. Aren't you happy about the baby, chérie?'

'I don't know, Gabby,' she answered honestly. 'I love Seth, but I didn't mean for this to happen. The future is so uncertain, and I don't have any idea how he'll react to the news that he's to be a father.'

'But surely you both realized that if you went on as you were this would inevitably happen.'

Charl shrugged. When Seth took her in his arms and made love to her, she ceased to think of anything: not the past, not the future, not the consequences she might have to face. All that mattered at that moment was the achingly sweet union with him, of yielding everything and receiving so much more in return. At the memory of their shared passion a delicious shiver of desire went through Charl, and the colour rose in her cheeks at the immodesty of her thoughts.

'Then you must tell him as soon as possible,' Gabrielle was saying, as she arranged the soft waves at Charl's temples.

'I've been trying to find a time, but he's been so preoccupied lately that I hate to bother him.'

'Yes,' Gabby agreed. 'I've noticed that, too. Shall I plait this all together?'

'A chignon, I think, with the flowers pinned at the sides,' Charl answered, considering herself in the dressing table mirror.

'Tell him tonight, Charlotte. There's nothing to be gained by waiting.'

'And when shall I tell him? As we're waiting to be presented to the Governor so he can't lose his temper? Or perhaps in the middle of a quadrille so that while I dance with another partner, he'll have a chance to accept his impending fatherhood?' Charl teased.

Gabby laughed, trying not to swallow any of the hairpins she held between her teeth. When the thick coil of hair had been secured, she went on.

'Perhaps you should wait until you've found a more private place, but tell him soon,' she advised. 'I'll wager that once he's accustomed to the idea, he'll marry you. He loves you, Charl, and being illegitimate himself I doubt he'll want his child to be born out of wedlock.'

Charl's chin came up angrily. 'I don't want him to marry me because I'm to bear his child. I want him to marry me because he can't go on without me!' she declared.

Gabrielle was diplomatically silent and busied herself pinning the clusters of silk camellias into Charl's hair. She added a quick dusting of rice powder to Charl's face and shoulders and a touch of lip salve. Charl's colour was already quite high, and there was no need for rouge.

As that was completed, there was a knock at the door.

Anxiously Charl rose from her seat in front of the mirror and slipped her feet into the white satin pumps with their glittering paste buckles.

'Am I ready?' she asked the older woman tremulously.

Swiftly Gabrielle handed her the elbow-length gloves and the tiny gilt reticule that hung at her wrist.

Charl took a deep breath and nodded for Gabby to open the door.

At the sight of Seth in his finery a tight feeling of pride and love rose in her chest. He was so handsome and dear to her. His dark blond hair gleamed amber in the candlelight, and the deep blue velvet of the matching coat and waistcoat seemed to intensify the colour of his eyes. The ruddy gold shade of his skin, in sharp contrast to his snowy linen and meticulously tied neckcloth, brought a vitality to his features and gave clear evidence of his active life. Dark grey faille trousers tucked into high black boots completed his costume, and he carried a black cape and grey top hat.

'Oh you look beautiful!' Charl exclaimed ingenuously.

Laughing, Seth bowed and kissed her hand.

'And you, madam, will undoubtedly be one of the most handsome ladies present,' he teased, his eyes bright with admiration.

'There is, however one more thing you need to complete your costume,' he told her, taking a long, narrow, velvet box from behind his back. 'Before I show these to you, you must realize that they are not a gift, but on loan, and they must be returned tonight.'

'Yes, yes, I understand,' she nodded, her eyes intent on the box in his hand which bore the name of a prominent Quebec jeweller. Smiling, he extended it to her. Inside on a bed of white satin lay a necklace of opals and diamonds. Simple in its design, the shifting pinks, blues, and greens were a stunning counterpoint to the brilliance of the diamonds.

'Oh Seth! This must be worth a king's ransom. Wherever did you borrow it?'

'Do you like it?' he asked, smoothly avoiding her question.

'Like it? Oh yes, but I can't wear it,' she said sternly. 'It's too valuable. What if I lost it?' But even as she spoke, her eager fingers were lifting the necklace from its case.

'Just try it on,' he coaxed, his eyes twinkling. 'Here, let me help you.'

Charl fidgeted impatiently as he worked the fasteners and then flew to the mirror to view the effect. At first she could hardly believe that the woman reflected in the glass was she. The upswept hair with its pale halo of flowers, the stunning ivory

gown, and the brilliant circlet of jewels around her slender throat
all combined to give back a portrait of some regal, beautiful
stranger. For a moment she stared at herself in wonder.

As Seth came to stand behind her, Charl met his admiring gaze
in the glass. 'Can I really wear the necklace?' she asked.

'Of course you may,' he assured her with an amused
smile. 'You may wear these, too, and you need not give them
back.'

He placed another, smaller jeweller's box in her hands, and as
she opened it, she gasped in surprise. Nestled inside were a pair
of opal earrings that matched the necklace at her throat. From
their ivory bed the perfect stones reflected the light in a rainbow
of shifting, iridescent colours.

'Oh Seth! They're magnificent!' Charl breathed.

'The Porterfield family jewels,' he mocked lightly, but his
words brought an inexplicable surge of bitterness that suddenly
outweighed the pleasure of giving the gift.

Turning towards him Charl gently laid a palm on his sleeve
and looked deep into his troubled eyes.

'Because you gave these to me, they are more precious than
anything in the world,' she said softly.

'Some day –' he began, but she silenced him with a finger on
his lips.

'No, you needn't promise me some day or brood about what's
past. These are beautiful and you've made me very happy with
your gift.'

From his lips her fingers skimmed across his cheek and tangled
in his hair to draw his head down for a light kiss.

'Thank you,' she whispered as her mouth brushed his.

Heedless of Gabrielle's presence, Seth gathered Charl in his
arms and held her close.

This woman had the power to banish the memories that came
back to haunt him, to neutralize the bitterness and ease the pain.
She would not let the doubts of the past trespass into their life
together. Instead, she filled his days with unutterable sweetness
that was a balm on his spirit.

Behind them Gabrielle cleared her throat, and they sprang
apart, both flushed with embarrassment.

'Hadn't you better be on your way?' she reminded them.

Quickly Charl put on the earrings while Seth retrieved the
deep turquoise pelisse from the bed and settled it about her

shoulders. Picking up the white fur muff, she tucked her hands inside and gave her escort a brilliant smile.

'Such a handsome couple,' Gabrielle commented, smiling benevolently as they descended the stairs. 'Have a wonderful time.'

Once inside the fashionable carriage that Seth had hired for the evening, Charl's uneasiness returned, manifesting itself in nervous chatter. Seth nodded indulgently, only half listening to what Charl was saying.

Perhaps it had been a mistake to involve Charl in his intrigues without her knowledge, but the ball had seemed the most logical place to display his bribe and make contact if his informant found the exchange to her liking. This time the price was high, but the information he sought was critical to the American cause.

'And Gabrielle says I'm to report on the gowns, too,' Charl went on, 'especially the ones worn by Mrs Prevost and a Madame Verreault.'

'Madame Verreault?' Seth asked sharply, his full attention shifting back to the woman at his side.

'Yes. It seems she's quite notorious. Do you know her?'

He settled back into the carriage seat, his brows drawn together.

'I know who she is,' he replied noncommittally.

'Gabrielle says she will be the most beautiful woman at the ball tonight. Will you point her out to me?'

Seth's smile was warm as he pulled Charl closer in the chilly carriage, and she could not see the expression of relief that crossed his face.

'Nonsense,' he said softly, 'it's you who will be the most beautiful woman there.'

The heavy stone edifice of the Governor's Mansion was illuminated by a score of torches, set in place along the high iron fence, that cast wavering shadows on the heavy fieldstone blocks. In the dark the façade seemed even more imposing than it did in daylight. Each window shone with a candelabra, and Charl stared in awe as their coachman waited for them to disembark.

Once they were inside the arched wooden doors, a liveried servant took their outerwear, and they advanced down a wide, vaulted corridor that opened onto a sumptuously furnished ballroom illuminated by three huge brass chandeliers down the centre of the hall. The walls were painted with English country scenes, and the tall French doors that opened onto the garden were hung with deep green velvet draperies, tied with golden cords. Delicate gilt chairs lined the dance floor and filled a gallery at one end of the room. Directly below it was a raised platform from which the musicians had already begun to play. On a dais at the opposite end of the room General Prevost was receiving guests. Charl and Seth joined the group of people who were waiting to be presented to him.

Seth could feel the iciness of Charl's hand in his even through the kid glove, and he was aware of her wide-eyed fascination with her new surroundings. In spite of all her poise, he reflected, she was still essentially a country girl. It was by no means the first function of this nature he had attended, but to her all this must seem overwhelming and intimidating. Nevertheless, when they reached the corpulent General Prevost and his wife, Charl made a neat formal bow before they proceeded down the line of dignitaries. Near the end they came face to face with Major Felix St James, resplendent in his scarlet tunic and buff breeches. He bowed low over Charlotte's hand, then turned to Seth, his expression hostile.

'Well, Porterfield, I hardly expected to meet you here tonight. Usually the general is more selective with his invitations,' St James greeted him.

Ignoring the thinly veiled insult with difficulty, Seth bowed and met the officer's gaze squarely.

'As a rule I don't enjoy a close association with the effete aristocracy, but it might be to your advantage to remember that occasionally I do turn up in unexpected places.'

St James' brows rushed together in a scowl as he measured the other man's words.

'What do you mean by that, Porterfield? Are you threatening me?' he demanded in a low, icy tone, his hand moving unconsciously to the hilt of the sword he wore on his hip.

In an instant the acerbic repartee had become something deadly and dangerous. Tension crackled between the two men as they faced each other like pit bulls, ready for combat: their bodies gone rigid and their eyes locked with hatred. In the depth of their mutual loathing the guise of civility dropped away, leaving only the savage emotions that demanded justice and, blood for blood.

Sensing the explosive confrontation that seemed imminent, Charl stepped between them.

'Seth, please!' she pleaded. 'Seth, please listen to me!'

With difficulty he tore his gaze from St James and looked at her. In the depths of his blue eyes she saw a murderous rage that terrified her, and it took all her courage not to shrink away from him.

'Seth, please. This is neither the time nor the place to settle whatever is between you. Be sensible.'

At first she was afraid her words had not reached him, but finally there was the dawning of rationality in his face, and she saw him loosen his knotted fists. Then he turned to Felix St James. His face had gone hard and impassive, but his eyes were molten.

'When we face each other on this matter, St James,' Seth said quietly, 'you will know I've made a threat. And you will have had adequate time to repent of your sins before I kill you.'

'Seth!' Charl gasped, her face pale, but Felix St James seemed unaffected by Porterfield's words.

He bent low over Charl's hand a second time, his russet gaze moving over her like a flame.

'You will have to forgive us both, my dear Miss Beckwith,' he apologized smoothly. 'It seems in the – ah – ardour of our reunion we both forgot the proprieties. Perhaps later you will allow me the pleasure of a dance and,' the smile on his lips was malicious, 'then I will be able to thank you properly for the note you sent me.'

The grip Seth clamped on her elbow was vicelike, but his expression did not change.

'Come, Charlotte,' he said coldly. 'I am sure you and I have taken up too much of Major St James' time already. Good evening, sir.'

'Good evening,' St James replied, and the stunning blond couple moved off across the ballroom.

As they walked in the direction of the garden doors, Charl tried to gather her scattered wits. She was both appalled by and curious about what had transpired between Seth and Major St James. From what Seth had told her, she would never have guessed the extent of the animosity they held for one another, and she wanted to know the cause. But before she could ask Seth about that, she would have to face his questions about her communication with St James. It was evident that he had only mentioned the note to pique Seth, but as she felt herself being inexorably propelled towards the relative privacy of one of the window alcoves, she wished fervently that St James had kept his thanks to himself.

Once in the concealing shadows of the curtains Seth spun her around to face him.

'What kind of note did you send to Felix St James?' he demanded in a furious whisper.

In spite of herself, Charl felt a ripple of annoyance at his high-handed manner.

'I wrote to let him know I would not need his assistance in booking passage out of Quebec and to thank him for his trouble on my behalf,' she replied evenly.

'If it was as innocent as all that, why didn't you tell me you were writing to him?'

'Because I knew you wouldn't approve.' She shook her head to silence the words he seemed ready to speak. 'I felt it was something I had to do. It would have been impolite –'

'Impolite!' he burst out. 'Good God, woman! Impolite!' He took a long breath.

'If you had any idea of writing him, you should have consulted me.'

'Why?' she asked belligerently, her temper no longer in check. 'Am I no longer capable of making my own decisions?'

For a full minute they stood toe to toe, glaring at each other. Then Charl closed her eyes in an attempt to regain control.

'Oh Seth,' she said softly, 'please, let's not quarrel. It was a simple note of thanks, nothing more. He had agreed to help me, and I felt I owed him that much. The only reason he mentioned the note was to make you angry and spoil this evening for us. Are you going to let him succeed?'

Charl could see his anger drain away as Seth recognized the sense in her words. Slowly, he loosened the grip on her wrists.

'Very well,' he apologized. 'I'm sorry, but I want you to promise that you'll never seek him out again, no matter what happens. St James is an unscrupulous blackguard, and I guarantee you'd regret it if you ever trusted him.'

Charl gave him her most dazzling smile and nodded, relieved that the argument was over. There was a moment of silence as they readjusted themselves to their roles of party guests and Seth took her hand.

'Would you care to dance, Miss Beckwith?' he asked with a slight bow.

'Most assuredly, Mr Porterfield,' she answered with a low curtsey.

A moment later he led her onto the floor, and they joined the swirl of dancing couples.

For Charl the rest of the evening passed in a golden haze. She was aware of the lights and the music, the colours and the laughter, the food and the people, but most of all she was aware of the tall, handsome man at her side and how much she loved him. They drank champagne and ate from the groaning buffet table that was set up in an adjoining room. Together they explored the Governor's mansion, danced for hours, and shared clandestine kisses in the same alcove where they had argued earlier. They lost themselves in the gaiety of the evening and in each other until St James turned up unexpectedly and Seth was forcefully reminded of his real reasons for attending the ball.

As the major approached across the dance floor, Seth immediately recognized the woman on his arm. She was exquisite, small and slender as a child but with a fragile beauty that dazzled the eye. Her icy blonde hair was dressed high and threaded with peacock feathers, and her porcelain face with its enormous silver-grey eyes heightened the illusion of her frailty. The gown she wore was jade green silk, embroidered heavily with gold on the filmy overskirt, and at her throat an emerald necklace sparkled brilliantly. From the corner of his eye Seth could see Charl's reaction to the approaching couple, and he wondered if the girl recognized the woman she had inquired about earlier.

When St James spoke, there was no hint of the animosity that had passed between the two men earlier in the evening.

'Good evening, Porterfield, Miss Beckwith,' St James greeted them with a bow. 'Do you know my companion, Madame Muzette Verreault?'

'I am sorry to say I've never had the pleasure of meeting her,' Seth answered smoothly, 'but certainly everyone in Quebec has heard of Madame Verreault's beauty.'

'You are very kind, sir,' the silver blonde woman demurred, flashing a flirtatious look in Seth's direction.

'If you don't mind, Porterfield, I've come to claim my dance with Miss Beckwith,' the officer said with a charming smile at Charlotte.

Before Seth had time to respond, Charl had agreed and was offering her hand to St James.

'It is all right, isn't it, Seth?' she asked softly.

He understood her reasons for acquiescing to St James' demand for a dance, but it did not make him any happier about the prospect of watching Charl go off on his enemy's arm. The curt nod he gave in assent clearly indicated that it was anything but all right. Frowning and frustrated, he realized that he had been neatly manoeuvred into compliance with St James' wishes.

'You will keep Madame Verreault company, won't you, Porterfield?' St James asked as he and Charl moved onto the dance floor.

'Of course,' he mumbled as he watched them disappear into the throng of dancers.

'I think I understand now why our meetings have been so businesslike in spite of my desire to make them otherwise,' observed the woman at his side. 'Aren't you going to ask me to dance, Seth?'

Automatically, he led Muzette Verreault out onto the dance floor to join a set of dancers. After Charl's tall, substantial body, Muzette was like a wisp of smoke in his arms. Although Seth had planned to make contact with her this evening, he had not intended to do so openly. But now that St James had thrown them together . . .

'I think Felix knows,' Madame Verreault whispered, breaking into his thoughts.

'About what?' he asked as he led her through a graceful turn.

'I think he knows about the papers!' she went on. 'He has hardly left me alone all evening, and he watches me as closely as a cat watches a mousehole.'

Could it be that St James had deliberately introduced them in order to gauge their responses to each other? Seth wondered. If that was so, he would be watching them closely now. A brief glance towards the other dancing couple revealed that St James seemed completely captivated by his partner and was quite oblivious to anything else. Feelings of mixed jealousy and relief assailed Seth.

'Perhaps you have only made a conquest, Muzette,' Seth suggested lightly.

Her laughter was brittle.

'Felix St James and I have been acquainted for some time. If

I was to make a conquest of him, I would have done it long ago.'

'Then it is fortunate that he unwittingly gave us this opportunity to conclude our business. If you are satisfied with the price being offered for the papers, I can come for them later tonight.'

'Yes, the bargain seems fair,' she replied, her eyes seeking Charlotte Beckwith and the jewels she wore. 'And the earrings, are they included with the necklace?'

'No,' he said flatly. 'The earrings are a gift to Miss Beckwith.'

She gave him a measuring look and sighed softly. 'Yes, I see. Lucky woman.

'At any rate, the necklace is quite satisfactory. Regrettably I will not be able to offer your government any more help in the future. These activities are becoming too dangerous, and I'm certain St James is suspicious. I spent some time in the prisons of France, as you know, and I would rather die than face such treatment again. Come for the papers tonight. I will be glad to be rid of them.'

Seth appreciated Madame Verreault's fear of St James, and he had more reason than most to know how cold blooded and cunning his sworn adversary could be. It had unsettled him to discover, through their informant at Château St Louis, that his old nemesis had been asked to look into the theft of certain secret documents by American agents. It would please Seth a great deal to do his part in spiriting the information out of Quebec. After tonight he would be prepared to leave Quebec forever, taking Charl with him.

'As soon as we can slip away, I will send Charl home and go to your apartments. See that you are not escorted home and that your maid does not attend you.'

'And when I find you alone in my room, will we complete our assignation?' she asked, peering flirtatiously over her shoulder as she made a turn away from him.

Although they had business to conduct, her meaning was clear, and Seth realized that if it had not been for Charl, he might well accept the invitation to spend the night in this woman's bed.

'It is a tempting offer,' he admitted as he put an arm around her waist for the next figure of the dance, 'but I must decline. Instead we will conclude our business and I will go.'

'I am greatly disappointed,' she pouted, 'but somehow I doubted you would stay with me.'

'No,' he answered almost absently as his eyes wandered to the

tall golden-haired woman and her partner on the other side of
the room. Charl seemed to be hanging on every word Felix said,
and St James was smiling boldly into her eyes. Seth's mouth
narrowed with irritation as he watched them, and he wondered
what they were finding to say to each other.

For some time Charlotte Beckwith and her partner had danced
in silence, moving in the precise, measured steps of the contredanse. In spite of the other couples in their square, she had been
aware of the intimacy of his attentions, and a rosy flush stained
her cheeks as he watched her.

'You are a complex woman aren't you?' he observed as he
drew her close for a moment. 'I sensed that the day you came to
my office.'

'I don't know why you have cause to think that,' Charl replied,
flustered by the personal nature of his comment.

'I think more goes on inside that pretty head of yours than
most people give you credit for,' he continued smoothly. 'And I
doubt that you do anything without a reason.'

She turned slowly away from him and curtsied to the man to
her right.

'You certainly do make me sound calculating,' she observed
as she returned to place her hand in his.

'Not calculating precisely, just logical.'

'Ah yes,' she replied, slanting him a look from under her
lashes. 'Women are seldom credited with that attribute, but it is
not the first time I have been accused of having a logical mind.'

St James smiled. 'I thought not. Then perhaps you will explain
why you came to my office one day, desperate to leave Quebec,
and only a few days later I received a note telling me you were
going to stay. After what you told me, I was very curious to learn
the reason for your change of plans.'

'Isn't it a woman's prerogative to change her mind?' she
inquired with a charming smile. St James inclined his head in
agreement, but beneath his speculative gaze the colour mounted
to her cheeks.

'There is no reason for me to explain myself to you,' Charl
went on tartly, aware that his fingers had tightened painfully on
her hand.

'It is undoubtedly true that you owe me no explanations, but
it intrigues me to see you here with my old friend Porterfield. Is
he your rescuer or the man from whom you wished to be rescued?'

'As long as we are satisfying our curiosities,' she countered smoothly, 'I want to know the reason why there is such bad blood between you and Seth.'

St James' craggy face broke into a wide smile, and his teeth flashed white in his dark face. 'Ah, Miss Beckwith,' he laughed, 'from our first meeting I knew you were a woman of rare spirit, but I would never have expected you to counter my questions with such a demand.'

'Indeed?' Charl responded as she made a slow turn and swept low in a curtsey to him. 'Then you're not going to answer my question?'

'Since your allegiance is obviously to Mr Porterfield, perhaps he should be the one to explain our differences.'

'And since you will not enlighten me about your relationship to Seth, I see no reason to explain myself to you.'

They moved through the last graceful figures of the dance in silence. As the music died away, St James offered her his arm, holding her hand in place on his sleeve with the intimate pressure of his warm palm. Inclining his head as he spoke, he met her eyes with his smouldering stare.

'I fear we have reached an impasse, my dear Miss Beckwith, but who knows what the future will bring? Perhaps someday we will both find the answers we seek.' He paused to watch her, then went on more lightly.

'I have enjoyed our dance and our little conversation. And now, regrettably, I must return you to your escort.'

They were moving towards the rear of the room where Seth and Madame Verreault waited. Charl could guess the tenor of Seth's mood by the grim set of his mouth and the stiff, wordless bow he made in response to the officer's polite thanks. With a deepened frown from between his brows he watched the other couple move away.

There was a tightness in Charl's throat as she looked up into his scowling face. She did not want such a wonderful evening to end like this. Tentatively, she laid a hand on his sleeve.

'I'm sorry if I made you angry,' Charl said softly. 'I accepted Major St James' invitation to dance in order to avoid more trouble between you.'

'I'm not angry,' Seth answered tersely, still staring after the British officer and the woman on his arm.

Charl drew a shaky breath and said nothing. The lump in her

throat seemed enormous, and tears prickled behind her downcast lids.

'It's time we left, Charlotte,' he said abruptly as his gaze shifted to the woman at his side.

'Oh Seth, no, please. I didn't mean –' she began, but he silenced her with a look.

'It's time we left,' he repeated, each clipped word harsh and clear although his voice was low. Firmly, he took her elbow and began to steer her between the couples moving in the steps of a spirited country dance.

Tilting her head stubbornly, Charl pulled her elbow from Seth's grasp and preceded him towards the door. As they traversed the ballroom, anyone might have read in her shiny eyes and tremulous smile the emotions that went unnoticed by the man at her side. She was precariously balanced on the ragged edge between anger and tears, and not even pride could keep her disappointment hidden. She had wanted tonight to be perfect, and it had been until now.

They waited in silence for the carriage to be brought around. Charl's brittle pretence held until they were inside its dark, anonymous interior, but then the silvery tears began to seep from between her thick lashes and roll down her hot cheeks. For a time Seth was unaware of her distress as he stared fixedly out of the window, but some small movement drew his attention, and he turned to regard her in amazement.

'What's the matter?' he demanded shortly.

She shrank away from him into the far corner of the seat, taken aback by his tone, and the tears fell faster.

'You're angry with me for dancing with Major St James,' she sniffed, accusingly.

'I told you before I was not angry,' he returned irritably. Then, as they passed a street lamp, he caught a glimpse of her face with its tear-smudged mouth and wet luminous eyes. Shaking his head in mixed tenderness and exasperation, he reached out and drew her closer across the slippery leather seat. At first she resisted, wishing only to be left alone, but he pulled her closer until she rested against his chest. The arms were both comforting and imprisoning, but for once she curved against him, accepting his dominion over her.

'I'm not angry with you, Charl,' he repeated gently. 'I understand why you agreed to dance with St James.'

'You do?'

'Yes, I do. What I don't understand is why you are crying now. You've certainly faced me when I've been in worse tempers than this.' His words were quiet and serious, but there was a hint of teasing beneath them, and a smile seemed to hover at the corners of his mouth.

She burrowed into his shoulder, feeling the prickly wool cloak against her cheek. It was not like her to dissolve in tears like this, she reflected, but lately she became upset so easily. Perhaps it was the child she carried that made her so sensitive.

This might be the right time to tell Seth about the baby. They were alone, and he seemed very solicitous and understanding, she reasoned. She raised her eyes to his face and tried to find the words, but at the last moment her courage failed her.

'Are you all right?' he asked.

'I'm fine now,' she answered, trying to give credence to the lie.

'Are you sure?'

She nodded.

'Then would you mind if I left you before we reached home? The necklace must be returned to its owner tonight, and I had planned to do that on our way. If you wish I will escort you home first and then –'

'No, go ahead. I'm fine, really,' she assured him.

'Good girl,' he said, giving her a quick hug.

After signalling the driver to stop, Seth drew Charl close once again, tracing her cheeks and jaw gently with his thumbs as he bent to kiss her. His hands moved caressingly down the column of her neck as the kiss deepened, and Charl melted against him, losing herself in the tenderness of his touch. It was not until she felt the opal and diamond necklace slide along her collarbones that she realized what he was doing. But before she could react, the jewels were gone.

'You rogue!' she laughed, pulling free of his embrace. 'You're still not above using any tactic to get what you want, are you?'

She made a grab for the necklace gathered in Seth's hand like some worthless trinket, but he stuffed it into his pocket out of her reach.

'I always fancied I might do well as a jewel thief,' he grinned, catching her seeking fingers against his chest.

'Well, I doubt you'll find many women as gullible as I was,' she told him.

'You think not?' he inquired, levering one eyebrow upward. 'Perhaps you're right. Come closer, pretty maid,' he invited, 'and I'll make recompense for your loss.'

'You're not after my earrings now, are you?' she asked in mock suspicion.

'No,' he answered, going suddenly serious. 'Those are yours forever.

'You'll be quite safe the rest of the way,' he went on, 'and I'll ask the coachman to see you to the door. Are you certain you don't mind going on alone?'

'I don't mind,' she told him. 'And you won't forget to thank the owner of the necklace for me, will you? It was a most generous loan.'

'I won't forget,' he assured her, his grin flashing in the dark.

As the carriage rolled to a stop, Seth drew Charl close for one last, lingering kiss. All evening she had been aware of his quicksilver changes of mood. At first he had been angry then gay, understanding then teasing; now there was an undefinable tension in him that leaped like a static charge between them. To Charl it seemed a dark and sinister force that filled her with a breathless dread. Suddenly she did not want to let him go, but she was at a loss to explain her rising panic. Her fingers closed over the edges of his cape as if to detain him, but he gave her a hard little hug and swung abruptly out of the carriage and into the street.

'Goodnight,' he said softly as he closed the door.

'Seth, wait!' Her voice rose to call him back, but the vehicle had begun to roll. Leaping to the window she looked back to where he stood in the pool of torchlight. Then he hunched his broad shoulders against the cold and disappeared into the swirling snow.

❋

It's finally over, Seth thought as he noiselessly closed the door to his room at the La Soeur house and leaned back against the stout wooden panel. All the pretence and intrigue that had governed his life for the past six years was over tonight. Not an hour ago he had exchanged the opal and diamond necklace that Charl had worn to the ball for the papers he carried inside his shirt. Tomorrow he would meet Joubert to collect some additional information; then he would be free to leave Quebec, and his life as a spy, behind him. He exhaled long and slowly, feeling as though he had been holding his breath since that night in Black Rock when Mitchell had blackmailed him into returning to Quebec. It was all over now, and he could not help but feel overwhelming relief.

Coming free of the door he moved towards the bed where Charl lay deeply asleep. Her hair looked dark against the white pillowcase, and in the moonlight that filtered between the curtains, he could dimly see the half smile that curved her lips. In sleep one hand had crept across to his side of the bed, as if she was seeking him in the empty space. She seemed so vulnerable and unprotected as she lay lost in dreams that he had an almost overwhelming desire to gather her in his arms and keep her safe. Watching her, an aching tenderness began to coil in his middle and nearly took his breath away, and he was forced to admit what he had tried to deny for so long.

This was his woman. This lovely, stubborn, quixotic creature was the one he wanted above all others. And now, at last, he would be able to claim her. In a few days they would leave Quebec and its pretence behind them. Once they were safely across the border, he would tell Charl the truth about everything and make her his wife. That thought brought a tranquillity to his mind that stilled all doubts and settled any questions about the future.

With slow, deliberate steps he went to the window, parting the curtains to look out at the snow. The hour was late and the quiet seemed infinite and all-pervasive. It had been snowing steadily since early evening, and the drifts at the corners of the buildings had begun to deepen. He frowned as he watched the flakes float with silent persistence past the window. He had hoped the heavy snows would hold off until they reached Plattsburg, a small town on the western shore of Lake Champlain. It would not be difficult to send his dispatches to Mitchell's office in Albany from there, and in the spring they could go to Youngstown if that was what Charl wanted. What was important now was that they leave Quebec and begin their new life together. Even though the journey to Plattsburg would not be easy with winter upon them, he knew Charl would not complain. She had faced the hardships of the trip down the St Lawrence with courage, and he was certain she would brave the wilds again to return home.

Closing his eyes he revelled in the silence. He was tired with a weariness that seemed to penetrate his bones. He no longer wanted to face the risks that had been so much a part of his life these past six years. Once he had found the intrigue exciting, but no more. Suddenly there was too much to lose if Mitchell's plans went awry.

His mouth thinned with determination. He would finish his business with Joubert tomorrow. Then, as soon as he could gather their provisions, he and Charl would leave Quebec to begin life anew, the question of his allegiance resolved for ever.

Breaking from his reverie, Seth slid the fingers of his left hand along the window sill, searching for the small round depression in the stone. He found it easily and pressed, pulling the sill forward in the same motion. As if by magic the shallow cavity below appeared. Unbuttoning his waistcoat and then his shirt, he drew out the leather folder he had received from Muzette Verreault. Inside were the final plans for the British offensive to begin in the spring. He scanned the pages by the light of the full moon, then tucked them back inside the envelope. There would be time tomorrow to commit the contents to memory. Silently he slid the envelope inside the compartment with some other papers and closed the sill.

Again, he stared out at the pristine snow reflecting in the bright lunar light. The night was peaceful and deathly quiet. For a long time he stood as if one with the night, mesmerized by the drifting flakes.

Charl was never quite sure what had roused her. Perhaps it had been some small sound or the midnight brightness in the room, but she was suddenly totally awake. When she opened her eyes, the first thing she saw was Seth, standing by the window so silent and still that it startled her. Against the dark shadows his features were etched with moonlight into a sharp linear portrait, and his hair seemed streaked with silver. For a moment she almost called out to him, but his expression was so intense and sombre that she changed her mind. Instead she lay watching him.

Would she ever really understand him? she wondered. Or would she ever know what he was thinking? He seemed to have so many secrets, so many complexities that she had yet to discover. Was it possible that she could ever fathom the intricacies of this man she loved?

He had been still for so long that when he moved it startled her, although his movement was neither sudden nor violent. With fascination she watched as his hand slid along the edge of the window sill until he found what he was seeking. To her amazement the heavy block glided forward, and she could see a shadowy compartment behind it. Under her curious gaze, Seth took a narrow envelope from his shirt. For several minutes he studied the contents with a frown between his brows, then refolded the documents and returned them to the packet. There was the rustle of other papers as he put them into the narrow opening and then pushed the stone smoothly back into place.

Her heart beat wildly as she watched him. Seth had never let her see evidence of his spying before, and even now she would not have known about it except that he thought she was asleep. Her mind buzzed with questions. Where had he gone when he left her in the carriage? Was the owner of the necklace somehow connected to Seth's sinister activities in Quebec? Or was the necklace itself some kind of bribe or payment for the papers he had just hidden? Charl lay watching him, her thoughts tumbling in confusion, questions rife in her mind. Then slowly came the conviction that she really did not want to know too much about his activities. She had no desire to be privy to his intrigues or know about the risks he took. She loved him beyond all else, but this was one part of his life she could not share. Minutes passed as he continued to stare out of the window, his eyes shadowed and far away.

Finally, she stirred as if she was just coming awake and called out to him.

'Seth? What are you doing? It's cold, come to bed.'

He started at the sound of her voice and whirled towards her, his features hardened with suspicion.

'Where have you been so late?' she went on. 'Did you just come in?'

He came towards the bed and sat down beside her, his tension visibly easing. With those two questions Charl had allayed his fears and convinced him that she had slept through his nocturnal activities. Tenderly, he brushed a strand of hair from her cheek.

'You looked beautiful tonight,' he said softly. 'I was proud to have you by my side.'

It had been a wonderful evening, one she would never forget. Years from now she would still recall the golden glow of the ballroom, the elegance of her gown, the sweet music in her ears, and Seth's strong arms around her as they danced.

'Oh Seth,' she whispered, her voice hushed with emotion. 'I love you so.'

'And I love you,' he replied without hesitation, surprising himself with the ease of the admission. He had never even considered saying those words to her, and yet he knew he had never meant any words more.

'I want to marry you, Charl,' he went on in a rush, 'and take you somewhere where nothing can come between us. I want to make up for all the times I've hurt you and build a future for us together.'

Charl searched his face, memorizing the tenderness in his features and the undisguised love in the depths of his eyes.

These were the words she had longed to hear from his lips: the words of commitment that would forever bind her to this man. In that moment her fears for the future subsided, and she felt secure for the first time since the night they had left Youngstown. Seth loved her and wanted her for his wife. A warm serenity began to seep through her veins, quelling the doubts that had plagued her since she had realized that she was to bear Seth's child. Now he had given her a gift of time, an endless future stretching vast and promising before them in which to share her secret.

Charl reached up to him, sliding her hands across his bare chest, under the loose folds of his shirt, until her palms caressed the strong column of his neck. Her fingers tangled in the silky hair that grew long and thick at his nape, and she stared into the fathomless blue of his eyes.

'Oh yes, Seth,' she whispered, 'that's what I want, too. I want to be your wife.'

His arms closed around her until she was held hard, almost fiercely, to his chest, and she tightened her grip around him in response. It felt so good to be hugged close in Seth's arms, her cheek pressed tight against his shoulder and her face hidden in the curve of his neck. Sighing, she surrendered to the contentment that settled over her and the warm sense of security and belonging she found in his embrace. Nothing could part her now from this man she loved. When his lips moved to cover hers in a hot, demanding kiss, she gave herself joyfully in return. Soon he was naked beside her, his fine clothes left in an untidy heap beside the bed as he sought the warmth of the covers and her. Charl's hands moved over his big body, stroking, encompassing, arousing until he trembled beneath her touch. His mouth explored her tenderest places, leaving her clinging to him, her limbs gone weak and watery with her need. Their ragged breathing tore the stillness of the night as they lost themselves in the intimacies of passion.

For all the times that they had come together, this time was sweeter and the satisfaction was manifold because of the commitment they shared. A tide of feeling rose in them both, and their husky voices mingled as they repeated the love words that were an affirmation of their mutual need. Then the sweeping delight was too great, and they clung together, dissolving in waves of sensation until their identities, their futures, and their very souls became one. They rode out the cresting of their passion and then slept, replete and secure in each other's arms.

Twenty-One

�֍ ✿ ✿

'Unnecessary, so unnecessary,' Felix St James muttered angrily as his gaze moved slowly over the familiar rose and buff chamber with its sumptuous furnishings. How well the room reflected the personality of its occupant. The ornate marble mantelpiece with its intricate china candlesticks at each end, the gilt-framed mirrors, the opulent silk couches, and the delicately carved bed disclosed much about the woman who had entertained in this room. It spoke eloquently of her excellent taste, of her love of luxury, and of her sense of style. And for the men who shared the intimacy of her boudoir, this room was an island of gentility in this godless wilderness called North America.

He shook his head as he made his way to the graceful Sheraton table and poured himself a brandy from a cut crystal decanter. Turning, he faced the room with its memories of a woman's throaty laugh, of a slender body moving under his, and of the wicked pleasures they had shared. He brought the snifter to his lips in silent toast. She had been a remarkable woman, but histrionic and melodramatic to the end. She was a whore, no doubt, but she carried off the role with rare panache, and he had admired her even as he plotted her downfall.

It was a shame and a senseless waste of a life, he thought as he knelt beside the slim body slumped on the plush Aubusson carpet. Even in death she was painfully lovely, lying as if she had arranged her hair and gown, like an actress in a tragedy who would awaken for her curtain calls. He pried the ornate perfume vial from her lifeless fingers and held it in his palm. Who would have thought that Muzette Verreault would drink poison rather than face questioning about her espionage activities? His grip tightened convulsively around the bottle in his hand.

They had broken into her apartment a scant hour earlier in the hope of apprehending the beautiful spy and her accomplice, as well as recovering the incriminating papers. Unfortunately, she had been alone, preparing for bed when they arrived. If only General Prevost had not detained him, they might have followed Muzette when she left the ball and accomplished his purposes, St James mused. His fingers tightened around the vial in frustration until his knuckles showed white against his olive skin. He was not a man used to failure.

When he accused her of the theft of certain documents from the Château St Louis, Muzette had not even bothered to deny it.

'You may search wherever you wish, my dear Felix,' she had said haughtily from where she reclined seductively on one of the silk divans, 'but you will find no papers here. And without these papers you claim I stole, you have no proof against me.'

He had chosen his words with care, watching the woman whose silver-bright image was seared indelibly into his memory.

'Even without proof I have the authority to arrest you,' he had said slowly, 'at least for questioning. It is imperative that we find your accomplice before these documents leave Quebec. You could be most helpful in this matter, Muzette.'

Her great silvery eyes shone diamond clear in her chalky face, but still she did not speak.

'And if you chose not to be helpful,' he had paused, 'I would be forced to incarcerate you. But then, I understand that is a situation you became very familiar with in your native France.'

The fear emanating from her was almost a tangible thing; but it did not show in her face, and he admired her composure.

'Come, Muzette,' he urged her, 'don't be foolish. Is your silence in this matter really worth the risk of languishing in prison?'

Rising from the couch, she moved unsteadily to stare into the fire, twisting her rings in mute terror. After several trembling seconds she turned to face him, but there was no mercy in his eyes, nor did she expect any.

'And if I confess the names of my associates, Felix, will I go free? I think not.'

'But you will not be hanged for treason and perhaps . . .'

'I need a guarantee, Felix, some kind of guarantee,' she told him fiercely as she faced him.

'You know I can't promise you anything, Muzette,' came the low reply.

A deep and impenetrable silence fell between them in which the sputtering of the flames and the draught blowing down the chimney were the only sounds. Watching her, St James wished he could read the thoughts behind her shaded eyes. When Muzette finally spoke, she seemed even more pale than she had been before, but her voice was strong.

'Very well. I trust you and your men will be able to make yourselves at home in the drawing room while I dress and pack a few things to take with me.'

'Certainly,' he had agreed, and closed the double doors to the room behind him as he left.

It was nearly half an hour later when they broke into the bedchamber to find Muzette collapsed on the floor, still dressed in the diaphanous gown and wrapper. Even as he knelt beside her, he knew she was dead, although the pallor seemed only to heighten her ethereal beauty. Regretfully, he had brushed a silvery strand of hair from her brow and noted that her skin was already growing cold. The poison had done its work quickly.

'Unnecessary, so unnecessary,' he said again as he rose from beside the limp form of Muzette Verreault. He loosened his grip on the vial in his hand and moved absently to the dressing table with its myriad of cut glass bottles. How many more of these contain poison, he wondered. At random he selected one and unstoppered it. The scent of jasmine filled his head as he passed the bottle under his nose.

Damnation! With Muzette's suicide his investigation was at a dead end. In the past three months he had been successful in tracing the American spies this far and no farther. Why hadn't he been able to discover where this group got its information? And how was it being passed to this man Mitchell in Albany? It was not as if a man could carry such complex facts and figures in his head. Papers must be passed; meetings must take place. Why, then, had he been unable to discover any of these connections?

And how long would the Americans continue to ignore or misinterpret the intelligence coming from Quebec? Was it possible that they did not recognize the weaknesses in the British line of defence? Because of the Peninsular War in Spain with Napoleon there were simply too few British troops in Canada. The conflict with America was very much secondary in the eyes of the War Department, and the best leaders and troops were employed in Spain. God knows, that was where he belonged, St

James reflected bitterly. In Spain a man could quickly advance his career; but instead of an assignment with Wellington, he had received this appointment. Because of his experience in Quebec ten years earlier, he had been sent here.

Thankfully, the Americans either did not recognize the British weaknesses or were too disorganized to act. Was it possible that they did not recognize the frailty of the supply lines to the Western outposts or realize how critical these supplies were to the loyalty of their Indian allies? Yet no serious attempt had been made to interfere with this vital flow. He shook his head, mindful of both the American incompetence and the tenuous British situation on this continent. Since Isaac Brock's death, there was no aggressive British leadership in Canada. Proctor in the West, Sheaffe in York, and Prevost in Quebec were like three old women unable to make a decision among them. Even the plans for the spring offensive outlined in the stolen documents were too conservative to accomplish anything decisive. It must only be a matter of time before the Americans acted on the information that was leaking out of Quebec and invaded Canada.

Frustration burned inside him, bitter and acid as gall. Why couldn't he discover the sources of information these people used? He felt as if he was casting about in the dark. He would sense that he was close to some pertinent discovery, and then its relevance would slip away. Who were these men who could carry out their business and never leave a trace of their activities? He had been sure he would trap them this time, but they had outwitted him again.

Carefully, he replaced the perfume vial on the dressing table and drew one long finger through the tangle of jewels scattered on the satiny mahogany surface. Muzette had such lovely jewels, he reflected, worth a king's ransom but no good to her now. Absently he scooped up a handful of the baubles and was aware of the cool, serpentine feel of them in his palm before he returned to his musings.

It was a pity that Muzette had killed herself, he thought, staring down at the necklace curled between his fingers. If only she had told him the identity of her visitor, he might easily have spared her the punishment she undoubtedly deserved. He had not been able to promise her anything, but surely a woman who sold her loyalty for a few jewels would realize how expedient it would be to change allegiance. Why, then, had Muzette Verreault taken her own life?

He stared intently at the gems in his hand, as if seeking an answer in the cloudy, rainbow-hued opals or the icy diamonds that flashed so brilliantly in the firelight. Their contrast seemed to mesmerize him, and he turned them slowly, watching the dancing reflections.

Using the plans for the spring offensive to trap the Americans had been a dangerous gamble; and, having failed to capture one of the spies, he could not hope to justify his actions to General Prevost. Still, he was less disturbed by the thought of the general's displeasure, and the inevitability of revamping the plans for spring, than he was by the fact that the Americans had thwarted him again. Was he dealing with incredibly lucky or incredibly skilful men? Why hadn't he been able to find out who they were? Why couldn't he catch them passing information? And how were the papers being sent across the border?

With an oath he clenched his fist around the necklace in his hand. But in doing so the force of his grip drove the sharp clasp into his flesh. Startled by the sudden pain, he drew back, as if the object had attacked him. Transferring the jewels to his other hand, he put the bleeding finger in his mouth in a primitive response.

It was a lovely piece, he reflected with appreciation as he inspected the offending article. Somehow it was oddly familiar. Slowly, he uncoiled the necklace and spread it across his palm. Perhaps poor Muzette had worn it just tonight. But no, Muzette had worn green to the ball, with an emerald pendant hanging between her breasts. Yet he was sure . . . His brows furrowed as he stared at the glittering stones. Where had he seen this necklace? The memory was suddenly very important to him although he was not sure why.

He closed his eyes, imagining the Governor's ballroom as it had looked this evening, aglow with hundreds of candles and alive with the élite of Quebec society. With meticulous care he searched his mind for the women who had attended the ball: those he'd greeted, those who had smiled at him at the buffet, those he'd noticed as he danced with Muzette. Every image that flashed through his head strengthened his conviction. He had seen this necklace tonight; if only he could remember. Then a slow smile curved his full mouth, and his eyes, behind their lowered lids, smouldered like live coals. Of course he had seen this necklace tonight. It had been curved around the slender alabaster throat of Seth Porterfield's beautiful mistress.

※

The morning was well advanced when Seth awoke and slid noiselessly from the bed so as not to disturb the woman who slept by his side. In the chilly room he washed and dressed hastily, deciding not to take time to shave. He was anxious to see Joubert and complete their business so he could get on with his plans to leave Quebec. Porterfield's mind was busy with lists of supplies he and Charl would need on their journey. As he buttoned himself into the rough woollen shirt, he considered the advantages and disadvantages of the various routes to Plattsburg, the small settlement where he planned they would spend the winter.

Had he intended to make the trip alone, he would have paddled upstream in a canoe, picking his way between ice floes. With this leg of his journey complete, he would have proceeded southward along the Richelieu River, on foot if the river proved impassable. However, a trek of this nature would be far too difficult and dangerous for Charl. Probably he would take her across the river on the ferry and travel one of the overland routes on horseback. With luck they would find ample game to augment their supplies and shelter at night in caves or abandoned cabins. He frowned thoughtfully. He would talk things over with Joubert. In the past months he had come to respect the wily Frenchman, and he knew the master spy might well be able to offer some alternative means of reaching the United States and safety.

Tucking his shirt into his breeches and donning a fleece-lined jerkin, he prepared to leave but paused long enough to lay and light a fire so that the room would be warm when Charl awoke. Moving to the edge of the bed, he watched her as she slept. Things were almost resolved between them, and their secure future was within his grasp. There was only this one last thing to accomplish, and then he could turn his thoughts completely to their life together. Brushing his lips against her sleep-warm cheek, he bid her good-bye and made his way downstairs.

In the kitchen Gabrielle was already busy with her chores, and they exchanged pleasantries while Seth drank a mug of coffee and ate several bran muffins fresh from the oven. Then he pulled on his heavy coat and left for his meeting with Joubert.

The day was crystalline with the sun glinting on the freshly

fallen snow and reflecting off the icicles that formed a jagged
fringe along the eaves of the stone houses. Beneath his feet the
snow scrunched as if in protest at his weight on its powdery
surface, and the air was as crisp and heady as a fine wine. Seth
breathed deeply, letting the frigid vitality fill him, and then
exhaled sharply, watching his breath turn to great clouds of
vapour. There was a sense of well-being in the clarity of the day,
and he whistled softly as he ploughed through the drifts that
reached well past his knees.

La Place Royale was busy as always, and he was just turning
onto rue Sous le Fort when two guards from the provost marshal
stopped him.

'Are you Seth Porterfield?' the shorter one asked as they
stepped from the shadow of the church at the head of the square.

There was a nauseating curl of apprehension in his belly as
Seth turned to face them that immediately dispelled any feeling
of well-being.

'Yes?' he replied coolly.

'Mr Porterfield, we have orders to escort you to the Château
St Louis for questioning in a matter of some importance.'

For a moment Seth was seized by an almost uncontrollable
urge to turn and run, but he suppressed it, knowing it was futile.
Instead he stood his ground and regarded the young soldiers with
a calm he was far from feeling.

'Who gave you these orders, sergeant?' Seth asked, certain
that the answer would confirm his worst fears.

'It was Major St James, sir.'

There was a quick leap of panic in his chest at the reply.
Muzette had been right, Seth realized. St James must have known
about their relationship all along. But if that were so, why hadn't
he made any effort to stop the flow of information until now?
And what purpose would it serve for St James to have him
arrested when he might otherwise have led the British to Joubert?
The initial shock of being stopped was wearing off, and his head
was full of questions.

'What is this all about?' Seth blustered. 'I demand to know
why I am being detained.'

'We were ordered to deliver you to the Château St Louis, sir.
That is all I know except that we are to shackle you if you refuse
to come peaceably,' the sergeant replied.

There was a long, brittle pause as Seth faced his would-be

captors while his mind churned with plans for escape. Both guards seemed to sense the trend of his thoughts, and they involuntarily tightened their grip on their muskets. Without being told, both recognized this man as a dangerous adversary should he decide to resist. Then the moment shattered and Seth suddenly agreed.

'Very well, I will come with you. I wish to talk to Major St James and get to the bottom of this nonsense.'

'Yes, sir.' The sergeant seemed relieved. 'If you'll follow me, sir.'

With the gusts of wind from the river at their backs, they made their way up rue Sous le Fort to the foot of the stairs to Uppertown. Above them loomed the heavy rock face, its weathered crevices frowning pessimistically on the slow progress of the three men who climbed the icy steps.

What had gone wrong? Seth asked himself as they walked. Had Muzette Verreault been arrested, too? If so, had she confessed to stealing the papers and then implicated him?

In spite of himself the metallic taste of fear rose in his throat at the sight of the Château St Louis towering above him. What awaited him behind those high grey walls? Was he to finally face the consequences of his treasonous acts, or would he be able to evade his guilt again? As he entered the Prescott Gate and turned left towards the Place d'Armes, he steeled himself for what might well prove to be the most dangerous encounter of his life.

※

The soft knock on the bedroom door caught Charl drowsing indulgently in the wide, warm bed as she watched the flames flicker over the logs in the fireplace.

'Attendez, s'il vous plaît,' she called out as she reached for the pale pink wrapper flung over the foot of the bed and slipped it on. She was reminded suddenly of a morning, not so long ago, when such a knock had filled her with dread and she had wished desperately to be able to say those few words in French. How much her life had changed in these few short months.

Belting the robe around her slim waist, Charl moved to the door, flinging it wide to admit the mistress of the house.

'Bonjour, Charl,' she chirped cheerfully as she entered the small room.

'Bonjour, Gabrielle,' Charl replied. 'Have you brought me breakfast?'

'Oui, I thought you might enjoy being pampered this morning after being out so late last night,' she answered, setting the tray laden with muffins and tea on the table. Efficiently she laid two places.

'Now, tell me everything about the ball,' Gabrielle demanded eagerly as she settled herself in a chair and poured their tea.

'I will, I will,' Charl assured her, 'but there is something else I must tell you first.'

'Oh?' the Frenchwoman inquired, her dark eyes wide with expectancy.

For a moment Charl hesitated. She knew she had not imagined the things that had happened last night, but the events still seemed unreal to her. Was it possible Seth wanted her for his wife? Had he really said the words of love that bound them inseparably together? A smile curved her lips as she remembered with unmistakable clarity the tenderness in his eyes and the passion of his touch. Last night had marked a new beginning for her, a future at Seth's side.

'Seth has asked me to marry him,' Charl said softly.

There was a momentary pause, and Charl began to wonder if Gabrielle had understood what she said.

'And what did you answer him, chérie?' Gabrielle finally asked.

'Why I told him yes! Of course I told him yes!' Charl bubbled, her quiet contentment transformed suddenly to merriment. 'I love him, Gabrielle, and he loves me!'

The Frenchwoman reached across to give Charl a hard, impulsive hug.

'That's wonderful! Wonderful!' she repeated, smiling broadly although there were tears of happiness in her eyes. 'Everything has turned out just as you had hoped, n'est-ce pas?'

'Everything,' Charl agreed, blinking back tears of her own.

Silence fell between them for a long moment as they smiled at each other, and then they were both talking at once.

'Seth says we'll need to leave Quebec once we're married, and as much as I hate to go, I think it's better . . .'

'How did he ask you? What did he say? We'll have to have time to make you a proper wedding gown, and I'll have a little party here after the ceremony . . .'

They paused, laughing joyously together even while the tears glistened in their eyes.

'Oh, chérie! I am so happy for you. Seth is a fine man.'

'I know.'

'He'll make you a good husband.'

'I know.'

They laughed again, a little breathlessly.

'There's so much to do!' Gabrielle observed. 'Did you tell him about the baby?'

'Not yet,' Charl answered. 'It was late last night when we returned home, and there was no time to discuss anything. Tonight I'll tell him. There is so much we need to talk over, but there is no hurry. We have the rest of our lives.'

*

For a long time Seth stood with his captors in the draughty stone corridor outside Major St James' office in the Château St Louis. They had removed his coat when they searched him for weapons, taking the knife he habitually carried in his boot, and he was glad for the protection the heavy jerkin offered against the chill. He was calm now and watched the comings and goings with veiled interest, hoping to catch a glimpse of something that would offer a clue to the reason for his arrest. His brain teemed with unanswered questions, and he tried to isolate anything that he had done to make St James suspicious of his actions.

Mentally, he reviewed the events of the preceding evening, searching for the one word or action that had tipped his hand. He had danced with Muzette only at St James' insistence. Was it possible that their conversation had been overheard? Did someone follow him to Muzette's rooms? Since he had entered and left through the garden, it seemed unlikely that anyone could have seen him. Could it be that Muzette had betrayed him? But why? His thoughts went back to other missions, other meetings he'd had in the months since he'd come to Quebec. Where was his mistake? What had he done that alerted St James to his real reason for being in Quebec?

He shifted uncomfortably where he stood between his two stoic guards. It was well past noon. Surely Joubert was no longer waiting at the abandoned farmhouse a mile or two beyond the Kent Gate where Seth was to have met him this morning. Word of his arrest would soon reach Joubert through the network of informants, but what of Charl? She would have no idea of what had happened to him. Could he convince St James to send her word of his whereabouts? And what would she think when she learned that he had been captured as an American spy? He smiled inwardly. He had been right not to tell her his real reasons for being in Quebec, as difficult as it had been to keep them from her these past months. Regardless of what happened to him now, Charl could not be implicated. By keeping his activities secret, he had protected her.

The door to St James' office opened abruptly, and the young lieutenant who was the major's aide came out carrying a pair of manacles and moved towards them.

Seth straightened. The waiting was over now, and he was almost glad. He would be confronted with his crimes, and that could be no worse than the uncertainty.

'Major St James has ordered the prisoner shackled before the questioning begins,' he told the two guards.

Seth stood docilely as the manacles were clamped around his wrists only because it seemed pointless to resist, but a slow, dangerous rage had begun to simmer inside him. Undoubtedly St James had ordered the chains to humiliate and degrade him, but his pride would not be bowed. With shoulders squared and eyes blazing he followed the young lieutenant into St James' office.

He was left in the centre of the room, flanked by his two guards, while the major stood with his back to them as he contemplated the Place d'Armes. The office was befitting a man of his rank, with its dark wood-panelled walls, a wide, leather-topped desk, and an obligatory portrait of George III over the fireplace. Slow, silent minutes ticked past before Felix deemed it necessary to acknowledge their presence. He turned from the window and let his gaze move over Seth, finally coming to rest on the arrogant Porterfield features. How it would please him to discredit this man and bring disgrace to his name.

A malicious smile played at the corners of his mouth before he spoke.

'Ah yes, Porterfield. Somehow I've never seen you looking better.'

Seth stiffened at his words.

'What the hell is this all about, St James?' he demanded.

'Easy, easy, my impetuous friend. I doubt we'll need your guards in attendance for our little conversation.'

He turned to the two soldiers.

'You may wait outside,' he told them.

When they were gone, Felix sat down in the ornate, high-backed chair behind his desk and studied Seth over his steepled fingers. His expression was lost in the glare from the windows at his back, but the younger man was aware of the close scrutiny.

'Whatever else Porterfields are, I never expected to find one who was a traitor,' he said baldly.

Seth felt colour rise along his cheekbones but said nothing.

'Not even a denial? You surprise me, Porterfield. I expected a denial.'

'Then I am sorry to disappoint you,' he replied coolly in spite of the tension singing in his veins.

'Are you?' St James asked as he receded thoughtfully into the shadow cast by the high chair back.

For a long time neither man moved, letting the billowing silence fill the room. Sounds from the corridor seemed to eddy around them, and Seth's own breathing seemed loud in his ears. He knew that St James had set out to unnerve him, and he kept his face carefully impassive while his mind raced on towards the interview to come.

St James must not have proof of the charges against him, Seth reasoned, or he would not resort to these tactics: the silence, the insults, the shackles. The major must hope to wring a confession from him or convict him by his own admission. If that were so, perhaps he had a chance. There was still no clue to the charges that St James would make, but Seth must be ready to defend himself whatever they were. No one knew St James' guile and cunning better than he, and Seth realized that every question asked would have to be carefully weighed and analysed before a response was given.

Seth's muscles ached with tension as he fought to maintain his outward composure while his mind was clamouring for the confrontation. In spite of himself, the silence was having its desired effect. Once again, Seth reminded himself sternly that he must remain in control, calculating every word, every gesture, every inflection, or his life would be forfeit.

'So you will not deny that you are a traitor, eh, Porterfield?'

'It is only that I have no idea what you're talking about when you make that accusation, major.'

'No idea? Even when I know you have been trafficking in stolen government documents? That you have been smuggling them to the Americans?'

So that was it, Seth thought with relief. He cocked an eyebrow in St James' direction and smiled.

'This sounds like a fascinating story, major. Tell me more.'

St James' lips thinned with irritation, and his eyes were like agate as he watched the tall, blond man who stood before him. He remembered Seth as William Porterfield's young, impulsive nephew and later as the impertinent scout who had forced his way into command headquarters demanding an explanation for his uncle's death. In those days Seth had been rash and reckless, so different from this cold, arrogant man who was his prisoner. Yet every man had his weaknesses, Felix knew, and he must find Porterfield's quickly before the orders for the spring offensive were smuggled out of Quebec.

What were Seth Porterfield's weaknesses? And could they be used to manipulate him into a situation where he would incriminate himself? St James noted the other man's bearing: the proud set of his jaw and the icy challenge in his eyes. It would be impossible to force information from this man by the usual means. Still, there must be something that would destroy his composure and precipitate a slip that would expose Porterfield for the traitor he was.

It would give him such pleasure to discredit the Porterfield name, Felix mused, although it could not begin to rectify the wrong that had been done to his own family. That final satisfaction would come only when the line was exhausted, when every descendant of Alistair Porterfield was dead. Over the years he had moved towards that end until now only the man who stood before him remained: the old man's only living descendant. How ironic it was that fate had delivered Seth into his hands, and all he needed was some proof of his activities to hang him for treason.

But what ploy, what device could he use to find that evidence? St James puzzled. What would bring this man to his knees? Carefully, he studied the prisoner. He was a strong man, a stubborn man, a proud man. He would accept total responsibility for his acts, the major was sure, and he would endure torture rather than betray his associates. But if he took it upon himself to attempt to protect the others that were already implicated, then perhaps the unfortunate Madame Verreault and Charlotte Beckwith would prove to be his undoing.

'Then, Porterfield, since you know nothing about government

documents being smuggled to the United States, you will probably also deny that you went to Madame Muzette Verreault's apartments last night with the express purpose of exchanging stolen military plans for these jewels.'

As if playing a trump card, St James spilled the opal and diamond necklace from his palm on to the top of the desk, where the perfect stones winked and sparkled in the sunlight.

So it was the necklace that had betrayed him, Seth thought in the seconds after Felix's accusation. Then a second, chilling realization came to him. If Felix had connected the gems with him, then Charl must be implicated as well. He could not ignore the danger of the situation, but at least now that he knew where he stood, he could begin to act.

'I only met Madame Verreault last night at the Governor's ball,' Seth explained evenly. 'You introduced –'

'Damn it, man! Did you exchange this necklace for military secrets?' the major thundered.

He must discern the source of St James' information, gauge the seriousness of the charges, Seth decided coolly. Did he have additional evidence of his involvement, or was he casting around in the dark?

'Did Madame Verreault tell you I did? Did she give you this necklace?'

'Madame Verreault told me nothing. Madame Verreault is dead,' St James answered slowly.

The meaning of the major's words washed over Seth with stunning force, leaving him momentarily disoriented and off balance. He remembered Muzette's silver-bright eyes smiling up at him last night as he prepared to leave.

'Stay with me, Seth,' she suggested seductively. 'We could find such pleasure together.'

She had been so vital, so beautiful. If it had not been for Charl, he would have agreed.

'Dear God! What happened?' he demanded of the officer, aware that his tone was revealing too much.

'You seem very concerned about a woman you met only last night,' the major observed.

God damn St James if he ordered Muzette killed, Seth cursed silently. And God damn me if I was somehow the cause.

'What happened?' he demanded again, his voice husky.

'She took poison,' came the unemotional reply.

Unwanted visions of a writhing, painful death flashed through
Seth's mind, leaving ghosts of images that would haunt him all
his life.

'But why?'

What had driven Muzette Verreault to suicide? He could see
that St James would give him no explanations. What had this
man threatened that made Muzette choose death instead?

Over the years he had seen other agents die, but this affected
him more profoundly than any of them. They had known the
risks, but Muzette was an innocent in this world of intrigue. She
had not realized the chances she would be taking or the danger
she would face. She saw this all as a game with the jewels as her
prize for winning.

The thought of what had happened filled him with remorse.
Although he had tried to warn her of the risks at the outset, she
had not believed him, and for all her worldly experience she was
surprisingly naive. He should have found a way to protect her,
he chided himself. He should have . . .

St James watched his prisoner's face, wondering if the news
was having the desired effect. There was a pinched look around
the man's mouth, but Porterfield gave no other outward sign of
distress. Perhaps it was time to see if his ploy had worked.

'Then you deny that you went to Muzette Verreault's apartments last night.'

'Yes,' Seth answered distractedly.

'And you will not admit that you exchanged this necklace for
military secrets?'

'I will admit nothing.'

'Then where did you go after you left the Governor's Mansion?'

'I . . .' Seth paused to consider the ways he could respond to
that question. Logic dictated that he claim to have gone home,
but he would not involve Charl in this. He had taken too many
chances with her safety already. 'I sent Miss Beckwith home in
the carriage and then went to a tavern for a drink. I stayed quite
late . . .'

'And you were not with Miss Beckwith after the ball?' St James
persisted.

'No,' Seth answered.

He should have stopped at a tavern to establish an alibi. What
had he been thinking about? Why had he been so careless?

A slow, self-satisfied smile came to the corners of St James' mouth, and he looked as if he had suddenly succeeded in gaining the advantage in this dangerous game. Involuntarily, a shiver of premonition skittered down Seth's spine, and he wondered what mistake he'd made. He found out almost instantly.

'Since Miss Beckwith was the only other person to have access to the necklace, she must have been the one who met Madame Verreault in her rooms last night to exchange the papers for this,' he reasoned aloud, running one slender finger through the pool of gems that glittered coldly in the sunlight. 'As difficult as it is to believe, Charlotte Beckwith must be an American spy.'

Time seemed suspended as Seth stared uncomprehending at the British officer who sat smugly on the opposite side of the massive desk. The man's words and logic made little sense to him, but the essence of the accusation was appallingly clear. Seth tried to make himself respond, tried to think of some denial that would turn St James' suspicion from Charl, but his brain was dulled with shock, and he knew it was too late to spare either of them what was to come.

'I knew I had seen her wearing the jewels at the ball, and I mistakenly assumed that you were the one who took them to Madame Verreault,' Felix went on. 'Sometimes we forget the treachery of the female . . .'

First Muzette and now Charl, Seth thought wearily as he listened to the other man's words, so lovely, so vulnerable. Somehow he should have been able to protect them from St James. Muzette was dead, but Charl . . .

The thought of the treatment Charl would receive at St James' hands began to cauterize his mind. At least Muzette had understood the reasons for her arrest, but Charl would not. She would be confused, angry, terrified.

St James was moving around the corner of the desk, coming towards where Seth stood. With an effort he brought his attention back to what the officer was saying.

'As soon as we have questioned Miss Beckwith, you will be released. And once you are, I advise you to leave Quebec. If you stay, Porterfield, you will die, either by my hand or on the gallows. Your actions are suspect, and I will be watching you, waiting for one step outside the law.'

Roughly, he prodded Seth towards the door and jerked it open. 'Jenkins!' he called sharply.

This was a bluff, Seth thought, his mind racing. St James had given in too easily, believed Charl's guilt too readily. It had to be a bluff, but could he be sure? And even if it was, did he want to subject Charl, his sweet Charl, the woman he loved, to St James' ruthless questioning? The need to protect Charl grew inside him.

'Jenkins!'

'Yes, sir!' the young lieutenant answered, scurrying down the corridor from another office.

'Inform Sergeant Sass and Private Moore that they are to arrest Miss Charlotte Beckwith.' He turned. 'Where will we find her, Porterfield?'

It was a trap. He was sure of it. All his instincts urged him to brazen it out, but Seth was very aware that he was no longer gambling with his own life. Everything was moving too fast; his emotions were too involved. He needed time to think, but his time had run out. Irrelevantly, he remembered the warning Mitchell had given all those months ago in New York. He had said that Charl would be the death of him. Seth smiled grimly to himself. Those words might well be his epitaph.

'Well, Porterfield? Where is she?' The major's voice was harsh, impatient.

In the end the capitulation was easy. If he loved Charl, he had no choice.

'Don't send them to arrest Charlotte,' he answered.

'What did you say, Porterfield?' There was a note of triumph in St James' tone, and Seth knew that with his next words he would seal his doom.

'I took the necklace to Madame Verreault's house last night,' he said simply.

St James slammed the door in the startled lieutenant's face, guided Seth to a chair in front of the desk, and leaned thoughtfully on one corner regarding his prisoner. The once-proud man before him slumped in his chair, his head down. A thrill of satisfaction came over the British officer at the realization of his success. He had forced a confession from this man, had broken his spirit, and when he saw this one hang for his treachery, he would finally have his revenge on the Porterfields. They were such an arrogant breed, comporting themselves as if they were above the laws of England and of society itself. A smile twisted the major's countenance. He had brought this Porterfield down. He was no longer the insolent bastard he had been an hour ago. He had confessed to his crimes; next he would tell the location of the documents and then name his associates here in Quebec. There were many questions that needed answers.

'Where did you take the papers you received in exchange for the necklace?' St James inquired conversationally.

The blue eyes that came up to meet his gaze were cold and defiant.

'I never received any papers,' he said.

The blow came with unexpected speed and brutality. It was only the restraining chains that saved St James from retaliation as Seth surged to his feet.

'You lie!' Felix snarled.

In spite of the swelling that was already beginning to show along his cheekbone and the blood that flowed freely from the corner of his mouth, Seth's eyes remained defiant.

'You will tell me what I want to know,' the officer assured him. 'Just as you admitted to taking the necklace to Muzette's, you will admit to your other crimes.'

'I doubt that,' came the reply.

For a long vibrating moment they stood eye to eye, their contempt and loathing for each other like an animate force in the room. Felix broke the stare abruptly and strode to the door.

'Very well, Porterfield, we'll see how cocky you are after a few days in that hellhole on Cape Diamond.' With a single move he swung the portal wide.

'Guards!' he snapped.

The two who had brought Seth from Lowertown trooped in and went to flank him where he stood before the desk.

'You are to take Mr Porterfield to the prison upon Cape Diamond,' St James ordered with a malevolent glare fixed on Seth. 'See that he gets one of our finest cells.'

'Yes, sir!' Sergeant Sass responded as the private draped Seth's coat around his shoulders capelike to cover the shackles on his wrists. If either of the guards noticed the fresh blood on the prisoner's face, they made no move to staunch the flow before they led him out.

St James went to the window to watch their progress across the square.

Damn that Porterfield bastard, he cursed furiously. He carried himself as if he was on his way to see the king instead of on the way to the gallows. He might well be defiant now, but soon that insufferable pride would be broken. And when it was, Seth would confess not only his part in the spy ring but the names of his associates as well. But first there was the matter of the papers. They must be found before they could be spirited out of Quebec, and they would be necessary to prove the charge of treason against Seth Porterfield.

The question under consideration now seemed to be: how would he obtain this information? The major frowned thoughtfully, oblivious to the snowy square before him and the people who had braved the cold to go on about their business. He pressed his palm against the glass, watching the condensation etch its shape in frosty white.

The girl, Charlotte Beckwith, was the key; that was certain. Whatever their relationship, Porterfield would not see her come to harm. The most obvious solution was to continue to threaten her, perhaps even have her arrested. St James pondered the possibility. Regardless of Porterfield's feelings for Charlotte Beckwith, he was no idealistic schoolboy and would not be duped again. Nor was St James himself anxious to hurt the girl. In the back of his mind he still planned to make her his. No, this time the manoeuvre would have to be more subtle, more devastating. He wanted Porterfield to die a broken man, his pride and will obliterated by his defeat. That would take more than threats, more than physical pain. Perhaps betrayal by the woman he loved would bring Porterfield to his knees.

St James took his fingers from the glass, suddenly aware that the chill was creeping towards his wrist. It would take time and cunning to arrange such a ruse, but he was content to let Seth live a few more days if it led to the ultimate satisfaction of his dreams of revenge.

Twenty-Two
✤✤✤

The two women sat by the fire in the small room on ruelle du Porche until the morning was well spent, sharing an intimacy it might have taken years to establish in another circumstance. Before, Charl had always been too busy or too independent to seek a friendship with another woman, but now she shared an instantaneous understanding with Gabrielle and valued her candid Gallic wisdom. In many ways there was a sharp division in Charl's life marked by the moment she noticed Seth at the Crow's Head Tavern. The pleasant existence she had known in Youngstown seemed remote and far away, and she felt as if she had only come alive in the time she had spent with Seth. She was different now: calmer, settled, more content, finding in his love a more complete happiness than she had ever known. Her friendship with Gabrielle was an outgrowth of that change in her and, as Gabby gathered the dishes to go, Charl was pleased to have someone with whom to share her thoughts.

In spite of the brief respite from work, it was laundry day. By the time Charl came downstairs into the kitchen, Gabrielle had already set the great cauldrons of water on to boil over the fire and was scrubbing the first garments with harsh lye soap. They worked efficiently together, washing, rinsing, and hanging clothes on lines strung between the rafters. While the clothes dried, they moved on to sweep and dust the other rooms.

As hard as the chores were, Charl was too lost in daydreams to notice. Gabrielle smiled indulgently at the girl's vacant state, finding it both romantic and amusing – the spilled wash water and the minutes Charl spent staring into space as she swept and reswept the same place on the floor. With reminiscent understanding she realized that Charl's thoughts were too much on the events of the previous night to be bothered much by the mundane tasks of the day.

And regardless of her good intentions Charl's mind continued to wander, returning again and again to the promises they'd made in the dark. Even now she could not believe that Seth wanted to marry her, after all that had happened between them. Yet somehow, in the stillness of the night, he had asked her to be his wife. She smiled dreamily, her face soft with the memories she would treasure the rest of her life.

There was so much that she needed to discuss with Seth, so much that there had been no time for last night. The wedding should take place as soon as possible, she decided. And in spite of the fact that she had lived as his mistress, Charl wanted to marry Seth in a church, not in a ceremony read by some town justice. How he would react to her request she could not guess, but she hoped that he would agree, if only to please her. These days Seth was a different man from the one who had carried her off to Quebec: considerate, thoughtful, gentle. Charl smiled tenderly at the thought. She did not fool herself that their life together would always run smoothly, though. Seth's basic nature had not changed, nor had hers. She realized that conflicts would arise, as they did in any marriage, but she was confident that they would make the necessary compromises because they loved each other.

There were many other questions in her mind, too. Seth had said last night that he wanted to go away and start a new life with her. Did that mean that he was giving up his work for the English? In this time of war where could a British spy and his American wife settle to find peace? And more important, would the life he had planned for them have room to include a child?

A quiver of uneasiness ran through her. She would have to gather up her courage and tell Seth about the baby growing inside her. Now that they were to be married that should be easier. Still, she felt distinct panic at the thought of facing him with the news. Did Seth either like children or want any of his own? In spite of the trepidation she felt at the thought of telling Seth, Charl was happy about the child. Somehow, its conception represented the joining of their two lives and the confirmation of their future together. Charl wanted a life with Seth more than she had ever wanted anything. She did not want to go on without him, and even if he had not offered the respectability of marriage, she would have stayed with him gladly. Her love for him was a bond that would endure forever.

That evening Charl dressed with particular care for the dinner Marie was preparing to celebrate the occasion. She selected the dark green faille gown with black piping that Seth had given her for Christmas. The dress was cut in a slim military style with a high collar and a double row of buttons down the front. Humming softly to herself, she had taken extra time with her hair, arranging it in gentle waves around her face with a braided coronet high on her head, and she was well pleased with the effect.

'Everything smells marvellous!' she exclaimed as she joined the others in the kitchen. 'Are we ready to eat?'

'Yes, except that Seth is not home yet. This morning he didn't mention that he would be late for dinner. Did he say anything to you, chérie?' Gabby asked.

Charl shook her head. 'I was still asleep when he left,' she admitted.

'We can wait another half hour,' Marie announced. 'It would be a shame for Seth to miss his dinner.'

At that moment Waukee entered, his dark face beaming with pleasure. Charl had gone out to the stable that afternoon to tell him the news of her marriage to Seth and to invite him to dine with them when it appeared that the meal was to be something of a celebration.

His face had been totally still when he heard the news, and then he had spoken in profound seriousness of his friend.

'This is what Seth has needed all these years and what I had hoped would happen from the moment I saw you together. You are right for him, Charl, and I know you can make him happy. He is very lucky to have found you.'

For a long moment he had searched her face with eyes so dark and solemn that they seemed to penetrate her very soul.

'I can see that Seth is what you want, too, and I know he will take good care of you. But if there is ever anything you need that Seth cannot provide, come to me.' His voice had been very low. 'I will always be your friend, Charlotte. If there is anything you ever want, you need only ask.'

Impulsively, she had thrown her arms around him, and he had hugged her back, sharing a bittersweet understanding that transcended words.

That serious man in the stable that afternoon seemed unrelated to the one who entered the noisy, crowded kitchen seeking to congratulate his friend.

'Seth is not home yet,' she told him gaily, 'but I'm sure he will be along soon.'

An hour later, when they sat down to burned venison, the festive air had evaporated. Conversation was strained, and each person was acutely aware of the empty place at the table. Although she did not intercept the look of concern that passed between the Indian and the mistress of the house, Charl knew that there was something amiss. It was not like Seth to be gone without letting someone know.

The evening stretched on unendingly, and Charl sought refuge in her music, but even the intricacies of Bach could not take her mind off her worry. When the clock in the hall struck nine, she retired with the others, hoping to be awakened by Seth's return. She slept fitfully, rousing at the slightest sound and listening fruitlessly for his familiar step on the stairs. But when dawn arrived, she was still alone.

She washed and dressed quickly in the chilly, grey light and made her way to the kitchen where she found Gabrielle in the company of Emile Savard. It was his day to deliver a wagonload of his goods to the shops in Uppertown and Lowertown, and he had stopped for an early breakfast with Gabby. Charl poured herself a cup of tea and sat down at the table, pulling the cashmere shawl more tightly around her against the morning cold.

'Seth didn't come home last night?' Gabrielle asked, although her words were more a statement than question.

The blonde woman shook her head and continued sipping her tea in dejected silence.

'This isn't like Seth,' she said finally. 'I know it's silly, but I'm worried about him. He may have had an accident or been set upon by ruffians . . .' her voice trailed off and her eyes shone with tears.

'I don't think it's foolish to wonder where he is,' Gabby comforted her. 'I must confess I'm a bit concerned myself.'

'If you would like, Mademoiselle Charlotte, I will make some inquiries for you. I have quite a few acquaintances in town. Perhaps one of them will have seen or heard something,' Savard offered.

Charl looked into his round, earnest face. 'Thank you, monsieur, I would be most grateful.'

He reached across the table and patted her hand.

'Don't worry, mademoiselle. We'll find out where he's been,' he assured her as he rose to leave. 'Thank you for the breakfast, Gabrielle. If I find out anything about Monsieur Porterfield, I will stop on my way home.'

When Savard was gone, Charl turned to Gabrielle.

'I can't stay here all day waiting for Seth to come home, Gabby. I'll go mad. I've got to go out looking for him.'

'But, chérie, where will you look?'

'I don't know. I'll start at the Ursuline Convent. If he was hurt, he might have been taken to the hospital there.'

'Then ask Waukee to accompany you. He will be glad to do it, and Seth would not be pleased to hear you have been wandering the streets alone, no matter what the reason. And perhaps by the time you return, he will be here,' she added with a conviction she did not feel.

Charl nodded and rose, heading purposefully towards the stable.

They were gone for the best part of the day, stopping first at the hospital that was run by the Ursuline nuns and then at a multitude of inns and taverns that seemed the only places that might offer a man a bed for the night. There was no sign of Seth anywhere in Quebec, and by dusk when they returned to the La Soeur house, Charl was exhausted and distraught. How could he have vanished so completely, she wondered. And where would they look for him next?

Gabrielle met them at the door when they returned, her usually serene face marked with worry.

'Before you go upstairs, I want to warn you . . .' she began.

'Is Seth back?' Charl demanded. 'Is he hurt?'

Before Gabrielle could put her answers into words, Charl was running down the hall towards the stairs in a frenzy of excitement and concern.

'Oh no!' Gabrielle breathed as she bolted after her.

'What's the matter, woman?' Waukee demanded, catching her arm and pulling her roughly to a halt.

'I knew this would happen,' Gabrielle babbled, her eyes round with terror. 'I tried to warn him!'

At that moment Charl's harsh cry sounded through the house, and both the Indian and the Frenchwoman rushed for the stairs, their conversation forgotten.

They found Charl leaning faintly against the door, her hands pressed to her lips and her face pale. The room itself was a

shambles. The table and one of the chairs had been upset, and
the contents of the campaign chest were scattered across the
floor. The bed had been torn apart, and the mattress was upended
against one wall.

Charl moved dazedly across the room, pausing to retrieve the
silver tankard with the Porterfield crest from where it lay on the
hearth. Seth was so proud of this tankard; he would not be
pleased to see it misused, she thought dully. Then, closing her
trembling fingers around the smooth silver surface, Charl turned
to face Gabrielle.

'Who did this?' she wanted to know.

'I tried to tell you when you came in. This afternoon a detachment of redcoats came to search the room.' She did not go on to
say that they had wanted to search the rest of the house as well,
but she had refused to let them. She had drawn herself up to her
full height and told them, as Seth had coached her so many times,
that Mr Porterfield was a boarder and had no access to the rest
of the house. After a cursory look into other rooms and in the
stable the soldiers had left.

'Did they take anything?' Charl asked. 'With the room in such
turmoil it is hard to tell.'

'They took some letters from the campaign chest, but nothing
else that I could see.'

Charl nodded. 'They must have been William's letters,' she
reasoned aloud.

'Yes, I think so,' Gabrielle agreed.

Shaking her head at the destruction around her, Charl sank to
the edge of a chair.

'What is happening? Where is Seth? Why are British troops
being sent to search our rooms?' Tears of fear and confusion had
begun to slip down her cheeks. 'I don't understand. I don't
understand.'

Gabrielle went to where she sat and put her arms comfortingly
around Charl, stroking the girl's tousled hair.

'Hush, chérie, hush. You must not become so upset in your
condition. Come to my room and lie down. You are tired
and overwrought. Things will seem brighter once you've had a
rest.'

Still compulsively clutching the silver tankard, Charl allowed
herself to be led downstairs and put to bed.

When Gabrielle emerged from her room, she found Waukee

sitting at the head of the stairs, his dark brows drawn together in concern.

'Is Charl going to be all right?' he asked.

'She's fine for the moment,' Gabrielle answered distractedly. Then she turned to Waukee with a frown.

'I intend to put that room to rights before Charl sees it again. Come upstairs with me. There are some things we need to discuss.'

Once the door to the room under the eaves was closed tightly, Gabrielle turned to face the Indian.

'Do you know what Seth is doing in Quebec?' she demanded.

'Not specifically, but I know he has been working for the Americans for a long time.'

There was a long pause before the woman spoke again, the words coming on a sigh.

'Yes, I thought so. I am beginning to fear that he has been found out and arrested.'

Waukee agreed gravely. 'I have wondered about that myself.'

'And if that is true, what are we to do?' Gabrielle finally asked.

Waukee shook his head. 'I don't know, but we must not tell Charl what we suspect. For the first time I agree with what Seth was so determined to do. He never told her his real reason for being in Quebec because he wanted to protect her. And I'm beginning to think that perhaps he was right. As long as she knows nothing about his activities, there is a good chance she will be safe.'

'You're right, of course,' Gabrielle agreed as she bent to pick up some of the clothes at her feet. 'But heaven help Seth if he has been arrested for treason because he is as guilty as Cain and there is no one in the world who can save him from the gallows.'

They gathered in the kitchen for a late supper of Marie's thick bean soup and chunks of hearty dark bread, but no one was very hungry. The room was strangely quiet for a mealtime, and the only noise came from the children who were studying aloud at the opposite end of the long table. Charl's rest seemed not to have helped her at all, and she looked even more pale and haggard than she had been before. All three adults seemed to draw protectively closer to the girl as if they could somehow shield her from misfortune, their concern evident on their faces.

As they finished the meal, a loud knock rang through the quiet kitchen. Charl was on her feet instantly, flying across the wide-planked floor to fling open the back door. The firelight that filtered into the snowy night illuminated the squat figure of Emile Savard.

'Good evening, Mademoiselle Charlotte,' he greeted her as he stepped inside, stamping his feet and shaking his furry coat to dislodge the snow. Charl closed the door behind him, shutting off the icy wind that had followed him indoors, and turned to face the Frenchman, her heart in her eyes. One quick glance at her disappointed face told him how it was with her, and he reflected that the news he brought would do little to cheer her.

'Emile!' Gabrielle smiled as she rose from the table. 'I did not expect to see you tonight. Let me fix a cup of tea to warm you.'

'Thank you,' he said, seating himself at the trestle table and taking the proffered cup. 'I had not planned to stop, but I have news of Monsieur Porterfield although I fear it is not good.'

'Oh tell us, please,' Charl said softly.

'I had several stops to make at La Place Royale, and in each shop I inquired if they had seen Seth recently. He has lived in Lowertown long enough so that most of the shopkeepers know him, and I thought –'

'Yes, go on,' Charl encouraged.

'At the last one, Monsieur Bourêt, up near the church, said he had seen Seth yesterday. He noticed him because two British soldiers stopped him in the square and they stood talking for some time. He said that at one point it looked as if they were arguing about something, and then Seth nodded and went with them.'

Gabrielle and the Indian exchanged worried glances.

'Did he say where they went?' Waukee asked intently.

Savard shook his head.

'Towards Uppertown, but they could have been headed any-where.'

'What does it mean?' Charl asked, her voice tight.

'I don't know, Charl, but don't worry,' the Indian reassured her. 'I'll make some inquiries in the morning and see what I can find out.'

He looked sympathetically at the girl, noting the strain in her pale face.

'Why don't you go to bed? You look exhausted. There's nothing more we can do tonight.'

Charl resisted the suggestion although she knew it was born of his concern for her.

'I don't want to go to bed,' she began, the tears rising in her eyes in spite of her best efforts to hold them back. 'I want to do something. I feel so helpless. I want to know where Seth is. I want to be sure he's safe.'

'I know. That's what we all want. Charl, you've got to get hold of yourself,' Waukee urged, taking her icy hands in his warm ones.

'Gabrielle, bring Charl a glass of brandy. And you, young lady, are going to drink every drop of it and go straight to bed.'

His tone was protective and gentle, but it was stern as well; it seemed pointless to argue when he had her welfare at heart.

'Very well,' she finally agreed.

'And you are not to worry any more. Is that clear?' he persisted.

Charl nodded as she took the glass of spirits.

'I'll try,' she promised.

Alone in her room, she found that the liquor had helped her. It had smoothed out the harsh contours of reality and eased the tense knot of anxiety that she had carried inside her all day. Sighing, she blew out the candle and climbed into bed, pulling the covers up to her chin. With wide eyes she watched the shadows cast by the moonlight on the ceiling. In the stillness her mind was very clear.

Finally, she had some idea of what had happened to Seth. Regardless of how serious his arrest might be, it was a relief to know. It had been torture waiting for the door to open and constantly listening for his voice in the hall. Even knowing that he was in prison was better than imagining him lying somewhere, hurt and helpless. Somehow he had run foul of the provost marshal here in Quebec, that much was obvious. But what had he done?

She stirred uncomfortably and rolled over, noticing the dull sheen of the silver tankard in its proper place on the mantel once more.

What could Seth have done that the provost marshal would have him arrested? she asked herself again. Why would the British incarcerate someone who was working to further their cause? Surely they were aware of Seth's activities here in Quebec, whatever they were. But if they knew what he was doing why had their rooms been searched? What had the soldiers been looking for? William's twelve-year-old letters were obviously not what they were seeking.

At least now that she knew what had happened to Seth, she could begin to act. With her thinking slightly fogged with brandy, the enormity of the task she was undertaking did not occur to her. Instead, her mind began to order the steps that would be necessary to effect his release.

First she would need to discover the charges against Seth. But how? She knew so little about the military system of justice. She searched her mind for anyone who might be able to answer her questions. The single possibility was obvious: Felix St James.

She drew the covers more closely around her.

Felix St James would be able to help her if only he would agree. She knew that Seth had warned her about the major's treachery, and she was aware that St James hated Seth, but she had no alternative. Since the major had been willing to help her once before, surely she could appeal to him again.

Caught in the intensity of her planning, Charl's mind moved smoothly over the things she would say to St James, calmly ignoring the possibility of failure. She smiled to herself with satisfaction, knowing that finally there was something she could do to help Seth.

Nestling into the pillow, she rested one cheek on her hand. Tomorrow she would go to see Felix St James and set her plan in motion. She sighed softly as the deep quiet night closed around her, and at last she slept.

❉

The name that Jenkins brought him first thing Wednesday morning surprised him, and Felix St James was not a man easily taken unaware. It was that much more of a shock to hear the name enunciated in Jenkins' crisp tones because he had spent a good deal of time in the past several days thinking about this same Charlotte Beckwith and how he might use her to extract the information he wanted from Seth Porterfield. In spite of intensive questioning, the prisoner had remained stubbornly silent. Now time was running out, and St James would have to find the plans for the spring offensive soon or face Prevost's certain displeasure. He had ruled out any direct threats to Miss Beckwith as too unsubtle to break Porterfield's spirit. Still, St James knew there were other ways to play on a man's weakness for a woman. He intended to see Porterfield devastated and

ready to answer any questions he cared to pose before this thing
was over.

The major smiled to himself. What an incredible stroke of luck
it was to have Charlotte Beckwith come forward like this. And
if she came to him seeking favours, she would be even more
easily manipulated. If he was clever, he might well find a way to
gain the advantage over Porterfield and fulfil his carnal plans for
the lovely Charlotte as well. At the very least this would be an
interesting interview.

'Send her in, Jenkins,' he nodded.

As usual, he was struck by her physical beauty: by the lush
body revealed by the fashionable gown, by the dewy skin and
the golden masses of her hair.

'Won't you be seated, Miss Beckwith. I am surprised to see
you so soon after the other evening. It was a delightful party,
was it not?'

He could see she was flustered by the casual turn of the
conversation, so intent was she on her own mission to his office
this morning, but she responded quickly.

'Yes, it was a wonderful evening. I certainly enjoyed myself.'

'And might I say, Miss Beckwith, you were one of the loveliest
women in attendance.'

She flushed at his rich words of praise.

'Well, thank you, major,' she managed to stammer. 'I am very
flattered that you think so.'

'Indeed I do,' he went on. 'Any man would have been proud
to be your escort. I was most pleased that you consented to dance
with me.'

Like many beautiful women, Charl had difficulty accepting
such flowery compliments; even though she was suspicious of
his motives in giving them, she was taken aback by his words.
She had intended to greet him formally and come directly to
the point of her visit, but his effusive flattery had disconcerted
her.

Charl broke in sternly, 'You must save your praise for those
more deserving.'

'Does that mean, Miss Beckwith, that you doubt the sincerity
in my words?' He sent her a wounded look from beneath his
slashing brows. 'I assure you –'

'It is only that I have a pressing reason for seeking you out this
morning,' Charl interrupted him.

'Indeed? I had hoped it was my company you sought.'

She was very aware of those glowing, red-brown eyes upon her and the simmering intimacy in their depths.

'I came to see you about Seth Porterfield, major,' she said crisply, wondering for the first time about the wisdom of this visit.

'How extraordinary that you should come to discuss that blackguard with me!' His voice was cold and stilted. 'I assure you, we have nothing to say to each other if he is to be the subject.'

Unconsciously, Charl moved forward in her chair, and her grip tightened on the reticule in her lap.

'Several days ago Mr Porterfield disappeared without explanation,' she persisted, undaunted by his words. 'I have reason to believe that he has run foul of the provost marshal and has been arrested.'

'My dear Miss Beckwith, Porterfield has always been something of a rapscallion. If he has been detained by the provost marshal, it is probably with just cause,' he interjected.

Charl shook her head slowly in a mute denial of his words. 'Please, Major St James, I need to know what has happened to Seth and what charges have been lodged against him.'

The sincerity in her voice struck Felix, and he wondered for the first time if Charl really was ignorant of Porterfield's reasons for being in Quebec. He had assumed that she was aware of his activities, even if she was not a party to them. After all, she admitted to being an American citizen and she had worn the diamond and opal necklace to the ball. Was it possible she did not know the man was a spy? The thought crossed his mind that this visit was some sort of trick, but he quickly discarded the idea. Her concern was too genuine.

It would be like Porterfield to keep his activities from her: a foolishly noble gesture to protect the woman he loved. In the light of this discovery, it was small wonder that he had been willing to admit his meeting with Madame Verreault rather than implicate his Charlotte. And in her innocence, would Miss Beckwith be able to tell him more, or less, about Porterfield's moves? he wondered.

'And can you tell me why I should lift one finger to help Seth Porterfield? He and his breed have brought me nothing but trouble. Not more than three or four nights ago he made threats upon my life. And now you want me to look into this matter for his sake. Why should I trouble myself to do it?' St James blustered angrily.

Charl had expected this argument from him and had prepared herself for the only tactic to refute it.

'Why, major,' she said simply, 'I had hoped you might do it for me.'

A vision of her lying willingly beside him ran through his head, and he was pleased that she would be so accommodating as to put herself in his debt. It would be so easy to control her once she owed him this favour. He frowned at her darkly, knowing that he must not agree too readily to her demands.

'I may not be able to find out anything about Porterfield,' he told her, the lies flowing easily from his tongue. 'It will depend on the nature of the complaint, where he is being held –'

'I would be forever indebted to you if you made the inquiries or at least sent me to someone who could help me find out about Seth,' she prompted him.

In her need to be assured of Porterfield's safety her tempestuous nature had been subdued, but now there were flickers of anger in her eyes as she waited for his agreement. It would be to his advantage, he realized, to keep her in a submissive situation where she would be compelled to answer all his questions. And if she did not know about Porterfield's spying, then she would not understand the need to guard her words. Perhaps he would learn much of value.

Even as he watched her, he began to order the events that would ultimately lead to the girl's seduction and Porterfield's demise.

'Very well,' St James finally agreed with false reluctance. 'I will look into the matter today. And since I know you are anxious for whatever news I can discover, I am sure you will not mind coming to my rooms tonight.'

Charl's mouth formed a wordless 'O', and St James knew she had not thought further than this interview or considered the price she would pay for his help. She might have been Porterfield's mistress, but she was still an innocent in so many ways.

Hastily, he scribbled the address on a piece of paper and gave it to her, knowing that she would dare not refuse him.

'Do you know where rue des Jardins is?' he asked.

'I'm – I'm sure I can find it,' she answered dazedly.

'Well, until tonight then. And I hope I will have some good news for you by then,' he said, escorting her to the door.

'Thank you,' she mumbled.

'Bonjour, my dear Miss Beckwith,' he smiled. His lips were hot against her icy fingers as he bid her good-bye.

'Bonjour, major,' she responded automatically.

Twenty-Three

Charl prepared with particular care for her evening meeting with Felix St James, selecting the deep green dress Seth had given her and arranging her hair in a neat chignon at the nape of her neck. Carefully, she adjusted the opal earrings in her ears and stepped back to assess her appearance in the shaving mirror she had propped up on the campaign chest. The effect was as she had hoped: attractive, yet demure and businesslike.

The fact that she was to meet Felix St James in his rooms troubled her greatly. She had planned to trade on his obvious attraction for her because there was no other reason for him to do as she asked, but she had hoped to trade in some less tangible coin than the one he must have in mind. She had been a fool not to realize the obvious ramifications of her request, and she wondered if the major would have demanded a similar price if he had helped her to return to Youngstown. Charl was only beginning to realize how naive and unprepared she was to deal with a man like Major Felix St James, and the thought of what she was planning to do plainly frightened her. Still, she had no choice. Once she had begun this task, there was nothing she could do but see it to its completion. She would try to get through the meeting without compromising herself; but in the end if anything she did ultimately led to Seth's release, she would not have any regrets. When Seth was free and safe, she would just have to find a way to make him understand that whatever sacrifice she made was well worth it.

She propped a carefully worded note on the coverlet for Gabrielle, explaining where she was going. She had kept to her room much of the day to avoid both the Frenchwoman and the Indian, knowing full well that either one of them could easily dissuade her from keeping her appointment. With a final glance in the mirror, Charl swung the turquoise pelisse around her shoulders and tiptoed down the stairs. Everyone was in the parlour, and as she slipped noiselessly down the hall and out of the back door, she was thankful that she had been able to get away undetected.

Charl found the number on rue des Jardins with little difficulty and stood before the whitewashed house for several minutes before she went to the door. The heavy brass knocker was icy cold, and the hollow sound it made seemed to reverberate thunderously up and down the narrow street. She felt exposed and conspicuous standing on the doorstep, as if everyone knew her errand, so that she was almost glad when an impeccably groomed servant ushered her inside. She gave him her name, and he escorted her wordlessly up an elegantly curved staircase. Taking her pelisse from her in the upper foyer, he indicated a pair of glass doors that opened to reveal a small drawing room. She had the impression of elegance and beauty around her, and then St James was advancing on her. His auburn eyes burned into hers as he took her hands in his, and Charl felt a rush of primal fear deep within her. In his office he had never seemed so sinister, so elemental, and it took all her courage not to turn and run.

Holding her hands tightly, as if he could read her thoughts, St James led her towards the tapestried sofa in front of the fire and smiled encouragingly at her.

'I am glad you came tonight,' he said warmly. 'It is not often that such a lovely lady graces these humble rooms.'

Charl allowed herself a brief look around although nothing she saw made much of an impression on her.

'These seem like lovely apartments,' she observed automatically.

'That is most kind of you, Charlotte. It is said I have something of an eye for beauty although, of necessity, I cannot indulge myself as freely as some.'

It startled her to hear her Christian name so freely on his lips, but she supposed that in these circumstances that was to be expected. Still it sent a new wave of panic churning through her, and she rose and moved around the corner of the sofa for protection.

'Let's not spend our time in idle conversation, major,' she began bravely. 'The only reason I came here tonight was to see what you found out about Seth Porterfield.'

His dark eyes narrowed slightly for a moment, and then he reached over the back of the sofa to catch her wrist.

'Come sit down, Charlotte. This needn't be an unfriendly conversation.'

She eyed him warily, then carefully resumed her seat, ready for flight if necessary.

'Before I tell you what I discovered, there are some questions you must answer,' he told her.

'Questions? But why?' she demanded.

'A few questions in exchange for your information. Is that too much to ask?' St James cajoled.

'Why?' she persisted, her face full of suspicion.

'Because information is not free even to a major in the British army,' he snapped.

She regarded him mistrustfully, measuring his reply. St James frowned. For all her pretence of ignorance in this matter, she was still a very canny woman. If he was to get what he wanted from her, he would have to be very shrewd.

'What is it you want to know?' she asked reluctantly.

'What is the nature of Seth Porterfield's business here in Quebec?'

'I don't know.' She answered truthfully for she was not really sure.

'Come now, Charlotte. You've lived with the man for six months. Surely you know what he does,' St James said with exasperation.

'No, really I don't know. He was gone a good deal: sometimes for a month or more, sometimes for only a few days.'

'And do you know where he went?'

Twice, she thought. Once he had gone to New York with the American refugees and once to Queenston. But if Seth was working as a spy for the British, why wouldn't the major know that?

'No,' she lied, uncertain why she did so. 'Seth was secretive, and for the most part he and I were not getting along. I didn't care where he went as long as he left me alone.'

'But that has changed of late, I take it,' St James observed dryly.

'Yes,' she answered with downcast eyes.

'Did you ever meet any of his associates? Did he ever bring anyone to the house where you've been staying?'

Charl shook her head.

'Never.'

'You're not being very helpful,' the major said irritably.

'I'm sorry. I can't tell you things I don't know.'

His glowing eyes moved over her, but he could find no hint of a lie in either her answers or her demeanour. He frowned again. Perhaps Porterfield had been successful in keeping his activities from her. Still he persisted.

'Had you met Muzette Verreault before I introduced her the other night at the ball?'

'No. I had heard gossip about her, though. They say she is a very wicked woman.'

St James smiled to himself, remembering that wickedness firsthand.

'Did Porterfield know her?'

'No, I don't think so.' The brief conversation they had in the carriage on the way to the ball flashed through her mind. Be careful, admit nothing, a voice inside warned her.

'Madame Verreault met with a fatal accident only hours after the ball,' St James told her, awaiting some response. It came as anyone's would on hearing of the death of a stranger. Charl was sombre but unaffected.

Silence fell between them as St James tried to reconcile the fact that the girl could be of no help to him in trapping Porterfield. As difficult as it was to believe, she seemed to know nothing that could incriminate the man. Still, there had to be something: something he had let slip, something she had unwittingly observed.

'I've answered your questions, major,' Charl broke in with her most businesslike voice. 'Now I'd like to know what you've learned about Seth.'

She would not be held off any longer, and besides he had accomplished one of his purposes. He had introduced Muzette Verreault's name into the conversation, and perhaps that would be sufficient to connect her with Porterfield in Charlotte's mind. He reached for a cigar from the humidor on the table at his elbow and made a show of lighting it with a splint from the fire.

'The charges against Porterfield are rather serious,' St James began. 'He was arrested in a case of theft.'

'Theft!?' Charl echoed. 'Seth wouldn't steal anything!'

'I'm afraid you don't know your light-of-love nearly as well as you think you do.'

'What do you mean?'

'I mean that he has already confessed to part of his crime.'

What could Seth have stolen? Charl asked herself as she stared uncomprehending at Felix St James. Unconsciously, her fingers went to her throat, and the major smiled at her obvious train of thought. In one way this proved that she did not know about the papers, but it also confirmed Porterfield's connection with the necklace. If only he knew where Porterfield had gone when he left Muzette's, he might be closer to locating the plans. Was it possible the girl knew? Glancing over at her stricken face, he knew he would have to wait to ask her. Clearly, she would answer no more questions now.

Charl's thoughts were spinning: moving too fast, drawing what she prayed were all the wrong conclusions. Surely Seth had not stolen the necklace and earrings she had worn to the ball. He had refused to tell her where he got the gems, but they were obviously beyond his means. And why had the major asked about Madame Verreault? Had the jewels been hers? Of course, if they were, she would have recognized them instantly. Was that why Seth had begun to act so strangely and why he had been so anxious to leave the ball? But why would he have insisted that she wear the jewels if he had known that they belonged to one of the guests? It made no sense to her, and yet she could not imagine what else Seth might have stolen. Then an even more terrible thought came into her head. St James had told her that Madame Verreault was dead. Was it possible that they suspected Seth of her murder?

'Oh no!' Charl gasped.

'My dear, you must not take it so hard. You are not the first woman to be taken in by a scoundrel,' St James said, solicitously patting her hand.

'But there must be some mistake,' she persisted.

'There are few mistakes when a confession is made.'

'But why would Seth confess? And why would he be arrested by the provost marshal?'

St James' eyebrows levered upward.

'In times of war many civil cases are handled by the military police,' he explained smoothly. 'In a way it is very fortunate that this is being handled by the provost marshal,' he went on, 'because I believe I could help your Seth if I were given the proper incentive.'

In the past minutes Charl's initial fears had been forgotten as he led her to believe the answers to his questions would be payment enough for his help. Now things had changed again.

'What do you mean?' she stammered.

'What I mean is quite plain to both of us, I think, don't you, Charlotte? I will be willing to see what I can do to help Seth Porterfield in exchange for your favours.'

Once the words were spoken, the transfer of words into deeds seemed imminent, and Charl was filled with panic.

'What's the matter? I am an attractive man. Is it possible that you profess to love Porterfield and yet you are not prepared to make this sacrifice on his behalf?'

Her chin rose sharply, and her green eyes snapped with anger.

'Of course, Seth's safety is of paramount importance to me, but I am no whore, sir,' she told him.

'I won't play word games with you, Charlotte. Will you come to my bed in the hope that I can help him, or not?'

There was a long, agonizing silence that stretched between them, filled with the girl's indecision. Her pride was not easily conquered, but in the depths of her luminous eyes he saw the anger turn to resignation, and he knew he'd won.

'I haven't any choice, have I?' she answered softly.

He drew her unresisting body across the sofa into his arms and tipped her face up to his. In the instant before his mouth closed over hers, Charl searched the depths of those mahogany eyes for even one flicker of warmth or human compassion. She found none.

His lips were hot, like a flame against her flesh, but they ignited no excitement in her. The kiss became more demanding as he bent her back, fitting her to the length of his body. She felt the strength of his desire and shrank from him with growing panic. How could she go through with this? she asked herself wildly. Could she open herself to this terrifying stranger when she had only known the touch of the man she loved? And how could she sell her body for his freedom when she knew that Seth would never understand the reason for her sacrifice? Finally, St James drew away and glared down into her frightened face, his hooded eyes smouldering.

'Surely you showed more fire than that with Porterfield,' he observed sarcastically. 'Perhaps a glass of sherry will warm your response.'

And loosen your tongue, he added silently as he went to the sideboard to prepare two glasses. He returned to the sofa with the glasses, making certain to offer his guest the one in his right hand.

'Major, please!' she began.

'Drink, Charlotte,' he snapped. 'It will give you courage.'

With trembling hands she put the glass to her lips and took a long swallow. It left a dry, stale taste in her mouth.

'Major, please,' she began again. 'There must be some other way . . .'

Slowly St James shook his head.

'There is no other way, Charlotte. I've wanted you from the moment I saw you, and I'm only sorry that I've had to employ these tactics to get you to agree to share my bed.'

Tears rose in her eyes. 'I can't,' she said simply. 'I can't.'

'Then finish your sherry and be gone, but I'll not be responsible for what happens to Porterfield if you leave,' he threatened.

With a single move she swallowed the sherry and came to her feet. Heart hammering, she faced him in a frenzy of fear and confusion. If she left, she would forfeit her only chance to help Seth, and yet she could not stay. Beyond the guilt and shame she would feel if she surrendered to him was that basic, primitive fear she had felt from the first time she had seen him. There was something about this man that terrified her beyond all reason; as much as she wished to agree to his demands for Seth's sake, she could not let him touch her.

He came to stand before her and caught her hands.

'Well, are you going to leave or remain?' he asked, his voice strangely resonant in her ears.

As she stood staring up into his inscrutable face, a ripple of dizziness moved over her, followed by a second stronger wave. As if weakened by the sensation, Charl found she could only stare into those molten eyes, robbed of the power to think or move.

'I – I must go,' she whispered desperately, but his hands on hers held her immobile, and she had no strength to pull away.

A curious light-headedness assailed her as if she were floating free in space. Then she realized that St James was helping her to the sofa.

'The sherry –' she mumbled. 'I'll be all right in a moment.' But the room continued to spin and waver before her eyes. She could see St James' hawklike face just above her and could read a strange satisfaction in the depths of his eyes.

'I'm sure you'll be fine. But before you go, just a few more questions, please,' he was saying.

'Oh no, please. No more questions.'

'I just want you to tell me where Seth went when you left the ball,' he coaxed.

'The ball,' she repeated, knowing with the last thread of rational thought that there were things about that night that no one, especially St James, must know.

From where she lay on the sofa the ceiling looked miles away, partially hidden in a wavering blue mist. There was a faint rushing in her ears, like the sound of wind through the trees or a brook running over stones. She had the sensation that she was floating, and yet when St James spoke, it was an effort to turn her head to look at him.

'After the ball,' he reminded her.

Quite beyond her ability to control it, that evening began to spin out before her, like a playlet in which she was both audience and actress.

'I don't know where he went, but Seth came back very late,' she said softly, seeing their moonlit room as it had looked three nights ago. As if in a dream she watched Seth move to the window and open a secret place under the sill. There were papers in his hands that Seth securely tucked away before he came to her. His lips were hot and frenzied when he kissed her, and then his arms, strong and sinewy, were beneath her shoulders and her knees as he carried her to his bed. She responded with abandon, as she always did, pressing kisses along his throat and whispering his name over and over.

'Seth, Seth, Seth.'

❉

A growing brightness assailed her, and she stirred slowly in response, moving sluggishly between the soft sheets, rolling over to escape the insistent sunlight in her face. Her mind was still mired in sleep while her body was beginning to respond to the demands of a new day. She came to consciousness with difficulty, penetrating layer after layer of drowsy fog. Her eyes fluttered open reluctantly, seeking some familiar object, and when she found nothing she recognized, she came awake with a start. In a rush of panic she sat bolt upright, ignoring the sickening dizziness that came with her sudden movement. Incredulously, her gaze swept the blue and gold bedchamber, her sense of disorientation growing. She could not recall how she had come to awaken in a strange room this morning.

Bridling her growing apprehension with difficulty, she looked carefully around her in the hope that she would remember where she was. There was no doubt that this was a man's room for the shaving stand by the wall and the triangular cocked hat box on the bureau were unmistakable masculine touches to the décor. But to what man did this room belong? She put her fingers to her temples trying to banish the residual cloudiness from her brain. What had happened last night that she should wake up here?

The memories came creeping back one by one. She had gone to Major St James' apartments on the promise that he would have word of Seth. Instead, he had asked harsh, unsettling questions and had given her little information of Seth's whereabouts. Then St James had told her quite boldly that he would use his influence to help Seth only if she made certain concessions to him. With unmistakable clarity she remembered the guilt and confusion she had felt at the untenable decision he had forced on her. As she tried to reconcile her feelings with her inevitable decision, they had shared a glass of sherry. She pressed her fingers to her head and began to massage the aching tension, hoping to clarify the jumbled residue of impressions. She vaguely recalled St James bending over her and carrying her somewhere. But interwoven with those memories were the wisps of a passionate dream where Seth had made love to her endlessly, long into the night.

She blinked away the unsatisfactory recollections and looked around once more. This must be Felix St James' bedroom, she realized uncomfortably. In some ways it reminded her of him. The furnishings were elegant, expensive, understated. It was devoid of clutter, and yet it was neither spartan nor austere.

Her musings were interrupted by a brief, sharp knock at the door, and Charl was suddenly aware that beneath the sheets she was naked. In panic she looked around for her clothes and noted them piled neatly on a chair across the room.

'Attendez, s'il vous plaît!' she cried out and made her way

towards them on strangely unsteady legs. What was the matter with her this morning? she wondered as she tucked the sheet more tightly around her.

The door burst open, and St James reached her in three long strides, sweeping her into his arms for a fiery kiss. When it was over, he looked down ardently into her startled face and smiled.

'I'm glad to see you up, my dear. After the excesses of last night I was glad to let you sleep, but today is a new day and there are things to be done.'

'Last night?' she stammered, nonplussed by the familiarity with which he was caressing her hip through the thin sheet that was all she wore.

'Ah, yes, my darling Charlotte. It is a night I shall remember always. Who would have thought that beneath that cool exterior of yours was hidden such a tempestuous nature.'

'Last night,' she repeated, unable to believe what he was saying.

'You are an extremely passionate woman, my dear,' he went on. 'Any man would consider himself fortunate to . . .'

'But, major, I don't remember anything that happened last night!' she broke in, a bright flush glowing along her cheekbones.

'You don't? Would you like me to refresh your memory?' he asked with a purely lecherous smile. 'Surely you recall something, madam. You were very vocal about my . . .'

Her blush deepened, and she drew the sheet a bit higher to cover her nakedness.

'I assure you, major,' she said with a stubborn tilt to her chin, 'my mind is totally blank. But it seems I behaved in a most uncharacteristic and lascivious manner. And I am sorry.'

He reached up to stroke one flushed cheek with his knuckles.

'You must never apologize for that, Charlotte. But then perhaps you can't remember anything because, I fear, we did imbibe a bit too freely before we adjourned to the bedroom.'

She retreated a step, flustered and confused.

'I recall having one glass of sherry.'

'One glass?' he said incredulously. 'We finished two bottles and started on a third.'

'Oh!' she breathed, trying without success to recall any scrap of memory about what had gone on the night before.

'Charlotte, are you all right?' he inquired gently. 'Have you suffered ill effects from the wine?'

'I do feel rather peculiar this morning,' she admitted.

'Perhaps you should return to bed,' he suggested solicitously.

'No, I'll be fine once I've washed and dressed.'

'Good,' he nodded. 'Since you fulfilled your portion of our bargain so admirably, I have arranged a brief visit with Porterfield this afternoon.'

'You have!' Hope leaped in her eyes. 'Oh, thank you!'

Then Charl caught her breath suddenly as another thought struck her.

'Oh, major! You won't tell Seth what happened last night, will you?'

Some bright spark flashed briefly in his eyes, and then his face was a mask of outraged dignity.

'A gentleman never reveals his trysts,' he replied stiffly.

In spite of her compromising position, a smile quirked one corner of her mouth at his outraged tone.

'I am sure you are the soul of discretion,' she assured him. 'Now, if you will excuse me, I would like to dress.'

Her words were clearly a dismissal, but he stood over her for several moments, as if he was considering taking advantage of her déshabille, before he turned to go.

'Very well,' he said abruptly. 'I have some papers to look over.'

'Thank you,' she replied and waited until the bedroom door was securely shut before she moved.

She found a washstand behind a stencilled screen and absently went about her ablutions as she tried to make some sense out of what had happened. But try as she might, she could not remember a thing after they drank the first glass of sherry.

If only she could remember what she had done. Was it possible that she had deliberately overindulged in the sherry in the hope that it would help her endure St James' attentions? This morning she felt much as she had the time she and one of the boys from town had liberally sampled his father's moonshine, the summer she was thirteen. She had experienced this same weakness in her arms and legs, and her head had ached abominably just as it did now. Smiling ruefully, she remembered how her father had laughed, saying that the way she felt was worse punishment than any he could mete out for the youthful escapade.

She sighed deeply. Was it the wine that fogged her memory this morning, or had she deliberately put the things that had happened with St James out of her mind? A blush mounted to her cheeks as she recalled the pleasure he had voiced at her behaviour. She knew that her relationship with Seth had always been deeply satisfying, and she was appalled to think that she could share that intimacy with any other man. She loved Seth, had loved him ages before she had been willing to admit her feelings for him, and she knew her response to him was based on that love. If that were so, then how could she have given herself so freely to St James, a man she both disliked and feared? And the more pressing question was: how could she face Seth after the passionate night she had spent in his enemy's arms?

She had been so preoccupied with trying to remember how she had come to awaken in St James' bed that she had not even considered what must have happened there. A dizzy swell of nausea rose in her, and she sank to a chair, her knees gone weak. She was revolted by the idea of St James' kisses, of his hands on her body, and of what must have inevitably followed. She moaned softly, sick with shame.

Dear God! How could she possibly face Seth now? She was soiled, unclean, tainted after her night with St James in a way that Seth would surely recognize. And even if he did not see the change in her, everything that passed between them from now on would be based on something less than the truth. Silently, she began to weep, dissolving in her despair, pressing trembling hands to her cheeks and letting the tears slip freely through her fingers.

She had betrayed Seth last night. He would never have wanted her to go to St James for help; he had warned her against that himself. That she would go against his wishes was, in itself, a kind of betrayal. The fact that she had sold her favours for his sake would be even more abhorrent to him. In those shady, half-dreamed memories of last night Charl knew she had tried to leave St James. Driven by the certainty of Seth's disapproval and her own fear of the British officer, she had decided to go. If that were true, then why was she still here? If only she could remember.

'Charlotte? Are you almost ready?' St James' voice came from outside the bedroom door, cutting across her troubled thoughts.

'Just a few more minutes,' she called out unsteadily.

With deliberate steps she went back to the washstand and poured fresh water into the basin. She brushed away the tears with one hand and began to wash again, scrubbing vigorously in an effort to remove the taint of Felix St James from her body if not from her soul.

Twenty-Four

✳✳✳

Ten paces in one direction and six in the other; with an endless repetition of those measurements Seth Porterfield marked both the perimeter and the extent of his confinement. He had never liked being shut in, but this subterranean cell was like his own tomb. At the far end, over the raised platform that served as a bed, was a small barred window built at ground level. When they had thrown him into this cell at the end of the long, damp corridor, even that window had been dark, covered over with drifted snow. Once he had discovered it, though, he had set out to clear away the drift, digging at it until his hands were numb; and after several hours' work, he had been able to see the sky.

Today that sky was a shade of blue that was like a reward after so many days of winter grey. Climbing on to the platform and gripping the icy metal bars, he pulled himself up to see outside. It looked as he had known it would, with the sunlight bright and golden on the snow and the trees frosted with white. From his window he could see the crest of the opposite bank across the river gorge and a spidery fringe of silver-brown branches against the sky. Satisfied for the moment, he lowered himself and resumed his pacing.

He'd only been locked up for four days and already it seemed like an eternity. Nor could he find much hope for an early release. Neither Mitchell nor Joubert could help him without exposing themselves, and he feared that St James would continue to hold him until he found proof enough to hang him. Briefly, he wondered about the man's blind hatred for him, as he knew William had done, but there were no answers. If anyone but St James were investigating the disappearance of the documents, Seth might have been able to wait it out, but the major was too determined. At least as long as the papers lay undetected in the secret compartment under the window sill in his room, he retained a modicum of safety. Still, it was frustrating to know where the documents were and be unable to send them on to the Americans when he knew the need for such information was great. But to tell anyone, even Waukee, would be to risk discovery. As long as he was the only one who knew about the secret compartment and its incriminating contents, there could be no charge of treason proved against him.

The major came every day in the late afternoon to continue questioning him about the papers and his other activities in Quebec, but Seth had divulged nothing more. He had begun to take perverse pleasure in these verbal duels although he knew there was danger in every word he uttered. Since that first day he had been the one to remain coolly silent while he watched St James chafe under the demands made by his superiors to find the documents. Seth had begun to nurture a faint hope that if no evidence of his guilt came to light, they might force St James to let him go in spite of the major's personal desire to see him executed.

Restlessly, Porterfield moved to a spot below the window and stared up at the sky.

There had been no more threats against Charl since the day in the major's office, and Seth could not help but wonder why the man had not pressed his obvious advantage. Even now Seth did not know what he would do if St James returned to that tactic. He loved Charl and felt responsible for the dangers he had subjected her to by bringing her to Quebec. Somehow he must keep her from harm.

In the past days his thoughts had turned to Charlotte with increasing frequency, sometimes with concern for her safety but more often in hazy daydreams that banished the realities of hunger and cold.

He wanted to take Charl west, he decided as he shivered alone in his cell. He would like to show her the wonders of this wild free land: the grandeur of the snow-crowned mountains, the silent reverence of a pine forest, the vastness of the plains where the sky was the most dominant force in all nature. In his mind he planned the home he would build her one day when their travels were over, a solid enduring place where they could live out the rest of their lives. In his mind he furnished it with rich carpets and glittering chandeliers, with desks, beds, chairs, and tables of mahogany and rosewood, with the finest linens, china, and silver. Finally, he populated that home with children, golden haired like their mother, but with their father's blue eyes. He even dreamed of taking her to Seahaven, of standing beside her on the hill behind the house at sunset, watching the blue-grey shadows that veiled the sea at dusk. He could clearly remember how the breakers rose from the dark to catch the fading light, then rushed like molten copper to foam in lacy whorls upon the beach. All this he wanted to share with Charl in the future, but he took comfort in the fact that regardless of what happened, they'd had these past weeks together. Now if only he could keep Charl safe, Waukee could take her back to Youngstown in the spring. In the spring, perhaps that would be after he was dead.

The heavy wooden cell door grated on its hinges and swung wide to admit the gaunt British officer. His adversary was early, Seth observed. Was this a good sign or bad?

St James' gaze swept the squalid cell with disgust, coming to rest on the blond man who lounged negligently on the stone platform, the blanket thrown carelessly over his shoulders. Slowly Felix advanced on his prisoner. His eyes were flashing with triumph, and the colour in his hawkish face was high. There was to be nothing devious or subtle in the manoeuvres today, Seth decided.

From inside his tunic Felix withdrew a long, narrow leather folder and extended it towards the other man. Recognition was instantaneous, but Seth managed to hide his shock and accepted the folder with apparent indifference.

'What's this?' he inquired mildly.

The sparks in the major's eyes were like a bonfire now.

'You know damn well what it is!'

With outward calm Seth removed the leather slipcase and glanced over the papers.

'Are these the documents you claim I got from Madame Verreault?' His expression was bland in spite of the sickening certainty that churned through him.

'They *are* the documents you exchanged for the necklace, taken from the place where you hid them yourself.'

'Really?' Seth replied. 'I've never seen those before in my life.'

St James' smile was malignant.

'I find that hard to believe,' he said, withdrawing several more papers from inside his coat, 'because these were found in the same place.'

Seth unfolded the top ones, knowing full well that the British had somehow discovered the cache he had guarded so carefully. He stared at the white parchment sheets in his hand and knew he was trapped. Slowly, he traced the raised seal in the lower corner with his thumb. They were his citizenship papers.

He looked up at St James ready to acknowledge his defeat.

The major's eyes were hooded.

'Don't you want to know how we found the documents?' he asked.

'I suppose so,' came the weary reply.

'It was Charlotte Beckwith who told me where to look.'

There was a flicker of disbelief in the blond man's eyes, but the meaning of St James' words was inescapable. Still he stared at the other man for a long time without comprehension.

It was as if someone had blown a jagged, gaping hole in the middle of his chest when the realization came to him, and it was a full minute before Seth remembered how to breathe.

He did not want to listen to the rest of the major's words, but the sense in them penetrated his brain in spite of the turmoil that engulfed him.

'She's been keeping an eye on you all along, ever since she came to me about passage to the United States. I can't imagine what you did to make her hate you so, but her information has been invaluable. It was a stroke of luck that she knew where you hid your papers.'

His pain was suddenly transformed to rage by St James' jeering words, and Seth surged to his feet driven by a desire to kill that banished all reason and all caution. The officer had anticipated the response and with a quick move brought his sword up. He stopped Seth short, balancing the blade against his chest, ready for the thrust into his heart.

'I warn you, Porterfield. It doesn't matter to me if I kill you now or watch you hang tomorrow, but I'll warrant those extra hours mean something to you. Sit down and live until dawn or stand where you are and prepare to die.'

As suddenly as the rage had come upon him, it dissipated, leaving Seth strangely spent. Wordlessly he returned to the stone ledge under the window, dazed and dispirited.

'Besides, the lady wants to see you,' St James added.

'What?' Seth raised his head.

'Charlotte wants to see you,' he repeated.

'Why?'

St James shrugged. 'To gloat perhaps?' he suggested.

'I don't want to see her.'

'I'm not sure you have a choice in the matter. She wants to see you, and I've never been known to disappoint a lady.'

There seemed to be no point in arguing. Seth nodded mutely and continued to stare blankly ahead. Watching his prisoner's despondent behaviour, St James felt a surge of satisfaction. The man was clearly demoralized. By tonight, after his interview with Charlotte, he would be ready to tell everything. A smile flickered at the corners of the major's mouth. He had been right about Porterfield's weaknesses; an ordinarily insular man, he had not been able to accept the apparent betrayal by the one person he had come to love. This emotional maelstrom would leave him submissive and pliable as neither threats nor torture would. Tonight Porterfield would answer any question he was asked.

Then at dawn, with that fierce, arrogant pride in ruins, they would hold the execution. After a brief hearing earlier this morning, the judge had unhesitatingly signed Porterfield's death sentence. The major smiled again. It was so easy to speed justice in such a clear case of treason. By daybreak on the first morning of 1813, Felix St James was convinced he would have both the answers he needed and his revenge on the last of Alistair Porterfield's progeny.

Breaking from his thoughts, the officer moved towards the door.

'Well, prepare yourself, man. Miss Beckwith will be down in a few minutes. I'll have the jailer bring you some water. You won't want to greet Miss Beckwith as filthy as you are.'

'That's very kind of you, sir,' Seth snorted.

St James could not miss the sarcasm in the reply, but he chose to ignore it. Porterfield's rebellion would not last long.

When the bucket of lukewarm water arrived, Seth washed absently as he tried to steel himself for Charl's visit. One part of his mind refused to accept the obvious reasons for her betrayal; nor was he able to believe that she could feign what had passed between them. Yet St James' explanations had begun to erode that certainty. Everything had changed between him and Charl the same day he had seen her leaving the Château St Louis. Was it possible that she and St James had struck a bargain? After all, how could she have resisted the opportunity for the revenge she had so often threatened with the offer of passage as her reward? The logic was inescapable. Then, too, there was the damning fact that St James had recovered the stolen documents.

Seth closed his eyes, resting his palms on the rim of the bucket, and hung his head as the pain swept over him. What a fool he'd been to trust Charl, to open himself to her, to love her. For the first time in his adult life he'd let down his guard, and now he would pay dearly for his stupidity.

It had always been his misfortune to underestimate Charl. She had been stronger, more determined, more cunning than he expected her to be. He frowned, remembering how well she had withstood the rigours of the trip up the St Lawrence, that night in Youngstown when she had tried to take him captive, the way she had tried to escape by setting out across the lake in the mackinaw while he was asleep. Why hadn't he learned his lesson? Charlotte Beckwith was a danger to him, not only because he continued to underestimate her, but because she could cloud his judgement with one smile. And so beguiled he had lost his objectivity, then his heart, and finally his freedom as he had blithely walked into the trap she had laid for him.

'Bitch!' he whispered in a voice raw with pain. 'Lying bitch!'

For a few terrible minutes Seth hunched over the water bucket, too shaken by the events of the past half hour to think. Then slowly he straightened and forced his brain to work.

How had Charl come to know about the secret compartment under the window? Could she have inadvertently discovered it as he had years ago? Had she been searching the room for something else and stumbled on it? Or was she feigning sleep the other night when he returned with the papers? He remembered her voice in the dark, sounding drowsy and soft. Had she been awake and watching him all that time?

He combed his damp hair with his fingers and rebuttoned his shirt.

What possible reason could Charl have for wanting to see him? he wondered. And when she looked at him, would he see hatred in her eyes since there was no longer a reason to conceal it?

In his anguish he wanted to shake her and ask her why she had done this to him, but he would not. It would be easier to slide his fingers around that soft, slender throat and choke the life from her body than to admit how much her betrayal had hurt him. He wished he could hate her with an intensity that would blot out all his other emotions, but that would come later, if he lived. Now he had only the remnants of his pride to shield him from whatever gloating, venomous things Charl was coming to say. He had reached no point of resolve when he heard the rasp of the key in the lock to his cell and the door swung wide to admit his betrayer.

Charl paused at the doorstep for a moment while her eyes probed the dimness, and then, with an inarticulate cry, she ran across the tiny room and threw herself against him. Her arms reached up to tighten around his neck, fitting her full length of breast and thigh against him. It was the last reaction he had expected from her, and all his hastily made preparations crumbled with her nearness. Involuntarily, his arms closed around her, and with a low groan he buried his face in her hair. Still, some semblance of rationality remained in him.

An hour ago he would have kissed her: bent her head back and lost himself in the sweetness of her response, forgetting the cold, the hunger, and the loneliness. An hour ago he could have done that, but he could not do that now.

His body stiffened in her embrace, and she was instantly aware of his withdrawal. With difficulty he put her from him and looked down into her tear-glazed eyes. Her expression of compassion and anxiety was not what he had expected, either, he reflected irrelevantly. Then his hands tightened on her arms so she could not escape him.

'You betrayed me,' he said softly.

Shock flickered across her features at his quiet accusation, and then the tears spilled over. In spite of what he knew she'd done, she still seemed incredibly vulnerable when she cried.

'He promised he wouldn't tell you,' she began in a quaking voice. 'Oh Seth, you must try to understand. He said if I slept with him, he would try to help you. Can't you see that I had no choice?'

As Seth stood staring into the face of this woman he thought he knew, the world seemed to spin a full revolution around him. So she had taken St James as a lover, he thought grimly. Well, what did it matter now? And why did she feel compelled to explain it with such an obvious lie? Was there no end to her treachery?

Then there was an icy rage growing inside him that froze his blood in his veins and crystallized his thoughts. For a moment his fingers tightened on her arms and then, abruptly, he shoved her away.

'You know that's not what I mean. Who you bed with and why is no longer my concern,' he whispered frigidly, 'but you told St James where he could find the papers, and that's going to cost me my life.'

She stared into the face of the man she loved, gone suddenly cold with fury, reading the contempt in his eyes.

'What are you talking about?' she demanded through her tears. 'What papers?'

'The papers hidden in the window sill,' he prompted angrily. 'Really, Charl, there's no point in lying to me.'

'Under the window sill? I didn't tell him about . . .'

There was a dawning terror in the depths of her eyes, and her face was pale.

'Dear God!' she breathed. 'Seth, what were the papers in the window sill?'

Her heart thudded painfully, each beat sending dread coursing, like a numbing poison, through her veins.

Last night she had dreamed, or thought she dreamed, of Seth standing by the window, taking papers from inside his shirt and hiding them under the sill just as he had done the night after the ball. She sought some explanation in his face, but it was like a mask, excluding her from all his thoughts. Something was terribly wrong, she knew, something she did not understand.

'Seth, please, you must explain what has happened. I know you are angry with me about St James, but you must not shut me out! Please, Seth! What were those papers?'

Watching Charl, he could hardly believe that she was not sincere in her confusion and concern. But then she must be a consummate actress to have lain in his arms night after night professing to love him when she had always meant to betray him. With numbing detachment he wondered what St James hoped to gain by sending Charl to him. Did the major think he was fool enough to believe this innocent pretence she had adopted and tell her his secrets? Could St James think he was so slow-witted that he would try to send word to Mitchell or Joubert through her? He had been taken in by her once, but he would never be duped again. He turned away, not willing to look into that lovely face, innocent even in her betrayal.

'I don't know what you hope to gain by pretending. You know

very well what those papers were,' he accused, his voice frosty
with anger. 'Surely St James told you what to look for. They're
evidence enough to get me hanged.'

'Hanged!' she echoed.

'At dawn tomorrow, judging from what St James said.'

'Dear God!' she gasped.

He tried to concentrate on the small square of blue sky visible
through the barred window and the silvery white cloud that
skimmed along just above the tree branches.

He wanted Charl to go now while he maintained some semblance of composure. He could not listen to her lies and denials
any longer.

'Seth?' The hand she laid gently on his arm seemed to sear
into his flesh, and he spun around to face her.

'Damn you, Charl,' he began in a voice so low and resonant
that it seemed to penetrate her very being. 'Don't pretend you
aren't aware of my reasons for being in Quebec. St James must
have told you. I know you probably went to him that first time
to see about leaving Quebec, but then you saw your chance to
get even with me for the things I'd done and you decided to stay.
Perhaps I even deserve what you've done for the way I treated
you. But tell me, Charl, how do you reconcile the betrayal of
your country with your revenge on me?'

'My country?' she stammered.

'You're a fool, Charlotte, if you think you can convince me
that you didn't know who I was spying for all along.'

'Oh!' she said softly, exhaling the word as she stared at him,
shaking her head in silent negation. Only a fraction of what he
had said made any sense to her, but she was beginning to
comprehend what he thought she'd done. Suddenly she was
angry, even angrier than Seth was, because she realized the
terrible injustice of his accusations. She had freely given everything to this man: her virtue, her heart, her future. And until
this moment she had joyfully carried his child in her womb. Yet,
in spite of everything that had passed between them, he had
chosen to believe the lies that St James told him and not her.

She turned on him like a tigress, her green eyes narrowed and
flashing with unbridled rage. She was unable to refute charges
she did not understand, but she could try to convince him of her
loyalty with the only proof that should matter between them.

'Damn you!' she shouted at him, heedless of the tears streaming down her cheeks. 'How can you believe St James when you know that I love you?'

'Oh God!' he groaned, as he tried to turn away from her, but she would not let him. Her fingers tightened on the hard muscles in his arms, and she held fast, determined to have her say.

'Seth, Seth,' she said softly, 'surely you know that I love you.'

'I don't want to hear this,' he ground out.

'But you will hear it! The question is whether you'll listen to me or what that blackguard St James has told you. If you are going to the gallows, at least it will be with the truth ringing in your ears.'

'Damn you, woman! Why are you doing this?'

'To make you realize that in spite of what you think I've done, I love you. And if I love you, I could not knowingly do anything to harm you.'

He moved under her hands, trying to break her grip on him, but she would not let him go.

'I'm not sure when I fell in love with you. Maybe it was that first day at the tavern or on the escarpment when you kissed me. I only know that when you came to me that night after the party, I felt something for you that I have never felt for any other man!'

'Stop it!'

'I loved you even when you dragged me off to Quebec. And when you lied to me. And when you left me without explanations. I worried about you. I cared about you and I missed you.'

Her words were punctuated by sobs now, and he had gone quiet and still, no longer trying to stop her.

'Oh God! And then there came a time when I knew you loved me, too.'

'Charl, please.' His voice was tortured.

'I loved you then, and I love you now. I'll love you till the day I die and beyond that! Oh Seth, please. You can't believe I would deliberately betray you. To betray you would be to betray myself.'

She stood before him trembling and panting with the raw emotion of her words, but he was impassive, his eyes opaque and expressionless to hide the turmoil within him.

The thoughts went around and around inside his head until he was sure he would be torn apart by the conflict he felt. Why was Charl doing this? What could she possibly hope to gain by these empty declarations of love when he knew full well what she had done? Did she feel remorse now that she knew he had been sentenced to die? Was she seeking some sort of absolution from him for her part in this affair?

And why did he still want her? It took every ounce of his strength not to take her in his arms and use passion to block out everything that had happened. It did not even matter that the source of his solace was the source of his pain as well. He must be mad to want that. Just as he must be losing his mind to consider that there might be truth in anything Charl said when the evidence against her was so strong. With the last shred of sanity he tore his eyes from that sweet, treacherous face that would haunt him for all eternity.

'Guard!' he bellowed.

'No, Seth!'

'Guard!'

'Seth, please!'

The key scraped in the lock, and the door creaked open. 'Miss Beckwith wishes to leave now,' he said, forcibly prying her fingers from his arms and pushing her towards the guard at the door.

'Seth, no, please. You must listen.'

He looked down at her, his eyes icy and impersonal, and it seemed impossible that those deep blue eyes could ever have sparkled with warmth and love.

'It's too late for that, Charlotte,' he told her. 'Your actions belie any words you might devise to explain. I die at dawn tomorrow. I hope you're satisfied.'

He spun around to face the window, staring at the square of blue with desperate concentration. Behind him he heard the scuffling of feet as Charl was taken from the cell and the muffled slam of the door. For some minutes Charl's voice drifted back to him through the corridors, and his name grew less and less distinct the farther she was led away.

He made his way to the stone platform and sank down in the fetid straw, his knees suddenly too weak to support his body. He hung his head and felt the smothering weight of black depression settle over him. It came like bats out of a twilight sky, awakening some deep, primitive panic he could not control. He began to tremble.

Dear God, he thought, Charlotte had betrayed him. The full realization of what that meant devastated him. Earlier, he had been shocked and angry, but now there was an overwhelming wave of pure grief that engulfed him. He had loved the girl with a depth of feeling he had never thought possible. He had opened himself to her and had planned for their future together. Now suddenly all the sweet, golden memories and the bright hopes for the future that had sustained him were crumbling in ruins around him.

He recoiled from his own thoughts, but there was no ease for his hurt. For a time he kept his mind carefully blank, but he could not sustain the effort of will it took, and his thoughts moved tentatively to probe his shattered emotions. Slowly realization and acceptance came, but neither acted as an anodyne for his pain.

Charl had betrayed him to St James. She had not revealed his secrets accidentally or in anger. Instead she had deliberately set out to trap him. In her thirst for revenge she had made him want her, trust her, love her before the débâcle. How coldly calculating she had been to beguile him and seduce him, demanding from him the one thing he had never been able to give. How long had she been dividing herself between the nights in his arms, making him love her, and the days with his enemy, planning his downfall? Charl had plundered his vulnerability and laid waste to his emotions. In that was the germ of the hatred that would sustain him forever.

He lay back on the straw, shading his eyes from the light with one crooked arm. The acceptance of what had happened was agony, but he had no choice. Charl had betrayed him. He could not believe otherwise. His mind hurt, his body hurt, and his spirit was crushed under the weight of his depression. He closed his eyes and drew a long painful breath, wishing for oblivion. And in the depths of his despair sleep claimed him, closing like a comforting blanket around him, mercifully offering a retreat from his tortured thoughts.

✼

Charl allowed herself to be led back down the long stone corridor towards the entry hall where St James waited for her, only because she was blinded by tears and too distraught by the disastrous interview to offer much resistance. So much of what Seth had said and so many of the accusations he had made meant nothing to her so that she did not fully comprehend what had happened. Still, she understood that St James had lied to Seth, and for some reason Seth had believed those lies. With difficulty she brought her ravaged emotions under control and tried to make some sense out of the things Seth had told her.

He was angry, not just because she had sold her favours to St James, but because of something else he thought she'd done. He kept saying she had betrayed him, kept talking about the papers she had seen him hide under the window sill in their room. What were those papers? And what made them incriminating enough to condemn him? It seemed incomprehensible, but Seth seemed to think that she somehow sought his death in revenge for what he had done to her and that she was responsible for delivering him into St James' hands. Oh God! How could he think that of her? How could he believe that she would do anything to harm him?

Her tears were subsiding, and it was very clear that St James had used her for his own nefarious purposes. As she and the jailer rounded the corner into the entry hall, she was filled with questions and gnawing, half-formed suspicions that terrified her.

Heedless of the others in the hall, she went to where St James sat waiting, advancing on him like a duellist with a dangerous glitter in her eyes.

'I want to know exactly what's happening here and what you've told Seth,' she demanded.

'Whatever do you mean, my dear?' he asked calmly.

'You know very well what I mean, and I want the answers now!' she said fiercely.

The others in the hallway stirred uncomfortably in the face of her anger, but St James was unperturbed.

'May I take it that your interview with Porterfield went badly?' he inquired.

'You know it did! You told him lies, and I intend to find out what they were.'

It was obvious that the guards and other officers waiting to see prisoners found her ferocity unsettling, but St James enjoyed the fire. She was like a lioness with her mate: aggressive, protective, primal. He watched her covetously, noting her thick, tawny hair; the fury in her green eyes; the regal pride and sinuous grace in her bearing. She was magnificent in her anger, passionate, wilful, wildly exciting. Last night she was all those things; and he knew he must possess her, drinking deep from the wellspring of passion that existed in this woman. But at the moment she must be controlled, especially in the presence of the guards and other officers.

In a single, fluid motion he rose, bringing one hand up to slap her while he held her wrist with the other so she could not escape. Undaunted she glowered at him, her eyes teary with pain and rage. The second blow was harder than the first, causing her hissing intake of breath as she tried to squirm away.

'We will discuss these matters in private, my dear, when you are yourself again,' he told her. 'I know how taxing a visit to a condemned man can be. Now get your cloak. I am ready to leave.'

Glaring at him murderously and trembling with hatred and agitation, she did as he had ordered her to do, unaware of the men in the room who would have readily championed her cause if only she had turned to them. Instead, she followed him outside to the carriage. In hostile silence they drove down the hill and into town, coming to a stop in front of his apartments on rue des Jardins.

'Why are we stopping here?' Charl demanded.

'I thought you wanted to know what I told Porterfield,' he answered. 'Come inside and have some tea to calm you. Perhaps then we can discuss this rationally.'

Charl eyed him mistrustfully, wary of an invitation to the place that had been her downfall only the night before. Belatedly she was finding out that everything Seth had told her about St James was true. Still, the enticement of finding out what lies he had told Seth was too strong.

'Very well,' she relented, 'but I can't stay more than a few minutes.'

St James nodded in agreement and helped her out of the carriage.

Some time later, when tea had been served by St James' servant, Charl set aside her porcelain cup and turned to the major.

'All right. Now that we've observed the pleasantries, why don't you tell me about Seth?'

'Please, Charlotte,' he said with a slow smile. 'Must you be so abrupt? I had hoped we might enjoy a friendly cup of tea before we went on to discuss this unpleasant business.'

'Don't delude yourself, major, that there ever has been or ever will be anything remotely resembling friendship between us,' Charl told him tartly.

'Oh, but you were more than friendly last night,' he reminded her.

'I – I do not wish to talk about last night,' she stammered. 'I do not remember any of what happened, and I was clearly not myself.'

'That is to be sure,' St James observed sarcastically.

Her blush darkened.

'I came here to find out about Seth and the trouble he is in. If you don't intend to tell me what I want to know, I will leave this minute!' As if to reinforce the words, she gathered up her reticule and came to her feet.

'Oh, sit down, Charlotte, for what I have to tell you may come as a shock.'

Charl sat down abruptly.

'What do you mean?'

'Porterfield is to be hanged at dawn tomorrow,' he said without preamble.

She nodded mutely as helpless tears rose in her eyes.

'I know. Seth told me, but I don't understand the charges against him.'

'He is being hanged for treason.'

'For treason?' she echoed. 'But how can you hang him for treason when he's been working for you British all along?'

'Is that what he told you?' St James interrupted incredulously.

'Yes. When he left Youngstown . . .' she began, but St James cut her short as he burst into gales of laughter that fairly rocked the walls. Charl stared at him in total confusion. What kind of monster was this man to find humour in so dire a situation?

And how was it that Seth had been convicted of treason? At the jail he had said that the documents she had seen him hide under the window sill had been the proof of his guilt. What were those papers, she wanted to know. And was it really possible that last night she had told St James where to find them? If only she could remember.

St James' laughter was dying away, and he slowly shook his head from side to side.

'No wonder he was such a successful spy,' he observed, 'if he was such an accomplished liar.'

'What do you mean?' she asked through stiff lips.

'What I mean, my very dear Charlotte, is that while he told you he was working for us, he was really acting as a courier for the Americans, carrying all kinds of information to a man named Mitchell who is employed by the United States War Department.'

'But Seth is English!' she exclaimed.

'Oh, he may have been born in England, but he has been a citizen of the United States for nine years,' he told her.

Her eyes were wide with shock as she tried to digest what Felix St James was saying. Could it be that she and Seth had been on the same side in this war all along? Was that what he meant when he accused her of betraying her country? But how had she done that?

'But why didn't he tell me? Why did he lead me to believe he was a British spy instead?'

The major shrugged. 'Maybe he was trying to protect you,' he suggested. 'Or perhaps he did not trust you.'

The realization that Seth had not trusted her with his secrets was a painful one; but then she had never given him any reason to believe she would not betray him. From the night war was declared she had loudly pronounced her hatred for him, making threats of revenge and scheming to escape. She had reviled him for his allegiance with her enemies and fought him bitterly because of it. No wonder it had been so easy for St James to convince him of her treachery. Still, what had passed between them lately should have allayed any doubts of her loyalty.

'Are you certain he was spying for the Americans?' Charl persisted. 'Did you find proof of his activities?'

'We found proof enough to convince a judge.'

St James' slender fingers reached between two buttons on his tunic and withdrew a narrow leather folder.

Although Charl could not be certain, it seemed strangely familiar, and her mouth was suddenly dry with apprehension.

'We found these papers in his rooms,' the major went on. 'They were stolen from General Prevost's office at the Château St Louis about a week ago.'

'What are they?'

'It does not matter what they are. Suffice it to say that it would have been very inconvenient if Porterfield had succeeded in passing them to his associates across the border.'

'Did Seth steal them?'

'No. Muzette Verreault stole them. She gave them to him in

exchange for the necklace you wore to the ball at the Governor's mansion.'

'And was Madame Verreault hanged for treason, also?' Charl's voice was unsteady.

'No.' St James paused as if anticipating the effect his words would have on the girl. 'Muzette Verreault killed herself rather than face the gallows.'

Charl was very pale, but there was one last question she needed to ask even though the answer would surely confirm her worst fears. She moistened her lips and tried to draw a calming breath, but anxiety bound her tightly.

'How – how did you come to find those papers in our room? Your men did not find them the first time they searched.'

St James' mouth curved slightly in a mocking smile.

'You told me where they were yourself, just last night,' he said softly.

'Last night!' she whispered, hating the realities that were hidden from her by a blur of dreams. 'Why can't I remember anything about last night?'

He watched her tortured face, knowing that there must be impressions, half-memories of what had happened. In time she would come to realize what he had done.

'There was a drug in your sherry,' he told her blandly. 'It was very mild, but it served its purpose.'

'You!' she breathed, the depth of her loathing evident in that one syllable.

What a fool she had been to trust him. Felix St James was everything Seth had said he was: evil, treacherous, cunning. How cruelly he had played on her naïvety. How viciously he had manipulated both of them to gain his ends. Then an even more infuriating thought came to her.

'You never intended to help Seth when you demanded that I sleep with you!' she exclaimed, her voice deep with accusation.

St James laughed.

'My poor, dear innocent,' he said. 'It is little wonder that Porterfield deluded you with his lies. You believe everything anyone tells you. Undoubtedly, you even believed that I would let you leave here when we finished our tea.'

The implied threat in his words was appallingly clear, but Charl had no intention of spending another moment with this despicable man. Springing to her feet, she raced towards the door. From the shadowed hallway St James' burly servant appeared to check her flight, and the major came up from behind to close the trap.

'Of course, you will accept my invitation for a short stay, won't you, Charlotte?' he drawled.

'Never!' she spat as she whirled to face him.

'Then I fear it might be necessary to detain you,' he threatened as he swept her up in his arms and turned towards the bed-chambers. But Charl was a strong woman and not easily subdued, as St James readily discovered. She twisted furiously in his grasp and struck viciously with her free hand, raking her nails across his cheek.

St James swore vehemently and abruptly dropped his squirming burden. There was no time to get her feet under her, and Charl landed heavily on the floor at his feet.

'Blasted bitch!' the major muttered as he stood over the stunned girl, pressing one hand to his wounded cheek. His manservant came to stand beside him.

'I'm going to put something on this. Take her to the guest bedroom and lock her in. I will deal with her later,' he said.

Charl struggled ineffectively against the other man's hold, but she was still dazed and breathless from her fall and it took too much effort to fight him. He dumped her roughly on the bed in the smaller bedchamber, then left, turning the key in the lock.

For a very long time Charl lay as he had left her, too devastated to even move.

Twenty-Five
✵✵✵

Seth came awake all at once, rising from the depths of sleep like a cork coming to the surface from far beneath the water. He opened his eyes into pitch darkness, and there was a moment of total confusion when he had no idea of where he was. Then his memory returned.

With a start he sat upright, gripped by a gnawing panic. What time was it, he wondered wildly. And how far gone was the last night of his life? He sprang to his feet and peered anxiously out of the barred window, seeking anything that might indicate the hour. Far to the west he could see the last pearly grey hint of twilight and he drew a deep breath. It was just after sunset, and he had until dawn to live. How many hours, how many minutes, how many heartbeats until they led him to the gallows? And how should he spend those last hours, he asked himself. He could review his life, wallow in his hurt, repent his sins. Perhaps it would have been better if he had slept until dawn, he thought bitterly.

As many times as he had risked his life, there had never been time to reflect on his own mortality. Now death loomed ahead, vast, unfathomable and inescapable; there was no way he could find to grapple with the idea of his own end.

Instead, he contemplated his life, wondering if there was anything he would change if he could. Unexpectedly, his grandfather's face floated before him, an unwelcome reminder of his past. He was sorry that there had never been an opportunity to make peace with the old man. He momentarily considered asking for pen and paper to write to him but quickly gave up the idea. What would he say?

Dear Grandfather,
    I'm to be hanged for treason in the morning, coming to the bad end you always predicted for me.

Your obedient grandson,
Seth Porterfield

His laugh was bitter for the regret was very real.

For a long time he stared up at the cold stars that appeared like pinpricks in the muffling fabric of the winter sky, and he took strange comfort in the infinity of the cosmos. For this brief time he had been part of a greater whole. He had lived too long with nature not to believe in some unity of purpose, some divinity of plan. In that belief he found peace.

In the cold and the stillness he became very aware: of the air that moved rhythmically in and out of his body, of sounds previously insignificant and far away, of the clarity of his own thoughts. Memories returned with startling reality, and he found he did not regret the life he'd led. It had been filled with travel and adventure, with friendship and loyalty. He had played a small part in the exploration of the new lands to the west and had helped to open them to settlers. He had served his adopted country well, and he was not afraid to die to protect those who served it. It had been a good life, he decided, if too short by half.

He was surprised by this unexpected philosophical side to his nature, and he smiled to himself, thinking of the other things he had discovered in these past weeks. He had been stunned by the capacity for love and tenderness Charl had brought out in him, by the burgeoning desire to settle down and live in peace. He never thought he would feel the same loyalty to America as he had felt towards England, but suddenly there was no question of where his allegiance lay. It was a pity, he reflected, that he would never have the opportunity to explore these discoveries to the fullest. But for now he was alive. He shivered in the icy wind that whistled through the bars and ached with the pain of Charl's betrayal, realizing that those things were part of living. And for the brief time left to him Seth Porterfield planned to revel in his humanity.

He was aware that he was to have a visitor long before the single pair of footsteps was discernible in the corridor outside his cell. Although he could not say how he knew who it would be, when the door swung wide, he was ready.

St James swept into the room, his long dark cape swirling around his boot tops, casting strange, shifting shadows on the wall by the light of the lantern he carried. He paused to stare at the tall, blond man who was sitting on the stone platform much as he had left him. The man's features were smooth and impassive, his eyes cast down and hidden by their thicket of lashes. His shoulders were slightly hunched as if in weariness or acceptance. By all outward appearances, Charlotte Beckwith's visit had had the desired effect. Porterfield seemed subdued and resigned.

'Good evening, Porterfield,' St James greeted him.

'Good evening, major,' Seth returned softly, without glancing up.

St James took several steps closer, peering at Seth's face, raising the lantern so he could see the other man's expression more clearly. It was one of defeat.

The major smiled.

'I need a number of answers from you, Porterfield,' he began, an intent look on his gaunt face. 'I want to know who it is you report to here in Quebec and where I can find him.'

Seth mumbled an unintelligible reply that the major could not hear, and the officer stepped even closer.

In that split second when St James bent over him, Seth brought his fist up from where it had lain innocently in his lap, with every ounce of his strength behind it. He caught the officer squarely on the chin, and St James fell as if he had been poleaxed. The lantern flew up against the wall with a loud clatter of breaking glass and went out.

After the lantern's brightness Seth was nearly blind in the dark, and he fumbled forward, searching the man's prone body for the key to the cell. He felt in the pockets and folds of St James' clothing, then on the rough stone floor around him, searching for the familiar shape of the key. Apprehensively, Seth crossed the cell and peered through the grille in the door. The key was still in the lock on the outside. St James had not even bothered to relock it after he had entered.

Seth grimaced. The other man had been so confident that he would find Seth cowering in his cell after Charl's visit that he had not taken the most basic precautions. He had come alone, carrying the key himself, and had not been wary enough to lock the door behind him. Seth felt a momentary rise of contempt for the other man until he realized that only a few hours ago he had been in exactly the state St James had expected.

With a new concentration he stared through the grille down the long corridor. He tried to remember every detail he had observed the day they had brought him to this place, hoping to recall anything that might help him in his escape. The hallway was dead straight, and the doors along its length were nearly flush with the walls. There were shadowed sections where the light from the torches did not penetrate, but really no place to hide. Once he stepped outside his cell, he would be plainly visible.

The stone building that housed the prison was three storeys tall, with two levels above this one. The only entrance, as far as Seth knew, was from the anteroom at the end of this corridor. Each level was patrolled by two guards who took turns making the rounds on the hour and half hour. At the main door there were two armed sentries, stationed one on each side, to monitor visitors or act as a second line of defence.

Seth frowned. He could not say he liked the odds against him: eight guards armed with muskets or black jacks. Still he would have the element of surprise on his side. It was well worth the gamble. He would be alive until the trap door to the gallows gave way beneath his feet. If there was any chance he could avoid that fate, he would have to take it. The warm, familiar surge of excitement was in his veins, and already a plan was simmering in his mind.

After relieving St James of his cape and sword, he dragged the man to the stone platform and covered him with a blanket to disguise his identity. Then he tightened the sword belt at his waist, slung the cape around his shoulders, and bent to retrieve the cocked hat, settling it on his head at a rakish angle. He was several inches taller than St James and considerably broader, but he did not plan to impersonate the major. Instead, the borrowed clothes would allow him to approach the guards before they realized what was about to happen.

But first he would even the odds against him. For several minutes he had been aware of the plodding footfalls from the far end of the corridor. As they drew closer, he flew to the door.

'Guard,' he said in a muffled tone. 'This blasted lantern's gone out. Can you bring me a light?'

The guard could see the outline of the cocked hat silhouetted in the narrow grille and lit a twig of straw from one of the torches, carrying it behind his cupped hand towards the man he assumed to be the British major. Seth inched the cell door open as if to accept the flame, but his sword rose in the space. It was an easy thing to push the thrust home. There was an instant of confusion in the jailer's eyes, and then he crumpled obligingly into Seth's outstretched arms. Porterfield dragged the unconscious man into the cell and laid him beside St James. The officer groaned softly, and Seth knew there was no time to waste in making good his escape. He went to the door, took one quick look through the bars, and began the long, slow walk down the seemingly endless hallway. He made no attempt to hide the ringing of his footsteps on the uneven cobbles, and the other guard glanced up from the battered cards in his hand as Seth rounded the corner into the entry.

'Evening, sir,' he said pleasantly; then a look of recognition crossed his pudgy face.

'You're not . . .' he began, but Seth's sword struck swiftly, leaving the man slumped over the table.

At the sound of voices the sentry inside the door turned. He was momentarily shocked by the spectacle of a British officer attacking one of the guards. Then he recognized the blond man, too. His brief hesitation had given Seth time to spring at him. As the man raised his musket to waist height, Seth was upon him. The shot he got off before Seth knocked him to the floor passed harmlessly through the folds of the heavy cape, but the sound reverberated in the stone chamber. It was only a few seconds later that there was the thundering of feet on the stairs.

Seth glanced around quickly, planning his strategy. The long corridor, where his cell had been, intersected the entry hall at the end farthest from the main door. Opposite it was a storeroom or office, its doorway hidden from above by the slope of the stairs. It was here in this recessed doorway where he would await the others, swinging around so his back was to the corridor once they had reached ground level. The odds were better now, he thought as he huddled under the stairs, but he had lost the advantage of surprise.

Then there was the pounding of footsteps directly above his head. When he was sure that all the guards had reached the foyer, he stepped out of his hiding place. He caught the nearest one in the folds of his cape and kicked him savagely in the groin as the second man approached on his right. The ground shifted unevenly beneath his feet as he stepped into the depression of a drain grating, and for a split second he lost his balance. With a curse he thrust at this second man. Catching him high in the shoulder, he turned to ward off the third. This one brought his heavily weighted sap down on Seth's forearm with a force that left it numb. Dropping the sword, he brought his other hand up to catch the guard's wrist, forestalling a second blow that had been aimed carefully at his head. As they grappled in the centre of the foyer, the door burst open and the other sentry entered. He aimed his musket at the struggling men; but as he fired, the battle shifted, so that the guard's body blocked Seth at the crucial moment. The musket ball caught him squarely in the back, bringing his full weight against Porterfield as he died and nearly dragging him down.

From the corner of his eye Seth caught a movement in the corridor behind him, and for an instant he could see the shadow of this man cast on the opposite wall by the wavering light of the torches. He tried to turn to defend himself, but there was no time. Something came crashing down on his skull, and he sagged to his knees in a dazzle of shimmering colours. He did not lose consciousness altogether, but by the time his head cleared, the remaining guards had subdued him.

He blinked hard to bring his eyes into focus and found himself looking up into St James' murderous face.

'You may or may not tell me what I want to know this night, Porterfield, but I'll be damned if there will be more than a scrap or two of you to be hanged in the morning.'

He turned to the guards.

'Take him inside and chain him,' he ordered.

The room beneath the stairs that Seth had mistaken for a storeroom had a much more sinister purpose. Chains were set into the walls, ropes hung from the rafters, and there was a collection of devices whose use Seth did not care to contemplate. With a sudden dryness in his throat he realized that this was where troublesome and uncooperative prisoners were questioned.

Two guards stripped off his shirt and dragged him towards the farthest wall, where they made him stand while his wrists were shackled high above his head. What was to happen next was patently obvious even if Seth had not seen St James take the heavily corded whip from a peg on the wall.

'Have you ever seen what a whip can do to a man, Porterfield?' St James asked silkily as he unbuttoned the scarlet tunic and laid it aside. 'It's not a pretty sight.'

Years ago, when he was a boy sailing to Quebec for the first time, Seth had seen a man flogged. He never knew what the sailor's crime had been, but at the time he could not imagine one to justify the brutality of the punishment. With appalling clarity he remembered the man's bloodstained breeches riding low on his hips; the tattered ribbons of flesh and muscle, where once a strong, brown back had been; the hoarse, pitiful cries of pain.

A tremor of terrible anticipation moved over his flesh like a cold wind across the still sea.

From behind him, Seth heard St James approach.

'Answer my questions, Porterfield, and you will spare yourself much discomfort.'

As if to underline the threat, St James ran the nub of the whip along Seth's ribs. Involuntarily, his muscles knotted and jumped at the touch, and he clenched his teeth to control the swirl of panic that rose within him.

'I will tell you nothing!' he ground out.

'Would your fellows do as much for you?' the major taunted. 'Would they endure torture in the name of loyalty?'

'Muzette Verreault gave her life. Can you expect less of me?'

'Muzette gave her life in fear, not for loyalty,' he scoffed.

Seth's broad shoulders rose in a shrug of resignation and acceptance.

'You aren't going to overlook my attempted escape. It doesn't matter if you call this beating interrogation or punishment, the outcome will be the same.'

St James' boot soles scraped across the stone floor as he moved away to speak in low tones to one of the remaining guards.

With difficulty Seth controlled his breathing and tried to fight the mind-numbing fear that threatened to overwhelm him. The stones were icy cold against his chest, but his body was clammy.

He had to get hold of himself, he knew, or he would surely disgrace himself in front of his oldest enemy. But now the philosophical complacency and resignation that had sustained him were gone. Those few, brief moments of almost freedom when escape had seemed possible had destroyed what little peace he'd found. The galling bitterness was back, and he cursed this war that had sundered his loyalties, the blackmail that had forced him to return to Quebec, and his own damnable vulnerability. He hated St James for his incomprehensible, single-minded thirst for revenge, Mitchell for his uncompromising demands, and Charl for her insidious duplicity. All the raging hurt returned when he thought of her and the cruel games she had played with his emotions.

Behind him, he heard St James' footsteps come closer, and he was aware of the whip uncoiling and slithering across the floor in preparation. He lowered his head, pressing his face hard against the uneven stones in the wall before him, and deliberately slowed his breathing. He let his conscious mind float free and mentally retreated from the talons of pain that would grip his body. Deliberately, he lost himself in a senseless void that would allow him to endure the unendurable.

The Indians had taught him well how to bear physical pain. He would be aware of what was happening to him, but it would not matter. It was the kind of pain Charl inflicted for which he had no defence.

*

From somewhere in the darkness Seth heard his name being repeated insistently. The voice was oddly familiar, but he fought the dawning consciousness, as if he sensed the pain awareness would bring. He let himself drift free in a sea of blackness, but the voice continued to assail him, forcing him to rouse. Slowly, he opened his eyes, blinking in the torchlight. Standing above him was Waukee, his face drawn with concern. Seth tried to rise to greet his friend, but the pain that accompanied the movement threatened to smother him in the billowing darkness again.

'Seth!' the Indian repeated sharply, bringing his attention back to the present, 'Seth, can you hear me?'

'Yes,' he answered slowly, trying without success to focus on where he was.

'Seth, we must leave here. Do you understand?'

'Yes,' he replied. His eyebrows puckered as he tried to make some sense out of what had happened. 'Waukee, what's the matter? Did the bear come back?' he asked hazily.

Waukee paused and stared down at his friend, comprehension dawning in the depths of his dark eyes. In the pain and confusion, Seth's memory had returned to the incident all those years ago when their roles had been reversed. Determinedly, he continued.

'Seth, you must get on your feet. I'll help you.'

Waukee's arm was sliding gently around him, and Seth tried to think what the Indian wanted him to do. But the darkness seemed to linger at the edges of his vision and fog his thinking.

'Now, I want you to get up,' Waukee said, half-ordering and half-cajoling the man who lay in tatters on the floor beside him.

Seth nodded and tried to do as he was told, but the pain that went with the movement sent pinwheels of light dancing before his eyes until the heavy black clouds rolled in, threatening to obscure everything.

White and panting with effort, Seth fell back on the fetid straw. His eyes were wide and glazed with confusion.

'Waukee?' he asked. 'Was it the bear?'

'Seth, you must get up!' There was an edge of desperation in the Indian's voice.

'I can't; you'll have to go and get help.'

'Seth, Seth! Listen to me. If you stay here, you'll die,' he insisted, knowing full well what he was asking of his friend. Seth was in pain and weakened by the brutal things that had been done to him, but Waukee knew he could not relent and leave his friend here to be hanged in the morning. He owed this man his life a dozen times over. They had grown to manhood like brothers of one blood, and he could not desert Seth now. The friendship that had begun in that creek bed fifteen long years ago made him lay one hand gently on Seth's brow and speak softly to him.

'You're right. It was the bear, and if she returns while I'm gone, you'll be helpless. You must come with me.'

The blond man seemed to consider the logic in that for a long moment, then nodded gravely.

'I'll try.'

With great care Waukee worked his arms around Seth, knowing that his lightest touch was hurting the other man.

'Now get your feet under you,' Waukee instructed. With great effort Seth rose from where he had lain on the floor. He leaned heavily on the Indian while the room stopped spinning. He was pale and sweating and his knees seemed ready to buckle under him, but his head was beginning to clear.

'Where are we going?' he asked finally.

'Just trust me,' the Indian whispered back as he moved towards the door.

As they made their way unsteadily down the long corridor, Waukee wished there was some way to revise the plan he had made for their escape. He had not expected to find Seth in this

condition when he had raised the drainage grating in the entry
hall and silenced the guard. Now their escape hinged on whether
Seth would be able to climb back down the cliffside, for Waukee
knew there was no other way out.

It had been easy for the Indian to get information about the
prison on the Citadel once he had found out that was where Seth
was being held. There were many along the docks and in the
taverns who had served behind those stout stone walls; however,
their information had been far from encouraging. The place
seemed impregnable to fewer than a dozen men. In desperation
Waukee had wandered along the riverbank, staring up at the
building on the cliff. Below and slightly to the left of the end
wall, he had spotted a shadowed opening, slightly overgrown
with brush and hung with icicles. Just before dawn Waukee had
returned to scale the rocky wall and explore it. To his delight,
what appeared to be a cave was the mouth of a drainage tunnel
that ran steadily uphill to end below a grating in the floor of the
prison itself. Jubilantly, he had returned to the La Soeur house
to make plans and preparations for Seth's rescue.

In his absence St James had come to search the house again.
Evidently, he found what he was seeking because it was a scant
two hours later when word reached Waukee that Seth had been
sentenced to hang for treason at dawn. The Indian paid his
informant well and hurried to complete his preparations for
leaving Quebec. Charl had not yet returned from wherever she
had gone, and both he and Gabrielle were uneasy about her
absence. Unfortunately, there was no time to look for her if
things were to be ready for an escape tonight. At moonset
Waukee set off, knowing that by dawn either he and Seth would
be far from Quebec or they would both be dead.

In the dark Waukee had guided the canoe through the ice floes
to the base of the cliff and secured it to a tree. Climbing noiselessly
up the steep rock face, he reached the mouth of the opening in
a matter of minutes, then followed the slope of the tunnel up
another thirty feet until he came to the place he had discovered
the day before. Through the grille he could see a solitary guard
asleep at a worn desk. There had been no way to be sure that
the grate would move once he got this far, and as he pressed up
against the bars, he prayed the fates would smile on him. The
grille moved easily, and he was able to raise it and set it aside in
spite of its weight. After that, it had been an easy thing to hoist

himself up and slit the sleeping man's throat. Finding Seth's cell without rousing the other guards had proved more difficult, but he had discovered it eventually. It was what he found inside the cell that destroyed the plans he had made. He stood for a full minute, sickened by the sight of what they had done to his friend. Yet, even as he bent over Seth's prone body, he realized that there was no choice but to go back the way he had come.

Seth seemed to understand that, too, as he stood over the dark recess in the floor of the entry hall. He wavered slightly on his feet, but he was totally cognizant.

'Can you make it?' Waukee whispered.

'I'll be all right,' he assured the Indian as he came to sit on the rim of the opening.

'Let me go first to help you down,' the Indian offered.

'No, you need to lift the grate into place,' Seth answered as he braced himself against the edge of the hole. The flexing of the muscles in his shoulders turned his back to a sheet of flame and made him light-headed again. Determinedly, he continued inching downward until he disappeared into the opening.

The drop was no more than five or six feet, but Waukee was aware of a muffled groan from below as Seth landed. Waukee followed, sliding the grille into place behind them.

The descent from the mouth of the tunnel was a slow and difficult one, and they arrived at the base of the cliff just at dawn. Seth's hands and knees were scraped raw from the rough stones, and he was swaying with weariness when Waukee loaded him into the canoe and tucked a blanket around him. With a quick glance over his shoulder, the Indian manoeuvred the craft into midstream. He had hoped to be far from Quebec by now, but with luck they might still get away. Few would think to look to a river swollen with ice floes as a means of escape, but with care and skill the waterway was still passable. There was no sound from the bow as the canoe bucked wildly in the choppy water, and Waukee smiled grimly. Seth had earned his rest.

Twenty-Six

✷✷✷

It was dawn, the dawn she had prayed would never come. She had listened to the dying wind, had watched the morning stars fade into silver. Then the first stealthy streaks of grey had crept beyond the horizon, and the birds had begun to circle in the ever-lightening sky.

Charl shivered and hugged herself closer, as if to keep from coming apart because she knew she must endure what was to be endured.

It was the dawn that Seth was to die.

She stared blindly at the walled garden below her window, lit by the first grey light of the winter day. Then, reluctantly, she turned her eyes to the crest of Cape Diamond, rising above the streets of Quebec. St James had asked her to accompany him to the execution, but she would not go. She knew all too well how it would be. There would be the hollow ringing of Seth's tread upon the stairs as they led him to the gallows. As he waited, he would stand erect and strong for his pride would allow him no other course. Even when the noose was tight around his throat, his eyes would be bright and fearless. She did not have to be there to see. It was all too vivid in her mind.

'Oh, Seth,' she moaned as she leaned her head against the cold window pane.

How had they come to this? she wondered in despair. Could it have been less than a week ago that she and Seth had danced at the Governor's ball, lain together in the dark as they pledged their love, and planned their future together? Surely those wonderful things had happened to someone else, not to the man who was to hang for treason on this cold winter morning or to the woman who had betrayed him.

Tears slid unchecked from the corners of Charl's eyes as the first flickers of sunlight caught the edges of the grey clouds, etching them with gold.

This was the dawn that ended the night that seemed to have no end, a night of rage and violence. St James had come to her in a frenzy, his eyes burning with emotions she had never seen, raving like a madman about the Porterfields and his conquest of them. He had used her as if he was a victor in some savage battle and she the spoils to be plundered and defiled. When he left her bed in the pre-dawn darkness, she had huddled beneath the covers, shattered by his hatred and brutality.

In addition to that terrible devastation was the numbing fear that St James would never let her go. In the aftermath of his lust Charl realized that she was no longer just a desirable woman whose attraction would pall in time. She had become a symbol of his success. For as long as he could use her at his will, she would remain a tangible reminder of his final revenge on the Porterfields.

As if from far away, she was aware of a door opening and closing. She straightened and dashed the tears from her cheeks, listening to the sound of muffled footsteps approaching her door. The key turned in the lock, and St James spoke her name. Charl did not turn at the sound of his voice but stared all the more resolutely at the garden below. St James came to stand behind her, so close that she could feel the cold of outside emanating from him. She tried to draw a deep breath, but the air seemed trapped in her chest. Finally, she turned to read of Seth's death in his eyes.

St James' face was grim in the grey-tinged daylight, and the broad, chiselled bones seemed harsh and more pronounced. With difficulty she met his eyes. They were unfathomable, neither bright with victory nor dark with remorse.

Feeling suffocated by his nearness and the thing he had come to tell her, she moved away, standing erect and unbowed.

'Yes? What is it?' she asked in a voice that was soft but rock steady.

St James watched her for a long moment. Then, choosing his words with care, he spoke.

'Porterfield is gone,' he said simply.

Charl went pale, but her eyes blazed like emeralds out of the parchment whiteness. Moving with painful deliberation, she brought one hand up to her throat.

'So Seth is dead,' she whispered, drawing the conclusion his words had intended. 'God rest his soul.'

The thudding of her heart seemed to reverberate inside her ribs and at her temples. A crushing pain in her chest made it impossible to breathe. From the very centre of her being a cold, foggy darkness began to spread, leaving her limbs tingling and icy in its wake. It rose to her head in ever-thickening whorls, filling her vacuous brain and clouding her sight.

'Oh Seth,' she heard herself moan, and then her senses slipped away as she sank down into nothingness.

For a long time the British major stood above the slender figure slumped on the carpet. He watched the lovely face, now devoid of colour, the thick, dark lashes fanned out on her pale cheeks; the almost imperceptible rise and fall of her shallow breathing. Finally, he bent and lifted the unconscious girl and carried her gently to the bed.

Obviously, she had drawn the conclusion that he had meant for her to draw: that Seth Porterfield was dead. It had been a nasty shock to arrive at Cape Diamond prepared to see his old enemy hanged, only to find that in the night someone had somehow spirited the prisoner away. Porterfield had been in no condition to travel far, but St James had been a soldier long enough to know that men were capable of great feats when their lives were forfeit. He had instituted a search for the man, but he held little hope of locating the prisoner.

At least he had recovered the papers, he reasoned philosophically, and the girl was his. In time he would have another chance at the man; he was sure of it. For now he was content to have sullied the Porterfield name with a charge of treason. Even if things had not turned out as he had hoped this time, he had achieved much in the way of revenge on Alistair Porterfield. He had seen William dead, and the heir, Simon, had been killed a little more than a year ago in a hunting accident. The daughter, Elaine, had succumbed to her own vices. Only Seth Porterfield was left of the once-proud line, and St James could wait to kill Seth. He was a very patient man.

And now he had the girl. He ran his fingers across her pale cheek, amazed anew by her beauty. Now that Charlotte believed her lover dead, she would be more cooperative. He would give her time to grieve for Porterfield, but in the end he would make her his mistress. She was the prize in his battle with Porterfield, and as victor he would never let her go.

Last night she had been a hellion, struggling desperately against him, and he had lost all control. The events in the prison had honed his nerves to a fine edge, and her resistance had pushed him beyond restraint. As she fought him, his desire had flamed to frenzied heights, driving him madly until he spent himself between her thighs. In time she would gentle to his touch or at least bow to his control over her. He toyed with one thick golden curl and smiled. When that time came, she would be the perfect mistress.

※

They stopped at noontime by the outlet of a stream, pulling the canoe up on the ice and making a small fire on the bank. Waukee brewed tea to warm them both and they ate Gabrielle's biscuits with salty strips of smoked venison. When they had finished, Waukee boiled up a herb potion and dosed Seth liberally with it, knowing it would ease his pain and make him sleep.

Once Seth had drunk every drop of the bitter concoction, the Indian began to cleanse the wounds in his friend's back and apply an ointment that would speed healing. Although Seth remained stoically silent, he flinched involuntarily at even the gentlest touch, and Waukee could guess the pain his ministrations were causing.

As he worked over his patient, the Indian spoke softly, telling Seth about the inquiries he'd made that had led him to the prison on the Citadel, about the discovery of the drainage tunnel high on the cliffside and of the plan to go on to the American settlement of Plattsburg where Seth would be safe. Porterfield nodded in agreement, feeling strangely ambivalent and detached from the decisions being made.

'And once you're safe in Plattsburg, I'll go back to Quebec and search for Charl,' the Indian added as he fastened a light dressing over the wounds to protect them from contact with the furs and blankets.

'No!' Seth growled as he turned to the other man. Every trace of indifference was gone from his face, and in his eyes there was such naked, undiluted pain that Waukee was taken aback. This was a hurt that seemed to burn from his soul and had nothing to do with the physical mistreatment he had suffered.

'But why?' the Indian asked.

Seth's voice was raw. 'Because it was Charl who betrayed me to the English, to St James.'

There was a lingering moment of disbelief between them as Seth's accusation sank in.

'You must be mistaken,' Waukee said flatly. 'Charl couldn't have done that. She had no idea of why you were in Quebec.'

Seth shook his head.

'She knew. She knew. Charl made a bargain with St James. She gave him proof of my activities in return for passage back to Youngstown.'

'You don't believe that!' Waukee exclaimed.

'Of course I believe it,' Seth answered, but the effect of the drug Waukee had given him was suddenly evident, robbing his voice of conviction. His eyes looked cloudy and unfocused, and noting this Waukee helped Seth to his feet, intent on settling him in the canoe before the potion rendered him helpless.

'They were lovers,' he went on, his voice soft and slurred, 'Charlotte and St James. They set out to trap me.'

'Seth, be sensible . . .' the Indian began, but there was no reasoning with him. Porterfield was convinced of Charl's guilt, and the drug had begun to dull his senses. There would be a time in the future when they could discuss this rationally.

Ignoring the tirade of muffled accusations and curses, Waukee guided Seth back to his place in the bow of the canoe. Almost immediately Seth's eyes flickered closed, and Waukee knew he would sleep long and deeply.

'You are wrong about Charlotte,' he told his friend as he tucked a blanket around his shoulders, 'for there are few women in this world who love their men as she loves you.'

There was more than a hint of regret in the Indian's quiet words, but Seth slept on unaware of it. Nor was he aware of the icy wind that buffeted them, the snow that blew in blinding sheets, or the miles they travelled struggling upstream against the churning water towards safety.

*

It was nearly dark in the room when Charl awoke, but she knew instantly where she was and why. Her first emotion was breathless fear for with the darkness came St James and his vile demands on her. If he came tonight, she would surely go mad. She would kill herself before she would let Seth's murderer lay his hands on her.

She flew to the door and found it locked from the outside. The window offered no escape either, and she cast about wildly for some way to subvert the inevitable. Dread ran through her veins and panic clutched at her throat as she stared helplessly at the door. Then her eyes came to rest on a tall, mahogany chest of drawers that stood just to the left of the panel. Carefully she surveyed it, measuring its height and width, assessing its worth as a barricade against her captor's unwelcome intrusion. Although it equalled her weight and more, she determinedly set her shoulder to it and gradually inched it across the polished floor until it effectively blocked the entrance.

Once her privacy was assured, Charl gave way to her grief, sinking to the floor, huddled with the pain of her loss. The tears were torrential at first, and sobs spasmed her body in response to the emotions that writhed within her. Finally spent, she slept where she lay, only to awaken to that same all-encompassing grief. For three days she cried and slept, only marginally aware that St James beat at her door demanding entry.

In those three days and nights Charl was barely sane. She conversed aloud with a dead man and retreated from the terrible reality of her loss into memories of the happiness they had shared. At times she eyed the curtain cords, imagining them a noose around her throat, and fingered the letter opener, wondering if it hurt very much more to die than to live.

In a haze of despair, she relived the brief time she and Seth had had together. Even as she took comfort in those memories, she tried desperately to accept that she would never see him again, never hear his laugh, never feel his caress. During those bleak hours she came to realize the truth in the things she had shouted at him in his cell. He had not believed her then, but she had told him no lies. As long as she lived, she would never love another man.

At dawn on the fourth day, Charl awoke slowly and turned on her side to stare out of the window at the pink-streaked sky. Her eyelids were thick and swollen from weeping, and her body was heavy with lethargy. She curled closer, drawing her knees up to her chest, and was aware of a strange fullness inside her. Then, with a start, she realized why she felt as she did. She was carrying Seth's child. Until now there had been no real signs of her pregnancy, and the all-encompassing grief had driven everything else from her mind. Turning on her back, she ran her palm over the imperceptible rounding of her belly and smiled. Seth might be dead, but he was not gone from her altogether. He had left a child as his legacy.

As she lay listening to the cries of the birds that wheeled in ever-widening circles across the wintry sky, she felt at peace for the first time in days. All was not lost. Seth had left his child to nurture and protect. He had given her a trust more difficult and sacred than any she had ever undertaken.

Slowly, her mind made the transition from the past, where it had been mired by grief, towards the future she would make for herself and her child.

Her first concern was to escape St James. The thought of facing him after everything that had happened filled her with a mixture of fury and dread. She wanted to flee from him: running so far and so fast that he could never find her. But she knew, at the same time, that if she gave any hint of her intention, he would continue to lock her up and she would never get away.

Instead, she needed to trick St James into thinking that she would agree to his demands. Then, when he let his guard down, she would have the opportunity to escape. As difficult as it would be for her to comply with his wishes, she had no choice if she was to succeed.

She pulled the blanket higher against the encroaching morning cold and the chilling prospects that awaited her. But even as the dread rose inside her, so did the conviction that this was the right course to take.

In the brightening daylight Charl lay thinking about the child she carried. Would it be a boy who would grow strong and courageous like his father? Or would the child be a girl with her own passion for life? Either way, Charl would protect it from the doubts that had marked Seth. This child would know that it was loved and wanted. She would see to that.

As she lay quietly contemplating the future that seemed suddenly more hopeful than it had in days, she was struck by the delicious irony of the situation. Perhaps her reason to escape St James might prove her deliverance as well. Once he discovered that she was carrying Seth's child, he would let her go. He would be furious, but he would have no choice for the only way he could keep her as his mistress was to acknowledge Seth Porterfield's bastard as his son. And he would never do that. Once her condition became obvious, he would be glad to be rid of her. She had only to wait, and St James would be forced to set her free.

When that happened, there was no question of where she would go. Gabrielle would let her return to her little room on ruelle du Porche. And in the same room where she and Seth had known such happiness, their child would be born. Afterwards, she would make a life for herself and her child just as Gabrielle had done.

Charl sat up slowly, feeling light-headed from lack of food, and went to wash her hands and face with the last of the water in the ewer. The pale wraith who stared back at her from the mirror shocked her, but there was a set to her chin and a clarity in her direct gaze that spoke of her determination to escape.

If she was to live out this charade as St James' mistress, she must school herself to acquiesce to his demands, as difficult as that might prove to be. For a short time she must disguise her hatred for this cruel man behind a semblance of compliance and do everything he asked.

Charl had been given back her reason to live, entrusted with a life beyond her own, and she realized the price she would pay to honour that commitment.

With great deliberation she brushed out her tangled hair and smoothed her wrinkled gown. She struggled to push the chest from where it had guarded the door, then sat calmly, waiting for St James.

Twenty-Seven
✷✷✷

For the first time in several days Seth Porterfield's head was clear, and he watched the activity in the corridor outside his room with interest. On the previous evening they had arrived on the western shore of Lake Champlain and he had been given accommodation at Fort Moreau. Waukee's herb potions had done their work well during the journey, and Seth had little recollection of either the passage up the St Lawrence and Richelieu Rivers or across the lake. He had accepted the Indian's ministrations with uncharacteristic complacency, welcoming the drugged sleep that obliterated his pain and allowed him to retreat from his thoughts. He was better now, and the wounds left by the lash were healing. There would be scars, he knew, but they would fade in time. It was the memory of his betrayal at Charl's hands that would always mark him.

He stirred restlessly beneath the blankets as the memory of his last meeting with her played and replayed in his mind. Charl had seemed so earnest in her concern for him, and yet he knew she had given St James the papers that proved his guilt. She had never denied it. Her only defence for any of the charges he made was that she loved him and would never knowingly do anything to harm him.

She loved him! At least he was no longer fool enough to believe that lie. Once he had believed it readily enough, though. When she had pampered him and cooked his favourite meals, he had no cause to doubt her. When she had lain in his arms and quickened to his touch, he had believed her. When she had listened to the stories of his past and eased his bitterness, he had loved her in return. And all of it, the caring, the passion, and the understanding, had been a lie.

His throat was tight.

Everything between them had been lies. That was bad enough;

but now he realized that the lies had been meant to delude, manipulate, and trap him. And how well Charl had succeeded.

He had been blinded by her smiles, deafened by her sweet words until he lost all wariness, all caution. Gradually, he had come to trust her and then love her. She had encouraged that trust, accepted his love, and insidiously woven her web around him until he could not hope to escape. He had been too guileless, too unsuspecting to even guess her game, but in retrospect her purposes became very clear. She had stayed with him only long enough to find proof of his activities in Quebec and then gone over to his enemies.

A spy might expect that kind of betrayal, but a man in love did not. He might have forgiven her if only she had been honest with him. Instead she had chosen to mask her intentions with the pretence of love. And for that deception he would always hate her.

A weight seemed lodged in his chest, and his breathing was ragged. Once he had loved Charlotte, and now he hated her. In these past days that change had become complete. But what he must do if he was to retain his sanity was to forget her. He could not let himself think about the joy he had found with her or the hurt she had caused him. He must put Charl out of his mind until the time came when he could think dispassionately about everything that had happened in Quebec, a time far in the future.

'Seth?' Waukee's inquiry came from the doorway.

He turned quickly, then struggled to sit up, clenching his teeth against the pain that came with the movement. He was glad to see the Indian and welcomed the diversion from his thoughts.

'Good morning,' the dark-haired man greeted him. 'I can see you are much better today.'

'Thanks to you,' Seth returned.

Waukee mumbled a reply and bent to examine Seth's back and shoulders. The healing was progressing well, and the less serious welts were closing, but he was still appalled by the cruelty of the act. Gently, he applied more of the herb ointment to the deep, raw furrows that remained.

When he was finished, he pulled a chair over beside the bed.

'Lie down,' he ordered gruffly. 'You are still weak but too stubborn to admit it.'

Seth complied gratefully and settled himself gingerly on the cornhusk mattress.

'You saved my life by rescuing me when you did,' Porterfield began. 'They planned to hang me at dawn.'

Waukee gave a brief definitive nod of acknowledgement.

'Your hanging was general knowledge in Quebec an hour after the sentence was pronounced. It is fortunate that I discovered a way into the prison in time.'

They talked quietly for the best part of the morning, sharing the warm camaraderie that had bound them together since boyhood. For nearly half their lifetimes they had ridden together: through adventure and danger, across half a continent. They had learned to trust and depend on each other, and each knew the other man well. Perhaps it was for that reason that Waukee hesitated before he spoke, studying Seth intently.

'I am returning to Quebec tonight to find Charlotte,' he finally stated softly. 'With your escape she may be in danger.'

Seth struggled to rise on one elbow.

'You'll do nothing of the kind!' he exclaimed. 'Charl is in no danger, believe me. And I'll not have you risk your life to rescue someone who does not wish to be rescued.'

'Are you sure Charl is safe in Quebec?'

'Charl betrayed me to St James. She is the one who gave him proof to convict me of treason.'

'You said as much before,' Waukee observed calmly in the face of Seth's agitation, 'but I was sure you were delirious to even consider such a thing. You can't honestly believe that Charl would do anything to harm you.'

'There is no doubt of her treachery. St James had the papers that I hid in our room, papers only Charl could have seen me hide.'

'Charl wouldn't have given them to St James,' Waukee stated flatly. 'You don't know how emotional she was when you were missing. She was frightened, distraught . . .'

'Then you were as taken in by her performance as I was, my friend. She was neither frightened nor distraught when St James sent her to my cell although she attempted to convince me she was both.'

Waukee observed him gravely.

'When? When did you see her?'

'That last day in Quebec, in the afternoon. She came to my cell, contrite, pretending not to understand –'

The Indian came to his feet in a rush, nearly upsetting his chair, and began to pace the floor at the foot of the bed.

'If Charl is with Felix St James, then she is in danger!'

'Damn it, man! That's where she wants to be. She made her choice.'

Waukee ignored him and made another circuit of the room.

'She's where she wants to be,' Seth repeated. 'She's taken St James as a lover.'

'I'll wager she sold herself to him to help you,' Waukee fired back.

'Don't attribute any nobility to what she's done,' Seth advised bitterly.

In spite of himself, Charl's memory came back to haunt him. Her eyes had been wide and glazed with tears, her voice soft and tremulous. What was it she had said? 'Please try to understand. St James said if I slept with him, he would try to help you. Can't you see that I had no choice?'

Seth smoothed the rumpled blanket on his lap without really seeing it.

Surely Charl knew that he would face any fate rather than have her choose to share St James' bed. But if he had succeeded in forcing himself on Charl, wasn't it possible that he had made her tell him where the papers were hidden as well?

His hand stopped in mid-motion and curled slowly into a fist.

As much as he wished to find explanations for Charl's betrayal, he knew there were none. She was undoubtedly guilty. If he let even the smallest doubt encroach now, he would be lost.

Sympathetically, Waukee watched the warring emotions on the blond man's face and the pain and confusion in his eyes. Perhaps there was something Seth should know that might temper his judgement of the girl, yet the Indian hesitated to tell him. After overhearing a conversation between Charl and Gabrielle, and from his own observations, he had come to believe that Charl was carrying Seth's child. Still, he did not know it for a certainty, nor was he sure what effect that news might have on his friend. Would it change Seth's mind about Charl, or would it only serve to deepen his disillusionment and bitterness?

Waukee decided to remain silent, but his decision only underlined the need to get Charl out of Quebec. Even if she was not pregnant, these two needed to resolve their difficulties face to face.

'I'm going to Quebec tonight,' Waukee repeated softly, but before he could finish the sentence, Seth had snatched a pistol from an open pack beside the bed and was levelling it at the Indian.

'No! You're not going anywhere!' His voice wavered slightly, but his aim did not.

'Give me your word that you will not go to Quebec!' he demanded.

Slowly Waukee spread his palms in an age-old gesture of acceptance and shook his head sadly.

'Would you shoot me, my brother?' he asked.

Seth lowered the pistol to the bed, his hands trembling with the realization of what he had done. He shook his head slowly.

Neither man moved for a very long time, and when Seth finally spoke, his voice was thick with regret.

'I'm sorry. Surely you know that I would never have hurt you. Please don't go back to Quebec. Charl is where she wants to be. And I never wish to see her again.'

With difficulty, Waukee held his tongue. Seth was wrong, but it would do little good to argue with him now. He was like a horse with blinkers on, unable to see any path but the one laid out before him.

In spite of what Seth said, the Indian was convinced that Charl was in danger, and he intended to return to Quebec regardless of what he told Seth. If Seth did not want to see Charlotte, then Waukee would offer her the opportunity to return to Youngstown. Either way, he could not rest until he knew she was safe.

Lies did not come easily to his lips, but he nodded as if he had finally agreed.

'Very well. If you wish, I will not bring Charl to Plattsburg,' he said carefully, 'but I will leave tonight in any case.'

Seth glanced up in surprise.

'Where will you go?'

'It has been a long time since I have slept in the land of my people. I have been thinking about going home for some time.'

There was a long pause before Seth spoke his thoughts.

'Will you fight with Tecumseh?' Seth asked, dreading the answer.

Waukee smiled.

'No. I will not fight. I have come to know my enemies as friends, and I have always been a man of peace.

'I will build a lodge near the joining of the two rivers where we fished as boys. Do you know the place?'

'Near the sycamore grove?'

Waukee nodded.

'I will live quietly there, at one with the land and the sky. In the past I have been known for my skill with herbs and medicines. Other tribes will seek me out for my skills. And in time you will come, too.'

Seth glanced up to where the Indian stood at the foot of the bed. His face was open and unguarded.

'Are we still brothers, then?' he asked softly.

Waukee looked at the man who had shared so much of his life, and his smile was soft with understanding. He could read the sadness in his friend's face, the regret and vulnerability that had never been there before. What Seth had done changed nothing between them, just as Waukee's half-truths would change nothing. This would pass as so many other things had passed, and their friendship would remain strong.

'We shall be brothers for all our days,' Waukee replied solemnly as he gathered his belongings. At the doorway he paused and looked back at the man in the bed.

'I wish you could find the peace you seek, my brother, as easily as I find mine,' he said softly.

His words hung in the silence; then he turned on his heel and was gone.

※

Glancing up from the letter he was reading, Felix St James paused to listen appreciatively to the intricate melody that filled the room. The complex passage moved towards its crescendo, effectively obscuring the sound of sleet splattering against the windows. In spite of the foul weather outside, the room was cosy with the roaring fire and the warm mellow glow of candles. Everything about this quiet evening at home heightened his sense of well-being. Slowly his gaze moved over the rich, tapestried furniture; the glowing satinwood tables; the plush, crimson carpet; and came to rest on the woman who played the pianoforte with such skill. Her pose was one of deep concentration as she laboured over the Beethoven concerto, and he could study her unobserved.

Her thick, fair hair streamed loosely down her back, bright in sharp contrast to the amethyst gown. The expression on her lovely face was intent as she studied the maze of notes before her.

She played exceptionally well, if a bit too single-mindedly, and her mastery of the pianoforte pleased him. In truth, everything about his new mistress pleased him.

In the scant month since Charlotte Beckwith had been his, he had come to consider himself a very lucky man. She was undoubtedly one of the most beautiful women in Quebec, now that he had bought her a suitable wardrobe of rich gowns, and he knew he was the envy of his fellow officers. Her refined manners and innate elegance afforded her notice at any gathering, and she moved within the social circles he frequented with a quiet grace.

Of course, a mistress, like most of his other luxuries, was something he could ill-afford. But Charlotte, at least, was well worth the price. Her new gowns had set him back nearly a month's wages, but a fortuitous bet had paid off and saved him from ruin. Thankfully, he had not needed to buy her jewels, since she came to him wearing an impressive pair of opal earrings that complemented any gown.

Charlotte had indeed become the perfect mistress as he'd intended. It was the ease of the transformation from rebellious prisoner to accommodating concubine that amazed him. He did not know how she had exorcized her grief over Seth's 'death'; but when she had emerged from her locked room four days after Porterfield's supposed execution, she had been pale and drawn but utterly calm. She had quietly expressed her willingness to do as he wished, and she had acquiesced to all his demands since then. Of course, the fiery nature that had intrigued him from the first was no longer in evidence; but her equanimity was a plus in the day-to-day business of living, if not in the bedroom. Still he found her one of the most exciting women he had ever known. Even when she lay silent and unresponsive, he knew the passion and fire of which she was capable, and that stirred his soul. In time he would make her writhe and cry out as she had that first time. Only now it would be his name on her lips and not Porterfield's.

He was well pleased with her, if somewhat puzzled by her bland aceptance of her role as his mistress. In this past month he had begun to see her innate value. She had become more than the spoils won from a vanquished foe. It was almost as if she had become more beautiful: her skin more glowingly translucent, her body more lush and womanly, her eyes brighter. He had come to recognize her poise, her grace, her accomplishments. And in doing so he realized he had come to possess something to be treasured.

With difficulty he turned his eyes from the lovely woman at hand and the pleasant contemplation of approaching bedtime to the more tedious demands of a letter from his father.

It was another fruitless plea for funds to maintain the small estate in Essex. The property and the renowned surname had been the only legacy Brice St James had received from his father Martin, Earl of Besswick. It had represented only a token of the extensive family fortune; but as second son it had been his place to enter the military, the clergy or marry for monetary advantage. Brice had attempted the latter, but with neither land nor title behind him he had not made a very successful match. The girl, Elizabeth, had brought a large dowry, it was true. But Brice, with the same love of luxury he had passed on to his son, quickly squandered it, and they were forced to retire to the small estate to live in genteel poverty. It had been this complete lack of capital that had forced Felix into the military. With the influence of the St James name behind him and a loan from his uncle, he had purchased a commission in the hope of winning the glory and fortune his birth had denied him.

As he stared at the closely written pages, the old familiar bitterness came back to haunt him. His father deserved better. Brice St James should have been the Earl of Besswick, with the manor in Hampshire and the vast income from the family holdings across England. It was only a bizarre twist of fate that had robbed him, and Felix also, of their heritage. Nor was there any hope of rectifying the situation. Martin's heir, Alexander St James, had married early and quickly sired four sons and a daughter to insure the future of the line.

There was nothing to be done but accept the lives fate had planned for them and to contemplate revenge on the man whose actions, all those years ago, had altered both their lives.

St James was so caught up in his own thoughts that he was not aware when the music broke off in mid-bar and began again with a more familiar tune. Charl had suddenly had enough of the difficult piece for one evening and set it aside for another time. Instead she began a tune she had played since childhood, letting her fingers skim over the keys almost of their own accord. Her music had become a solace in these dark days since Seth's death, and it was the forgetfulness she found in it that enabled her to stay with St James.

She had expected that by now her condition would have become evident and that St James would have sent her away. But even as she neared the end of her third month, she did not look pregnant. Her figure had grown fuller and rounder but her height and carriage concealed much.

He had been considerate and solicitous in the weeks that she had been with him, but it was growing increasingly difficult to hide her loathing. He was the man who had tricked her into betraying Seth, who had turned the man she loved against her. And, in the end, he had finally seen Seth executed. She detested Felix. His touch and the vile things he expected of her made her skin crawl though she had no choice but to endure them. For the sake of her unborn child she must go on pretending. But how much longer would it be before her condition began to show, she wondered. Once her pregnancy became obvious, he would be forced to claim Seth's child or let her go.

There was no question of which he would choose. St James was a proud man and his hatred of Porterfields was deep. He would send her away; Charl was sure of it.

In these past weeks she had learned a great deal about him. It was clear by the proprietary air he effected when other men came near that he was pleased with her as a mistress. And she was aware that he could be jealous and possessive. He would be furious when he discovered that she was carrying Seth's child, but she was counting on that to speed his decision to let her go.

She would be no great loss to him, she reassured herself as she contemplated the simplicity of her plan. Other women responded easily to his intensity and his smouldering attraction. He would have little trouble replacing her if he chose to do so. If only she could maintain her pretence of cooperation until her chance for escape came. Still, he frightened her.

He was too intelligent, too aware of what went on. She was not even sure how she had managed to fool him thus far. St James was not an insensitive man. He clearly saw and understood the myriad of emotions that stirred his fellow men and women, but for all his sensitivity he had no sympathy, no warmth, no compassion for them. It was only a matter of time before he realized that there was a purpose behind her cooperation. When he did learn her reasons for deceiving him, he would show no mercy. She must be prepared for that.

Charl suddenly realized that Felix was standing beside the pianoforte watching her. Startled, her fingers froze on the keys, bringing the music to a discordant halt.

'You play beautifully, my sweet, but too intently. I have never known anyone to lose herself in music the way you do.'

'My father used to complain of the same thing,' she admitted, wondering how long he had been standing there and if her thoughts had been evident on her face.

'At any rate it is time for bed,' he told her. He could not quite mask the eagerness in his voice or the glow in those mahogany eyes.

'Then you've finished your reading?' she asked as she gathered up the sheets of music and arranged them in a neat pile on the music stand.

'It was a letter from my family in England.'

Somehow it was hard to imagine this ruthless man as part of a family. Had there been a mother to pamper and gentle him? Or brothers and sisters to teach him compromise? And a father . . .

The thought of her own father made her throat constrict.

'Is your family well?' she asked softly.

A frown crossed his gaunt face. 'Well enough,' he answered, taking her arm and leading her towards the bedchamber.

She paused and looked up at him. 'Is there any news from Fort Niagara?'

He did not need to ask her reason for wanting to know. 'There is seldom much military activity at this time of year,' he reassured her.

'If there is any word of Fort Niagara or Youngstown, will you let me know?' she asked.

'Certainly,' he assured her, struck by the intensity in her eyes. 'Now come to bed.'

※

Waukee had been discreetly watching Felix St James' rooms for nearly three weeks waiting for an opportunity to speak to Charl alone. But thus far one had not presented itself. When he slipped back into Quebec and found that Charl had not returned to Gabrielle's house, it hadn't been difficult to locate her. A few inquiries gave him the information he sought: that Felix St James had a lovely new mistress, one Charlotte Beckwith. In a variety

of disguises he had carried out his surveillance of the house on
rue des Jardins; but on each of her infrequent outings, Charl had
been accompanied by either St James or his servant. Pulling his
collar up against the bitter January wind, Waukee frowned in
frustration. If he did not get a chance to talk to her soon, he
would have to try more drastic measures.

He stepped back behind a fence as the door to the narrow,
white house opened and St James' servant emerged. The man
was laden with parcels and could be seen to be mumbling irritably
to himself as he moved up the street. No sooner was the servant
out of sight than the door opened again and a tall woman in a
turquoise pelisse came out. The hood was drawn up, against the
wind or to hide her features, but Waukee recognized her instantly. With a quick glance up and down the street that failed
to disclose the Indian in his hiding place, she moved off in the
opposite direction from the one the servant had taken. There
was a set to her shoulders and a determination to her stride that
hinted at the importance of her mission. Waukee, his curiosity
aroused, followed silently behind her. There would be a chance
later to talk to her, he decided, but now he wanted to know her
destination.

For the next hour and a half Waukee followed Charl, first to
the Banque de Quebec and then to Fournier and McIver, the
firm of guides and surveyors that had sent Seth west for the first
time.

What was Charl doing? he wondered, as he clamped the
broad-brimmed hat more firmly on his head and turned his back
against the wind that whipped along the ramparts. There were
so many unanswered questions. What had happened between
Charl and his friend? Was there any truth in Seth's accusations?
She was openly living as St James' mistress. Was she happy? Did
she still want to return to Youngstown?

He had followed her long enough to appease his curiosity, he
decided. When she came out of the office, he would talk to her.
His wait was not a long one. Less than twenty minutes later Charl
came into the street, but before he could get close enough to call
to her, she saw him. She must not have recognized him in the
strange clothes for, after a moment's hesitation, she bolted in
the opposite direction. He hurried after her as she fled through
the web of streets and alleys that took her back across Uppertown.
As they approached her destination, Waukee began to sprint,

determined to overtake her before she reached rue des Jardins. Charl must have heard his running footsteps behind her because she suddenly took to her heels, moving with surprising speed in spite of the long cloak and gown.

As quickly as he could he followed, but in spite of his greater speed, Charl managed to slip away from him in the maze of paths that crisscrossed the Ursuline Convent. Much to his consternation, Waukee found himself standing in the courtyard of the small chapel a few moments later with no idea of where Charl had gone. He gave the church a cursory inspection and then moved back through the complex until he reached the opposite end at rue Ste Anne.

As he stood watching the ebb and flow of daily traffic, a wild frustration came over him. After all these days of waiting, Charl had somehow managed to elude him. Who could know when he might have another chance to talk to her?

Twenty-Eight

Charl was in better spirits than she had been for weeks, and St James attributed the change to an unexpected letter from her father and the abrupt break in the bleak winter weather. For the first time since the New Year, the sun that streamed in across the table where they breakfasted was warm and bright.

'It looks a fine day,' Felix commented as he poured more tea from the silver teapot.

'Even for all that sunshine, I'll warrant it's still cold out,' Charl returned as she set down her porcelain cup and glanced at him across the elaborately laid table.

Felix smiled proprietorially. Charl was spectacularly lovely this morning in her mauve and ecru gown, with the sunlight glinting in the pale, golden hair that tumbled over her shoulders in artless abandon. Watching her, he was seized by a sudden desire to show off his prize to the rest of Quebec.

'Shall we chance the weather anyway?' he proposed. 'I can get away from my duties this afternoon. Would you like to join me for a ride? You've been cooped up in these rooms for weeks.'

She considered his suggestion for a moment. A diversion from the endless round of reading, practising the pianoforte and embroidery that she had adopted to fill her days would be welcome. How good it would be to feel the wind against her face and move to the familiar rhythm of a horse's gallop. It would be wonderful to exercise the muscles stiff with days of inactivity, and revel in the sense of freedom that always came when she and her mount bounded across the countryside.

'That sounds lovely,' Charl agreed. 'What time shall I be ready?'

St James laid his napkin aside and rose in preparation for his departure. 'About three, I should think. Is that all right with you?'

'Fine. I'm looking forward to it,' she told him.

Smiling, he came around to her chair, and she steeled herself to accept his kiss.

'A bientôt, my love,' he called as he left, clattering down the stairs and slamming the lower door behind him.

Turning back to the window, Charl's gaze moved across the rooftops of the city. At the end of the street she could see the bulky, grey buildings of the Ursuline Convent and the spire of a church that soared skyward, dwarfing the houses nearby. The upper storeys of the Governor's Mansion, where she had danced so gaily, and the Château St Louis were visible, too. The crest of Cape Diamond, the site of Seth's execution, rose to the southwest outside the stout stone wall that encircled the city. Beyond her vision was the steep, rugged rockface that divided Upper and Lowertown and the wide ice-clogged river that swept eastward to the sea.

There was a time when Quebec had been exotic and compelling with its strong French influence and rich history. Once, viewed through the eyes of love, it had seemed a paradise where she and Seth could make a life together. Because of those sweet memories of this high-walled city she was reluctant to leave even though she knew there was no longer a future for her here. In a matter of hours she would meet her guide and leave Quebec, with its joys and sorrows, behind her. Only then would she be free to begin a life for herself and her child.

Promptly at three Felix arrived on his big grey stallion with a spirited bay mare in tow. The day had fulfilled its early promise. The sun was unseasonably warm, melting the snow from the roads and rooftops and allowing Charl to discard her heavy cloak in favour of the new habit St James had bought her. The maroon velvet jacket was cut close to emphasize her lush curves, and a jabot of creamy lace rose above the high collar; the skirt was black faille, as was the narrow-brimmed hat with its maroon cockade. Felix gave an approving nod for her attire as he helped her into the saddle.

'Where shall we ride?' the major asked agreeably when he had mounted.

Charl shrugged. 'Out across the Plains of Abraham, I suppose,' she answered as she let him take the lead.

Apparently many of Quebec's citizens had decided to take advantage of the fine weather, for rue St Louis was lined with coaches and carriages, making the road nearly impassable for those on horseback. As they made their way along the crowded thoroughfare, St James nodded greetings at various groups and paused from time to time to speak to someone. As Charl waited for him, she could not help overhearing snatches of a conversation between two overdressed matrons who occupied an adjacent calèche.

'. . . a most handsome man, and from a fine old family, I understand,' one was saying. 'It is a pity about his taste in women, though. They say Muzette Verreault killed herself when he rejected her, poor little tart. The blonde in maroon is his latest mistress, you know.'

The colour flamed in Charl's cheeks, and she averted her head so that she missed the second woman's comment. But when the first matron spoke again, her voice rang clearly above the street noise.

'Oh, she's pretty enough,' she said, 'but no matter how fine her trappings, a whore's a whore.'

Tears came to Charl's eyes unexpectedly, and she clenched her teeth to keep from turning on the two old cats with unbridled rage. The realization that she had indeed become St James' whore tore through her. She had lain with Seth for love and desire, giving herself to him freely with no thought of any return for her favours. But she had sold herself to St James: first for Seth's life and then because of her own cowardice. In her heart hatred for St James warred with disgust for her own weakness. She had come to him cheaply, for he had kept none of his bargains. Seth was dead and though she had once deluded herself, she knew now there would be no safety once he found out about her child. Blindly, she turned her horse into the flow of traffic, bent on escape.

St James looked up just in time to see her ramrod straight back disappearing into the crowd. Hastily, he said his good-byes and followed her. They were some distance beyond the St Louis gate when he caught up to Charl.

'What the deuce possessed you to go galloping off like that without me?' he demanded as he caught the reins of her horse with one hand.

She turned to him, her green eyes flashing.

'How dare you speak to me as if you owned me, you bastard,' she spat.

His dark eyebrows shot up in surprise at her venom. He did not know what had precipitated this change in her, but it both angered and excited him. She seemed suddenly more the woman who had intrigued him that first day in his office, a woman with fire and spirit. It was almost as if he had been living with an impostor these past weeks, and now the real Charlotte Beckwith had returned. He nudged his horse closer to hers.

'You are wrong, Charlotte. I do own you,' he told her as his russet eyes blazed into hers. 'I won you from Porterfield. You are my prize, and I shall keep you forever if it suits my purposes!'

'No! Never! You shall never own me!' she cried as she pulled the reins from his grip and dug her heels into her mount's sides. The horse bolted away, and she turned it skilfully from the crowded roadway into the open fields. She bent low over her mare's neck, urging her on with singleminded determination. The horse responded, lengthening its stride until they fairly flew across the snowy fields. Her single thought was to outdistance St James, and she used every bit of skill she possessed to meet that purpose.

At dizzying speed they traversed the wide flat plain at the crest of the river gorge, where the British had defeated the French and where Abraham Martin had planted his fields more than one hundred years before. Charl's hat was torn off as they thundered over the frozen ground, and her hair tumbled free, tossing in the wind like a golden banner. She had no idea of where she was going, but at St James' words some inner control had snapped and her need to escape had become overwhelming.

St James had been startled by her sudden flight, and he watched her for an instant before he turned his horse and galloped after her. She had already taken a long lead, and he spurred his grey stallion mercilessly.

Through the blur of sound Charl was aware that he was calling her name, and she chanced a look over her shoulder. The big grey was still some distance behind her, but he was coming up fast. In desperation she bent lower over the mare's neck, pressing her face into the flapping mane as she gave the horse its head. In spite of the mare's valiant effort, Charl sensed that her mount was tiring, and she realized that she could not hope to outrun St James' stronger horse. Still she would not give in. Through tear-glazed eyes she could see St James bearing down on them.

'Rein in!' he ordered as he drew close beside her.

When she did not obey, he gathered himself and leaped from his horse to hers. At that moment her horse wheeled suddenly and St James' momentum carried them both out of the saddle. They landed heavily a dozen feet from the base of one of the barren oaks that dotted the winter landscape.

St James had fallen on top of her, driving the breath from her body, and it was some time before Charl managed to raise her head.

When she did, he was standing over her, glaring down with fury in his eyes.

'What was it you hoped to prove by that little display?' he demanded angrily.

Charl put one hand to her throbbing head. Her fingers came away sticky with blood from a deep gash at her hairline.

'I don't know,' she mumbled and lay back dizzily. Her chest had been crushed by his weight on top of her, and it hurt to breathe. Then suddenly, a pain twisted through her that overshadowed her other hurts, and she writhed helplessly on the frozen ground.

'Oh please, no!' she whispered as a stronger wave of pain wrenched through her.

Felix dropped to his knees beside her.

'What is it, Charlotte?' he asked sharply. 'What's the matter?'

'Oh God! It's the baby!' she sobbed.

St James bent closer, his eyebrows drawn together over the bridge of his nose. 'What baby?' he demanded.

Charl's face was devoid of colour except where the blood had trickled across her temple, and, in spite of the cold, beads of sweat stood out on her brow as another spasm caught her in its tenacious grip.

'Seth's baby! I'm going to lose Seth's baby,' she managed to gasp before she fainted.

St James stared down at her in disbelief, but even as he tried to deny the truth in her words, he knew he could not. Rage and jealousy filled him. Somehow Porterfield had thwarted him again. Charlotte was his, and yet her former lover had retained a hold on her stronger than any he could claim. She had been carrying another man's child all this time, and he had never suspected. Had she planned to pass off Porterfield's bastard as his own? What a final irony it would have been if she had succeeded. This explained why she had been so agreeable and cooperative these past weeks. The bitch had been planning to tell him the child was his.

Yet today she had been different: angry, defiant. What had happened to cause that change?

Grimly, he lifted her limp body from where it lay on the icy ground, aware of how pale and still she was. How badly was she hurt, he wondered, ignoring the alarm that flashed through him. Surely Charlotte would recover once she was cared for properly. Still, he quickened his pace towards the road. He would send someone back for their mounts, for he could not safely transport Charlotte on horseback. When he reached chemin de St Louis, he would flag down a wagon to return them to the city.

His hold tightened around the girl in his arms. Charlotte was the most beautiful possession he had ever owned, a prize among women and a symbol of his victory over the Porterfields. He would not give her up, either to the memory of a man he had defeated or to the unborn child that might claim her life.

'Damn you, Porterfield!' he mumbled as he gathered Charl even closer to protect her from the rising wind. 'I'll see you in hell for this. I swear I will.'

❖

The fine, warm January day that had beckoned Charl and Felix outdoors for a ride changed suddenly. The wind abruptly stirred to life and the temperature plummeted, refreezing the puddles at the sides of the roads. A pelting snow began to fall just at dusk, but even that could not force Waukee from his post across the street from St James' rooms.

He had been about to leave when a farm wagon turned into the street and pulled up in front of St James' house. Felix had leaped down from the wagon and ordered the driver to call for his servant. Then, with concern etching his gaunt features, he carefully lifted a woman's body from the back of the cart. A profusion of golden hair spilled across his arm as he held her, and for a moment Waukee glimpsed a familiar face, smudged with dirt and blood, but otherwise devoid of colour. At the sight his mouth went dry, and it was only by the greatest effort of will that he controlled the impulse to rush forward to find out what had happened. With his heart in his throat, the Indian watched St James carry Charl into the house. Only then did Waukee cross the street to question the driver.

The man's knowledge was frustratingly sketchy. The pair had

been by the side of chemin de St Louis when he came past in his wagon. There had been a riding accident, and the girl had fallen from her horse. She remained unconscious for the entire trip, and the major seemed very agitated by her condition.

As they talked, St James' servant bustled past them and some time later returned with a man who appeared to be a doctor. In a frenzy of frustration and concern, Waukee watched them enter the house, wondering about the extent of Charl's injuries. For the next hours the Indian waited grimly, maintaining his silent vigil as the daylight faded and the weather worsened. The hour grew late and the lamps that had been lit at dusk in the houses up and down the street were extinguished one by one. Still Waukee waited, for, in spite of his hunger and the bitter cold, he could not bring himself to leave until he knew Charl would recover.

It was after midnight when the door to the narrow, white-washed building opened and the doctor emerged. His shoulders were hunched with weariness, but he straightened abruptly when Waukee called to him from the shadows.

'Doctor!' he repeated as he crossed the street to where the doctor had paused beneath a street lamp.

'Yes?' the man replied warily, eyeing the tall figure. 'What is it you want?'

'Charlotte Beckwith, the girl in Major St James' rooms, is a friend of mine,' Waukee began. 'I saw them bring her in this afternoon, and I wanted to know how she was faring.'

The doctor gazed up into the Indian's face in amazement. Had this man been waiting in the cold all these hours for word of his friend? There was no doubt of his sincerity for his face was drawn with concern. The more intriguing question was how one of Felix St James' fancy women had come to win such loyalty from an Indian.

In truth he probably shouldn't tell this man anything, the doctor reasoned. But there was a quiet desperation in the Indian's dark face that touched a sympathetic response in him. He could at least answer the man, though God knows the news wasn't good. The smaller man sighed and his shoulders drooped once more.

'Miss Beckwith had a bad fall from her horse this afternoon,' the doctor said quietly. 'She has two broken ribs and a nasty gash on her head. Any other time we'd have her right as rain in a couple of weeks. But she was pregnant, and as a result of the accident she lost the child she was carrying.'

He paused, watching a dazed look come into the Indian's eyes. He laid one hand against the dark man's sleeve, sensing the pain that would come in response to his next words.

'I've tried everything I know to stop the haemorrhaging but nothing helps. I doubt she'll live until morning. I'm sorry.'

Waukee stared wordlessly at the doctor for a full minute, waiting for something, anything, that might offer him hope for Charl's recovery. When the man remained silent, Waukee turned blindly and stumbled off into the night.

In a haze of sorrow and disbelief he made his way back to the La Soeur house. Perhaps if he had overtaken Charl the other day, she would be well and safe now, he reflected bitterly. He had been able to get Seth out of Quebec in time, but for Charl he had come too late.

Waukee let himself in the back door and paused on his way to Gabrielle's room only long enough to stir the fire in the kitchen hearth to life and put the kettle on to boil. Gabrielle would want to know what had happened, and he needed her understanding. In these past days, while he awaited his chance to rescue Charl from St James, Gabby's support had been invaluable. Now he wanted the company of someone who would feel this loss as deeply as he did.

Gabrielle answered the knock on her bedroom door at once although her eyes were heavy lidded with sleep.

'What's the matter?' she asked immediately, taking in Waukee's ravaged expression.

'It's Charl,' he said softly.

Some time later, they sat at the planked oak table in the kitchen staring morosely into the wavering fire. Waukee had been half frozen from the hours he had spent waiting outside St James' apartments, but the brandy Gabrielle had poured into his tea and the food she had set out before him had helped.

'Seth never even knew about the child,' Waukee mused, swirling the remaining tea in his cup absently.

Gabrielle pulled her wrapper tighter against the winter chill that seeped through the doors and windows.

'Charl was afraid to tell him. She thought he would be angry.'

'She was mistaken. It would have pleased him to know that Charl was carrying his child. It might even have given him reason to believe in her when St James told him lies.'

Gabrielle poured more tea from the pewter pot and then added a tot of brandy to each cup.

'Will you tell Seth what happened?' she asked, glancing into his bronzed face. His expression was bleak, empty, and she understood the reason for his pain.

'In time, when he's ready to hear it,' the Indian answered. They sat in silence as the fire died to embers and the storm worsened outside. The timbers creaked in the gale, and the wind roared down the chimney as snow fell in blinding waves of white across Quebec.

'What will you do now?' the woman asked finally.

Waukee shrugged.

'I told Seth I was going west, back to my people. That still seems like a good plan. I will return to my homeland and try to live in peace,' he answered slowly.

'And what about you, Gabrielle? Will things go on as always for you here?'

The dark-haired woman's lips curved in the slightest of smiles.

'I am going to tell Emile Savard that I will marry him,' she told Waukee. 'He asked me weeks ago, but I have been putting him off. Now I am going to tell him "yes".

'Oh, he's not all I wished for once. But he's a good man: kind, resourceful, hard working. We understand each other. And I do not want to spend the rest of my days alone.'

She paused as she gathered up the cups and spoons they had used, then went on, as if to confirm her decision.

'I had my time with William, but with love there is no promise of forever. Forever is a condition man tries to force upon fate, but with little success.'

She turned to Waukee.

'You must not be sad. Charl had her time with Seth. She knew the sweetness of their love and the joy of carrying his child. There are many women who live far longer than Charl has, but few who know more happiness.'

Waukee nodded and slowly came to his feet. His wide shoulders sagged with weariness, and his dark eyes were ringed with shadows.

'I will try to remember that for my own comfort, and for Seth as well. When he hears what has happened, his pain and regret will be very great, I fear.'

Gabrielle nodded in agreement.

'You are a good friend to him, Waukee,' she said softly.

He smiled, resting his palms lightly on her slight shoulders.

'And you are a very wise woman, Gabrielle. You deserve every happiness.'

There was a long silence between them as they stood together in the dawn. Then Waukee straightened and turned to the door. With a hard knot of tears in her throat, Gabrielle watched him trudge through the snowdrifts towards the stable to rest before he gathered his gear for the trek west.

Twenty-Nine

✥✥✥

In those long, bleak, pain-filled hours after they had brought her back to St James' rooms, Charl had wanted to die. They must have expected her to die, for a priest had come to administer last rites. And she had tried to die. Having lost the child that had become her one reason for living, she had willed herself into endless oblivion to escape her despair.

In the shadowy, half-memories of that first night she could hear her own voice pleading:

'Doctor, you must save my baby. Please. I want to keep my baby.'

His reply had come impatient and yet gentle as he bent over her.

'I'm sorry, my dear. It's too late. There's nothing more I can do. Now lie still and let me bandage your head.'

There were feverish dreams that wove through her consciousness, leaving her as spent as the pain that twisted through her body. In her head visions came and went: of her father, calling to her from the front steps of their home as he had done when she was a child, of Stephen Langley with a pistol in his hand, of Gabrielle and Waukee. Then Seth rose up before her, his blue eyes cold and his voice filled with accusation.

'You betrayed me. You betrayed me . . .'

Even in the depths of her torment she accepted his reproach. It was true. In a moment of anger and madness she had miscarried his child. She had failed to guard the sacred trust he had left in her care. Seth was dead, and now there was nothing of him that would live on in his child.

'I'm sorry. I'm sorry,' she had whispered endlessly through lips parched with fever, while tears slipped from the corners of her eyes to trace glistening tracks into her hair.

Charl turned her head listlessly from the sunlight that intruded on her sickroom and spilled with cheery brilliance across the foot

of her bed. It was more than three weeks since her accident, and
her body had begun to mend. The fever and the headaches were
gone and her ribs seldom pained her, but the aching emptiness
inside her could not be assuaged. For as long as the doctor would
allow it, she was content to lie in bed, staring fixedly at the
ceiling, her mind blank.

There was one recollection from those first days, though, that
haunted her. Try as she might, she could not put it out of her
mind.

Late one night she had awakened to find St James sitting beside
the bed, holding her hand. His face had been drawn with fatigue,
but he was smiling.

'Felix!' she had mumbled in surprise.

His smile deepened at the sound of his name on her lips and
he moved closer.

'The doctor says you are better,' he told her.

Her eyes filled with tears as she nodded.

'But I lost my child.'

He smoothed her tumbled hair.

'I know, Charlotte. I know,' he comforted her. 'You must not
cry any more. It's just as well that you lost the child. The St
Jameses would never claim another Porterfield bastard. Now you
must sleep, Charlotte, to regain your strength. I am anxious for
you to recover.'

Now that she was better, that conversation puzzled her. Nor
could she dismiss it as a dream. What had Felix meant by 'another
Porterfield bastard'? Was he talking about Seth? But Seth had
no claim on the St James family. The conversation nagged at her,
but she could not bring herself to ask Felix for an explanation.

The doctor came daily and finally expressed the opinion that
she was well enough to be out of bed. She greeted that news with
the same apathy that had marked all her days since the accident.

'You should be happy to be making such fine progress,' he
chided her. 'In no time you will have recovered completely.'

His face softened.

'I know you grieve for the loss of your child, but there can be
other children.'

Charl turned away in panic. Other children. The thought
overwhelmed her. There could never be another child with Seth
as its father, and she had no desire to bear another man's children.

It was not long before Charl's physical recovery was complete.

By the bitter blustery days of mid-March she was able to take up the threads of her life with St James. She played at musicals, dressed in the elegant gowns Felix bought for her with the winnings at the gaming tables. They were guests at half a dozen parties and balls in the gay week before Lent began. And when the doctor told St James it was safe, Charl returned to his bed.

Now Charl moved through every phase of her life with the same vacant complacency, acquiescing to all of Felix's demands because nothing mattered. To survive the double loss of Seth and their child she had been forced to deny her emotions. In her need to retreat from her pain and grief she had no choice but to forfeit anger, outrage, and pride as well.

A strange, haunted look came into the depths of her sea-green eyes, and she moved like a pale shadow of the woman she had been. Yet there was something compelling about her frail, almost painful beauty. It was as if the distance she kept between herself and her world served only to draw men closer. Men came to her side with a need to protect her. Yet each one hoped to win a response from her that had been denied to all the others.

Nor was Felix St James immune to Charl's appeal. He was as seduced by her indifference as the others, but he was secure in the knowledge that she belonged to him, by right of possession and conquest. Still, as often as he plundered her body, the essence of her remained untouchable, ever elusive and ever compelling.

During the first week in April, he received orders to go west. Since he had long chafed under the monotony of his duties in Quebec and General Prevost's reticence, he was delighted by the prospect. For as much as he enjoyed the luxuries and social life Quebec had to offer, he preferred the promise of action. He had been assigned to Fort Malden, on the Detroit River near Amhurstburg, under General Proctor. It was Henry Proctor who had assumed command of the Northwest forces from General Isaac Brock after the American defeat at Detroit the previous October. The garrison was not a large one, but with the help of several thousand Indian allies under Tecumseh, the English presence was evident along the entire Western Frontier. The hope of confrontation with the Americans, and the probable career advancement that would result, was a challenge St James welcomed.

The supply train with which the major and several companies

of reinforcements were to travel was scheduled to leave on 15 April. Thus, he had only slightly more than a fortnight to conclude his affairs in Quebec and prepare his household for the trip. There was never any question that Charl would accompany him. She had come to be a possession he would not relinquish easily, and she was expected to follow him wherever he went. Charl received the news of their impending departure with her usual apathy, asking only how long the journey would take. Primarily, through the Herculean efforts of his servant, Ellis, everything was ready when the wagon they had been assigned rolled out of Quebec just before dawn on the appointed day.

Charl drew her cloak closer against the brisk April wind and looked back at the city, knowing she would never return. Her life in Quebec was over, and she was filled with grave regrets. For the first time in many weeks tears came, sliding silently down her flushed cheeks, eroding the icy wall she had built around her heart.

Because the St Lawrence would not be passable until mid-May, the supply train jolted along on a road that ran in full view of the swollen, raging river. They passed through Trois-Rivières, Montreal, and arrived at Kingston at the head of Lake Ontario after many days' travel.

Charl tried not to remember the journey she had made along this same route less than a year before with Waukee and Seth, just as she tried to forget the strange mixture of camaraderie and antagonism that marked their passage. Still, many of the things she had learned on that journey to Quebec stood her in good stead as they travelled west. Felix was pleasantly surprised that she did not complain about the rough way they were forced to travel and their nightly stops in the forest. He had arranged for her to have a narrow bed in their wagon, but there was little he could do to provide other facilities for her comfort. Still Charl did not seem to mind.

When it became obvious that Ellis could not cope with cooking over an open fire, Charl voluntarily began to prepare their meals, amazing Felix with her skill and the variety of the menus. Still, it rankled with him that she had willingly assumed tasks no lady would consider performing, and while he appreciated the meals she prepared, he was appalled by her knowledge and skill. She even welcomed the addition of game to the larder, skinning and preparing the animals with an efficiency that any man would envy. She even selected greens from the forest itself to relieve the tedium of dried corn and beans.

At Kingston they turned on to a less-travelled road that rimmed the lakeshore. Normally, supplies would have been loaded into boats for transport to Newark and Fort George via York, but the lake was not safe for travel. Both the British and the Americans had spent the winter preparing to battle for control of the vital Great Lakes water system. Now that the lake ice had melted with the coming of spring, an attack could be expected at any time.

As they travelled, Charl was torn between melancholy memories of this same journey with Seth and the inevitable joy spring always awoke in her. The trees were bursting into leaf, the lacy, green whorls popping almost overnight into broad, emerald leaves that moved restlessly in the insistent wind off the lake. Mornings were masked with cold fog that shrouded the treetops and turned the lake steamy and mysterious. Yet by midday Charl was able to doff her heavy cloak and bonnet and turn her face up to the sun. Verdant, earthy smells were in the air, and the trees were noisy with chirping birds. Crisp, white dogwood blossoms were like swarms of butterflies against the budding greenery, and the forest floor was alive with yellow cowslip and starry trillium. For the first time in months, Charl was intensely aware of the beauty of life around her, and she reached out to it with unqualified eagerness.

Word of an attack on York came by way of a rider sent east to rouse militia units. Immediately St James and the troops prepared to march, but they reached the small settlement too late to repel the enemy raiders. The Americans had already retreated, leaving in their wake devastated fortifications and burned-out buildings.

The next morning when Charl arrived in York with the supply wagons, she came face to face with war, and the confrontation left her heartily shaken. In the still-smouldering rubble and in the ravaged faces of the citizenry, she recognized the terrible futility of fighting. The political issues, the expansionist philosophy, and the fiery rhetoric that had begun this conflict had never seemed less viable than when she looked out over this ruined town. It did not matter that these people were her enemies, for in their haunted eyes she saw the fate of countless numbers of her countrymen. During their stay in York, Charl offered what aid and comfort she could to the hurt and homeless. Even when York was far behind them, the image of the destruction she had seen there haunted her.

After York she grew strangely restless. Her perch on the high seat at the front of their wagon beside Ellis became intolerable. Except for the condition of the road, she would gladly have walked beside the wagon. Instead she began to wander off into the woods or along the lakeshore while the men were making camp. St James was understandably suspicious of her periodic disappearances. Convinced that she was about to run away, he began to monitor her movements more and more carefully. They were only a day and a half from Fort George and the Niagara River when Felix made his decision. That night after dinner he sought Charl out, with a bottle of wine for them to share. Three days later she awoke to find that the wagons were preparing to leave on the trek along the shore of Lake Erie.

'I'm glad to see you're finally better,' he told her as he finished shaving, using the mirror she had hung from one of the ribs that supported the canvas top. 'You've had a fever for several days.'

Her eyelids were heavy, and her head felt stuffed with cotton.

'I want you to stay in bed all day today,' he went on solicitously. 'Perhaps tomorrow you will be well enough to get up.' Bending, he straightened the covers and tucked them snugly around her. 'Now just rest.'

As the wagons creaked on, Charl slept again, awakening at midday. For a time she lay watching the shadows of branches move across the arched canvas above her head.

There was no question of what Felix had done, she reflected, as she brushed the tangled hair from her face. He had been afraid she would try to slip across the river to Youngstown when she had the chance, so he had drugged her – drugged her just as he had in Quebec, the night she had betrayed Seth.

Restlessly she moved beneath the blankets. How naïve she still was when it came to dealing with St James. And how ironic it was that he had gone to all this trouble when escape had never entered her mind. Would it have, she wondered, if she had been able to look across the river gorge and see the chimneys of her father's house poking through the trees? Or had she lost all desire to be free? She had fought Seth so long and hard for a chance to return home. Why didn't that seem to matter to her now? Why didn't she feel anything but weariness and resignation? She closed her eyes again, unable or unwilling to see the answers to her questions. Instead she took refuge in sleep.

The next day dawned warm and fresh, renewing Charl's restlessness until she could barely tolerate the confines of the wagon seat.

'Felix, please, may I ride for a while this afternoon?' she begged when he drew rein beside their wagon just before midday. 'I know there are some extra horses with the wagon train.'

He frowned deeply at her request.

'Really, Charlotte. This is a military convoy, not a social outing. None of our horses are equipped with sidesaddles. Besides it would be most unseemly for a major's lady to behave in such a manner.'

'Felix, please –' she began, but he spurred his horse away, effectively closing the subject.

However Charl was not without resources of her own. The next morning she appeared astride one of the extra horses, having convinced an attractive young ostler that she was indeed capable of handling the beast. It felt wonderful to ride again after months of inactivity, and she managed to avoid Felix until just before their noon stop.

He pulled up beside her, eyeing the expanse of shapely leg that was exposed where her skirt had ridden up.

'Just what do you think you're doing?' he demanded, his dark eyebrows drawn together.

'I just couldn't bear another day in the wagon,' she told him. 'Please, Felix, don't be angry.'

He took in her flushed cheeks and sparkling eyes and said no more. But at midday he drew her aside to continue the conversation.

'You're a major's lady and I'll not have you disgrace me by riding with your skirts hitched up like some hoyden. Do you hear me, Charlotte?' he blustered at her.

'Yes, Felix,' she had answered, her eyes cast down obediently.

'Good! Then it's settled,' he concluded.

But the matter was far from ended, for the next morning Charl emerged from her wagon dressed in a pair of white breeches she had borrowed from one of the more slender soldiers. Wearing a frilled blouse and high boots, she made a most fetching picture that the men readily appreciated. She managed to elude St James until late in the afternoon, and when they stopped for the night he pulled her roughly into the wagon. His face was flushed red with rage as he stood over her.

'You disobeyed me!' he began in a voice that could be heard throughout the camp.

'Oh no, Felix!' she answered meekly as she sat before him with lowered eyes. 'I didn't mean to disobey you. You said I couldn't ride with my skirts hitched up. I thought that the breeches seemed like a perfect solution!'

'Breeches! Good God! Breeches! Women don't wear breeches. What's possessed you?'

The deep green eyes that rose to meet his were wet and filled with contrition.

'I'm sorry, Felix,' she apologized soberly.

He drew a long breath. She certainly seemed contrite.

'Very well, Charlotte. Tomorrow you will ride in the wagon. I won't have you asking my men for their extra clothes. God knows they'll need them in this wilderness. Now take off those garments and give them to me.'

Wordlessly she obeyed, undressing before his stormy eyes and putting the offending article into his outstretched hand.

'Charlotte, I wish you to remember who you are and act accordingly. I will not tolerate a woman who is an embarrassment to me. Is that clear?'

'Yes, Felix,' she replied softly.

'Good,' he snapped as he left the wagon.

He was aware that most of the camp had been privy to the conversation between him and his mistress, just as he had intended them to be. Charl had accomplices in this escapade. Although she would never tell him their names, he wanted them to realize his displeasure. With great ceremony he stalked to the central campfire, which was now burning brightly, and made a show of casting the offending breeches into the flames. Then he stood silently, watching them slowly turn to ashes.

The next day Charl returned to her place beside Ellis on the high wagon seat. Dressed in a demure lilac gown with its lace ruching and fluttering black velvet ribbons, she looked every inch the lady. With a small smile St James congratulated himself on his success in handling what might have become an embarrassing situation. Women were like horses, he reflected. They needed to be reminded occasionally who wore the spurs, no matter how loosely the reins were held.

It was several days later, after Charl had resentfully resigned herself to riding on the wagon seat for the remainder of the journey, that she discovered a plainly wrapped package in her trunk. With her curiosity aroused, she tore open the bundle. To her amazement she found a pair of pale grey breeches inside that seemed just her size. Without hesitation she dropped her skirt and petticoat, then pulled them on, buttoning them snugly at her waist. She had no idea who the anonymous donor could be, but the implications of the gift were clear. Someone had approved of her attire the day she had worn her borrowed trousers as much as Felix had disapproved of it. Now whoever that was intended to offer her another opportunity to savour that same freedom.

She should not consider wearing them, she realized. It would surely cause her nothing but trouble and Felix would be livid. But then, what more could he do to hurt her?

Charl's chin rose stubbornly, and for the first time in months defiance flickered in the depths of her eyes. She would wear the breeches and ride freely along the length of the convoy once more before they reached Fort Malden. And when Felix found out, he could do as he pleased with her.

As it turned out, St James spent most of the next day attending to a wagon that had broken an axle on the rutted road and did not discover his mistress's defiance until he returned to camp that evening.

For one long, golden day Charl revelled in the freedom Felix's absence afforded her. At first she was content to canter along beside the slow-moving convoy. But by mid-morning she was galloping further and further afield, like a feckless colt cavorting in the spring sunshine. Only when she was far ahead would she draw rein and wait for the ponderous progression of wagons to catch up to her. Nor was there a man, common soldier, or officer, who did not appreciate the sight of her galloping along, laughing and carefree, with her thick, yellow hair tumbling around her shoulders.

Charl's face was bathed in the warm, amber glow of firelight as she sat tending the stew she was making for dinner. From across the clearing St James noticed her at her task and stopped to smile to himself. A hot meal would be welcome after the aggravations of the day. Then, as he watched, Charl rose to add something to her pot of stew, and he became aware of her attire.

He glared at her for a full minute across the flickering flames as his anger grew inside him. Charl was wearing men's breeches and had undoubtedly spent her day astride a horse. Nor was the worst of it that she had been behaving like a hoyden. In donning breeches, against his expressed instructions, she had defied him before the entire company. For that he could never forgive her. Rage swirled in his head until he was aware of nothing but Charl's disobedience. He took the space that separated them in three long strides and dragged the startled girl to her feet.

'I thought I made my views on women's attire abundantly clear, Charlotte,' he hissed as his grip tightened on her shoulders.

As she stood before him, trying to muster her defences, St James became aware of the crowd that had begun to gather around them. Without losing his hold on Charl, he glanced around at the faces illuminated by the firelight. They were tense with anticipation, anger, concern, or filled with contempt and disdain. As angry as he was, Felix realized he dare not punish Charl for her defiance because each of these men considered himself her protector. To give Charl the beating she so richly deserved would be to turn his own men against him. Yet to ignore her insolence would be to undermine his authority and open himself to ridicule.

Impotent rage churned through him as his narrowed eyes came to rest on the woman who stood half cringing and half defiant before him. Whether he chose to ignore or punish her, Charl's open rebellion could cost him his command. There was but one choice left to him.

Slowly he released his hold on her shoulders and masked the searing hatred in his eyes.

'I thought I made my views on women in breeches quite clear, Charlotte,' he reiterated, 'but perhaps I was too hasty. You look very fetching tonight. If you want to continue to wear your borrowed attire, I have no objections.'

St James was only able to say those words by reminding himself sternly that retreat was often as valid a manoeuvre as attack. The time would come when Charl would be in a more vulnerable position than she was tonight. And when that time came, he would take his revenge for this defeat at her hands. With what grace he could muster, he turned and stalked off into the darkness.

Part Three
✳✳✳

The West

Thirty
✼✼✼

From behind a screen of pipe smoke, General William Henry Harrison, revered Indian fighter and commander-in-chief of the American forces in the northwest, observed the newest addition to his military staff. The captain's sturdy, sun-browned hands moved across the carefully drawn map to indicate the possible deployment of the new British troops that had arrived at Fort Malden only the week before. With sapient insight, he outlined the advantages and disadvantages of each position and what countermeasures might be undertaken to prevent the enemy from gaining any more control over the lands to the west of the Maumee River in Ohio. The crisp, precise answers that he gave to the other officers' questions gave evidence of his understanding of the seriousness of the situation.

Harrison sat back in his chair with a frown and drew raspingly on his pipe as he watched the younger man. This Captain Porterfield was certainly a puzzle, he mused. He seemed English to the core. His deep, cultured voice, the casual polish to his manners, the way he carried himself all spoke of an upper-crust English background and a proper education at Oxford or Cambridge. Yet his loyalty to the American cause was unimpeachable. The papers that had accompanied him were quite extraordinary, consisting of a brief note from Secretary of War Armstrong and a longer letter from Malcolm Mitchell, one of the secretary's special advisers, enumerating Porterfield's qualifications.

There had been no indication of previous commands or assignments, and as Harrison observed his new officer, he began to suspect that the commission had not come in the usual way. Seth Porterfield was too intolerant of the chain of command and too ignorant of protocol to have had much experience with military life. But then, it was not unusual for officers to have been appointed for friendship or political reasons. It was one of the things that undermined any real effort on the part of the Americans to gain a victory. Well, perhaps once Perry had secured Lake Erie, they could press on into Canada and defeat the British.

From somewhere, though, this Captain Porterfield had picked up an extensive background in military history and an unerring grasp of battle strategy. Harrison's frown deepened. Then, too, Porterfield knew the terrain around Fort Meigs as if he had been born here, and he was an accomplished woodsman. Nor was Harrison surprised to learn that Porterfield spoke the Indian language as well as any of the translators the Army employed.

There was no question that Porterfield was ideally suited to the nebulous post of officer-scout that Mitchell had suggested for him. Officially he was a member of the general's staff, with the same duties as the other officers, but he had been given the freedom to ride out on his own. When he did, it was a safe bet that he would return with detailed maps or invaluable bits of information about British plans. Harrison never questioned him about his sources, but it was common knowledge that he rarely rode out in uniform. Speculation ran high that he travelled freely into British territory and to Fort Malden itself.

Harrison watched Porterfield take a seat at the far side of the table, and another officer rose to give his report. But the general could not put the Englishman out of his mind. He was avidly curious about his background and how he had come to be assigned to Fort Meigs. But Porterfield's demeanour did not invite questioning. It was not that he was unfriendly exactly, just intensely private and aloof. Even Anna, the general's wife, had not been able to draw him out. With women he was icily formal, although his looks could easily send feminine hearts aflutter. And if he had not attended the few social functions the fort had to offer, it was not for lack of encouragement from that quarter.

The general stirred in his chair and tried, with little success, to turn his attention back to what was being said.

He should thank his lucky stars for a man as superbly capable as Seth Porterfield was. Wasn't it enough that his men liked and respected him? Or that he had proved himself courageous and cool-headed in battle? It was as much to his credit as anyone's that the party, sent to spike the cannon on the south bank of the river during Proctor's attack earlier in the month, had succeeded. Seth Porterfield embodied the dashing, invincible, romantic image of a soldier at war; but there was more to him than that. And the general wanted to know what secrets were hidden behind those shaded blue eyes.

The last officer sat down when he had completed his report, and Harrison cleared his throat.

'Thank you, gentlemen. Now if there is no new business,' Harrison paused, and his gaze swept from face to face around the table, 'I believe we can adjourn, as it is nearly dinnertime.'

They rose with a scraping of chairs and a tumult of voices and made their way out of the stuffy smoke-filled room. Seth paused only long enough to roll the map he had used and tuck it under his arm before he followed the others.

'Captain Porterfield.' Harrison's voice halted Seth at the doorway, and he turned slowly to face his commanding officer.

'Yes, sir.'

'That was a mighty fine map you used for your report – clear but with good detail. Who was it that drew it for you?'

Seth smiled. 'I draw my own maps, sir.'

Harrison's bushy eyebrows rose as another of this man's accomplishments came to light.

'I should have known,' the general muttered, then went on more loudly. 'And where was it you learned mapmaking?'

'My first trip west was with a party of surveyors,' Seth told him. Harrison waited for the younger officer to elaborate, but Porterfield remained silent, his eyes hooded and opaque. It seemed that instead of being flattered by the commander's interest, as most men would have been, this captain preferred his privacy.

After a full minute of silence, Seth spoke.

'If the general has no more questions, there are some matters that require my attention.' His tone was carefully polite, but the message was one of dismissal.

Harrison could find no fault with Porterfield's manner, and yet irritation stirred through the older man.

'Very well, Porterfield,' he replied gruffly, 'go on about your business. Good evening.'

'Good evening, sir,' Seth replied as he closed the door behind him.

The late afternoon sun slanted across the compound, casting long irregular shadows on the dusty parade ground and the crisp breeze sent small whirlwinds scurrying across the grassless expanse. Inside the small canvas tent he shared with another officer, Seth removed his coat and bicorne hat and hung them on a nail in the main tentpost. With a long sigh he stretched out on the cot.

Lord, he was tired, Seth thought as he crossed his arms beneath his head. He'd been in the saddle nearly three days, meeting various informants who kept him abreast of British activities around Detroit. When he returned to the fort just before noon, there had barely been time to complete the map and prepare the report he had presented at the staff meeting.

What he was doing now, in the guise of an American army captain, was not so different from what he'd done in Mitchell's employ. He gathered, interpreted, and passed on information. But this time his information went directly to Harrison, who could act on it, rather than to Mitchell, who only passed it on to the War Department. He wore a uniform now, but his role and the risks were very much the same.

Seth closed his eyes and drew a long breath, allowing himself to think for the first time about one scrap of information that he had seen no reason to include in his report to Harrison. It would be of little interest or importance to anyone but himself that among the officers who had arrived with the new troops at Fort Malden was one Major Felix St James. Seth had been momentarily stunned when his informant had mentioned the name. He had not expected to encounter his old nemesis so soon, and he could not help wondering what quirk of fate had brought him west.

Under careful questioning, he had learned from that same source that several women had accompanied the wagon train. One tall, yellow-haired girl had scandalized the entire encampment by arriving astride a horse and dressed, most becomingly according to his informant, in men's breeches. There was not a doubt in Seth's mind as to her identity.

The idea that Charl was only a matter of miles away, rather than half a continent as he had thought, unsettled him. As he remembered the way she had looked the last time he'd seen her in Quebec, he was torn between anger that she had somehow managed to follow him here and an almost overwhelming desire to brave Fort Malden to see her for himself. Of course, it was madness to even consider such a thing, he chided himself. There were any number of people, besides Charl and St James, who might recognize him. He had travelled frequently in this area before the war and was known to the Indians who were now allies of the British. And if he was discovered out of uniform, behind British lines, they would not even bother with a trial before the hanging. Obviously, Charl's power to lead him into danger was not diminished by all that had passed between them.

Seth sighed again and moved restlessly.

What would he hope to gain by going to Fort Malden? he asked himself. Charl had betrayed him, and he hated her. Was the chance to confront her worth risking his life?

He had not let himself think about Charl these past months, except to fan the fires of hatred, but as he floated free, just outside the realm of sleep, a vision of her came to him. There was the feel of her thick, golden hair between his fingers; the sound of her soft, clear voice in his ears; and her sweet lemon fragrance all about him. He remembered how those wide, sea green eyes would look up at him, alight with love and laughter, and how soft her body felt in his arms. With haunting clarity he recalled the silky warmth of her skin and the taste of that sweet, coral mouth against his own. Desire for her throbbed through him, sweeping away all considerations of danger in his reckless need for this one woman.

'Porterfield? Are you coming to dinner?'

The voice from the doorway jerked Seth awake, and he sat up suddenly, feeling light-headed and disoriented.

'What?' he asked dazedly.

It was Captain John Bartlett, whose tent he shared.

'I'm sorry,' Bartlett apologized. 'I didn't realize you were asleep. I asked if you were coming to dinner.'

'Yes, I am. In a minute. You go ahead,' Seth answered as he sat at the edge of the cot, caught between dream and reality.

Bartlett's dark head disappeared from the tent flap, and Seth was left alone with his thoughts.

For several minutes more, he sat hunched on the edge of the bed, waiting for the thudding of his heart to slow and for the images from his dream to fade.

He could not go to Fort Malden, that much was clear. For if the memory of Charl could send his blood racing, what would happen if he confronted her?

He shook his head as if to clear Charl from his brain, then hauled himself to his feet. At the washstand outside the tent he poured cold water into the tin basin and doused his head. Still her presence remained, woven through every level of his consciousness.

Bracing his hands at the edges of the basin, he stared down into the water.

'I hate you, woman,' he whispered huskily. 'For all your treachery I put you from me. Now leave me alone. Just leave me alone!'

Thirty-One

�֍✫✫

The life at Fort Malden was very different from the one Charl and St James had lived in Quebec. Their accommodation in a rustic, two-room cabin was a far cry from the luxury of the rooms in rue des Jardins. Furnishings were sparse, consisting of a table and three chairs, a dilapidated trunk, and a low rope bed in the curtained alcove that served as the second room. It took three days of sweeping, scrubbing, and whitewashing to make the place habitable, but with curtains on the windows and rag rugs on the floor, the place began to take shape.

St James, and Ellis as well, had been pressed into immediate service for the multitude of projects underway to strengthen the fortifications along the Detroit River, and Charl was left primarily to her own devices from the start. It did not take her long to realize that in spite of the myriad of goods the wagon train had carried west, supplies were short. From what she could gather, the sheer number of Indians who had built encampments around the fort and who demanded food and other goods in return for their continued loyalty quickly depleted whatever stockpiles the British managed to amass. Nor was the overland trail they had followed west the most efficient route of transportation. But until the Great Lakes were secured by either the British or the Americans, neither country dared use the waterways.

Charl adjusted surprisingly well to her new role. But then, she had kept house for her father, shared Gabrielle's duties, and was no stranger to frontier living. She worked hard at her chores: cooking and cleaning, mending and washing, until she fairly lost herself in the never-ending work. She accepted her new life easily, welcoming the sense of accomplishment and mind-numbing exhaustion she'd earned by the end of the day. She drove herself mercilessly, so that there was no time to think about Seth or the child she had carried. As she struggled to rebuild her life, hard work filled the void that had been created by their loss.

The only leisure she allowed herself was a daily ride, taken early in the morning while the world was lit with dawn. While most people lay snug in their beds, Charl thundered across the dewy countryside, enjoying the crisp morning air. She did not confine herself to the well-travelled roads around the fort or to the streets of Amhurstburg, but galloped along the river or picked her way through the forest on overgrown trails.

It was one morning, as she made her way silently through the trees, that she came upon two men who had paused in a clearing. With the sun in her eyes she could see no more than their dark silhouettes, but their pose suggested a clandestine purpose to their meeting. One of the men was an Indian, with a fan of feathers in his hair and a quiver full of arrows slung over his shoulder. Judging by the cut of his clothes, the other was a white man, his face obscured by a slouch-brimmed hat. For no reason she could name, she drew rein and sat watching them from behind a bank of wild grape vines. Then, quite suddenly, an overwhelming swell of tears rose in her throat as she realized how strongly this second man reminded her of Seth. She could not say if it was the set of his shoulders or some small, unconscious gesture that awakened her memories. But if she had not known better, she would have sworn it was Seth Porterfield who sat astride his horse not fifty feet from her.

If she made a sound, she was not aware of it, but both men started suddenly, then moved off through the undergrowth in opposite directions.

Unsettled by the incident, Charl gave up her morning rides for the best part of a week. But finally restlessness overcame her, and she reluctantly resumed them. After that, however, she confined herself to riding on the riverbank below the town or the main roads.

St James was having a good deal more difficulty adjusting to life at Fort Malden than Charl. He missed the luxuries Quebec had to offer and the leisure that an officer at a frontier outpost could ill afford. He had been accustomed to working somewhat independently for General Prevost and now found the tedium of a regular command weighed heavily on him. It was to his eternal frustration that he had missed Proctor's siege on Fort Meigs in May, indecisive though it was, and he chafed under the command of more seasoned officers who had been involved in the operation. Initially, he had rejoiced in this assignment in his quest for action and advancement, but now Proctor seemed as mired in indecision as Prevost had been. As the fine, fair days of early summer slipped past, he railed against his commander's inactivity.

But in mid-July the Indians began to gather. There had always been a number of Indians who moved freely in and out of the fort, but now that number doubled and tripled. Then one day as Charl stood watching from the doorway of their cabin, Tecumseh rode in.

Flanked by his chiefs and a small band of warriors, he made an imposing figure. He was a tall man, obviously in the prime of his life, built solid and strong as an oak. In his fawn-coloured buckskins he stood out from the rest of his band and the red-clad British officers who had come to welcome him like gold in a bed of rough stones. His features were hard and uncompromising, and he sported an ostrich plume in his hair as a symbol of his authority.

In those first few moments Tecumseh equalled and surpassed everything Charl had expected, and she could hardly keep her eyes off him. Then to her left there was a small disturbance from a group of officers' wives who had gathered to watch the ceremony. There was much fluttering of fans and rolling of eyes, as if they were discomfited by the Indian presence in the fort.

'Silly fools,' Charl muttered as she levelled a quelling look at the other women. Didn't they realize this man's importance? Without the Indian allies the British could never hope to hold the Western territories, much less force the Americans back over the Appalachian Mountains, as St James had explained was the British goal. With the greatest difficulty she restrained the impulse to speak to them sharply.

Then, as she turned back to the scene before her, she caught the disapproving eye of one young warrior. In his expression was a reprimand as sharp as any she had ever received, and she longed to protest her innocence in creating the uproar. Pointedly he turned back to the greeting General Proctor was offering his chief, but Charl continued to glare at him over the heads of the crowd.

He sat proudly astride his horse only three rows behind Tecumseh, in a place of honour for one so young. Undoubtedly he had won distinction in battle against the Americans, and in truth he

looked as fierce as any man she had ever seen. Dressed in black
leather leggings and a dark woven shirt, he seemed forbidding
and dangerous. He had a bullish build, with heavy arms and
shoulders and short sturdy legs. Charl doubted that he would
stand much taller than she, but there was leashed power in every
line of his body.

The Indian must have sensed Charl's gaze upon him, for he
turned suddenly and looked directly at her. His coal-black eyes
raked her from head to toe as Proctor concluded his speech.
Then his party dismounted, and he was lost from her sight in the
milling crowd.

The influx of Indians did indeed mean that something was
brewing, that within a few days the garrison was preparing for
an attack on the American supply depot on the Sandusky River.
The attack was to serve a dual purpose. Initially it would deprive
Harrison and the men at Fort Meigs of supplies, but in doing
so it would also conveniently refill depleted British coffers as
well.

The troops' destination became common knowledge at Fort
Malden in the days before they planned to march. As Charl
galloped her horse along the grassy riverbank beyond Amhurstburg one morning, she wished she could find some way to warn
the Americans of the forthcoming attack. Seth had given his life
in an attempt to send just this kind of information to her country.
Perhaps if she could get word to General Harrison at Fort Meigs,
it would somehow rectify the blunders she had made in Quebec.

Farther down the bank the greenery fell away, leaving a long
grassy slope down to the water. At a point directly before her in
this clearing, a man stood watching her intently, almost as if he
had been waiting for her. The rising sun at his back cast his
features in shadow, but it caught in his fair hair, turning it brilliant
gold.

At the sight of him Charl drew rein so sharply that her horse
reared up, and it took all her horsemanship to retain her seat.

With difficulty she controlled her skittish mount and stared
across the space that separated them. There was something about
the angle of his head and the contours of his body that set her
pulses throbbing. And even from this distance her eyes seemed
to catch and hold his deep blue ones.

'Seth!' His name was torn from her lips in a ragged whisper.

There was an interminable moment when she could do no

more than stare at him. Then she jerked her mount around and thundered back the way she had come, bent on escape.

She flew along the deserted streets of Amhurstburg and through the fort gates, never slowing her pace until she neared the stables. Her hands were trembling as she led her horse into the stall, and she fumbled clumsily with the cinch and bridle.

Then with quavering breath, she leaned her head against the mare's neck and allowed the tears to come.

Oh God, she thought as she pressed one hand against her mouth to muffle her sobs, I must be going mad. I must surely be insane to have imagined that Seth was at the river this morning.

A tremor shook her and the tears came harder still.

'Seth is dead,' Charl told herself brutally, as if hearing the words aloud could help her accept the horrible reality. 'He has been dead all these months.'

But then why had he seemed so real to her this morning?

She swallowed hard and tried to quell the emotions that flooded through her. She had been thinking about Seth just before she had seen the man on the bank. Was it possible she had conjured him up from longing or projected her loneliness on some stranger?

Charl shivered involuntarily. It was almost as if she had seen his ghost.

'Why are you weeping, woman?' came a deep, male voice from the foot of the stall.

Dashing the tears from her eyes, she turned to face the intruder.

She recognized him instantly. He was the young warrior who had ridden in with Tecumseh.

Charl squared her shoulders. 'I'm not weeping,' she answered stubbornly.

One black eyebrow rose at her barefaced lie.

'And why did you ride into the fort as if Satan himself was at your heels?'

Charl frowned, as she had no intention of answering his questions.

'Who are you?' she countered.

'Black Feather. I ride with Tecumseh.' He paused, watching her with unwavering black eyes. 'And who are you, white woman?'

Moving closer, Charl studied him intently. Although he topped her by less than two inches in height, he seemed massive, thick-bodied and broad. Somehow the features of his bronzed face seemed to match his stature. They were hard and blunt, with a width at his cheekbones and jaw that spoke of an uncompromising nature. Still, there was something in the curve of his full mouth that hinted at gentleness beneath his frightening exterior.

At least she was not afraid of him. Perhaps it was her friendship with Waukee, or that she sensed she had nothing to fear from this bear of a man, but Charl exhibited none of the usual trepidation white women showed when confronted by an Indian. This both pleased and amazed Black Feather.

'Who are you, white woman?' he repeated, his voice shaded with new curiosity.

'My name is Charlotte Beckwith,' she replied.

'Are you the wife of the English major?' he proceeded bluntly.

Charl's cheeks flushed pink. 'No,' she said and wondered how he had come to that conclusion.

Black Feather's expression did not change, but Charl's face grew warmer still under his candid black gaze.

'I – I must rub down my horse,' she stammered and turned away to end his silent perusal of her.

'I will help,' he offered and set to work.

They completed the task without further conversation, and when they had finished, she thanked him.

His only acknowledgement was a curt nod before he stalked away.

As Charl crossed the compound from the stables, the various units were beginning to assemble for morning parade. Inside their cabin St James was nearly ready to join them.

'You were gone rather a long time this morning,' he remarked as he buckled his sabre around his waist.

Charl shrugged and went to stir the embers in the hearth.

'I rode further than usual,' she lied.

'I've told you before that I don't like you riding all over the countryside unescorted,' he began, 'especially before proper daylight.'

'The water's hot. Do you want me to make you some tea?' Charl asked, hoping to divert St James and avoid another of his frequent lectures on her behaviour.

'No respectable woman rides alone,' he continued, warming to his subject. 'I don't see why we don't join the other officers and their ladies for a ride at sunset. It seems as if we could take advantage of what little society this place has to offer.'

With difficulty Charl bit back her reply.

'They don't seem very anxious for our company,' she said quietly.

'Nor am I surprised. You arrived here astride a horse like a man. And your behaviour since then has been –'

'I asked if you want me to make some tea,' she repeated sharply, breaking into his tirade.

He stood for a long moment, fixing her with his molten stare: transmitting both anger and disapproval in that one long meaningful look.

Even after all these months he still had the power to send a shiver of fear down her spine when he eyed her in that manner.

'I'll take something at the officers' mess,' he replied, turning towards the door.

'We move at dawn tomorrow. Tell Ellis to prepare my equipment.'

'With his other duties I doubt Ellis will have time to –' Charl began.

'Damn it, Charlotte. Then do it yourself,' he ordered as he slammed out of the door.

Furiously, she glared after him.

Dear God! How she had come to loathe that man. And how well grounded that hatred was. The odd part was that he seemed to feel almost that same animosity for her. Yet he had forced her to accompany him west.

Absently, Charl made herself a pot of tea and settled down at the rough pine table to breakfast on honey and biscuits left from dinner the night before.

The altered state of her relationship with St James puzzled her. In Quebec he had been pleased with her, taking pride in her beauty and her accomplishments. But the further west they had travelled, the more dissatisfied he seemed to become until she wondered why he had bothered to bring her to Fort Malden at all. He found fault with everything she did. She worked diligently to keep the cabin spotless, when she could have hired an Indian woman to cook and clean. She was too friendly with the troops and did not quake when Indians approached, as civilized women were expected to do. She rode alone, dressed simply, and failed to aspire to the society of the other officers' wives.

In truth, the other women had avoided her and pointedly rebuffed her initial attempts at friendship. It did not take her long to realize the cause. She was Felix's mistress, not his wife, and as such was unfit for their society. In Quebec they had associated with other officers and their mistresses, but on the frontier no half-world existed. Felix should have realized what would happen if he brought her west. Or had he been so blinded by his need to possess her that he had put all other considerations out of his mind?

Charl sighed softly and stirred her tea, watching the whirlpool subside before she put the cup to her lips.

She had changed, too. In Quebec it had been easy to do what Felix wanted her to do because nothing had mattered to her. But now there was work to fill her empty days and places to go that were not filled with bittersweet memories. There were soldiers, happy for a few minutes' conversation with an attractive woman, and new sights, smells, and sounds to excite her senses. Charl had begun to rebuild her life, slowly becoming aware of her world once more.

As reluctant as she had been to put away her memories of Seth and the life they shared in Quebec, she had done it. Yet this morning that life had come back to haunt her.

Charl frowned as she thought of the man she had seen. She wished now that she had ridden closer, if only to satisfy her curiosity. How could anyone have been so like Seth? she wondered, as she sought to recall every detail of this morning's encounter. She knew Seth's face and body as well as she knew her own. His gestures and mannerisms were indelibly etched in her mind. The man on the riverbank had been like Seth in every way, and she could not dismiss him as an illusion. Desperately, she fumbled for an explanation of his presence, but if one existed, it eluded her. And it was a very long time before she was able to put the incident out of her mind.

At dawn the next day, Felix St James left Fort Malden with a sizable force of British regulars and Indians under General Proctor's command. At the last minute the objective of their mission had been changed from the supply depot on the Sandusky River to Fort Meigs itself. En route the plan underwent further revisions, on insistence from the Indians, and they detoured east to attack the small American garrison at Fort Stephenson. Marred by indecision, the expedition seemed doomed from the start.

Fort Stephenson resisted the British attack and, with a large number of casualties, Proctor retreated, seeking the safety of Fort Malden.

Frustrated by the aborted plans, and demoralized by the need for retreat, the men dragged themselves back to Amhurstburg to wait out the hot, endless summer. The Indians who had arrived with their families for the Sandusky River campaign stayed on, further depleting the fort's dwindling stores.

In those sweltering days of mid-August, after the retreat, Charl thought she might go mad. The move west had been meant to advance Felix's military career, and when his dreams of glory were thwarted by Proctor's retreat, he lashed out in frustration at those over whom he had control. With his subordinates he was inflexible and even more demanding than usual. But it was Charl who took the brunt of his ill temper. He found fault with everything she did and was not above abusing her for imagined mistakes and misbehaviour. He suddenly found great sport in tormenting her so that Charl was never sure when he might trap her with his inconsistencies and extract a suitable punishment. Orders were given that she was not to leave the compound, effectively forestalling her one pleasure, her morning ride. The days blurred together as the unremitting August sun beat down on Fort Malden, and it was only Charl's unflagging determination that kept her from being overwhelmed by the heat and the loneliness.

On the first crisp, clear day of late August, as Charl was returning from the well at the far side of the parade ground, a deep, male voice halted her sloshing progress.

'White woman, I have a great thirst. Would you offer me a drink of your water?'

Charl turned slowly and stared up at the man who had addressed her. She recognized him instantly, even without the elaborate buckskins and the ostrich feathers in his hair. It was Tecumseh himself, and beside him was the young warrior she had met in the stable, Black Feather.

She inclined her head slightly in greeting.

'I would be honoured to offer the great Chief Tecumseh a drink. If you will follow me to my cabin, I will gladly extend my hospitality to you and your brave.'

'I would like that,' he agreed. 'Show me the way.'

With the two Indians on horseback moving sedately behind,

Charl led them across the parade ground to her small cabin, aware that most of the garrison was watching curiously.

'Won't you come in and sit down?' she offered as they tied their horses to the porch rail.

'You are very kind,' Tecumseh accepted as Charl led them inside.

After setting the pail of water beside the hearth, Charl turned to her two guests.

'What may I get for you?' she asked.

'A drink of water is all we want,' the chief answered as he eyed her speculatively. He had never been treated with such courtesy by a white woman. They usually chose to ignore Indians or reacted with fear. But this fair-haired girl showed neither fear nor reticence. He nodded almost imperceptibly to Black Feather as Charl bustled to ladle water into two wooden mugs. Then she set them before her guests at the rough pine table.

Both men made a show of politely drinking the water and then rose to go.

'Thank you for your hospitality,' Tecumseh told her.

'It has been my honour to serve you and your warrior,' she replied as she followed them out on to the porch of the cabin. Then she watched as they moved slowly across the compound towards General Proctor's office.

By the time the general's staff had assembled at the long conference table to await Tecumseh's arrival, news of his detour to Major St James' cabin was common knowledge. Flushed with anger and agitation, St James sat silently in his chair fuming, as he'd had reason to do so much of late, at Charl's impossible behaviour.

Didn't the girl have any sense of propriety? he wondered as he stared with smouldering eyes at the papers before him. Didn't she know that any proper Englishwoman would scream and faint at the prospect of opening her home to one of these savages, even Tecumseh himself?

By God! The girl had done her best to humiliate him in front of the general and the other officers ever since they'd arrived. She had worked like a common charwoman, scrubbing and cleaning, when she could easily have hired an Indian squaw for those duties. Even after their journey ended, she persisted in wearing those blasted breeches, knowing full well that her attire displeased him. It was small wonder the other officers' wives shunned her. Although she had not been openly defiant, Charl had done everything in her power to embarrass him.

She had never been like this in Quebec, he reflected. Why was she so difficult now? For a moment a vivid image flashed in his memory of Charl and the way she had looked when she came to his office that first time. There had been a fiery determination about her, a will of iron beneath feminine trappings. He had seen that tenacity again on the road outside Quebec, the day she had miscarried her child. And he realized suddenly that those brief glimpses of her strength had been more the real Charlotte Beckwith than the reticent woman who had become his mistress. In Quebec she had been demoralized by Porterfield's supposed death, and out to curry his favour so he would accept her bastard as his own. But now, by slow degrees, she was returning to herself: growing stubborn, wilful, independent. And St James found himself wondering if any man could bend her to his will.

Porterfield had succeeded, but then Charlotte had loved Seth: loved him enough to willingly sell her body for him. But even when she had come to him freely, Felix had not possessed her, for it was Seth's name, not his, that she had cried out in her passion. With sudden insight he realized that in all the months since then, while he had considered her a symbol of his triumph over the Porterfields, he had won an empty victory. In the end he had never really possessed her. And now it was Charl's own indomitable spirit that was defeating him.

Felix was shaken by his own realization, but he had no time to ponder its meaning. For at that moment Tecumseh entered the conference room, and the British officers rose to greet him. The Indian selected a chair at the far end of the table and seated himself, while the brave who had accompanied him remained standing several paces behind his leader.

'Why is it that the great Chief Tecumseh has requested this meeting?' Proctor began when he had resumed his seat.

'There are several reasons,' Tecumseh answered. 'The wise men of my tribe have noticed signs of a hard winter to come, and there is already a lack of food and blankets. No crops have been planted, no hunters sent out, and no meats smoked because you promised to feed and clothe us in return for my warriors' skill in battle. When will you see to the needs of my people?'

'Tecumseh must realize that the British always see to their friends' needs,' Proctor soothed, though he knew that supplies were critically short and that his own men were underfed and unpaid. 'Soon we will win control of Lake Erie, and then the goods will flow freely again. I myself have given Commander Barclay some of my best men to see to his victory over the Americans. The deed will be accomplished in a matter of days.'

The Indian looked frankly unconvinced by Proctor's assurances.

'And when the commander has won control of the lake, will we again unite to drive the Americans from the Indian homelands?' Tecumseh asked, voicing his most sincere wish.

'It is as we agreed long ago, Tecumseh,' Proctor promised. 'Until the supplies come again, is there anything you wish for yourself and your people?'

It was obvious the chief knew he was to be placated with a few baubles, and he set the price accordingly high.

'We have a great need of corn and blankets,' he began enumerating, 'and gunpowder and flints for our rifles. My women wish heavy cloth so they can begin to make winter clothes, and beads for decoration.' The list grew. 'And we will take the yellow-haired woman who lives in the cabin of the British major,' Tecumseh finished, indicating St James with a nod of his dark head.

Felix's mouth dropped open with shock, and Proctor gasped, 'Preposterous!' before he regained control of himself.

Flushing brightly, the British general turned on the Indian. 'We do not deal in women, sir!' he informed Tecumseh curtly. 'As for the other things, they will be loaded on a wagon for you at once.'

With a brief nod to the assembled officers, Tecumseh left, trailed by Black Feather.

'Damned savages!' Proctor blustered when they were gone. 'Imagine the effrontery, asking right out for a white woman! Curse the day his majesty's forces got tied up with the likes of him. My apologies, Major St James, and to your lady.'

But Felix had not heard the general's words, for he had already stormed out of the room in a rage.

Charl was sitting quietly by the fire working on a bit of quilting when he burst into the cabin and hauled her roughly to her feet.

'What have you done?' he demanded of her. 'What damned bit of mischief have you contrived this time?'

'Nothing! I've done nothing,' she cried. 'Please, Felix, whatever is the matter?'

He struck her an open-handed blow that sent her staggering, but caught her arm before she could move away.

'What was it you did this morning to make those two Indians offer to trade for you?'

'What? Me?' Charl gasped incredulously. 'What Indians?'

'Tecumseh and his brave asked for you, along with a dozen blankets, a few sacks of flour, and some other trinkets. They want to take you back to their camp, for God knows what purpose.'

Charl stared at him in disbelief.

'Don't play the innocent with me, Charlotte. You must have done something to make them offer for you. What happened while you were alone here with them?'

'Nothing! Nothing at all!' Charl stammered. 'They asked for a drink of water, and I gave it to them. That's all!'

His fingers tightened on her arm until she cried out in pain. His russet eyes blazed with rage. 'Don't lie to me! You must have said or done something to make Tecumseh ask General Proctor for you.'

Abruptly, he released the hold on her arm and shoved her away.

'Good God! The humiliation you've brought me since we came west. You've behaved like a common strumpet and done everything in your power to embarrass and discredit me with the other officers. I curse the day I ever set eyes on you!'

All at once Charl's own rage surfaced, and she felt dizzy, as if she'd been holding her breath for a long time. With it came a strange kind of power that infused her and she turned on him with eyes narrowed.

'You curse that day no more than I,' she said in a low, husky voice. 'I'd gladly go with Tecumseh and Black Feather now than spend another moment here with you!'

There was silence in the cabin as they faced each other: a roaring, echoing silence, like the quiet after a clap of thunder. And then St James spoke in a voice as soft and dangerous as Charl's had been.

'Then get your cloak, Charlotte, for go with them you will!'

Felix reached for Charl, but she turned away, jerking her cloak from a peg on the wall, and preceded him to the door.

They crossed the compound at an angry pace and approached the small wagon that was loaded with a variety of trade goods and foodstuffs. Before any words were spoken, it was evident why they had come. The woman's chin was tilted with stubborn pride, and her eyes flashed defiance, while the major's hawkish features were flushed with ire.

'I give this woman to you, Tecumseh,' St James announced as they drew up to where the two Indians stood beside the wagon. 'I give her to you, as you asked, though I admit she is a gift of questionable value.'

With appraising eyes the chief looked from the man to the woman, returning his gaze to the British major as he spoke.

'Perhaps the value of such a rare jewel goes unrecognized in an imperfect setting,' he offered quietly.

Slowly Tecumseh turned to Charl again, noting the angry red mark that ran along one cheekbone, marring the symmetry of her features. Then he understood the desperation that had driven her to this course.

'Would you go with me, golden woman?' he asked simply.

There was no hesitation in her reply.

'Yes,' she responded as simply.

There was a flicker of approval in Tecumseh's hazel eyes, and he gave her a brief smile.

'Very well. You will ride with me to the village,' he told her.

Black Feather had already taken his place on the wagon's narrow seat and watched the other three with a curious expression of mingled pleasure and anticipation in his dark eyes.

With one final nod at St James that acknowledged the exchange of the woman between them, Tecumseh mounted his horse. Wordlessly, he offered the blonde woman his hand, a speculative look on his swarthy face, as if at this last moment he doubted her intent. It was Charl's last chance to change her mind.

St James smiled confidently to himself. Charlotte Beckwith was the most stubborn and difficult of women, but in bringing her here to confront the Indians, he had called her bluff. Now she had no choice but to go with the savages or beg him to let her stay at the fort. And when she inevitably turned to him, he would make her pay dearly for this final transgression. She would return to their cabin chastened and subdued, and he would have established his control over her once more.

But then she was reaching up to catch Tecumseh's hand, swinging into the saddle behind him. It was with stunned disbelief that Felix St James watched the little procession move across the parade ground and through the gate.

For her part, Charl never looked back.

Thirty-Two

They had not ridden far from the fort when Tecumseh drew rein.

'We will walk for a while,' he told her as he dismounted. Then, with great care, he helped Charl to the ground, also. Behind them Black Feather slowed the team of horses to a walk and followed at a sedate pace.

The sunlight that filtered through the trees cast a dappled pattern on the lane, and the slow, rhythmic jangle of the horses' harnesses was the only sound that intruded on the tree-shaded stillness.

Finally Tecumseh broke the silence. 'Why was it you agreed to come with us, white woman?' he asked without preamble.

Before she answered, Charl's chin rose in a gesture of determination that the Indian easily understood. 'Why was it you offered for me when you spoke to General Proctor?' she countered.

There was a glimmer of surprise in Tecumseh's hazel eyes at the speed of her retort, and the hint of a smile touched his lips.

'You must realize that life with my people will be very different from your life with the British major,' he went on.

'Yes, I realize that,' she agreed.

'Then why did you come with us?' he persisted.

'Why indeed?' Charl paused for a time as if sorting out her reply. 'With the British major I was a prize he had captured. He admired my beauty, but it was the prestige I brought him that determined my worth. For a moment today I made myself worthless to him. I became, by my unacceptable behaviour, a liability instead of an asset. And while he seemed willing to give me up, I saw my chance and fled. In leaving Felix St James I've regained my freedom.'

Tecumseh nodded at the eloquence of her explanation. 'Do you imagine that life with my people will offer you freedom?' he asked. 'Or will you flee from us as you have fled from the British major?'

Charl considered his question for a moment, then shrugged. 'I don't know what life with your people will be like,' she answered frankly, 'but I know what it was like with Major St James.'

Tecumseh nodded more thoughtfully this time, and they walked on in silence.

'Why did you offer for me when you spoke to General Proctor?' she asked after a time.

'I offered not for myself,' Tecumseh replied, 'but for Black Feather.'

'Black Feather?' Charl echoed as she turned to stare over her shoulder at the man who sat stoically on the wagon seat.

'Tonight you will become his second wife,' he went on.

'His second wife!!' Charl was appalled.

'The Shawnee brave may take more than one wife,' Tecumseh explained. 'Black Feather was first married to Singing Waters. They were very happy, and from their union came a son, Pale Wolf. But Pale Wolf's birth was a difficult one, and Singing Waters never regained her strength. When the boy was five winters, his mother sickened and died. As is our custom, Black Feather married his wife's sister, Bright Bird. He had hoped that Bright Bird would be a good mother to her sister's child. But Bright Bird proved barren, and as the years passed, her love of Pale Wolf turned to jealousy and then to hate. In you Black Feather hopes to find a good mother for his son.'

'How old is the boy now?' Charl asked, her concern for a motherless child she had never met evident in her voice.

'Eight winters,' Tecumseh informed her, his eyes intent on the white woman's pale face. In her expression he read her compassion and smiled with approval. Black Feather had chosen well.

'When we reach camp, you will be prepared for the wedding. When a man gains a woman in trade, they must be married and joined before moonset on that same day. It is a great dishonour for both the man and his wife if this is not accomplished.'

Charl digested Tecumseh's explanations in silence.

'I have not yet agreed to marry Black Feather,' she said finally.

Tecumseh gave a gust of laughter.

'When you came with us, the choice was made for you,' he replied.

Again silence came between them, and again Charl broke it.

'Will Bright Bird accept me when I become Black Feather's second wife?'

Tecumseh's eyes narrowed as he studied her. The question showed acceptance of her new role as a warrior's wife and a great perception of human emotions. This golden-haired woman was rare among her sisters and worthy of a brave like Black Feather. With every word she spoke and every question she asked, the Indian's esteem for her grew. He was glad now that he had decided to explain what was to transpire. For if he had failed to make her understand and accept her fate, she might well have fought against it. And a formidable foe she would be.

'Some women welcome a second wife to ease the burdens of work and share the care of the children. I fear that Bright Bird will not be such a woman,' Tecumseh told her honestly. 'But do not fear. Black Feather is a fair and strong man, well capable of dealing with the jealousies of two wives.

'Now come mount up for the day is quickly spent and there is much to do before moonset.'

They rode into the village a few minutes later. It was a gathering of conical-shaped structures, covered with bark and skins, pitched upon a wide meadow beside the river. At their approach a crowd began to gather near the central campfire. A moment later Charl found herself surrounded by unfamiliar people who reached out to pluck at the ribbons and lace on her lilac mull gown or stroke the silky cascade of golden hair.

The noisy tumult of voices that had risen with their arrival in the village subsided as Tecumseh began to speak. Eyes shifted to the wagon laden with supplies, then to Black Feather, and finally back to Charl as he spoke. And in spite of her ignorance of the Shawnee language, Charl easily followed the trend of his speech. At the end of his explanations, Tecumseh issued several orders, and an Indian woman made her way through the crowd.

When she reached him, Tecumseh spoke to her in English.

'Bright Bird, you will take the golden-haired woman and prepare her for the wedding ceremony. See that she is washed and clad in the finest buckskins so that she will make a worthy bride.'

The Indian woman eyed Charl with open hostility but dared not refuse. She motioned for Charl to follow and turned back into the crowd.

As Charl moved to follow Bright Bird, she glanced once at Black Feather and noticed that he stood with his palms resting gently on the shoulders of a boy who was in every way his father's miniature. Charl paused long enough to meet the child's wary eyes. In the briefest instant, understanding flashed between them, and Charl gave him a reassuring smile before she turned away.

The clearing where Bright Bird took her was soon filled with babbling women who had come either from curiosity about this white woman or to see the confrontation between Black Feather's two wives. They began to circle Charl slowly, touching her experimentally at first and then harder: tugging at her hair and pinching her through her clothes. Even as her tormentors' attacks became more overt, Charl stood perfectly still, showing no emotion.

Then Bright Bird descended upon her to unfasten the gown, tearing at the tiny buttons with rough hands, until the dress was stripped away and Charl stood clad only in her petticoat and chemise.

Defiantly, Charl tossed her head to signify that she was unbowed by the treatment she had been subjected to by the Indian women. But as she did, the opals she had worn in her ears for so long flashed in the sunlight. Instantly Bright Bird reached for them, but when Charl realized her intent, she jerked away.

The Indian woman tried for the stones a second time, catching Charl's chin with her left hand as she sought one of the fiery opals with her right.

'No!' Charl said firmly as she fended the woman off with one raised hand. 'You will not take those from me!'

But Bright Bird was not to be put off and reached for Charl again.

This time as she tried to touch the shimmering stones, Charl reached too, quickly unsheathing the knife the Indian woman wore at her waist. With the weapon in her hand, Charl stepped back to face Bright Bird and the other women.

The clamour of the women's voices rose sharply with alarm as Charl glared at them. But even as they backed away, Charl realized she was hopelessly outnumbered. Anger and determination steeled her resolve, even against these odds, when she realized what those opals meant to her. They were the last link with the life she had shared with Seth in Quebec. Tears constricted her throat when she remembered the night he had given them to her.

She could almost see the tenderness in Seth's eyes and hear her own voice as she thanked him for his gift. 'Because you gave these to me, they are more precious than anything in the world.'

Charl tightened her grip on the knife as she faced her tormentors. She would never give up the opal earrings.

Then suddenly Tecumseh materialized from behind one of the wigwams with Black Feather only a step behind him.

'What is this?' he demanded, taking in the scene before him. The white woman, clad only in her underclothes, stood brandishing a knife, fearlessly facing Bright Bird and the other women. 'What is it that has happened here?'

For a long moment no one spoke. It was unseemly that the great Tecumseh should concern himself with women's squabbles, and the squaws were reluctant to answer.

'She wears sparkling stones in her ears,' Bright Bird said defiantly, at last. 'By rights, as first wife, those stones should be mine.'

Tecumseh considered this, looking from Bright Bird's truculent face to the white woman whose features were moulded in stone. It was true that no gift could be given to the second wife without a gift of equal or greater value being presented to the first. But if the second wife already possessed something of great value at the time of her marriage . . .

'What are those stones worth to you, golden woman?' Tecumseh addressed Charl.

She lowered her weapon as she faced the chief.

'They are worth my life,' she stated softly, 'for to lose them would be to break my heart.'

Tecumseh read the truth of her words in her sea-green eyes.

'And you, Bright Bird,' he asked.

'They are my right,' she replied.

Tecumseh glanced briefly at Black Feather before he made his decision. 'Then you must fight to settle the question. Bright Bird, draw your knife.'

A dark flush rose under Bright Bird's dusky skin, and it was immediately obvious to all who did not know that the weapon the white woman wielded so skilfully belonged to Black Feather's first wife. Quickly, someone thrust another knife into Bright

Bird's hand to end the embarrassed silence, and she advanced on Charl.

The Indian girl struck quickly, certain that in this dangerous game she held the advantage. For where would a white woman learn the subtleties of handling a blade? But as she reached to draw first blood, Charl spun away in a whirl of petticoats and a flash of golden hair. The thrust had all of Bright Bird's strength behind it, and when it encountered nothing more substantial than thin air, she sprawled heavily on the ground. She rose with hatred flashing in her dark eyes, but she did not make the mistake of charging her opponent a second time. Instead she circled slowly to the right, and Charl matched her movements.

It had been months since Waukee's lessons, but Charl fell immediately into the loose-jointed stance he had taught her. With deliberation she watched her opponent as they circled: assessing, planning, preparing. And when Bright Bird attacked again, those lessons stood her in good stead. All the things she'd practised on those warm afternoons a year before came back to her, and she easily eluded the other woman's blade until Bright Bird was panting with her exertions. Then Charl went on the offensive, reaching across to nip the leather thong that held the other woman's bead and shell necklace and spilling the baubles to the ground. But as she retreated triumphantly, her feet tangled in the wide petticoat and she fell backwards. Bright Bird was on her instantly, her knife poised above Charl's cheekbone, her intent clearly to disfigure the white woman. Charl caught the other woman's wrist before the blade could descend and forced the squaw's arm inexorably downward away from her face. But as the knife moved lower between their two bodies, the point snagged the tender skin below Charl's collarbone and opened a deep ugly gash. A murmur of approval moved through the assembled village, and Bright Bird raised her eyes from her opponent to acknowledge it. In that split second Charl shepherded her strength, and with a single whipcord movement, heaved the Indian woman over, reversing their positions. A wild, sweet rush of pure, feral joy swept over Charl as she glared down into Bright Bird's eyes. With deliberation she tightened her grip on the Indian's wrist until the knife fell from her nerveless fingers. Then she moved to pin Bright Bird's shoulders to the ground, holding her in place as she drew a calming breath.

The Indians in the circle that surrounded the two women

remained motionless, watching the blonde girl expectantly. In confusion Charl's eyes went to Tecumseh's dark face. What was it they expected her to do? With a movement that was hardly a movement at all, he drew one finger along his cheekbone as Bright Bird's knife had meant to cut. Charl's eyes widened as his meaning struck her, and he nodded almost imperceptibly.

For a long moment she stared down into Bright Bird's flushed face and saw that same anticipation. Then suddenly she understood: in winning her right to the opals she had been bloodied. If she allowed Bright Bird to emerge from this confrontation unscathed she would bring dishonour to them both. Slowly Charl raised her knife but she could not bring herself to mark the other woman's face. Instead she pressed the point of her blade into the tiny hole where an earring was meant to hang. Then with one swift motion she drew her knife downward, opening the hole to a slit that ran the length of the woman's earlobe. Bright Bird did not cry out, but a murmur of appreciation ran through the crowd at the irony of the wound the white woman had chosen to inflict. With bile rising in her throat, Charl completed the job and sprang to her feet.

For a moment she stood panting, fighting down the wave of nausea that threatened to overwhelm her. Then Charl felt Tecumseh's eyes on her, and she raised her head to read his approval in their depths.

He turned to an elderly woman to his left and spoke to her clearly in English.

'Take the golden woman and prepare her for the wedding. Treat her with respect and honour, for she has indeed proven herself worthy of our tribe this day.'

✳

. The wedding of the Indian brave to the beautiful white woman took place just at dusk. As the glowing, crimson sun melted into the horizon, turning the darkening sky cerise, mauve, and powder blue, the couple stood on the river bluff, amidst a group of well-wishers, to be joined together. The words of the ceremony were completely foreign to the bride, and she found her mind wandering as she watched the muted reflections of the sky in the gently rippling river.

What improbable turn of events had brought her here? Charl wondered. Why had she come to this Indian village on the edge of the frontier, to be wed to a man she hardly knew? This morning she had elected to give up everything comfortable and familiar, to embrace a life and people who were completely alien. Even now she was not sure why she had done it. Had freedom from Felix St James been worth all she had left behind? And had she merely given up one kind of prison for another?

Her eyes moved from the river to her new husband's dark face, wondering at his thoughts. Why had he chosen her to be mother to his son when there must be maidens from his own village perfectly willing to accept this role? And why had she agreed? It always came back to that.

Charl was suddenly aware that everyone was looking at her, and she realized that it was time for her part in the ceremony. Carefully she opened the beaded pouch she wore at her waist and removed the cob of dried corn that had been placed inside. The corn, she had been told by the old woman who had bandaged, bathed, and dressed her, was symbolic of her body being offered to her new husband. It represented a wish for happiness and bounty in their marriage. With hands that trembled ever so slightly, Charl offered the corn to Black Feather. Solemnly he took it, holding the ear of corn as if it was truly the essence of her. Then with his other hand he reached to claim her pale, slender fingers and clasp them tightly in his own. She looked down at her hand where it lay entwined with his, unaware of the prayers being offered for their happiness. The deed was done now, and for whatever the future held, she was Black Feather's wife. Then the ceremony was over, and they were immediately the centre of a babbling throng of well-wishers who escorted them back through the encampment to the conical wigwam where they would spend the night.

Inside a fire was burning brightly, and dishes of food had been set nearby for them to eat. Charl followed Black Feather through the door flap, but as she did, she noticed Pale Wolf standing uncertainly at the edge of the crowd.

'May I ask Pale Wolf to join us?' Charl asked her new husband.

A look of surprise flickered across his face, and then he nodded. 'For a time at least,' he agreed.

Charl went to the doorway and beckoned to the boy, who came happily into the tent. He seemed relieved to at last be included in the events that would so profoundly affect his life.

The boy's presence did much to ease the tension between the new man and wife as they ate and drank the things that had been

prepared for them. Charl had never been alone with Black
Feather, except for that morning in the stable, and she was
acutely uneasy in his presence. But somehow her natural warmth
for the child transmitted itself to the father as well, and she found
herself exchanging smiles with him as she talked quietly with the
boy. By the time that Black Feather rose to escort his son to
another wigwam where he would spend the night, the seeds of
the unity that would bind them together had already begun to
grow.

The fire had died to embers when Black Feather returned, and
Charl watched with trepidation as he fastened the tent flap behind
him.

'Already my son grows fond of you,' Black Feather told her
approvingly. 'In time he will be as bewitched by you as I am.'

He had moved silently to the near side of the campfire and
beckoned her to rise. Slowly she obeyed, her wide eyes mirroring
her uncertainty.

'Do not fear me, golden woman,' he said in a voice as dark
and velvet soft as his eyes. 'I will not harm you.'

Charl opened her mouth to deny her fear, but he silenced her
with his lips on hers as he drew her inexorably closer. His kisses
were warm and gentle, pressing lightly along the curve of her
cheek to her temple and then back to claim her parted lips once
more. His tongue softly sought hers, moving tantalizingly against
it until she willingly gave him her response.

In her months with St James she had forgotten that such things
as tenderness and patience existed. But with the Indian's arms
around her, she rediscovered their meaning. Of their own volition
her arms crept around his back, measuring his bulk against Felix's
rapier-thin proportions and Seth's broad strength.

After a time Black Feather's hands found the fastenings at the
shoulders and sides of her dress, and he drew it from her body.
He laid it carefully aside to be worn by another Shawnee bride
sometime in the future, then turned back to look at her. In the
wash of the firelight, the fine, strong lines of her body were
readily visible: the lush, swelling breasts; the slender, curving
waist; the sleek fullness of her hips and flanks.

'You are very beautiful,' he whispered as he ran one calloused
palm along the roundness of her breasts.

In the silence that followed he loosened her plaited hair,
spreading its thickness across her shoulders, and removed his

own finery. By the steady red glow of the embers, his body was revealed to be broad and rugged, but with a symmetry and grace that was not unattractive.

With a tender smile he pulled Charl down on a bed of skins beside him and began to kiss her again. For all the strength and power of him, he was surprisingly gentle. His mouth moved slowly against hers and across her pale golden skin until it flushed with warmth. His hands skimmed skilfully along her body, bringing her nipples erect with the gentle persistence of his touch. His hands moved lower, across her abdomen to the sweet, warm recess between her thighs. Her body was stirred by his skill, and she responded as she had thought never to respond again. But for the pleasure of his touch, there was none of the bone-melting desire that she had known so briefly with Seth.

She responded in kind: touching and stroking Black Feather's broad body, employing sensual skills she had learned in those rapturous nights with Seth and at St James' hands. In his dark eyes she saw a fire grow bright and hot until it consumed him, but she was not touched by its flames. And when Black Feather came to take his pleasure, hoarsely mumbling words of love in English and Shawnee, it was Seth who claimed her thoughts even as the Indian warrior claimed her body.

As Black Feather curved contentedly against her in the drowsy aftermath, Charl lay staring into the dark. In spite of the Indian's skill and tenderness, she had remained unaffected by his passion. Would it always be so? she wondered. Would she always remain untouched and untouchable by any man, save the one who had died by her unwitting betrayal? Black Feather stirred and pulled her close against his broad chest before he slept. At the gentle, protective gesture, tears rose in her eyes, and she fought hard to blink them away. Black Feather's breathing grew deep and even in the silence that followed, but Charl lay awake. What was she doing here? she asked herself again. And why had she agreed to marry this strong, gentle man when she had no love left to give him? Awake in the midnight darkness, she finally allowed herself the luxury of tears. But even as she wept, she was not sure if it was for Seth or some lost part of herself that she grieved.

❋

When the first fusillade of gunfire shattered the morning stillness, Charl and the rest of the Indian women and children were well behind British lines. They had been on the trail for some days, following the British forces' retreat, that continued in spite of Tecumseh's repeated demands that General Proctor turn his forces and make a stand. The Indian had threatened, cajoled, and finally accused the general of cowardice, but Proctor remained adamant. Retreat was the only option open to him once Perry had won control of Lake Erie for the Americans. And since the fates of the British and Indians were inextricably mixed, they had followed Proctor north and east along Lake St Claire and the Thames River. Now, belatedly, Proctor had elected to face his enemy.

As the sound of that first blast of gunfire died away, Charl found herself thinking that in spite of the turbulent times she had found a kind of peace in her life with the Indians. Her initial confrontation with Bright Bird had established her place in the tribe and had gained her an acceptance that might otherwise have taken her months or years to establish. As it was, she had been absorbed into the flow of daily life in the village without difficulty. The other women had voluntarily schooled her in her tasks as Black Feather's wife and shyly welcomed her into their society. Even Bright Bird had come to recognize Charl's place in the community. Though she chose not to hide her animosity, the Indian woman was wise enough not to plot against one who had so quickly earned the tribe's favour.

Her new husband seemed pleased with her also, but in spite of his nightly visits to her tent, the bond that was growing between them was one of friendship and not passion. But it was with Pale Wolf that she was the most content. His acceptance of her was instantaneous and complete, as was hers of him. For it was in Charl that the boy found the mother he had lost and in him that Charl found the child she had been denied.

Now, with the sounds of battle echoing through the forest, Charl looked around for Pale Wolf, seeking to reassure him that all would be well. He had been as unsettled as the rest of the tribe had been by Tecumseh's premonition of his own death in the forthcoming battle. But Pale Wolf had transferred much of that apprehension into fear for his father's safety. As her gaze moved over the group that sat nearby, she was surprised to find that he was not with his friends. After a moment she decided it was better to seek him out than leave him to face his fears alone. Rising, she handed the infant she had been holding to one of the other women and went in search of him.

It did not take her long to make a circuit of the temporary encampment, and when she did not find the boy, she was terrifyingly sure of where he had gone. With anxiety twisting inside her, Charl turned towards the sound of the fighting and began to run. With every step the sound of gunfire seemed to grow louder, until it echoed in her head and shook the ground beneath her feet. Still she dodged through the trees, driven by a fear for Pale Wolf's safety that overcame her own terror. As she darted through the billows of dense smoke and between groups of struggling men, she called Pale Wolf's name, but her voice was lost in the cacophony of the battle. Soldiers on horseback flashed past, and she noted, quite irrelevantly, that the uniforms they wore were militia brown and dark blue, not British red. At that moment neither politics nor personal safety mattered in her compulsion to find the Indian boy.

Then above the din, she heard a small voice that she instantly recognized as Pale Wolf's raised in a war whoop. She struck out blindly in the direction of the shout, stepping over and around men who had tossed their useless firearms aside and faced each other at close range with bayonets, tomahawks, and drawn knives. Both Indians and Americans let her pass: one recognizing her buckskin clothing as Shawnee, the other seeing her yellow hair and believing that she sought nothing more than safety from her captors behind American lines. But at that moment Charl was so intent on finding the boy that the possibility of escape never occurred to her.

Topping a slight rise, she caught sight of Pale Wolf, his sturdy young body firmly entwined with one of the blue-coated infantrymen who had followed behind that first mounted charge. It appeared that Pale Wolf had attempted to tackle the man but had lacked the strength to wrestle him to the ground. Now he clung tenaciously to the man's legs, while the soldier tried unsuccessfully to beat him off with the butt of his musket.

As Charl swiftly drew her knife from her belt, her only thought was to protect Pale Wolf. With a war cry of her own, she raced down the incline and launched herself at the soldier's back. Frantically, she clung to the man's shoulders as she brought the blade of her knife around beneath his chin.

'Leave him alone!' she demanded in a voice that quivered with fury.

'What the hell?' he exclaimed as he reached back to dislodge this new attacker. But as he moved, Charl brought the knife down in a deadly arc that sliced the man cleanly from ear to ear.

He crashed over backwards as he died, pinning Charl beneath him with his crushing weight. Pale Wolf leaped up from where he had fallen and somehow rolled the heavy body away so Charl could extricate herself from beneath the corpse. For a long moment she stood staring down in horror at what she had done.

'Oh God! No!' she cried and might well have sunk to her knees beside the dead man if Pale Wolf had not pulled her away.

Then they were running, hand in hand, across the battlefield to the safety of their encampment.

All around them men came together in mortal combat, killing and maiming for principles that had somehow lost their meaning in the heat of the battle. They fought now only for survival. And as they ran, Charl understood their reasons with new clarity.

At the end of their endurance, they staggered into a clearing and stopped, leaning against a boulder as they gulped air into their burning lungs and waited for the pounding of their hearts to ease. Finally, as her breathing slackened, Charl looked down at her bloodstained hands and realized, with fresh horror, what she had done to protect Pale Wolf. The sharp, long-bladed knife she had used to kill the American was still clutched tight in her hand, and she cast it away with a moan of revulsion. Then the clearing seemed to spin and waver around her and she stumbled forward violently sick.

Thirty-Three

It was a dream. Even as Seth watched the scene unfold before him, he knew it but was entrapped, held powerless to control the images that by now were all too familiar. There was the mist, streaked with sunlight, casting pale rainbow hues across the landscape and the vague shape of trees. The air was cool and clean as on a spring morning, soft and fresh upon his face, scented with honeysuckle. And all about him was stillness, a quiet so profound it seemed to assume a presence of its own.

Then from the mist came a woman, clothed in a gown as soft and translucent as the day. Her hair hung like a golden cloak around her, tumbling in softly curling masses to her waist. Her body was lush and strong, and she moved towards him with liquid grace until she stood before him. Mesmerized, he stared into her face, stunned by the perfection of her features and the pale ivory glow of her skin. As he looked deep into those wide, sea-green eyes, recognition came and with it a thrill of fear. But even as that fear grew, he knew it was too late to turn away. For she was already touching him, awakening a need that only she could satisfy.

Huskily, he whispered her name as he drew her closer. Then with a low moan he buried his face in her hair, expecting to breathe the sweet citrus scent that was so much a part of her. Instead it was musk – stale, rancid musk – that filled his head.

Seth's eyes fluttered open, and he raised his head from the rumpled pillow with its cloying smell of stale perfume. It took another moment for full consciousness to dawn, but when it did, he hauled himself from the bed and went to the window, flinging it wide to admit the crisp winter air. Bracing his hands on the sill he breathed deeply, letting the cold clear his head and dispel the last hazy tendrils of the dream from his mind.

Outside the window the world was the colour of putty, with

banks of clouds rolled up that mirrored the bleak landscape under its coat of greying snow.

It was the day after Christmas, and Seth could not remember when he had spent two more miserable, lonely days than the last two had been. Try as he might, he had not been able to suppress the memories of the previous Christmas: the one he had spent in Quebec with Gabrielle's family and Charl. Nor did it help that it had been the most nearly perfect Christmas he had ever known. There had been a goose dinner, wassail, and carols, both French and English, sung to Charl's accompaniment on the pianoforte. They had all gone to midnight services, and he and Charl had walked home hand in hand through the newly fallen snow. This year he'd bought himself a bottle and a whore and had found no solace in either.

'Enough!' he said aloud, determined not to waste any more time feeling sorry for himself. Not that this place and the weeks of inactivity weren't enough to drive any man half mad, he conceded as he turned back to the room and stirred the smouldering fire to flames. Perhaps today would bring his orders at last, and he could be off on some new assignment.

Half an hour later Seth had finished dressing and was preparing to leave for headquarters when there was a knock at his door. Somehow he was not surprised to find Mitchell outside. They had met by chance in a tavern a week or more ago and had swapped news of the war over a mug or two of ale. It was from Mitchell that Seth had heard the first, sketchy bits of information about the raids on the American towns along the Niagara River.

The stocky grey-haired man took a turn around the spartan chamber, carefully noting the tumbled bed and the empty rum bottle on the floor beside it. Then he lowered himself to the single straight-backed chair before the fire.

'Not the best accommodation they've given you,' Mitchell observed as he stretched his palms towards the feeble fire.

'I was lucky to get any accommodation at all when Harrison's staff disbanded,' Seth replied philosophically, aware of the room's many deficiencies.

'I hear General Harrison has gone back to Ohio,' the smaller man went on conversationally.

'So they tell me,' Seth replied.

Without glancing up Mitchell continued. 'It seems that things along the Niagara are even worse than we first thought. Reports from refugees have been filtering into my office, and two of my best men have ridden through. Between the British and the Indians, they burned everything they could find between Buffalo and Fort Niagara. Whole settlements have been wiped out: Black Rock, Lewiston, Youngstown.'

Thank God Charl's safe with Waukee, the thought intruded as he recalled the scrap of news Felix St James had imparted during the battle at the Thames River. With his dying breath, Felix had said that Charl had left Fort Malden with an Indian. Surely that meant Waukee had sought Charl out in spite of the promise he had made at Plattsburg. That realization brought a surge of relief before Seth mastered his emotions. Charl was the last person whose safety should concern him, he chided himself.

'Do you think they'll rebuild?' Seth asked, remembering the bustling main street of Youngstown and Lewiston's grassy town square with its neat fringe of buildings.

'Sure they will. Some of those folks moved to the Niagara frontier when it was no more than a wilderness. They built their cabins in forests full of Indians, when the only other white men were French and English fur traders. They saw the towns spring up and watched them prosper. Some may wait until the war's over to return, but in spite of the hardships and the memories they'll be back.'

'And when will this war be over, Mitchell?' Seth asked wearily.

'By this time next year, I'd say,' the older man prophesied, his eyes intent on the flames.

'Will we have won by then?'

'We aren't going to win this war.' Mitchell seemed resigned. 'We have never fought to win it.'

Seth drew a sharp breath in disagreement.

'Surely you don't think the British –'

Mitchell cut him short, though his voice was barely audible even in the quiet room. 'Oh no – no. No one will win it. Nothing will be resolved. We will have struggled two years and more and gained nothing. This was a political war, declared with much optimism and oratory. But like all wars it was fought with bloodshed and destruction. Even now our ambassadors, Adams, Gallatin, and Bayard, are in St Petersburg suing for peace. A few fortunes will be made in this war, a few men will come to prominence, your General Harrison for one. But otherwise nothing, nothing will have been accomplished.'

Seth had never heard Mitchell speak so frankly or with such bitterness. He was like a man who had lost the last of his illusions. As for himself, Seth reflected darkly, hadn't he lost some of his illusions, too?

For a long moment they were silent as they struggled to deal with the difficult realities of war that had cost the nation so dearly. In the harsh winter daylight the strain, weariness, and disillusionment were evident in both their faces. But even as they accepted the ultimate outcome of the war, both knew they must fight on.

Seth stirred first, taking his bicorne hat and cloak from a peg on the wall.

'Well, Mitchell, not that this hasn't been a fascinating conversation,' he began, 'but I was just on my way down to headquarters to check on my new orders. So if you don't mind . . .'

It took Mitchell a moment longer to rouse from his thoughts, and even then the bleak expression did not leave his black eyes.

'Go down there if you wish,' Mitchell replied, making no move to leave his seat by the fire, 'but I doubt you'll find your orders have arrived.' The bitterness was gone from his voice, and in its place was a quiet certainty that made Seth immediately wary.

'How do you know that?' Seth demanded, suddenly suspicious of Mitchell's intentions in seeking him out this morning. 'Have you tampered with my orders? I told you before I was finished with your schemes.'

'Now hang on a minute, Porterfield. It's not what you think. I just happened to hear about something, and since I knew you were between assignments, I thought of you. If you're not interested in it, just say so and we'll drop it.'

Damn the man, thought Seth furiously. This visit had been no more than a ploy. But then Mitchell had always known just how to manipulate a situation to get what he wanted. If he didn't agree to do what Mitchell had in mind, there was no telling how long he would be kept waiting for his orders to come. Nor did he imagine that Mitchell was above delaying those orders himself, just to be spiteful. But, then, anything would be better than the way he had spent the last month.

'All right, Mitchell. I'll hear you out,' Seth conceded, 'but if you plan to send me skulking around behind British lines again . . .'

'It's nothing of the sort,' Mitchell denied irritably.

Seth laughed at the other man's tone. 'All right! All right! You needn't look so wounded by the accusation.'

Almost immediately Mitchell's expression changed from one of irascibility to one of shrewd intelligence: an expression Seth had come to know well and distrust.

'There's a man in Tennessee who's made quite a name for himself in this past year or so by fighting the Creek Indians,' Mitchell began. 'Andrew Jackson's his name. Do you know him?'

Seth took a slender, dark cheroot from his pocket and made a show of lighting it, to buy time to catalogue what he knew about Jackson. If the tales were true, the man was a hothead. He had fought any number of duels and made more than his share of enemies, both public and private. But in spite of the unsavoury aspects of his reputation, he was known as a man of great personal courage and conviction. He had been nicknamed 'Old Hickory' by the men in the campaign to Natchez because of his tough and unwavering discipline. But in the chaos that reigned in the aftermath, he had proved himself a shrewd and resourceful leader. Seth was frankly intrigued by the mention of his name.

'Jackson?' Seth asked coolly as he exhaled a slender stream of cigar smoke. 'He's the commander of the Tennessee militia, isn't he? What's your interest in him?'

Mitchell frowned. He had hoped that Seth would know more than that about Jackson and would be able to express an opinion about him one way or the other. It was difficult to get an unbiased view of the man when half the people you talked to could not abide him and the other half championed him.

'There's a possibility that he'll be given Harrison's commission when the general resigns,' Mitchell admitted reluctantly.

Seth was stunned by the revelation of Harrison's imminent resignation, and he had the feeling that he had somehow forced Mitchell's hand.

'What does that have to do with me?' Porterfield inquired coolly.

'I want to have you assigned to his staff. We need to know his qualifications now, not after he's been appointed.'

'So you want to send me to spy on him, do you?' Seth's eyes were flinty as he regarded the smaller man.

'Damn it, Porterfield, don't make this any worse than it is.'

'I should think Andrew Jackson's qualifications speak for themselves. He's the only one who's been able to deal with the Creeks
after Tecumseh incited them.'

'Then since you've already made up your mind about Jackson,
it shouldn't be difficult serving under him,' Mitchell snapped in
return. 'If you agree, we can have your orders issued before the
new year.'

Seth threw the remainder of his cheroot into the fire and stood
staring into the flames. Wouldn't any assignment be better than
being stranded in this backwater outpost? There had been nothing
but waiting to fill his days, and even less to fill his nights. And
he knew he couldn't go on like that much longer. Jackson sounded
an interesting character at least, and the idea of going west again
appealed to him. It was the deception he didn't like.

'One condition, Mitchell,' he said without glancing at the other
man. 'Don't pass me off as something I'm not. I'll accept the
assignment if you send me as an official observer, uniform and
all. The man has a right to know why I'm there. We are fighting
on the same side, after all.'

Mitchell glared at the blond man, an expression of consternation on his round face. He would rather have sent Porterfield
anonymously, but then, from what he knew of Jackson, the man
would do as he pleased regardless of who was observing or for
what purpose.

'All right, Porterfield. You'll be assigned as an official observer,' the smaller man conceded. 'I want you to start at the
end of February.'

'I'd rather start immediately,' Seth began, but Mitchell cut him
short.

'I was hoping you'd agree to check on something else for me
on your way south. We've had reports that the winter has been
very hard for the tribes that followed Tecumseh; there's said to
be no food and much sickness. You have friends among those
Indians. I want you to stop in a few of those villages to see how
they're faring.'

'Not well, I'll warrant. Those Indians have been almost completely dependent on the British for the past year or more. I
doubt that your reports on conditions are far from wrong, now
that the British have left the Northwest.'

'You'll look into it, though?' Mitchell asked.

Seth nodded. 'Will there be aid for them if things are as bad as you say?'

Mitchell looked dubious. 'I doubt that there will be much sympathy along the frontier for Indians who were raiding and burning only a few short months ago.'

'What good will my reports do, then?' Seth asked testily.

'They'll probably help set Indian policy for the next year or two.'

'I'm not interested in influencing policy if those people are starving. Or is suffering the ravages of cold and deprivation their penance for their loyalty to the British? Of course, if that is the case, we must ask ourselves: Whatever happened to the virtues of Christian charity and the admonitions that we're to love our enemies?' Seth's words were liberally laced with sarcasm as he faced the other man.

Even in the reflected firelight, Mitchell's face was strangely grey.

'Damn it, Porterfield. I don't see that you can afford to be so judgemental. How was it you learned to love your enemies, that you can set so fine an example for the rest of us?' Mitchell countered with cynicism that matched Seth's own. 'I understand that one Major Felix St James was found dead on the battlefield beside the Thames River. And what about the beauteous Charlotte Beckwith? Surely you won't let your Christian virtues stand in the way of whatever revenge you have planned for her.'

Seth went pale with fury at Mitchell's unexpected attack. Their relationship had always been a volatile one, but the clashes they'd had in the past were over policy or assignments. Now, without provocation, Mitchell had dredged up a personal matter that was clearly none of his concern. Even through the anger, Seth recognized the inconsistency in Mitchell's behaviour this morning, but that realization did not check his response.

'You've gone too far this time, Mitchell,' Seth warned. 'What I do with my life is no concern of yours.

'I'll follow through with this assignment, if only to get out of this hellhole. But don't approach me again!'

'As you wish, Porterfield,' the man replied, his voice suddenly without the rancour it had held only a moment before.

Seth's brows snapped together in a frown as he gave the other man his undivided attention for the first time since his arrival. Mitchell suddenly seemed almost measurably older than he had only a few nights before, and his face was newly eroded by lines of pain, worry, and responsibility. His shoulders had lost the set that had always marked him as a man of power in spite of his unremarkable appearance. But most of all the change was evident in his eyes. There was still the spark of shrewd intelligence in their inky depths, but somehow there was no look of calculation and watchfulness left. Instead there was only bitterness.

Until that moment Seth had been too wrapped up in his own thoughts and considerations to see the change, but now it became obvious that something had irrevocably altered Mitchell in the past days.

'Send the information through the usual channels,' Mitchell instructed as he rose stiffly from the straight-backed chair and moved towards the door.

'Mitchell,' Seth said, halting the other man where he stood, with one hand on the door latch. 'Mitchell, is there anything wrong?'

There was a very long pause before the older man responded; and when he did, the words seemed almost wrenched from him.

'Wrong?' Mitchell replied softly without turning to face the blond man. 'Why, yes, Porterfield, there is something wrong. You are not the only one with interests along the Niagara. My father came to settle there before I was born, and my own family lived in Black Rock. When the British and the Indians came through, they killed anyone who crossed their path. My son and elder daughter were killed, as were many of my neighbours. Then those bastards threw the bodies into the burning buildings so that there was no trace left of who they might have been. My home was torched, my livestock slaughtered, and it is only by the grace of God that my wife and younger daughter escaped.

'What's worse, I know that all this death and ruin will serve no purpose. In a year's time the war will be over, and we will be asked to forgive and forget. Forgive and forget. Love our enemies. Practise Christian charity.' The words came on a reedy gust of laughter. 'What empty phrases those are now.'

Mitchell turned momentarily to face the blond man, his black eyes burning with naked pain.

'You must do your duty now, Porterfield, just as I must do mine. We have no choice about that. But if you ever do learn how to love your enemies, you let me know.'

Seth stared at the smaller man, stunned by his words. In all the years he had worked for Mitchell, there had never been any hint about the man behind the businesslike façade or the life he lived. He had been an enigma who seemed to exist only at those times and places where their paths crossed. His moods and his feelings had always been carefully masked behind his power and the strength of his will. Now quite suddenly he had exposed not only his life, but his pain as well.

In that stunning moment, Seth groped for words of comfort: for something, anything that might ease the other man's grief and bitterness. But even after Mitchell had left, closing the door silently behind him, Seth could not think of anything that would help.

꙰

He could hear the wind raging outside as the storm that had been threatening all day swept in from the Northwest, with pelting snow and plunging temperatures. Inside the wigwam Seth Porterfield sat on the thick rug of skins replete and drowsy from the warmth and food. But even as he puffed contentedly on the slender, dark cigar, his thoughts were on the many who were not as fortunate this night as he.

The weather for his trip west, thus far, had been perfect. The days had been cold and clear, and the trails had remained frozen and passable. But this weather was not good for the Indians, who depended on game, easily stalked through light snow, for their livelihood at this time of year. Still, neither that, nor Mitchell's preliminary reports, had prepared Seth for the want that was evident in the Miami and Shawnee villages. He was appalled by the silent, hollow-eyed children and the withered faces of the elders of the tribe. And as he travelled from place to place, he found that conditions were worse than he could ever have imagined. The Indians had believed the British promise, made over and over to their chiefs, that there would be ample provisions for the tribes in return for their warriors' skills. As a result, no game had been smoked or dried, no crops had been planted and put by for the winter. But with Proctor's retreat to Burlington, at the western end of Lake Ontario, those promises were as empty as Shawnee stomachs. The people were subsisting on seed corn, set aside for spring planting, and what little game they could track over the frozen earth.

Seth had bought what supplies he could before he left Pittsburg and loaded them on two scrawny pack animals. But the meagre amount he had been able to carry was as nothing in the face of the need. In the third village, where he had dispensed the last of the grain, he left the animals also, knowing full well that by nightfall they would be slaughtered to feed the hungry.

There was sickness in the Indian villages, too: old wounds unhealed from past battles and other illnesses aggravated by the deprivation and the cold. These illnesses sapped the strength of the tribes and robbed them of their warriors and hunters when the need for their vigour was great. There was a desperation in both old and young, as the winter dragged on, that hung over entire villages like the grim, grey pall of death.

Seth had arrived at Waukee's camp in the grove of sycamores well after nightfall the day before, exhausted and disheartened by what he had seen. They had talked briefly while Seth ate his meal. Then he had wrapped himself in a blanket and lain down by the fire. When he awoke at midday, Waukee was already gone to a nearby village with his bag of healing herbs. Seth had eaten a hasty breakfast of johnnycake and jerky and gone hunting. He'd been lucky enough to bring home a rabbit for supper and Waukee had turned it into a marvellous, spicy stew.

Just then the door flap was swept open to admit Waukee and an icy gust of wind that bore a few stray snowflakes into the cosy structure.

'I hope you've nowhere you must be for a day or two. It will take at least that long for this storm to blow itself out,' Waukee said as he dumped his armload of logs onto the pile beside the door.

'Are the horses all right?' Seth inquired as Waukee hung his coat on a peg and came to sit beside him.

'Fine,' the Indian assured him. 'Now, tell me what has brought you so far west.'

There had been no time for talk until now, and as Waukee brewed spicewood tea for them both, Seth explained what had transpired since they had parted in Plattsburg.

'And are you to ride with this Jackson?' the Indian asked when Seth had finished.

'Yes, then send my reports back to Mitchell,' he confirmed, sipping his tea.

'He is a hard man, this Andrew Jackson,' Waukee went on. 'The Indians, the Creeks and the Chickasaw, are afraid of him and his soldiers.'

Seth nodded thoughtfully, his curiosity aroused by this man about whom he had heard so much. A companionable silence settled between them, filled with the crackle of flames and the rushing of wind through the sycamores outside the wigwam. They were peaceful sounds that made a man thankful for the comfort of a cosy shelter and the company of an old friend, Seth thought contentedly.

After a time Waukee broke the silence, his voice oddly deep and troubled. 'You spoke Charlotte's name last night as you slept,' he said softly.

The intrusion of those words and the disturbing images that accompanied them were in variance with Seth's mood. He sighed heavily and only nodded in reply.

'Is she very much with you?' Waukee asked, his eyes intent on Seth's shadowed face, as he tried to judge the impact his unhappy news would have on the other man. If Charl was still so much in his thoughts, it would be very difficult for Seth to accept word of her death. And it would be harder still for him to accept the cause.

Seth nodded again and stared all the more persistently into the smouldering fire. 'I was all right for a while after I left Plattsburg. She had betrayed me, and there was no reason to think about her. But then I learned that she was at Fort Malden with Felix St James.'

'What!?' Waukee gasped in shock as he stared at his friend's profile, awaiting some kind of confirmation from the other man. Could Charl still be alive? he wondered anxiously. What was it the doctor had said that night almost a year ago when they stood in the deserted, snow-clogged Quebec street? The words came back to him so clearly it was as if no time had elapsed: 'I'm sorry. I don't expect her to live until morning.' But somehow Charl had survived the loss of Seth's child. A fierce gladness grew in the Indian, and deep inside him some ever-painful hurt was miraculously healed.

Seth was unaware of the emotions that flickered in quick succession across his friend's dark face. Instead he continued his musings, his voice husky with memory and regret.

'After I found out where Charl was, I couldn't get her out of my head. I met my informants in the shadow of the fort. I took chances I never should have taken just to get a glimpse of her. Then I found out that she rode along the river below Amhurstburg every morning, and I decided to meet her. I don't know what I wanted to prove to myself, or to her; but one morning I waited for her, and she came.' Seth paused for a moment, staring wide-eyed into the fire, but seeing instead a woman on horseback galloping along a wide swath of riverbank.

'Dear God, she was lovely,' he went on, 'lovelier than I remembered. But it must have frightened her to see me because she turned and spurred her horse away as if she'd seen a ghost.'

'You did not speak to her?' Waukee inquired intently.

Seth shook his head and looked up almost as if he was surprised to find the Indian beside him.

'Do you know where she is now?' Waukee persisted.

'No,' the blond man replied. 'That day at the Thames St James told me she had left Fort Malden with an Indian. When I rode in yesterday, I half expected to find Charl here.'

'Since she's not here, where is she?' the Indian demanded.

'How the deuce should I know?' Seth snapped defensively. 'She was probably evacuated from Fort Malden with the rest of the women and children. It would not surprise me if she's already found another protector to take St James' place. If ever there was a woman who could see to her own interests, it's Charlotte Beckwith. Perhaps she's even gone home to her beloved Youngstown.'

The moment those last words were out of his mouth, Seth knew there was no comfort in them. They had both heard of the destruction wrought by the British and Indians along the Niagara. In spite of himself Seth was chilled by the thought that Charl might have been caught up in that disaster.

'But why would Felix St James have told you that Charl went with an Indian if it was not so?' Waukee continued.

'I don't know why St James did anything, much less why he would lie to me about Charl,' Seth stated flatly, unaware of the penetrating look the Indian sent in his direction. 'But regardless of what St James said, I'd much rather believe that Charl is in Youngstown now than in one of those Indian villages, half frozen, starving and dying by degrees.'

His voice broke off abruptly as he remembered the deprivation he'd seen these last few days. Charl would be better off almost anywhere than with the Indians.

He frowned darkly at his own thoughts. He was being swept along by Waukee's concern for Charl, he told himself. He was worrying needlessly about her welfare. After all, why should he give a damn about Charlotte Beckwith? She had seduced him and deliberately betrayed him to St James. He had every reason in the world to hate her. And yet . . .

Waukee broke into his whirling thoughts.

'I'm going to try to find Charl,' Waukee told him, an odd light in the Indian's dark eyes. 'If she is with Indians, she must be a captive. And a blonde-haired captive should not be difficult to locate.'

There was a long pause, and then he went on more quietly. 'And if I find Charl, shall I send word to you?'

Seth hesitated as a brief, difficult battle went on inside him.

'No,' he answered finally. 'I don't care where she is. Charl doesn't matter to me anymore.'

But even as he spoke the words, both men knew they were a lie.

Thirty-Four

✳✳✳

The tall Indian moved easily along the well-worn trail between the banks of autumn bright foliage. There was a feeling of pleasant anticipation in him as he approached the wide meadow where many of his tribe had gathered in celebration of the successful harvest. This year there was much to celebrate, for not only had the harvest been plentiful, but many saw its bounty as an omen of better times to come for the Shawnee. The preceding year had been blighted by the British retreat from the Northwest, leaving all the tribes who had followed Tecumseh without provisions for the winter. There had been privation and illness in the scattered villages. But now there was hope again for Shawnee survival, and the celebration would reflect that optimism.

Abruptly the forest fell away as Waukee topped a rise, and he looked down upon a sunny basin, filled with conical wigwams. They were pitched in an orderly fashion along the banks of the swift-running river, fanning out from the central campfire in precise arcs. He had been detained in his own camp, far to the south; and as he watched the activity below him, it was evident that the festivities were well underway. With boyish excitement he started down the slope towards the large encampment. For too long he had lived a solitary life or in the company of white men. Suddenly he was anxious for the companionship and society of his own people.

As he made his way through the clusters of wigwams, he saw the familiar faces of long-absent friends, smiling their greetings at him; smelled the welcoming smells of herbs and roasting meats; and heard the shouts and laughter of a happy people. Contentment touched his heart as he looked around him, and he felt as if he was coming home. Through the babble of voices, crying children, and barking dogs he caught the sweet, familiar tones of an Indian flute. Its warm, mellow sound was a subtle counterpoint to the clamour of daily life in the village. He stood for a time, quietly watching and listening, being absorbed again into the mainstream of Indian life after nearly two years of self-imposed exile. The sense of belonging was strong in him, and he felt as if he too had new hope for the future.

The flute slowly faded as the last notes were played: then it began again with a familiar tune, far different from the first, although he could not place it. Intrigued, he moved in the direction of the sound, feeling oddly compelled to seek its source. He moved slowly, following the elusive melody through the camp until he traced it to a protected clearing between two wigwams. There in the warm October sunshine sat the woman he had been fruitlessly seeking for nearly a year, contentedly playing her carved wooden instrument.

He stood, hardly breathing, as his eyes moved over her: lingering on her pale golden face with its closed eyes and intent expression. She was thinner than she had been in Quebec, but no less beautiful. And suddenly he recognized the tune she was playing; it was the one Seth had taught her on the way up the St Lawrence River, so long ago.

Silently, he slipped behind a wigwam so that he could watch her unobserved. In the months since Seth's visit to his camp, Waukee had inquired wherever he travelled about an Indian captive with yellow hair. But as often as he asked, and as intently as he searched, there was no word of the woman he sought. Eventually, he had written to Seth that Charl was not with the Indians, that for some reason of his own, Felix St James had lied about her fate. Now, when he had given up hope of ever seeing Charl again, he had unexpectedly found her.

As Waukee watched, an Indian boy of nine or ten burst into the clearing, and Charl laid aside her flute to talk to him. From the pouch at his waist he drew several spiral shells and a handful of shiny stones and spread them out on the grass for her to admire. As she bent her golden head beside the boy's raven-dark one, Waukee caught a glimpse of her face. It was soft and tender, with a gentle smile curving her lips. He knew instinctively that this child was her adopted son.

Feeling oddly short of breath, he turned and made his way back through the encampment, unaware of the sights and sounds that had given him such pleasure only minutes before.

As he moved aimlessly along, Waukee pondered what he had seen. Charl now made her life with the Shawnee, assuming what must be a role as wife and mother and obviously finding some measure of happiness with his people. Somehow that realization badly unsettled him although he could not say why. He paused, staring vacantly around him. Perhaps it would be wisest for all of them: Charlotte, Seth, the boy, and even himself, if he simply went back the way he had come and never acknowledged that he had found her. But even as he considered that possibility, he knew he could not leave until he had seen and talked to her one last time. Circling back towards where he had left Charl and the boy, he made inquiries until he found someone who could tell him her husband's name and where he could be found.

Several minutes later Waukee approached the wigwam that belonged to Black Feather's first wife, where he found the man he was seeking and his obviously pregnant woman, Bright Bird. Waukee greeted the well-known warrior, introduced himself, and was offered a place by the fire. Bright Bird bustled to set food before the two men, then disappeared silently, leaving them alone. They conversed on general topics as they ate, and it was only when Black Feather offered Waukee an ornately carved pipe that he revealed the true reason for his visit.

'I was told,' Waukee began, exhaling a long slender stream of tobacco smoke as he eyed the other man, 'that you claim a yellow-haired woman of great beauty as your second wife. Is this true?'

Black Feather shot the stranger a suspicious look before he replied.

'Why is it that you ask about her?'

Waukee paused to weigh his answer. Would it be wiser to acknowledge that he had known Charl in a different time or to pretend that he had seen her for the first time today? Predictably he chose the truth, selecting his words with care.

'Once, long ago in Quebec, the yellow-haired woman and I were friends. When I saw her today, I wanted to know how she had come to be with the Shawnee and if she has found contentment with this life.'

Black Feather did not answer immediately, and a frown came and went between his blunt brows as he weighed the other Indian's words.

'Golden Woman is a fine wife and has proved to be an excellent mother to my son,' Black Feather reported with pride in his voice.

'But how did she come to be with you? When I last received word of her, she was at Fort Malden,' Waukee persisted.

'She came with us by her own choice,' Black Feather replied defensively, 'to escape the British major.'

'St James,' Waukee breathed with loathing.

'St James,' Black Feather agreed, sharing Waukee's emotion. 'Golden Woman was much mistreated by him.'

Then, as if their mutual hatred for the Englishman established some common ground, Charl's story began to unfold. Black Feather spoke first of her defiance in leaving St James, and of her battle with Bright Bird for possession of the opals. Then his voice softened as he went on to tell of Charl's courage in protecting Pale Wolf at the battle of the Thames River and her unstinting care during the terrible winter that followed, when both he and Bright Bird had fallen ill.

'She is a fine woman, a fine woman and a credit to her tribe,' Black Feather finished emphatically.

Waukee sat for a moment, taking the measure of the other Indian's words.

'Has she found contentment with you?' he asked again.

The frown that had come fleetingly before returned to settle on Black Feather's brow, marring it with doubt and indecision. It was a long time before he replied, and then the words seemed almost forced from him.

'Do you know the man for whom she grieves?' he asked.

There was a strange heaviness in Waukee's chest as he met the other man's eyes. In that brief moment he understood the concern that prompted the difficult question, and he recognized that they were both bound by the same frustrating emotions.

'What has she told you?' he wanted to know.

Black Feather shrugged. 'Not much. He gave her the opals she always wears in her ears, and they meant enough to her to fight Bright Bird in order to keep them. I know that for a time she carried his child. But what is more important, I know that she will never get over his death.'

'His death?' Waukee echoed softly. 'He is not dead!'

The silence stretched on almost endlessly before either man spoke.

'I will buy her from you,' Waukee offered huskily. 'I am not a rich man, but . . .'

'A token. I will give her to you for a token. She has never truly belonged to me, and she will never belong to you either. Golden Woman has given her heart, and there is only one man who will ever be able to claim it.'

'I know,' Waukee agreed as he took the bear claw necklace from around his neck and extended it towards the other Indian. 'Even so, this is the price I offer for the Golden Woman, this and a promise of my enduring friendship.'

Black Feather took the necklace from Waukee, noting its weight and size. 'I accept both as offerings of great worth,' he said solemnly.

Again silence fell between them, a silence that was broken only when Black Feather stirred to take the ear of corn that Golden Woman had given him on the night of their wedding from his medicine bag. He held it for a moment in his broad, dark hands as he thought of the woman who had brought such kindness and understanding to their union. Then he turned abruptly towards the doorway.

'Come,' he said. 'We will tell Golden Woman of her good fortune.'

As the two Indians crossed the makeshift village in the direction of Charl's wigwam, Waukee voiced another concern.

'Will she want to leave the boy?' he asked.

Black Feather considered this before he replied. 'Times were very difficult when Golden Woman came to me. Bright Bird would not accept my son because she had no child of her own. Now all that has changed. Then Pale Wolf needed a mother; Golden Woman as desperately needed a child, and the bond grew strong between them. But soon Pale Wolf will become a man and leave her behind. It is as it must be, but she would grieve for her loss. If she stays here, there will be only loneliness for her. If she goes with you, she will have her chance at happiness.'

They halted outside a small, neat wigwam at the perimeter of the camp. Black Feather called Charl's name, and after receiving a reply, he preceded Waukee through the door opening.

'I am glad you have come, my husband,' Charl began without glancing up from her sewing. 'I have nearly finished the beading on this jacket, and I am anxious to see –'

Her words came to an abrupt halt when she realized that there was a second man with her husband. Then slowly her eyes widened as she recognized who it was.

'Do you know this man, Golden Woman?' her husband asked.

Not trusting her voice, Charl nodded in reply.

'This day he has offered, and I have accepted, a price for you,' Black Feather stated matter-of-factly. 'In deference to this, I return to you the symbol of our union. You have been a good wife, Golden Woman. I hope you will find happiness in the future.'

There was a sudden constriction in her throat as she accepted the ear of corn that Black Feather placed reluctantly in her outstretched palm. So her life was changing once more, Charl found herself thinking. Fate was taking her from these people who had accepted her and given her time to heal her hurts.

'May I speak to Pale Wolf about what has happened?' she asked in a voice that quivered with emotion.

In his way, Black Feather was both pleased and saddened by her acceptance of what had transpired, and he stood for a moment weighing her response to his decision. Then he nodded, as much in agreement with the course he had chosen for both of them as in assent.

'I will send him tomorrow,' he told her. After one long, final look at the pale beauty before him, Black Feather left, securing the tent flap behind him to ensure their privacy.

Even when he was gone, Charl sat motionless, staring at Waukee.

'Charlotte?' He spoke her name hesitantly.

Then suddenly, as if she had been released from her immobility by that single word, she was across the tent and in his arms. He held her hard against him, feeling her body shake with silent sobs and ignoring the tears that wet his shirt front. Her arms held him as tightly, clamping around his waist as if she was afraid he would escape her. Smiling with strange contentment, Waukee rested one cheek in her pale hair and drew her even closer. They stood that way for a very long while, without words or explanations, in a greeting as old as time.

At last she stepped away from him and wiped her eyes self-consciously. Her nose was red and faintly mottled with crying, and her long lashes were clumped and spiky with tears. All in all, she had never seemed lovelier to him.

'Well,' she began with a watery smile, 'I suppose it isn't necessary to say I'm glad to see you. But how did you find me?'

He looked down at her standing before him, so soft, trusting, and vulnerable, and he realized he could not just blurt out the whole story. If seeing him unexpectedly after so long had been such a shock to her, hearing that Seth was alive would tax her already strained emotions even further. Instead he wanted to take her back into his arms and keep her safe for ever.

For a moment, as he stood there, temptation nibbled at the edges of his conscience. He knew Charl loved him in her own way. Perhaps if he never acknowledged that Seth was alive, she would turn to him. He might wake up every morning with her beside him, pass each day in her sunny presence, and drift to sleep at night holding her in the protection of his arms. But as quickly as the thought came to him, he forced it away. He had known, from that first moment he'd seen Charl and Seth together, that there would be no happiness for either of them apart. It might well be the hardest thing he would ever do, but he must tell Charl that Seth was alive and then help her find a way to win him back.

Waukee had been silent for so long that Charl laid a hand on his arm, conveying both her curiosity and concern. For a moment more he seemed mired in his own distant and unfathomable thoughts; then he smiled down at her.

'How did you find me?' she repeated when she realized that he had no idea of what she had asked.

Before he answered, he motioned for her to resume her seat by the fire and came to sit beside her. There was so much to be said between them. As he looked into her pale, earnest face, he only hoped that he could help her accept and understand the difficult and painful things he must tell her.

'I found you quite by accident,' he replied at last, 'though it seems I have been seeking you ever since you left Gabrielle's house in Quebec.'

Briefly, he reviewed the days and nights he'd spent outside St James' rooms waiting for a chance to speak to her alone.

As she listened, her face clouded with confusion that gave way to bitter disappointment.

'Was it you I ran from on the ramparts that day?' she asked, remembering the tall, dark figure that had pursued her across

Uppertown. 'I was so sure it was one of Felix's men sent to spy on me.'

In the depths of her eyes a haunting melancholy replaced the recollection.

'How different things might have been if only I had recognized you,' she mused.

Her distress was so evident that Waukee considered waiting until she was calmer to tell her the rest. But in the end, it was the growing temptation to keep his peace forever that forced him to go on.

'The next day, I watched them bring you back to St James' rooms. It was evident, even from a distance, that your injuries were serious. I waited outside for hours until the doctor left. And when I stopped him to ask how you were, he told me you were not going to live.'

Charl was silent as she stared vacantly ahead, seeing other days.

'I didn't want to live,' she finally admitted in a voice that was all but inaudible. 'Seth was dead on the gallows. I had lost his child and with it my last link to him. For a time after that nothing mattered, nothing . . .' Her voice trailed off into memories and her green eyes were dark with sorrow.

The moment for truth had come, but Waukee could not force the words from his lips. He knew, as he sat only inches from the woman he loved, that he had only to keep silent and offer Charl comfort for her to be his. He had only to forfeit his honour to find happiness. He had only to betray his friends to gain what he most desired.

Beside him the girl was oblivious to his struggles, so lost was she in her own thoughts. Frowning darkly, the Indian gripped her arms and shook her, as if forcibly freeing her from memories of the past. For a moment her eyes fluttered as she returned slowly from other times and other hurts.

'How did you learn that Seth was dead?' Waukee asked intently.

Charl went suddenly pale with the memory.

'St James told me,' she answered on a trembling breath. 'He returned from the execution just after dawn. "Seth Porterfield is gone," he said, and I –'

Waukee inhaled sharply at the terrible treachery of the words St James had chosen for the lie. Fresh hatred for the Englishman flashed through him. He was glad the man was dead, glad that this villainy, along with all his others, had been avenged. He shook her again, more gently this time, and looked deep into her sea-green eyes, conveying strength, compassion, and truth in his dark gaze.

'Charlotte, Charlotte, listen to me! St James lied to you,' he said tensely, knowing that with his next words he would relinquish her for ever.

'What do you mean?' she whispered, her face going paler still, until her cheeks and even her lips were totally devoid of colour. From the stark whiteness her eyes blazed intense and emerald dark.

'St James lied to you,' he repeated. 'I helped Seth escape from the prison on Cape Diamond the night before he was to be hanged. By dawn we were on our way to Plattsburg and safety.'

There was a faint roaring in her ears, and spangles of colour danced before her eyes as the meaning of his words washed over her. With difficulty she marshalled her scattered wits.

'Are you telling me that Seth is alive?' she breathed.

'Yes, yes,' Waukee confirmed. 'Seth is alive. The last time I heard from him, he was serving with Andrew Jackson near Mobile.'

He watched first comprehension, then acceptance, and finally joy dawn in her face as the colour came flooding back.

'Seth's alive?' she whispered in wonder as she remembered the warmth of his touch, the tenderness in his sky blue eyes, his teasing smile flashing white in his sun-darkened face. 'Thank God! Thank God, he's alive.'

The Indian watched her, a bittersweet current of emotion flooding through him. Charl was lost to him. If ever there had been a moment when he could have claimed her for himself, it was gone now. In telling her that Seth had escaped from Quebec, he had made her whole once more; but he had also forfeited his last chance to make her his. Looking into her luminous face, he realized he'd had no choice. He had done what he must to ensure her happiness and in doing so had preserved his honour. But even as she spoke her halting, tremulous words of thanks, he knew that in the loneliness of the night, his honour would be small comfort compared to what he had given up.

Then, slowly, Charl turned to him, asking the question he had been sure would come.

'Waukee? Why did Felix lie to me?' she asked, her voice strained and husky with tears. 'How could Felix lie to Seth about my loyalty and to me about his death?' Knowing he had no answers, she went on fiercely as the tears came again.

'Damn St James! Damn him! Damn him! Everything – everything changed between us because of St James' lies!'

Her words shuddered to a halt as sobs wrenched through her. Somehow she was in Waukee's arms again, burrowing against his broad chest seeking solace. His hands moved gently over her: patting, stroking, in an effort to calm and soothe her. But Charl was beyond comfort.

She wept noisily now in an outpouring of emotion that expressed not only her grief and hatred for St James' treachery, but in some odd way her joy at finding Seth alive as well. In the storms of tears Charl sought, and found, a release for the terrible spectrum of feelings Waukee's revelations had aroused in her.

As he held her, Waukee understood the reason for her tears. Keeping her safe within the bulwark of his encircling arms, he let her cry. And when her sobs began to subside, he cradled her gently, murmuring comforting monosyllables against her hair. After a time her ragged breathing began to ease, becoming deeper and more regular. The tension left her slowly. Bit by bit her body went slack, sagging against the Indian's chest and shoulder as the deep, dreamless sleep of emotional exhaustion claimed her.

For a while Waukee was content to hold her as she slept, fancying that somehow his strength and compassion could penetrate her exhaustion to make the sleep more restful and nourishing. Then quite suddenly, his sympathy and concern became something else; and the mounting emotions that claimed him were quite outside his role as comforter and friend. He was newly aware of the womanly softness in his arms; of the sweet, golden fragrance that was Charl's alone. Without volition his lips moved to press tender kisses along her temple and across her cheek. When she did not stir at his touch, he settled her on her bed of skins, lay down beside her, and took her in his arms once more. So deep was her slumber that Charl was unaware of the way he held her: close and tenderly as his hands moved over her, gently and cherishingly as a man might hold his wife. Even as he touched her, he could not condone his own actions; but neither could he help himself. His blood ran thick and hot in his veins, and his heart thundered in his chest. As his need and desire for her grew, he whispered all the things he'd never dared say: words and emotions he would never voice again. Still Charl slept, unaware that the Indian had poured out his love and the secrets of his heart to her. He held her for a long time: softly and intimately, sadly and longingly, as he would never be able to hold her again. Slowly, so slowly, his tension ebbed away. It was as if in saying the words he had held inside himself for so long he had found a release that left him spent but, in some odd way, stronger. And somehow, in those hours before moonrise, Waukee found a way to give Charl up forever.

❊

Charl awoke slowly, feeling as if she was drifting back to awareness on a long, slow-moving river of dreams. Her mind was still laced with foggy wisps of sleep, and she stirred sluggishly, blinking at the moonlight brightness in the wigwam. The door flap was open admitting the pure white light of the autumn moon, the scent of burning leaves, and the murmur of nearby voices, discernible above the persistent drumbeat from the harvest ceremonies being performed at the central campfire. She stretched, feeling languorous, slow-witted, and vaguely confused. Why had she slept so hard and so long? she wondered. Then her memory returned in a rush, like a splash of ice water that instantly cleared her head. And with her memory came a sweet serenity, unlike anything she had ever known. She smiled slowly as her mind embraced the wondrous truth Waukee had come to tell her: that Seth was alive. He was alive and strong and somewhere waiting for her.

Her eyes were dry and thick-lidded from weeping, but in a way hers had been cleansing, healing tears. She felt stronger now, calm and determined, as if she might never find reason to weep again. Her life was before her with its conflicts and problems. But Charl knew that life held its joys and compensations as well. And tonight she was brave and sure, ready for whatever was to come.

Nimbly, she came to her feet and, taking a moment to find a shawl and smooth her hair, went to the door.

'Waukee?' she called, aware that the voices she had heard from outside the wigwam earlier had come to an abrupt stop. 'Waukee?'

As she stepped out into the crisp night air, she caught a glimpse of a slender figure moving swiftly along the arc of tents pitched to the north of her own.

'I'm here, Charlotte,' he answered from the shadows to the left of her doorway.

As she moved towards him, she asked, 'Who was that you were talking to? I didn't mean to interrupt . . .'

'You didn't,' he replied, sounding faintly distracted. 'That was Silver Sky. Her brother and I hunted together when we were boys. She has grown up so much since I last saw her that I can hardly believe it. I remember when she was born.' His voice faded on an odd note of wonder. Charl sent a speculative glance at him, puzzled by his reaction. Then his manner changed, and there was no chance to question him further.

'Are you feeling better now?' he asked.

'Yes, much. I want to thank you for everything you've done: for buying me from Black Feather and for . . .' she began, but he silenced her with a single motion.

'There is no reason for thanks. Black Feather knew he could not hold you if you chose to go. Nor can I. You are free, Charlotte. You belong to no man.' He paused to smile at her. 'Now that there are no holds on you, what is it you wish to do with your freedom?'

She came to sit on the blankets beside him, savouring the truth in his words.

'I don't know if there has ever been a time when I have known true freedom,' she answered slowly. 'Though it seems I have been bound more often by love and responsibility than by chains.'

Charl drew a long breath, exhaling it as she contemplated what that freedom meant.

'For as long as I can remember, I have wanted to return to my father's house,' she said finally. 'When Seth first took me to Quebec, and later when I believed he was dead, all I could think about was going home. Then I lost Seth's child and neither that, nor anything else, mattered. There were times while I was travelling west to Fort Malden with St James when I might have tried to escape. I'm not sure now why I didn't attempt it. But in those days just living – getting up in the morning, putting one foot in front of the other, going through the motions of being alive – took almost more effort than I was capable of mustering. And since I've been with Black Feather and Pale Wolf, home and my father have seemed impossibly far away. It is as if

Youngstown, my father, and the store were part of someone else's life, not mine.' Charl paused, and in the faint glimmer of moonlight that penetrated the shadows Waukee could see the wonder in her luminous eyes.

'I suppose the wisest thing to do would be to return to my father's house. Now, while I have the chance,' Charl went on reflectively, 'but in spite of the prudence of making that choice, Youngstown is not where I want to go. Now that I know Seth is alive, I cannot rest until I have seen him.'

In the darkness it was impossible to read the Indian's expression, but there was approval in his tone when he spoke. 'I thought that was what you would want to do though it is not an easy road you've chosen. The way is long to Mobile, and your welcome there probably won't be a warm one.'

'Does Seth hate me?' she asked reluctantly.

'He thinks he does,' Waukee replied.

'Then he still believes Felix's lies. He is convinced that I betrayed him to the British in Quebec.' There was sharp disappointment in her tone.

The Indian's nod confirmed her worst fears.

Charl fell silent again. Across the encampment the celebration at the central campfire reached a throbbing crescendo, and slowly Indian families returned to their wigwams for the night; but she was unaware of them. Instead, her mind was busy with the dilemma at hand. She had dared to hope that time would alter Seth's perception of what had transpired in Quebec. She had thought that in the ensuing months he might gain a new perspective on the whole affair, but it appeared that he had not. For a moment her resolution failed her. How could she bear to face the hatred and scorn she had found in him that last time when she had seen him in his cell on the Citadel? The hostility in his blue eyes had all but broken her heart. But if she could not find the courage to confront him, what choice did she have except to give him up forever? Slowly, resolve seeped through her, flushing her cheeks and steeling her will. She had finally come to accept her loss when she thought Seth was dead; but now that she knew he was alive, she would be damned if she'd resign herself to being without him because of her own cowardice.

'What must I do to convince Seth I did not betray him?' she asked at last.

Waukee was both startled and pleased by the strength of the

determination in her voice. He hesitated as he sought an answer to her question, and silence fell between them once more.

'You must make Seth listen to his heart,' he told her when his contemplation was over, 'for in his heart, he still loves and believes in you. But in order to do that, you must first understand why he chose to accept Felix St James' lies, and not your love for him, as truth.'

Waukee paused momentarily, peering into the girl's shadowed face, searching for, and finding, the strength and intelligence to accept and heed what he was about to say. Satisfied, he went on.

'Seth learned as a boy not to trust his emotions and to rely only on logic and proof to guide him. Detachment became a habit with him, adopted early in life, that both protected him from those who would hurt him and marked him forever after. For as long as I have known him, Seth has lived as half a man: trusting only when logic decreed it and caring only for those who had proved their worth. It was a lonely existence, but he did not recognize it because he had never known any other. Nor did he realize the thing he had always been seeking, wherever he wandered, was the lost part of himself.'

Charl nodded slowly in agreement and comprehension at hearing Waukee voice the observations and conclusions she had arrived at on her own.

'Then you came into his life,' the Indian went on, 'making demands on him and stirring up unfamiliar emotions: arousing anger, exasperation, tenderness, and finally love. I do not know how you managed to reach him, but it was evident by the time I joined you outside York that he had begun to acknowledge his emotions at last. You made him whole, Charlotte, and the change both pleased and terrified him.'

'I did not mean to upset him,' Charl put in thickly. 'I only wanted to love him. In truth, I don't think I had any choice.'

Waukee nodded. A germ of what would grow between Charl and Seth had been there from the first. He had been aware of it, but had given it no heed until it was too late. By then he had begun to care for the girl, in spite of the fact that she was bound to his friend.

'Those last weeks in Quebec,' he went on, 'Seth was constantly off balance. His world had changed almost overnight. He was happier and more content than I have ever known him to be, but he needed time to adjust and accept the alterations your love had made in his life. He was unsure, and just when he was most vulnerable, St James came to him with proof against you. He confronted Seth with irrefutable logic and accusations that you did not even deny.'

'Would it have made any difference to Seth if I had denied St James' charges?' she countered quietly.

Waukee shook his head. 'It is hard to say,' he conceded. 'Logic and proof have always been reality to Seth. St James offered him something that had always been basic to his life, while you expected him to act on his own new, uncertain emotions. Do you understand what I'm saying, Charlotte? Another man might have been able to refute St James' accusations, but Seth could not.'

He waited for her reaction, but when she only nodded, he went on more softly.

'Seth could not let himself believe you, but neither has he been able to forget you. You have been with him all this time, in his head and in his heart. To convince him of your innocence and your love for him, you must make him acknowledge that he still cares for you. Only then will he be able to set aside his need for logic and proof. Once he's done that, he will be able to listen to the truth.'

'It isn't going to be easy to make Seth expose his feelings, is it?' she asked ruefully.

Waukee smiled at her tone. 'No. It will not be easy for him to admit that he still cares for you. He will be angry and bitter. He'll probably accuse, curse, and storm at you. But you must remember, the harder he fights, the better your chance of victory. The more cutting and venomous his words become, the closer he is to acknowledging that he still loves you. And once he does that, you need only to remain strong and constant to convince him of your intent.'

'You make it sound simple, if not easy,' she replied on a sigh. He smiled again.

'It will neither be simple nor easy. And it is not a task for the faint hearted. Seth is a stubborn man at the best of times. Even when he realizes that he still loves you, it will put everything he believes in and lives by in jeopardy to tell you. Be patient and persistent with him, and in time he will be yours again.'

Charl reached out to touch his arm, conveying her appreciation and understanding.

'You are a good friend, Waukee, to both of us,' she told him solemnly. Then a smile came to her face, and her tone changed as she went on.

'As Seth well knows, I can be stubborn, too,' she assured him. 'In that respect we are well matched. If I am ever to be happy, if either of us is to be happy, I must convince Seth that we still love each other.'

Waukee nodded slowly.

'And in that, Charl, I believe you will succeed.'

There was a moment when they sat together, listening to the night sounds, the crackle of the fire across the clearing, and the hoot of an owl in the woods that rimmed the meadow. Then Waukee stirred.

'If we are to begin this journey south tomorrow, to find Seth, you must get some rest, and so must I.'

'Come in and sleep by my fire,' she offered shyly. 'The nights are getting colder.'

But even as she spoke, he was shaking his head. 'No, I'll sleep here under the stars as I have these past nights. Now go inside; it is late. The moon is already high.'

She rose gracefully and went obediently to the wigwam. In the doorway she paused.

'Good night, Waukee. And thank you.'

'Good night, Charlotte,' he replied.

He watched Charl's dim silhouette cast on the translucent wall of the wigwam as she prepared for bed and lay down. For a long time afterwards he remained motionless, watching over her as she slept.

Finally he spoke aloud, addressing the sleeping woman, although he did not intend for her to hear.

'Yes, Charlotte, I do believe that you will win Seth back. If I did not, I would have lied to you this afternoon and kept you for myself.'

Finally, he wrapped himself in his blankets and lay down, but the birds had already begun to announce the approach of a new day before he slept.

✳

By midmorning Charl and Waukee were ready to begin their trek south. They would stop first at his camp, to pick up horses and supplies, then move on towards Mobile, where Jackson's troops had last been assigned. Charl reluctantly said her good-byes to Black Feather, Bright Bird, and several other Indian women who had befriended her during her stay with the Shawnee. But it had been most difficult to leave Pale Wolf. Her feelings for the boy had grown deep and tender, as had his for her. In the months since she had left Fort Malden they had shared a special warmth that was somehow more than friendship. And as Charl put the shells and stones that Pale Wolf had given her into the rough burlap sack with the rest of her meagre possessions, she knew that she would miss the boy terribly.

The Indian girl that Charl had seen fleetingly the night before also came to see them off. As she bid Waukee a safe journey, Charl watched them surreptitiously from beneath her lashes. Even from a distance, the admiration in Silver Sky's huge, golden eyes was evident when she looked at Waukee. Beside his towering height she seemed slight and fragile, but there was a strength and serenity about her that impressed Charl. And in spite of her impatience to find Seth, she wished that they had planned to stay until the end of the celebration to give these two more time to become reacquainted.

From the site of the Indian gathering it was a two-day walk to Waukee's camp in the sycamore grove. There they spent another day preparing for the main part of their journey. At dawn on the fourth day they set out, while the dew still clung to the fragrant grasses and wild flowers growing in clumps along the edges of the trail. It gave them a shimmering, jewel-like beauty that seemed clear and crystalline as the day itself. As they rode along, the trees met overhead, forming a canopy of gold and red and brown that matched the softly rustling carpet beneath their horses' hooves. The sky, when it was visible in patches through the trees, was clear cerulean blue, brilliant and cloudless in the sunshine. They moved steadily southward through varying terrain, keeping the wet autumn weather that heralded the approach of winter at their backs. But it was not long before the nights grew colder; and in the mornings it was frost, not dew, that etched its designs on the woods and fields. The days continued to be warm and fair, excellent weather for travellers like themselves who wanted to move quickly.

The foretaste of winter finally overtook them somewhere north of the Tennessee River, with sheeting, wind-whipped rains and bitter temperatures that added immeasurably to the discomforts of frontier travel. After two days of continuous rain, Charl awoke the next morning trembling with chills, though her skin was hot.

Waukee tied her on her horse when it became evident that she could not sit erect, and by midday he had found an abandoned cabin in the hills where they could rest. For the next two days Charl raged wildly in delirium, as Waukee tried everything he knew to reduce her fever. On the third day she was better, but it took the best part of two weeks for her to regain strength enough for them to continue.

The days were cold now, and the skies leaden with clouds that threatened snow. They could see white-topped peaks far to the east, and the trees that overhung the trail had been stripped of their leaves by the persistent wind. At night they sought shelter in abandoned cabins if they could find them, or built makeshift lean-tos as protection from the weather.

During the first week in December, they met a peddler at a river ford who told them that Jackson had been ordered to New Orleans at the threat of a British attack on that city. After that they moved on a more southwesterly course, reaching Natchez, on the Mississippi River, only slightly more than a week later. From there they might easily have taken a packet boat downstream to New Orleans, if there had been money to do so. As it was, Waukee spent the last of his hoard of coins for some clean second-, or perhaps third- or fourth-hand clothes for Charl in a disreputable establishment in Natchez-under-the-Hill. A lump rose in her throat when he presented them to her, because there was something touching that she could not explain about his determination that she would not meet Seth for the first time, after so long, dressed in her grimy, travel-stained buckskins. That night she tried on the clothes and modelled the often-mended garments as if they had been the finest silks and satins. Then she packed the things away and donned her buckskins to continue the journey south.

As Waukee and Charl travelled, they exchanged stories, filling the gaps in time and distance since they had all been together in Quebec. It was from the Indian that Charl learned of Felix St James' death at Seth's hands during the battle at the Thames River. Charl accepted the news with mingled satisfaction and dismay. She was glad her tormentor had paid with his life for his treachery and for William Porterfield's murder, but she cursed the fates that had brought her so close to Seth without reuniting them. Waukee also confirmed Seth's presence in and around Fort Malden, and admitted that Seth had been waiting for her on the riverbank below Amhurstburg that morning so long ago. The fact that she and Seth had missed each other by inches, time after time, firmed her resolve. She would find Seth in New Orleans and never let anything come between them again.

The night before they were to reach the city, they stayed in a friendly Choctaw camp some distance south of Lake Pontchartrain. For days they had heard rumours of the impending British attack on New Orleans, and of the gunboat battle that had taken place on Lake Borgne that resulted in the capture of the American ships. But as Charl slipped off into the deepening twilight to bathe in the creek, the military situation was far from her mind.

Over the long days and silent miles they had travelled, Charl had been framing the explanations she would offer Seth for her behaviour in Quebec. She had practised and repeated them over and over to herself, hoping and praying that somehow she had found the words to convince him of her sincerity. In a day or two she would face Seth for the first time in nearly two years, and she quaked at the thought. How would he look? How would he react when he saw her? That night when she had sat beside her own wigwam with Waukee, safe and secure in the Shawnee camp, she had been so certain that this was the course to follow. But now she was not sure. Suppose Waukee was wrong and Seth did not still care for her? What would happen if Seth refused to listen to her explanations? What if he heard her out and still did not believe her? Where would she go if he sent her away?

The icy cold water in the creek drove all other thoughts from her mind as she concentrated on finishing her bath as quickly as possible. She dried herself vigorously and then began to dress in the clothes Waukee had bought for her in Natchez. The chemise seemed tight and constricting after the loose-fitting Indian garments she had grown accustomed to in the last months. Had there been a time when she was comfortable in the long trailing skirts and the narrow shoes that pinched her toes? With every article of clothing she put on, she was moving farther and farther from her life with the Shawnee. Would she be sorry? she wondered. She had found a measure of contentment in her life with the Indians. Should she have remained as Black Feather's wife, or offered herself to Waukee?

She sat down wearily and began to brush out her damp hair. How many different roles she had played in her short life, she reflected. She had been an obedient daughter, a rebellious captive, a willing mistress, an expectant mother, a grieving lover, an accommodating concubine, and an Indian's wife. After all that, how much of the woman Seth loved was still in her?

With a sigh she came to her feet, pulled on the drab, blue gown, and fastened the myriad of tiny buttons that ran up the front. She had been too deep in thought to notice the cold, but now she shivered and pulled a blanket around her shoulders for warmth. Tomorrow her transformation to freed Indian 'captive' would be complete, and she would leave the protection that Waukee had afforded her all these weeks. But tonight she could still seek his reassuring presence and his unwavering friendship. She gathered up her belongings and determinedly pushed her questions and fears for the future to the back of her mind. She meant to find Waukee, to sit with him beside the fire, and enjoy his warm, soothing company one last time.

As Charl moved quietly towards the hut she would share tonight with several other women, she became aware of an oddly discordant voice rising above the others from the direction of the central campfire. It drew her attention, not because of its sheer volume but because of its cadence: slurred and flowing, sounding suspiciously like a Scottish burr. Intrigued, Charl slipped through the shadows to the perimeter of the firelit clearing. The speaker was a small, ruddy-faced frontiersman, who had obviously been sampling liberally from the earthenware jug that was being passed from Indian to Indian around the circle.

'I tell you,' he continued raucously to the Indians with bleary-eyed enthusiasm, 'that it would be to your advantage to join up with the British for the attack on New Orleans. This upstart Jackson has given you nothing but trouble since he took command of the Tennessee militia. You would do well to ensure his defeat. After the battles at Fort Mims and Horseshoe Bend you must know that these Americans will not rest until they've taken over every acre of Indian lands for their damn farms and plantations. Soon there will be no game to sustain your tribes. In time all the ancient hunting grounds will be cleared and ploughed. Join with us now to ensure a British victory at New Orleans. Then together we will drive the Americans back over the Appalachian Mountains.'

In spite of the crude and drunken delivery, Charl recognized the validity of the Scotsman's argument. She knew the Shawnee had been driven further and further west by encroaching civilization. To her it seemed a sad inevitability that the Indians would continue to lose their ancient lands to the superior forces the white man could bring to bear on them. If it were her decision, she might well heed the little man's words, though she was not sure that the British offered a much better alternative.

Then as she was about to turn and go, the Scotsman's voice reached her again.

'And do the Britishers have a plan! Good Lord! It's such a sweet plan that it will bring the entire British army to within a spitting distance of the city without the Americans suspecting a thing!'

At his words Charl sank deeper into the shadows and pulled the blanket more snugly around her to hide the telltale blue dress.

For the next minutes she listened breathlessly as the plan was explained in the Scotsman's slurred, melodious voice. Because she was unfamiliar with the area around New Orleans, there were parts of his descriptions that made no sense to her. But as she hunched beside one of the huts that rimmed the central clearing, she memorized the names and places, the landmarks and directions that the Scotsman mentioned. And as she crept off to her bed at last, she knew that before she could attempt to find Seth, she must warn the American forces of the planned attack.

✳

It had rained most of the night, leaving the air dank and cold. A heavy mist rose from the lowlands on either side of the roadway, obscuring all but the track itself in creeping banks of fog. It was difficult to say if it was the early hour, the inclement weather, or the threat of British attack; but the track was deserted except for an occasional freight wagon, loaded with military stores, that rumbled out of the murk on its way to New Orleans. At the side of the road, beneath the drooping branches of a scrubby tree, a tall Indian and a blonde-haired woman stood together. They had been there for some time, standing without speaking or without really looking at each other: postponing and prolonging the inevitable moment of farewell.

The woman shivered and drew the dark, woollen cloak she had traded for one of the skins more closely around her; though it was hard to say if it was the chill or her own apprehension about the future that made her quake. In the burlap sack, with the rest of her meagre possessions, was a small pouch of money that was to be used for her expenses in the next days. The sum had come from the sale of the horse she had ridden all these weeks. In spite of her protests, the Indian had insisted that she take the whole price to sustain her until she was able to locate the man she had come so far to find. In his generosity she recognized his concern for her, even though he steadfastly refused to accompany her further than this. Nor was the reason for his refusal unknown to her. She only wished, as she stood on the brink of the future, that she shared his conviction about what she would encounter in New Orleans. Determinedly she squared her shoulders and forced the doubts from her mind. Somehow she would brave whatever joys or sorrows the future held for her, she resolved. But her fate awaited her in New Orleans, not on this foggy strip of road.

Earnestly she turned towards the tall Indian, looking up into his dark, rugged face. It was time to thank him for his help and bid him farewell. But as she looked deep into his eyes, the words caught in her throat. Was there any way to express what his friendship meant to her? How could she thank him for what he had done? What could she say to him when she knew that part of the reason for his kindness lay in his unspoken love for her?

Thus, it was the Indian who broke the silence that lay between them.

'You must go, Charl,' he said regretfully. 'The rest of your life is at the end of this road.'

Though she knew he spoke the truth, she hesitated, searching for some way to voice her feelings. Instead of the words she sought, a question came to her lips.

'What will you do now?' she asked huskily.

He shrugged and looked away. In the past weeks he had not let himself think beyond this moment of parting. He had long been resigned to giving Charl up, but until now he had not realized how much he would miss her. He had grown used to her daily presence. As he looked down into her pale face, he realized it would be a long time before he stopped listening for her soft voice, stopped waiting for her ready laugh, stopped expecting to find her beside him. He had known this moment would come, but the scope of his loss left him desolate. They might well meet some time in the future, but things between them would never again be as they were today.

She touched his arm gently, waiting until his troubled eyes met hers once more. And as she looked into their dark depths, she realized that no words were necessary for all the things she had been unable to say.

'Go back to your people, Waukee,' she advised at last. 'They need you, and you have lived alone far too long. Find a good woman for a wife and have a family of your own. You have so much, so very much to give them. If you do that, your life will surely be a long and full one, for I have never known a man more deserving of love and happiness than you.'

Charl's eyes shimmered with unshed tears as she hugged him: holding him fiercely for one long moment before she turned to go. With swift, resolute strides she walked down the road in the direction of New Orleans. Never once did she allow herself to look back, but Waukee watched her retreating figure until it was obscured by the shifting banks of fog.

Part Four

✽✽✽

New Orleans

Thirty-Five

✳✳✳

As he bent over the maps spread out across the field desk, in Major General René Arnaud's makeshift headquarters in the marshy district to the west of New Orleans, Seth Porterfield tried hard to hide his growing irritation. Why the general insisted on wasting their valuable time in idle speculation about the probable route of the British attack, when they all might have been about more productive activities, he could not understand. Surely Arnaud must realize that all of General Andrew Jackson's staff had spent hours poring over maps such as these since their arrival in the city on 1 December. They had studied the approaches to New Orleans, both by water and by land, and devised means to block, monitor or defend each one. Since then they had begun to implement these plans: establishing outposts; building earthworks; reinforcing existing fortifications, like Fort St Philip at English Turn on the Mississippi River, or Fort St John on Lake Pontchartrain. In addition, Jackson had encouraged the training and deployment of new militia units such as those under Arnaud's command. Outside the cabin, the troops of Arcadian trappers and fishermen that Seth and Colonel Will Hubbard had ridden out to inspect continued to drill in the rain and cold as their officers attempted to transform them into a fighting unit worthy of the name. And precious little time they had to succeed, Seth reflected grimly. Already the British had been sighted and a battle fought on Lake Borgne in which five American gunboats had been lost. After that, panic had seized the city, and Jackson had been forced to revise his original opinion of Jean Lafitte's 'cut-throats' and accept their offer of help. Since then, however, John Coffee and his Tennessee militia had arrived from Baton Rouge, and William Carrol's Tennessee volunteers were expected at any moment to swell the American ranks. For the first time since he had marched into the city, Jackson seemed to have the situation under some kind of control. Still there was much to be done, and Seth was impatient with Arnaud's endless speculation.

Across the table Seth exchanged glances with Will Hubbard, who was nodding attentively as Arnaud prattled on in rapid French. Will had joined Jackson's staff in May, shortly after the general received his commission from the Army. Since then he and Seth had resumed the friendship that had begun when they were both in Mitchell's employ, and had worked closely on several projects for Jackson. Seth frowned as he listened to the Creole's words, and reflected that it was fortunate that Will had elected to accompany him this morning to review Arnaud's troops. Will had been in New Orleans since October, working with several other officers to prepare a defence of the city. In that time he had developed the necessary patience for dealing with these old-fashioned, stiff-necked Creoles, and Seth was glad to defer to Will's more diplomatic nature in this matter.

As the general droned on, Seth became aware of a disturbance on the wide porch of the house.

'I tell you, mademoiselle,' he could hear the sentry's words drift down the hallway from the front door, 'the general is very busy just now and can't be disturbed.'

'Please, corporal,' came the reply in a low, musical voice that Seth would have recognized anywhere in the world. 'I have come with some information of great importance. Please, I must see the general.'

At the woman's words Seth's heart gave an uncomfortable lurch and began beating an erratic tattoo inside his chest. He knew that voice as well as he knew his own, but he drifted to the window anyway to confirm the speaker's identity.

She stood before the adamant militia corporal, her face pink with cold and her golden hair tumbling across her shoulders where the hood of her shabby, dark cloak had slipped back.

Charl. Seth nearly said her name aloud as his eyes moved hungrily over her. It had been all of two years since that day in the prison in Quebec, and he still found her almost unbearably beautiful. She was thinner than he remembered, and her face had lost the last hint of girlish roundness. Instead her fine, strong features had become more pronounced beneath her flawless skin. But otherwise she had not changed.

'Please, corporal,' she was saying, her sea-green eyes wide

with entreaty in a deceptively innocent expression that Seth instantly recognized as anything but innocent. 'I must talk to General Arnaud now. I am sure that once he hears what I have to say, he will bless you for your perceptiveness in letting me in to see him.'

'I'm sorry, mademoiselle,' the soldier persisted. 'My orders are . . .'

But as he spoke, Charl allowed the burlap sack she carried to slip from her fingers to the floor, spilling its contents across the porch. As the young soldier bent to help her retrieve her belongings, she brushed past him, rushed down the hallway and burst into the main room of the small house.

'General Arnaud!' she exclaimed as she bore down single-mindedly on the startled officer.

'What is the meaning of this intrusion? Who are you?' he demanded, recovering himself slightly.

'Please, General, I beg only a few minutes of your time. My name is Charlotte Beckwith, and I have come by some information that might well save New Orleans from the British!'

Seeing Arnaud's startled expression, Charl seized the moment and continued.

'A companion and I spent last night in an Indian camp some miles from here. As you must know, British agents have been circulating through the villages in an attempt to incite the Indians to rise up against the Americans and aid in an attack on New Orleans. Such a man was in the village where we spent the night. He plied the Indians with liquor in order to gain their favour and in the process became quite intoxicated himself. In that state, he let slip some information that might well provide General Jackson with advance knowledge of British plans.'

As Charl addressed the general, Seth had done his best to compose himself for a confrontation with this beautiful and treacherous woman from his past. He was vaguely aware of the expression of mingled recognition and astonishment on Will Hubbard's angular face, and he shot a quelling look at his friend before he spoke.

'I know this woman, General,' Seth drawled, amazed by his own casual tone of voice and offhand manner, 'and I'd not believe her word for something I'd seen with my own eyes.'

Instantly Charl recognized the voice with its rich, mellow tone and clipped words and whirled around to seek its source.

For an interminable moment her eyes met Seth's deep blue ones, and they stood staring, as if suspended somewhere outside time and space. Her first impulse was to reach out and touch him, to be sure he was real. But the expression in the sapphire-dark depths of his eyes placed the yawning chasm of his doubt between them. Before she could try to span it, Seth looked away, breaking the unbearable intimacy of the communication that had flowed so briefly between them.

'I knew this woman in Quebec,' Seth went on to Arnaud. 'She was a British informer, ruthless and shrewd. She nearly cost an agent or two their lives. Although she'll probably claim to be an American citizen, I warn you not to believe a thing she says. I don't know what purpose she has in approaching you today, but whatever she tells you will be suspect for I have no doubt that Miss Beckwith is here to act as a British spy.'

It had been with great difficulty that Seth had turned his gaze from Charlotte to Arnaud as he stated his charges, but Will Hubbard had continued to watch her. He had been aware of the spark that had ignited between these two people at the initial contact, and knowing something of what had transpired between them, he was curious about the girl's reaction to this unexpected encounter. Judging from what he'd been told about her treachery in Quebec, he was unprepared for the sequence of emotions that crossed Charlotte Beckwith's flushed face. At first there had been disbelief in her expression, that changed gradually to pure joy. Her eyes moved slowly over Seth, touching him everywhere: gently, caressingly, filled with unabashed wonder. A tender, bittersweet smile touched her lips, and her face glowed with emotions that were the antithesis of what he expected of this woman.

Good Lord! She's in love with Seth, Will found himself thinking in confusion as he watched her. Surely he could not be mistaken about that when her feelings were so evident. Nor did he believe that any woman could pretend the warmth he saw in this girl's eyes when she looked at his friend. But why didn't Seth realize how she felt? Why was he so adamant in his belief that she had betrayed him? And how could he claim to hate her when Will had seen the strength of her effect on him? Then Will had no more time to wonder because Arnaud was speaking, drawing his attention.

'What do you make of these charges against you, mademoiselle? This man has named you as a British spy.'

Charl turned her gaze reluctantly from Seth to the Creole and took a moment to collect her thoughts.

'I am no spy, sir,' she said softly, 'though this gentleman may well have reason to believe otherwise. But perhaps it would be best to tell you what I overheard and let you judge for yourself if it would be of value to General Jackson.'

Arnaud exchanged glances with the two other officers, then nodded.

'Perhaps I could show you on a map,' Charl offered, indicating the ones spread out across the field desk.

'By all means,' the general agreed and stepped aside to allow her access to the pile of charts.

Charl took a moment to study the carefully drawn documents as the three men looked on. Finally, she indicated a point somewhere south of Lake Pontchartrain.

'I believe this is the location of the Indian village where we stayed last night,' she began.

'That could be true,' Arnaud confirmed. 'There is an Indian village near there.'

Encouraged, Charl went on.

'The man who came to the camp said that after the gunboat battle on Lake Borgne the British troops were landed on an island called Ile au Pois. There,' she said, pointing triumphantly.

Will confirmed this with a nod of his head. 'We've heard reports to that effect,' he said, but Seth broke in.

'This is all common knowledge,' he challenged. 'Surely you realize that a British agent would offer enough genuine information to make her lies seem plausible.'

Charl looked up into his sceptical face; her eyes were calm and steady but she was troubled by his doubt. What an effective job St James had done of turning Seth against her. What chance did she have of convincing him that she had not willingly cooperated with Felix in Quebec if she could not make him believe her in this matter, where her word could be checked for its veracity? With determination she fought down the surge of hopelessness that threatened to overwhelm her. She could only pray that this time the truth she meant to set before Seth would be stronger than St James' lies.

'I agree with you, Captain Porterfield,' she answered levelly.

'If I came here to deliberately mislead you, information that was half fact and half fiction would prove the most effective course. Thus far you've been able to confirm what I've told you. Surely it cannot hurt to hear me out. Then it will be up to you to judge or verify what I have to say. Either way, you have everything to gain and nothing to lose.'

'Go on,' Will encouraged her.

'The British agent told the Indians that the troops would row across Lake Borgne to a bayou that wound around and eventually came out at the river. Some sympathetic Spanish fishermen that the two English scouts found in a village at the mouth of the bayou showed them the way. The man laughed when he told the Indians that, and said that the scouts drank a toast to a British victory with water from the Mississippi when they reached the river.' Charl paused and bent over the map.

'Ah. This must have been their route: Bayou Bienvenu. There's the fishing village, and if you follow the southern branch of the bayou, it connects to several canals that run to the river.' Triumphantly, Charl traced the route with her finger as the men watched, their faces frozen in various attitudes of interest, consternation and scepticism.

Will Hubbard broke the silence, whistling low under his breath.

'Good Lord! That can't be more than eight or nine miles below the city,' he breathed.

'And you say the scouts found no impediment to their journey down the bayou?' Arnaud inquired, an odd note in his voice.

'Apparently not,' Charl replied. 'This is the route the British agent described to the Indians as the one the troops would use for their attack.'

Slowly, Arnaud straightened, his Creole features flushed with anger.

'I fear you have made a grave error, mademoiselle, in bringing this story to me,' Arnaud began in a voice that was low with outrage. 'Earlier you asked us to test the authenticity of your information by challenging us to discredit it. That was a bold bluff, but one I am forced to call. For as certainly as we were able to verify the location of the Indian village where you claim to have passed the night, I can refute this last. I know for a fact that the route you have just shown us is indeed carefully guarded by my neighbour, Pierre de la Ronde, and my son, Jacques. Both are fine Creole gentlemen who would not shirk their duty. To intimate that British scouts could pass without question through bayous that I know to be blocked and guarded negates everything you have told us.

'I fear you are, as Captain Porterfield claims, mademoiselle, a British spy. And we deal harshly with spies here.'

'My God, Arnaud. How can you be so sure it's a lie?' Will found himself coming instinctively to the Beckwith girl's defence, although he had as much reason as the others to doubt her.

'I heard Jackson make the assignments himself, Will,' Seth put in. The expression on his drawn face was one of mingled pain and satisfaction, as if this evidence of Charl's guilt was both vindication and further betrayal. As he went on, he could not bring himself to look at the girl.

'The British must be planning their approach from another quarter, and they have sent this information on as a feint. If we are fools enough to believe this woman's lies, our troops might be drawn off to the south and east, leaving us open to attack from a different direction.

'Though if Miss Beckwith's purpose was to gull us into swallowing her lies, why she chose to affect this preposterous story of overhearing British plans in an Indian village, of all places, I am at a loss to understand,' Seth went on. 'Still she is a creditable actress and in other circumstances might prove to be quite persuasive.'

Seth's words were purposefully cutting and cruel, and Charl might have reacted with anger if she had not been so frightened. It had not occurred to her that her information might be suspect or that she would be branded as a spy. But beyond concern for her own safety, Charl was terrified and devastated by the strength of the resistance she found in Seth. Could she ever convince him that she loved and needed him? Or that what had happened in Quebec had been St James' doing, and not hers?

'Have you anything to say in your own defence, mademoiselle?' Arnaud asked.

In that moment of despair, she shook her head, never raising her tear-glazed eyes from the floor.

'Very well,' the general continued, adopting an officious tone. 'Then for treason against the United States and the Louisiana territory, I sentence you to death by firing squad. The execution will be carried out at three o'clock today. And may God have mercy on your soul.'

There was a moment of stunned silence in the cabin. Then Charl and Will Hubbard were both speaking at once.

'What I told you is the truth! I swear it!' Charl began in a quaking voice.

'Now wait a minute, Arnaud! You can't sentence Miss Beckwith to death without a trial. And an execution by firing squad, it's barbaric! Let me take her to General Jackson's headquarters. There may well be more she can tell us, whether she's a spy or not.'

The militia commander brushed their words aside. Drawing himself up to his full height, Arnaud faced Hubbard angrily.

'Martial law has been declared, Colonel. I am well within my rights to judge and sentence this woman as a spy. You of all people should know that. As for the means, that is at my discretion also. As both you and your General Jackson have been so quick to point out, we Creoles cling to our traditional ways. Just consider execution by firing squad one of our quaint, old customs. Perhaps you will even wish to extend your visit with us until three o'clock to judge for yourself the effectiveness of this antiquated practice!'

Will opened his mouth and closed it again. There was nothing he could do to help the girl. Arnaud outranked him and seemed bent on making an example of her.

Arnaud turned to address Seth.

'Captain Porterfield, since you seem to have a particular interest in this woman and her past misdeeds, I am giving you the honour of commanding the execution detail. There is a storehouse on the far side of the creek where Miss Beckwith may be detained until her execution. The officer of the day will give you the key and some men to guard her. Now see to your prisoner, Captain.'

Seth turned to Charl, his face impassive and his blue eyes impenetrable. Without a word he took her arm and led her towards the door. As they left the room, she broke away and turned back to Arnaud.

'What I told you is the truth!' she blazed at him, her face flushed with anger and frustration. 'Some day soon you will awaken to find the British at your gates. Then, when it is too late for both of us, you will know I did not lie!'

Almost gently Seth took her arm and spoke to her directly for the first time. 'Come on, Charl,' he said softly.

For an agonizing moment she looked up at him, the morass of her conflicting emotions evident in her eyes. Finding nothing in him that might offer her comfort, she wrenched her arm from his grasp, squared her shoulders and preceded him down the hall.

❖

Will waited for Seth to return from the storehouse on the narrow wooden bridge that crossed the creek. He was more than a little disturbed by what had transpired in the past hour and meant to confront Seth for his part in it. Frowning, he watched the stream, swollen by the persistent rains, swirl over its bed of mossy stones. He could not explain why he felt so strongly about what was happening to the Beckwith girl; but he knew he could not stand idly by and let her die. He had dealt with intrigue long enough to know better than to judge a situation by what it seemed or to be swayed by feminine allure. Still, he was irrefutably sure of Charlotte Beckwith's innocence in this matter by the naïve and earnest way she had presented herself. Even if the information she brought proved to be false, Will could not convince himself that she had come to Arnaud's camp for any sinister purpose.

With mild surprise he realized that it had been the unguarded expression in the girl's eyes in that first moment when she had turned to Seth, that had won him over to her cause. No woman could counterfeit the emotions he had seen in her, and he could not fathom how Seth had come to believe so strongly that she could.

Just then Will heard footsteps on the path and turned to see Seth approaching from the direction of the stone storehouse. His tanned face showed no emotion, but he moved as if unspeakably weary.

'Is Charlotte settled?' Will asked.

Seth came up to where Will stood and leaned heavily against the wooden railing.

'For the moment,' he answered, then paused before he said more. 'God! That storehouse is a wretched place. I'm sending someone back with a lantern and some blankets in the hope that these will make it more comfortable for her.'

'Do you really think that will help her much?' Will asked.

'No, no . . .' his voice trailed off.

'You can't go through with this, you know.' Will's words were half statement and half question.

Seth shrugged, moving his broad shoulders as if they bore a tremendous weight.

'I have no choice,' he answered flatly.

Will was momentarily stunned by the other man's complacency. Of all the ways Seth might have reacted to Arnaud's order for Charlotte Beckwith's execution, Hubbard had not expected indifference. There should have been some emotion in Seth besides this icy detachment: a thrill of revenge if he truly hated her; despair if he cared for her; and even if he felt only impersonal compassion, there would have been regret.

'Good God, man! Tell Arnaud you won't go through with this,' Will urged him.

'They'll only find someone else to carry out the orders,' Seth pointed out dispassionately.

'Then tell him you were wrong about her. Tell him you confused her with someone else you knew in Quebec. Tell him anything, but don't let him execute the girl on this flimsy kind of evidence.'

Porterfield turned cold eyes on the other man.

'What you don't seem to grasp is that Charlotte Beckwith is guilty. She collaborated with the British in Quebec, and I have no doubt that she's working for them here in New Orleans. If we hadn't happened on her today and spoiled her little game, there's no telling what kind of harm she could have done.

'And how is it you've suddenly become her champion? It's not like you to be taken in by a pretty face.'

It was the same question Will had asked himself only a few minutes before.

'I think you're wrong about her,' he stated quietly after a moment. 'I think Miss Beckwith is telling us the truth as she knows it. She overheard a man she believed to be a British agent telling the Indians about a route through the swamp. If you ask me, her only intention in coming here was to warn us.'

Seth gave a rough approximation of a laugh.

'And next you'll be telling me you believe in fairies,' Seth scoffed. Still, Will's stubborn insistence on Charl's innocence played on his own doubts. The other man's judgement had proved right so often in the past that Seth found his resolve weakening. After all, didn't he want to find a way out of this for Charl, and for himself?

'Why do you believe her?' Seth asked intently, as if he wanted to be convinced.

Will knocked the ash from the bowl of his pipe and slid the meerschaum into his pocket before he replied. If he tried to explain how he'd come to the conclusion that Charlotte Beckwith was to be trusted, Seth would not believe him. His opinion of the girl was based on intuition and a knowledge of human nature. Seth wanted, and needed, cold, hard facts to overcome his suspicion and distrust. But then, what course did he have open to him, Will reflected, but to lay the truth before Seth and hope his friend could see past what had happened in Quebec?

'This may sound odd, but I believe Charlotte Beckwith is here for the purpose she claims primarily because what I've observed does not mesh with what you've told me about her.' Sensing the coming interruption, Will hurried on. 'I saw the way she looked at you in those first few moments. When she turned and saw you, it was evident that nothing else mattered to her: not your accusations, who else was in the room or why she'd come.'

Seth gave a rasp of bitter laughter. 'I'd never have taken you for such a romantic, Will,' he frowned.

Hubbard was undeterred.

'The basis for your certainty about her guilt is what happened in Quebec, not what's happening here in New Orleans. And somehow, Seth, I can't help but think you've got it all wrong. Besides, wouldn't it be wise to at least check on Bayou Bienvenu to be sure it's as carefully guarded as Arnaud says? Damn it, Seth! There are too many holes in this thing to let the general go ahead with his plans.

'If you allow yourself to be a party to this execution, and do nothing to stop it, you'll regret it for the rest of your life. You don't want Charlotte Beckwith's death on your conscience, do you?'

'When it comes to Charl I've never known what I wanted!' Seth admitted vehemently, turning to stare at the swirling water so Will could not see the sudden anguish in his eyes. But his voice: low, husky, filled with pain, told the whole story.

Will was quiet for a time while he determined his own course of action apart from whatever Seth chose to do.

'I'll tell you what you want from Charlotte Beckwith,' he finally offered. When Seth did not stop him, Hubbard continued. 'You want to take her in your arms and have her convince you, beyond any doubt, that in spite of how it seemed in Quebec she was innocent of any complicity. If she could do that, you'd be damned sure to find a way to save her from Arnaud.

'Seth! For the love of God! Can't you see that half the reason Arnaud wants to see her dead is because Charlotte cast a slur on his family's name and honour by suggesting that the bayous and canals his son was assigned were not properly guarded?'

Seth continued to watch the water as if mesmerized by its froths and swirls.

'And don't you see there's nothing I can do?' he replied softly.

'Then I am riding to New Orleans to get a stay of execution from General Jackson since he's the only one who outranks Arnaud. I think 'Old Hickory' might be quite interested in what Miss Beckwith has to say. Then he can judge whether or not she's a British spy. You'd just better hope I can get back by three o'clock. And if I'm not, you're a damn fool if you don't find a way to stall that firing squad.'

With those parting words Hubbard turned on his heel and stalked in the direction of the stables. He was well out of earshot when Porterfield finally spoke.

'Good luck, Will,' he said softly.

Seth stood on the bridge a while longer, unable to bring himself to move on. With deliberate concentration he watched the water as he tried desperately to sort out the shambles the last hour had made of his life.

He'd been moderately content since he'd been assigned to Jackson's staff. He liked the backwoods commander with his fiery temper and his blunt language. The friendship he'd resumed with Will Hubbard was warm and satisfying. But in the past year there had been little in his life but his duty. Most of the time it seemed enough. It was only when he awoke alone in the middle of the night or saw Will's pride in his young family that he realized how empty his life had become.

It had been one evening, after dinner with Will and Janette, that he'd got well into his cups on Will's imported brandy and had unintentionally poured out the whole maudlin story of what had happened in Quebec. Most likely it had been the almost tangible contentment of the quiet domestic scene that had opened old wounds and prompted the uncharacteristic disclosure. It had been a mistake, of course, and he wished that he had kept his peace. But then he had needed their consolation and understanding.

Now today, suddenly and unexpectedly, Charl had been thrust back into his life, forcing an agonizing conflict between his already fragmented emotions. One angry faction of his mind sought to destroy her for her treachery, while another cried out a joyous welcome and counselled forgiveness. The only thing he was certain of, as he stood staring blindly at the water, was that he still wanted her. He still wanted Charl with the same single-minded compulsion that had driven him to take her to Quebec. Even as he stood there gripping the bridge railing until his knuckles went white, he realized that to succumb to his desire would be to condemn himself to an endless circuit of self-pity and regret. For his own sanity he must stay away from Charl until – until three o'clock.

Resolutely, he turned towards the main camp. He needed to dispatch someone to the storehouse with a lantern and some blankets. God knows it was the least he could do for Charl in that dungeon, he thought wearily.

He had nearly reached Arnaud's headquarters when a sentry stopped him.

'The lady left her bag,' the man informed him as he thrust a rough burlap article at him.

Seth had been so busy with his own thoughts that he accepted the torn and dirty item without comprehension.

'What?' he mumbled in confusion.

'The lady, the pretty lady that was taken to the storehouse, she left her bag on the porch at headquarters.' Slowly understanding began to dawn, and Seth recognized the adamant young corporal who had tried to block Charl's entry to General Arnaud's office. 'I thought she might be wanting her things.'

'Yes, thank you,' Seth managed to reply. 'She might well want her things at that.'

After sending an orderly off to the storehouse with the supplies for Charl, he found a campfire with a coffeepot steaming over the coals. He helped himself to a cupful and sat down on a log beside the fire to enjoy its feeble warmth. He'd go through Charl's bag to be sure that it contained no weapons and then send it along to her for what comfort it might offer.

He dumped the contents of the bag on the ground between his feet and stared down at the treasures Charl had managed to amass since he'd last seen her in Amhurstburg. It was not an impressive store of possessions, he reflected. First he removed the long-bladed knife from the pile, balancing it between his fingers for a moment before setting it aside. In addition to the knife, there was a bag of coins; a yellow shawl, nearly as tattered as the cloak she had worn for warmth; a tortoiseshell comb and brush, three delicate spiral shells and a handful of pretty stones; a buckskin pouch with a quill design and a pair of moccasins. Seth picked up one of the doeskin shoes, turning it over and over in his hands. It was soft and well worn.

Was it possible that Charl had been with the Indians all these months as St James had said? he wondered. Or had this array of objects been gathered purposefully to mislead anyone who was thorough enough to check the girl's belongings?

He set the shoe aside and picked up the drawstring pouch. Opening it, he dumped the contents into his hand. There were a number of packets of herbs, their fragrances mingling sharply in the fresh air. Instinctively he knew their source. But when had Charl seen Waukee? And hadn't Waukee told her that he was with Jackson? If she had known that, why had she come to New Orleans with her lies? Hadn't she seen the danger?

The last object from the pouch sent a sickening curl of recognition through him. It was only an ear of corn, but Seth had lived with the Indians long enough to know its significance. Charl had been a warrior's wife. The custom was a common one. A woman could be passed from warrior to warrior as easily as the ear of corn, symbolic of her fertile body, could change hands. A searing flame of anger and pain swept through Seth. How many other men had Charl welcomed into her arms just as she had welcomed him? How many times had she given herself in passion just as she had abandoned herself to him?

Impulsively, Seth cast the corn into the fire and watched as the flames embraced and engulfed it, feeling strangely cleansed by the act. Then the terrible symbolism of what he had done came to him. In a matter of hours he would be called on to end Charlotte Beckwith's life with the same merciless detachment he had used to destroy this token of her being.

Suddenly, his breath caught in his throat as the terrible reality of what he was expected to do raged through him.

Dear God! He did not want to see Charl die, or, worse, be the instrument of her death. In spite of what had passed between them and the hatred for this woman that he had nurtured for so long, he could not countenance what was to happen. Was it possible that he had no choice? But even as he considered going to Arnaud, he knew the general would see the sentence carried out even if he refused to do the deed. Nor would he abandon Charl to ease his own conscience.

Regret washed over him in waves as he clenched and unclenched his fists in silent agony.

Damn! He had no idea that things would come out as they had when he accused Charl of duplicity this morning in Arnaud's office. But in good conscience could he have done otherwise, when he was certain that Charl had come from the British with false information meant deliberately to mislead Jackson? He wished that he could somehow make her understand what he'd done. He did not want Charl to die thinking that his motive in exposing her was revenge for her treachery in Quebec and not loyalty to the country she had once claimed as her own.

If only he could talk to her, he found himself thinking feverishly. There was so much he wanted to tell her and explain.

His mind teemed with questions, too. Had she lived with the Indians as her belongings seemed to indicate? When and where had she seen Waukee? And why hadn't the Indian written that he'd found her? Where had she been since the fall of Fort Malden? Did she know that Felix St James was dead? And above all, there was the one question he dared not ask: Why had she betrayed him?

But even as he considered approaching her, he realized he dared not. For stronger than his wish to make her understand, or his own need to know, was his staggering physical desire for her alone. In all the time since they were together in Quebec, and with all the women he had sought, he had never satisfied the craving that Charl aroused in him. If he was fool enough to confront her, there would be no questions asked and no understandings reached. If he went to her now, there would only be his lust and the sweet damnation of his body on hers.

Instead of going to her he stared down at her belongings with an expression in his eyes as sad and bleak as the promise of an early grave.

Thirty-Six

✳✳✳

As three o'clock approached, rational thought became impossible for Seth. He had vowed he would stay away from the storehouse across the creek where Charl was being held. But in spite of his best resolves he could not keep his eyes off the place or banish from his mind the traitorous, glorious woman locked inside. Like a siren she called out to him, urging him to come closer and be destroyed. He fought the need to see her and talk to her one last time, but her memory seared his brain and his desire for her was so strong he ached with it. It didn't matter that she had betrayed him in Quebec, or plotted with Felix St James for his downfall. He burned for her, so desperately needing the corrupt softness of her body to soothe him.

As the hour of the execution approached, he tried to tell himself that Charl deserved to die for the treachery she had wrecked on him and for the deadly deception she had tried to work on them all. Perhaps if she was gone, he could force her from his mind and the dreams that left him hot and trembling in the middle of the night would finally cease. But if Charl was dead, he would never know her sweet body again.

Without volition and tortured by his own actions, he found himself approaching the storehouse on the far side of the creek.

'I've brought Miss Beckwith her belongings,' he heard himself tell the guard and was surprised that his voice could be so calm.

A moment later the bolt was slipped back, and the door opened beneath his hand. Inside the storehouse, huddled in a circle of lamplight was Charlotte: his Charlotte, Charlotte the traitor, Charlotte the whore. Dear God! Why was she so beautiful?

She came slowly to her feet, letting the cloak and blankets slide to the floor as she faced him.

His breath was coming in quick gasps as he entered and closed the door behind him.

'I brought your bag,' he said thickly as his eyes moved hungrily over her. Her hair was like a curtain of gold silk tumbling across her shoulders. Her body was lush and full beneath the tight gown. Her green eyes were wide and luminous, locking with his as he stepped closer.

He would have her, he thought dizzily, as if the decision was not already made. He would have her before the bullets tore her silky flesh, before her blood stained the parade ground, before her body was broken and ugly.

He knew Charl could read his thoughts, for her eyes went wild with mingled outrage and anger. In the moment before he flung himself at her, he heard her whisper: 'Oh, Seth, please no. Not like this, not this last.'

But there was a roaring in his ears, and he was beyond caring about anything except satisfying the wild, driving lust in his blood. When he reached for her, the bodice of her gown came open under his hands, sending a rain of tiny buttons around the room. Incoherently mumbling a jumbled string of endearments and curses, he pressed his face to her breasts as he pushed the remainder of her dress and shabby underclothes to the floor. A moment later he found her taut nipples with his lips and he pulled her against him as they collapsed together on to the tumbled pile of clothes and blankets. She was pale gold all over just as he remembered: her arms, her legs, her hair. Holding her still with his weight, he devoured her. His lips moved across her chest, paused in the hollow above her collarbone, nibbled gently along the curve of her throat to the sensitive pulse point just below her ear. With trembling hands he explored her; stroking her back, her hips, her thighs. He tugged at his own clothes, working out of them as he held her, until he could sense, feel, enjoy her with every part of his body. Pulling her more tightly against him and moaning softly, he finally kissed her mouth, savouring its remembered sweetness.

Charl fought him madly at first, hitting his shoulders and chest with her fists, but she had been too long without him. Seth's body was warm, hard, and vital against hers and in spite of her hasty resolutions to resist him, her body was working its own betrayal. Under the onslaught of his kisses her anger, disappointment and despair were dissolving in a flood of sensations. Her mouth clung to his in an eagerness she could not control, and her hands moved over him compulsively and tenderly, urging him on. The sweetness of this reunion staggered her, searing through her, leaving a pain in her chest that both frightened and enraptured her.

She knew his big body well from those glorious nights in Quebec, and she responded instinctively, touching, stroking, caressing him in the ways that pleased him most. Sensing her surrender, Seth opened her thighs and entered her with a stroke that was torture and bliss for them both. He moved deeper, claiming her and being claimed by her as her legs tightened around his waist, locking them together. For a long moment their gazes held, and she could read the need, the hurt and the confusion in the sapphire-dark depths of his eyes. There had never been any pretence between them in the tender moments when they were one, she reflected dizzily, and suddenly she understood the terrible conflict of emotions that drove him. Then his mouth came down to claim hers, his tongue probing, sweet and demanding. She surged against him in response, arching upwards to take him deeper still, carrying them beyond restraint. Suddenly their motions were too violent and frenzied to prolong the moment, and they crashed together through the barrier of sensation and emotion and love. And for that trembling moment nothing else existed.

Seth fought his way back to coherence, rolling away from Charl and resisting the impulse to hold her close. He had told himself over and over that he hated this woman, but for this moment she was the most precious thing in his world. Her hand reached out to touch him, to hold him there beside her, but he resisted.

'Wait, Seth, please wait. We must talk,' she pleaded, her voice bleak. 'It will be our last chance.'

He tensed at her words, then pulled away seeking to rise, but she would not allow him to go. Instead she held him tightly until he sank back against his will. He did not want to hear what she had to say.

'Seth, please. I need to explain –' she began.

'Damn it, Charl. Don't you know that nothing you can say will mean anything to me?'

'Listen to me!' she demanded.

'No!' he replied.

But before he could gather himself to stand, she was on top of him, straddling his hips with her knees, pinning his shoulders with her hands as she leaned forward to kiss him. He tried to flinch away, but she would not let him. Her seeking tongue explored his mouth as she kissed him ardently, and she moved lower to allow her breasts to brush his chest with maddening slowness. She felt him respond involuntarily, as she knew he must. For he was no more immune than she to the mysterious attraction that existed between them. His breathing was deeper, faster and he went suddenly very still. She moved to lie beside him, knowing that in spite of the turmoil she was creating within him, he would not leave her. With teasing reluctance her lips left his mouth and skimmed across his cheek to find the pulse point that beat just below the line of his jaw. Her fingers slid slowly across his broad shoulders and down his arms, tracing the pattern of blue veins on the sensitive inner surface. She wove her subtle magic around him: caressing his thighs, his loins, his abdomen, then ploughing upward through the soft, fair hair on his chest.

'Oh God,' she heard him mumble and smiled to herself, aware of his escalating desire for her.

Nor was she untouched by the sensations that consumed him. They were like flint and steel, the contact causing sparks of desire flashing between them.

In the enclosing haze of feelings she could not say what emotions drove her to arouse him and shatter his self-control. Perhaps it was anger at her fate or at this man, for whom she had sacrificed and endured so much, that made her determined to seduce him. Maybe she sought to show him that they were controlled equally by the other: that they had both shared the same needs, emotions, and desires. She might have wanted to stamp his memory with the sweetness of her kisses, the suppleness of her body, the tenderness of her touch; so that there would be no night in his long life when she would not be there to haunt him. Or it might have been love that compelled her to prove their mutual need to him this one last time.

With a long-drawn breath that ended with a trembling sigh, she rose above him. Her hair was a shimmering mass of gold in the lantern light; her eyes, shaded by her thick lashes, were dark and unfathomable, but a slight, sweet smile curved her lips as she watched him.

'I love you, Seth,' she said softly. At that moment, there was nothing in him that questioned the sincerity of her words.

She lowered her head to kiss him gently as her body slid the length of his. She was molten, moving with agonizing slowness against him, searing his flesh with her fire. She left a blazing trail of kisses across his throat and chest, pausing to fondle each of his nipples with her tongue, bringing them erect as he had so often done with hers. She moved slowly downward, across the rise of his ribs, then on to his stomach, his hips, his thighs.

At the juncture of his legs she looked up, smiling at him almost shyly. For a moment she seemed the guileless innocent he had known in Youngstown so long ago. She had been so eager then, so incredibly fresh and lovely. But abruptly the illusion shattered when he saw the flaring passion in her eyes and felt her warm mouth close around his erect manhood. A low moan rose in his throat, and his senses reeled in delight. Bone-melting pleasure swept through him, leaving him momentarily weak and dizzy with the strength of his own desire. And as Seth abandoned himself to the exquisite sensations Charl was evoking, all memory of the doubts and conflicts that had come between them blurred and vanished into nothingness.

Then an overwhelming need began to build in him, and he was urging Charl upward once again, turning her gently on to her back so he could be one with her. He heard himself mumbling love words, whispering her name between kisses as he took her tenderly. He made love to her with consummate gentleness, sharing this ultimate act of life in the dark face of death. His movements were slow, sensual, meant to please her. Holding back his response, he gazed deep into her eyes, watching the delight and despair that mirrored his own feelings. For a few seconds he seemed at the edge of discovering some long-sought truth. Then the crest of his passion reached him and took him beyond thinking. Together they spiralled up into some spangled universe beyond their own that dazzled, expanded and shattered their senses. They hung there suspended for an infinite moment of mutual wonder. Then they plunged downward, clinging together for the dizzying descent into oblivion.

Seth stirred first to find his face buried in fragrant, luxuriant hair, and for a moment was utterly content. Then reality rushed in and he sat up wondering what time it was. Still curled among the blankets, Charl stretched and smiled, sloe-eyed with spent passion.

Watching her, he was suddenly overwhelmed with confusion. Until a few hours ago he had never thought he would see Charl again, never imagined he might hold her soft in his arms, never dreamed he could hold her life in his hands. What had transpired in these last few minutes had changed everything between them. And yet it had changed nothing. Charl was still as she had been this morning: an agent for the British who was sentenced to die for her intrigues. She was treacherous, underhanded, deceitful. But regardless of her faults and deceptions, how could he reconcile what had passed between them with the fact that he had been ordered to conduct her execution? It could not be much longer before the firing squad would assemble outside the storehouse to lead her to the parade ground where, under his command, they would take her life. And no matter what he wanted, there was nothing he could do to prevent it.

It was because of his own damnable weakness for her that he found himself in this position. Once he had carefully erected barriers of hate to shield him from her, but now passion had destroyed his resistance. Rage at his own impotence and vulnerability rose in him. In the first swell of panic he lashed out at Charl, selfishly seeking to place anger between them once more so that he could endure what was to come.

'Where did you learn all those whore's tricks, my dear?' he asked silkily, hating the terrible injustice and cruelty of his own words. He heard her hissing intake of breath before he continued. 'You've become quite accomplished since our days in Quebec.'

Charl sat up quickly, the languorous satisfaction gone from her eyes. With a toss of her hair, she faced him, magnificent in her rampant nakedness.

'And who was the first to make me a whore, but you?' she purred, answering his cruel question with one of her own.

'My whore, St James' whore. How many other men have known that soft seductive body of yours? What does it matter if I was the first of so many?'

'And the last,' she reminded him bitterly. 'Tell me, Seth. Is revenge as sweet as they say?'

'It's not revenge –' he began, rising to stand over her, but she cut him short.

'Of course it's revenge, revenge for something I didn't even do!'

He turned on her fiercely.

'Damn it, Charl! How can you deny that you betrayed me in Quebec? St James had the papers I'd hidden in our room as proof!'

'And you believed Felix St James, your sworn enemy, and not me!' she cried furiously.

'I don't want to discuss this now!' he said, tugging on his white breeches and buttoning them with trembling hands.

'If not now, then pray tell me, when do you think we will have another chance?'

He did not answer but went on dressing, stamping into his high boots and buttoning up his white shirt. Finally, she reached up and frantically caught his hand.

'Please, Seth, please! I want to tell you what happened in Quebec before it's time to go. I don't even ask that you believe me, but at least hear me out.' She looked up at him with her heart in her eyes. 'Please, Seth, you can't deny my last request,' she finished softly.

Knowing he was defeated, he let her pull him down to sit beside her. Now she would tell him her lies. They would renew the terrible hurt inside him, and the even more terrible confusion that made him want to believe her. He closed his eyes for a long moment: too aware of her beside him, too aware of time passing, too aware of his own turmoil and regret.

'Very well,' he agreed wearily.

Facing him at last, all the smooth, sure explanations she had practised deserted her. Instead, she drew one of the blankets close around her, both for modesty and for warmth, as she became aware again of the chill in the storehouse and the even colder expression in Seth's eyes. Now that she had her chance to explain to him at last, she did not know how to begin.

'Well?' he prompted.

Without warning Charl began to cry, angry and appalled by her own treacherous emotions.

'I don't know how you could believe that I would deliberately betray you to St James when you knew how much I loved you!' she began voicing her entire argument in one sentence. She heard him exhale sharply in disbelief. Holding his hand possessively between both of hers she hurried on, heedless of the tears that spilled down her cheeks. 'I told you that I loved you for the first time the night of the Governor's ball. Do you remember?'

Seth said nothing, but his face had gone tight as he fought against the memories.

'You came in very late and were standing by the window when I awoke.' Her voice was soft, clouded with reminiscence. 'I could see you so clearly in the moonlight. You looked tired, determined, relieved, but you seemed so deep in thought that I dared not disturb you.'

Charl had read his expression exactly; that was just how he'd felt. He had completed his last job for Mitchell. He would have been free to pursue a life with Charl, away from Quebec, away from the war.

'Then you opened the window sill somehow and took a leather folder from inside your shirt. You checked the contents and looked them over for a few minutes. You put them inside the sill and closed it tight.' Her voice was suddenly lower, softer, more tender as she went on. 'Then you came to my bed.'

'I remember,' he answered hoarsely, as a wave of feeling swept him. She had been so desirable that night: soft, responsive. He had asked her to marry him.

'The next day you were gone: suddenly, inexplicably gone. Waukee and I searched everywhere, until Emile Savard found someone who thought he'd seen you being arrested. I went to St James in desperation. What could I do, Seth? I had no highplaced friends in Quebec to turn to for help or money to hire solicitors. St James offered to do what he could in return for my favours.'

She watched his face for some sign of understanding or acceptance, but there was none.

'Please, Seth, you must believe me! I wanted you safe. The rest didn't matter.

'St James lured me to his rooms that night on the promise that he would tell me the charges against you. And, like a fool, I went. He asked me questions at first.'

'What questions?' he inquired intently, his eyes narrowed.

'Oh, I don't know. They were questions about you: what you were doing in Quebec, if I had met any of your associates –'

'I should think you would have been keeping him informed about those things all along,' he put in.

'Damn it, Seth! Why is it you are so determined to think the worst of me?'

When a few moments had passed with no response, she went on.

'He told me that you had been charged with theft, though he did not tell me what you had stolen. Then he offered to do what he could to help you – for a price. I agreed. What choice did I have?

'We drank a toast to seal our bargain, but he put something in my sherry, a drug of some sort. My memories are hazy after that. He asked me more questions, I think. And I dreamed, or thought I dreamed, about that night after the ball. The next morning I awoke in his bed and was told that I would be allowed to see you as a reward for my, for my –' Charl's words faded into silence and her face flamed with her shame.

To cover his own discomfort, Seth gave a snort of derisive laughter.

'You can't possibly expect me to believe that blatant fabrication!?' he exclaimed.

'I did not ask you to believe me,' she said precisely, 'though I suppose I had hoped you would. I only wanted you to hear the truth this once.'

He looked at her long and slowly. Wrapped in nothing more than the rough, woollen blanket; with her face dirty and tear-stained; she seemed unbearably vulnerable. There was something infuriatingly stubborn and yet so achingly familiar about the angle of her head and the set of her chin that it wrung his heart.

Dear God, he thought fuzzily. How could he possibly believe what she'd told him?

A thunderous knock echoed through the silence, startling both of them. There was no question of what it meant. As they sat frozen in place, it sounded again.

'One moment!' Seth turned and shouted towards the door. 'I – I've not finished questioning the prisoner yet!'

Reluctantly, knowing there was no help for it, he came slowly to his feet and picked up the blue coatee from the floor. His fingers were clumsy on the long row of brass buttons that ran up the front, and he seemed to focus his entire attention on the task of fastening them.

How very different both their lives might have been, Charl reflected sadly as she watched him, if Seth had been wearing this uniform when he came to Youngstown instead of the guise of a spy.

'You may take your time getting dressed,' he said awkwardly when he was ready to leave.

Charl carelessly brushed the hair from her face and looked up at him, an odd brightness in her eyes as she spoke.

'That's very kind of you, Captain Porterfield, but you needn't fear that I'll be late, even for my own execution.'

Initially, her aplomb startled him, and then he realized the brittle courage beneath her bravado.

'Now if you don't mind,' she went on brusquely, 'I prefer to dress in private.'

Although her words were clearly a dismissal, he hesitated, watching her as if he meant to etch her image into his memory forever. There were still so many things left unsaid between them, he found himself thinking. If only there was time –

More pounding came on the door.

For a few timeless seconds he looked deep into her eyes, then turned abruptly and left.

✳

Outside a few streaks of sunlight had begun to penetrate the overcast.

'Miss Beckwith will be out directly,' Seth said quietly to the half-dozen men who were under the command of a wiry Creole sergeant. 'Have a smoke if you like. This is damn grim business and can well be put off for a few more minutes.'

As if taking his own advice, he produced a cheroot from inside his coat, lit it with a twig from the sentry's fire and ambled in the direction of the stream.

How could he go through with this? Seth asked himself when he had moved far enough downstream so that the men of the firing squad could not read the conflict in his face and guess at his emotions. Regardless of what she had done or what had passed between them, this was Charl's life he held in his hands. How could he march her to the parade ground, give the order and watch her die? He passed one hand wearily across his eyes.

Will Hubbard had been right about one thing: there was precious little proof that Charl had been lying about the route of the forthcoming British attack on New Orleans. If anyone else had made these same claims, they would have investigated the allegations without questioning the source. It was his accusations that had condemned her, his accusations and Arnaud's injured pride. And those damning charges were based solely on what had transpired in Quebec, not on anything that had been said or done here.

He puffed absently on the slender, dark cigar, his thoughts on the day long ago in his prison cell when he had last confronted Charl. He had seen proof of her cooperation with the British and had heard her admit to her own infidelity with St James. But if there was even a gram of truth in the account of her actions during his imprisonment, then perhaps his judgement of her had been too harsh. Was it possible he had been wrong in believing the worst of her? Charl's story seemed preposterous and yet –

Seth threw down the half-smoked cheroot and ground it out with his foot. There would be time enough later to debate the ramifications of Charl's actions in Quebec. But as long as there was any question in his mind about her reasons for coming to New Orleans, he could not let her die. But how could he prevent it?

It would do no good to appeal to Arnaud; the man's mind was made up. He might try to help Charl escape from the firing squad en route to the parade ground, but they would not get far in the swamp before they were retaken by the general's troops. If only Will Hubbard would return with a stay of execution from General Jackson, Seth found himself thinking, Charl would be spared. Where was Will anyway?

Seth took a fresh cheroot and clamped it between his teeth. Since a stay of execution appeared to be Charl's only chance, he would have to play for time until Will arrived. But how could he stall the execution when Arnaud was obviously out for blood.

'Think, damn it!' he muttered under his breath as he paced along the bank of the stream, wracking his brain for every detail he had read or heard about the protocol of executions. Considering how close he'd come to hanging in Quebec, he should be better informed, he reflected wryly.

After a few moments of concentration a plan began to form. With that germ of an idea came the familiar tingle of excitement that suffused him with confidence and strength. He realized that if Will was somehow detained or returned without the stay of execution, all would be lost. Still he was spurred on by a heady recklessness that sent his pulses racing. What he planned was a long shot that depended for success on Hubbard's imminent return and his own ability to play a role. As he began to elaborate on his idea, he allowed himself the slightest of smiles. This was a gamble for desperately high stakes; but if Charl was to survive, it was her only chance.

'Captain Porterfield,' the Creole sergeant called, 'the mademoiselle is ready.'

Turning, Seth tossed aside the unlit cheroot and started back up the bank.

Charl stood before the stone storehouse with her tattered cloak clutched tightly around her. Seth suspected that she had been crying, but now her eyes were dry. Two spots of bright pink glowed along her cheekbones and her mouth was set in a grim, angry line that spoke of her resolution.

'Bind her hands, sergeant,' Seth ordered gruffly, and the dark-haired soldier jumped to obey.

They moved down the slight rise and across the bridge at a sedate pace. The sergeant led the small procession, Seth fell in beside the prisoner and the six marksmen brought up the rear.

As they approached the muddy parade ground, Seth was appalled by the number of men who had turned out to witness the execution. Even Arnaud waited on the porch of his headquarters, his dark face filled with the same fierce anticipation that marked the faces of his men.

'You are late, Captain Porterfield,' Arnaud snapped as they halted at the foot of the steps to the main building. 'It is well past three o'clock.'

'I'm sorry, sir,' Seth apologized. 'I was questioning the prisoner one last time to see if she could tell us anything more about the British positions.'

'And did you learn anything of value?' the general asked.

'I'm afraid not,' he replied. 'She is undoubtedly one of the most stubborn women I have ever encountered.'

There was an odd echo of recognition in those words, as if Seth had used them to describe Charl more than this once, but he did not pause to consider the circumstances. Instead, he lowered his voice seriously as he went on.

'However, sir, it has come to my attention that Miss Beckwith has not been allowed the benefit of a visit with a priest. Surely you did not intend to have her executed without the opportunity to make a last confession and receive absolution.'

Charl was startled by Seth's request on her behalf since he knew she had been raised in the Anglican church, just as he had.

A faint note of suppressed excitement in his voice puzzled her as well. What was Seth up to?

'Is this absolutely necessary?' Arnaud demanded irritably.

'I only thought, sir, that since there is bound to be some inquiry at General Jackson's headquarters about this execution, we might better carry it out to the letter of the law. However, if –'

The Creole officer cut him off, recognizing the wisdom of his words. 'Do you wish to make a confession, mademoiselle?' he asked.

'Yes, General,' she replied, uncertain of Seth's reasons for making the request but trusting him instinctively. 'A few moments with a priest would be a great comfort to me.'

Arnaud hesitated, and for a split second, Seth feared that he would deny Charl the chance to talk to a priest and the delay it would cause.

'Very well,' he finally agreed, knowing that if he had refused the request he would answer for his actions at his own confession. 'Send for Father Marrisiou at the infirmary.

'And you, Mademoiselle Beckwith, you will make your confession a brief one.'

'I will try, General Arnaud,' she replied as she allowed herself a long speculative glance at the tall, blond man who stood by her side, 'but I have lived a wicked life, as Captain Porterfield will readily confirm. I fear there is much for me to confess and many things for which I must seek forgiveness.'

While Charl spoke with the priest in the privacy of Arnaud's office, Seth waited nervously on the porch with the rest of his detachment. Where was Will Hubbard? he wondered as he cast another surreptitious glance in the direction of the road from New Orleans. If Will did not return soon, the execution would be held in spite of anything he could do to prevent it.

To Seth it seemed only a short time later that Charl emerged from the headquarters building and was led down the steps.

'Now if there is nothing else that has been overlooked, Captain Porterfield, may we get on with the execution?' Arnaud inquired sarcastically.

'Well, sir,' Seth broke in as he took his place beside the prisoner, 'there is one more detail that should be taken care of before we proceed.'

Arnaud scowled. 'And what detail is that?'

'A list of charges against Miss Beckwith should be prepared

and signed first by you as commanding officer and then by me as officer in charge of the execution squad.'

'Very well,' growled the general, cutting the other man short, 'but I will tolerate no more delays. I thought when I put you in charge of this detail, Porterfield, that you were as anxious as anyone to see this woman come to justice.'

'Be assured that I seek nothing more than justice for Miss Beckwith,' Porterfield told him. 'But I know General Jackson. If there is anything irregular about this entire affair, there will be hell to pay. And I'd rather face the entire British army than the general's wrath!'

With a brief nod of agreement and understanding, Arnaud turned to one of his aides.

'Bring the document from my desk and an ink pot and quill as well. In a few minutes' time the death sentence would require Captain Porterfield's signature anyway.'

The aide returned a moment later and General Arnaud read the charges aloud in his heavily accented English. The stiff, official phrases did not adequately convey the reality of what was about to happen, but Seth was all too aware of what they meant in human terms. He was going to have to give the order, then stand stoically and watch Charl die. There was nothing more he could do to save her.

His gaze moved over those strong, familiar features and he wondered at her thoughts. Had there been time to come to terms with death and find peace, as he had in Quebec? Did she realize how abhorrent he found his role in this? And could she understand that he had no choice?

As Seth scribbled his name at the bottom of the page Arnaud handed him, he cast one last, desperate look in the direction of the New Orleans road. Still there was no sign of Will Hubbard.

'Now if there is nothing else, Captain Porterfield,' Arnaud instructed, 'do your duty.'

A terrible sense of unreality assailed Seth as he escorted Charl the length of the muddy parade ground. The hoots and catcalls of the attendant soldiers roared in his ears, though everyone and everything but Charl seemed to exist only at the periphery of his senses.

This can't possibly be happening, he argued with himself. Yet he could feel the brittle straw beneath his palms as he pushed aside the hay bales that had been painted with a crude crimson

bullseye for use as a makeshift target. He could see his own
fingers moving nimbly on the rope as he bound Charl to the
rough wooden post where she would die. From far away he could
hear his own voice inquiring dispassionately: 'Will you have a
blindfold, Charlotte?'

She was trembling ever so slightly and that, more than anything
else, brought home the agony of his own helplessness and the
strength of his regret. Her sea-green eyes came up to his face
and in their luminous depths he watched the last of her hopes
die. Then, in their place the fires of pride and defiance sparked
to flame and her chin rose stubbornly.

'No thank you, Captain,' she replied coolly. 'I prefer to employ
all my faculties until the last possible moment.'

He was amazed by her ability to marshal her wits when his
own seemed to have fled and he struggled to match her calm as
he went on.

'And do you have any last words, Miss Beckwith?'

There had been a moment, as they stood by Arnaud, when
she thought that Seth had meant to do something to help her.
But now, as she stared up into his impassive face, she realized
she'd been wrong. Nothing she'd said had made any difference
to him. Not one word she'd spoken had changed his mind about
the past. Anger and despair mingled in her chest, making her
voice soft and tremulously vibrant when she answered him.

'I have no last words for the world,' she said as she looked
deep into his fathomless blue eyes. 'My last words are for you,
Seth Porterfield, only for you.' She paused, breathing deeply,
before she went on. 'For doubting my loyalty and my love, you
shall carry the memory of this day with you into eternity.'

Her quiet words, half statement and half curse, shook him to
the depths of his soul. And never, for a moment, did he doubt
either their sincerity or their truth.

Gently, moving as if in a dream, Seth brushed a few tangled
strands of golden hair from her cheek before he turned to go. In
doing so he noticed for the first time that she still wore the opal
earrings that he had given her. As he stood there, with one hand
poised above her satiny cheek, the memories came rushing back.

The night he had presented her with the opals Charl had been
intoxicatingly lovely. She had worn the splendid alabaster gown
he'd bought her and looked like a queen with the shimmering
gems at her throat and ears. It was then that he'd promised her

a future for them together. How clearly he remembered her answer.

'You needn't promise me some day or brood about what's past. Because you gave these opals to me, they are more precious than anything in the world.'

Had those been the words of a woman who, in a few days' time, would betray him? Had she meant to warn him of her treachery or merely soothe his feelings?

'Captain Porterfield, sir,' the Creole sergeant spoke from beside him, interrupting his thoughts. 'General Arnaud wants to know if there is anything wrong?'

'Wrong?' Seth replied absently, unable to look away from Charl's upturned face. 'No.'

'Then, if there's not, the general orders you to get on with the execution.'

Woodenly, Porterfield turned and followed the smaller man back to resume his place beside the firing squad. Across the length of the parade ground Charl's eyes met and held his, just as they had that first day at the Crow's Head Tavern. An angel with the temperament of a shrew, he'd called her then. Little had he known the heaven and hell she would put him through between that day and this. Regret washed over him in waves. He had never meant for it to end like this.

Dear God! How could he give the order for Charl's execution after all that had passed between them for good or ill?

'Get on with it, Porterfield!' came Arnaud's voice from somewhere behind him.

'Take your place, sergeant,' Seth finally said as the crushing weight of his own helplessness settled over him. He had absolutely no choice but to proceed with the execution.

'Yes, sir.'

There was nothing more he could do.

'Ready,' came a voice Seth did not, for a moment, recognize as his own.

He'd never meant for this to happen.

'Aim.'

His heart was thundering in his chest and his mouth was dry.

'Sir?'

'Yes, sergeant. Aim.'

How could he say that one final word that would end Charl's life with the taste of her kisses fresh on his lips? How could he give the order, hear the musket fire and watch the light die in those sea-green eyes? The moment seemed suspended in eternity.

'No!' he cried suddenly, as if in answer to the score of questions that had plagued him since that day in his cell on the Citadel. 'No! No! At ease men!'

At the far side of the parade ground Charl sagged against her bonds, her eyes closed. Has she fainted? Small wonder if she had, Seth found himself thinking. He felt weak kneed himself.

Then from behind him he heard Arnaud's furious voice. 'Damn you, Porterfield! What have you done? The woman is sentenced to die. How dare you countermand my orders?'

Without thinking Seth whirled and hit Arnaud with all his strength, sending the general crashing backwards. In that moment of irrationality he might have gone after the fallen man if two soldiers from the firing squad had not restrained him.

Just then Will Hubbard pulled up his lathered horse and vaulted into the centre of the mêlée.

'For the love of God! What's going on here?' he demanded turning to where Seth was still struggling with the two militiamen. 'You didn't go ahead and execute the girl, did you?'

'Where the hell have you been?' Porterfield demanded in return, recovering himself slightly and shaking off his two guards.

'This man attacked General Arnaud,' reported one of the Creole officers, indicating the prone figure sprawled in the mud.

'So I see,' Will replied gravely as he eyed the general's assailant. 'I suggest that you see to your commander's welfare and leave the rest to me. I will see that General Jackson gets a full report on this incident. In the meantime I'll keep Captain Porterfield in my custody.'

As several men bore Arnaud's limp body in the direction of the infirmary, Will turned to the blond man.

'Good God, Seth! I should think you've been in the army long enough to realize that you can't go around hitting generals when you don't agree with their orders. You can get yourself into real trouble that way.' He dropped his voice as he went on. 'Now I don't doubt for a minute that Arnaud deserved what you did. But when Jackson hears what's happened, after all the trouble he's gone through to win over these people, he's likely to throw a fit. You'd just better have a damn good explanation for this attack on Arnaud and for going through with this execution when I told you I'd be back in time to prevent it.'

'Then you got the stay of execution?' Seth asked breathlessly.

'Of course I got it. I told you I would. All you had to do was stall the firing squad until I got back,' Will pointed out as if the task had been an easy one.

At that moment Porterfield was so light-headed with a strange euphoria he let the comment pass. Instead, he turned abruptly and stalked across the parade ground, leaving Will staring after him.

At the far end of the field Charl was beginning to stir against her bonds, raising her head and blinking in confusion.

'Dear God!' Hubbard muttered under his breath as he realized, for the first time, that the girl was alive. In the end Seth had not gone through with the execution. And until that moment, Will had no idea what his friend had risked to save Charlotte Beckwith from death as a spy. It was entirely possible that Seth would face a court-martial, and perhaps even prison for countermanding Arnaud's orders. But as he watched Seth draw the girl gently into his arms, he suspected that her safety was all that mattered. With an approving nod and a grim smile Will started out across the parade ground towards the man and woman who stood together.

Thirty-Seven

✳ ✳ ✳

From the depths of the copper bathtub, Charlotte Beckwith surveyed the cosy, well-appointed room she had been given in Will and Janette Hubbard's house in New Orleans. After her months with the Shawnee, the lacy curtains and crocheted canopy and coverlet on the high poster bed seemed the height of luxury. Sighing, she closed her eyes and settled back into the fragrant water, letting it both warm and soothe her. The ride from Arnaud's camp on the back of Will's horse had been a cold and uncomfortable one and she had arrived in the courtyard of the neat yellow-stuccoed house trembling with both chill and fatigue. Will's wife had taken one look at her unexpected guest and led Charl straight to the bedchamber, issuing a stream of exclamations and orders in rapid French as they went. The two servants scurried to obey their mistress and in a few minutes they had produced a decanter of sherry and a glass on a silver tray, clean clothes to take the place of Charl's torn and tattered things and a bathtub filled with lavender-scented water.

Now, watching the shimmer of reflected firelight through the crystal wineglass and sinking lower into the tub, Charl found it difficult to reconcile the calm, capable woman she had met today with the shy, retiring girl she had known briefly in Youngstown when Will was commander at Fort Niagara. It was hard to imagine that girl railing at the two tall men for their mistreatment of her as Janette Hubbard had done today. Will had defended himself with good-natured bluster but Seth had remained silent, his eyes focused on some point far in the distance.

'Seth.' Charl whispered his name on the breath of a sigh. What could she expect of Seth now? Their reunion had been the antithesis of what she had hoped it would be. Though Waukee had tried to warn her, she had stubbornly clung to her illusions, but the Indian had been right. Seth's accusations had been harsh and hurtful, and even in the face of their all-consuming passion he had remained steadfast in his condemnation of her. And yet he had risked his career and perhaps even his freedom to save her from the execution Arnaud had ordered. She put the glass to her lips and took a last long draught of sherry, letting the liquor's warmth seep through her veins, bringing languorous calm. Long ago she had come to accept that Seth was the only man she would ever love, and she knew she must find the strength to be patient with him now. For as agonizing as she found his inconsistencies, she was no more tortured by them than Seth was himself.

The logs in the fireplace collapsed into a glowing rubble at the bottom of the grate, sending a shower of sparks up to the chimney and startling Charl from her reverie. With a sigh of reluctance, she set aside her empty glass and went on about the business of completing her bath. After she had dried herself with towels warmed by the fire, she put on the clothes Janette Hubbard had laid out for her use. The green silk gown fitted remarkably well, Charl reflected as she tied the drawstring beneath her breasts and adjusted the flowing skirt. The delicate whorls of lace that rose at her throat and trimmed the narrow sleeves of the fashionable gown were the perfect foil for her fair skin, and the deep green fabric darkened her eyes to emerald. As she appraised herself in the gilded mirror, she found herself wondering if Seth would notice how well she looked in her borrowed attire.

When she was dressed, she located her brush and comb in the burlap sack she'd carried and began to brush out her tangled tresses. From the tall French doors that opened onto the wide gallery with its ornate ironwork railings, she could see the garden below. As she stood looking out, Seth appeared from the stable. He moved irresolutely across the brick-paved path to the small fountain that nestled in one corner of the courtyard. Resting one booted foot on the low balustrade, he puffed thoughtfully on a cheroot. As he stood there lost in his musings, the last coppery rays of winter sunlight came slanting over the garden wall to illuminate that corner. In the warm amber glow the planes of his hard face were sketched in saffron and ochre, and his fair hair shone a rich, tawny gold. Even from the distance Charl could see the frown that tightened the corners of his mouth and drew his brows together. What was he thinking? she wondered. If only she could read his thoughts, she might be able to understand how he could risk everything to save her from being executed as a spy and then, when her safety had been ensured, retreat from her so completely.

This afternoon she had watched in confusion as Seth approached her across the muddy parade ground. For a moment she was uncertain what had transpired and why she was still alive, when by rights she should have been dead. As he came closer, she could see the emotions blazing in his face and hear them in his husky voice as he spoke.

'It's all right, Charl,' he murmured as he cut away the ropes that bound her to the rough wooden post. 'It's over. Will Hubbard brought a stay of execution from General Jackson. We stalled them long enough. It's all right. You're safe now.'

Seth held her gently against his chest as he chafed her hands between his own to restore the circulation. All the while he continued to mumble a comforting litany of phrases that she sensed were meant as much to relieve his own uncertainties as to quell her fears. As she accepted his ministrations, a fierce gladness raged within her. Seth would not conspire to save her life if he still hated her. But when she tried to thank him, he recoiled from her, dropping her hands abruptly and stepping away as if he could not bear to touch or speak to her. After an uncomfortable moment's hesitation he turned on his heel and stalked away from her, muttering something about seeing to their horses.

Since then he had neither looked at her nor spoken to her directly. She had ridden into the city on the skirt of Will's saddle, with her arms clamped tight around his waist to maintain her seat. And the entire time the impression Seth gave was that of a man who desired nothing more than escape, but who was inextricably bound.

There was a discreet knock on the door behind her, and Charl turned to greet her hostess.

'I can see that you are feeling better,' Janette Hubbard observed as she entered the room. 'That gown is most becoming. I knew that shade of green was just your colour.'

Smiling, Charl regarded the other woman. There was a sweet-faced serenity about Will Hubbard's young wife, evident in the huge, bottomless, dark eyes and the gentle, almost child-like mouth that showed both compassion and understanding. Her hair was a mass of barely suppressed ringlets that haloed her fine features with deepest sable.

'I'd like to thank you for your kindness, Mrs Hubbard,' Charl began. 'It can't be usual for you to have houseguests thrust upon you –'

'You'd be surprised what is usual,' the other woman replied with a laugh. 'I am an innkeeper's daughter and one more or less in my household means nothing to me. Anyway I am pleased to return the favour. You were one of the few people who treated me with kindness when we lived in Youngstown. And as lonely as I was then, that meant a great deal. Now please, call me Janette, as if we have always been friends.'

As she spoke, Janette had come to stand beside Charl at the French doors.

'Ah, the elusive Mr Porterfield,' she observed, glancing down into the garden. 'Is it you that has made him so unhappy?'

For a moment Charl floundered in confusion, seeking an answer to the unexpected question. But the other woman went on, sparing her the necessity of a reply.

'But no, I think it is Seth himself who refuses to make up his mind.'

With eyes narrowed, Charl studied the other woman, seeing the shrewd intelligence in her face.

'Have you known Seth long?' Charl asked, suddenly determined to learn as much as she could about Seth's life here in New Orleans before she confronted him again.

Janette nodded.

'We met nearly five years ago in France. Both Seth and Will were unofficially attached to an American delegation that was negotiating with Napoleon's government. They stayed at my father's inn outside Paris. The two of them go back even further, to the time when Seth began to work for Mr Mitchell and the War Department.'

'Then you knew Seth when he came to Youngstown?' Charl questioned.

'Of course, but Will cautioned me not to let on. Seth was busy with intrigues of his own, and it would have been most unseemly for an American officer's wife to be acquainted with a British spy.'

Slowly a vague half-memory emerged from the recesses of her mind, and Charl nodded with new comprehension. The night of the party at her home, she had detected an undercurrent of familiarity when she had introduced these two, but she had allowed herself to be diverted by a question from Colonel Hubbard. Now the reason for her impression came clear.

'Why didn't Seth tell me?' Charl whispered, voicing the ever-present question, more to herself than to the other woman. With an expression of understanding in her dark eyes, Janette Hubbard offered her the comfort of an answer.

'Seth is like Will,' she explained softly, 'a man not given to easy confidences. He would have told you if he felt he could; you must believe that. But you must also realize that it might well have been worth his life to tell you the truth.'

As Charl pondered Janette's words, Will and his two-year-old son Benjamin emerged from the house into the garden. At their appearance, Seth tossed away the stub of his cigar and sank down on his heels, opening his arms invitingly. With a squeal of recognition Benjamin let go of his father's hand and ran unsteadily across the lawn towards the blond man. His small legs churned as he moved, and at the last moment he dived into Seth's outstretched hands, shrieking in delight as Seth lifted the child high over his head. The broad grin of enjoyment on Seth's tanned face was evident even from where the two women stood together.

Then Janette's quiet words cut across Charl's contemplation of the pleasant domestic scene below as she continued with the thought she had begun some minutes before.

'Perhaps if you wish to understand why Seth failed to trust you with his secrets, you should consider if you kept faith in confiding all your own,' she advised as she turned to go.

The frank words of counsel bore a pain that Janette could not have foreseen, and Charl reeled with the irony of the unwitting observation. For a long time after the other woman had gone, Charlotte Beckwith stood watching the two men and the child in the garden below as silent, bitter tears seeped down her flushed cheeks.

※

They did not eat their evening meal in the formal dining room on the first floor of the house, with its ornate brass candelabra and fine mahogany furniture, but en famille at the long trestle table at one side of the kitchen on the ground floor. The doors to the garden were open in spite of the December chill, in deference to the heat from the roaring fire that blazed on the wide brick hearth. The meal was a simple but tasty one consisting of a spicy fish stew, thick with pompano, crayfish, okra, and rice, served with fresh loaves of crusty bread and sweet butter. They passed the dinner with companionable chatter in a mixture of French and English that dealt primarily with Janette's trip to the market, the weather and Benjamin's latest feats. At the conclusion Janette excused herself and took her son up to bed, while Charl and a serving maid washed and put away the dishes. On her return, Will set aside his pipe and produced a decanter of ruby-dark port and four glasses. After pouring them each a glassful, he leaned back in his chair and turned to Charl.

'Very well, Miss Beckwith, perhaps now that you've had a rest and a bite of dinner to restore you, we could prevail upon you to tell us how you came to be in New Orleans this morning. The last any of us knew for certain, you were at Fort Malden with Major St James. Since Amhurstberg is a long way from here, I am sure yours is a fascinating story, and one it would do us all good to hear.' Hubbard's tone underlined the last words, and Seth stirred uncomfortably, then rose to stand in the doorway to the garden as if he wished to disappear into the dark but dared not. Instead, he lit a cheroot from the taper in the wall sconce, braced one broad shoulder against the door jamb, and stared out into the night.

All along Charl had known this moment was inevitable, when she would be forced to account for her life during these past two years. She had only hoped that when it came, things would be settled with Seth so that she would have nothing to fear from her disclosures. Nor would she be able to gauge Seth's response to her words if he continued to stare so intently into the dark garden. Still, there was a tension in his stance and a set to his broad shoulders that assured her of his attention in spite of his desire to escape.

'I was never with Felix St James by choice,' she began at last, 'neither in Quebec nor at Fort Malden. In a way I was as much a prisoner in his house as Seth was in his cell on the Citadel. But if you are to understand how Seth came to suspect me of complicity, and why I did not understand the need for caution when I spoke to Major St James, this story must begin not in Quebec but in Youngstown, on the night that war was declared.'

Charl told the story simply, touching only on those things necessary to set the tenor of the relations between Seth and herself. In the telling Porterfield did not interrupt, nor did he give any other sign that he heard her words.

'You see,' Charl continued after taking a sip of port to steady her, 'the night St James questioned me, I had no idea that anything I said could be used against Seth. If only he had trusted me with his reasons for being in Quebec, I would have done my best to protect him. But it was from St James, not Seth, that I finally learned the truth. By then, it was only a matter of hours before Seth was to be executed and the damage had been done.'

There was no reason to chronicle the degradation St James had forced her to bear during that endless night before Seth was to die, but the distress that those memories brought was evident.

'The next morning St James returned from the prison and told me Seth was dead. And though he lied, I had no reason to doubt him. For a time I was nearly mad with grief, with grief and guilt for my part in sending the man I loved to the gallows. I think all that kept me alive in those days when I was St James' prisoner was the knowledge that I was carrying Seth's child.' As she spoke, she watched the blond man, hoping for and yet dreading any sign of response. For several endless moments she waited, but he did not move. Instead, he continued to stare out into the night as if he had been turned to stone.

Her throat worked hard on the next words, and when they came, her voice had begun to fray with emotion.

'How much I wanted that child so that something of Seth would live on. But there was a riding accident just outside Quebec and I –'

Charl fell silent on the breath of a sob, her face streaked with tears.

From across the table Janette Hubbard reached to pat Charl's hand comfortingly, offering an understanding that only two women could share. Even Will's dark face was drawn with sympathy and concern. It was only Seth's reaction she could not guess.

With trembling hands she put her glass to her lips and drank deep, setting it aside empty a moment later. Then, as if the port had fortified her for the rest of her story, she went on, her voice steady, clear and calm once more.

'Nothing mattered after that,' she stated, 'not St James' cruelty or his abuse. I went to Fort Malden with him because I had no strength to oppose him. But later, in a moment of anger when he threatened to trade me to the Indians, I saw a chance to escape him and I took it.'

'Dear God!' Will breathed, but Seth's voice cut across the quiet exclamation.

'Felix St James paid for his treacheries,' he stated coldly without turning to face them. 'He died by my hand at the battle of the Thames River.'

Charl watched him, trying to guess what emotions had driven him to speak when he had remained silent for so long. He seemed strung between the two doorposts in a tortured pose that clearly defined the hard, strong muscles of his back and shoulders beneath the fine linen shirt. And suddenly she was aware of the terrible tension in him that was half anticipation and half hard-won control.

'I know about St James,' she replied. 'Waukee told me.'

'Waukee?' Seth echoed, though his voice was only slightly tinged with surprise.

'Go on, Charlotte,' Will urged.

'The Indians were good to me. They made me welcome in their way and in time accepted me as one of their own. I married a warrior named Black Feather and adopted his son, Pale Wolf. I was at the Thames, too, but with the Indians. For them it was the end of their world. Tecumseh was killed along with so many others.' Her voice faded to a whisper, and her eyes were clouded, as if her thoughts were far away. Then after a moment she picked up the thread of her story.

'The winter after the battle was very bad. There were no blankets, no food, no supplies of any kind. Black Feather fell ill and I nursed him. With Tecumseh's death the allegiance to the British wore thin, and in the spring most of the tribe returned to more peaceful pursuits. At the harvest festival I met Waukee again. He bought me from Black Feather and told me that Seth was still alive. When I decided to come to New Orleans to find Seth, he accompanied me. He was with me last night in the Choctaw village when I overheard the British plans. If I had known that you would be so quick to doubt me, I would have insisted that he escort me into the city.'

Her last words were a challenge flung at Seth, and the other two people were suddenly acutely aware that there was much to be settled between Seth Porterfield and this woman who had once been his mistress.

'Um – yes. That might have been a good idea,' Will agreed lamely when the silence between the other two grew past enduring.

With a questioning look at his wife, he continued. 'If you two will excuse us, I think Janette and I will retire. The hour is late, and my son is an early riser.' Will stood up abruptly, unfolding his tall form from the chair he had occupied all evening, and moved to the far end of the table to help his wife to her feet.

'Make coffee if you like,' Janette broke in smoothly. 'There's a parlour on the floor above if you prefer to talk there.'

As she passed Charl's chair, she laid a hand on her shoulder and gave her a reassuring smile. 'Good night,' she said as she turned to join her husband at the foot of the stairs.

'Good night,' Charl echoed in reply.

The two people in the kitchen were frozen in place until Will and Janette's voices were muffled by the closing of a door somewhere on the floor above. Then Charl rose slowly and went to where Seth stood intently watching the trees in the garden as they moved sluggishly in the light breeze.

'Would you like some coffee?' she asked softly.

'I suppose so,' he replied, still without looking at her.

Charl went about making the coffee, setting out cups and spoons, sugar, and cream, strangely content to be doing things for Seth once more.

Abruptly he turned from the doorway to watch her, his eyes dark and unreadable. Finally he moved over to where she stood.

'Was the child really mine?' he asked without preamble.

Charl was totally unprepared for the question and fumbled in confusion, torn between wonder that he would want that answer above all others and anger that he could think her capable of deceiving him about the paternity of their child.

'Of course,' she stammered. 'Who else's child would it have been?'

'Felix St James'?' he suggested.

Blind fury stung her to action, and she struck out at him as hard as she could, leaving an ugly, white handprint on his tanned cheek. He accepted the blow stoically, knowing full well that if she had indeed carried his child, he richly deserved whatever recriminations she cared to offer.

'I knew I was pregnant long before Felix ever –' She broke off abruptly and drew a ragged breath as she struggled for control.

'I tried to tell you in the carriage after the ball at the Governor's Mansion, but I was afraid of what you'd say. And you were so damned anxious to be on your way to Muzette Verreault.'

'I'm sorry –'

'I'm glad you killed Felix,' she went on in a low voice, ignoring his apology. 'He was pleased when I lost the child. I think I hated him more for that than for anything else.' She paused thoughtfully, her brows knotted in a frown. 'When I was ill, after miscarrying the baby, he said the most peculiar thing to me. Of course, I was in a lot of pain, and I might have misunderstood.'

'What did he say?' Seth asked quietly.

'He said, "It's just as well this happened because the St Jameses will never claim another Porterfield bastard." I always wondered what he meant. Do you know?'

Seth shook his head, his expression blank and troubled. 'No. I haven't any idea.'

He was silent for a moment, then went on slowly.

'Then St James was telling the truth that day at the Thames. You really were with the Indians.'

'Oh yes,' she sighed, her eyes blank and unfocused. 'I was with the Indians that day. I saw it all: how the British broke and ran leaving the Indian warriors to fend for themselves. I saw the Americans take their vengeance on the Shawnee for a hundred years of Indian trouble. They showed no mercy, no mercy at all. But then it was not a day when civilized behaviour prevailed in any of us.'

Seth's frown deepened as he regarded her. 'What do you mean?'

'I killed a man that day, too,' she told him. 'A trooper was beating Pale Wolf with the butt of his musket, so I killed him. I killed him with my knife, blessing you and Waukee for teaching me the skills to protect Pale Wolf.'

'Dear God!' he mumbled, stunned by her words. Unconsciously he laid a hand on her shoulder, whether to steady himself or comfort her he was not sure.

'We all do things in battle that we live to regret,' he offered in consolation.

She shrugged his hand away and stepped back to look at him speculatively. 'Do you regret pushing Stephen Langley over the cliff at Queenston?'

His heartbeat staggered with shock at her words. There was no one in the world who knew about the incident with Charl's former suitor, and the question stunned him.

'No, I – dear God! How did you find out about that?' he demanded in confusion.

'A letter from my father came shortly after your escape from Quebec. He wrote that Stephen had been horribly crippled in a fall from the heights during the battle at Queenston, and that he claimed you pushed him over.'

For a moment Seth digested her words and then nodded thoughtfully. 'In truth it was nearly the other way around. Langley found me behind the American lines during the retreat and tried to force me over the edge of the escarpment. In the struggle he lost his footing and fell.' A shudder passed through Porterfield as he remembered. 'I could hear him falling, crashing through the trees and undergrowth. It never occurred to me that he might survive.'

'Why didn't you tell me?' she asked as she searched his face for an answer she knew she would not find.

'How could I tell you, Charl, without explaining why I was with the Americans that day?'

Her eyes held his as she replied. 'You could have trusted me,' she suggested softly.

He looked away from her with a short breath of laughter. 'Trusted you? And have you report every word I said to Felix St James?'

Anger, mingled with despair, came back in a rush.

'Damn it, Seth! How can you believe that I would plot with Felix against you?'

'It's very easy, Charl, when there's so much evidence of your cooperation.'

'Tell me then. Tell me what convinces you so absolutely that I willingly betrayed you. Tell me why you chose to believe St James' lies.'

'It's not just what St James said –' he began.

'Then tell me,' she challenged. 'Let me at least know why I am being accused!'

He swung away from her and moved towards the door as if he meant to leave. But before he reached it, he turned to face her once more, as if he had decided to settle things between them once and for all.

'The night I returned from Queenston I saw you coming from Felix's office in Château St Louis.'

'I swear to you I was there only to see if I could find a way back to Youngstown,' she explained.

'Oh, I believed that then,' he admitted, 'but in retrospect it was clear what you'd done. You'd made a bargain with St James: my life and proof against me as a spy in return for your passage home.'

'Then I made a poor bargain, don't you think? For as many places as I've travelled in these past two years, I've never once been home!'

'Perhaps St James betrayed you too, or you decided to stay with him for reasons of your own. All I know is that everything changed after that night. You were suddenly warm and accommodating when before you'd done nothing but fight and oppose me. I was a fool to be taken in by your charms. I should have known that no one changes so quickly, but I was beguiled by your sweet words and your even sweeter body. God knows I wanted to believe you. You offered me everything I'd ever looked for in a woman: tenderness, understanding, love. But I should have realized that you'd been bought, bought for a chance to even the score with me and a promise of passage to Youngstown.'

'You were different, too,' she protested. But Seth would not let her finish and went on determinedly.

'And then there is the question of your communications with St James. You admitted to writing him at least one note. How many others passed between you undetected?' he asked with the air of a lawyer making a case.

'You have a convenient memory,' she countered in her own defence. 'You clearly recall evidence to damn me but blithely overlook anything that might serve to prove my innocence. If you care to remember, it was St James who mentioned that I'd written a note to him. Does it seem likely that we would allow you to learn about messages passed between us if we were in collusion? If we were truly plotting against you, wouldn't we have tried to hide any communication between us rather than flaunt it?'

Seth was silent for a moment, weighing her words and the irrefutable logic behind them. Finally he nodded as if forced to concede this one point. Still he plunged on, undeterred by the lapse in his own reasoning.

'Can you deny that you were awake that night after the ball when I returned from Muzette Verreault's rooms? You saw that I hid the papers I'd received from her in the window sill, and yet you chose to feign ignorance of my activities. There can be only one explanation for your actions; you didn't want to show your hand until you'd had a chance to report to Felix St James. You wanted me to think my mission had succeeded. Otherwise I might have begun to suspect the real motive behind the calm acceptance of your role as my mistress.'

There was such conviction in his tone that the now familiar feeling of futility rose in Charl, bringing the sting of tears beneath her eyelids. What could she ever say or do to convince Seth of her innocence in this matter?

She moved to brush a stray strand of hair from her cheek and took a long, steadying breath. At least now she was facing his accusations one by one. Finally she was learning the spectrum of the charges against her and was being given a chance to refute them. Perhaps now that his reproach had been given voice, the anticipation of it would cease to loom like a sinister, dark cloud over her mind, and the terrible, festering doubt in him would ease.

After a long taut moment of silence she found words to explain.

'Yes, I was awake that night, and I did see you hide something in the window sill, but I had no idea what it was. In truth I didn't want to know.' She raised a hand to forestall the interruption he was ready to make. 'You had taken such pains to conceal your intrigues from me that I hated to let you know you had failed. You asked me to trust you and I did. I didn't want to know what you did for the British. I didn't want to know anything that might force me to compromise either the loyalty I felt for my country or the love I felt for you. To this day I don't know what those papers were beyond the fact that they were used to prove the charge of treason against you.'

His tone was incredulous when he replied. 'You knew. Why is there reason to deny that now? You knew.'

She came a step closer and lay one hand on his arm as if to convey her sincerity. 'I swear to you, Seth, I was never told what they were.'

He looked down at her, waiting for a flicker of guile or duplicity in the depths of her eyes. For as long as he could bear to watch her in silence there was none. There was only hope, and a fleeting glimmer of understanding for his confusion and doubt.

'They were the British plans for the spring offensive against the Americans,' he told her at last, uncertain of why he felt compelled to speak.

'Dear God!' she whispered, one hand coming slowly to her throat as she backed away.

'I'd have given my life gladly if there had been some way to get those plans to Washington intact.'

'And I,' she agreed.

'And you?' His laugh was scornful. 'You told St James where I'd hidden them. There is not another person on earth who could have known that. When St James came to the prison with the plans, my citizenship papers and a number of other things that were nearly as damning, there was no doubt in my mind about who had betrayed me.'

'Seth, please. I told you –' she began, but her denial was cut short by a hiss of steam and the sputtering of coals on the hearth as the long-forgotten coffeepot boiled over. As Charl hurried to snatch up a wad of towelling and remove the coffeepot from the fire, Seth dropped into the chair he had occupied earlier. A moment later Charl set a steaming cupful of coffee before him and seated herself across the table.

For a time they sipped their coffee in silence, each intensely aware of the other. Speaking the accusations aloud had been both an end and a new beginning. The doubts that had lain so long between them were exposed at last. And suddenly they seemed not so immense, so terrible, or so insurmountable as they once had. Though nothing was settled, some prearranged condition for resolving their differences had been satisfied.

Over the rim of her coffee cup Charl watched Seth. Without his accusations to shield him, he was wary of her. From the tentative, almost pensive set of his firm mouth she could sense his unease. And that, she reasoned, was a good sign. If Seth was wary of her, it must be that she could still hurt him. If she retained that power, it was because deep inside he still cared for her.

Though Waukee had prepared her for Seth's anger, his cruelty and his accusations, they still wounded her, tearing agonizingly at the fabric of her being. Yet in spite of what Seth said or did, nothing could change her love for him. Neither time nor distance, nor the despair of thinking him dead had diminished her feelings,

and his recriminations could not change them either. She understood Seth's emotions, just as she had come to understand the
man himself. Charl recognized the bond that held him even now.
And she knew if there was even one spark of his love for her
alive, in time she would win him back.

She raised her eyes to Seth's face and found him watching her:
cautiously, speculatively, with grave anticipation.

'I was surprised to find Will Hubbard here in New Orleans,'
she said softly, a slight sweet smile on her lips. 'How long has he
been with General Jackson?'

Seth almost visibly relaxed at the innocuous question, answering it in the warm, deep tones she associated with their happier
times in Quebec. The conversation flowed from there to other
fairly neutral topics: her time with Waukee, his friendship with
Will and Janette, the wonders of New Orleans.

As she sat watching him and listening to the sound of his voice,
Charl knew a peace she had not felt since those last golden days
in the La Soeur house. It seemed so good just to be able to look
at Seth, real and tangible, before her, after all the days of living
with a memory. In the tranquillity of the cosy kitchen, she
devoured him, absorbing all that her senses could hold: the faint
scent of shaving soap and tobacco that clung to him; the soft,
mellow accent that threaded his speech; the reassuring presence
of him close beside her that transcended any single perception.
Charl watched him totally entranced, drinking in the essence of
this man she'd travelled so far to find.

He seemed older, she decided as she studied him. The sun-
bronzed skin seemed stretched more tightly across the width of
his cheekbones, and the lines were deeper at the corners of his
eyes and mouth. His expressions had changed, too. In the depths
of his azure blue eyes some of the recklessness was gone, and in
its place had come a kind of steady strength. During the past two
years Seth had matured, taking both life and himself more
seriously. And in some strange, satisfying way that pleased her.
Their separation had subtly changed them both, but she was
suddenly sure it had not altered the need that bound them
together.

Charl wanted to make love with Seth again, not hurriedly and
violently as they had in the storehouse, but slowly and with great
tenderness. With an almost physical ache she wanted to join his
warm, strong body with her own. But she could not, not yet. She

could not let herself touch him until they had settled all the doubts and buried all the ghosts that stood between them.

His words went on less haltingly now: asking, telling, explaining. Together they were building bridges from everyday conversations towards the things that needed to be said between them. As the time passed, Charl poured more coffee, laughed softly, and answered his questions truthfully. She took time to explain when he frowned, calmed his anger and made light of their problems until he could smile again. Nor had he forgotten how to tease her or the things that made her laugh, but he never quite forgot the deadly serious things that lay just beneath the surface of their easy banter.

At times it was as if they had never been apart, as if fate and the war and their own doubt had not separated them. When Seth's eyes would light with laughter or when his voice went soft and deep with tenderness, Charl was sure they would find a way to reconcile their differences. When his grin flashed white in his tanned face or he moved unconsciously to touch her, she knew new hope for their future together. But as easily as that warmth flowed, and as readily as Charl was willing to believe that they could rebuild what they'd once shared, communication would cease. As if suddenly aware of his vulnerability, Seth would retreat. He would go silent, his face hard and implacable to exclude her purposely from his thoughts and his irresolute emotions. In despair, Charl would realize the extent of the rift between them and the enormous effort it would require from both of them to heal it.

They did not notice when the first pale hint of dawn lit the eastern sky or when the darkness outside the windows turned silver, mauve, and finally apricot with full sunrise. They were aware of nothing but each other: his dark, unfathomable emotions; the infinite depths of her tenderness; the vast gulf of doubt that separated them and their mutual need to span it.

Then came a stirring from the floor above, followed by the sound of voices. A moment later there was the noisy clatter of Will's boots on the stairs and his cheerful 'good morning'.

Charl looked at Seth, her eyes clouded with regret, and for the briefest instant his hand covered hers in silent consolation. Their solitude was gone now with nothing settled between them.

'Is there coffee in that pot?' Will asked as he took his place at the table and settled Benjamin on his knee.

Charl came to her feet in a rush. 'I'm sure it's cold by now. I'll make more.'

For a few minutes the two women bustled to prepare the morning meal. There was fruit, hot cereal and cream, toast, butter and preserves, coffee, milk, and tea. With daylight streaming through the windows, they sat down together where they had gathered the previous night. But to Charl it seemed like days or years, rather than hours before, that Will had asked her to recount her recent life. Even now too much remained unsettled between her and the man she loved so desperately for Charl to accept the intrusion of mundane life on their precious time together. The early-morning conversation swirled around her as she watched Seth across the table. He seemed so distant and remote sitting there, as if he was able to divorce himself from all that had passed between them in the hours before dawn. Then he glanced up and met her eyes. With a sweet thrill of satisfaction, she realized he felt the same disappointment that she did.

'I'll send a carriage for you, Charlotte,' Will was saying, breaking into her thoughts. 'Jackson's so busy these days that there's no sense in having you sit at headquarters all day waiting for a chance to see him, though I'm sure he'll be anxious to hear what you have to say.'

Then abruptly he was rising, pulling on the coat of his uniform, buckling on his swordbelt, and picking up his hat. Janette wrapped Benjamin in a shawl and followed her husband into the courtyard where a groom was holding the two officers' horses in readiness. Seth followed suit, but more slowly, as if reluctant to give in to the demands of a new day.

Together the blond couple approached the horses, where they stood waiting patiently at the far side of the garden. Already Will was bidding his wife a tender farewell, and Charl found herself being pulled gently into Seth's encircling arms. Smiling she turned her face up for a parting kiss. His lips came sweet and warm on her mouth, but then a ravishing intensity swelled between them. His arms closed tight around her as if he would meld them together forever.

As he held her against the length of his body, tenderness rose within him. It was like a growing thing inside: a delicate unfurling of emotion inside his chest; a soft constriction in his throat; a gentle budding, stretching ache along his limbs until every part of him seemed filled with this delicious new sensation. He felt intoxicated, light-headed with the pure delight he found in her. He was unprepared for the intensity of his own feelings and was totally consumed by the welcome in her response.

Surely this was his woman: this soft, warm, strong, beautiful woman was his beyond all others. How could he doubt it?

He turned his face into her hair and closed his eyes, savouring the pain and ecstasy she brought him. There had been a time when he would have been a happy man with nothing more than what he held close in his arms. God! Charl would have more than satisfied him now if only –

He drew a steadying breath and set her from him, though his gaze lingered in the depths of her eyes. Then, without a word, he turned, mounted his horse and followed Will through the gate to the street. The two women stood silent, listening to the hollow ring of the horses' hoofs on the cobbled street.

After a moment Janette came to where Charl stood. 'Were you and Seth able to come to an understanding?' she asked quietly.

Slowly Charl turned to smile at her. 'Not yct, Janette, but we will. I'm certain now that we will.'

Thirty-Eight

✳✳✳

The two men had moved barely beyond sight of the house in the direction of General Jackson's headquarters on rue Royale when Will reined in beside his friend.

'Well, is it safe to assume that you and Charl did manage to settle your differences last night?' Will asked with a hopeful smile.

Seth had not been expecting an inquiry into his private life, especially from this quarter, and the blunt question took him by surprise. As Will waited for a response, Seth was abruptly reminded of the myriad of things that remained unresolved between Charlotte Beckwith' and himself. The realization was like a splash of icy water that immediately dispelled the faint, warm aura that lingered after Charl's tender good-bye. With irritability he recognized that Charl had somehow succeeded in weaving her subtle magic around him again, making him forget all reason and all caution. He would never understand why this one woman had the power to make him believe whatever lies she cared to tell, even when his instincts warned him of betrayal. At least Will's words had broken her spell, he reflected, and he could view the events of the past twenty-four hours with a modicum of rationality. He welcomed the return of a certain detachment and control, even though he realized it would likely serve to intensify his doubt. He must learn to listen to the voice of reason where Charlotte Beckwith was concerned, he chided himself, and not to her siren song.

With a frown between his fair brows, he replied to Will's question.

'It's not all that easy to resolve things between us. I don't know if I can trust Charl. I'm still not convinced that she's in New Orleans for the purpose she claims. God knows she's still as beautiful, still as appealing as she's ever been and I want to believe her, but she betrayed me once –'

Will snorted in disgust, cutting him short. 'Charlotte Beckwith came all this way just to find you. What would drive a woman to do that if not love?'

'You don't understand,' Seth retorted, his eyes flinty.

But Hubbard did understand, far better than his friend knew. Will had been every bit as wary of attachments as Seth, and he realized, as few other men could, how difficult it was to trust when your life had depended for years on constant suspicion. Still, the girl obviously loved his friend; there could be no doubt of that. Briefly he wondered if he could find it in his heart to trust Janette if the situation was reversed. With relief he brushed the thought away. He was more than a little thankful that he would never face the dilemma that confronted Porterfield.

'Why don't you ride out towards the Arnaud place and see for yourself if the canals are as carefully guarded as the general claims?' Hubbard proposed. 'It might ease your mind to determine the truth of Charlotte's information, and I'm sure Jackson will welcome a report on your findings once he's talked to the girl.'

Seth considered the suggestion for a moment and then agreed. It was the only logical way to prove or disprove what Charl said she had overheard at the Indian camp. And perhaps it would enlighten him as to the truth of her other revelations as well.

'That's a good idea,' he conceded. 'Will you let them know at headquarters where I've gone?'

'Certainly, and I'll see to your duties myself,' Will assured him. 'I'll expect to see you at headquarters or back at the house this evening.'

He paused, watching his friend and noting the strain on his face. 'Good luck, Seth,' he added softly.

The blond man acknowledged the words with a brief nod and turned his horse down a side street that led to the edge of town.

Once he'd left behind him the morning traffic that clogged the narrow streets and turned onto the levee road, he gave his horse its head. The cold wind that sent waves dancing on the surface of the wide, murky river felt good against his flushed face and brought with it a clarity of mind that he welcomed. He felt tired but utterly calm as he reviewed the past day's events and their devastating effect on the comfortable life he had been leading.

Who could have foreseen that Charl would return so suddenly and unexpectedly as to destroy all the defences he had so painstakingly built to protect himself from the hurt she had caused him? And who could say if the account she had given of her life these past two years was fact or fiction?

Unwanted visions of her filled his head: Charlotte with her golden hair streaming across her naked breasts as she made love to him; Charlotte bound to the wooden post, terrified but defiant in the face of death; Charlotte, her blue-green eyes soft with understanding and tenderness this morning when she'd told him good-bye. Unbidden, his thoughts slid back further to those halcyon days in Quebec City that he'd tried so hard to put out of his mind.

Why was it he had never been able to banish Charlotte Beckwith from his memories? he wondered. What had passed between them that had never happened with any woman before or since? There had always been the sweet intensity of their unions, but he knew it was more than his physical need for her that made Charl impossible to forget.

As he turned his mount off the levee road onto Arnaud family holdings, the answer came to him clear and irrefutable.

During those days in Quebec Charl had demanded, and he had freely given, a part of himself. He had allowed her to ease his bitterness, touch his soul and claim his heart. At the time it seemed that she had given as freely in return, creating a unity of mind and spirit between them. But when Charl had betrayed him, and he had been forced to flee for his life, he had left that part of himself with her. Since then there had been an emptiness within him, an emptiness that, for all her treachery and betrayal, only Charl could fill. She possessed that vulnerable, trusting part of him and he could never hope to claim it for himself again. Even if he hated Charl, for the rest of his life he would be incomplete without her.

That revelation shook him, making him realize that there was more at stake now than just the veracity of the information Charl had offered to the Americans. Hanging in the balance was his entire future, and hers. If her story about the proposed route of the British attack proved false, she might very well face renewed charges as a spy. And unless he could find a way to trust her, he would continue living as half a man: damned by her to a solitary life, robbed of his capacity to love. Yet even if he was able to prove that Charl had told the truth about the British plans, could he be sure that she had not fabricated all the rest of her story for his benefit?

The road to the Arnaud plantation branched ahead of him. The left fork, he knew from previous inspections, ran towards the fields where indigo, rice and cotton would be planted in the spring. The right led down a tree-lined drive towards the single-storeyed château. At this hour, Major Jaques Arnaud might well still be at breakfast, Seth decided as he urged his horse down the right-hand lane.

As the arching tunnel of branches closed overhead, he turned his thoughts once more to Charl and the dilemma her sudden reappearance had caused him.

'Damn the girl!' he muttered irritably.

How could she expect him to believe that she had crossed half a continent to find him because she loved him? Yet if that was so, what more proof of loyalty did any man need? Still he felt compelled to put his doubt between them because there was something inside himself that would not let him believe her. Some scrap of cynicism, some remnant of suspicion was so deeply ingrained in his character that he feared that nothing Charl could ever do would prove her innocence to him.

If Seth had been less preoccupied with his own musings, he might have noticed the unnatural stillness in the morning air and the absence of the usual traffic on the road that led to the Arnaud plantation. But as it was, the first gunshot that whined passed him took him by surprise. As he wheeled his mount and reached for the pistol before him in the saddle holster, the second shot slammed into his chest. The impact knocked him from his horse and he landed heavily in the rutted road. Dazedly he forced himself to a sitting position and scanned the woods to the left of the road. What devilry was this?

Gingerly, he pressed his hand to his right shoulder and watched as his fingers came away dark with blood. There was no pain yet. That would come later, but he was dizzy and it was damnably hard to breathe.

'Damn!' he muttered under his breath. If he'd kept his mind on his mission instead of mooning over Charl, he might never have ridden into this ambush for an ambush it clearly was.

Just then the foliage to his left rustled and two British infantry-men stepped onto the road not ten feet ahead of him.

Somehow, in spite of his fall, Seth had retained his hold on the heavy saddle pistol. As the troopers advanced, he tried desperately to raise his right hand to fire at them, but his muscles refused to obey and the gun slid from his nerveless fingers.

'Damn!' he mumbled a second time. Without the pistol and the use of his right arm he was very nearly helpless.

'Well, what have we here?' asked the taller man of his companion. 'An American officer out for a morning's canter?'

Seth glared at him silently.

'And who might you be, captain?' the Englishman went on.

'Looks like general staff, judging by the insignia,' the other man put in.

'Are you on "Old Hickory's" staff, captain?' When Seth made no reply, the infantryman continued. 'Well, talkative or no, I suppose General Keane will be wanting a look at you. He may even send you off to Cochrane himself, like those fellows last night. On your feet!'

With an abrupt movement he grabbed Seth's tunic and hauled him upright, sending an agonizing flash of pain searing through the injured man. Deftly he confiscated the American's dress sword.

'Up the road, captain,' he ordered, indicating the direction with the point. 'We arrived less than an hour ago ourselves, so don't expect much hospitality.

'John, you gather up his pistol and his horse and keep them out of sight. I think our visitor here was alone, but watch to see if he has friends nearby.'

When they arrived at the verandahed plantation house some distance up the tree-lined road, they were escorted into a parlour where a tall, black-whiskered man was conferring with two subordinates.

'Yes, corporal?' the officer asked as the infantryman and his prisoner halted before him.

'This man came riding up the drive, sir. It appears that he may be one of General Jackson's staff.'

Major General John Keane turned from the other men at the soldier's words, and studied the tall, bloodstained American officer who stood, somewhat unsteadily, before him.

'Was he alone, corporal?' he inquired, his narrowed eyes never leaving the prisoner.

'As far as we can tell, sir,' the soldier answered.

Keane made a long, slow circuit around the wounded man, noting the full dress uniform and the ornate scabbard.

'And he came riding up the main road, you say?' he continued. 'Then it's doubtful he's one of Jackson's scouts. What is your business here, captain?' Keane finally asked.

The walk to the plantation house had taken its toll on Seth, but he tried to compose himself to reply, in spite of the throbbing pain in his shoulder and his inability to get his breath.

'I was just out for a bit of exercise,' he lied smoothly, speaking for the first time.

The British officer's eyebrows rose in surprise at the American's obviously English accent and offhand manner. He was not sure that this man was telling the truth. Yet he could not believe that one of Jackson's officers would blunder into their hands if there was the slightest suspicion that the British had attained a position so near the city.

'Very well,' Keane said after a moment's consideration. 'It is immaterial to me what you're doing here as long as Jackson didn't send you. And we have too much to do to take time for a prolonged questioning. But perhaps Admiral Cochrane would like a word with you, as he did the men we captured last night.

'Lieutenant Seawell,' Keane spoke, addressing an aide who had been hovering by the door. 'See that our prisoner's wound is dressed and then have him rowed back to the Admiral's schooner.'

Wordlessly, the young officer obeyed, leading Seth out of the room and down a hall towards the back of the house. As they walked, Seth tried to formulate a plan of escape, but his thoughts were the consistency of treacle and the pain in his shoulder pounded relentlessly at him, weakening his resolve.

There was a makeshift hospital in the yard beside the cook-house, and a bandy-legged orderly came immediately to his aid.

'You're me first customer today, mate,' he told Seth cheerfully as he cut away the front of the blue coatee to expose the wound. 'I see you've lost a bit of blood,' he observed as he worked.

Dispassionately, Seth looked down at the deep, jagged furrow the ball had torn in the flat muscle of his chest and wondered vaguely if he was going to die. Then the orderly was bending over him, cleansing and packing the hole with lint and bandages to stop the bleeding. With those necessary ministrations the pain came again, like a fire in his flesh that obliterated all thought and left him shaking and clammy with sweat.

Afterwards he managed somehow to walk to a longboat drawn up at the edge of Arnaud's canal and settle himself against one of the gunwales. Someone had given him a cloak to wear, and he adjusted it against the cold before he closed his eyes. As he lay in the bottom of the boat, each short, panting breath brought a new twitch of pain, and he was forced to concede that the escape he had been contemplating was, for the moment, beyond him. Then there was the rattle of rowlocks as they got underway, and he realized it was too late to try to break free. Seth felt the smooth pull of rowing and the persistent rhythm of movement up the canal. Dimly he realized that it would be several hours before he would be called upon to face further questioning. With a long sigh of acceptance and relief, he let his tenuous hold on consciousness slip away.

For a time awareness of his surroundings came and went, like a world viewed from a lazily swaying hammock, leaving him dizzy and confused. Then someone was prodding him awake, forcing him to climb a rope ladder that hung from the side of a gently rocking ship. The exertion of the climb sent a tearing pain through the clotted wound that brought Seth abruptly back to full consciousness. It took only one look towards the Union Jack snapping crisply above the stern of the vessel for Seth to realize that they had reached their destination. As his captors conferred with the ship's first officer, Seth tried to marshal his scattered wits. An interview with Admiral Cochrane seemed imminent, and he knew he could not let slip any of General Jackson's secrets. Under the cover of his cloak, his left hand probed up along his shoulder to confirm that his wound was bleeding again, even more freely than before.

Then the first officer was coming towards him, pushing him roughly and painfully in the direction of the main companionway. At the bottom of the steps he was led into what appeared to be the officers' wardroom. At the far end, dressed in the splendid gold and blue uniform of the British admiralty, stood Admiral Sir Alexander Cochrane himself. There were a number of other officers in the cabin, but Seth took no note of them. With instantaneous recognition of his adversary, Seth's eyes came to rest on Cochrane, taking in the crisp, white hair and stiff military bearing. As if rising to the challenge, Seth became aware of the familiar quickening in his blood that gave him at least a momentary renewal of strength.

'This man was captured by General Keane's men, near the landing site below New Orleans,' said the man who had escorted Porterfield belowdecks. 'His insignia led them to believe that he is a member of Jackson's general staff.'

Slowly Cochrane stepped from behind the wide table strewn with charts and advanced on the blond man who stood silent and unbowed before him.

'What is your name?' the admiral asked with a low rumbling tone.

'Captain Seth Porterfield, United States Army,' came the even reply.

A flicker of surprise crossed the older man's face as he noted the familiar cadence and intonation of the prisoner's voice.

'And is it true that you are a member of General Jackson's staff?'

Seth made no reply but stood stiff and still, conveying his total lack of cooperation.

'If you choose, Captain Porterfield, you could be a great help to us.' Cochrane paused, watching the other man. 'You see, as a member of the American's general staff you could clarify a number of things for us. For example, we've had conflicting reports on the number of men Jackson's managed to amass for the defence of New Orleans. As someone privy to that kind of information, it would be very convenient if you chose to cooperate. You might even be able to suggest how those men have been deployed.'

Seth remained silent, staring stoically ahead, his concentration divided between the Englishman's questions and the task of remaining on his feet.

'Come now, captain,' Cochrane went on. 'It's not as if you're defending the land of your birth, for I'd recognize an English gentleman's speech anywhere on this earth.'

Seth made a valiant effort to smile. 'I assure you, sir, that while I do speak the King's English, I am no traitor to the American cause.'

Cochrane frowned and continued undeterred, noting that the prisoner before him seemed markedly paler than he had been only moments before.

'We've had reports from other captives that Jackson has between ten and fifteen thousand men in and around the city. Is that true?'

Seth met the admiral's eyes for a long moment before he answered.

'I will neither confirm nor deny the truth of your information. If Jackson's force is indeed more than fifteen thousand men, why should I confirm it and allow you to prepare to face superior numbers? On the other hand, if his force is fewer than fifteen thousand, it would surely be to my advantage to keep my peace, in the hope that those sheer numbers would discourage you from attempting an attack on such a well-defended city. In short, Admiral Cochrane, even if I answered your questions, you would not know if I spoke the truth or was merely trying to manipulate you.'

Seth saw the expression of consternation on Cochrane's face and was amazed that he had managed to sound so glib and sure when he remained erect only by an act of will. Under the cover of the enveloping cloak he could feel the sticky wetness of his own blood crawling slowly from the reopened wound in his shoulder down across his chest and along his ribs to soak the waistband and leg of his breeches. The pain was stronger, too, pounding relentlessly in his chest and at his temples with each thunderous beat of his heart.

'You're damnably unhelpful, Captain Porterfield,' Cochrane complained, though there was grudging respect in his tone. His words were strangely resonant and seemed to be coming to Seth from far away.

'I'm terribly sorry, sir,' he managed to mumble in the seconds before his knees gave way. A strange tingling sensation passed along his limbs, and a shimmering golden mist swirled around him, dragging him down.

From somewhere beyond his vision he heard voices and felt hands probe his clothes.

'Good Lord!' someone exclaimed. 'If something's not done, this man will bleed to death!'

Then Cochrane's voice came deep and clear. 'Have them send for the surgeon or, better yet, carry Captain Porterfield to the sick bay so he can be treated properly.'

'Pardon me, sir,' another man interrupted. 'Don't you think we should have the American doctor, who came out after the gunboat battle, care for him?'

'Good God, no!' came the admiral again. 'I'll have my own man look after him. Underneath that damned American uniform Captain Porterfield is still an Englishman!'

As they carried him down to the surgeon's quarters, the blood ran even more freely from between Seth's pressing fingers, leaving a trail of red on the polished floors. When he was settled on a straw pallet a doctor bent over him, a frown on his lean face.

'What's your name, son?' the grey-haired man asked, cutting away the clotted bandage.

'Porterfield,' Seth managed to mutter from between clenched teeth. He was fully conscious again and intensely aware of the surgeon's lightest touch as he probed the bullet hole.

'Are you having any difficulty breathing, Captain Porterfield?' he asked as he felt Seth's brow, checking for signs of fever.

He nodded in response to the doctor's question, and the older man's frown deepened with concern. He did not like this young American's colour, and his skin was cold and clammy. If the man was to survive, he would need to act quickly.

'Would you like a drink?' he asked his patient.

'Please,' Seth replied in a whisper.

The doctor moved away, but returned a few moments later and held a cup of cool water to Seth's dry lips. There was a peculiar taste to the water, but Seth could think of nothing but assuaging his thirst. When he had drunk every drop, the doctor set the cup aside.

'You've a nasty wound there, Captain, and you've lost a good deal of blood. The ball broke a couple of ribs, I'd say, but if you're lucky, it's not lodged in your lung. I've given you a drug for the pain, and when it has taken effect, I'm going to have to remove that ball before the lead poisons you.'

As the doctor went on, his words began to sound slurred and indistinct, and he seemed to be regarding Seth from a great height. All at once his head was swimming as he gave himself to the drug and the ease it brought. Seth's last coherent thought before the dizzying darkness closed in was of Charl and how much he wished he'd told her he still loved her.

Thirty-Nine

✳✳✳

After the men had gone, Janette convinced Charl to lie down on the sofa in the parlour until the carriage Will had promised to send for her arrived. But as it was, Charl slept well into the afternoon for the carriage never came. Instead she was jerked awake by the sound of cannon fire from Fort St Charles and the pealing of bells from the Old Cathedral in Place d'Armes. She went immediately in search of Janette and found her standing in the kitchen doorway listening.

'What does it mean?' Charl demanded as she came to stand beside the other woman.

Janette's dark eyes were huge. 'I don't know exactly. The bells are the alarm. The British must have been sighted somewhere.'

Charl's heart leaped. 'Where?' she breathed.

'I don't have any way of knowing,' Janette replied sharply, an undercurrent of fear in her voice. 'I'd better go and see to Benjamin. The noise has probably terrified him, poor thing.'

As Janette Hubbard turned to go to her son, Charl snatched a cloak from a peg on the wall and ran across the garden to the gate that opened onto the street. In every doorway and along the banquette people stood still as statues, their heads cocked to one side as they waited. It was almost as if they expected the next peal of bells to bring comfort, explanations, reassurance. Charl stood for a long moment caught in the same spell, her breathing suspended, her expression blank. Then abruptly she shook off the feeling of dread and moved swiftly towards the busier avenue that intersected their own to find out what this alarm meant. As she approached the corner, she could hear the sound of marching feet and martial music in the air. Near the centre of the next block a militia unit was forming up. They looked fine in their bright, fresh uniforms, and they moved smartly, as if on parade, very aware of the citizens who paused to watch.

With curiosity and a breathless certainty prodding her, Charl approached a young lieutenant who was at the head of his column of men awaiting the order to march.

'Pardon me,' Charl began in her best French. 'Where is it you are bound? Is it true that the British have been sighted?'

The young Creole officer smiled down at her, noting that this comely American spoke French very well indeed.

'Ah, mademoiselle, those are such serious questions for so lovely a lady,' he observed, his grin widening wickedly. 'You would perhaps prefer to discuss some more pleasant topic than the impending intrusion of war on our pleasant life here in New Orleans.'

His cavalier manner took her off guard, but she recovered quickly. 'As much as I would like that, monsieur, it is the answer to those two questions that I seek.' She responded in kind, with a flutter of her thick lashes and a flirtatious smile, as if they stood on a dance floor exchanging pleasantries instead of at the head of a unit of men bound for battle.

'War makes for such grim conversations,' he complained with a slight Gallic shrug. 'Rumour has it that the British have landed near the Arnaud plantation, but we are not certain yet where we will be assigned.'

'The Arnaud plantation!' she echoed with growing satisfaction. If this young man told the truth, she had been vindicated. She was right about the route of British invasion, and Seth would know she had not lied to him about this at least. But even as a slow smile came to her lips, she realized what must inevitably happen next. It was obvious that militia units were being mustered all over the town, as this one had been. There was no doubt that there would be a battle soon, pitting Andrew Jackson and his hotchpotch of units against crack British troops fresh from the continent and victory over Napoleon. What chance did this handful of ragtag Americans have against such odds? Suddenly she became aware that the Creole lieutenant was addressing her again.

'Except that we are on our way to battle, mademoiselle, I would not presume to approach you,' he began, his black eyes twinkling with mischief, 'but I wish to ask the favour of a kiss, a sweet memory of your beauty to carry with me as I offer my life for my country.'

Charl was startled by his proposition and his pretty speech, and in the split second when she could have refused, she did not. Instead, within full view of his men and with their clamorous approval, the Creole lieutenant took Charl into his arms and kissed her soundly.

When he had set her on her feet again, she turned to him with mock severity. 'You are a rogue, monsieur, and your men are no less so to condone such behaviour. But let it not be said that the women of New Orleans send their men into battle without the proper incentive for victory. So I will pay you twice the price in the hope that you will fight twice as gallantly to protect us.'

Amidst hoots and catcalls she rose on tiptoe to brush her lips against the young lieutenant's smooth-shaven cheek. Then, with a twitch of her skirts, Charl turned and went back the way she had come, followed by the appreciative roar of the militia.

But Charl's bravado, like the raucous good humour exhibited by the troops, was no more than a half-hearted attempt to disguise the fact that New Orleans was a city poised on the brink of panic. As the citizen soldiers rushed past on their way to join their companies, and the women and children scrambled for safety, the atmosphere in the streets was a mixture of carnival gaiety and stunned disbelief. Nor could Charl help being caught up in the mounting confusion about her. There was no way to know the outcome of the impending battle, and even as she retraced her steps to return to the Hubbard house, she knew there was nothing to do but wait.

The bombardment of British positions began just as dusk was turning to full dark, with a thunderous roar that rattled the shutters in the parlour where the two women sat together. That first startling noise had scarcely died away when another deep-throated boom took its place.

'Mon Dieu! It has started!' Charl heard Janette Hubbard whisper from where she sat gripping the arms of the rocking chair.

'I think Benjamin is crying,' Charl whispered back, hearing the child's frightened wail between choruses of destruction.

Janette moved swiftly to see to her son and returned a moment later carrying him in her arms. He blinked once or twice in the light, put his thumb in his mouth, and rested his silky dark head against his mother's shoulder. The peaceful expression on the sleeping child's face, in contrast to the damage being wrought only a few miles away, brought unexpected tears to Charl's eyes.

'It's a pity we can't all find comfort and consolation as easily,' she mused, almost to herself.

The barrage continued with volley after volley of cannon fire until the intermittent silences rang in their ears. The two women sat frozen for a time, dreading and yet anticipating each new clash of guns. As they listened, Charl could begin to discern the different tones and pitches, the different voices, of the various cannons that spoke with such deadly rhythm and cadence.

It's not at all like thunder, Charl found herself thinking. There was no growling rumble of sound skittering across the sky to end in a resounding, satisfying crash. There were no ear-shattering cracks that seemed to vibrate in the air. There was only the steady thudding that seemed to go on endlessly and the knowledge of what each of those blasts meant.

'I don't know if I can bear this,' Janette said in a strained whisper. 'I've always accepted the dangers that Will faces as a career officer, but this is the first time I've been close enough to hear the sound of battle. Tonight every time I hear a cannon I wonder –'

'I know!' Charl agreed, not allowing the other woman to finish the thought. 'I think it must be worse to sit here waiting than to be in the battle itself.'

'Do you suppose Jackson's lines will hold?' Janette went on seeking reassurance.

Charl shrugged. 'I think the element of surprise is on his side. The British can't have been expecting an attack tonight.'

All afternoon rumours had run rampant in the city as to Jackson's plans for defence, but no one knew for sure what to expect from him. Someone had claimed that Jackson had received the news of the British landing with fury and had exclaimed: 'By the Eternal, they shall not sleep upon our soil,' then set about organizing this night attack. No one knew if the general's hastily laid plans would succeed, and there was the unspoken fear throughout the city that if Jackson's defences fell, he would retreat, leaving New Orleans to British plunder. Neither Will nor Seth had come near the house all day, and while both women understood that they were busy with preparations for the attack, each hungered for a few last words with her man before he went off to battle.

In reality, the bombardment did not last very long, though it seemed like an eternity to the women who had gathered all over New Orleans for mutual support. It was only after the guns had stopped that they realized that the silence was a subtle and far more excruciating torture than the sound of cannon fire had been. The quiet of the night became an endless pause: suspended, unfinished, without resolution as New Orleans waited. Eventually the groups began to disperse as the women went home to lie sleepless in their lonely beds.

Shortly after dawn the dead and wounded began to arrive in the city, along with the news of the encounter between the Americans and the British on the plains of Chalmette. The battle had been a brutal one, fought at close quarters, as was evidenced by the horrendous character of the wounds inflicted. With the arrival of the casualties, the women who had cowered in the dark calmly and efficiently manned the hospitals set up for those in need. Although there were many families in the city touched with grief, American losses were fairly light.

All that same day companies of slaves with picks and shovels over their shoulders were seen moving through town towards the southeast. It was rumoured that the work crews would be used to prepare earthenworks to strengthen Jackson's defences. Bombardment of the British positions picked up towards midday. But unlike the terrifying roar in the darkness the previous night, these cannonades were accepted as something benign: a thunderous background to daily life in New Orleans.

By nightfall Charl and Janette had established that neither Seth nor Will was among the dead or wounded. Though they had received no word from either man, they both slept soundly that night. The next day, Christmas Day, passed uneventfully, and though a few friends came to the Hubbard home with gifts for Benjamin, his father did not.

Just before noon on the twenty-sixth Will did arrive, looking gaunt, hollow-eyed, and staggering with exhaustion. But before Janette helped him to their bedroom, Charl managed to ask him about Seth.

'Damn it, Charl,' he told her irritably, his voice slurred with weariness. 'We've been working around the clock. If he's wise, he's found a place to get some undisturbed sleep!'

During the early evening Will awoke long enough to eat from a tray Janette had prepared for him, then slept again. Looking much refreshed, he appeared at the breakfast table the next morning, and only then did he give any account of the battle.

'The gunship "Carolina" began the engagement by bombarding British positions from the river,' he told them between mouthfuls of bacon. 'Then the land forces attacked with mounted troops flanking the British right and those of us with Jackson moving up in the centre. It was black as pitch by the time we reached the British line, and except for the man beside you, you couldn't tell friend from enemy. Guns became useless as we closed in, and for the most part we fought with swords and bayonettes. In the confusion we captured one squad of British infantry by pretending to be their comrades. The redcoats employed the same tactic to take some of our men. When it was over, we Americans had well proved that we can protect our own.

'Jackson has established field headquarters at the McCarty plantation house and has settled in quite comfortably. Someone gave him a telescope that he's set up on the first-floor gallery. From there he can keep an excellent watch on our enemies across the way. We've also been working to construct breastworks along the Rodriguez Canal at the edge of the McCarty property. Since General Packenham has joined Keane's troops, we are expecting an attack at any time.'

'Has Seth been working with you on these preparations, or has the general sent him scouting as he did at Pensacola?' Charl asked. It had been necessary for her to swallow her pride to make the inquiry, but she was willing to seek word of the man she loved from any source, since Seth had not seen fit to send her reassurance of his safety himself.

Will paused almost imperceptibly before he answered her, but Charl was chilled by the hesitation.

'I haven't seen Seth since the morning we left here,' he admitted reluctantly. 'He decided to ride out towards the Arnaud place to see if the canals were being as carefully guarded as the general claimed. I'm sure we've just missed each other at headquarters. It's been a madhouse these past few days.'

Charl paled at his words, and he hurried on.

'Now, Charl, don't you worry about Seth. He's like a bad penny and turns up in the most unlikely places. I don't doubt he's scouting for the general and will return with lots of valuable information and some outlandish story about having had dinner with General Keane, or polishing General Packenham's boots so he could get a look at his papers.'

Charl had gone paler still and was frankly unconvinced.

'All right!' he conceded. 'I'll make a point of finding Seth when I get back, and I will force him, at sword point if necessary, to send you word –'

Will's promise was roughly abbreviated by the sudden, ear-shattering renewal of shelling. But as they listened, a strange new sound was discernible above the persistent rumble of cannonades. It was this new, high-pitched whine that sent Will rushing up the stairs to the rooftop with the women at his heels.

'Dear God! Those must be Congreve rockets!' he muttered breathlessly as they watched the shells burst, with flashes of colour, over the river to the southeast. The bombs rose like flaming comets from the British positions to streak across the sky towards where the 'Carolina' bobbed helplessly becalmed near the opposite bank. As they watched, flames burst from the American ship, followed by a deafening blast and a reverberating concussion that shook them even where they stood.

'I've got to get back to headquarters!' Will exclaimed as he watched fire sweep the ship.

'Oh, Will! I'm afraid!' Janette cried suddenly, throwing herself into his arms. 'What if Jackson's lines do not hold? Is it true that he plans to blow up the city if he is forced to retreat?'

'Jackson isn't going to retreat,' he reassured her, dodging the question. 'Anyway you have Charl with you. You'll be all right together. Janette, you must know that I cannot stay with you!'

Over his wife's bent head Will Hubbard met Charlotte Beckwith's blue-green eyes. For a moment his expression was of mingled desperation and entreaty.

'It will be all right,' Charl said gently after a moment as she stepped closer, 'honestly it will. Please, Janette, you've got to let Will go.'

Janette clung to her husband for one last moment, then slowly and reluctantly relinquished her hold on him. Immediately he turned and clattered down the long flights of stairs, calling for his horse.

After Will was gone, the two women remained on the roof, watching, waiting, and wondering what the future held for them and the rest of New Orleans.

On the morning of the twenty-eighth, the British attacked Jackson's line. When the smoke cleared and the rumble of gunfire was silent, the army that had defeated Napoleon was itself repulsed by the American 'dirty shirts' and their Indian allies. The defeat was a great blow to British pride, and they retreated to lick their wounds and prepare for the next confrontation.

In the ensuing days Will sent several notes to Janette with a young sergeant from the quartermaster corps on his frequent trips to the city. But never once in any of them did he mention Seth or his whereabouts. On her own Charl revisited both the hospital and the morgue searching for, and yet loath to find, any sign of the man she loved. Though it cheered her to know that he was not in either place, she could not dismiss the cold knot of uncertainty in the pit of her stomach.

The celebration of New Year's Day in New Orleans was every bit as important an event as Christmas was, and in deference to the old French customs, General Jackson authorized a full dress parade at the McCarty plantation to mark the occasion. Thus, on the first day of 1815, Charlotte Beckwith, Janette Hubbard, and her son Benjamin set out along the levee road in a small carriage to attend. As Charl piloted the gig through the early morning fog, her thoughts were, as they had been for days, on Seth. The waiting had been torturous, and she had sought reassurance of his safety through every means she could think of but had received no word. She could not understand why Will had ignored the promise he had made her. Surely he must realize that any news would end her terrible uncertainty. A frown settled between her brows as she tried to penetrate the thick fog that all but obscured the road. She only knew that she did not intend to leave the encampment today until she had found the whereabouts of Seth Porterfield, even if it meant confronting General Andrew Jackson himself.

Finally, she pulled the gig to a stop beside a row of trees where other carriages had been left. While Janette and Benjamin clambered down, she skilfully unhitched and tethered the horses. Together they made their way across the frozen fields, treading carefully on the roughened terrain and finding their way through the mist primarily by following the sound of voices.

Already the units had begun to assemble on the field behind the main house. As they formed up, the diversity of Jackson's army was readily evident. The crisp blue uniforms of the United States Army seemed severe in contrast to the more varied and flamboyant colours worn by the units of Louisiana Militia. The rough garb worn by the Tennessee and Kentucky volunteers seemed appropriate to the name the British had given them, 'dirty shirts', for their clothes were worn, rumpled, and spotted with mud. As if on cue, the fog rolled away and the band struck up the familiar tune, 'Yankee Doodle'. The troops moved smartly, stepping in unison to the lilting rhythm. A flutter of applause rose from the civilians who had gathered to witness the review. Then without warning the morning air was split with the sound of cannon fire. For a second all movement was suspended and the musicians broke off in midbar. It was the abrupt arrival of the first cannonball that ploughed a furrow across the field not twenty feet from where Charl stood that sent everyone running. Dodging soldiers on the way to their posts, Charl dragged Janette and Benjamin to shelter behind a stone smokehouse. They cowered there for a few minutes trying to think what to do next. Benjamin was crying loudly, frightened by the noise and confusion, but above the roar of opposing cannon he was barely audible.

Then from nowhere Will appeared.

'Dear God!' he shouted at them. 'Don't you realize they're probably using this smokehouse as a benchmark to judge their range? You'd be safer lying in a ditch!'

From the three pairs of wide, frightened eyes that stared back at him he realized the answer.

'Come on!' he ordered. 'I want to get you out of here so I can get back to what I'm supposed to be doing.'

Snatching Benjamin around the waist like a sack of grain, he led them on a zigzag course towards the trees where the horses were tied. As they ran, the sky seemed to shatter with deafening thunder and the earth trembled beneath their feet. Once they reached the trees, the skittish horses proved difficult to harness, and Will and Charl struggled with them for some minutes before the task was completed. With Janette and Benjamin safe in the carriage, Will turned to go but Charl would not let him.

'Where is Seth?' she demanded, holding tight to his forearm, determined to have her answer in spite of the battle that raged around them.

He looked down into her pale, mud-spattered face and knew

he could not put her off. He only wished there was time to be gentle and sympathetic; but there was not.

'No one has seen him since the morning he rode out to Arnaud's,' he told her, his voice hard. 'He must be either dead or captured.'

It was what she had expected to hear, but the news stunned her.

'Charl, I'm sorry,' he went on. 'When it comes time for the exchange of prisoners, I'll do everything I can to get him back. I swear I will. Now, please, will you get out of here?'

Woodenly, Charl nodded and turned to climb into the gig. With practised hands she turned the skittish horses back towards New Orleans. But now the levee road was obscured, not just by fog, but by billows of smoke from the battle and the swiftly falling tears that she could not seem to control.

The British were repulsed a second time in the attack on New Year's Day, and the residents of New Orleans breathed a collective sigh of relief. They did not delude themselves that the threat was gone, but they seemed more confident and determined about the outcome of the battle or battles ahead.

More Kentuckians arrived under the command of General John Thomas, but to Jackson's dismay they came unarmed, ill clothed, and without provisions. Immediately, the women of the city set to work cutting and sewing literally thousands of coats and trousers from blankets provided by the Louisiana legislature. Charl threw herself into the project with single-minded fervour, stitching far into the night until her eyes stung with the close work and she fell into bed exhausted.

As the women sewed and the men continued to build and reinforce the breastworks along the Rodriguez Canal, more British reinforcements arrived. Everyone knew that the enemy was massing for an all-out attack, and they braced themselves as best they could to withstand it.

The attack came on Sunday, January 8 1815, with wave after successive wave of British soldiers throwing themselves against the American defences. Repeatedly they were driven back by the brilliant artillery work of the American gunners and the unerring aim of the backwoods sharpshooters, until the plain before the earthworks was carpeted with British dead and wounded. In the end it was not a battle won or lost by brilliant tactical skill. Jackson had the advantage of superior position and hung on tenaciously, employing each of his diverse units to the best advantage. Yet the legendary British valour could not be faulted. It was only the extent to which it had been fruitlessly employed that might be questioned. The cost to British forces was staggering, with nearly two thousand dead and wounded. Meanwhile the Americans, safe behind their earthworks, had lost very few men. Skirmishes continued along the western bank of the Mississippi, but ten days later, on January 18, the British began to withdraw the way they had come: up the bayous and across Lake Borgne to the ships that awaited the drastically depleted numbers.

With riotous good spirits the people of New Orleans cheered the victors. On January 23, they held an elaborate ceremony during which Andrew Jackson was repeatedly crowned with laurel wreaths befitting the hero of such a battle, and the Place d'Armes resounded with cheers for everyone connected with the British defeat. Rachel Jackson was sent for from Nashville to join her husband for the festivities and was regally entertained by New Orleans society.

But of far greater importance than the noisy adulation of the crowd and the raucous celebrations, at least to Charlotte Beckwith's mind, was the unremarkable passage of letters and lists of prisoners' names between the American, Edward Livingston, and his British counterpart, Major Harry Smith. During the several weeks of negotiations she waited with brittle courage, studying each new list, waiting patiently for one particular name to appear. She maintained her hope until the very last list was made public, but Seth Porterfield's name was not on it.

Charl accepted the inevitable conclusion with silent reserve. There were no tears for Seth now; she had cried them all in Quebec, so long ago. There was only the familiar cold ache that seemed lodged in her chest. Indeed she found it difficult to believe that the hurt had ever really gone away. That same devastating emptiness that she had come to know so well, after she had lost both Seth and his child, returned to her. But now she knew better how to combat the loneliness.

On the day that the British hoisted anchor and sailed out of Lake Borgne, Charl went down to the New Orleans waterfront with a loan from Will Hubbard in hand. She had thought long and hard about what she must do next, and it seemed as if there was only one alternative. With deliberate determination she booked passage on a ship bound for New York. Charlotte Beckwith was going home at last.

Forty

In the main salon of Admiral Cochrane's flagship, the 'Tonnant', were assembled the captains of the British fleet and some of the remaining army officers, several still recovering from their wounds. The occasion was not a convivial one for there was nothing to celebrate after the retreat from New Orleans and the bad weather that had prevented them from getting underway. They had gathered as a final farewell to fallen comrades before the new plans for an assault on Mobile, and eventually New Orleans, were set into motion on the morrow. They had eaten a satisfying meal and had now settled down to enjoy their port, raising their glasses occasionally in melancholy toasts to absent friends that inevitably led to stories and remembrances of glories past.

As the officers hoisted their wine for another salute, the ship's surgeon, Doctor Mulgray, resumed his place near the middle of the long table, having excused himself some minutes before to check on his patients. Noticing him, Cochrane emptied his glass and asked:

'I say, Mulgray, how fares our prisoner today?'

Major Harry Smith, whose negotiations for the exchange of prisoners were nearly complete, stirred at his words and glanced questioningly at the admiral.

'I was not aware that there were any prisoners aboard this ship,' he said quietly. It was obvious that Smith had been too busy, first with the manoeuvres on land and later with supervising the exchange of prisoners, to hear the stories of the admiral's concern for the young American captain who had been brought to him for questioning. With a few words Mulgray sketched out the details of the story, then went on to answer Cochrane's original question.

'He's no better, sir,' the doctor replied. 'In fact, he's somewhat worse. We had the blood poisoning nearly under control, but now congestion of the lungs has set in. His fever's up and he's having difficulty breathing. It's nearly a week since he's been fully conscious. Another man less fit would be dead by now, but Captain Porterfield determinedly clings to life against all the odds.'

'Yes,' Cochrane agreed, remembering how the captain had bandied words with him in spite of the fact that he was barely able to stand. 'I doubt that one will leave this world without a fight.'

'What's the man's name again?' Smith inquired, puffing thoughtfully on his cigar.

'Seth Porterfield,' Cochrane replied.

Whether the admiral spoke the name with more emphasis than usual or whether the other voices ebbed at that particular moment it was difficult to say, but the name carried clearly to those who sat at the far end of the table. In response one of the more junior captains glanced up with a start, an expression of mingled recognition and disbelief on his tanned face.

'I beg your pardon, sir,' he began, somewhat reluctant to break into the admiral's conversation, 'but the name you mentioned just now is one I've not heard in a number of years.'

'Seth Porterfield?' Cochrane repeated. 'Do you know the man, Captain Barrows?'

Devon Barrows was aware that the conversation at the long table had subsided, and the other officers, as well as Admiral Cochrane, were awaiting his reply.

'If it is indeed the same man, he was in my house at Eton,' he said quietly.

'At Eton!' Cochrane echoed. 'That explains a great deal.'

'The Seth Porterfield I knew was Sir Alastair Porterfield's bastard grandson,' Barrows went on.

'Sir Alastair Porterfield's grandson. Good God. It was Sir Alastair and my older brothers who first taught me to sail.' Then Cochrane's eyes narrowed, and he frowned thoughtfully. 'Now that I think about it, I do remember the story. Sir Alastair's daughter had an affair with a duke the year she was presented at court. The man was married, of course, and in the end she was left to bear the shame alone. Pretty thing she was, too – Eliza, Elaine, or something like that,' the admiral recalled. 'I never heard what happened to the child. I suppose she left him with

Sir Alastair at the estate in Yorkshire when she moved back to
London. Just as well, too, considering the life she was leading.'

Cochrane eyed the younger man. 'Would you recognize this
Seth Porterfield if you saw him, do you suppose?'

Barrows paused. 'I don't know, sir. I haven't seen him in more
than fifteen years. He was blond, as I recall, with very blue
eyes.'

'It must be the same man,' the doctor put in somewhat excite-
dly. During the weeks while he'd cared for the American he'd
come to like and respect the man who had remained stoic in spite
of his obvious discomfort. Mulgray was curious too about the
snatches of conversations Porterfield had whispered in his delirium and the woman whose name was continuously on his
parched lips.

'But what is Sir Alastair Porterfield's grandson doing with
Andrew Jackson's forces in America?' Cochrane mused.

'I'm sure I don't know, sir,' replied Barrows, who felt the
burden of an answer to his commander's question fall to him.
'As I recall, he was sent down from Eton and with good cause.
I doubt they ever had a more rebellious student. He smuggled
in liquor and cigars for us once,' he went on, the echo of his
boyish awe still evident in his words. 'Porterfield was the only
boy I ever knew who dared to defy old Fielding, the Latin
master. He would cane Porterfield almost daily for not having his
declensions done properly, but when it was Seth's turn to read
in class, his translations were always flawless.'

Barrows paused, slightly embarrassed by the indulgence in
reminiscence. But when he realized that the admiral was still
eyeing him attentively, he continued.

'From what I heard later, Seth was sent off to join his uncle's
artillery unit in Quebec when his grandfather discovered that, in
addition to his other faults, he'd been a bit too friendly with the
serving girls at the manor.'

'Sir Alastair Porterfield's grandson,' Cochrane mumbled to
himself. 'I'll be damned if there isn't a family resemblance.

'Before you go, Captain Barrows, would you have a look at
the man in the sick bay? I am very curious to know if you are
right about our prisoner's identity.'

The evening wound down slowly for it had been a long time
since such a group of officers had gathered for a purely social
purpose. But eventually the men began to disperse, leaving on

launches for their various ships to prepare to sail on the morning tide.

※

Once back in his cabin, Major Harry Smith considered the conversation he had heard earlier in the evening. Reluctantly, he picked up the final list of prisoners he would send to Edward Livingston the next day. The paper had been completed and sealed earlier that afternoon, and he was loath to reopen it. For a moment he toyed with the list and then abruptly set it aside, his decision made. There was little point in opening it to add one last name. After all, this Seth Porterfield might very well be dead before the papers even reached New Orleans. And if the man lived, he would see to his release himself.

Putting the thought out of his mind, Major Smith prepared for bed.

※

Just after dawn, having completed the last of their business with Jackson's representatives, the British fleet set sail. With a fresh wind from the west at their backs and the green sea before them, the ships of the line fell into their respective places with crisp precision that was a credit to the greatest sea power in the world. Admiral Sir Alexander Cochrane stood on the quarter-deck of the 'Tonnant' watching the manoeuvres with almost fatherly pride. It was here that Doctor Mulgray found him, standing by the rail, his spyglass in hand and his head cocked ever so slightly to the side as he listened contentedly to the hum of the wind in the canvas.

'It's good to be underway,' Cochrane observed after they had completed the morning pleasantries.

'Yes, sir, it is. I'd begun to think we would never quit New Orleans and these environs.'

'Mmm,' the admiral nodded in agreement. 'And how did our American guest pass the night?'

'Very well indeed,' Mulgray told him. 'Captain Porterfield's fever broke early this morning, and barring more complications he should recover. He seems a fine young man in spite of his association with the United States.'

'My sentiments exactly,' the naval officer agreed. 'And I am glad he's doing so much better. When time permits, I will write to Sir Alastair Porterfield myself to advise him that we'll be bringing his grandson home to convalesce.'

❖

The news that a peace treaty had been signed at Ghent on
Christmas Eve, 1814, ending the war between Great Britain and
the United States, reached Seth Porterfield as he lay on his pallet
in the sickbay of the British flagship, the 'Tonnant'. The orderly
who brought him his midday meal had told him of the truce
with great excitement, obviously expecting some extreme
reaction from the American captain. But Seth disappointed him
by staring blankly ahead, numbed by the unforeseen turn of
events.

Mitchell was right, he found himself thinking, as he remembered the conversation they'd had that bleak winter morning
when he'd agreed to accept this one last assignment to Jackson's
staff. Incredibly perceptive, as always, the man had predicted
the end to the war almost to the day. In his mind's eye he could
recall every detail of that meeting: Mitchell's bitterness, his own
desperation, the angry words that had passed between them, the
disillusionment that they'd shared. He rubbed his left hand
wearily across his eyes, wondering how the older man had reacted
to the word of peace. In the year or more since they'd talked,
had Mitchell found a way to live with the pain of his loss? Or
had the war left its indelible mark on Mitchell as it had on Seth
himself?

He leaned back against the pillows and closed his eyes. Dear
God, what would happen to him now? he wondered wearily. He
was still a prisoner on this British ship, though with the news of
peace it was more his own damnable weakness that held him
captive than his former countrymen.

'Have you heard the news of the treaty, Captain Porterfield?'
asked a familiar voice from beside him.

Seth opened his eyes to find the doctor sitting beside his bed.

'Yes, sir, I have. As a matter of fact, I was just considering
my position in all of this. If our two nations are no longer at war,
is it safe to assume that I am no longer a prisoner?' he asked the
older man.

'My dear Captain Porterfield,' the doctor began, 'in the strictest
sense you have never been a prisoner. Admiral Cochrane has
long since arranged for your parole and return to England when
your health permits.'

'He has?' Seth breathed in astonishment.

'As soon as he found out you were Sir Alastair Porterfield's grandson, he made the arrangements and drafted a letter to your grandfather advising him of your imminent return.'

'He did?' Seth managed to gasp.

'It seems that your grandfather knew Admiral Cochrane when he was a boy, and your families have long been on friendly terms. The admiral was pleased to advise Sir Alastair of your safety once we were sure you would recover from your wound.'

'Oh,' Seth mumbled as he tried to take in this last turn of events. 'But how did Admiral Cochrane know I was Alastair Porterfield's grandson?' he managed to ask.

'It was Captain Barrows who recognized you.'

'Captain Barrows?' Seth repeated.

'Devon Barrows,' Doctor Mulgray provided helpfully. 'You knew him when you were at Eton,' the doctor prodded.

'Devon Barrows.' There was an image of a thin, serious-faced boy forming slowly in his memory, but he pushed it aside in the light of more pressing matters.

'But I don't want to go to England!' Seth announced after a moment.

'I am sure you are a man, Captain Porterfield, who is used to ordering his own life; but this once let fate play its part. If it is your wish to return to America once we reach England, that will be easy enough to accomplish. For now, accept the things you cannot change. Do not struggle so. Your destination has been decided, and there is nothing more you can do.'

With the doctor's words echoing in his ears, Seth slept, allowing himself to trust, for the moment at least, in whatever future fate had in store for him.

When the supply ships arrived at the British anchorage in the Gulf of Mexico, preparations for the voyage to England began in earnest. It had been decided, primarily at Captain Barrow's insistence, that Seth would be transferred to his ship the 'Anaconda' for the journey. In the days since he'd discovered his former schoolmate's whereabouts, the young captain had come to the sick bay often: first making short visits that did not tax Seth's strength and later for longer periods to raise the American's flagging spirits, until the flicker of a long-ago friendship had been kindled anew.

❧

Was it the sun, the sky, or the ever-changing colour of the sea, the wind that ruffled his hair, the persistent whisper of the water against the hull, or the hours and days without demands that lent themselves to endless reminiscence? Seth Porterfield leaned his elbows on the rail and watched the waves boil up against the bow of the ship as it cut through the swells under the press of heavy sail. At least his health seemed to have been slowly re-established, with the long days of rest, nourishing food and the sea air.

What would happen when he reached England? he wondered for what might have been the hundredth time. All those years ago he had left his homeland under a cloud and had never voluntarily gone back.

It seemed impossible that people would remember a scandal that had rocked London society nearly thirty-four years before. But if Devon Barrows and Admiral Cochrane had recognized him as Sir Alastair Porterfield's bastard grandson, others would, too. And with that recognition would censure come as it always had when he was a boy?

His mother's death several years before would at least spare him her familiar recriminations for the disaster he had made of her life. Seth was not sure when he had begun to understand the whispers about what his birth had unwittingly made her, but eventually he had begun to accept the blame his mother had heaped on his innocent head. Logically, he knew he had not been the one to make her accept a string of temporary alliances with protectors unworthy of the name, nor had he been responsible for the dimming of her beauty that made her an unacceptable mistress. But even now, though he could see his mother for what she was, half spoiled child, half calculating bitch, those same desperate feelings he had known as a young man returned to haunt him. And neither the years, nor the rationality distance provided, could protect him from what he felt.

Only the recollections of his time at Seahaven and the strange, tenuous relationship with his grandfather brought him any pleasure. In those days he had lived for school holidays when he would return to the imposing stone house by the sea. There he would be able to gallop along the shore and over the rolling hills of Yorkshire; ride the swells in an open boat; swim in the cold clear sea; and savour his freedom. With mixed feelings he remembered the meals he'd taken with his grandfather at the long, walnut table in the dining room at Seahaven. Too often those meals had ended with a catalogue of Seth's recent sins, with his grandfather's face set in lines of disapproval as he frowned down the table at his recalcitrant charge. But occasionally, as the older man lingered over his port, Alastair Porterfield would recount the adventures of his youth, when he had travelled the earth on sailing ships to establish the complex trade routes that were the basis of the Porterfield fortune. Those stories had always left Seth enthralled and dreaming of mysterious places far away.

After visits to Seahaven, Seth would earnestly try to apply himself at school in order to win the older man's favour, but things would inevitably go awry. And no matter how Seth tried to earn his love, Alastair Porterfield had always managed to remain aloof: for ever demanding but never approving, eternally judgemental and seldom accepting, always stern with no hint of pleasure or affection for his daughter's son. In time, Seth came to see himself as a responsibility his grandfather had grudgingly accepted but never sought. He was an obligation forced on the older man, a constant reminder of the shame his mother had brought to the Porterfield name.

Since Admiral Cochrane had written to his grandfather to advise him of Seth's imminent return to England, it seemed unlikely that he could avoid a confrontation with the older man. Perhaps it was time to make peace with Alastair after all, Seth reflected.

He drew a long breath and watched the spume leap high and shimmer in the sunlight as the ship flashed through the grey-green waves. If he found the uncertainties of the future unsettling, he found the memories of his past no less so.

That Charlotte Beckwith had told him the truth about the route of British attack opened an endless number of possibilities for review and consideration. The fact that he had refused to believe her and had ridden into an ambush as a result infuriated him, but that was his fault and not hers. It also made him question how much of the rest he had dismissed as lies was also true. Doctor Mulgray had confirmed that Felix St James could have used a drug to gain the information he sought from Charl. If that was possible, might Seth also need to reconsider all the things that had seemed such ironclad proof of Charl's complicity in Quebec?

Dear God! How much of what Charl told him during the few hours they'd had together in New Orleans could he believe? The things he'd found in her bag that day at Arnaud's headquarters seemed to confirm that she had lived with the Indians. And if she'd told the truth about going to the Indians to escape St James, it hardly seemed likely that she was working with the English in Quebec to trap him as a spy.

There were suddenly so damned many unanswered questions: questions whose answers Seth both wanted and dreaded. And how could he weigh the truth in the things Charl had told him without wondering about all she had elected to omit?

The fact that she had willingly given herself to St James for any reason, much less for his sake, ate like acid at his insides. Blind jealousy filled him at the thought of another man's hands on her soft, alabaster flesh; another man's lips on that sweet, coral mouth; another man's body moulded to the long, sinuous length of her. Had Charl gone to Felix willingly after that first night, or had she been forced to submit to him time after time in the months she was his mistress? Had she shrunk from St James' touch, or had she gone numb at last, ceasing to fight, ceasing to feel?

'I'm glad you killed Felix!' Charl said that night in the Hubbard's kitchen. Would she have felt such loathing for a man she had gone to willingly?

He had been the one to take St James' life, but even that ultimate price seemed cheap in the face of all the pain the man had caused. Nor did Seth know if the scars he and Charl both bore would ever heal.

Christ! He had not been the one to make his mother a whore all those years ago. Instead, it was Charlotte Beckwith who had been forced into the final degradation for his sake. And even if he could not accept what she had done, he recognized the inner strength that had enabled her to survive the descent into hell that life with Felix St James must have become. Charl was a woman of strength and passion, a woman of warmth and beauty; she was a woman any man would consider well worth having. Then why was it so difficult to simply claim her?

Seth stared intently eastward, watching the nebulous point where sky became sea. Somewhere beyond that horizon lay England and the need for decisions he did not know how to make. He only knew that Charl would be lost to him for ever unless he chose to seek her out.

He loved her, of that there was no doubt, but the final acceptance of his feelings brought him no joy. He loved Charl and would love her until the end of his days. Dear God! Why wasn't that enough?

He expelled his breath slowly and closed his eyes, realizing that the decision that had tortured him for weeks had somehow been made. Because he could not live with Charl and forget the past, he would have to learn to live without her. Since he was afraid to trust her with his love, he could not claim her for his own. Numbing resignation moved through his blood and with it a sense of relief.

Well, at least there was the satisfaction of knowing his own mind, Seth reflected bleakly. Even if this course offered him no promise of happiness, it was resolution.

He would make a new life for himself when they reached England. He could not have contact with anyone in America, nor could he return to the land he had fought for and loved. But it would be a small price to pay in the end. Charl would believe him dead and find a man who could accept her love as he could not. He would stay in England to ensure her happiness.

It was hard to say how long he stood at the rail staring out at the rolling sea, but when he turned at the sound of his name, his muscles were stiff and cramped.

'We've sighted land, Seth!' Devon Barrows announced as he offered the spyglass to the man at the rail. 'There she is, Seth. England, sweet, green England!'

Taking the telescope, Seth followed the captain's gesture and sighted on a pale grey-green fringe along the rim of the sea, nearly obscured by the mist and the distance.

'England,' Seth echoed, but with none of the joy of homecoming that was evident in Barrow's voice. To Seth Porterfield England had suddenly become a place of self-imposed exile, a life sentence he had committed himself to serve without complaint.

❧

Seth and Devon Barrows sat in companionable silence in Porterfield's new rooms at the Warren Hotel in St James' Square after an evening of gaming and women in London's most exclusive establishments. The night was nearly gone, as was the decanter of brandy on the small table between their two highbacked chairs. In them the men slumped low, watching the fading embers of the fire. At that moment, there existed between them a mellow camaraderie that was one part liquor haze and two parts honest emotion.

'I'm going to miss you, Devon, when you go back to sea,' Seth told the other man, amazed at the ease of the admission.

'And I you, Seth.'

'I want to thank you and your family for all you've done –'

Barrows made a dismissing gesture. 'It's odd, isn't it, that we should meet after all these years?'

'Seth?' Devon's voice was a lazy drawl. 'Seth, do you think you'll ever return to America?'

The blond man stirred and poured more brandy into the bottom of the glass.

'No,' he said slowly, his voice like a requiem. 'My life there is over.'

His future was in England now or in any of the thousand places in the world that would welcome the man of money and ambition that he had become. His life in the United States was over forever.

✳

The insistent knocking woke Seth, and he sat up in bed wishing he had imbibed somewhat less freely the night before. Slipping from beneath the covers, he tugged his rust velvet dressing gown over his nakedness and padded barefoot across the sitting room, fully prepared to chastise his early morning caller for his lack of manners. But the angry words were never to be voiced as he flung open the door and stared in stunned silence at his visitor.

The man who stared back at him with equal intensity was one he would have known anywhere in the world. It had been twenty years since he had seen his grandfather, and yet Alastair Porterfield hardly seemed to have changed at all. The lines in his granite-hard face were more deeply etched, and his hair had gone from blond to grey, but the things that marked these two men as the same blood were unaltered.

Recovering himself to some degree, Seth opened the door wider.

'Come in,' he offered.

'I heard you were in London and decided to call to see how you'd turned out,' Alastair explained, to his grandson's unasked question.

'Have a chair, sir. I'll ring for some tea.'

'Surely your valet should take care of such things,' the elder Porterfield observed.

'I have no valet, sir. I never have had one,' Seth responded, then added as he saw Alastair's eyebrows rise, 'America is a very egalitarian country, you know.'

Sir Alastair accepted the chair his grandson had offered, and Seth began to stir the fire on the hearth to life.

There was a knock at the door, and Seth rose from tending the fire to answer it, moving with the sinuous grace of the Indians with whom he had elected to live.

Taking a box of biscuits and two cups from the cupboard, Seth laid the table and poured the tea that had been delivered, never once breaking the silence that lay like a gauntlet between his grandfather and himself.

Sir Alastair took the proffered cup and stirred it absently.

'I never heard one word from you after William died,' Alastair finally said and then instantly wished to recall the words. There had been more than a shadow of reproach in his voice, and that, as much as what he said, sent warmth creeping along Seth's cheekbones.

After a protracted silence the older man tried again. 'Did you make your fortune in the new world?' he asked.

'My fortune?' Seth asked softly in return. 'No, but I found friendship, acceptance and adventure. And to some men those things are more precious than gold.'

Alastair was surprised by both the insight and the bitterness in the younger man's words. Old age had brought him wisdom, if not happiness. Now he understood, as twenty years ago he had not, the forces that drove Seth to rebel against all forms of control.

'Admiral Cochrane wrote to tell me that you were wounded in New Orleans and for a time were not expected to live.' Alastair paused.

'Admiral Cochrane wrote to you without my knowledge or consent,' Seth said stiffly, 'but I thank you for your concern.'

'I also heard that you have done quite well financially since you have returned to London: that though your initial good fortune was at the gaming tables you have a fine head for business investments as well.'

'You seem to know a great deal about me,' Seth observed.

'Well, of course, I would make inquiries,' the older Porterfield blustered.

Finally Alastair cleared his throat, ending the uncomfortable silence that followed his outburst. 'You must be wondering why I came today,' he began, 'and it's high time I got to the point. I came to offer you an invitation to Seahaven.'

'Seahaven?' Seth echoed, aware of a warmth rushing through him at the mention of the place where he'd grown up.

'Well, it was your home once, and I thought you might welcome the chance to see it again.'

Seahaven. To Seth the name itself was an invitation, a cool, soothing balm for his weary spirit. His face softened as he thought of his childhood home. It was the one place on earth where he might find peace.

❧

Seahaven. How long he had cherished memories of the place: the wide meadow carpeted with wild flowers, where the house stood; the green, velvet hills on either side; the sunlight shimmering on the water; and the broad, blue sweep of sky. He had steeled himself for disappointment, knowing full well that the things of childhood often paled when viewed through the jaded eyes of an adult, but Seahaven was exactly as he remembered. They arrived from London in his grandfather's coach just before dusk on the third day of travelling. As they rounded the last curve in the road, the house came into view, strong and stately, silhouetted against an endless panorama of sky and sea. The buff-coloured stone was turned bronze in the sunset, and the house shimmered like a moonstone in a setting of deepest turquoise. It was as Seth had seen it a hundred times in his mind's eye, and a strange poignancy enveloped him with the realization that he was coming home at last. The enchantment of this stark, beautiful place had lost none of its potency for Seth, and he was forced to swallow hard to master his emotions. Nor was the softening of the lines in his grandson's face, or the wonder in his eyes, lost on Alastair Porterfield.

As the days passed, the tempo of life at Seahaven absorbed Seth and the peace he had been fruitlessly seeking settled over him.

Slowly, the estrangement between grandfather and grandson began to ease. Initially, there was the business of the manor to discuss; then the scraps of local news and gossip that Seth heard in his travels were shared. Later Alastair began to explain the affairs of other Porterfield holdings to his grandson, finding in Seth a well-honed business sense.

In return for the older man's confidences, Seth began to talk of his life in America, sketching the tales broadly to conceal as much as they revealed. For as pleased as he was by the change in his relationship with his grandfather, there was still something of the boy he had been in Seth.

Life continued at a sedate pace through the summer with the routine of daily chores, with sails on the blue-green sea, with days spent fishing in an open boat, and with parties and pastimes at neighbouring estates. Through Sir Alastair's solicitor, Seth sent for the clothes and keepsakes he had left at Gabrielle La Soeur's in Quebec.

The burl campaign chest and several other boxes arrived early in August, and with them came painful reminders of the life he had elected to leave behind. For along with his clothes, his silver tankard, and his books were Charl's things as well. There was the creamy cashmere shawl he'd bought her, the modest night-dress she'd insisted on wearing in the hope of cooling his ardour; the softly ruffled aqua gown, with Charl's clean citrus fragrance somehow clinging to the fabric. At the bottom of the trunk was a letter from Gabrielle herself.

Dear Sir Alastair,
    These are the things you requested. Along with your grandson's effects, I have included the possessions of his mistress, Charlotte Beckwith. To the best of my knowledge, she died when she miscarried Seth's child during the winter of 1813.
    Missing from the trunk are some letters that were written to William Porterfield while he was stationed here in Quebec. I do not know what they were, or why Seth kept them, but they were seized the first time the British troops searched your grandson's room.

'The first time?' Seth mumbled as he reread the sentence. How many times had St James searched his room? And why would he bother to search it if Charl had told him where the papers were hidden, as Felix claimed? There was an uncomfortable knot of uncertainty in the pit of his stomach as he finished the letter.

    Since you have requested his effects, I assume Seth is dead. In that case I offer you my condolences. Seth was a fine man and a good friend to my family and me. I grieve for his loss.
        Your obedient servant,
        Gabrielle La Soeur Savard

In the months since he'd decided to stay in England, Seth had exiled thoughts of Charl to some far corner of his mind so he could survive each day as it came. But now, with her belongings spread out across the library floor beside his own and with the question of her loyalty fresh in his mind, he could not deny her.

'Damn you, woman, and damn me!' he muttered, balling up the pale aqua gown and throwing it across the room with all his might. But the angry gesture had relieved none of his frustration.

He could not escape her. Charl might well be an ocean away, but she was a part of him: in his heart and in his head until no thought of his own could exist without a coupling thought of her. If he closed his eyes he could see her before him, her honey blonde hair streaming like molten gold to her waist, and feel the soft lush body beneath his hands. Why was she still so real to him after all these months? When would his memories fade?

The sound of the door opening startled Seth, and he turned to watch as Sir Alastair made his way to the decanters on the table. The elder Porterfield nodded in greeting, and with drink in hand moved towards where Seth stood in the window alcove.

'Hiding from your ghosts, boy?' Alastair asked, his voice strangely sympathetic.

'We all have ghosts of one kind or another,' Alastair went on, settling himself in a chair not a dozen paces from Seth, effectively cutting off his escape.

'I'll warrant your ghost is a woman, just as mine is,' the older man observed. 'I've watched you, boy. No matter where you are, you watch the women. But you don't watch them appreciatively like most men. No matter how lovely the woman on your arm is, you seek the others. It's almost as if you expect the one you want to appear at any moment.'

Seth remained silent and stared blankly out of the window, thinking how close his grandfather had come to the truth.

'Is the girl an American?' his grandfather asked softly.

Seth nodded and the older man read the sadness in his grandson's face.

'She's not dead in the war is she?' he persisted.

'No.'

'Is she another man's wife?'

Seth shook his head.

'Then, boy, if you want her, why don't you claim her?' Seth searched his soul for the answer.

Sensing his grandson's anguish, the older man returned to his musings.

'I loved a woman like that once. I loved her more than life itself, yet I was too much a fool and coward to claim her.'

The moonlight that streamed in the windows caught and shadowed the furrows in Alastair Porterfield's face, but his eyes were the soft, dreamy blue of a young man's. Seth saw himself in that face forty years hence: regretting his mistakes; remembering one brief, joyous interlude in Quebec. He hated the vision of his future, and suddenly his chest was tight as if its inevitability had already begun to suffocate him.

'Lavinia Langford St James.' The elder Porterfield spoke the name almost caressingly, and Seth's attention was drawn to his grandfather's words.

'St James?' Seth echoed. 'William served with a Felix St James in Quebec.'

'Yes,' Sir Alastair nodded. 'Felix St James was Lavinia's grandson. Ironic, isn't it, that her grandson and my son should be comrades in arms.

But it was Felix St James who was responsible for William's death! Seth longed to shout the accusation aloud, but he restrained himself, realizing it would do more harm than good. Alastair Porterfield's face was engraved with lines of grief when he spoke of his son's death, and it would be unnecessarily cruel to deny him the comfort of his illusions.

As he waited for Alastair to continue, Seth felt a tremor of anticipation race through him. The hairs on the back of his neck and along his arms stirred in primitive reaction, and his heart was suddenly loud in his ears. He felt balanced blindly on some precipice, as if his grandfather's next words would either offer him safety or send him hurtling off into oblivion.

'I received a long letter from Felix St James when William died. He spoke of William's valour, of what a capable officer he had been. They were fine words and they offered me a great deal of comfort in those dark days.' The older man's voice broke and ebbed away.

In the silence that followed, Seth's anger grew, expanding and bubbling until it filled him with hot, seething rage. Common sense bridled his words as he struggled with his own emotions.

Let Alastair take what comfort he could from Felix St James'
lies, but Seth knew the truth. Lavinia Langford St James' grandson had died by his hand at the Battle of the Thames River, and
with that act, William Porterfield's murder had been avenged.

A momentary contempt flickered through Seth. Of course, St
James had known just what to write Alastair Porterfield after
William's death. Felix had always possessed an uncanny ability
to manipulate people, to make them think or feel whatever he
wanted them to think or feel, regardless of the truth of the
matter.

A shiver of recognition passed through Seth's body as that
thought thundered in his brain, awakening echoes of understanding until his world trembled with dawning comprehension. He
drew a long breath and was giddy with the implications of his
own thoughts.

Dear God! How well Felix had been able to manipulate people,
he reflected angrily, his contempt turned inward now. For he had
been St James' victim, too. He had been cruelly duped into
thinking that he had been betrayed.

'You would believe Felix St James, your sworn enemy, and
not me!' The words Charl had spoken in the storehouse in New
Orleans came back to him as if the woman stood before him. He
had been wrong to doubt her, wrong about everything.

Alastair began to speak again, and Seth drew closer to listen.
For the moment he put his own thoughts aside, to be examined
and analysed at his leisure.

'Felix St James must have been a fine officer and a fine man,'
the elder Porterfield mused. 'And he could well have been my
grandson, just as you are. If I had married Lavinia when I had
the chance, Felix might have been my flesh and blood, just as his
uncle was.'

It took a moment for the implications of this last statement to
reach Seth. 'What did you say?' he finally breathed.

'Alexander St James, Felix's uncle, was my son.' Alastair
studied Seth in the dim light but was at a loss to explain the
strange tension in the younger man.

'Lavinia was betrothed to Martin St James when I first met
her,' he went on. 'Beautiful she was: all flaming red hair and
slender as a sapling, with eyes as deep and green as forest pools.'
His voice was tender with the memory. 'I loved her from the first
moment I set eyes on her. It was not long before we were meeting

secretly for lovers' trysts. Never have I been as happy or content as I was for that one brief summer. In the autumn her banns were posted, and she begged me to take her away. But I had nothing to offer her. Martin St James was the Earl of Besswick, and I was nothing but a merchant's son. I put her off, doubting I could make her happy once she realized all she was giving up. Instead of staying and claiming her like a man, I went away. I spent nearly five years travelling the world, establishing new trade routes for the Porterfield fleet and making my fortune. When I returned, I had everything, a title for my efforts, a place in society. I was an unqualified success, but it all came too late. Lavinia was dying and Martin St James had accepted my son as his heir.' The bitterness and self-loathing etched Alastair Porterfield's face with lines of pain, and he raised his eyes to Seth's as if seeking forgiveness for this one tragic mistake. 'If I'd known she carried my child, I would have married her gladly. I'd have stayed with her and devoted my life to making her happy. But she never told me, not until it was too late for both of us. I'm not sure that the Earl ever knew the truth, but the knowledge that Alexander St James is my son will be with me for ever.

'I married your grandmother out of a sense of family duty, but it's Lavinia Langford I'll love until my dying day!' Alastair's tone was husky as he made the final declaration, and he rose slowly to refill his glass.

Seth watched him intently, considering all he had heard.

Too many revelations had come too quickly, and he needed time to sort things out. Still Seth could not ignore the implication that this fifty-year-old love affair was the basis for Felix St James' hatred of the Porterfields. What was it he'd told Charl when she'd miscarried Seth's child? Wasn't it something about the St Jameses not claiming another Porterfield bastard? When she had asked him about it in New Orleans, he hadn't understood, but suddenly, in the light of what had happened long ago, the meaning came clear. Was that why Felix had sought William's death and then his own? Had they all been hopelessly trapped in a web of hate that had grown more tangled and treacherous over the years? Dear God! How venomous and futile revenge could be.

Alastair returned to his chair. 'So that's my story, boy. I've told you so that you might learn from an old man's mistakes.

I sit here nights without sleeping, wishing and remembering; imagining that soft, sweet woman I once held in my arms. I ache for my Lavinia, boy, just as you do for your lady. Only for you, Seth, it's not too late!'

Alastair Porterfield's eyes were a bright, piercing blue in the moonlight, and he spoke with the conviction of a man who had seen a vision of the future.

Suddenly the room seemed too close, too confining, and Seth knew he had to find somewhere to be alone with his thoughts.

'You've given me a great deal to think about, sir,' he said. 'And now, if you will excuse me, I believe I will go for a walk.'

Alastair gave a slight nod and a smile of acquiescence that lingered on his lips long after Seth was gone.

❧

Seth came into the dining room at Seahaven the next morning dressed for travelling. He had left his single valise at the front door and had ordered his horse for the long ride to London. It was his intention to bid his grandfather a brief good-bye and set off immediately on the quest for his future, but Alastair Porterfield clearly had other plans.

'Are you going somewhere?' Alastair inquired, glancing up from the three-day-old newspaper that had arrived from London that morning.

'Yes, sir, I am,' Seth replied briskly.

'You're going to America, I suppose,' the older man observed blandly, setting the newspaper aside.

'Yes, sir, to America.' Seth took a deep breath and began to voice all the appropriate, impersonal phrases that would enable him to take his leave, knowing that he had suitably expressed his gratitude for the invitation to Seahaven. 'I'd like to thank you for your hospitality these past weeks. It was very pleasant to return to Seahaven –'

Alastair broke into the crisp, well-rehearsed speech. 'You have time for a cup of tea, at least,' he said, pouring from a sterling silver pot into the cup at Seth's place.

'Really, Grandfather . . .' Seth began to demur.

'Oh, sit down, Seth!' Sir Alastair spoke in a tone that brooked no resistance, and the younger man obeyed, more startled by the tone of voice he'd not heard since childhood than intimidated by it.

'I suppose you've decided to take my advice and seek out your young lady?' he inquired, fixing his grandson with his unblinking stare. 'And just what is it that you plan to do when you find her?'

'Well, sir, I plan to ask Charl to marry me.'

'And will she have you, boy?' the older man asked bluntly.

Seth took a shaky breath.

'I hope so, sir,' he replied honestly.

'You sound doubtful,' Alastair observed. 'Have you mistreated the chit somehow?'

'Grievously so, I'm afraid,' his grandson admitted. The need to leave was burning bright within Seth, fanned to flame by this discussion about why Charl might refuse him.

Alastair was silent as he frowned across at Seth. In that quiet moment the younger man came to his feet, pushing aside the untouched cup of tea his grandfather had poured for him.

'Really, sir,' he began. 'I must be on my way. I want to ride as far as –'

'Damn it, boy!' Alastair roared. 'Sit down! There are things to be discussed between us, and it is doubtful that I can wait another twenty years for you to return.'

Seth sat down stiffly and watched his grandfather with narrowed eyes.

'I'm sorry I spoke to you so,' Sir Alastair made an almost unprecedented apology before he went on.

'So you love this girl, and you plan to marry her, is that right?'

'Yes, damn it, one way or the other I do!' Seth snapped.

Alastair nodded and withdrew a small velvet box from his pocket.

'Then you had better take this with you,' he said.

Seth picked up the box from where his grandfather had set it on the polished tabletop and opened it slowly. Inside was a ring, a circlet of blue-green emeralds set in gold, resting on ancient yellowing satin. With confusion in his eyes he looked up to where Sir Alastair sat.

'The ring has been in the family for generations,' he began to explain. 'For nearly two hundred years it has been passed down to the bride of the heir when he married. I'm not surprised that you don't remember seeing it. No one has worn it since your grandmother died, and you were little more than an infant then. Now it has come to you, to your bride, since you are the last of the Porterfields.'

It took Seth a moment to catch his breath after this unexpected gift for Charl and his grandfather's perplexing words.

'But you said this ring was passed on to the bride of the Porterfield heir,' he began doubtfully.

Alastair nodded again. 'That's right,' he confirmed. 'I have made you my heir, Seth. I went directly to my solicitor's from your rooms in St James' Square to make the arrangements. Even in the few minutes I was with you that day, it was evident the kind of man you had become. It's legal now. When I die, Seahaven and all the Porterfield holdings will come to you. I made my decision impulsively that day in London, but I've never once had a moment's regret.'

Alastair smiled at his grandson, the warmth of his feeling for the younger man eroding the lines in his granite-hard face. Seth smiled in return as he struggled to accept this last, and perhaps most unexpected, turn of events.

'I never thought –' Seth stammered. 'I never expected –'

'I know, boy. I know. But it's what's right; I'm more certain of that every day,' Alastair assured him as he rose from his place at the table. Seth followed suit, more from force of habit than from earnest desire to go. It seemed as if there was so much left to say. Clapping his grandson on the back, the elder Porterfield led him towards the door.

'Go find your Charlotte now, boy,' Alastair advised, 'and perhaps she'll look on you more kindly if you offer her that bauble and a place in society.'

Feeling on familiar ground again, after all the somewhat dazzling things his grandfather had told him, Seth made a wry face. 'If Charl decides not to have me, neither the crown jewels nor the promise of King George's throne would sway her.'

Sir Alastair gave a low chuckle. 'She sounds like a bit of a tartar but a lass well worth having. You must bring her to meet me when you've made her your wife.'

There was a note in Alastair's voice as he spoke those last words that made Seth abruptly aware of the older man's isolation. Many of his grandfather's contemporaries were gone now, and the woman he loved was long dead. There was only his tenuous hold on the future through Seth himself, and perhaps his wife and children, to offer the older man comfort in his loneliness. Instinctively, Seth moved to hug him close in an expression of affection that had never before passed between them.

'You will bring her, won't you?' Alastair asked in a choked voice. 'And your children, too?'

Seth's hands moved comfortingly against his grandfather's broad back, aware of a certain frailty in spite of his deceptive size and proud carriage. 'Of course I'll bring them,' he managed to reply.

'You've grown to be a good man, Seth, a good man,' Alastair went on. 'And I'm proud of you.'

'Thank you, Grandfather, for those words and everything else,' Seth whispered simply.

They stood for a long moment without moving, unashamed and unafraid for the first time to expose the soft core of feelings deep within them both. They were so alike, both inside and out, that when they parted at last, the expressions of tenderness and affection on their faces were nearly identical.

Alastair watched as his grandson rode away, waiting on the steps of the house until he was long out of sight. He would miss Seth terribly in the weeks to come since he had grown used to the younger man's company. But Alastair took comfort in the knowledge that this morning a bond had been forged between them that would never be broken again.

Part Five

✳✳✳

Youngstown, New York

Forty-One

Charlotte Beckwith glanced into her mirror as she adjusted the flowing white gown so that it fell in graceful folds from the demure neckline to the deeply ruffled hem. Its pristine lace and soft flounces complemented her pink and gold beauty, and though she had objected to the overly youthful style of the dress, she knew it looked well on her. At any rate Stephen had insisted on it, and she had acquiesced rather than fight a pitched battle over such a trivial matter. After all, it was their wedding day.

Sighing softly, she leaned closer to the glass and wondered why these last months had not left their mark on her. There was still the same pliant vulnerability to her pale coral mouth, the same womanly roundness to her cheeks. In spite of the hours of poring over the books in the backroom of her father's store by the light of a flickering candle and the months of hiding her loneliness and her pain, no lines marred her flawless skin. If there was any change, it was in the determined set of her jaw and the coldness that was evident in the depths of her blue-green eyes.

Charl had returned to Youngstown during the almost-spring of early April 1815 while the ice floes were still nudging their way along the banks of the river and the willows were turning pale yellow with a promise of new life after the hard winter. The town was much altered in her absence, due primarily to the fact that it had been all but levelled by the British and the Indians during the winter of 1813 in retaliation for the burning of Newark by the Americans some months before. The main street had been partially rebuilt, though the buildings looked somehow less substantial to her than the original ones had been. Nor did she find the people the same, especially her father.

The day she arrived, he had been waiting on customers in his rebuilt store, a mere skeleton of the vigorous man he had formerly been. A letter advising him of her safety and her wish to return home had preceded her, but the reunion had been rending for both father and daughter in spite of it. Charl was as unprepared for the hollow-eyed, one-legged man who greeted her with tears on his flaccid cheeks as Henry Beckwith was for the strong, self-possessed woman his little girl had become. He had been shot in the knee while defending the frontier with the rest of the militia. After he was wounded, he had lain in a hospital in Canandaigua, where the leg had festered, rotted, and eventually been amputated, but Henry Beckwith had never recovered from the ordeal. And the man Charl found in her father's place that early spring day was a man awaiting permission to die.

After the disillusionment of the reunion with her father, Charl was loath to return to the house she remembered so well, but when she rode up the tree-lined drive, she found it battered but still solid. Only Harriet, their long-time housekeeper, remained of the servants that had once been employed by the Beckwiths, but the meeting between the two women had been joyous and tearful.

The house was certainly not as Charl remembered it to be; but it had changed in the ensuing years no more than she had herself. As she fell into the routine of her old life, there was a certain satisfaction, a certain sense of continuity that came with living in the rooms she had known as a child and following the paths she had walked then. If she had stopped to consider, she would have realized it was that consistency that provided Charl with the strength to resume her life in Youngstown.

Too much had befallen the entire populace during the course of the war for her experiences to be remarked upon. But there was something about Henry Beckwith's prodigal daughter that held everyone at bay. It was only Stephen Langley who dared to seek her intimidating presence, and the people of Youngstown found him even more forbidding than Charlotte Beckwith had become.

In the weeks after her return Charl took over more and more of the duties at the store as Henry failed before her eyes. Soon he gave up going to work at all and eventually kept to his bed all day. It was hard for Charl to accept that her father had given up, but nothing she did could spark his interest in the world around him. As he worsened, Charl tried to get him to discuss the business with her. She asked specifically where he had found the money to rebuild and restock the store after the original building had burned, but Henry flatly refused to talk about it. And in spite of the nights Charl spent poring over the account books, she could not find a clue.

Instead, Henry preferred to deal in reminiscences of the happier days when she was a child, talking about their rides in the woods and their sails on the lake. While it pleased her that Henry could derive such contentment from their close relationship as father and daughter, she was alarmed to realize that he had lost touch with the present. When the time came that Henry Beckwith died peacefully in his sleep, Charl found she was neither surprised nor totally sorry.

A soft knock at the door broke into her thoughts, and Charl was pleased to see Janette Hubbard peek into the room. She, Will, and Benjamin had come to the wedding en route to Will's new command at Pittsburgh. Charl welcomed their visit, especially now, for she was feeling the loss of her father very deeply. During the short time she had spent in New Orleans, a very real affection had grown between her and the Hubbards. Their support as she awaited news of Seth and later when she found that he was dead had been invaluable to her. The fact that Will had reluctantly agreed to give her away at the ceremony this afternoon would make her feel that much less alone when she faced Stephen.

'You are far too beautiful for him, Charlotte!' Janette exclaimed in exasperation as she bustled into the room.

'Janette, thank you,' Charl broke in. 'I know you are only trying to help, and truly I appreciate your concern. But this marriage is what I want, honestly it is.' Taking a circlet of silk flowers and filmy lace from where it lay on the bed, she turned back to face the looking glass. 'Will you help me with this, Janette?'

With her lips set in a disapproving frown, the Frenchwoman took the ornate headpiece and settled it in place, arranging the sheer fabric to frame Charl's flawless features. When the ensemble was complete, both women realized that no matter how inappropriate the veil and gown were, they highlighted the bride's own beauty. These pieces, like the rest of her trousseau, had been fashioned to Stephen's exact specifications by a modiste who had been summoned from New York especially for the task. The wardrobe that was the result of his choices was elegant and expensive. Yet Charl was uncomfortable in the new clothes for

she knew she was neither the innocent virgin whose role she
would play today nor the jaded harlot who would grace Langley's
bed tonight.

Forcing a bright smile to her lips, Charl cast one last look into
the mirror. 'That looks fine, don't you think? Is Will waiting
downstairs with the carriage? Now I must go.'

At the foot of the stairs Will, Benjamin, and Harriet waited.

'Charl is pretty, Daddy!' the child crowed, summing up the
sentiments of the group concisely.

'Why, thank you, Ben,' Charl acknowledged the compliment
with a smile before she turned to the housekeeper with last-
minute instructions for the party that would follow the ceremony.

'Don't you worry about a thing, Miss Charlotte,' Harriet broke
in to assure her, though her face was set in the same disapproving lines that the Hubbards' were. 'If you're determined to
marry Stephen Langley, the least I can do is see that
your wedding celebration goes smoothly. Lord, child, you sure
are the prettiest bride I've ever seen. Your papa would be so
proud.'

Charl hugged the older woman close, blinking back the sudden
tears that threatened to overwhelm her.

'Thank you, Harriet,' she whispered as she struggled for control. Then, without daring a moment's hesitation, she turned
from the hall and went resolutely to the carriage that awaited
her.

The ride to the church would be a long one, Charl reflected as
they turned from the drive onto the River Road, especially with
Will Hubbard scowling across at her as he was.

The formal church wedding was another of Stephen's dictates,
and since the only church for miles around was the one that
recently had been rebuilt in Lewiston, the service was to be held
there. He had been obsessive in his concern for the details of this
wedding.

Oh, damn, Charl thought wearily, glancing out of the window
at the passing greenery. Perhaps she was mad to agree to marry
Stephen Langley. But then, what choice did she have?

Stephen had come to her the night they had buried her father.
With a smug expression on his swarthy face he had given her a
bank draft drawn on one of his accounts at a New York City
establishment. It was made out to her father for the amount of five
thousand dollars; on the back was Henry Beckwith's signature as

proof of receipt. For a moment Charl stared at the paper, then raised her eyes to Stephen's face.

'So it was you who lent Father the money to rebuild the store. I have wondered where it came from since we lost nearly everything in the fire.' She waited a moment for him to state his business, already certain of why he had come. But when he did not speak, she set aside the draft and faced him squarely.

'I suppose you have brought this to me because you want immediate repayment of the loan,' she began. 'Well, Stephen, I'm afraid that's out of the question. The store is a paying concern, and it will do even better in the future with everyone rebuilding. But at the moment I haven't got five hundred dollars ready cash, much less five thousand.'

'To tell the truth, Charlotte, I had no intention of demanding the money,' he drawled. Through the haze of cigar smoke Charl could not read his expression, but she was suddenly alert to a more sinister purpose for his visit. 'Actually what I had in mind was something in the nature of an agreement between us.'

'Then I will be happy to sign a note for the balance of the loan, Stephen,' she told him coolly.

He blew a long plume of smoke towards the ceiling as he eyed her.

'That's not quite what I wanted either,' he said softly.

With apprehension knotting her stomach, she glared at him. 'Then just what is it you want?' she had asked.

He paused and smiled.

'I want you to marry me, Charlotte,' he said simply.

His words caught her unprepared, and conflicting emotions stirred in her heart: surprise, pity, revulsion, fear.

'You have not given me your answer, Charlotte,' he prodded, a parody of a smile curving his cruel mouth.

Eyeing him levelly she replied, 'I don't intend to marry anyone, Stephen. Not ever.'

The silence became thick and threatening between them.

'Is that because you are saving yourself in the sanctified memory of Seth Porterfield?' he demanded.

'Seth Porterfield has nothing to do with this,' she denied vehemently, though her fists were clenched tight in her lap as she fought for control of her emotions to give credence to the lie.

'Oh, I believe he has everything to do with this,' Langley

countered. 'You came to love him in the end, didn't you? You even sold yourself to an English officer to save his life?'

'How do you know that?' she gasped.

'It doesn't matter how I know it!' he went on. 'It just seemed to me that if you were willing to sell yourself once for the life of a man you loved, you might sell yourself again for the honour of another.'

Charl stared at him in confusion. 'What do you mean?' she asked, her voice quaking in spite of her efforts to steady it.

Stephen smiled again, his calm certainty sending a tremor of dread racing through Charl.

'I brought the bank draft to you, not because I wanted to foreclose on the loan, but because it is proof that your father was paid off for his cooperation in a scheme to sell supplies to the British during the war.'

'That's a lie!' Charl blazed at him, her face flushed with ire.

'Are you sure?' he responded undeterred. 'I could make quite a case against him with this bank draft, some invoices, and orders signed by various British officers.'

'But, Stephen,' she asked after a long moment, 'why would you do that? And how could you prove a case against my father without implicating yourself in these same transactions?'

It was clear that she still possessed the same fearlessness he had admired in her when they were children, he reflected as he watched her. But in this game her bravado would be to no avail for he held all the winning cards.

'I am doing this, Charlotte, because I want you. I have always wanted you, but you know that. And I realize that you will never come to me in any other way. To put it plainly, my dear, either you agree to marry me, or I will sully Henry Beckwith's name for ever.

'As for implicating myself, I do not care. I've been considering a trip to Europe for some time. They say the baths of Germany and France can be quite restorative. At any rate, I will be far from here when the scandal breaks. It will be a pity if you must remain here to bear the burden of your father's intrigues with the British. Nor would it surprise me if public sentiment turned quite sharply against the daughter of a conspirator, a woman who lived openly with both an English officer and an English spy. There is no telling what might happen.'

There was no doubt of the threat in his words, and Charl

trembled with impotent rage as she tried to grapple with her choices. Each was as repellent as the other.

'This is a low, despicable deed, Stephen, to slander a man who cannot defend himself,' she whispered, her voice thick with loathing.

Langley shrugged, unaffected by her rancour.

'Nevertheless, whatever I must do to claim you at last will be well worth it, my dear,' he told her. 'You see, I want you very badly.'

'Why?' she had breathed, mesmerized by his determination.

Stephen's black eyes moved over her slowly, unclothing her with a look that simmered with contempt, desire, and something else she did not recognize.

'Because, my dear Charlotte, you are very, very beautiful.'

She had not understood then or seen deeper than his words. That night she had thought only of protecting her father's good name, though she was not so naïve that she did not demand some concessions of her own.

'If I agree to marry you, Stephen, I want the store and the rest of my father's holdings to remain in my name,' she had begun, stating her terms coolly and dispassionately.

Langley watched her from beneath lowered lids, amazed that though he had cornered her, she still had the temerity to dictate her terms. But then, if it meant possessing her at last, wasn't it prudent to agree?

'Very well,' he had nodded, 'the store and your father's holdings shall be my wedding gift to you.'

For a moment Charl was angry both at Stephen for his galling condescension in returning what was, after all, her own property to her and at a society that forced her to barter herself to retain her rights. With difficulty she swallowed her irritation and hurried on.

'And I want your word that you will not interfere in the way I run the store or handle the property.'

Stephen shrugged. 'As you wish, my dear. Is there anything else?' Charl had shaken her head. 'Then I think we should set a date for the wedding, perhaps sometime in September.'

Reluctantly she had agreed. It was only later that the doubts came to plague her. In marrying Stephen she was salvaging the two things she had left that she valued: her father's good name and the store that was his legacy. Seth was gone, their child was gone, and beyond that nothing mattered. She knew too that she was a colder, harder woman for having survived the descent into hell that life with St James had been, and she would not allow Stephen to destroy her. In that light marriage to Langley did not frighten her, at least not at first. But in time she came to realize that as obsessed as Felix had been, he was always in control; Stephen was not.

Stephen's hatred of Seth ran deep, based not only in the incident on Queenston Heights, but in the duel the two men had fought that sullied Langley's honour for ever. Slowly Charl came to understand that she was as much a symbol to Stephen of some kind of victory over Seth Porterfield as she had been to Felix St James. In truth her beauty, her desirability, her capacity for kindness and love meant little to Stephen. He was stirred by darker emotions. Charl's tenure as Porterfield's mistress and her repeated refusals of his suit before the war, coupled with his childhood infatuation, drove him to make her his own. And as she came to realize his true motives for the marriage, Charl became desperate to refuse him. But she knew she dared not.

Will Hubbard's gentle touch on her arm returned her abruptly to the present and alerted her to the fact that they had reached the church. Stephen was waiting in the doorway of the small brick structure as the carriage pulled up, and he descended the steps with his dragging gait as he came to greet her. He had insisted on wearing his militia uniform for the ceremony, complete with cocked hat and sabre, though he had not served with the unit since the fateful battle at Queenston Heights.

'Stephen, don't you know it is bad luck for the groom to see the bride before the wedding ceremony begins?' Charl chided him as her betrothed helped her down from the carriage.

'That's superstitious nonsense, my dear,' he replied, his dark eyes glowing with undisguised lust as he regarded her. 'Besides I make my own luck, as you well know. Now go into the church and see to your gown. The others will be arriving soon.'

She obeyed silently, finding a small sunlit chamber at the end of the church's foyer where she could wait for the ceremony to begin. Once inside, she turned to Will, chattering nervously in an attempt to drown out the warnings of her conscience and the clamour of her doubts.

Hubbard came to stand beside her, catching her cold hands in his and peering intently into her face.

'You mustn't go through with this, Charl,' he insisted softly. 'I don't understand why you ever agreed to marry Langley. I know what he is, and I'm sure now how you really feel about him. Damn it, Charlotte, this is wrong. You see that as clearly as I do!'

Ruthlessly he forged on. 'Seth would want me to look after you, Charl,' Hubbard said, 'and he would never forgive me if I let you marry this man.'

Charl blanched at his words but faced him squarely, her eyes accusatory and full of pain. 'Seth is dead, Will,' she said bitterly, 'and my life goes on. I will do what I must, and you cannot dissuade me. Now please, Will, I need to be alone.'

Will Hubbard was not a man to easily admit defeat, but there was something in Charlotte's soft voice that convinced him he had lost. Quietly, he left the room and closed the door behind him, feeling as helpless as ever he had felt in his life.

※

Seth was awakened just before dawn by the sound of birds chirping noisily in the trees above his head. He stirred sluggishly on his bed of pine boughs and closed his eyes resolutely against the fading night. After well over a month of constant travel on the swiftest ships and strongest horses, he was within a day's ride of Youngstown and the woman he had come so far to find.

Giving up on sleep, he rolled onto his back and tucked his arms beneath his head as he watched the silvery sky across the still, dark lake. Since that night in the library at Seahaven, he'd had so much time to think, to plan, to rehearse the things he would say to Charl when he found her. He loved her, and she had only to reach out to him to seal the bond between them for ever. It was this bright and daring dream that had sustained him as he travelled. And today, well within his grasp, was the means to make that dream a reality.

Seth reached Youngstown shortly after noon, riding down the main street without any sign that he had been recognized. He saw the town had changed dramatically since he'd been there last, but he found the evidence of its destruction unremarkable in the light of the reports he had heard from Mitchell. He was pleased that the Beckwiths' store had been rebuilt but disconcerted to find it closed at this hour of the day. With apprehension nipping at his heels he rode towards the Beckwith house at the edge of town. As he cantered up the drive, he noticed a carriage was drawn up to the front door and that two women were emerging from the house to board it. It was immediately apparent that neither one of them was the woman he sought, but as he came closer, he realized one of them was the Beckwiths' housekeeper and the other was Janette Hubbard. His uneasiness grew as he dismounted and approached them, wondering where they were bound.

'Janette?' he called out hesitantly.

The slender, dark-haired woman turned at the sound of her name, and when she recognized the speaker, her eyes became round as saucers.

'Seth? Seth, is that really you?' she gasped. 'Oh, thank goodness you've arrived in time.'

'In time? In time for what? Why are you in Youngstown, Janette? Is Will with you?'

'I'm here for the wedding. Oh, Seth, you must hurry!'

At the word 'wedding' a jolt of panic raced through Seth.

'Who – who's getting married?' he demanded.

'Charl is getting married,' Janette exclaimed. 'Charlotte and Stephen Langley!'

Seth flinched as if the words had been a blow, and he fought the overwhelming despair of knowing he had come too late. There was nothing for him now but to accept Charl's choice of husband and wish her well.

Looking up into Seth's sun-bronzed face, Janette Hubbard could see his expression solidify and she felt as if she was watching water turn to ice. When he finally spoke, his voice was controlled and his words carefully chosen.

'I hope you will convey my best wishes to the happy couple,' he said as he turned to go.

Desperately Janette caught his arm.

'No, Seth, you must listen!' she implored. 'Though Charl won't admit it, Stephen Langley is forcing her into this marriage somehow. I'm sure of it.'

Seth paused, frankly unconvinced, and Harriet chimed in, nodding in agreement.

'I reckon Mrs Hubbard's right, though I have no proof of it. Mr Stephen began coming 'round as soon as Miss Charlotte returned from New Orleans. He came to her the night after we buried her pa,' Harriet went on.

'Henry Beckwith's dead?' Seth gasped.

The housekeeper nodded. 'More than three months now. Wounded in the war he was.'

Porterfield shook his head slowly. 'Go on,' he encouraged.

'Mr Stephen came the night after we buried her pa. I didn't eavesdrop, mind you, but they were arguing in the parlour. Mr Stephen said he had proof that Miss Charlotte's pa had been dealing with the British during the war. But I know that's not true. Mr Henry wouldn't –'

'Then what happened?' Seth asked intently.

'Their voices got quiet after a while, and when they came out of the sitting room, Miss Charl was as white as paper. Later that night she told me she'd agreed to marry Mr Stephen.'

'Does Charl want to marry him?' Seth demanded.

'She's never said a word against him between that day and this, but I know she doesn't love him. She loves you, Mr Porterfield. It's just that she's thought you were dead all these months.'

'I can well imagine,' Seth put in, unable to meet the housekeeper's eyes.

'Mr and Mrs Hubbard were up half the night trying to change her mind about the wedding.'

'That's right, Seth,' Janette agreed. 'No matter what Will or I said, she just stared off into space and refused to listen.'

'Please, Mr Porterfield,' Harriet went on as if sensing his uncertainty, 'you must go after her. I'm afraid for Charlotte if she marries Stephen Langley, for as twisted and as ugly as his body is, his mind is even more so.'

The description chilled Seth to the marrow of his bones.

'All right, where will I find her?' he asked tersely.

The two women gave him directions to the church, and he raced for his mount. A few moments later he was thundering along the riverbank, bent low over his horse's neck. As he rode towards the church where Charl would take her vows, his thoughts were in a turmoil of self-loathing and burgeoning hope. While he had been in England pretending to be dead, Charl had been in Youngstown, living with the harsh realities of war and its aftermath. While he had drunk and gamed in London's most exclusive clubs, she had come home to an ailing father and a struggling business that was their only livelihood. While he had tried to deny his love for her, she had been fighting Stephen Langley and her own devastating loneliness. Yet both Harriet and Janette had assured him that Charl still loved him. And as undeserving as he was, he wanted to believe them.

'I'll make this up to you, Charl. I swear I will.' He whispered the promise as he urged his horse to greater speed. 'I'll make this up to you if it takes the rest of my life.'

Forty-Two

Will Hubbard was standing on the steps of the little brick church smoking his pipe as he waited for the carriage with Harriet and Janette to arrive so the ceremony could begin.

The thunder of hoofbeats broke into his troubled thoughts, and he glanced up just as a lone rider drew up and leaped from his saddle.

'Dear God!' he muttered, afraid to believe his eyes. 'Seth! Where the devil did you come from?'

'Quick, Will,' Seth gasped, 'where is Charl? I must see her before she goes through with this marriage to Langley.'

Nodding, Will grabbed the blond man's arm and led him through the double doors into the church and past the startled wedding guests who were still milling in the vestry. At the doorway to the anteroom where Charl was waiting for the ceremony to begin, Will stepped aside.

Seth opened the door and paused for a moment, transfixed by the sight of Charlotte Beckwith after so long. In the sunlight that filtered through the windows, there was an ethereal quality to her beauty that was highlighted by the pure white gown and filmy veil. She semed pale and fragile in the brightness, as if she was almost translucent. And he wanted to touch her, but he was suddenly afraid.

Instead he said her name softly, his tone deep and gentle as his voice caressed the single precious syllable that was the essence of the woman he loved.

Charl turned from the window slowly, raising wide tragic eyes to where Will Hubbard should have been waiting. But as she looked at the man in the doorway, recognition came, and for one wild joyous moment her heart soared, hammering hard in her chest. Then abruptly, reality closed in, and she knew the man she saw before her could not be real.

I must be going mad, Charl thought as she stared at this apparition in frozen contemplation.

'I always thought that brides were supposed to be happy,' he said, taking a step closer.

At his words her sea-green eyes filled with tears.

'Dear God! Is it really you?' she whispered, bringing one trembling hand up to her throat. Charl could feel the blood recede from her face as she spoke, and her world was suddenly dissolving around her.

Seth reached her in two long strides and swept her up in his arms, holding her gently as reality wavered and swam before her disbelieving eyes. Dizzily, she tipped her head back against Seth's strong shoulder to look into his face, and somehow his nearness penetrated her spinning brain. She well knew the feel of him, the scent of him, the hard uncompromising look of him. And as he held her, crushed close to his chest, she recognized, with a rush of pure joy, that this was no ghost but the man she loved, real and solid beside her.

'Seth?' she whispered in disbelief.

'Yes, Charlotte?' he smiled into her eyes.

'Seth!' The word was a revelation, and then his lips claimed hers with a hunger and intensity she knew too well to doubt. Her arms came around his neck, and she clung to him as if she never meant to let him go. Her tears wet both their faces as he held her. For the two of them time ceased to be, and they existed in a world unto themselves where the gentle touching, the murmured words of endearment, and the depth of their feelings for each other recreated and confirmed the wonder of their love.

Slowly and reluctantly they drew apart, and Seth set Charl on her feet once more. But as they stood there, their eyes held in that same unmistakable way they had across a tavern on that day long ago.

Then, abruptly, Charl's chin came up in an expression he instantly recognized and knew all too well. Taking a step away from him, she fixed him with an unwavering stare.

'Where have you been?' she demanded.

Seth had nurtured some vague hope that when he took her in his arms, there would be no need for explanations. And in truth she had come to him as joyfully and eagerly as he had dreamed she would. But he should have known that even the elation of this reunion would not make Charl completely accepting. He chuckled softly and drew her back into his embrace. This woman, with all her contradictions, her sapient insight, her fiery spirit, and her unquenchable passion for life, was the one woman in the world he wanted. And perhaps it was just this stubborn, indomitable part of her that made it so. At any rate, Charl wanted and deserved to know the truth.

'I was wounded and captured at the Arnaud plantation the same morning I left you in New Orleans,' he told her.

There was a puzzled expression on Charl's face as she looked up at him.

'But if you were captured, why didn't your name appear on any of Edward Livingston's lists of prisoners for exchange?'

Seth was suddenly intensely aware of the warm, vibrant woman he held in his arms and the incredible sweetness of being alive.

'I doubt they thought I'd live long enough to be exchanged: but as you can see, I proved them wrong about that.

'When the fleet left for England after peace was declared, I was too weak to be put ashore. And after all that had happened in New Orleans, it seemed better to go with them.'

Her pale face was earnest and solemn with the need to understand. And as he lost himself in the shimmering blue-green depths of her eyes, he could not recall any of the reasons he'd invented to keep them apart.

Gently, he cupped her face between his palms and found the courage to continue in her luminous eyes.

'Oh, Charlotte, I thought I could forget you if I made a life for myself in England, but I was as mistaken about that as I was about all the rest. In time I came to know what a fool I was to believe St James' lies and how wrong I was to doubt you. I love you, Charl, and I want you with me always. After the way I've treated you, I know you have every right to send me away. And if that's what you want, I'll go. But I swear, Charl, if you agree to be my wife, I'll spend the rest of my life trying to make these last months up to you. Marry me, Charl. Please will you marry me?'

There was a breathless quality to his words, as if he had thought long and hard about what he would say when he faced her and was determined to get everything exactly right. She was even mildly amazed that the proposal had been voiced as a question. No one knew better than Charl what Seth was capable of doing in order to get what he wanted. But the earnest request for her promise confirmed his love for her in a way that even his declaration did not.

Tenderly, she looked up at the man she loved, watching the play of emotions on his tanned face. His expression was serious and resolute, but there was a flicker of uncertainty in the depths of his brilliant blue eyes.

'I have things to offer you now,' Seth went on quickly, non-plussed by her silence, 'things I never dreamed of in Quebec. There's so much to tell you –'

'For God's sake, Charl!' Will Hubbard's voice came from the doorway where he had obviously been keeping watch for some time. 'Tell the man "yes" and get away from here before Langley comes looking for you. The music has already started.'

'Oh, Seth,' she said softly. 'I told you once before I'd marry you. How could you think that I would change my mind?'

Seth bent to seal her promise with a kiss, but Will caught his arm.

'If you're wise, you'll get Charl out of here quickly, my friend,' he advised. 'I doubt Langley will take this well, and I don't think you want to confront him here. I'll do my best to keep him busy until you're safely away. Now hurry, and good luck.'

Taking Charl's hand in his, Seth led her out of the anteroom and down the hallway. Through the open sanctuary doors the wedding guests could clearly see the bride leaving with someone other than the groom. From his place before the altar, Langley saw this too and advanced down the aisle, his face scarlet with fury. He had easily recognized the tall, blond man who had returned from the grave to steal his bride from him.

'Damn you, Porterfield!' he bellowed, his rage echoing in the chancel as he turned and ran up the aisle towards the doors. Will tried to intercept him in the vestry, but Langley drew his sword and slashed at the Army officer, forcing him to jump aside as Stephen made his way out of the church with a swarm of wedding guests behind him.

Hampered by her full skirts, Charl had been unable to mount Seth's horse, so he was already in the saddle, preparing to pull her up to sit behind him, when Langley reached the street. Snatching Charl's arm, he dragged her out of Seth's grasp.

'I'll not let you have her, Porterfield. Charlotte has agreed to be my wife!' Langley snarled, tightening his grip on the woman's wrist so that she gasped in pain.

'Oh, Stephen, please!' Charl whispered, knowing even as she spoke that her plea would be futile.

'Never, Langley, she'll never be yours!' Seth replied, dropping lightly from the horse's back to the dusty churchyard where they would play out this drama.

'Charl belongs to me. She doesn't love you, Langley. She loves me. She wants me. Let her go.'

Stephen's eyes were glowing with hatred for the blond man who faced him. Porterfield had stolen the love of this woman from him, defiled his honour, scarred his pride, and finally made him a cripple. He would not lose to this man again.

'By God, Porterfield, if I cannot have the girl, then neither shall you!' he raged, moving the sword from before him, where it had protected him from Seth's stalking, to Charl's throat. Grimly he pulled her against him with his left arm and adjusted the blade so that its point rested against the pulse that tapped just below her ear.

An audible gasp moved through the crowd, and Porterfield froze where he stood.

In that split second as they stood like some grotesque tableau, Seth took in the rapid rise and fall of Charl's breathing, the tears that trickled helplessly down her pale cheeks. Somehow in these past minutes Stephen had taken the last step over the final line between sanity and madness. Possessing Charl was no longer the question between them, and Seth knew that in Langley's quest for revenge Charl's life would be forfeit.

'Come no closer, Porterfield,' he warned. 'She can be dead before you take a step.' To emphasize the threat he pricked her tender skin with his sword point until a single scarlet drop of blood began to trace a path down Charl's silky throat.

Charl whimpered softly, and Seth knew it was a sound that would echo in his nightmares forever after.

Langley read the raw fear in the other man's eyes and laughed.

'It's good to have you at my mercy this once,' he taunted. 'I'm going to enjoy killing her, Porterfield. This way you will always carry a vision of her last moments with you. It will haunt you every day of your life, just as my hatred for you has haunted me.'

He saw the muscles in Langley's forearm flex and bunch as he prepared for the final thrust that would end Charl's life. Instinctively, Seth reached across the space between them to

catch the glinting silver sword, heedless of the blade that bit deep
into his palm as his grip tightened. The action had been born
of desperation, and as Porterfield glared into Langley's eyes,
measuring the man's strength against his own, he knew only that
if he allowed the sword to move even a fraction of an inch, it
would mean Charl's life. Slowly he began to force the point down
and away from the terrified girl's throat, but the momentary
advantage cost Seth dearly. The old wound in his shoulder
throbbed with the strain, and his arm began to tremble with the
force of his exertion. The blade returned a quarter of an inch,
and he heard Charl moan. Then from reserves of will he did not
know he possessed came the strength to force the blade outward.
Fear began to show in the depths of Langley's eyes as the sword
moved another inch and then two. Abruptly, Stephen whirled
away, thrusting Charl towards Seth. The force of the movement
sent her stumbling to the ground where she lay sobbing silently.
Seth stepped between Langley and the woman he was prepared
to defend with his life.

In a frenzy of frustration and hatred, Stephen slashed wildly at
him with his sword, but Seth was able to sidestep the swoop of
deadly steel. The moment it took Langley to recover himself gave
Porterfield time to draw the broad-bladed hunting knife he habitually carried in his boot. With it firmly in his grip, he confronted his
adversary. There was a terrible concentration in his face as he
parried the first thrust Langley made at his chest, and the next and
the next, turning them aside with the blade of his knife.

As the two men struggled, Will came to stand protectively over
Charl where she huddled in trembling terror, watching the battle
before her with blankly staring eyes.

As the duel continued, Will could see that Porterfield was
fighting a tightly controlled defensive battle against Langley's
wild, broad attacks.

Then recoiling from a wide arcing slash of the blade, Seth
stepped inside Langley's guard and caught the wrist of the man's
sword arm in the vicelike grip of his left hand. For what seemed
like an eternity, the men stood poised and silent as Stephen
struggled to break Porterfield's hold. Bit by bit his hand went
limp, and his grasp on the sword hilt withered under the pressure
of Seth's steely fingers. Slowly the weapon tumbled to lie in the
dusty road beneath their feet. With a grim smile of satisfaction
Porterfield kicked the sword aside, sending it scudding across the

ground. Drawing a long calming breath, he gradually released his grip on Langley and turned to where Charl lay weeping at Will Hubbard's feet.

It was her frightened cry that gave Seth a moment's warning before Langley leapt on him, dragging him down with the drawn hunting knife between their two bodies. For an instant Seth caught a glimpse of Langley's face, with its rage-red eyes and bared teeth, before Stephen's hands closed around his throat, cutting off his air. The two men rolled over and over in the dusty street as Seth struggled against Langley's frenzied strength. The world had begun to fade and spin around him before he managed to break Stephen's choking grip. Almost immediately the focus of the battle changed to the control of the hunting knife that Seth still held tightly in his right hand. With inexorable tenacity the deadly blade was forced down towards the blond man's heaving chest.

Clouds of dust swirled around the thrashing men as they turned and twisted in mortal combat.

With an echoing cry of total despair, Charl buried her face in her hands.

Stephen's body began to move, rolling slightly sideways as if he meant to rise. Then abruptly he pitched onto his back to expose the knife that was buried to the hilt at the apex of his ribs. Dazedly, Seth raised himself on one elbow, still breathing hard There was one more moment of stunned silence, and then the spell that had held the assembled wedding guests in the thrall was abruptly broken, and several men rushed forward to help Seth to his feet. Almost immediately he shook them off and went to where Charl was huddled, weeping inconsolably.

He came to his knees beside her and put one arm gently around her trembling shoulders. 'Charl?' he said softly, 'Charlotte, it's all right now.'

Trapped in her own shuddering world of terror, she seemed totally unaware of the man beside her. With apprehension and concern in his eyes, Seth turned to Will Hubbard.

'Charl's been through a lot today,' Will replied to his friend's unspoken question. 'She needs time to realize that you are real and safe and that there is no longer a threat to your future together.'

'Then I must take her away from here, perhaps back to the house where she will feel secure.'

Will nodded in agreement as he came to his knees. 'Let me see to your hand before you go,' he offered, binding the gash with a clean handkerchief. 'This should have treatment and stitching,' he went on.

'I know,' Seth agreed, 'but that can wait until later. Now I think Charlotte needs me.' Rising, Seth stripped off his blood-stained coat and waistcoat, then bent to gather Charl's trembling body in his arms. With Will's help he mounted his horse and turned towards the River Road.

As they cantered in the direction of Youngstown, along the familiar trail between the trees and the sun dappled ribbon of green water, Seth held Charl close. But in spite of the physical contact and the low soothing words he whispered in her ear, she seemed hardly aware of him. Somehow she had retreated and sat weeping softly in the echoing world of her own terror. She seemed so lost and broken that she frightened him, and Seth pulled the horse to a stop, plainly unwilling to subject her to the questions and confusion that were inevitable if they returned to the Beckwith house. Just ahead was an overgrown path that led down the steep bank to a clearing by the river well out of sight of the road. With no more than a moment's consideration, Seth turned his horse onto it. The clearing was just as he remembered, a broad grassy slope overrun by wild flowers and hidden from above by the overhanging bank. Slowly he dismounted and set Charl on her feet. Then, moving quickly, he hobbled the horse and spread a blanket beneath the trailing branches of the willow. Seating himself on the blanket he took Charl into his arms. He cradled her gently like a frightened child as his hands moved over her in a tender soothing caress. Still she wept, seeming oblivious to him and to the beauty and serenity about her.

Dear God, he thought desperately, he had almost lost her so many times. Was this the last cruel twist of fate? Now that he had realized his love for her and Charl had agreed to share his life, was she to be taken from him by something more difficult to accept than death?

Then he felt her nestle against him like the small, frightened creature her fear had made her, and he knew she was no longer completely indifferent to him. Quietly he began to talk, speaking to her of all the things that he had heard and seen since they had been together in Quebec. Unaccustomed endearments that came with astonishing ease to his tongue threaded his speech. And though he knew it was more his tone than what he said that reached her, he was certain he could sense a response to the caress in his voice.

As he spoke, her tears ceased and gradually her ragged breathing returned to normal. Her head was pillowed on his shoulder so he could not see her face, but one hand had come up to encircle his neck. With a wave of pure relief surging through him, Seth realized that the worst was past.

Still he continued to speak softly as his arms tightened protectively and possessively around her. His touch was gentle and soothing as he told her of his capture and what he could remember of the events thereafter. He spoke briefly of his life in England and told her of his reconciliation with his grandfather. It was then that his voice went husky, fading to little more than a whisper, and Charl responded by drawing closer still. Finally he told her of the conversation that explained Felix St James' hatred and made him realize how wrong he'd been about her. His last words were an apology so deep and sincere that there was no doubt that the suspicions of the past were gone forever.

For a long time he simply held her, watching the starry reflections of sunlight on the water, listening to the murmur of the wind through the grass and the hush of the river's passage. Charl seemed content to sit nestling close in the circle of his arms, and the peace of the place affected them both.

At last Charl raised her head from the shoulder where it had rested for so long and looked up into his face. Her eyes were wide and luminous, and they touched him everywhere. Wonder and delight and love mingled in their sea-green depths as she watched him. Her trembling fingers gently skimmed his cheek, traced the line of his jaw, and came to rest on his shoulder once more. Then with a smile of pure joy, she stretched up to taste his lips with hers.

His senses swam at the contact of her soft, questing mouth against his own, but he sat very still, fighting down the ravenous desires that raged through him. Too much had happened to her, too many demands had been made on her for him to make any more. He knew that, and yet it was exquisite torture to hold her close and not make love to her.

Slowly, Charl drew back to watch him, revelling in the hard, stubborn line of his jaw, the fathomless depths of his blue eyes,

and the firm narrow lips that were now softened with tenderness
and the hint of a smile.

'This is real,' she said hesitantly. 'You are real.'

But the reality evaded her until Seth's mouth claimed hers
again in a kiss that set her soul afire. Surely she could not be
dreaming this melting, sweeping weakness that came only with
Seth's touch. Her lips moved against his skin to his temples and
the corners of his mouth. She found the tender hollow below his
ear and tasted the tang of his skin, more intoxicating than any
wine. She breathed the scent of him, the mixture of shaving soap,
starch, and tobacco, and knew that this was Seth, real and solid
beside her. Even now she was not sure what miracle had returned
him to her, but in the face of that sweet truth everything else
blurred and faded to nothingness.

Seth lay back on the blanket, taking Charl with him. Tiger lilies,
buttercups, and Queen Anne's lace bent above them beneath the
canopy of willow branches, forming a haven for the two of them.

Charl's fingers soon found the space between two buttons on
his shirt and gradually widened the opening to expose the bronzed
plane of his chest. For a time she was content to touch him gently,
playing in the soft mat of golden hair that covered his chest and
crept down across his belly. Then she looked up and saw that his
eyes had gone dark and smoky with desire.

'Oh, Seth, love me,' she whispered. 'Please, please love me.'

'Oh, yes, my darling. Yes,' he murmured in reply.

She turned so he could unfasten the myriad of buttons at the
back of her gown and then helped him undress. And when they
were naked side by side, with nothing but the sky for a coverlet,
they came together in a shuddering tenderness that was achingly
familiar and yet completely new.

His tongue was a sweet seeking presence in her mouth, and
she responded to him, dissolving in pleasure. Once more there
was the wondrous quickening in her that came only with Seth,
only in his arms, and with no other man. His kisses came harder,
faster, more demanding, but she was his equal in desire and met
them with a hunger and need of her own. Her hands moved over
him, rediscovering the texture of his skin, pausing to caress,
stroke, encompass, and arouse. And with the same mixture of
tenderness and frenzy his hands moved over her. It was as if in
this one act they meant to make up for all the time that had been
stolen from them, for all the months they'd lost.

He paused to touch her breasts and kiss her nipples with his eager mouth. His hands moved lower to stroke the softness between her thighs that was already moist and aching with her need for him. Charl sighed and caressed his rigid manhood, as aroused by his ardour as by the wicked pleasures that left her trembling at the brink of sanity. When they were both beyond restraint, Seth spread her thighs and entered the moist, welcoming softness of her body. In that union there was a satisfaction that momentarily quelled all other sensations.

Charl's sea-green eyes were wide and tender as she looked into his, reading in the smoky blue depths an intensity of feelings that matched her own.

'I love you, Seth,' she whispered. 'I'll love you until the end of time.'

'I know that, Charlotte,' he whispered back. 'In my heart I think I've known that all along.'

She could sense the stirring in him that would take them to the cresting of their passion. Deliberately he held back.

'Charl,' he continued, his voice deep and husky with emotion. 'I love you, my darling. As hard as I tried to convince myself that I had, I never stopped loving you.'

Then the sensations they had held at bay came to claim them. She felt his smouldering passion flare as he moved within her and she was consumed by her own need for him. Prickly tension danced along her nerves, and then they were united in a sweet splintering of reality that carried them upward together. Dizzily they surged higher to the pinnacle of sensation where they hung suspended for an incandescent infinity. Trembling and sated, they spiralled downward to lie spent but united in the blissful aftermath.

It was the wetness of Charl's tears upon his skin that roused Seth, but her weeping no longer threatened him. Instead, he drew her closer and let her cry. These were healing tears, he reflected as he waited patiently for the storm to pass, as unifying in their way as making love had been.

Finally Charl raised her head. Her face was tear streaked and her nose was red from crying, but her eyes were calm.

'Seth?' she said in the tone of voice he had come to know so well.

With difficulty he smothered a grin.

'What is it you want now, woman?' he asked.

'Seth,' she hesitated, not quite meeting his eyes, 'do you still want to marry me?'

He was utterly astonished by the question.

'Yes, of course I do!' he assured her.

She took a deep breath. 'Then will you marry me now, tonight?'

He looked down into her earnest face and suddenly saw her vulnerability and her strength. With that insight came an understanding of her that matched the new, hard-won understanding of himself. She was like him: hard and soft, frightened and courageous, independent and yet bound by emotions too compelling to deny. Tenderness swelled within him, and he knew that he would love Charlotte Beckwith until the end of his days.

Without answering, he fumbled in the pile of their discarded clothing until he found the pocket of his breeches and withdrew a small velvet box.

'If I did not intend to marry you immediately, would I have brought a wedding ring with me?' he asked softly as he extended the box to her.

She took it gingerly and with trembling hands removed the circlet of emeralds from its bed of ivory satin.

'Seth, truly, is this to be my wedding ring?' she said as she examined the ring that shimmered in her palm. 'It's so beautiful and so very old.'

He reached out to caress her cheek, emotions welling within him that made it hard to speak.

'It's been in the Porterfield family for generations,' he told her at last. 'And now it comes to you, as my wife. I will slip it on your finger as soon as we can find someone who will hear us make our vows.'

'Thank you, my darling,' she whispered as she bent to kiss him. 'Oh, Seth, I love you so.' That single kiss had led to another and another until they were both flushed and giddy with renewed desire.

'I warn you, woman,' Seth told her huskily as he rose above her, covering her soft body with his own, 'if you want to find a preacher, we'd best be about it. For if you dally with me one minute more, thoughts of a wedding will be far from my mind.'

Slowly and reluctantly they dressed, sorry to abandon their secluded retreat and the solitude it had provided, but anxious as well to begin their new life together.

❧

They were married just at sunset, standing in the golden glow that streamed through the windows of the Beckwith house. As they repeated their vows before a travelling parson Will had found for them at the fort, Charl revelled in the tender emotions in Seth's face and the undisguised love in his eyes. These were the things she had longed to see there, and the words of commitment were the ones she had waited so long to hear on his lips. But even as he slipped the circlet of emeralds on her finger, she knew the bond that held them had been forged long ago: in the dark taproom at the Crow's Head Tavern, during those sweet, blissful days in Quebec, and even in the doubt – and suspicion – filled night in New Orleans. It was a bond that had joined their hearts and their lives for ever that was being sanctified today. And as the ceremony ended, Charl turned to her new husband with a soft smile on her lips and the promise of their bright future shining in her eyes.

MORE ABOUT PENGUINS, PELICANS
AND PUFFINS

For further information about books available from Penguins please write to Dept EP, Penguin Books Ltd, Harmondsworth, Middlesex UB7 0DA.

In the U.S.A.: For a complete list of books available from Penguins in the United States write to Dept DG, Penguin Books, 299 Murray Hill Parkway, East Rutherford, New Jersey 07073.

In Canada: For a complete list of books available from Penguins in Canada write to Penguin Books Canada Limited, 2801 John Street, Markham, Ontario L3R 1B4.

In Australia: For a complete list of books available from Penguins in Australia write to the Marketing Department, Penguin Books Australia Ltd, P.O. Box 257, Ringwood, Victoria 3134.

In New Zealand: For a complete list of books available from Penguins in New Zealand write to the Marketing Department, Penguin Books (N.Z.) Ltd, Private Bag, Takapuna, Auckland 9.

In India: For a complete list of books available from Penguins in India write to Penguin Overseas Ltd, 706 Eros Apartments, 56 Nehru Place, New Delhi 110019.

A CHOICE OF PENGUINS

☐ *Further Chronicles of Fairacre* **'Miss Read'**

Full of humour, warmth and charm, these four novels – *Miss Clare Remembers, Over the Gate, The Fairacre Festival* and *Emily Davis* – make up an unforgettable picture of English village life.

☐ *Callanish* **William Horwood**

From the acclaimed author of *Duncton Wood*, this is the haunting story of Creggan, the captured golden eagle, and his struggle to be free.

☐ *Act of Darkness* **Francis King**

Anglo-India in the 1930s, where a peculiarly vicious murder triggers 'A terrific mystery story . . . a darkly luminous parable about innocence and evil' – *The New York Times*. 'Brilliantly successful' – *Daily Mail*. 'Unputdownable' – *Standard*

☐ *Death in Cyprus* **M. M. Kaye**

Holidaying on Aphrodite's beautiful island, Amanda finds herself caught up in a murder mystery in which no one, not even the attractive painter Steven Howard, is quite what they seem . . .

☐ *Lace* **Shirley Conran**

Lace is, quite simply, a publishing sensation: the story of Judy, Kate, Pagan and Maxine; the bestselling novel that teaches men about women, and women about themselves. 'Riches, bitches, sex and jetsetters' locations – they're all there' – *Sunday Express*

PENGUINS ON HEALTH, SPORT AND KEEPING FIT

□ *Medicines* **Peter Parish**

Fifth Edition. The usages, dosages and adverse effects of all medicines obtainable on prescription or over the counter are covered in this reference guide, designed for the ordinary reader and everyone in health care.

□ *Baby & Child* **Penelope Leach**

A fully illustrated, expert and comprehensive handbook on the first five years of life. 'It stands head and shoulders above anything else available at the moment' – Mary Kenny in the *Spectator*

□ *Vogue Natural Health and Beauty*
   Bronwen Meredith

Health foods, yoga, spas, recipes, natural remedies and beauty preparations are all included in this superb, fully illustrated guide and companion to the bestselling *Vogue Body and Beauty Book.*

□ *Pregnancy and Diet* **Rachel Holme**

With suggested foods, a sample diet-plan of menus and advice on nutrition, this guide shows you how to avoid excessive calories but still eat well and healthily during pregnancy.

□ *The Penguin Bicycle Handbook* **Rob van der Plas**

Choosing a bicycle, maintenance, accessories, basic tools, safety, keeping fit – all these subjects and more are covered in this popular, fully illustrated guide to the total bicycle lifestyle.

□ *Physical Fitness*

Containing the 5BX 11-minute-a-day plan for men and the XBX 12-minute-a-day plan for women, this book illustrates the famous programmes originally developed by the Royal Canadian Air Force and now used successfully all over the world.

PENGUINS ON HEALTH, SPORT AND KEEPING FIT

☐ *Audrey Eyton's F-Plus*

F-Plan menus for women who lunch at work * snack eaters * keen cooks * freezer-owners * busy dieters using convenience foods * overweight children * drinkers and non-drinkers. 'Your short-cut to the most sensational diet of the century' – *Daily Express*

☐ *The F-Plan Calorie Counter and Fibre Chart*
Audrey Eyton

An indispensable companion to the F-Plan diet. High-fibre fresh, canned and packaged foods are listed, there's a separate chart for drinks, *plus* a wonderful selection of effortless F-Plan meals.

☐ *The Parents A–Z* **Penelope Leach**

From the expert author of *Baby & Child*, this skilled, intelligent and comprehensive guide is by far the best reference book currently available for parents, whether your children are six months, six or sixteen years.

☐ *Woman's Experience of Sex* **Sheila Kitzinger**

Fully illustrated with photographs and line drawings, this book explores the riches of women's sexuality at every stage of life. 'A book which any mother could confidently pass on to her daughter – and her partner too' – *Sunday Times*

☐ *Alternative Medicine* **Andrew Stanway**

From Acupuncture and Alexander Technique to Macrobiotics and Yoga, Dr Stanway provides an informed and objective guide to thirty-two therapies in alternative medicine.

☐ *Pregnancy* **Dr Jonathan Scher and Carol Dix**

Containing the most up-to-date information on pregnancy – the effects of stress, sexual intercourse, drugs, diet, late maternity and genetic disorders – this book is an invaluable and reassuring guide for prospective parents.

ENGLISH AND AMERICAN
LITERATURE IN PENGUINS

☐ *Main Street* **Sinclair Lewis**

The novel that added an immortal chapter to the literature of America's Mid-West, *Main Street* contains the comic essence of Main Streets everywhere.

☐ *The Compleat Angler* **Izaak Walton**

A celebration of the countryside, and the superiority of those in 1653, as now, who love *quietnesse, vertue* and, above all, *Angling*. 'No fish, however coarse, could wish for a doughtier champion than Izaak Walton' – Lord Home

☐ *The Portrait of a Lady* **Henry James**

'One of the two most brilliant novels in the language', according to F. R. Leavis, James's masterpiece tells the story of a young American heiress, prey to fortune-hunters but not without a will of her own.

☐ *Hangover Square* **Patrick Hamilton**

Part love story, part thriller, and set in the publands of London's Earls Court, this novel caught the conversational tone of a whole generation in the uneasy months before the Second World War.

☐ *The Rainbow* **D. H. Lawrence**

Written between *Sons and Lovers* and *Women in Love*, *The Rainbow* covers three generations of Brangwens, a yeoman family living on the borders of Nottinghamshire.

☐ *Vindication of the Rights of Woman*
Mary Wollstonecraft

Although Walpole once called her 'a hyena in petticoats', Mary Wollstonecraft's vision was such that modern feminists continue to go back and debate the arguments so powerfully set down here.

A CHOICE OF PENGUINS

☐ **West of Sunset** Dirk Bogarde

'His virtues as a writer are precisely those which make him the most compelling screen actor of his generation,' is what *The Times* said about Bogarde's savage, funny, romantic novel set in the gaudy wastes of Los Angeles.

☐ **The Riverside Villas Murder** Kingsley Amis

Marital duplicity, sexual discovery and murder with a thirties back-cloth: 'Amis in top form' – *The Times*. 'Delectable from page to page . . . effortlessly witty' – C. P. Snow in the *Financial Times*

☐ **A Dark and Distant Shore** Reay Tannahill

Vilia is the unforgettable heroine, Kinveil Castle is her destiny, in this full-blooded saga spanning a century of Victoriana, empire, hatreds and love affairs. 'A marvellous blend of *Gone with the Wind* and *The Thorn Birds*. You will enjoy every page' – *Daily Mirror*

☐ **Kingsley's Touch** John Collee

'Gripping . . . I recommend this chilling and elegantly written medical thriller' – *Daily Express*. 'An absolutely outstanding storyteller' – *Daily Telegraph*

☐ **The Far Pavilions** M. M. Kaye

Holding all the romance and high adventure of nineteenth-century India, M. M. Kaye's magnificent, now famous, novel has at its heart the passionate love of an Englishman for Juli, his Indian princess. 'Wildly exciting' – *Daily Telegraph*

A CHOICE OF PENGUINS

☐ *Small World* **David Lodge**

A jet-propelled academic romance, sequel to *Changing Places*. 'A new comic débâcle on every page' – *The Times*. 'Here is everything one expects from Lodge but three times as entertaining as anything he has written before' – *Sunday Telegraph*

☐ *The Neverending Story* **Michael Ende**

The international bestseller, now a major film: 'A tale of magical adventure, pursuit and delay, danger, suspense, triumph' – *The Times Literary Supplement*

☐ *The Sword of Honour Trilogy* **Evelyn Waugh**

Containing *Men at Arms, Officers and Gentlemen* and *Unconditional Surrender*, the trilogy described by Cyril Connolly as 'unquestionably the finest novels to have come out of the war'.

☐ *The Honorary Consul* **Graham Greene**

In a provincial Argentinian town, a group of revolutionaries kidnap the wrong man . . . 'The tension never relaxes and one reads hungrily from page to page, dreading the moment it will all end' – Auberon Waugh in the *Evening Standard*

☐ *The First Rumpole Omnibus* **John Mortimer**

Containing *Rumpole of the Bailey*, *The Trials of Rumpole* and *Rumpole's Return*. 'A fruity, foxy masterpiece, defender of our wilting faith in mankind' – *Sunday Times*

☐ *Scandal* **A. N. Wilson**

Sexual peccadillos, treason and blackmail are all ingredients on the boil in A. N. Wilson's new, *cordon noir* comedy. 'Drily witty, deliciously nasty' – *Sunday Telegraph*

A CHOICE OF PENGUINS

☐ **Stanley and the Women** Kingsley Amis

'Very good, very powerful . . . beautifully written . . . This is Amis *père* at his best' – Anthony Burgess in the *Observer*. 'Everybody should read it' – *Daily Mail*

☐ **The Mysterious Mr Ripley** Patricia Highsmith

Containing *The Talented Mr Ripley, Ripley Underground* and *Ripley's Game*. 'Patricia Highsmith is the poet of apprehension' – Graham Greene. 'The Ripley books are marvellously, insanely readable' – *The Times*

☐ **Earthly Powers** Anthony Burgess

'Crowded, crammed, bursting with manic erudition, garlicky puns, omnilingual jokes . . . (a novel) which meshes the real and personalized history of the twentieth century' – Martin Amis

☐ **Life & Times of Michael K** J. M. Coetzee

The Booker Prize-winning novel: 'It is hard to convey . . . just what Coetzee's special quality is. His writing gives off whiffs of Conrad, of Nabokov, of Golding, of the Paul Theroux of *The Mosquito Coast*. But he is none of these, he is a harsh, compelling new voice' – Victoria Glendinning

☐ **The Stories of William Trevor**

'Trevor packs into each separate five or six thousand words more richness, more laughter, more ache, more multifarious human-ness than many good writers manage to get into a whole novel' – *Punch*

☐ **The Book of Laughter and Forgetting**
Milan Kundera

'A whirling dance of a book . . . a masterpiece full of angels, terror, ostriches and love . . . No question about it. The most important novel published in Britain this year' – Salman Rushdie

PENGUIN OMNIBUSES

□ *Victorian Villainies*

Fraud, murder, political intrigue and horror are the ingredients of these four Victorian thrillers, selected by Hugh Greene and Graham Greene.

□ *The Balkan Trilogy* Olivia Manning

This acclaimed trilogy – *The Great Fortune, The Spoilt City* and *Friends and Heroes* – is the portrait of a marriage, and an exciting recreation of civilian life in the Second World War. 'It amuses, it diverts, and it informs' – Frederick Raphael

□ *The Penguin Collected Stories of Isaac Bashevis Singer*

Forty-seven marvellous tales of Jewish magic, faith and exile. 'Never was the Nobel Prize more deserved . . . He belongs with the giants' – *Sunday Times*

□ *The Penguin Essays of George Orwell*

Famous pieces on 'The Decline of the English Murder', 'Shooting an Elephant', political issues and P. G. Wodehouse feature in this edition of forty-one essays, criticism and sketches – all classics of English prose.

□ *Further Chronicles of Fairacre* 'Miss Read'

Full of humour, warmth and charm, these four novels – *Miss Clare Remembers, Over the Gate, The Fairacre Festival* and *Emily Davis* – make up an unforgettable picture of English village life.

□ *The Penguin Complete Sherlock Holmes* Sir Arthur Conan Doyle

With the fifty-six classic short stories, plus *A Study in Scarlet, The Sign of Four, The Hound of the Baskervilles* and *The Valley of Fear*, this volume contains the remarkable career of Baker Street's most famous resident.

PENGUIN OMNIBUSES

☐ *Life with Jeeves* **P. G. Wodehouse**

Containing *Right Ho, Jeeves*, *The Inimitable Jeeves* and *Very Good, Jeeves!* in which Wodehouse lures us, once again, into the evergreen world of Bertie Wooster, his terrifying Aunt Agatha, his man Jeeves and other eggs, good and bad.

☐ *The Penguin Book of Ghost Stories*

An anthology to set the spine tingling, including stories by Zola, Kleist, Sir Walter Scott, M. R. James, Elizabeth Bowen and A. S. Byatt.

☐ *The Penguin Book of Horror Stories*

Including stories by Maupassant, Poe, Gautier, Conan Doyle, L. P. Hartley and Ray Bradbury, in a selection of the most horrifying horror from the eighteenth century to the present day.

☐ *The Penguin Complete Novels of Jane Austen*

Containing the seven great novels: *Sense and Sensibility*, *Pride and Prejudice*, *Mansfield Park*, *Emma*, *Northanger Abbey*, *Persuasion* and *Lady Susan*.

☐ *Perfick, Perfick!* **H. E. Bates**

The adventures of the irrepressible Larkin family, in four novels: *The Darling Buds of May*, *A Breath of French Air*, *When the Green Woods Laugh* and *Oh! To Be in England*.

☐ *Famous Trials*
   Harry Hodge and James H. Hodge

From Madeleine Smith to Dr Crippen and Lord Haw-Haw, this volume contains the most sensational murder and treason trials, selected by John Mortimer from the classic Penguin Famous Trials series.

ENGLISH AND AMERICAN
LITERATURE IN PENGUINS

☐ *Emma* **Jane Austen**

'I am going to take a heroine whom no one but myself will much like,' declared Jane Austen of Emma, her most spirited and controversial heroine in a comedy of self-deceit and self-discovery.

☐ *Tender is the Night* **F. Scott Fitzgerald**

Fitzgerald worked on seventeen different versions of this novel, and its obsessions – idealism, beauty, dissipation, alcohol and insanity – were those that consumed his own marriage and his life.

☐ *The Life of Johnson* **James Boswell**

Full of gusto, imagination, conversation and wit, Boswell's immortal portrait of Johnson is as near a novel as a true biography can be, and still regarded by many as the finest 'life' ever written. This shortened version is based on the 1799 edition.

☐ *A House and its Head* **Ivy Compton-Burnett**

In a novel 'as trim and tidy as a hand-grenade' (as Pamela Hansford Johnson put it), Ivy Compton-Burnett penetrates the facade of a conventional, upper-class Victorian family to uncover a chasm of violent emotions – jealousy, pain, frustration and sexual passion.

☐ *The Trumpet Major* **Thomas Hardy**

Although a vein of unhappy unrequited love runs through this novel, Hardy also draws on his warmest sense of humour to portray Wessex village life at the time of the Napoleonic wars.

☐ *The Complete Poems of Hugh MacDiarmid*

☐ Volume One
☐ Volume Two

The definitive edition of work by the greatest Scottish poet since Robert Burns, edited by his son Michael Grieve, and W. R. Aitken.